SEX SESSIONS *Bundle*

CHARISSE SPIERS

Cover Art © Clarise Tan
Edited by Jessica Grover
Formatted by Nancy Henderson

CAMERA TALES BOOK ONE

SEX SESSIONS
Uncut

CHARISSE SPIERS

PROLOGUE

"Can you believe we did it? We graduated high school! Thank God. It's finally over and we can start living our lives free from parents."

I sit on Meredith's bed and watch unfocused as she continues to bounce around her room as she packs her bags. Wish I were that excited.

"Maybe for you," I say, sulking, unashamed. "My parents are making me go to junior college within driving distance so I can't get into trouble. I can't even go to a university and live in a dorm like normal college kids, or crap, even my brother. I wish my parents were cool like yours, or at least somewhat understanding. You tell yours you want to give acting a shot and they find you an apartment and hire an acting coach. I tell mine I want to move away to any of our state universities to find out what I want to do and I'm told I'm being ungrateful. *Some kids don't even get to go to college, Kambry,*" I mock the line my mom has used way too many times. "I just want out of Coffee Springs. I envy you, Meredith."

She sits beside me and bumps her bare shoulder against mine. "Come with me then. I've already asked Mom and she said she would rather us do this together. Plus, she agrees that you need to spread your wings and experience life a little, and as much as she loves your mom, that won't happen living with them. They can't see past their own noses to realize how ridiculous they're being." She grabs my hand in hers. "Could you picture us being on the big screen? People driving to the bigger cities to watch us while they shove popcorn in their mouths would be amazing. Think about it: movie premiers, celebrity events, and all the parties we could ever dream of. We can do this Kambry. We just have to want it bad enough."

Alabama summers are hot and humid. It's part of living in the south. The fewer clothes you can get away with the better. My choice of wardrobe, though, is a reserved version of Meredith, but not necessarily by choice. My parents are very conservative—churchgoers fulltime. My dad has probably paid for our small town church by now. He wants the perfect little cookie-cutter family and holier than thou, daughter included. Everything is about appearance with him. No daughter of his is going to be dressing skimpy for the whole town to see and running around acting wild or partying. Dating? Having fun? Not until you're grown. I would give anything to be like normal kids. It's embarrassing. Who goes to prom and has to be home by ten as a senior? The bad thing about small towns— everyone talks. You do one thing and it spreads like wildfire, so I'm always walking around on my tiptoes. I, Kambry Rivers, have never gotten drunk, cursed, or had sex. Sounds fun doesn't it? I didn't think so.

"That all sounds great, Meredith, but you've always been the dreamer, the rebel. I mean, how exactly do you propose I do that? If I can't even move into a girls only dorm where you have dorm moms, do you really think my parents are going to jump at the idea of me moving to Los Angeles, California, full of clubs, boys, alcohol, and sin? And with no parental supervision . . . Yeah right."

She slides off the bed and stands on her knees in front of me, grabbing my face in her slender hands. "Do you hear yourself, Kambry? You're eighteen years old. So what if they don't agree. You're an adult now. Sometimes as kids we have to cut the umbilical cords ourselves, even if our parents won't hand over the scissors. It's time to live our own lives, Darlin'. You and Kyle broke up last week. We all knew that was coming without you giving up the V-card." In her newfound ability to inspire, I don't have the heart to tell her I'm the one that broke up with him. "I'm surprised the two of you made it two years with your parents trying to turn you into Mother Teresa. You don't keep the most wanted baseball player on the team without sex to hold his interest. He hasn't even gotten to dip a finger in the *Fun Dip* for crying out loud. Baseball players know about bases, and to be such a good one he hasn't gotten very far."

My face begins to burn beneath her touch. "You don't think it's been hard? Every time we kiss, every time he touches me intimately when we're in his truck? Each time he looks at me with that sexy stare he's so good at? It'd be so easy to give in for me. The way he says my name when he's turned on drives me into a horny rage. It makes me feel good. And for a few moments every time it happens, I feel like dipping my wings into the fire just a little. You know why I can't have sex with him?" My voice is edging on yelling. "My dad monitors my phone calls and texts, social life, and the business of what is going on around town. He's like psycho dad on steroids. I wouldn't be surprised if he has a GPS on my car or has little spies around town to keep an eye on me. He would find out. I've been threatened with my life if I'm not a virgin when I walk down the aisle. He didn't even say anything when he found out Ben had sex and he was only like seventeen. All he did was storm out of the house and then spent a few hours at the church in prayer. He couldn't even hold out till graduation and he's like the golden child in my dad's eyes. It's completely unfair."

"Well, your brother is hot," she interrupts. "Someone was bound to get in those shorts at some point. Just saying." She pauses as if her mind is going off somewhere else. "If only we were closer in age to him back then . . ."

I grab the pillow within reach and smack her with it. "Don't talk about my brother like that, Meredith. Gross!"

She laughs briefly and then crinkles her face as if a different thought crosses her mind. "Ugh, I'm not trying to sound slutty, but you should always test drive the car before you buy it. All purchases are final. I'm not saying you have to sleep around, but damn girl, you need to sow some wild oats before you do that. We are only eighteen. I'm forbidding you from marriage until you're at least twenty-five. That shouldn't even work its way into our conversation. Wait for Mr. Right. Don't you dare marry some prick just to get away from your parents. None of that matters right now. All I'm saying is that all of our friends are leaving this hellhole behind by the end of the summer. I'm just leaving now so I can have a perfect summer on the west coast. There is no schedule for acting auditions like fall semester. The sooner I get started the better. We've been best friends since we discovered we were neighbors at five and then ended up in the same class in kindergarten. I would never steer you wrong. Come with me."

My mouth is salivating at the idea. Laying on the beach, getting a taste of city life, and doing something we've joked about since we both joined drama club freshman year. "How?"

She retakes her previous position beside me on the bed, throwing her arm around me. "I'm leaving at 4AM. I didn't want to fly because I want my car, and after very careful planning with my parents and promising I would stop at night to get a hotel, they agreed, but you know this. You can mention it to your folks if you want, but we both know what the answer is going to be. This is one time, sweet pea, that you're going to have to do what you know is best for you. If they love you, then they'll come around in time. If they want to choose social stigma over their daughter, then you're better off without them."

"I don't know. I have no plans at all. I'm not sure if I can do it on my own."

"Look. My mom and dad agreed to pay the apartment rent indefinitely and utilities until I find a part time job while trying to get a role. It'd be more affordable with both of us. What do you have to lose? A couple of semesters worth of junior college that you can make up later? You can always come home sobbing they were right and do it their way if it doesn't work out, but you can't undo regret, Kambry. You know both of us are meant for better things than being a young housewife with babies in a small town. Do you really want to be a preacher's wife? You know that's where your dad is heading unless you put your foot down."

I release a breath and a tear falls from my eye. Why? Well, because that's actually the truth. My mom just mentioned knowing someone yesterday at my graduation dinner that was leaving for seminary to become a pastor. I haven't even told Meredith yet. If I do this, though, I may not have parents anymore. They would probably disown me. "I'll think about it."

I stand, knowing my mom will be calling if I don't get home soon. It's getting close to ten, my curfew. I walk to the door. "Kambry?"

"Yeah."

"You know you're my best friend. I love you. I'm not telling you to rebel, but I know you're better than this. They are just too blinded to see it. I'll be waiting in my car until 4:05 if you want to come. We can do this together. It could be fun. An adventure. Just promise me you'll follow your heart either way."

"Okay. I love you, Meredith. You'll always be my best friend."

I leave and walk downstairs, knowing that if I don't do this I may never see my best friend again. If she leaves she'll never come back. I've always known this. Meredith and I are a lot alike. We've always wanted to leave this place, to move on to better places.

My heart is pulling me in one direction and my mind in the other. I've never disobeyed my parents. I'm also unhappy. This isn't what I want for my life. I'm not trying to be ungrateful for everything they've given me. I'm just different than them. I want nice things. I want to explore the world. I want to make something of myself. I want the big city life. I want passionate love that is good enough for storybooks or movie scripts. I want something that I'll never have if I stay . . .

CHAPTER ONE

Saxton

2 months later . . .

I go through the huge stack of fan mail in my dressing room as I wait for tonight's filming to start. They are always the same. Most stating they want to meet me or bang my brains out. Some even pouring out love confessions and that they'd throw away everything in their lives for one time with me like in my films, and they've never even met me. It's laughable most days. People have no shame. And what they don't realize is that it's nothing like what they see in those films. That's acting with no restrictions. Sex isn't the same to a porn star as most people. I have endless amounts of sex. To me, sex is a job, not a pastime.

A knock sounds at the door. "Mr. Maverick, filming begins in fifteen minutes."

"I'll be ready," I shout back. I look down at my erect cock to verify my promise, now in full stance from the medication and ready to perform. I toss my mail on the table and get ready for tonight's scene, adjusting my tie. Tonight, I'm a fucking billionaire working late at the office and she is a seductress bargaining for what she wants, but more importantly, what she needs. It doesn't matter how different the plot is, because it's still all the same. It's about the sex–what the viewer wants. Every pussy I fuck is still a porn star pussy. It's used, it's aged, and it's too experienced to be real, but it's my job to make it look real . . .

I have the best ratings of most male porn stars right now. I guess it's just my time to shine. I've worked my ass off since my life took this turn when I walked away from my junior year in college. Maybe it's because I started at a young age. Twenty-one to be exact, and here I am at twenty-five with enough money I could retire if I wanted and not have to worry about shit for a long time.

In this industry the younger the better, especially when it comes to the girls. This life is about fantasy and temporary pleasure. The viewers want to fantasize about what they aren't getting in their lives already, or simply to add to it, pretending they are the receiver of me, or the stallion fucking her brains out. I may have started out with limited experience, but today, there isn't anything about sex or a woman's body that I don't know. I am very good at what I do. My ratings and salary prove it. There is only one secret to knowing everything. Pleasing your partner is a learned art, whether staged or natural.

I walk to the door and open it, before making my way to the set. I pass by the hundreds of people that make this work, from the stage crew to the makeup artists and costume designers, to the directors, among many other roles that would take forever to name. In filming there are jobs for everything. It's fucking ridiculous, but I guess it's necessary or they wouldn't be here. Regardless, they will all watch me fuck her.

There are no secrets here. Your entire sexual experience is out in the open for everyone to watch. Every person here will know all of my tricks and skills when this night is over. Here, stage fright is nonexistent.

I walk on set and recall my beginning lines; the very lines that make no fucking difference because the majority of people that purchase this don't give a damn about the story . . .when there even is one. They only want the juice in the center. I take a seat at my desk and begin shuffling through the blank pages atop, as I listen to the director giving me my cue.

"Take one. Lights, camera, and action."

A knock sounds at the door and I look up, just before Veronica walks in wearing a trench coat cinched at the waist and heels. "I don't recall giving you permission to enter. Who are you?"

"I'm here to ask for a forbearance for Peter Davidson, my husband, or at least an extension."

"I'm sorry, Mrs. Davidson, but my hands are tied. There is nothing I can do. The bank is ready to foreclose. People like you cost me money I don't want to lose."

"Please, Mr. Adcock. There has to be something I can do to change your mind."

She pulls the tie at her waist and allows her coat to open, revealing her naked body underneath, before pulling the lapels over her shoulders and letting it fall to the floor. I allow my eyes to feast on her tits, and then veer down to her perfectly waxed pussy. *It's all about the eye movement.*

I sit back in my chair, leaning my arm on the armrest, before placing the tip of my pen to my lips, as if I'm actually considering it. "Does your husband know what you're doing?"

"Yes. It was his idea. We need more time. We will do anything."

"What makes you think I'm interested? I eat pussy like yours for breakfast. What exactly are you going to do for me to make yourself appealing?"

She walks toward me, wearing nothing but a set of pearls around her neck and black stiletto heels. Her chocolate brown hair hangs over her shoulders, pointing toward her tight nipples. She straddles me in my chair, before immediately going for the knot of my tie, loosening it. "Maybe we can work out a deal," she says and places her lipstick-stained lips to my neck. "I can give you a few sessions at the end of the day to relax you and you can give us an extension to get the money. I know you have more pull than you're letting on, Mr. Adcock." She kisses up to my ear. "The only man I've been with is my husband. And size is not his strong suit. It'll be tight enough for you," she whispers, rubbing her pussy back and forth over my hard dick, ruining a fucking expensive suit. "Are you in?"

I grab her hair in my hand, roughly pulling her head back. The tip of my nose touches the base of her neck and I inhale, breathing her in. There is no masculine scent present, only perfume. "You have three weeks and then there is nothing I can do. And you better be on your knees sucking my cock every day of those three weeks. I want to watch you swallow my cum so you'll remember what you had to do to keep that fucking mansion on the hill. I suggest you prove to me that your pussy is worth the hassle I'll have to go through to authorize it or the deal's off."

She breathes out, continuing to work the knot loose enough to reach the top button. I grab her ass and stand, before forcefully sitting her on top of my desk and pulling my tie over my head. I quickly pull the shirttail from my slacks. One by one I unbutton my shirt until it's completely open, letting it fall down my arms. Her eyes rake over my body as I pull the sleeves over my hands, letting the fabric fall to the floor. She licks her lips as my hands go for my black, leather belt. It doesn't take me long before each side is hanging apart, and the front of my trunks are visible through my unbuttoned pants.

I place my hands flat on the desk to each side of her hips, before enclosing my mouth around her nipple, flicking my tongue over the hardened center. She moans out, before grabbing my hand and pressing it between her legs. My fingertips brush over her wet entrance. I've barely even touched her and she's ready to go. They always are. Ratings would be shit if they weren't.

I pull her ass to the edge and slide two fingers inside, twisting them when they become knuckle deep before pulling them back out. She instantly pulls her heels up on the desk, opening wider for me. I suck harder, causing her to arch her back and press her chest into my face. I release her from my mouth and she leans back on the desk, grabbing her breasts in her hands.

Everyone knows prior to fucking her, what Veronica is known for. I kiss my way down her stomach, continuing to finger fuck her. I watch her as I descend. The lower I get, the harder she pinches her nipples, kneading her breasts in her hands. My lips become flush with her clit, before I suck her into my mouth, hard.

She screams out, her muscles tightening around my fingers as I curl them upward to drive the tips into her G-spot. "Suck me harder," she screams.

So I do.

When I feel her start to tighten around my fingers I remove them, but leave my hand cupped over her pussy. I start to rub my tongue on the underside of her clit, and that's when she starts. "Fuck yes," she screams out as she squirts into my hand, coating it with her orgasm. When she's done I remove my mouth from her body and stand upright, before rubbing my hand over her pussy to replace her orgasm on the exterior, ridding my hand of the excess.

She sits up when she notices me open the drawer to my desk and remove a condom. Like everyone knows her for squirting upon orgasm, everyone knows me to wrap it up. My only stipulation with every fucking contract I sign is to wear a condom. If they want me for the part, it's included in my contract. I will not sign it otherwise. I don't give a shit that every one of us have to go through extensive STD and HIV testing in between each new partner. I don't know what these girls fuck between jobs, and every somewhat smart person knows that shit can lay dormant for months and in some cases years. A pussy is nothing other than an incubator for shit you can't get rid of. I may be a fucking porn star, but I'm not nasty. Oral is as risky as I get, and most of the time I don't like it.

I hand it to her. "Sheathe me."

She slides off my desk and drops to her knees, before grabbing my trunks by the front waistband, stretching them out far enough to bypass my hard cock, and then pulls them down to my thighs with my pants. "Fuck, your cock is big," she says as she grips the base in her fist, not even covering half my length. "I want it in my mouth first."

Placing the condom packet between her teeth she tears it open, blowing the torn off section onto the floor, before sliding her index finger in the opening and hooking it over the rubber, removing it. She lets the wrapper fall to the floor and places her mouth over the head of my dick. It fills the width of her mouth completely. She moans as her tongue swirls around the head. Her glands release saliva, coating it, and then she takes me to the back of her throat.

The sounds coming from her throat cause a vibration against my head as she deep throats my cock, still not consuming my length fully; always the best part about getting your dick sucked. I grab the back of her head as she pulls back and shove it down the length of my dick until it hits against the back of her throat again. I can feel her throat contract from the slight gag of being caught off guard, but she controls herself. My fist clenches around her brown hair, close to the roots, to hold her head still. "Let me fuck your mouth."

She stills, preparing to take it, evening out her breathing through her nose. I pull back and thrust forward, then set a steady pace, but fast. "Fuck yeah." She suctions around me each time I pull out, making the fit tighter, and starts massaging my balls in her hand. My head falls back and I close my eyes briefly, before looking back down at her as she sucks my dick.

I pull out completely and grab the base of my long, thick cock. The veins are full, protruding to make room for the extra blood flow. She looks up at me, knowing I'm ready for her to roll the condom on. She does, and then stands. I turn her around and push her onto her knees in the chair, holding onto the chair back.

She pushes her ass out as I step behind her to give me enough of an angle that I can slide inside her pussy without coming out. I grab her hip in one hand to steady her as I position the head of my cock at her entrance, then thrust inside and move the hand from the base of my cock as I become buried deep inside of her. She screams out in a cry of pleasure. *Not tight enough for me.*

I can feel one of the alternate cameramen changing locations to get a different shot. I know enough that it'll be a body shot of me and a full shot of her while I fuck her, zooming in on the part that the viewers want to watch–her pussy being fucked to hell and back. The two different cameras will alternate between her facials as my big dick pleases her and my cock being shoved in and out of her pussy when this is all put together, making it all look seamless and nothing manipulated. Every viewer will have my dick and her pussy memorized.

I reach around her and place my finger on her clit, quickly rubbing up and down over it to bring her to a quick release. Her moaning becomes louder and verbally enhanced as she presses her ass against me to take me deeper, her pussy getting greedy for more. Entry becomes slicker as she comes again, lubricating my dick even more. It's slick, wet, and she's tightening around my cock. The tug in my balls starts. I pull out and remove the condom. "Turn around," I command.

She does as I grab my dick in my hand, her hands immediately taking residence on her tits, pushing them toward the center. "Open for me," I demand, as I begin stroking my cock.

Her mouth opens, watching me as I stroke myself to release. The warm semen starts to spurt from the head of my dick, landing in her mouth and around it, some on her chest. She holds her position until I'm done, before licking her lips and swallowing, then presses her fake tits toward her mouth as she brings her head down to meet them, licking what's coating her cleavage.

I immediately pull my pants up my legs, shoving my cock back in its place. "Three weeks is all I can give. At that point not even your pussy can bail you out. You're dismissed. I have work to do."

"Cut." I look up as the director shouts the cue that filming has stopped . . . for now at least. He stands from his chair and begins walking on set as a crewmember hands Veronica a towel to rid her face of my cum. "That was good, but something is missing. I'm just not fucking sure what. Take thirty and we will film again with the addition. Got it?"

I nod. "Alright, I'll be in my dressing room. Just let me know the changes."

"You need me to send a fluffer in twenty to get you ready?"

"Nope. Pills should have me covered for a few hours."

I walk past him, headed for some Listerine to wash my fucking mouth out. It's going to be a long night. I can see it already. By tomorrow I'll despise my cock and anything that most men crave shoving it into. This is only the beginning of what it takes to film porn . . . and to think some out there actually think it's easy. All there is to it is fucking, right? A free-for-all pussy that you get paid to hit. Wrong. I wouldn't even know what normal fucking is anymore. A few more days and this project will be done. Then I get a short break before my agent offers me something else and it starts all over again. Fucking has never been so complicated . . .

CHAPTER TWO

Kambry

I prop up on my elbows as I look out at the Pacific Ocean from behind my shades. "This is the life, isn't it?"

My head turns at the sound of Meredith's voice as she flips to lie face down on her beach towel in her bikini, her head facing toward me. I'm assuming her eyes are open behind her sunglasses. "It's different, that's for sure. We definitely aren't in Alabama anymore. Even after this long it's still kind of surreal."

That night I left Meredith's house I went home and talked with my mom, asking one last time if she would consider letting me stay in the dorm, even at the junior college so that I could get the full college experience. I barely got the word dorm out of my mouth before she narrowed her eyes at me and sent me to my room, not even acknowledging my request.

I laid in bed for hours, thinking and staring at the ceiling. I finally came to the conclusion that Meredith was right. I don't want the same things that my parents want for me. They should want to support my dreams and help me achieve them, not keep me away from living. They've sheltered me all of my life; protecting is what they call it, only it's been more like smothering. For me to not even be the preacher's kid you would think I was. Don't get me wrong, I love my parents and I was blessed with a loving family, but after eighteen years it's time to release their hold on me. Some parents are all but shoving their kids out the door at eighteen. Even my brother got to go off to college where he wanted.

It's not like I was asking for anything horrible. Geez, you would think I was begging for a boob job or something. I bet they would like that; food for thought. I just want to experience college like normal eighteen-year-olds. So what if I make a few mistakes. Isn't that how you learn? I may come home drunk or get heartbroken a few times. I'm sure I'll still live to tell about it someday. Isn't that what life is supposed to be about? To live with no regrets . . . You're supposed to reach adulthood with mistakes, with bad decisions, and with good.

Then I got mad. My entire life I've been good. I wasn't allowed to even go out with boys until I was sixteen—if that's what you call what I got to do—when I started dating Kyle. Let's face it, that's not the end of the world. That's just a difference in parents' opinions. I respected it, but even then my dad was a psycho about it when he let me go somewhere, which wasn't often, always watching and calling and ensuring he knew where I was, making me come home at nine until I was a senior, and then so graciously bumped me up to ten. I remember his exact words were, *nothing good happens after ten o'clock p.m.*, yet I never questioned him, came home late, or pushed his limits, and I still got treated like a child.

So I'm done. If he wants to treat me like a bad kid, I'll give him a reason to.

I waited till they went to sleep, got up and packed as much of my stuff that would fit in my luggage set my aunt bought me in hopes I could come visit when she moved. I only took what I was capable of carrying myself without waking them up. When I had everything ready, I quietly snuck out of my window, leaving a note on my pillow. It was probably the only moment in my entire life that I was thankful I didn't have a dog. It was the only way out of the house without tripping the alarm since I cut the wire last year when Meredith talked me into it. It was her scheme to get me to a party since we live next door to each other. I never was brave enough to sneak out, though, but my parents never even noticed that I did it.

I'm just glad that my parents don't have a two-story house, because escape was fairly easy. I waddled my petite frame loaded down with two duffle bags and a large rolling suitcase across my lawn to Meredith's black Honda Accord promptly at 4AM and chucked them in the backseat. I've never seen her cheese as big as when she pushed off of her car to give me a hand.

That was two months ago . . .

Shortly after we arrived in Los Angeles my parents disconnected my phone. They didn't even call me to see if I arrived safely. I could have died in a car crash and I guess they wouldn't have cared. I waited two weeks for them to call, thinking they would be worried and cut it back on, but they didn't. They act like they no longer have a daughter, all because I wanted to find out who exactly I'm meant to be.

I won't lie. It stung. I cried for a while, refusing to leave the apartment and only spending my graduation money on food. Then one Friday it clicked. If my parents want to act childish and not think about my feelings, then two can play that game. I'm going to live for me. I'm going to do what I want to do. My parents' morals can kiss my ass. I finally said screw them. I can make it just fine on my own.

That night was the first time I ever set foot in a nightclub. I had never seen anything like it. The music, the lights, and the carefree environment hooked me, even without being able to legally drink; although it really wasn't that hard to get alcohol. Every time I turned around some guy offered to buy me one. One guy even said he'd keep them coming if I'd just talk for him. Mississippi girl he called me. That's not even where I'm from. One southern accent does not make us all the same. It did make me smile, though, so I guess it wasn't so bad. The next day I went back and applied for a job, and to my surprise, after a few days the manager called me for an interview; my first one ever. And I had the nerves to show for it.

I've been working there ever since.

"Are you starting to regret coming with me?"

Her face remains serious, but I know she's baiting me. I smile. "Heck no. Are you going to come out tonight? I work till close."

"I will if you come to an open audition like you keep saying you will." She rolls over and props up to mirror my position.

I look back out at the water, glancing around at the bodies occupying the beach. My eyes pinpoint a surfer as he stands on the board and balances himself at the perfect moment that the wave folds. I'll never get tired of this place. "I don't know, Meredith. I'm kind of shy. You're the outgoing one. I would probably freeze and forget my lines, even if it is just one. Then I would look like an idiot and be embarrassed."

"That may have worked two months ago, and I've let it go till now. You work at one of the hottest night clubs in LA and you have come out of your shell more in the last two months than I've seen you your entire life. We've always been the blonde besties. You're gorgeous, Kambry. It's time you started seeing yourself in the mirror like everyone else has always seen you. You're hot, girl. What are you so afraid of?"

She turns on her side and raises her glasses on top of her head, a mischievous grin spreading. "I'll make a deal with you. We're going to play a little game: *How to lose a guy in ten days* style with a spin. You, Blondie, are going to play Kate Hudson's role. Tonight, I'm picking out one guy of my choice in the club. You have no say in the matter. I know your taste so he'll be cute. When I point him out to you, you have to go introduce yourself, serve up some drinks, and maybe start some small talk. Celebrity or not you're going to flirt, Meredith's way, which is shamelessly, and then turn and walk away. If he comes to find you, you have to give him a chance for more . . . like an extended night into the wee hours of the morning. If he tries to hook up and you're genuinely into him but don't go through with it out of fear, then you have to come to the next open audition with me, no questions asked."

"You're suggesting I hook up with someone I don't even know? Isn't that kind of slutty?"

"This is LA, baby. We can do whatever we want here. We can be free. Are you scared *Daddy dearest* will find out?" With a smirk on her face she pulls her shades back into place and rolls back onto her back, before tilting her head back to get some sun.

She knows that's my trigger. "As much as I love you, sometimes you're a bitch. How have I put up with you all of these years?"

"Because you want to be just like me. You just need a little push in the right direction. You'll thank me later."

"Fine. What are you going to be doing while all of this is going on? I could just lie, you know."

"But you won't. And you're a terrible liar." She hums her amusement. "I, love, am going to find the nearest hot bartender or bouncer and sweet talk my way into getting a wrist band, and maybe even a bedmate, since someone won't liven up and make some hot friends over twenty-one already. Must I do everything? We need connections, Kambry. Use your job for your benefit, for ours."

"You're doing my makeup then. I'm taking full advantage of all those hours you've put in working at Sephora. I'm glad they ended up letting you transfer. More free stuff for me." I grin in a sarcastic manner, and then become serious again. "You blame antisocialism on me, but it's not that easy to liven up when you're working and completely sober just like the other members of staff and everyone else in the club is drunk. It complicates things, and by the time it's closing most of us just want to go home and crash. I have to deal with guys trying to grope my ass all night."

She ignores my rambling as her face rises to the sight in front of her, as if she can smell the salty water mixed with man sweat from the heat. "Hello, gorgeous," she says, now totally oblivious to any prior conversation we were having. "I will never tire of looking at California boys." She's officially gone, her head now reeling in some fantasy that has a possibility of coming true depending on her mood.

I really envy her most days. It's so easy for her. I want to be that bold, and I could be, if I could just figure out how to break the ice. I mean, how does an eighteen, almost nineteen-year-old virgin go about ridding of her V-card when it's not my fault I'm even still hanging on to it. I've thought of just pretending it doesn't exist, but I fear that my lack of experience would give me away. Best friends have to be good for something, right?

I stand, quickly gathering my things. "Where are you going? We still have hours before you have to be at work. You cannot tell me you're done beaching it already. We pretty much just got here."

"If I'm going to have a chance in hell at winning this bet tonight I need all the prep time I can get. I've hooked up—okay made out, and maybe some heavy petting—with Kyle, and on several occasions, but I've gotten so good at pressing the stop button before sex that it's become a reflex. I need a tips and tricks session with Mer."

Her face takes on a star-struck expression and she stands so fast I'm surprised she didn't trip over herself before she's able to pick up her things. "I've never been so excited to help de-virginize someone. It's time my precious flower. It's time."

"Wow. You just took this to a whole new level of weird."

She laughs. "Shut up, asshole."

She reaches down for a handful of sand and I take off running through the maze of people before she can toss it at me. Work should be interesting tonight. In this strange, unexplainable way, I'm excited more than nervous. Maybe I do just need a push . . . Finally!

"I'm so jealous of your rack," she screams over the music while grabbing her drink off the bar, and then winks at Liam, the bartender, laying cash down for him to pick up. "How the hell do you get blessed with size D perky cups and a tiny waistline when you don't even use them? The universe is cruel sometimes. I'm getting a boob job. I swear it. That dress looks so much better on you. Keep it."

I look down at the short, tight, black dress that has a cutout pattern surrounding the very low-cut V neckline that twists with the bottom piece of fabric between my boobs, enhancing the visibility of my cleavage, as I wait on Liam to fill my drink order. I have always had a rather large bust size and a small waistline, very small, as in a size zero to two depending on the brand. That's why people at school have referred to me as a human Barbie since puberty. It's not the most common body frame, I'm aware, but my mother is a heavier set woman with a large bust as well and my dad used to be scrawny until middle age set in, so I guess I lucked out with the best qualities of the two. That could be one reason they never let me out of their sight. My body type has always made me look older than I am, drawing male attention, and topped off with the platinum blonde hair, well, you get the point. That term, Barbie, actually makes me cringe.

I glance at the neon wristband on her left arm only given to those twenty-one and up. I'm not sure how she got rid of the stamps that mark her age, but she's always been a partier, so I'm sure she has tricks most would never consider. Meredith was the flamboyant one in high school. Her parents aren't that strict, so she barely had to give any details at all on her whereabouts once we started driving. She's been sneaking into clubs with fake IDs since we were only sixteen. She's lied about one magical question to guys so many times I'm surprised she even remembers her real age anymore. The number of guys that have committed statutory rape without even being aware is mind blowing. "I take it you successfully seduced a member of staff into looking the other way while he upped your age a few years?"

She places the straw between her lips and sips. "I'll reward him later. No need to wait for me when you leave." She winks and then extends the drink to me. "Want some?"

"No. I can't get caught drinking. I'll lose my job. You need to be careful. There is an occasional undercover cop in here trying to catch people underage drinking."

She takes another sip and wraps her arm around my shoulders, pulling me to her. She kisses my temple. "No worries, love. My new ID will be in next week. This one is legit, with my face, state watermark, and all. I'm paying out the ass for it. Plus, it's all about confidence, boo. It can make you or break you."

"Kambry, your order is done," Liam says, interrupting us.

I turn to look at him and pick up my tray. "Thanks, Liam."

I've been assigned to Liam all night to fill my drink orders. The manager likes doing it that way. Makes it easier to split tips at the end of the night. I move it and get the weight of the tray balanced on my arm so that I can walk in my heels without spilling any drinks or toppling over. "I've got to deliver these. I'll be back after I circulate."

She places her clutch under her arm and continues to nurse her fruity concoction. "You do that, gorgeous. I'm about to scout myself. I have a man to pick out for you. You better bring your A-game."

I roll my eyes. "Please don't be mean. Make it a cute one. Karma is real."

"Oh, doll face, I would never pick out an ugly man. You just leave that to me. I have to give you some competition. Leaving."

We split in different directions and I make my way around my assigned section of the club, delivering the orders and collecting tips. With each new person I approach, I put on my best flirty smile as I introduce myself and ask if there is anything they want, occasionally running my fingers through my long, blonde, curled hair as I write down the order on my pad.

I notice the manager wave me over to the wall he's standing at, watching the club to ensure things run smoothly but out of direct sight. I tuck my now empty tray to my side and make my way toward him close enough I can hear and speak. "Yes, sir?"

"First of all, don't call me fucking sir. Understood?"

I nod, nervously. "Sorry. It's a habit I guess."

"Break it." Drake is about thirty-five, pretty hot, and cool as shit. He makes working here fun. Word is, among the other female drink servers, that if he likes you, you go far. If not, you won't last long. I'm still in my ninety-day trial period since I was hired. This is a popular club, and high-end celebrities utilize the VIP section because they can come here unbothered. Only the top servers get to work that section, and they each sign a confidentiality waiver prior to doing so. From what I've seen, those girls have the arrogance to go along with that job title. It intimidates me to be honest. I would probably stand there and gawk if I saw someone famous. I'm fine to stay away from there and remain with the normal people.

His eyes swipe down my body for the first time tonight, since I haven't seen him until now. "Good choice. You're blossoming beautifully since you first started. You ready to earn your stripes?"

I blink as I stare at him like an idiot. "I'll do anything you need. What's up?"

"Amanda had to leave suddenly and unexpected, throwing up, so she must have a virus or something. I can't have customers catching something at my club. Can you take her spot? I have a small section reserved that should be arriving within the next fifteen minutes or so."

My eyes widen. "Amanda, as in, Amanda Matthews, your best VIP server?" My stomach twists and turns. She's a bitch from what I hear, but supposedly all of the high-end clients like her. She has obtained a reputation for private sessions away from the club, but since she never talks about it, it's all hearsay. People that work downstairs talk, even when you're not conversing directly. Gossip gets around.

"Is that going to be a problem for you? I've been watching you over the last, what, couple of months, give or take? I think you'll be fine, but you have to leave nerves down here or they will eat you alive. Got it?"

My breathing heightens. What if I screw this up? I thought I was pretty good at my job, especially for it to be my first. My parents never allowed me to work in high school. In the entire time I've been here I've never gotten a complaint or an unhappy customer, but now I'm starting to doubt myself. "Are you sure I'm ready?"

He nods his head to the hallway at his left and starts walking. I follow him into his office before he shuts the door and pins me against the wall by placing his palms flush with the wall. He actually makes me comfortable, so it doesn't make me feel awkward. "This remains between us, but Amanda is pregnant. The second she starts to show she's gone. This club has an image to uphold. I need to start training her replacement before she leaves. If you can do this, I will more than double your hourly pay, but you'll also get bigger tips. You're a sweet girl, Kambry, but I need you to find your alter ego. I need you to be a nice bitch. Yes, it's a contradiction. When you go up there they are no better than you. Do you want it or not?"

I stare into his brown eyes, thinking. I don't know if I want this kind of pressure to do well at work, but then something Meredith said repeats itself in my mind. *We need connections, Kambry. Use your job for your benefit, for ours.* She's right. She gave me the chance to get out from under my parents, as well as her parents, by paying our rent. She wants to be an actress. It's why she moved here: her attempt at stardom. I'm just happy to be away from the sheltered little girl in Bama. Anything else is just a bonus to me, but I owe her to at least try.

Put your big girl panties on, Kambry.

"I'll do it. Just tell me what to do."

He smiles and pushes off the wall. "Good girl. For starters, go put on some lipstick. I want color on your lips." I nod as he opens the door to let me exit. "Which bartender do you work best with?"

"Liam, the one you've assigned me with this week. Why?" Liam is the only one that seems the most like people back home that I grew up with. It could be because he seems to be one of the youngest of the bartenders. Being around him gives me a sense of comfort; more so than anyone else I've met here. I like him. He's mentioned hanging out a few times so I could meet some people, I've just yet to actually do it in my attempt to sock away as much money as possible. I have been trying to form a cushion to replace what I've spent of my graduation money for emergencies before I really do anything fun.

"I'll send him up with you until you get used to it. The environment is a little different. Go touch up your face and meet me back at the end of the hall. I'll walk you upstairs."

I nod and walk out of his office, before making my way to my locker, barely able to breathe. To some people this may not be anything to freak out over, but to someone that has been smothered socially my entire adolescence it's terrifying. I'm still learning to live openly and uninhibited. I want so badly to not have to try in meet and greets with other people my age, but the truth is I was never allowed to go to sleepovers or parties. What time I got with friends was at school or monitored closely, but those are the people you grow up with. It's different. I'm that girl that stands there awkwardly not knowing what to say while Meredith draws all of the attention in the room to her. It's the main reason I haven't gone to any open auditions like she wants me to. I'm still shy and I hate it. I'm just not there yet.

My parents only allowed friends to stay over at my house, but by the time we were old enough to drive most people didn't have ten o'clock curfews, so most of the time it was me at home with my parents while everyone else was out having fun, and me wishing I was with them. Or I had Kyle sitting at my house in the game room within earshot of my parents. This job has helped me, but I still have a long way to go, and this is not a time when I want to sound stupid in front of important people.

I look up at the ceiling as I open my locker. "Please keep me calm. Don't let me freak out and look dumb. This once just let me be a natural." I quickly pull out my cell phone and send a quick text to Meredith before having to put it back up.

Me: Hey . . . there has been a change of plans. I have to work upstairs. We will talk later. I don't have much time to explain.

I toss it back inside of my purse and grab my makeup bag, before doing exactly as I was told. I'm going to show my parents and everyone else that I'm not the good girl they've tagged me as. I don't care what I have to do. No regrets from here on out, and innocent is a stigma I'm happy to lose . . .

CHAPTER THREE

Saxton

The car pulls up to the VIP entrance of the club to let me out. Filming finished on my last project a few days ago and I thought I was going to get a break; even thought about booking a plane ticket and just taking off for a bit. I don't even care where. I want to get out of LA for a while, to catch my breath, and to give my dick a rest. Sounds insane to most people I suppose. Then, as I was looking through flight options, I received a call from a producer about something he thought I might be interested in.

Yeah, good luck with that, I thought. Sex doesn't hold the same enticing thoughts for me that it used to. I don't even have sex anymore unless I'm getting paid for it. Hell, nothing gets me up anymore without a small pill. Come to think of it, I'm basically a legalized male prostitute. A dry laugh escapes.

Regardless of the title, this is my job and I'm good at it. What the hell else am I going to do? Not a damn thing. I walked away from college and I'm used to the money. I don't get paid for emotions. I get paid to fuck and to come, to make her come, and to make it good enough that people continue to buy my films, so I agreed to attend this meeting with him and a director I've worked with before, though I don't anticipate that it will be anything different than usual.

I open the door of the car and exit, before making my way to the club entrance. I give the doorman my ID, not having to say a word while he checks the list and lets me in. The stairs are located on the inside of the door. I climb them, knowing exactly where to go. This isn't my first time here. They will be waiting at a seating area they have reserved already.

The music is loud, drowning out the conversations of the familiar celebrities that came out tonight. Most of us know who the others are, and the few that may not, it doesn't take long to find out. The lighting is dim throughout the entire room, spotlights located above each section of seating that consists of two oversized, half-moon shaped couches surrounding a small round table.

I glance around the room, taking note of who's here, before picking out the correct table and making my way toward it. They immediately stand as I approach, holding out their hands for me to shake. I do, and then take a seat across from them as Michael, the producer, waves someone over, and then sits back down. "How are you," he asks. "It's been a while."

"Same shit, different day," I laugh mockingly. "But I'm sure you know that. I guess we should get straight to it. What's supposed to have me dying to get back in front of the camera so soon? I hear you have a new project in the works. What's the theme this time? College student bangs mother and daughter duo? Or are we going to find our own Mrs. Robinson with our very own mock Christian Grey . . . Isn't that what has every woman dripping wet these days?" I lean forward, lowering my voice some. "I'm not sure I'd make a good submissive trained dominant."

Michael rolls his eyes. "Can we try to remain professional?"

Someone approaches based on the sound of heels tapping against the floor that suddenly halts. My head slightly tilts, taking in a pair of black and hot pink stilettos pressed firmly against the floor. I shift my body to reach for my wallet as I take her in from the legs up, one slender inch at a time. "What can I get for you, gentlemen?"

"Refills on ours and whatever he wants," Michael says. "Keep them coming and put it on my tab."

"As you wish, sir." Her voice is soft and she has an accent. She sounds a little nervous, swallowing every few seconds to the point that it's visible. Small mouth. Long, enticing neck. I wonder if she's a screamer . . .

What the fuck?

I lean back against the couch and bring my arm to rest on the back, my eyes deciding to temporarily freeze on her cleavage as it rises and falls from her breathing. Nice rack. My vision finally ascends, taking in the pink splotchy patches on her chest and neck along the way to her face. "And you, sir? What would you like?"

No sound registers as I watch her full, pink-stained lips move with the words that exit. Those would be nice wrapped around a cock. "Saxton, are you going to order?"

I clear my throat at the sound of Michael's voice and my eyes meet her baby blue ones. "Shit. Bud light—bottle. Thanks."

She pauses briefly and then blinks, diverting her eyes away from mine. "Sure. I'll have that right out and then I'll get these empty glasses out of your way." Her eyes veer back to mine and her fucking lips draw my attention again as she rubs them together. "My name is Kambry if you need anything."

"I'll keep that in mind, Kambry."

Then she turns and walks away, slightly flipping her long, blonde hair off of her shoulder as if she doesn't really know what else to do. I clear my throat again, but a little deeper this time. My brows dip. It's almost an awkward action, unlike the majority of girls that do it, but her barely covered ass swaying dramatically from side to side immediately sways my attention, until she disappears from sight.

She's hot.

I pull my foot up to rest on my opposite thigh and grab my ankle, before turning to Michael and James, the director I'm assuming he's using for this project that he seems to think I won't want to pass up. They look at each other, as if they are having a mental conversation that I wasn't invited into, and then back at me. "What? So this project . . ."

Michael inches forward on the couch, before leaning forward, and then places his forearms on top of his thighs. "Not that the industry is really lacking in sales, but there is always room for expansion. Corporate wants to go in a different direction after coming together and surveying several hundred people about what it is they want to purchase, specifically, or what would it take to make them want to purchase if they're not already. In the past we've geared the films mostly toward men and their likes, because that was what our audience mostly consisted of. But after the recent survey responses were recorded, we found out that the industry actually has a pretty large percentage of couple viewers. Not only that, but also some women, which led them to the next question: what would you want to see differently in new material that isn't readily available in large quantities? And to our surprise the answer was fairly simple."

A napkin is sat down on top of the glass top table in front of each of them, followed by two tumblers filled with honey-colored liquid, and then a repeat action with the sweating dark brown bottle in front of me. I turn my head to a set of tits staring at me as she reaches for the empty glasses that were already here before I arrived. My mouth waters, wanting to lightly bite the smooth globe as I find her nipple. The scent of her perfume invades my nose.

Without thought I grab her hip. If she comes any closer my thoughts are going to become actions. Her skin jumps as my hand comes in contact with her body. Her eyes settle on mine. "I'm sorry. Please excuse me." Her tone changes to one of embarrassment and she immediately pulls away.

"Don't sweat it." I look up at her. Her cheeks are flushed, making me curious. I've never seen a server in a VIP section full of celebrities so . . . vulnerable and shy? "Are you always this nervous with customers or do I make you uncomfortable?"

Her expression freezes. She barely pulls her bottom lip between her teeth. That beautiful fucking mouth as her top teeth lightly skim the skin. Damn. "Uh. Again, I'm really sorry. I normally work downstairs. We were shorthanded so I'm helping out, and a little thrown off tonight being out of my element. It was a last minute change. I'll leave you to your meeting and keep an eye on your drinks."

There is something intriguing about her. She smiles and walks off to attend to her other customers, making a stop at Justin Talbert's table. He's looking at her exactly like I've seen him looking at the cocktail servers in here before . . . as if she's an easy lay and one he's planning to conquer. Last time it was that girl that's usually in this section the times I have been here. I'm sure the rich prick will use his star status to lure her into his limo later. *Not in my fucking lifetime.*

Jesus, I sound like a fucking psycho.

"Saxton, are you ready to continue?"

I look at Michael. Fuck. What is wrong with me? I'm way past unprofessional. I work to gather my thoughts. "Sorry. Yeah. Couple viewers . . . Go ahead." I pick up my beer and place the opening to my mouth, before turning it up, waiting for that first bite to the taste buds that is the best taste of any and all you'll drink after.

"They want to see plots more relatable: less fantasy and more realism. Something that can turn them both on instead of turning off the average woman when she thinks of porn. The viewers are requesting natural erotic scenarios that they can use in their own relationships as a spark or a guide. Men getting laid are happy men, and women that don't feel they have to compete with other women are more willing to want sex, so we did a panel interview with males and females. We wanted to get a feel for the best of both parties. And since you know a little something about *Fifty Shades of Grey*, then you'll understand the next part. The fact is, the romance book market is at an all-time high right now, spurring sexy images and gifs going viral on media platforms like *Tumblr* and *Instagram*, so we know there is an outlet to pull in more women. But to be okay with erotica, they need the story to go with it, and not some taboo shit like 'college student bangs a mother and daughter duo' or secretive in-house stepsibling storylines that you won't likely see with normal relationships. Men could give two shits less about the story, because we just aren't wired that way. The average male hates reading, especially romance, and prefers the visual images of what their partners are wanting from romance novels; the story with the erotic aspects weaved in. For most of us men, the closest we get to reading is *Maxim* magazine or *Playboy*."

He pauses as if he's gathering what else he needs to say, and I'm sure to take a breath, wetting his mouth with a sip from his glass. But also probably making sure I'm getting it like I'm fucking stupid. I have a lot of time to know what's going on in the world, guy related or not.

I raise my brows and my bottle in the air for him to continue, having nothing in particular to say at the moment. James is sitting quietly like he has this entire time, knowing his place in this meeting. Just like me he's chasing a paycheck. "If we can make it to where more women *want* to watch explicit material with their partners, sales will spike significantly, because men won't have to hide it anymore. I think we've been going at it from the wrong angle, because the problem is that each market seems to be geared toward gender, so we've decided to combine the two. There has to be a happy medium."

"How are you going to do that?" I ask.

He smiles, backed by what seems to be real excitement. "By taking the best of all those that have somewhat tried in the past. We are going to follow one couple in a mini, reality television series: a mock relationship. You remember those shows, *The real world* and *Jersey Shore*?"

I nod. "Chick T.V. at its finest with too much drama weaved in. How can I ever forget? My sister used to watch them all the time."

"Maybe if we listened to women more often we'd be a hell of a lot further already. Those formulas work for a reason. Anyway, there are always at least two roommates that end up hooking up and in a relationship, so just subtract the rest of the meaningless roommates and the camera doesn't stop filming or hide when sex happens. In the sense of porn—we want the sex to be more natural and the chemistry between the couple more believable, without it all being staged and scripted. The goal is to still allow the viewers to become immersed by following along week to week like the other shows before, from the perspective of watching a developing couple through reality TV—X rated. It's a proven fact that people need and thrive on gossip, drama, sex, and love for entertainment. It's why freelance photographers and paparazzi are everywhere. Public couples in the media go viral. Look at Hollywood. You remember all the big couples at one time: Justin Timberlake and Britney Spears, Reese Witherspoon and Ryan Phillippe, Paris Hilton and Nick Carter, Nick Lachey and Jessica Simpson, or Justin Bieber and Selena Gomez just to name a few. You get my drift. We want to give them the illusion of a real life relationship by letting them see every aspect with no censoring. The men get the sex and the women get the love story. Boom." His hand gesture mimics an explosion. "Happy couples everywhere."

He sits back after picking up his drink and drapes his arm over the back of the couch, waiting for me to give some input. I'm not really sure how to respond. Sounds a little whack to me, but I don't get paid to plot, I get paid to act. "Explain the stipulations."

He takes another sip of his drink to relieve his dry mouth from the long-winded talking. "We will provide the two of you with a house set up for filming that you will both live in for about six months. Like previous shows both of you will show up on the first day, meet, and get to know each other. Again, we want it to be natural, so there aren't any rules except for one. There are also a few things required that you'll find outlined in your contract if you decide to accept the role."

"What's the one rule?"

"During the term of your contract you will not be allowed to have sexual relations with anyone else. Again, couples in public eye go viral quickly, and one slip of you fucking another girl, even off set, has the potential to ruin the entire project. Hardly anyone buys the whole 'open relationship' thing. You and your costar should only have sex with each other where cameras are recording, which should be on the two of you at all times. Basically no trying to sneak to remote places once filming has begun. After all, we are paying you for the material. This project will be a real life simulation, so scenarios are still being discussed and will be given in more detail later."

I take another gulp of my beer and set the bottle down, straighten my posture, and then rub my hands over my face. "Let me see if I have this straight. So basically you want me to *pretend* to be in a relationship with another *porn star*, yet you want it to be *natural* attraction. I don't even buy it, much less normal people. Tell me exactly how you expect that to work. I may be an actor, but I don't think any of us are that good."

A smile spreads across his face as if he's about to sprinkle the sugar on top of the shit he's feeding me, expecting that to make it taste good. "We aren't using an established porn star. We are casting for a female that's never appeared in a film at all. It's the only way. We think that will make it more believable and raise the ratings, by sparking the curiosity of the viewer, giving them a sense of an emotional connection knowing she's raw. It shouldn't be too hard. Girls will do anything to gain fame—just look at *Girls Gone Wild*—but we need a young, attractive male to offer them. What better marketing strategy for fresh girls is there than searching for the girl that can make a porn star fall in love? Something mildly similar: *The Bachelor*. That's why we want you."

"I just don't think it's that simple," I interrupt. "You can't just put two people in a house and expect them to like each other. The difference in all those shows and this idea is that there are more people involved to give it an edge, to give you options. Haven't you ever heard of a blind date from hell? That's what this sounds like. I don't think I'm interested." I pick up my beer and finish it off, before setting the empty bottle back on the table.

He nods his head toward the center of the room. "Not even if we can get her?"

My head turns to one hot blonde walking with a tray of drinks in our direction. "You think you're going to get that girl . . . to film porn? She's awkward, shy, and nervous when she's the center of attention. I'm going to guess she's probably never had a one-night stand in her life. She acts like one that holds out for a while, and you seem to think she's going to jump in bed with a guy that's been with too many to count in front of a camera?"

"Yet the idea still appeals to you . . . doesn't it? Or have you not even noticed the boner you've been sporting since she walked up to this table?" Again, words being said with no meaning, because she's headed this way. Legs for fucking days, and length to height ratio is incredible. I've never seen a more perfect sized rack that would spill out of even a large-handed handful. She has a pair of lips that would wrap so tightly around my dick, and I imagine her pussy isn't as used as the ones I'm used to . . .

"Fuck," I mumble.

Two masculine chuckles occur. "Haven't seen that happen in a while."

I cover my face and close my eyes, a low moan escaping, when I realize exactly what the fuck just happened. My propped foot falls to the floor and I quickly lean forward so that my ass is flush with the back of the couch, trying to hide my arousal—the erection that occurred without a fucking synthetic pill. "Are you okay?" she asks as she sets a fresh cold beer down in front of me. "Is something wrong with the beer?"

I can't even remember the last time I lost control over my dick. I need a boner kill. Preferably sooner than later, because this is one time a guy with a smaller dick has the advantage over guys like me, and this meeting should be wrapping up. At least they can somewhat make it less obvious, but me . . . not a chance in hell. I'll be walking around with a rather large bulge next to my zipper, running down the inside of my thigh or toward my waistband, depending on which way it decides to lay.

When I say I have a big dick, it's not a shit-talking attention-seeking ploy to impress a girl. Actually those guys are usually the smallest. Guys with big dicks don't talk about it, because they don't have to. Those secrets never stay secrets for long. Genetics just decided I needed a longer and thicker dick than the average male for some reason. I didn't just up and decide I have a big dick. Girls have told me so since I started whipping it out in high school trying to get it wet. It's one thing that got me into porn so quickly. It's really not even anything to brag about like most would think, because any real man that's scored a few times knows that sometimes it's more of a fucking hassle than a good thing, especially with a tight pussy.

I do know of one thing that should rid me of a boner quickly. I have a guaranteed turn off. One thing that fucking disgusts me is blood. It's always made me weak in the stomach. I have no desire to earn my redwings or fuck in a warzone. Anything that bleeds for several days and doesn't die is immortal in my book, so I proceed with caution. My dipstick better come out just as clean as when I went for a lube check. It's nasty, it's unclean, it's uncalled for, and I get enough sex that I don't need it when a girl is on her rag.

I uncover my face and I'm again staring face to tits at her cleavage as she picks up my now empty bottle. So much for getting rid of my hard-on . . . What's funny is I really don't think she's doing it on purpose like a girl trying to draw attention to herself. "The beer is fine."

"Okay, then. Is there anything else I can get you?"

I'm just now realizing what kind of accent she has. One very different than what usually walks the streets of LA. It's sexy as hell in person to be honest. It's southern. It's been a long time since I've been around one of those. There is usually only a few reasons an accent like that is this far from home, the biggest being to come out west to try and make it onto the big screen. Chasing Hollywood . . .

I look at Michael, and then back at her nearly naked figure. "I do have a question."

She blinks, clearly caught off guard. "Okay."

"Are you here for an acting career, Kambry?"

"Not really." She gives me a half smile. "I'm just here for something different than I'm used to, but my best friend is, so I guess I'm really just tagging along."

I stand, finished with this conversation, and hoping like hell I'm not as hard as I think I am, but I'm about ninety-nine point nine percent sure that I am. When you go through twenty-five years with something attached to you, there is no guessing when it decides to do what it was intended for at the worst fucking time. The only thing that keeps this from being an awkward situation is that most of the people that would take notice have probably seen my dick in its entirety, and in use.

I place my hand on her neck, tilting her head back so that she is looking directly into my eyes. "That's unfortunate. Maybe you should rethink that answer."

I press my body closer to hers, and her mouth parts when she feels my dick pressed against her. Her cheeks are quickly changing in shade, deepening from any color of red they've been so far. She swallows. "If you're here then there's clearly a reason. Keep an open mind, Kambry."

I press my lips to hers to get a taste, a feel, because, well . . . I wanted to. My tongue slides into the crevice between her lips. She makes no attempt to move, to stop me. Instead, her lips conform around mine and she touches her tongue to mine, just before I let her go. She stares into my eyes and touches her fingertips to her lips as if she's deciding whether that really happened or not and then realized it was a very bad idea upon confirmation. "Just let it happen."

She'll figure out what that means. I look at Michael, and James—who makes no attempt to wipe the knowing smirk off his face—both staring, watching it play out as if I've lost my fucking mind but proving their point at the same time. Maybe I have. "I'll call you tomorrow and give you an answer, even though I'm pretty sure I just confirmed what it's going to be." I give them a cocky smirk in return. "Looks like you have your work cut out for you if you want me to sign that line. Ladies first." I wink. "Night boys. Thanks for the beer."

I place my hand against her hip and close in beside her ear, whispering where only she can hear me. "Maybe I'll see you later, beautiful."

Then I walk off, taking my fucking ass out of this club before I do something highly immoral to the general public, because that girl is not ready for me . . . yet.

CHAPTER FOUR

Kambry

I make it to my locker and grab ahold of the swinging door after opening it, steadying myself to remove my heels. My feet are killing me. Most heels are not made for wide-footed girls, and they're certainly not made to wear hours at a time. I have small feet—petite yes, narrow no. Walking around in six-inch heels while carrying a tray full of drinks without falling or spilling anything is not that easy. At this point I'm actually convinced it's a talent.

I grab both stilettos in one fist, letting the shoes dangle while I pull my duffle bag out of my locker, sitting it on the bench behind me. I unzip the bag and toss my heels inside, before digging around for my flip-flops and a ponytail holder. The fatigue sets in, proof from my yawn as I drop my shoes on the floor and slip my feet inside, letting the thong inch between my first two toes. The flat surface against the bottom of my feet yields a short moan of comfort.

I grab the bottom hem of my black dress and work the clingy fabric up my body, before pulling it over my head, leaving me in only panties since a bra is not an option with this dress. I need comfortable clothes. I've been walking around in this getup long enough. I'm not even sure where Meredith is. I didn't stop long enough when my shift ended to look for her. I'm just glad to finally be off. My head has been clouded for the last few hours. That doesn't have anything at all to do with a certain sexy stranger that decided to kiss me without asking or warning. No, not that.

I drape my dress over the bench and remove my bra from my bag, putting it on, followed by my coral, cotton, V-neck tee shirt dress that stops just below my ass. These dresses have become my favorite thing to wear. When I found them in a local store, and at a steal of a price, I bought one in just about every color. It feels like wearing pajamas without looking like you are.

I slip it over my head, dragging the fabric down my body until I'm fully covered. That feels so much better. The clean smell of laundry detergent causes me to turn my head to meet my shoulder. I sniff and close my eyes, letting it overwhelm my senses.

Home. I need to get going. My mattresses and purple satin sheets are calling my name. They're the only things aside from my phone and clothes here and there that I've purchased so far. My room is very much bare since I wasn't in the original plan when Meredith's parents made a trip prior to her move to set up her apartment. Until I can afford to buy the actual bed without dipping into my savings too much, my mattresses will remain on the floor in my room, but it's better than nothing, and it's mine.

I quickly toss the rest of my things into my bag and zip it up, throwing my hair into a messy bun before grabbing my purse and closing my locker. I'm ready to go. I haven't even had a chance to think about tonight, how I did, whether I liked it or if I want to continue. It's different from the lower level, like two different worlds. I feel more relaxed downstairs. I don't know. If the money is that much better maybe I'll just get used to it.

A tingling sensation runs across my lips, drawing my fingers to the site of origin to rub the tips horizontally across the bottom. I have a feeling making out with him would be fun, but it's just a hunch I have. He's so bold and confident, doing what he wants regardless of consequence. It's a turn on. What guy just does that? He doesn't know me. That one second touch of our lips was more of a rush than any kissing I've done with Kyle. My hand traces down my neck where he had his hand. It feels like it's still there.

You sound like a nutcase, Kambry.

I wonder who he is . . .

He doesn't look familiar, unfortunately. I'm pretty sure if I had watched a movie or something with him in it I would have remembered that face at least.

He has a broody sex appeal about him, and he's most definitely cocky. That I can tell. Maybe he's a model or something. *Or something* . . . reminding me that he's probably a celebrity and kissing me was more of a joke or pun for something said. I should just forget it even happened.

"What's up, Kambry?"

I jump at the sound of Liam's voice and turn around, grabbing my bag off the bench. "Hey, Liam. I was just leaving. I have to hail a cab. Thanks for not getting mad about having to be assigned to me. Babysitting sucks, but it made it easier having a familiar face around."

"Are you kidding? I made more tips up there than I would have made all week downstairs. I should really thank you. Wait up and I'll walk out with you." He glances down my body. "Even though that outfit is better than the first, I don't advise a girl that looks like you to walk around alone if you weren't born and raised around here."

"Oh, okay. Thanks."

He starts unbuttoning his white button-down that all bartenders are forced to wear unless we have a dress up night, and removes it, tossing it into the uniform hamper that will be picked up by the cleaning service. He doesn't even turn around before removing his black jeans. My eyes go directly to his torso, made of rippled perfection. Damn, they have some hot guys around here. It's a little different than most of the country boys back home that drink too much beer to keep their bodies in that good of shape. I'm still surprised that the locker room is co-ed.

He removes a pair of faded jeans and a tee shirt from his locker and pulls them on, a smile across his face when my eyes reach his. "So, I've been meaning to ask you something for a while. Do you have a boyfriend, Kambry?"

"Nah, we broke up before graduation. Different plans. You know how that goes. What about you?"

His smile broadens as he pulls on a flat bill baseball cap, adjusting it into place. "I most definitely do not have a boyfriend." He winks. "I prefer tits to pecs and holes to sticks." He sticks out his tongue, his top teeth pressed down in the center, showing he's being funny. "I also do not have a girlfriend either." His eyes have migrated to my chest. He's a nice looking guy and he's been nothing but friendly the few times I've actually conversed with him, but I get a weird vibe he's not as nice as he comes off. Not in the platonic friendly sense anyway. Like he's only friendly to get into your pants kind of thing. I don't know. It's hard to explain. That's probably judgmental.

He pulls on his high-top sneakers. "You have any plans? You could come hang out at my place for a little while. I have a sick view and a huge DVD collection."

"Thanks, Liam, but maybe another time. I wouldn't be much company tonight. I'm kind of tired. I guarantee ten minutes into a movie I'd be asleep. I think I just want to go home and crash. Sorry."

He nods and grabs his things from his locker, shoving his wallet into his back pocket and his phone into the front. "No worries. I'll ask again. A girl that looks like you has to be worth a second offer."

That's a little corny, even for me. "Uh, thanks."

He slams the metal door closed and walks toward me. "Let's go."

I adjust the strap of my bag on my shoulder and do a double check to make sure I have everything, before pulling my phone out of my purse and unlocking it as I follow behind him. There is a voice message from Meredith. I hold the phone to my ear as I play it back. "Hey, sexy bitch!" I laugh out loud at her drunken voice as it plays. "Don't wait for me. I kind of found someone interesting, so I'll just see you at home." She giggles shamelessly with the phone to her ear. I can't hear music in the background, assuming she called after she left the club. "Ohhhh, that feels nice."

"Just wait till I get you out of this cab and strip you," a male voice says back, my eyes widening. That's my cue to delete the message, because she has obviously already forgotten she is recording. What comes after that statement I don't want to hear.

I lock my phone as Liam holds the door for me to exit. Luckily, there is already a cab waiting curbside. Perfect. "Do you want me to give you a ride? I'm parked out back."

"That's okay. I appreciate the offer, but there is already a cab here needing to be utilized. Have a good night, Liam."

I start to walk toward the cab as he veers in the direction of the employee parking lot. "Hey, Kambry." I look back. "You coming to Drake's annual summer pool party next week for employees? You never did say. The guy has a pretty sweet crib."

I haven't really thought about it to be honest. "Um, maybe. I'll think about it and let you know, but probably." He did just offer me a raise. It would probably look bad if I didn't come.

"Sweet. Come ready to drink. There will be tons of alcohol and food. It's the one time Drake looks the other way for underage drinking." He smiles. "Goodnight, Kambry," he says and finally walks off. I need to make sure Meredith can come with me. I'll relax more and possibly even have fun if she's there.

I grab the door handle to the cab and open the door, before sliding on the back seat and rattling off my address without even paying attention as I shut the door, trying to situate all of my crap. "Driver, we're going to make a stop first."

My head jerks to the side at the sound of that now familiar voice. Him, just as I knew it would be before looking. God, he looks even better now than he did earlier. "What are you doing here? Saxton, was it? Didn't you leave hours ago?"

His eyes slowly roll down my body. I grab my ponytail holder and slide it out of my hair, quickly combing my fingers through my hair before his eyes return to mine. He smirks when our eyes lock. "Curious I guess. Beer or liquor?"

"What?"

The driver pulls out into the street, not even paying us any attention. "Do you prefer beer or liquor?"

"I prefer a bed and to stare at the back of my eyelids. I'm going home to sleep. Why?"

He checks me out again, not even hiding it. My stomach flips. "You may be going home, but you aren't going to sleep. I didn't get to talk to you earlier. You piqued my interest and now I can't sleep. Just so happens I'm bored and on a temporary vacation from work. Because of you I'm not ready to crash out yet."

"Your insomnia is not my problem. What makes you think I want to hang out with you? Do you really expect me to believe a guy like you wants to hang out with me and talk? I only let strangers in my panties on Friday. You're a day late. Darn." I snap my fingers in front of my face to be dramatic.

He laughs. "Believe me, sexy, if I wanted to fuck you I wouldn't have to try to con you. I would have already done it by now and I'd be sitting at home on my couch watching television by the time you clocked out, so relax, get drunk, and be my friend. I'm going to say you're probably a fruity wine cooler kind of girl. A gas station on the way should be fine."

"Uh, no it will not. I'm going home."

"That's fine. I'm coming with you."

"No, you're not. I don't even know you."

"I'm here and so are you. We are already going that way. You'll be fine. I've only been in jail once, for public intoxication back in college. Frat party and a bad prank on my friends' part. I solemnly swear I've never raped or murdered anyone." He winks.

I face-palm myself and shake my head. I'm not getting anywhere. "Who exactly are you, Saxton? Why on God's green earth would you want to hang out with a cocktail waitress so bad? You were in the VIP section of a popular club, among a few people there I recognized. I know how much it costs to get up there. From what I hear privacy here is costly. I may not know you, but I'm not stupid. Maybe I should just Google you. What's your last name?"

I hold out my phone in front of me and he grabs it out of my hand, sliding it into his pocket. "No the fuck you aren't going to Google me. Did it ever occur to you that maybe people here want to go back to being normal sometimes, even if only for a few hours? I may like it that you have no idea who I am. Humor me. Can you do that without being a pain in my ass?"

My head falls back against the seat and I close my eyes. A guy invades my night, forces me to stay awake to party, basically tells me I'm being an annoying pain in the ass by asking questions, and somehow I still feel guilty. What is wrong with this situation? I exhale abruptly. "Mike's hard lemonade."

I lift my head from the seat and roll it to the side so that I can look at him. My blonde hair forms a curtain over one eye as it falls toward the center of my face. His dirty blonde hair is sticking up all over the top of his head as if he's been running his fingers through the front. Good lord he's hotter than I remember. Maybe it's that I'm not at work and in the center of everyone watching me. "That's what I've been drinking lately when Mer—my roommate wants to party. By the way, if you turn out to be some kind of psycho killer I will come back and haunt your ass."

His smile comes back full force. "I knew you'd see it my way."

I roll my eyes. "You're just lucky that you're hotter than my last offer and my roommate decided to go party without me. Don't let it go to your head."

The cab pulls up to my apartment complex and stops. Saxton hands the driver a stack of bills folded down the center as I open the door and place one foot on the ground. I move the strap on my duffle bag to the opposite shoulder so that the weight is more evenly balanced across my body. Once I have all of my stuff, I exit the cab and automatically turn around to reach in and grab the six pack of Mike's hard lemonade so he can get his beer, but he waves me out. "I got it. You have enough of a load between that bag and your purse. Just lead the way."

"Okay." I adjust my purse strap on my arm and start walking toward the exterior stairs to the upper floors. I can hear the door to the cab shut and then his footsteps across the sidewalk.

We climb the concrete steps until we reach the third floor, almost immediately standing in front of my door since it's just past the stairs. When I am staring at the metal number that hangs on my door I look back at him briefly. He's waiting for me to open it. Well, this is a little more awkward now that we're here . . . with no middle-aged cabbie sitting up front. I purse my lips together. I cannot believe I'm letting someone in my apartment that I just met, literally. Doesn't this go against the grain of everything my parents have told me not to do since the day I could remember anything they told me?

With that thought . . .

I reach in my purse and shuffle things around until I can grab my keys. Shoving the right one inside the lock I glance back at him again. "Are you going to open it?"

"Don't judge, K?"

"One thing you don't have to worry about with me. Open the door. I'm tired of holding this shit."

I turn the key and open the door. The spotlights are on over the bar, but I remember turning them off before I left. I walk inside and set my bag down. "You can put those in the fridge," I say, as I walk across the living room toward

Meredith's cracked bedroom door. The light is off. Maybe she came home and crashed.

I press against the center of the wood and push it open to see if she's lying in bed. "Damn, Meredith! You have a lock."

She's standing in the middle of her floor, bent over with her hands on the floor, naked, while some guy equally as naked behind her has his hands clamped onto her hips and is pounding into her . . . and I'm still standing here, making no effort to leave, watching them, and slightly fascinated by it.

It's a small apartment, so the spotlights create a glow throughout the entire apartment without any other lights on, giving enough light into her room that you can see their entire silhouette. By looking at how intense they are and barely even registering me standing here, I'm going to say they're both wasted.

My body temperature is rising. I'm getting kind of dizzy feeling like I used to when Kyle and me found a way to sneak a heavy make-out session. The sounds she's making followed by a throaty groan from him soon after are spiking my curiosity on what that feels like. I'm slightly jealous. I'm really turned on. I'm also still watching them . . .

What is wrong with me?

"Do you like to watch other people have sex?"

I jump at the sound of his husky voice outside of my ear, verbalizing my surprise. "No," I say in a clipped tone.

"It's nothing to be ashamed of. Sex is a natural thing. Erotica through visual stimulation triggers the release of hormones in the brain for most people. It's a sexual stimulant."

He has one hand on the doorframe and places the other on my stomach, then aligns his back to my front. Meredith screams out and pushes up on her tiptoes. My thighs press together. "Then add touch."

His hand rubs down my front, and across my thigh, before slightly veering toward the inside, underneath my dress. My head falls back against his shoulder from the feel of his hand migrating up the inside of my thigh. A bulge starts to form against my ass. It's getting uncomfortable between my legs, wetting my panties.

"You want to join, beautiful?" the unfamiliar voice asks, bringing me out of my haze, and I knock Saxton's hand off of me.

Meredith stands slightly and grabs her boobs in her hands, then giggles. "You won't get her naked, sexy. She's not that kind of girl."

I know she doesn't mean anything by it in a malicious manner, and she's clearly had way too much to drink, but it stings. She knows that's my trigger. I loathe being called the good girl. Even worse, I despise that it's true. I hate that my high school years were wasted. I will forever regret that I don't have the memories she does, and she knows it. "Who's the guy?"

"Saxton. You can cont—"

"Horseman? Holy shit, bro. A girl? The Saxton Mav—"

"Don't go there, man. Not tonight."

I'm confused. He presses Meredith back down into her previous position and goes back to pounding into her, but harder this time. A slapping sound starts to occur against her skin. "Oh fuck. Did you just get harder? Hell yes."

Saxton grabs my hand and pulls me out of the doorway, before shutting her door and leading me toward the kitchen. "It's time for the alcohol now."

Saxton

I pull open the refrigerator and grab a beer from the six-pack after handing her a bottle of lemonade. I don't drink all that often so it should be enough without being too much. I wasn't really aiming for sloppy drunk anyway. More or less just to take the edge off. I took my ass home after I walked out of the club, sat on the couch, and scrolled through the never ending guide of reruns and stupid shit on TV with nothing to interest me. For the first time in a really long time I was bored.

Then I got to the porn channels. Occasionally I buy one to watch my competition, to see what else is out there, and to stay fresh, but then one caught my attention–Virgin girls gone wild. I kept scrolling then went back. Before I knew it I had confirmed the purchase.

Okay, so I caved. Normally, just the sound of the title would have turned me off, because to me that's stupid. Plus, why watch something that clearly doesn't relate to you? There is no way in hell I'd ever fuck a virgin. Been there and done that. I personally don't see the hype. It was horrible. Some things are just not made to fit no matter how many different ways you try to shove it. That was also when my dick was still growing. The length isn't even the problem, because that's adjustable during penetration, but something that always has the potential to increase in size, even in a full-grown male, is girth. Smaller dicks do serve a purpose and are very much needed. I do not take them for granted.

Add in a man with raging hormones and it's going to fit in some hole in one way or another. She'd probably end up in a hospital. Besides, no girl that looks like those girls are really virgins anyway. The title is a marketing ploy to make people purchase, but her awkward attempts of being sexy in the club started rolling in my mind. Then I watched it and it was just as bad as I figured it would be, but now I'm here with no idea why aside from morbid curiosity.

I twist off the cap and toss it in the trash, before turning the bottle up. She places hers on the counter and lays her palms on top as leverage to lift herself up until she's sitting on the counter. Her flip-flops fall from her feet when she starts swinging her legs back and forth. She grabs her bottle and tilts the neck toward me with a pleading grin. "What's the matter? Can't do it?"

She shakes her head. "Hurts my hand."

I down a few gulps as I walk closer, then set mine down, already half empty. "Here, I'll show you a trick." Gripping the bottle over the top of her hand, I lower it between her legs and beneath the fabric of her dress. I push the bottle against the fabric, making it conform to the shape of the bottle opening, then reach for her free hand and place it atop the dress-covered cap. "Now try."

She does, and the seal to the cap breaks, allowing her to twist it off. "Huh. Well that would have come in handy a while ago. Thanks."

She places the opening to her lips and tilts back, allowing the yellow liquid to flow into her mouth, before parting with it and swallowing. "That's good."

I'm staring at her damn lips again, now moist from the drink. For the life of me I can't figure out why I keep staring at her full lips. I like the way they naturally pucker . . . She takes another drink, looking away from me, and making no effort to drink slowly. I grab my beer to finish it off in silence, tossing it in the trash when I'm done. "Where are you from, Kambry?"

"Alabama," she says, before covering her lips with the bottle again, drinking faster with each sip. "You?"

"Oakdale." I grab her behind the knees and pull her closer to the edge of the counter. "How old are you?"

"I'll be nineteen in September."

"That's a bit young for my taste."

"Yet you're sitting in my apartment, forcing me to hang out with you."

I smile at her attempt to be a smartass. "That I am, beautiful. I suppose you're old enough."

"Define old enough."

"Legal. I like my freedom. Though I am contributing to a minor."

"I won't tell if you won't. How old are you?"

"Twenty-five."

"Kind of old for my liking."

"Yet you kissed me back and then allowed me to come home with you, willing to be a participant. If I recall, you never said no."

Her mouth starts pursing together, her eyes narrowing as she looks into mine. I can tell she's thinking of a quick comeback, but then a smile breaks free. "I guess I did." She shrugs her shoulders. "I suppose you're young enough," she quips back to my earlier comment.

"Define young enough."

"Under the ten-year line in age difference. If you're old enough to be my daddy, you're too old." She winks. "I need someone that can at least keep up with me. I have a lot of years left for partying and getting into endless amounts of trouble."

My hands take residence just above her knees, before rubbing up the length of her thighs beneath her short dress. Her muscles jump; a reflex action from being caught off guard. She takes another sip of her drink, this time a drop being left behind. I lean forward, stopping just outside of her mouth. "The question is, can you keep up with me?"

I lick up the center of her bottom lip, across the opening of her mouth, and then the top, before pressing my lips to hers. Her hands go to the back of my neck, combing up into my hairline as she kisses me back. I allow myself more this time. She kisses soft and slow, mesmerizing me. She tastes and smells sweet.

My hands inch up further, stopping on her hips, over the thin string of her panties. My fists close around them, ready to rip them from her body. The girl from the other room gets louder, causing her to break the kiss first this time. I pull back to look at her. Kambry's face starts to redden. "This is awkward."

She chugs the rest of her drink and pushes me back on the chest so that she can hop off the bar. She passes me and opens the refrigerator to grab two of her bottles by the neck in one hand, then hands me two more beers. "Here, we're going to the pool. I can't stay here and listen to that. If we're going to attempt a serious conversation I can't have orgasms as the music in the background without laughing or blushing. Surely they'll be done by the time we get back."

I can tell by looking into her eyes that she probably has little experience. She most likely dated the same guy the majority of high school, which means the probability of her actually committing to this little project they have worked up is slim to none, but regardless, I have beer to drink and time to kill. I'm not ready to give up on the possibility just yet. There is something puzzling about her, and I'm going to find out what it is.

Kambry

I swipe my gate key at the pool entry. The green light confirms it unlocked. I pull the wrought iron gate open and walk inside, immediately chasing the aqua tinted water created from the pool lights reflecting from the bottom. It looks inviting. I haven't been out here at night yet–only during the day–but not as often as the beach. "I doubt we're supposed to have glass or alcohol in here," he says from behind me as I take a seat on the edge of the pool, lowering my legs into the cool water.

I set one bottle down beside me and open the other, before immediately drinking from it. "I guess I just feel like living on the edge," I retort. A few seconds pass before he sits down beside me, mirroring my position. From the corner of my eye I notice tan, bare legs covered with a thick layer of blonde hair that matches the color on his head . . . yet moments ago he was wearing jeans.

"That's the best way to live. I was just fishing."

I turn to look at him, my mouth running dry. I want to close my eyes and memorize the hot guy sitting beside me kissing me again, but I refrain. His legs are more muscular than I imagined they would be. I'm assuming he's one of those guys that stay in the gym at least once a day. How exactly did I end up here, in this situation?

"What are you doing?" I follow my words by drinking more, and quickly, trying to quench this sudden thirst I've developed with him sitting poolside in boxer-briefs and the polo he's been wearing. That is one enticing view.

"I'm sitting beside you. What does it look like I'm doing?"

"You're in your underwear . . . at a public pool. Where are your pants?"

He twists off the cap to his beer, completely unfazed, before taking a sip. "On the lounger. I'm not getting them wet and you clearly wanted to get wet, so I took them off." His lips draw up into a smirk, noticeable even with the rim of the bottle pressed against them.

My buzz starts to hit me . . . already. I rarely drink, even living on my own. It's not as easy for me as it is for Meredith to just throw caution to the wind, living in a new place and scared to get caught drinking underage. Plus, I work as much as I can to save money, and that's okay, because I choose to.

Not eating dinner probably didn't help me with this scenario. Now I'm drinking on an empty stomach. I probably should slow down . . . because the truth is it tastes watered down now. That absent bite of alcohol should tell me I've had enough, or this could turn into an unattractive situation, and fast.

My eyes rake down his body, taking notice of the bulge running down the inside of his leg from the center. It doesn't even look hard, but it's noticeable . . .

My eyes lose focus. *Stop looking at his crotch, Kambry!*

I turn my eyes away, downing the rest of my drink. A laugh sounds–an amazing, manly laugh–dry but sexy. I shiver. "This makes you uncomfortable, doesn't it?"

"What?"

"Me this close to you; half naked. Sex in general. Being alone with a guy that you just met. Flirting. Take your pick."

He sounds amused. Asshole. This is embarrassing. This is the elementary stuff that I should have down by now. I should be confident around a guy . . . like Meredith. Even after two years with Kyle I was still a nervous wreck half the time, because we were never alone long enough for me to be bold, or to get comfortable in my own skin and sexuality. The way I feel right now should have been smothered by freshman year. It's time to ditch this girl–for good this time.

Enough talk about it. My parents have ruined me. I may have to fight for the girl I want to be, but dammit I'll at least be happy in the end. "No. Why would you make me uncomfortable?"

I grab my last bottle and uncap it, before pulling my legs out of the water, standing up, and making my way toward his jeans with it in hand, drinking along the way. "I can just tell. Body language screams a lot louder than words. Where are you going?" I can hear the water slosh, as if he changed his position.

"Wouldn't you like to know?"

I grab his jeans off the lounger and stick my hand in the pocket, pulling out my phone that he has yet to return, then throwing them back down. Unlocking it, I find the playlist I want in my music app–a country party mix–and toss my phone down on top of his pants as the first song starts to play: *Hell of a Night* by Dustin Lynch.

Now that the alcohol has taken control, all of my inhibitions are gone, and I welcome the freedom from my mind. Halfway through my last hard lemonade, I set it down on the ground beside the lounger. Staring at him, I crisscross my arms in front of me and grab the bottom hem of my dress, slowly pulling it up my body until it's off, leaving me in only my bra and panties. He's looking at me, one leg in the water and one out, bent, with his forearm resting on top of his knee as his fingers rub together. That small muscle in a person's jaw is working overtime on the side of his face that's facing me.

His eyes slowly scan down my body with this serious look, a hypnotic one, making me feel sexy. It feels so good for someone to look at me that raw, that sexually explicit, like he's trying to find his words so he doesn't come off as a jerk, with no knowledge of anything more about me. It may be shallow, but I need it. "So, Saxton . . . what really made you come back?"

"The thoughts of this." I love that he has no reservations about anything he says. It's nice for someone to just be . . . real.

I smile, a real smile, for the first time in a long time. "I like your honesty."

"Why lie?"

"Most do."

"Most aren't like me."

"Which is?"

One side of his mouth pulls up, revealing the start of a dimple I haven't paid much attention to until now. "The kind a girl like you would probably steer clear of."

I walk to the steps of the shallow end, taking them one at a time, letting my body get used to the water temperature as I descend. I bite my bottom lip. "What kind of a girl am I? To you of course . . . I'm curious."

"The kind of girl I want to corrupt. The kind I want to drag into my world and hold hostage for a while, even though I know better. The kind that is nothing like me, and needs to stay away from me, because I know you're too good for me, yet one I still want to turn bad, tainting you one orgasm at a time." He grabs the back collar of his shirt and pulls it over his head, tossing his polo and undershirt aside.

My breathing ceases. The water is no longer cool, but warm. I continue forward toward the middle of the pool, my face remaining on him until I'm far enough out to turn my body, then step a few feet backwards, still watching him. He grips the edge of the cement in his hands and pushes himself off into the water, landing on his feet.

I lower myself into the water, mouth underneath, looking over the surface and watching him wade toward me as the slope touches the bottom of my feet, signaling the beginning of the deep end. It takes him no time to reach me. He grabs ahold of my waist, halting me. "The problem is . . . I don't care enough to stop." I place my arms around his neck to hold on.

His hands continue around my waist and then move downward, before settling on my butt. He squeezes, pulling my body toward his and lifting me slightly to match his height. Without thought, I wrap my legs around his waist as he migrates as far as he can walk and still remain head above water. "What if I want to be corrupted?" I question in a whisper.

The ends of my hair are wet, sticking to the middle of my back. My insides feel like they are twisting in a million knots, but being pressed against him like this makes it hard to even acknowledge. "Be careful what you wish for. With a body like this you may be . . . corrupted by me."

Feeling bold, I lower my head closer to his and kiss him. He allows me to. His lips are full, but the top not as much as the bottom. They're soft. My tongue slowly inches inside of his mouth, and when it meets his, it's as if a fire has been lit within my core, building for an explosion. I don't really understand it, and it's not something I can explain, because I've never felt it before, not even with Kyle. It's an anxious need for more of him, more of this.

The second our tongues tangle he raises one hand to the side of my face and his movements become rougher, faster, and needier. A masculine growl sounds inside of his throat, instigating me further. I lightly bite his lip and the feel of something hard presses between my legs, making me nervous but turned on.

His hand drops from my face and disappears under the water. I feel it again at the edge of my panties, before he slips his fingertips underneath them. My breathing becomes rampant, loud, my nerves sending out warning signs and consuming my body as his fingers touch me somewhere I've never been touched by someone else. It's a foreign feeling, but I like it. I continue to kiss him, trying to sway my mind and nerves, shutting them out. I can feel my body shaking, but I'm hoping he doesn't notice. I want this. I will not quit because of fear.

When I don't stop him he continues, rubbing his finger over my entrance. His chest expands as he does, confirming it must be a good thing when he slips his finger inside. My mind, body, and soul quickly becomes enraptured for the first time in my entire life, not able to think about anything but the feeling of his finger inside me. As he pushes inside of me, my fingers claw into his neck.

As quickly as it started he stops and places my panties back in place, then removes his mouth from mine. "I can't do this. Fuck."

"I want you to. It's okay."

"No, Kambry, I can't. You don't understand." I look at him. He actually looks like he's harboring guilt.

"Why? Are you gay?"

Silence.

"What?"

His tone sounds angry.

"Are you gay? Is that why? You said I don't understand. I'm trying to. It's okay to tell me. I would never judge you."

He glares at me, but doesn't release me. Instead, he grabs my hand and places it on his . . . My eyes widen as he clamps my hand around it, but my fingers don't meet on the other side. "Does this fucking feel gay to you?" His voice is low, but harsh. "Are you fucking serious? If I were gay you wouldn't make me hard, Kambry. I don't think your pussy is even loose enough for me to get two fingers in."

He strokes my hand down the full length of his dick. "Do you really think that's going to go in without hurting you, or possibly hurting me? Fuck that. I figured you weren't as wild as the girls I'm used to, but I didn't think you were that good, and I really don't know how good that is. You work in a nightclub–a place primarily for quick lays and one-night stands. It's normal to make assumptions."

My breathing quickens. I unwrap my legs, but he grabs on to me. I push him back as I kick my legs underwater to stay afloat, unable to touch the bottom from the spot I'm in. I'm also drunk. "Screw you. Since when did the guys you meet in the before mentioned nightclub care? You don't know anything about me. You're the one that suggested we hang out, in case you have forgotten. I went along with it. I even gave you a green light to have a little fun, and instead of passing go you sat there, acting like every other douche bag. Go pretend to be a man with someone else. I'm over it."

I start to swim past him but he grabs the back band of my bra in his fist, pulling me back and turning me around. He continues walking in the direction I was swimming, holding on to me until I can touch bottom. "A man, huh?" He grits out the question between his clenched teeth. "The only pretending I do is when the camera is recording, and even then it's only fifty percent fake. You want me to distinguish between a man and a douche bag for you? Then I'll be happy to give you what you want, but even as fucked up as my sex life is I still have limits."

I'm not sure what exactly any of that means, but I don't really care when all I can think about is my bra straps separating at my back as he walks me further into the shallow end. His fingers grab ahold of the straps lying on my shoulders and he pulls them down my arms, baring my upper half.

A mild remembrance that we are in a public pool at a pretty big apartment complex crosses my mind, causing me to cover myself as my bra falls from my body, exposing me. I look around, but see no one. At least the pool is in a private area, enclosed inside of a fence, somewhat away from the apartment buildings, but every resident has a gate key.

He grabs my wrists, pulling my hands away from my boobs, his eyes immediately diverting as he does. "Fuck, you've got a beautiful rack."

My heels meet the first step, causing me to slightly stumble, but he doesn't let me fall. I climb the steps backward until I reach the third step from the top. "Sit down," he demands, no longer being playful or flirty. Oddly, I kind of like it. I do as he says, sitting in just enough water to keep my lower half somewhat hidden by the rest of the pool wall beside the steps.

He stands on his knees, straddled over my fully straightened legs, then cups my breast in his hand and lightly shakes it, letting it jiggle as it spills over. The second he stops he squeezes, pretty hard. "And they're fucking real? Damn. They're so big for your frame size. Fuck." I watch him as he stares at it in his hand, now rubbing his thumb back and forth over my nipple, hardening it more than it already was.

He leans in, placing his mouth over the center, the tip of his tongue immediately making contact with my nipple, lightly flicking over it. My back arches, altering me into a somewhat lying position across the steps as the back of my head touches against the cement. The step edge pressing into my back isn't comfortable, but am I going to chance saying anything that could possibly make him stop doing that? Uh . . . no. I moan, unable to help it, immediately biting my tongue to stop.

He licks horizontally across my body to the other side, doing the same to my other nipple, keeping the opposite side in his hand as if he doesn't want to let go. My hand rises above me and I grab onto the metal rail in the center of the wide steps, as his lips trace down the vertical curve of my body.

His hand fists the side of my underwear at the moment his lips reach my pelvis, pulling them down my hips. I lift, allowing him to work them over my butt; what little fabric there is to them. No panty line is imperative when I have guys staring at my ass all night. Thongs are the only panties I wear to work.

He pulls them down to my thighs, before altering his position to remove them completely, and then drops them in the water. His hand becomes flush with the back of my knee and he pulls my leg to the side. When he doesn't immediately touch me, I lift my head and nervously look down. He's staring between my legs, making me self-conscious, even under the influence of alcohol. "What is it?"

"You have one beautiful pussy."

Without another word he spreads my legs and bends over between them, before he places his tongue over my opening and swipes it up the center. My body does a roll and I scream out, not expecting it, and then slap my hand over my mouth. That felt so good, but I don't even have time to let it fully register when his tongue starts pressing firmly against my clit, roughly rubbing it back and forth. "Oh . . . shit."

My legs start to close together, but he blocks them with his hands, pushing them wider than they were before. The sensations are too much to bear. I've given myself orgasms on a few occasions after my parents went to bed, usually on nights that Kyle and I had heated make-out sessions, but none of those times ever came close to feeling like this, and I always felt dirty afterwards for doing it because of the way my parents are.

He thrusts his finger inside of me, amplifying the sensation. My breathing is out of control. He grips my hip with his other hand, slowly migrating it up my body, until he reaches my breast. He pinches my nipple between his fingers and the three-in-one points of pleasure are driving me mad.

I use the rail and pull up my head enough to look at him, watching his tongue moving against my body. This is kind of a sexy view. As if he can sense me staring at him, he looks at me from beneath his lashes, never letting up on any of the three places. "I can't take that much. It's too much," I say breathless.

That only motivates him to increase his speed. My head falls back and my hand grips into his thick, blonde hair and pulls, trying to focus on something, anything besides the pleasure he's creating. He hooks his finger when he thrusts inside and I fail miserably, bringing my hand to my mouth and biting the side of it to keep from screaming again. An overwhelming sensation starts to build within my body, my lower area throbbing.

My eyes close and I moan against my hand as an all-consuming pleasure begins, making real time slow down. My mind goes completely blank and my toes curl. My body numbs. My pulse is pounding. The wave falls and starts to subside slowly, until the feeling is completely gone, leaving me in a state that I would imagine is similar to a drug high–completely relaxed and a little energized.

The movement of his tongue becomes slower. I giggle as it changes from feeling good to a sensitive tickle, pulling him by the hair. "Stop. Please stop."

He does. I move my arms to the step and prop myself up as he removes his tongue from my body. He leans back, slides his finger out slowly, and then leans toward me, before he places his hands palm down on the step and pushes himself up like he's doing a pushup on an incline. Our faces are mirrored at level height. The expression on his face is blank. I'm not sure what to make of it.

This would probably be extremely awkward for me right now if I didn't still have a buzz, knowing I just let a guy I don't even know go down on me in a public pool where any resident has access. That's also the beauty of it. That's most likely another reason I feel so high right now, completely free to do whatever the hell I want and not having to worry about it getting back around to my parents. What I just did would probably land me a front seat ride to the counselor or preacher at church, or even an appointment with the confessional for a confession and prayer of forgiveness, and we aren't even Catholic.

"Kambry . . ."

"Yes?"

"Please tell me you've had sex before." His eyes change. "Please," he repeats in a pleading whisper.

I blink, unsure of how to respond. I should just lie. What would it even hurt? He probably would never know the difference between virgin and not virgin with minor experience. "No," I blurt out before my thought even finishes developing. His eyes close. "Has anyone ever done those things to you?"

I'm starting to panic a little. Why would these even be questions he would ask? It cannot be noticeable. I don't know what to say. Do I lie, tell the truth, or plead the fifth? He opens his eyes again. One look into them and I know I can't lie. I don't even know why, but I want to tell him the truth. "No."

"Fuck. You kiss like you know what you're doing." He starts to pull away from me. "Fuck. Fuck. Fuck. I'm probably going to Hell."

I sit up and grab his sides, anxiously stopping him. I might as well get this out while I'm intoxicated and uninhibited. "But it's not because I didn't want to. I need to clarify before you jump to any conclusions of it being a righteous decision. I dated the same guy from the time I was allowed to have a boyfriend, and that's not saying much since we didn't really get to traditionally date. We kissed, groped, he asked and tried, but even if I would have been brave enough to say yes, we didn't have much of an opportunity anyway. I've wanted to for years, time and time again, but I didn't for reasons that have nothing to do with me. It's complicated, Saxton; my entire life has been."

He's still staring at me with no expression. "Please don't get all awkward now. I did this because I wanted to. This is what I needed, and now I want more. I don't want to do this with the right person, but a willing person that I'm attracted to, because I'm sure I'll suck at it for a while. I want to do this to break the curse, to finally do what I want with no restrictions and no one watching my every move. I'm completely fine with nothing more than a hookup. This isn't the kind of thing I want people to know, but since you do we could use it to both of our advantage, right? I solemnly swear I want nothing more from you. I just want your dick, pun intended."

I laugh at my own joke, attempting to break the ice of this suddenly awkward situation. He stands and I notice his extremely noticeable hard-on. He attempts to adjust it, but it doesn't do much. He then holds out his hand for me to take. "I should say fuck no, walk you to your apartment to say goodnight, and then leave, never to see you again, but the reality is I want more than that too. My reasoning is just probably a little more fucked up than yours, but before I answer that question you will know what you're getting into, who you are offering your virginity to, and there will be stipulations that are beyond my control; part of who I am, but it won't be tonight for reasons I'm not allowed to explain prematurely. Tonight, though, I'm going to take you to your room and lay with you until you go to sleep, then I'll be on my way. The rest I'll leave to happen at will. Come on, beautiful. Cover your body."

I take his hand and stand, allowing him to make the plans for the rest of the night, or morning in this case. Now, more so than before, I want to ask questions, but I will abstain . . . for now.

CHAPTER FIVE

Saxton

I walk in her room after I leave my wet, balled up briefs on the small entryway table to pick up on my way out. I glance around at the bare room. From the looks of it she's still living out of suitcases. It's been a long time since I've seen a set of mattresses lying on the floor. The plastic storage drawer is the only form of furniture in the room, serving as a nightstand, most likely from a local Wal-Mart or Target. This whole visual just seems off.

I want to ask more questions, but instead I keep them to myself until I can gather my thoughts. I don't really think now is the right time when they're still scattered. I have to squat to sit on the low makeshift bed as I watch her change into a tank and pair of short shorts that shows off her petite but curvy backside.

She turns around to face me when her breasts are covered, rolling the gray cotton down her stomach. "Come here," I command, already realizing I've fucked myself as I sit here in the fucking apartment of a girl I just met that has my complete attention. I shouldn't have come back to find her. I should have just taken the job with no stipulations and do what I do best: fuck and act, completely oblivious to the real world. I cannot believe I'm even intrigued by this idea, but I'd be lying if I said I wasn't; although I do have limits that I'll talk over with Michael before I go any further with this project.

She walks between my legs and drops to her knees. *A woman on her knees has never been sexier*. I shake the thoughts off. I'm losing my fucking mind.

I place my hands on her waist, attempting to pull her closer. Her hands move to her thighs as she sits on her heels and looks at me, the wavy ends of her blonde, wet hair hanging over her shoulders. "Sit on my lap."

I hold her in place and scoot back a little, pulling my legs together to give her room on the bed. "Okay," she says and stands on her knees, before climbing on top of me, positioning her legs to each side of me, and then lowers herself down on my lap. It's a little scary how good this feels.

"If I ask you something will you be honest with me?"

"Okay," she responds.

"If you waited this long, then why do you want it now?"

"I didn't wait this long by choice. I told you that. I just want my freedom."

"Why do you work in a nightclub?"

"Because it's good money that also contributes to me being able to live here." She shrugs her shoulders. "It's just a job like anything else."

"I have a feeling that thought will change, but I'll go with it for now. Are you running?"

"From what?"

"Home."

"I guess that depends on your definition of running."

"Why did you move here?"

"To leave a life behind that I didn't want; that wasn't mine. I just finally realized it was better to be happy in solitude than in misery with company. It's pretty simple really. I didn't have a bad childhood, I wasn't abused, and I've never been wronged or harmed in a way that would classify me as broken. I have loving —in a weird way—parents and awesome friends. I was just tired of being who they wanted me to be. I was tired of being left behind out of fear to stand up for myself. It's not really a secret where I'm from. My parents are very conservative people. When I say conservative I'm being mild. Seeing the outside of my house or school was a luxury."

My conscience is suddenly digging itself out of the grave I buried it in when I chose this life. I don't like it . . . at all. I want to laugh that I'm even having this conversation. My subconscious has lost its fucking mind. The age difference alone should send my ass back home, but it only intrigues me more. I haven't even evaluated the fact that my dick has suddenly decided to work without a synthetic drug forcing it to, not once, but several times. I'm becoming more fucked up the older I get, yet I just keep going. "Don't you want to do it with someone you're in a mutual relationship with? Don't you want it to be special?"

She presses into my lap further, and then starts rubbing her middle along my semi-hard dick, hardening it even more. I can feel the heat emitted by the friction, even wearing denim. "No. That's not what I want at all. I have my entire life to settle down and be with one person, and it's likely they will have had short flings or quick hookups. Right now I want to have fun, but it's a little embarrassing to be an almost nineteen-year-old virgin. It's really no different than being a forty-year-old virgin now days. The older you get the harder and more awkward it becomes to just do it."

I close my eyes, trying to drown out those hypnotic eyes as she grinds herself on my cock, making rational thought more difficult. I can hear her heart loud and clear, proving itself present in the silence. "Will you regret it? Because I'm not a virgin."

"No. I promise. I know most people aren't. I'm not that naïve." She pauses, her eyes changing, pleading with me before her words are able to. "Please, Saxton. You're the first person I've opened up to since I moved here. That I will regret if this goes badly. I don't want to be in this awkward situation again with someone else. You kind of forced yourself here. You opened up the door for this conversation, so now we deal with it."

My eyes snap open. She found my trigger. My hand fists in her hair at the back of her head, holding her as I turn us over, laying her on the bed. She wraps her legs around my waist. I thrust myself against her, pressing my hard cock between her legs as I kiss her roughly. I can't do soft after hearing her beg me, taking me back to a time when I used to hear it often. A time when I used to fuck angry . . .

That's one reason I stuck with porn once I ventured down that path. I only have expectations of physical performance premeditated by outside parties. Emotional shit is left out of the equation. What *I'm* running from . . .

She grabs the bottom of my shirt and starts to pull it up my body. I break the kiss realizing conditions aren't ideal. Not that the others are, but I have obligations. "Stop, Kambry."

I'm my own fucking cock block.

Her eyes widen as if she's in shock, maybe even a little embarrassed. I place my hand just above the back of her knee and rub it up the length of her thigh, underneath her shorts, to her ass. "I have to. I don't want to. You need to realize what you're getting into if you want this . . . with me. I'm not a normal guy. Do you remember what I said earlier?"

"Which part?"

"About reconsidering acting?"

Her forehead crinkles. "Yeah, but what does that have to do with this situation?"

"Those men I was with at the club were there for a business meeting with me. They were there to discuss a project. One was a producer, the other a director. He noticed me taking an interest in you and is very likely to act on it. Sometimes acting is more about chemistry than anything else. The right or wrong two actors can make a huge difference on screen, so he's probably going to come talk to you. If you really want this to go somewhere, then you'll have to keep an open mind. Like wide fucking open. Until then, we can't go any further. That is beyond my control, for reasons you'll soon figure out."

"Um, okay, but I'm still con—"

I stop her by kissing her, trying to end this conversation before I throw everything out the window and decide that I don't give a shit about that fucking meeting or this project and just do what I want. She moans into my mouth, and it's now that I realize I need to go home. This isn't cooling off. And the longer I'm here the more I want her in ways I don't understand.

I pull away and stand from the bed. She looks at me in a way that I know she's disappointed. "I need to go, beautiful. I have things I need to get done tomorrow. Get some sleep. Maybe I'll see you again soon."

I lean over and briefly kiss her lips, before walking toward the door. "How will I see you?"

I grab the doorknob but don't look back. "When you know everything, if you decide you still want to go forward, you'll know where to find me. Goodnight, Kambry."

I walk out the door and shut it behind me, leaving my briefs on the way out the front door, calling a cab on the way downstairs. It doesn't take me long to get to the curb before I pull up my email on my phone as I stand and wait. I probably should wait till at least morning to do this, but what the hell.

To: Michael_Prescott@kissntellfilms.com
Cc/Bcc:
From: Saxton_Maverick@gmail.com
Subject: Reality project (title currently unknown) update

Michael,

I have some information on the project that we discussed earlier. I'll do it if we can work out the terms of the contract. There are certain things I will require, just as I am sure you will. Get with me on time and place. I'll be there.

Regards,
Saxton

I press send and slide my phone in my pocket. The cab comes into view and pulls up curbside. I get in and shut the door, rattling off my address as I do. My thoughts immediately return to that fucking pool and how good her tight, wet pussy felt as we pull away from her apartment building. It was too good. I shouldn't have kissed her. I would have been better off dousing myself with gasoline and lighting myself on fire. Now, I feel like someone I've never met gave me a line of free cocaine. Instead of asking questions I sniffed, and now I'm fucking hooked, already looking for my next fix.

That could be a problem for me.

She could always say no.

Girls like her don't say yes to porn offers.

I have to make her say yes . . .

My phone vibrates once, signaling an email. I shift my position and remove it from my pocket. I unlock the blank screen and open my email to a reply from Michael; an odd time to reply, but who am I to judge when sending at this time?

From: Michael_Prescott@kissntellfilms.com
To: Saxton_Maverick@gmail.com
Subject: RE: Reality project (title currently unknown) update

Saxton,

To clarify, the project has been named Sex Sessions: Uncut. Meet me tomorrow at noon. That deli about a block from the studio is fine. Shit, I'm drawing a blank on the name, but it's late. You'll know which one; same as last time. Lunch is on me, but bring all your cards to lay out on the table. They are ready to move on this project, hoping it will give us an edge. If you don't take it they are pushing to move forward with open casting auditions. We need to do this. You need to do this. This could be a good change for you.

Until tomorrow,
Michael

I let my head fall back against the seat, trying to drown out all the visuals of the last several hours. It's easier said than done. All I seem to be able to think about is my finger, as in singular, pressed inside of her pussy, squeezing me tightly as it became wet from her arousal. I never think about sex. Not anymore. Feeling her, though, may very well change that. I'm not sure if I should be relieved or fucking terrified. I guess I'm about to find out.

BONUS

Kambry

I robotically walk to the bathroom and brush my teeth. My body is wired. I'm not the least bit tired and my heated skin doesn't even register the sixty-five degree temperature in the apartment. I'm hot, sweaty, and the feelings swarming inside of me I don't understand. If I were honest with myself I would admit that I'm really disappointed he backed out. I've wanted to lose my virginity more times than I can count, but none of those times had me to the point of begging someone to take it.

As I replace my toothbrush in the holder I notice the pink circles on my cheeks. I touch my palm to one side, staring at my reflection in the mirror. My chest is splotchy in a shade to match, and my fingertips migrate to my tingling lips. What's wrong with me? If I can't even give it away with no strings attached there has to be something.

Before I can stop them, a few unwanted tears fall. I'm not even sure why I'm crying. The way I feel is foreign. Do I like him? Am I just lonely? Or am I now paranoid because he's the first guy I've let see me naked and now the guilt is starting to settle because he blew me off?

Anger overcomes me. He didn't have to lie to me. He could have just said he wasn't into it and left instead of feeding me some bullshit story about why he had to leave. I feel stupid and every bit my young age. Maybe I gave it away too easily and it was a turn off. I did seem needy with that whole speech. I take a deep breath. "Better luck next time girly," I say in the most motivating voice I can muster. "No one ever rode a horse the first time they tried."

I walk to the kitchen for a bottle of water, staring off across the room as I down half of it quickly. Meredith's door opens, the mysterious guy from earlier sneaking out quietly, clothed this time. When he turns around he spots me, straightening his posture to look less like an asshole leaving after getting a piece of ass I'm guessing. The funny thing is Meredith probably faked sleeping and already knows he's gone and has turned over and smiled herself to sleep for not having to share a bed.

He stares at me for a second, before shaking his hair out of his eyes. His brown hair is a little longer, but only long enough to curl out from under a baseball cap. "You must be the watcher."

I can feel my cheeks heat, and in return he smirks. This is embarrassing. "About that."

"It's cool. Doesn't bother me." He walks toward me, into the spotlight above the bar so that I can see him better, and leans over on his forearms on the bar top. I cross my arms over my chest, suddenly very aware of what I'm wearing and how cute he is. "I'm a little curious as to why a girl like you was with that guy, though."

My defenses take over. "What do you mean a girl like me? And you say *that guy* like you're implying that you know him."

"And you do?" he quips. "Maybe I do and maybe I don't, but I'm pretty sure I know him better than you, and I'm going to go out on a limb and say you're not his usual type."

"I met him at work," I say defensively, as if I owe him any explanation at all. "He came here on his own free will. This is my apartment."

"I have no doubt," he says in a witty manner.

He glances over to the door and looks back at me smiling. I follow his previous line of vision to a pair of underwear balled up by the door. My lips line. "You're not in a position to judge me right now."

He holds up his hands and backs toward the door, still smiling. He grabs them and throws them at me like he's throwing a baseball. Luckily, I catch them instead of looking like an idiot. "Judgment isn't always a bad thing. Sometimes it's just the shock of something happening out of the ordinary." He winks.

"Goodnight, watcher."

He disappears out the door, leaving me more confused than I was when Saxton left. I open his underwear, staring at them, and then without will the fabric ends at my nose, memorizing the way they smell: clean laundry and chlorine. Today needs to end so that it'll become just a night in the depths of my memory. But to do that I actually have to sleep. Good luck with that.

They return to their original balled up state in my hand as I lock the front door and return to my room, no more tired than I was when I left.

CHAPTER SIX

Saxton

The glass door comes into view and I pull it open. It's pretty busy for a Sunday. I bypass the line waiting to order and find Michael sitting over in a corner at a high-top table, sipping on a glass of water with a leather book in front of him.

I make my way over and take a seat across from him. He looks up at me as I take my seat. "Thanks for meeting with me on such short notice. I appreciate it."

"Not a problem. I understand the need to think things over. What do you have for me?"

"Well, I was originally planning to take a break for a little while. I just wanted to go for a while with no projects. Maybe I'm fucking crazy considering all I've accomplished, but I'm just burnt out with the same old shit, same type of girls, and same ending no matter how many different plots you use. There are only so many ways—no matter how kinky or raunchy you get—to fuck, eat pussy, etc." He doesn't even crack a smile. "You get the point. The only reason I met with the two of you last night was because you're a friend. You helped me out when I was going through a shitty time, so for that I'll always kind of owe you."

"And now?" he says vacantly.

"I'll agree to do this . . . if you can get Kambry as the co-star."

"I kind of thought we already established that. Is there something I'm missing?"

He opens the book, revealing a pad of lined yellow paper. He removes the metal pen from the holder in the center and uncaps it, exposing the narrow, metal point; an expensive pen. I cross my arms and lean forward on my forearms. "You did, but I am confirming your prediction. I want her, and only her. If you can get her to do it I'll sign the contracts no questions asked, with the exception of two stipulations."

"Go on."

He readies his pen, aiming the point just above the paper, preparing to take notes.

"I did a little investigating of my own last night, to see if this was worth my time. I spent a little one-on-one time with Kambry. It may be a little harder getting her than you think."

"Why do you say that? Money talks."

"She's a fucking virgin, Michael."

His eyes widen slightly, before a gleam appears. I interrupt his thought.

"Before you get settled with those dollar signs in your eyes, hear me out."

"I'm listening."

"Against my better judgment, I'll do it. This goes against everything that normally turns me on." *Ha! I'm not sure I even know what turns me on anymore.* "I'll fucking take her virginity for you on camera, but there will be requirements. To make this easy they are as follows: lights out, one camera angle in the room toward the bed, from a distance, and no close-ups. We've all been there. We've experienced that in privacy. We know what it entails. It's not erotic in the least. Mostly it's sloppy. A person is awkward, some girls in pain even with a guy of normal size, and learning how to go about it with each other. I don't give a fuck what you film before or after, but during that one sacred moment she will have some damn respect. Viewers can go to Hell if they have something to say about it. Furthermore, on the size note, you've seen my cock. I don't really know how that's going to work, but I'll try it."

"Women are miraculous creatures, Saxton. Those areas are capable of transformation, like during childbirth. They were created to adjust in size when they're supposed to. Everything doesn't have to be a physics problem. Sometimes things just work." He starts writing; taking notes. "Per your request, I don't see why that's not doable, but I'll still have to run it by the others. That was one, but you said two. What's the other?"

"You match her salary with mine."

He drops his pen and looks up at me. "Are you fucking serious?"

"I never joke about work."

"You're an established and seasoned actor. You have a name established with buyers. Has she even auditioned for a role, at all? You expect me to authorize that kind of budget disbursement to an amateur? I don't know if I can do that. Do you know how many girls are lined up to do that for less? We want you for this role, because we think you're right for the part, but you're asking things outside of your jurisdiction. What does it matter to you what your co-star makes?"

I think back to her mostly empty room, to the girl that evidently wants to spread her wings and try to fly from the nest. She's young and has her entire life ahead of her. She should be in college or something, not working in a nightclub to scrape by. There is no guarantee she will do this, but like he said money talks, and maybe if she can make enough to give her a really thick cushion she will figure out what she wants, finish this project, and go after it.

The anger is written all over his face. He's not going to make this decision today. It's a process. I tell him what I want and he counters or approves it. That's the way this works. I've worked with him before. I stand from my seat, preparing to leave. "Because I believe she deserves it, and you and I both know I don't normally vouch for people. I've fucked my ass off to get where I am. I help no one. If you want me to do this film, that's what will get my signature on a contract. I don't make requests often. That's the only reason you met with me. In the end you do what's best for you just like I do, because you have a family. I'm burnt out, Michael. Girls just don't turn me on like they used to. She does. *She* turns me on . . . with *no* magic pill. I need something different or nothing at all. Take it or leave it. I have done enough films I can take a break if I choose. I'm sure there is a long line of eligible males waiting for me to decline or fuck up if this isn't doable, but knowing you I'm sure it is. You're good at your job. Take a break of your own and go home to your family. You know how to reach me when you decide."

I walk away, trying to figure out what the hell I'm going to do with myself now. A certain blonde sounds enticing, but I will not go there again. Now that I know where she lives and works, it's going to be hard to stay away, because just the peek I got into that girl has me wanting more. It's time to see if he can come through. For now . . . I wait.

BONUS

Kambry

Pool parties aren't always about swimming . . .

Meredith comes running out of her room, still dressing as she does. One thing that isn't messy is her makeup. Sometimes I hate that about her. "Shit, shit, shit. Why did you let me oversleep? My boss is going to fucking kill me."

I disregard her comment, finishing my sandwich by placing the top piece of bread on the turkey. "I wasn't aware I had somehow transformed into an alarm clock," I say sarcastically, secretly smiling at myself for a decent comeback for once.

She straightens her clothes into place and stops beside me, pulling me into a side embrace. "Ah, someone has her own personal brand of humor this lovely Sunday morning, but have you met the bitches that be wanting their makeup done? It's a crazy world in the land of cosmetics and they don't play nice. I'm starving. You're the best. Thanks, love," she says, grabbing my sandwich and kissing me on the cheek before starting for the door.

"Hey!" I call out, but she already has the corner of the sandwich in her mouth, taking a big bite of what is mine. I'm not even sure she chewed before swallowing.

"I'm working a full eight-hour shift today. Take your pale butt to the beach or hang out with some people besides me. It's okay to make friends." She winks. "I promise I won't get jealous or offended. You wanted to explore the world, babe, now is your chance."

And just like that she slams the door behind her . . . taking my lunch with her. I couldn't even get it out of my mouth that there is no more turkey for me to make another and she has the car so I can't just go get something like she can on the way. My stomach growls reminding me that it's empty, and it has been that way for a while. I bend forward, letting my forehead fall against the counter in a dramatic fashion.

A knock sounds at the door, sending me shooting into an upright position. "Who is it?" I work to clear my voice from the scratchy, dehydrated state it's in. Obviously food isn't the only thing I need.

"Liam. Open up."

Liam? How does he know where I live? My feet begin to move before I instruct them to, and before I realize it I'm opening the door, suddenly curious. The sight on the other side isn't so bad. Board shorts, tee shirt fitted against his muscles, flip-flops, messy hair and a bright white smile. Maybe I misjudged him. Or jumped to an assessment too soon . . . "You rang?"

He takes one look at my body . . .or maybe the slouchy tee shirt and active shorts I'm wearing. At least I'm not in what I slept in. "Not that I have any particular problem with this just rolled out of bed look, because usually when I see it on a girl it's early in the morning and I have a rather large smile on my face, but why aren't you ready?"

My brows dip. "Ready? Ready for what? And how did you know where I live?"

His hands grip onto the top of the doorframe and his upper body swings forward, inside of the door. "As much as most girls would love to think they have a stalker somewhere out there, I'm not him. Sorry to disappoint. You told me at work one night when you weren't busy blowing me off." He winks, his smile not fading in the least. "And when I got here I saw that blonde girl you're always with leaving so I asked which apartment was yours. Surprisingly, she gave it to me without question and a massive grin on her face as she pointed me in the right direction."

I lean back as he closes in on me. "That did not tell me why you're here."

"Drake's pool party."

"That's not today."

"Plans have changed, gorgeous, as they so often do. Found out last night when I got home. Did you not get the text? It's usually a chain type thing. He tells a few people and they pass the information down. You know, it's just easier that way."

I don't think I've gotten any texts, but then it dawns on me that I haven't even seen my phone since we left the pool last night. I wonder where that is. Saxton had pockets . . .

"I can't go." The words slip out of my mouth with no control. He walks inside, pushing me back with each step to avoid a collision. "I didn't invite you in."

"I'm not a vampire. I can walk over the threshold without being invited."

He's still smiling, and my traitorous mouth begins to mirror his. "That doesn't mean I want you inside."

"I'm not leaving this apartment without you. I've watched you long enough to know that you obviously need a forceful push."

"I don't want to go."

"Why not?"

"It's just not a good idea."

"And tell me exactly why that is?"

"I can't at the moment."

"Did your relationship status change overnight?"

I think on that question for a moment, remembering how he kept shutting things down, how he didn't tell me anything about himself yet had me spilling my guts to him. He clearly didn't want things to go further even when I offered it to him free of stipulations or he would have taken it. I may not know all that much about guys, but what I do know is they rarely turn down an easy hookup. Maybe I'm going about this all the wrong way. I wonder . . .

"No, but why are you so hell bent on me going? What does it matter whether I'm there or not?"

His eyes change and his smile disappears. "Why do I have to have an ulterior motive? Maybe I like you and just want to hang out for a while. Is that so bad?"

"Sometimes ulterior motives are welcome," I whisper, not stopping the inappropriate words that are flying out of my mouth. I'm not even sure I'm whispering them to the right person.

His smile returns and he takes a step toward me. This time I don't move.

He places his hand on the side of my neck, before angling my chin up. "Care to prove that statement?"

"Okay," I say, my breathing becoming a little short with him this close. His lips linger above mine for a second, before he lays them on mine. He stalls for a moment, my guess waiting on me to tell him to stop, but currently my mind has gone too far with wonder to stop.

I wrap my arms around his waist, not sure what else to do with them, and then he finally begins to kiss me; really kiss me. And although it's not the same as Saxton—melting me to my very core with one kiss—it's still enough to leave my heart racing, my body quivering, and my hormones speeding through every vein in my body. I'm at the phase of my life that I want this with a guy. I ignored it for too long. I want it more than I've ever wanted anything else.

He pulls away too soon. "Go put on a sexy little bikini, grab a towel, and meet me back here before I change my mind and take advantage of the situation like any turned on man would do."

"What if I don't want to go? I'd rather try option b."

"Fuck," he whispers. "I want to, but no. Not yet. Then you'll get your way and have me gone within an hour. I want more time."

I spin on my heels and head for my room. This is really becoming harder than I originally thought. It's like I have a permanent *good girl* label plastered to my forehead for every hot guy to see. I want it gone. I have to figure out where I'm going wrong here. Seduction cannot be that hard. Saxton didn't want it, well, someone else will. Today I'm getting rid of it . . .

I follow Liam through the gate, closing in on the laughter, screams, and yells about passing the ball with every step forward. He stops and looks at me just as I take a deep breath to calm down. My nerves are beginning to take over. There's no darkness for me to hide behind, or a room filled with loud music drowning out my thoughts, and there's not enough alcohol flowing in my sight to put me in my comfort zone.

The person I've become was born in a certain environment. In the light I'm exposed. The insecure girl with no social skill is the focus, and the fear returns that no one will like me. There is music—the one thing that can relax me no matter what state I'm in—but this time it's just in the background. "You're kind of shy, aren't you? That's why you didn't want to come . . . "

"Am I really Captain obvious?"

He smiles. "Maybe just a little."

"I guess you could call it that; at least in big crowds. I'm not so bad around one person at a time."

A smirk returns when he grabs the edge of my hand, pulling me a little closer. "Didn't anyone ever tell you how to fix that?"

I blink a few times, looking him in the eyes. "Guess not."

"Just picture everyone being naked. Then you'll start comparing body parts and it becomes funny. You'll laugh and it'll loosen you up some. After that everyone doesn't seem all that bad."

"That really works? I can't imagine anyone having funny body parts out of the people that work in a nightclub. Having a good body is kind of a requirement."

"Yes, it works, and you'd be surprised what people can hide behind a little clothing."

"How would you know all of this? You hardly seem like you'd ever be anything besides extroverted."

He places my hand at the top of his chest and slowly runs it down his front, letting my fingers ripple over each contracted abdominal muscle that he has. He's smooth, but I can tell he shaves his chest. No hair, no imperfect places, no sporadic acne. "Don't let something I've worked hard for fool you. I used to be a big kid. For a while I could wear the same size pants as my dad, and he was stocky himself. The locker room isn't a fun place for some of us."

"You were overweight?" I ask in disbelief, staring at the hard exterior just below my hand. I don't even see faint stretch marks around his lower portion. "I find that hard to believe. You can't even tell."

"Well I was. I was a lazy kid that liked food. Parents worked a lot and I stayed inside." He pulls my arms around his waist, as if he likes them there. I like it, but some inner part of me feels wrong. Saxton feels better . . . Ugh, I have to stop. It was one night with a beautiful stranger. It's over and I need to move on. "Let's just say rejection is very real for some of us, Kambry. We all have our fears and insecurities, but if you want to change something bad enough you will, no matter what it takes. And if you look hard enough you may realize we're not all that different, you and I, even if it's just a friendship," he says, whispering close to my lips as if he wants to kiss me again. ". . .with benefits."

I wonder how bad it is that I kind of want him to. My emotions are tangled up with my desires. I don't know one from the other at the moment. "You're beautiful, Kambry. I've had my eye on you since the first time I laid my eyes on you. I've just been waiting on an opening ever since."

This time I make the move, unable to help myself. He's saying all the right things to confuse me even more. He doesn't rush it. Instead, he slows down my pace. The sound of someone clearing his voice fills the warm air. I can feel Liam's lips turn up into a smile against mine. I pull back, my cheeks flushed and hot. "Would you two like to join the party or are you just going to hang out at the gate all day?" Drake says.

I turn around, slightly embarrassed, and then Liam puts his arm around me. Drake glances between us a few times, sipping from a Corona. I've never seen him so . . . comfortable, normal maybe. Flip-flops and swim trunks are quite a change from his professional attire I'm used to. He looks different like this, more his age. "We had a straggler. I wanted to make sure no one was left behind for your epic pool party," he says in a lighter tone than before, as if we didn't just get caught kissing on someone else's property.

"A simple phone call couldn't get the job done?"

"Didn't have her number, boss. Had to go old school and show up at her door."

The laughter is present within every word, but I don't get the humor. I obviously haven't met Drake's humorous side. I feel like I'm standing in the principal's office. "And it took your tongue to coax her here? That's a little offensive."

"What can I say, boss, I can be very persuasive when I need to be."

I glance between them, squeezing my fists to avoid biting my nails. Then, Drake laughs, making all of my tensed nerves fade away. "Shit, son, save your bullshit for someone that believes it." He holds out his hand. "Keys."

Keys? Liam pulls his truck keys from his pocket and passes them over to

Drake. He walks past us and grabs the wooden gate, pulling it open. I walk through and stop at the sound of Drake's voice as Liam gets to the opening right behind me. "You better respect this one. Got it?"

"Of course."

I look at Drake, and warmth I've never known runs through me. In this second I see him for more than a boss, but also like a friend, a protector, and kind of like I always wanted to see my brother. "Drinks are in the coolers on the patio, alcohol and nonalcoholic, along with food. There's a T.V. and I've got the grill handled. Pool house is open to use the bathroom and whatever else it needs to be used for. Have fun. I only have two rules. You don't drive out of here if you touch any alcohol to your lips till morning or I clear you first. Otherwise, you want to leave, you call a cab. House is off limits unless you have a reason to be in it and I know about it beforehand." He stretches out his arms to each side of his body. "Aside from that, what's mine is yours. And remember, what happens here stays here. Don't bring it to work."

I finally glance around for the first time. The pool is filled with many familiar faces. He has a rock feature that incases a waterslide, currently being utilized by one of the bouncers going down head first into the pool. Loungers are covered in towels and girls I'm assuming are too good to get wet, sunbathing as if that crystal clear water doesn't feel better in this heat.

Drake is no longer standing before me, but I can hear him shouting directions at someone supervising the grill and glass bottles clanking as they're tossed into the trash. My stomach growls from the smell of beef cooking and filling the air, reminding me that I've yet to eat anything, but it doesn't look like anyone is eating yet. I'm definitely not going to be the oddball.

Lips skim across my cheek. "Go find a place to put your stuff and shed some clothes. I'll bring you a drink."

Liam walks off, leaving me to myself with the opportunity of thoughts occurring that I don't want. I take a deep breath and walk toward the sidelines of doom. I've never been good at making new girl friends. It's terrifying to be honest. Girls can be mean with just a simple sentence aimed at your gut where your deepest insecurities lie. This was my intention of coming here though, right? To create a life for myself I didn't have back home.

I make my way to the empty lounge chair beside Amanda. I'm surprised she's here, considering the secrets she carries within her body. "Well, well, look who it is. I figured you'd be a flake."

Her chin is turned up toward the sun, her glasses creating a shield to her eyes. "It's no more surprising that I'm here than it is for you," I quip back. "Should you be drinking?" I ask, pointing at the beer in her hand.

Her head jerks toward me so fast it's surprising it's still attached. "Who told you?"

Whoops.

"Stomach virus? Convenient . . . just a guess."

"Well, mind your own business. What is a problem today can be easily fixed in a few days like I intend for it to. Don't get too comfortable in my job. It's not for sure that you'll be needed to replace me yet," she says in a bitchy tone, and then turns up the bottle of beer so she can prove her point.

I stare at her, quietly observing her disregard for the human life that is growing inside of her. I get that it's her choice, but I don't have to agree with it. I'm not used to being around someone so open about it like it's a quick fix for syphilis. Even if there is an option B it's still a big deal. I guess I just assumed it would be a more private matter for those that go through it and choose that direction.

I remove my shirt and step out of my shorts, tossing them on the empty lounger. "Whatever. I'm going to find Liam."

She raises her sunglasses. "Oh yeah, just a little tip, he likes it on bottom. You southern girls should know all about riding, right?" she toys and adds a dramatic wink for good measure.

And every bit of attraction I had toward him just took a dive into the cold pool of suckiness. It's one thing to assume someone is experienced, but to know a previous member on his roster, especially her, kind of ruins it. I stare at her, wide-eyed and mouth ajar. What if it's his baby? Hell to the no. "Wouldn't you like to know . . ." she taunts, as if already knowing my thoughts. "but no. It's not him. It was long enough ago that he's been in the clear by almost a year, and he gloved it, so go and enjoy a night of drunken sex. It's worth it. You're welcome in advance."

My insides are constricting. My thoughts are running wild. You know what, screw it. Why should I care? I'm in the minority here. No matter what way I slice it this won't be equal. I cannot deal with strike two.

I turn around and spot him standing at a beer pong table, holding a beer in his hand as he yells for the person guzzling a cupful. I've always wanted to play that game. I've heard enough stories that I've been curious for years. I haven't liked the taste of beer so far, but maybe if I think of it as taking medicine I can do it. Just down it without thinking. Yes, I think I will.

Everyone around me has become like my best friends over the past few hours, cheering me on as I prepare to take my shot. Finally starting my third round. It takes forever for everyone to get a chance to play since it's become the hit of the party, but I guess in the world of alcohol it's for the best or everyone here would have passed out by mid afternoon. Between, I just munch and sip, because after each round I feel more relaxed, laughter and fun coming with ease. The beer doesn't even taste anymore. Dark has fallen and lights from the patio beam down on the table with the multicolored changing pool lights in the background.

The world is amazing in this view. Nothing matters and everyone is nice. Liam takes the opposite side of the table as the cups of beer are filled and setup in front of each of us. First round we played two on two, allowing him to stand beside me and teach me how to play against what he said was another amateur—Samantha is her name—splitting the cups when I had to drink so I didn't get trashed my first time to play. Second time her and I played alone. This time, I'm on my own with a real player.

"Ready to see how it's really done?" The smirk on his face is no less than arrogant. His cocky stance proves that he's clearly done this many times. I really wish I could say the same, but there is no doubt that this is fun.

"You sound confident in the outcome, Liam," I say in what I hope is flirty verbiage and not drunken slurs.

"Oh, I'm just determined, that's all." His eyes veer to my busty chest and then back to my eyes, the smile giving away what he is saying without saying it disrespectfully. And I'll admit, it makes me feel confident and sexy instead of the nervous mess I was last night. I was definitely going about it wrong. No more verbal planning. No more embarrassing explanations. It's just going to happen, and I'm going to let it.

I hold out my hand for the small white ball, a poised and satisfied grin on my face. It takes me a while to get my aim the way I want it, and then with the flick of my wrist the ball is catapulted through the air toward the red Solo cups. It bounces off the rim and then the table, before he catches it and returns it with what seems like no aim or prep at all. The ball lands in the cup at the top of the pyramid, creating a small splash as it hits the amber liquid.

Yeah, I'm going to suck at this . . .

I contain my smile as I lift the cup and place the rim to my lips. He stares at me as I turn it back and quickly down the contents of the cup, minus the ball. And then we start the process all over again.

My head falls back as he sinks the ball into my last cup. I'm already drunk. My lips are numb. He started drinking some of his cups several pitches back just to keep it balanced. My aim blows about like the wolf's try on the third pig's brick home. His cups aren't moving by force. It's a good thing I didn't try out for softball.

After a few breaths to ensure my stomach can hold it, I down the last cup and replace it rim down on the table like only a champ would a loss. "I think I'm done, y'all. I gotta pee. Who's next?" The words come out a slur. Even I can tell. The funny part. I don't care. I'm living.

I walk past the table, my eyes locking with Liam's as I pass, headed for the pool house. Luckily, the layout isn't a maze and it takes me just a minute to find the bathroom. I plop down, barely getting my bikini bottoms down before my bladder takes revenge on what I've done to it. Elbow to thigh, cheek to palm, I stare at the floor, watching the pattern on the tile spin. Masculine feet intrude on my pattern making, leading my eyes up the lean legs, until they meet with the face I've been staring at off and on all day.

Not as fun to look at as the one last night . . .but it'll definitely do.

"I'm drunk, but not half as drunk as I'm going to be when I drown myself between your legs."

I laugh. Harder than I have in a long time. I fight to breathe, as I pull on the toilet paper in a sloppy fashion. It takes a lot of effort just to wipe, but somehow I figure it out and shimmy my bottoms up my legs with no care in the world that I'm flashing him. He walks toward me as I flush. "That's either really corny or I'm really drunk."

His smile proves he knows it's a drunk pickup line from Hell, but it works in this situation somehow. “I'd say it's half and half,” he says, “but I don't need you so serious right now.”

He grabs my waist and pulls me toward him. “Why?”

“Because it'll make things easier.”

His lips assault mine, a heat much hotter than any previous times we've kissed today. Blindly he leads me out of the bathroom, and before I know it my back is aligned against a mattress and my panties have disappeared. There is no time to think before my top, too, is gone. His lips descend toward my neck. “What if someone comes in?”

“I locked the door.”

Lips to nipple, any previous thought dissipates, leaving me careless, reckless. My breathing is embarrassing. I ignore it. It doesn't seem to be bothering him. His hand grips behind my knee, spreading my leg from the other. He tugs on my nipple between his teeth. “You're so fucking hot.”

With a quick move to the other nipple, a finger massages my entrance, and before he can even press inside, a revolting feeling occurs in the pit of my stomach, leaving no room for error. I press against his chest and take off in a sprint for the bathroom, barely making it to the toilet before expelling everything I've consumed today with an evil vengeance. I feel like I'm dying.

Strike two.

One more and I'm out.

“I'm really sorry about last night.” My hand is already on the door handle. I just want my bed and water. Then, surely, this punishment will be over. The nausea still raging full speed tells me otherwise. Then there's the headache. I feel like someone used my head for a piñata.

Despite my embarrassing behavior he's still smiling. Now I know what it's like being Meredith while he was me, babysitting me through the worst sickness I've ever encountered, and I've had a badass stomach virus a time or two. The regret is real. “Don't sweat it. I told you I'm not a dick like you think. Another time. Get some rest. I'll wait till work to get your number.”

"Okay."

My out. I waste no time lingering with nothing to say. With what little of my pride is still in tact, I open the door and walk to my apartment in shame. When I open the door Meredith is sitting at the bar eating a bowl of cereal, a mocking expression on her face. "Well, well, look what the cat drug in."

"Shut up. I want to hear nothing."

"So you don't want this back?" She waves my phone in front of her in the air.

"Where'd you get that?" I shout.

"First tell me, did you lose it?"

The awful photographs begin a slideshow in my mind, reminding me of a night I'll never forget, and not in a good way. "No. I was a second away from blowing chunks all over him. Forget it. Just keep the phone. I don't want to talk about it."

"Awe, Kam. Don't be hard on yourself. It happens to the best of us. It takes practice, babe. Here." She hops off the stool and hands it to me. "It was on the door with a note. I laid it on your bed." She kisses my forehead. "Advil, water, bed. We'll talk when you get up. I'm going to get out of here for a bit and let you sleep. Me and boredom don't mix well. Love you."

"Love you too." She goes in one direction and me the other. I trudge along until I fall face first on my mattresses. My hand makes contact with paper. I roll over, pulling it directly in front of eyesight, trying to read the handwritten note through the pounding in my head, loud, with every beat of my heart.

I came by to return it and you weren't home. My number is in the phone. Use it for any questions.
-Saxton

Saxton . . .

Maybe he really wasn't blowing me off.

Shit.

CHAPTER SEVEN

Kambry

It's been a week since I've seen or heard from Saxton. The note is all I have to hold on to. His number was there, but I've yet to use it. He said it was for questions, and I don't currently have any; at least, none that would qualify as anything other than fishing for information. I thought he would come to work or something by now, yet it's been oddly quiet.

I won't lie and say that I haven't thought about him, because I have, more times than I truly want to admit aloud. Actually, I've thought about him enough to keep Liam at a distance just to see if anything is there with Saxton. I'm trying not to be that girl; the one that hooks up with a guy one time and then gets attached, thinking it's going to turn into more than it is. I won't. I was about to let him take my virginity, but it was going to be nothing more. I need to remind myself of that, because I haven't thought about Liam this much since the night we went a little overboard, so what does it mean that I think of Saxton daily? Two different pools involved, two guys, two nights apart. I have to wonder . . . Am I taking my newfound freedom too far? Nah. I don't think so.

Work has been busy. Drake kept his promise and moved me to the VIP section to properly train with Amanda as her replacement for when she leaves soon—when she can't hide her super mysterious pregnancy any longer, assuming she's still pregnant—and she's not happy about it. She's a real bitch to work with most of the time, and reminds me constantly that this is just a precaution, but I don't really think this whole ordeal is all that mysterious at all. People talk. Rumors fly. Usually, there is always some truth behind most rumors. Just saying.

I miss it downstairs, but the money is better up here. Tips alone for one slow night is more than what I made down there in an entire busy weekend. The environment is a little different than the carefree young adults partying without a care in the world, but supposedly certain nights it takes off up here, depending on who is in house.

I walk up to the bar and set my tray down, ready to give my order to Zack, one of the full-time bartenders up here. I met him when Drake put Liam back downstairs, my shift immediately following the pool party. I'm not disappointed. It helps me to keep the distance between us when he's all too ready to have a part two. I did judge him too quickly, but things just don't click like they did with . . . I take a deep breath. This is ridiculous. Maybe I should go out with him to regain my sanity from this insane crush. He's cute enough and all, is a pleasant kisser, and has persistent hands, but I worry I'll regret it the second it happens if something does turn up with Saxton.

Amanda sets down her tray next to mine. We're working different sections tonight to give me more time alone to get comfortable without her looking over my shoulder. "Hey, Kambry."

I look at her. The expression on her face is a little too friendly to mean anything good. "Yeah?"

"Drake wants you in the conference room. He said someone is waiting for you."

I immediately start to get nervous. No one ever gets called to the conference room. It's merely there for important people that don't want their business out in the open or to counsel employees that are about to get fired. The last people rumored to have gone in there were Amanda herself and that Justin Talbert guy that is supposedly a regular, and that was not long after I started . . .

I swallow. "Do you know what for? Who's in there?"

She zones out slightly, a smirk spreading across her face. "He didn't say. I'll cover your tables. Run along now. You don't want to keep whoever it is waiting." She winks; being a bitch I'm sure. "I told you not to get comfortable up here." I've discovered since coming up here that sometimes she is cool to be around and sometimes you just want to stab her in the eye with the heel of a stiletto. Girls like her are hard to be friends with. It's like she has a split personality.

I roll my eyes, but remain as calm as possible. I wouldn't want her to think for a second that she bothers me. "Okay. Thanks, Amanda. I'll be back."

"Mmmm Hmmm. Sure thing, doll. Whatever you say."

I grab my tray and walk around the bar to store it underneath the bar top, before heading in the direction of the narrow stairway that leads to the third floor, consisting of Drake's office, the club owner's office, whom I've never met, and the conference room.

As I come to the bottom of the stairway I place my hand on the wall railing that leads to the top, placing my foot on the first step as I look up, trying to remember if I've done anything wrong or questionable. It's almost closing time and that's what makes me nervous. Of course they are going to wait till closing if you're going to get fired so you don't cause a scene. Drake didn't seem pissed off about anything. Shit, what if a customer complained? I knew I should have stayed downstairs. I can't afford to lose this job.

I close my eyes and take a deep breath, preparing to ascend the staircase. I might as well get this over with. One by one I climb, trying to calm myself down. Why am I freaking out over this? What if it's nothing? I'm being a paranoid little girl.

Find your woman balls, Kambry.

When I reach the top of the stairs Drake steps out of his office, meeting me at the top. "Kambry."

"Drake. Amanda said you wanted to see me. Is everything okay?"

"Do you remember that client you served last week? The three guys on your first night?"

Saxton . . .

My anxiety turns into excitement. Is he here? Why would he come up here? I glance down at myself, wondering if I look okay. Crap. I guess I look decent. I've dressed up more all week than I usually do in hopes I may see him again. The short, red dress compliments my platinum blonde hair. The killer black shoes make me the perfect height. I've even learned a lot about the art of makeup application from Meredith. Smoky eyes are my best look, complimenting my blue eyes.

"Yes," I answer, my voice hitching in the middle of the word. Dammit. "Why?"

"Well, he called earlier, asking if he could meet with you before closing. He said it was important, paid to occupy the conference room, and I agreed. Are you okay with it?"

"Sure." He raises a brow. I answered too quickly and with too much excitement in my voice. Reset. Let me try that again, making my voice seem more bored. "I mean, I guess. They seemed nice enough and they did pay, you say. I guess it would be bad business otherwise."

He places his hand at the small of my back and leads me to the end of the hall. "I'll be in my office going over some applications. I'm not leaving you up here alone. If you need anything at all come get me. Do you understand?"

"Okay, Drake. Thanks . . ." I pause. "For everything."

"Don't sweat it. You've earned what you have. Keep working hard and I'll probably be looking for your replacement at some point. This is no place for you permanently. Just give me enough time to enjoy not having to for a while."

I stop just before we reach the door and look at him. "That's the nicest thing someone has said to me in a really long time."

His brows bunch. "That you're a hard worker? I hardly think that's a compliment worth recognizing."

"You'd be surprised," I say and continue walking until the distance runs out. I place my hand on the doorknob, pausing for a moment before I twist it and open the door. I can already hear Drake's footsteps distancing.

Upon opening the door, all of my excitement and nervousness halts as he stands from the chair and walks around the table to meet me at the door. He holds out his hand for me to shake. My shoulders fall, slightly disappointed. "Kambry, I appreciate you agreeing to meet with me under no prior notice. I hope all is well since the last time I saw you."

I shake his hand to be polite. "It is . . .um."

"Michael. Michael Prescott."

"Sorry, I just meet so many people here. Sometimes I'm bad with names." I release his hand. "How are you?"

"I'm good. Just here to take care of some late night business."

I look around the room, confused. "You wanted to see me?"

"I did, Kambry." The way he says my name so professional makes my nose crinkle. I hate the way it sounds, almost as if he's being sarcastic, even though I know he's not. He turns, walks back to his seat on the other side of the table, and sits in the leather, executive style chair before placing his forearms over a folder lying on the tabletop. He's dressed in a suit with no jacket. He looks like he needs a drink. "Come, have a seat. We may be here a while."

I walk toward the end of the table and sit as instructed, the corner separating us. "Isn't it kind of late to be working?" The ring on his left hand says he has a family.

He gives me a half smile at best. "The film industry never sleeps. Work never ceases. There's always people to please and budgets to manage, countless and never-ending screenplays to read, and jobs to be distributed." He winks. "But it's a job I love, which brings me here."

That conversation with Saxton last week suddenly slaps me across the face. *He saw me take interest in you and he may very well act on it. Most of the time acting is about chemistry between actors . . .*

"Why exactly are you here, Mr. Prescott?"

"I'm here about a client, and a possible job opportunity for you, Kambry, or do you prefer to be called something else?"

"My name is Kambry Rivers, but Kambry is fine."

"Okay, Kambry. I'm here because of Mr. Maverick, whom I know you've had the pleasure in meeting on an intimate level. I'm going to ask you first to excuse me, because this is completely unorthodox of the way business is usually handled, but I'm trying to adjust."

"Who?"

"Saxton Maverick, the guy that was with me last week. You two did mingle a little more informally, did you not?"

My eyes widen, suddenly remembering what exactly intimate means, even if he doesn't; at least I hope he doesn't. I let a guy go down on me and I didn't even know his last name. My cheeks are probably turning red. I can feel them heating. "Something of that nature."

"Well, I'm here at his request, and completely against my better judgment, but I've worked with him before so I'm taking a risk. What exactly do you know of Mr. Maverick? I'm assuming you know he's in films."

He opens the folder and looks at me. I am starting to get embarrassed by my lack of information on Saxton, especially given the nature of that hangout session and the amount of thoughts that have occurred since then. "I kind of got that vibe based on some things he said, but he didn't really clarify."

His lips purse as he stares at me. "Let's just start from scratch. That may be easier. Then you can give me your thoughts. Does that work for you?"

"Okay."

"This is going to be long-winded, so bear with me. You can ask questions once I'm done."

"Okay," I repeat.

"First of all I'm a producer for a film company. I have several roles but I basically oversee the whole process, and some of that has to do with casting. Saxton is an actor, and a pretty popular one in this industry. He's currently one of our highest sellers. More people are starting to want him. He's established, meaning he usually gets most jobs between his agent and the companies that want him in their films. He doesn't really have to chase after them anymore."

That's funny, because I've never heard of a Saxton Maverick . . .

"That's also another reason this is abnormal. If we don't use an established male, or in this situation, girl that we already know we want to pursue, or one that doesn't have an agent readily finding open roles for scheduled auditions with the panel, we have open casting for people to audition. Those are usually free agents that have yet to find an agent to represent them."

He pauses. "Is this making sense?"

"Yes. I'm listening."

"The meeting with Saxton last week was to offer him the role for a project that begins filming soon. It's a reality T.V. segment that we're giving a trial run by filming for a short time and then premiering to the public to see what the response will be, and then based on the numbers we will decide if we want to extend the project to the full six months of filming currently being discussed."

When he pauses I take the opportunity to ask a question. "What kind of reality T.V. segment?"

"Roommates. It's a male and female living in the same house, but a couple that has chemistry since it will only be two of you versus a group."

"Kind of like *Jersey Shore*, *The Real World*, or that *Party Down South* show? I've watched those shows. They look fun, but why did you want to meet with me? I'm not an actor. Wait, isn't there a long process for choosing those people since it's reality T.V.?"

"Exactly, just subtract the rest of the roommates. The rest will be pretty much identical with a few exceptions. And yes, you're right, but because of the type of exceptions it limits the choices in open casting for reality television. They want Saxton to bring in anticipation and numbers, but because we are coming to him directly it gives him room to make requests, and his request is you."

My stomach flips. "He wants me to live in a house with him . . .on camera? I don't know. I'm not really camera friendly. I'm a little bit of an introvert. I doubt there would be anything interesting to watch. I don't really have that star personality."

My nerves start twisting and turning, firing off like fireworks. I tend to be shy around people I don't know for a while. After I get comfortable I won't shut up, but for a while I'm reserved, feeling the new person out to see if our personalities click. Meredith tells me all the time that guys don't approach me at bars and clubs because I have a resting bitch face. I just roll my eyes, because who in the hell wants to wear a smile all the time? I can be perfectly happy without having to constantly think of what my facial expressions look like.

My mind recalls some of the conversation with Saxton. If I don't do this, I don't get to hang out with him? Because he'll be hanging out with someone else. That thought immediately sours my mood. Why have I never heard of him before? That puzzles me. I was sheltered but I knew how to read and stay up to date with normal things like movies and music. If he were really this big shot actor that gets to make demands with producers surely his name would at least be familiar.

"What are the exceptions?" I blurt out the question before he even has time to respond to my previous response. I'm not even sure what made me ask it to begin with.

"Cameras never stop rolling, not even during sex." My eyes widen. "It's an adult film series basically. It will only air on specific networks that allow porn, readily available for consumer purchase with the click of their remotes."

I stand, my chair rolling backward from my sudden change in position. "Saxton is a porn star! Please tell me I'm hearing you wrong. I have to have heard you wrong."

"He is an adult film star, yes. Terminology is up to the user."

My eyes well up; trying their damnedest to spill over the tears. I feel so stupid. I will not let them. This is so embarrassing. That is disgusting. I let someone that has probably screwed hundreds of women touch me, kiss me, and almost fuck me. What if he has some kind of disease? I didn't even ask any questions. I almost gave my virginity to someone that has sex as a career. Don't get me wrong, I didn't want love and cuddles in exchange, but I wanted some form of normalcy. I wanted respect. He expects me to lose my virginity in front of the world? Aren't most guys jealous in some form of someone else experiencing what they're experiencing? He wants every damn pervert out there to see my body? To imagine screwing me instead of him or vice versa?

I back up toward the door and he stands. "I'm sorry. I can't do that. I just can't. I'm sorry."

I bump into the door and my ankle twists from my balance shifting. I quickly recover, trying to fumble for the knob. He grabs the folder off the table and makes his way toward me. "Kambry, wait. Just give me five more minutes."

"You have one." I feel sick to my stomach. The thought of someone wanting me to be a porn star upsets me.

He extends the folder out toward me. "Just take this and look the contents over. There is no harm in reading. It has a copy of the contract in it and everything else you need to know, including my business card. I know you're surprised. Saxton told me you're a virgin. For your age that's impressive, and I'm not even sure of exact in years. As long as you're a legal adult that's all that matters, and judging from your job I'm going to say you are."

His mouth lines. I feel betrayed. That was personal information that I told one person. I assumed common courtesy would keep it between him and me, not start a domino effect. "Look, I'm not going to bad mouth the industry. I work in it. I also know the stereotypes that most people associate with it, and I assure you ninety-eight percent of them are false. Just keep an open mind before you decide, because there are things in this contract that may actually surprise you. They surprised me . . .and I've seen it all. He isn't doing this project if you don't, so keep in mind that we are at a standstill if you decline the offer, as we will be looking for two new people instead of one."

I yank the folder out of his hand, aggravated that he is now trying to guilt trip me. I'm not even sure how I ended up here. "I wouldn't expect my call. That would take a miracle."

I move to the side and open the door. "Have yourself a good night, Mr. Prescott."

Without any further words I open the door and walk out, suddenly in dire need of a shower and sleep. I'll text Drake that I had to go home. It's close enough to close it shouldn't matter. I'll just have to live short of the tips I would have earned otherwise. I think I'm in need of alcohol myself. I really hope Meredith came through like she said she would.

I think what I actually need is to be with someone else in ways that'll make me forget this whole thing. I run straight to my locker and grab my things, texting Liam on the way out the door.

Me: Hey, I'm ready to take you up on that offer. I need some fun tonight. No interruptions this time. Call me when you get off. I'm leaving a little early.

I hit send and hail a cab. The bad part is . . .even with a plan of what I want I'm still thinking about him, and that night, as if none of the information I just received is sticking, and that's a terrifying thing.

I walk out of the bathroom with a towel wrapped around my damp body, and make my way into my room. I'm not sure where Meredith is. My guess is she stayed over with some guy after leaving the bar. I'm sure she'll come stumbling in doing the walk of shame around sunrise. I haven't heard from Liam yet either.

I sit on my mattresses and comb through my wet hair with my fingertips as I let my body finish drying. It drives me nuts to get dressed still damp. Something about my clothes clinging to my body makes me feel claustrophobic. Plus, the air is still cooling down the apartment from us being gone and turning it up to conserve power. California heat may be different than Alabama heat, but it's still hot nonetheless. It's still summer.

My MacBook charging in the corner captures my attention. It was my graduation present. I would say it was a form of freedom finally from my parents, but it wasn't. It was only for school and research purposes, so I took it when I left. A gift is a gift and it's mine.

According to my parents, things like social media are a failure of society, and only contributes to rises in sex trafficking and kidnapping of children, among other evils in the world. I wasn't to be caught with any of the above under their roof. I still haven't remembered to venture there. I guess old habits, or restrictions, die hard.

I stand and walk toward it, picking it up and pulling the charger from the port, carrying it back to my mattresses to lay down. I place it on the mattress and fall down on my stomach, raising the lower part of my legs into the air, and swinging them back and forth in opposing directions as I open my laptop.

The screen instantly lights up, bringing up my login screen. I quickly type in my password and the selfie photo of Meredith and I the first day we put our toes in the Pacific Ocean appears on the home screen. I stare at it for a moment, trying to remember why in the hell I got my laptop in the first place. *Maybe I should just Google you . . .*

"Can't stop me this time."

Without further thought my finger swipes across the Trackpad, moving the cursor to the Safari icon and I double tap to open it. My default search engine appears: Google. I place my fingers in position over the keyboard and begin typing in the letters without giving them any instruction on what to type: Saxton Maverick.

My hand starts to shake as I hover over the search button. "Why are you freaking out, Kambry? Put your big girl panties on and just do it."

I click the button, waiting as it quickly searches the web for that specific key phrase. My eyes enlarge as the list of clickable links start appearing.

Possible new secret XXX project starring Saxton Maverick. Who to costar? Details to be released.

Saxton "The horseman" Maverick in XXX film featuring sorority girls.

Saxton Maverick, the rising porn star, in college escapades part II.

Title by title I read the article headers, my eyes flaring with each one. I'm scared to click on one, afraid of what I'll find. I click on the images option instead of web. At least this way I can get just a preview of what may lie within the links.

The thumbnails begin to appear quickly. My heart starts to race, my cheeks heating. My breathing becomes uneven. "Shit," I whisper. "Is that his dick? No wonder he turned around when he took his boxer briefs off to pull his jeans on that night at the pool. What have I gotten myself into?"

Various photos appear. Some of him fully clothed at what appears to be premiers or events, some candid shots probably from paparazzi, and others of him completely fucking naked with a woman. And not all are the same. In fact, most are different. There are hundreds of photos . . .*hundreds*, and thousands of webpages in the hit.

A sudden feeling overcomes me; one I don't understand. I hate those girls; the girls that are with him like I was with him. I despise that they're feeling him inside of them, yet I didn't. It angers me to see him touching them, and they him, experiencing him in a way that I've experienced him, but more. What's wrong with me? Why didn't he want more with me?

Even though I don't want to I keep scrolling, mindlessly taking in each one. One in particular catches my attention. He's standing on the side of a bed, holding a girl by her hips, with his waist shoved between her legs. She's blonde, lying on the bed with her back arched, her chin turned up toward the ceiling, and her eyes closed. At brief glance she has similarities like me. Her hands are clenched in the sheets, her legs bent and pressed against her body, her toes curled. She looks completely mesmerized by the feeling, but that's not really what captivated my attention.

He's what captured it. The way he's looking away from her. I know he's probably looking at the camera, but it looks like he's looking at . . .me. Gosh, he's beautiful, all of him, reminding me of the way he looked between my legs, his tongue flush against my body, watching me while he made me feel good.

A surge of wetness occurs between my legs—a rise in hormones being the cause. My bottom lip pulls between my teeth as I remember that night. My eyes close. Instead of that blonde being another woman, it's me. He's fucking me . . .not her.

I roll over onto my back, one hand pulling my towel open. I grab my breast in my hand, my nipple already hard. I begin to knead it, pulling my nipple between my fingers. My legs pull into the same position hers just were as my free hand travels down my body, over my navel, toward my clit. My hand runs across it, to my entrance. I rub my fingertip in a circle over it, coating it in my wetness, before slipping inside. I moan, pretending it's him, just like when he did it.

I pull my finger out and run it between my lips, until it settles firmly on my clit. The pressure instantly causes my back to arch. My legs spread wider, opening my lips up a little more. I whirl my fingers in a circle, spreading the wetness thoroughly over my clit, making it feel that much better, making it resemble his tongue.

As if it were just an hour ago that night plays back in my mind vividly. The grasp on my breast gets harder, the pinch around my nipple tighter. My moans become more pronounced as my fingers pick up in speed, rubbing up and down over my clit. "Just like that, Saxton. Right there." I moan. "Don't stop. I can feel it. I'm close."

My muscles contract, squeezing tightly even though there is a void. My clit starts to sensitize the faster I rub. One look into those eyes as his tongue rubs my clit and my orgasm starts, consuming my world, my mind. "Damn," I whisper, as my toes curl under and every sensation changes pace, now in slow motion. When I become too sensitive to withstand my touch any longer I stop, removing my hand.

My feet lower back down to the bed. I stare at the ceiling for a moment, before rolling back over, screaming and slamming my laptop closed as I do. "That was the hottest fucking thing I've ever watched, and I'm a porn star. I've seen everything. You just masturbated to mental images of me."

Saxton is standing in my doorway with his arms above his head, no smile present, and gripping the doorframe. His arm muscles are flexed, his head and torso leaning forward. His eyes glance at my computer and back at me. "What images, Kambry?"

I. Am. Mortified.

"What are you doing in my apartment, Saxton? This is breaking and entering, not to mention creepy as hell. How did you even get in?"

He ignores my question completely.

"Just so you know . . .this is me refraining. I swear on my fucking life it is.

I want to give in. Right now I want to fuck your brains out, hard, making your pussy so sore you can't sit down for hours, days. This is me telling my dick no."

My eyes lower, taking in the massive bulge in his khaki shorts, because obviously holding it drunk just didn't have the same effects. That photo now makes so much sense. Those comments he made . . .agreed . . .but I still want it inside me. I don't care how much it hurts. "Why are you in my apartment, Saxton?"

His jaw is locked together. I can tell by the flexed jaw muscles. He's staring at me, as I lay on my mattresses completely nude, behind my closed computer. "Michael called."

"And?"

"He told me about your freak out. You ran. Why did you run?"

"He had just told me you are a porn star and that he wants me to be in a porno. What would anyone else have done?"

"I thought you wanted this. From the looks of it you still do," he says in a clipped tone.

"Don't be an asshole to me. You barely know me. Do not make me feel guilty over this. I've never had sex with anyone. You've probably been with hundreds of girls. Don't you dare come at me! I have a right to be upset."

"So it bothers you?"

"What?"

"The fact that I've fucked numerous women. It's not the film part, but the number, isn't it?"

I open my mouth, and then close it. I choose not to answer. "Fuck it."

He walks forward, toward me. My breathing hitches when he gets close. He grabs my computer and places it on the floor out of the way, then comes to stand in front of the mattress. I watch him the whole way, never moving. He reaches down and grabs me by the arm, pulling me up to stand on my knees. I do, but don't look up at him. He grabs my chin between his thumb and index finger, tilting it toward him. "Yet despite that, you still want me, don't you?"

I lightly nod my head, ashamed. I shouldn't want my first time to be with someone that's been with so many, but I do. Even worse, I hate that he knows it. Something about his occasional arrogance turns me on more. "Then what's the problem?"

"Why on film? Why can't we just do it here?"

"Because this is part of who I am. I chose this life a long time ago. Maybe if you agree, I'll tell you why. Are you afraid?"

"Shouldn't I be?"

"What are you afraid of?"

"Everything. Everyone. Why do you want to share me with the world? I'm not like those girls."

"That's exactly why I want you; because you're not those girls. I want to know you. This is how I can do that. Who gives a fuck about everyone else? Be original. Be you. Haters will always hate no matter what you do, so do what you want. Did you even read the contract?"

I shake my head. "Sometimes the answer lies within the small print, Kambry."

My phone starts to ring. We both glance at it at the same time.

Liam calling . . .

"Who the fuck is Liam?"

"A guy I work with."

He reaches over and declines the call with the text response. Seconds later, a return text comes through, and since I don't have the text body hidden, it shows up on the lock screen.

Liam: I'm done at work and just got your message. Want me to come over?

He looks back at me. My fingers are already in my mouth, my teeth chewing on the ends of my nails. "Trying to replace me already?"

"Trying to make it easier to forget a porn star. Besides, you declined the offer. Remember?"

His eyes change. He looks a little angry. "Has he touched you?"

"Define touch."

"Has he kissed you?"

"Yes."

"Is that all?"

"No."

"Has he seen you naked?"

"Yes. Well, once."

He glares at me. "Has he put his mouth on you like I did."

"No."

"What has he done, Kambry?"

"Why is this a conversation? You and I aren't anything. You're a *porn star*. It's none of your business."

"Answer me. I told you I'd be in touch. Fuck. Did his fingers fuck you? Did he feel how tight you were?"

I blow out. "He just touched me there and then I stopped it. I got sick. You really have no room to judge me or question me!"

His hands scrape down his face. "Goddamn women. Try to be a fucking gentleman . . ."

He removes his shirt, tossing it on the floor. "Unbutton my shorts."

My body is shaking. I grab each side in my small hands, slipping the button through the slit, followed by the lowering of the zipper. "Have you ever held one before, Kambry?"

"No. Not directly."

"Pull down my trunks."

My nerves are making me a wreck. I hesitate. "I'm clean. If you had read the contract you would know that. Besides that, I've never fucked any of those women without a condom. That's my choice. Okay?"

I nod, trusting him to tell me the truth, even though I know I shouldn't. Who really even deserves trust any more before they earn it in this day and age? My brain is telling me this is stupid, yet I don't listen.

My hands clench around the wide elastic waistband at his hips, my eyes veering to his rippled stomach. I sit back on the heels of my feet and begin sliding them down, pulling them out enough to bypass over his hardened dick, pushing them down to his thighs. My eyes take it in for the first time free from restriction, now standing at full attention, and widening as I get a close-up view. It's so much bigger in reality than in the photos, sending me into a slight panic, yet still appetizing all the same. I never saw Kyle's dick in the flesh, but I felt it through his jeans, and even I know there is a big difference.

"You still wet?"

My cheeks flush from his abrasive question. I totally forgot for a second what he caught me doing. This is forever going to be embarrassing. Leave it to me to be the girl who gets caught by the guy in her spank bank while saying his name aloud and getting herself off. I shrug my shoulders, trying to make this situation as painless as possible.

Heel to toe he removes his sneakers, and then his shorts and briefs, before lowering himself, placing one knee beside me on the mattress. One hand wraps around my opposite thigh, pulling it up to his waist while the other hand settles on my upper butt cheek. He then places his remaining knee on the mattress. My hands wrap around his neck to hold my balance steady. Our bodies are aligned, my breasts pressed against his chest. "I'm going to make you change your mind, but first I'm going to let you dip your toes in the water, because once you join the team we're going all in."

He leans forward and kisses me, immediately thrusting his tongue into my mouth slowly, without prior consent. He tastes like mint, as if he recently brushed his teeth. Mixed with his unique taste, it's delicious, forcefully becoming my favorite flavor.

His fingertips ascend, brushing up the curve of my back, before settling high enough that he can support me as he guides me back on the bed. He holds himself off of me with one arm, but continues to lightly rub up and down my naked body. It's a hypnotic feeling.

My legs bend toward me, the lower half flush against his sides. His hand disappears from my body, automatically leaving a void that I hate. Something presses against my entrance, completely blocking it. It's warm, the texture of skin, just like mine, but hard. It takes on a circular motion, rubbing in my wetness, making me realize that it's not his fingers. His kiss becomes needy, rougher, and the movements harsher.

He breaks the kiss, breathing hard, before sitting up suddenly and pressing his weight into the back of his heels like I was earlier. "Fuck, Kambry, your pussy feels so good. It's fucking hot and wet. I don't want to stop."

"So don't. Do you have a condom?"

He shakes his head. "I meant what I said. I'm going to change your mind. I want you bound within the terms of a contract. I want time; time to do with your body as I please. I'm going to break it, and then I'm going to mold it . . .for me."

He bends over and kisses my belly, before running his tongue toward my breast, sucking my nipple into his mouth, hard, causing a verbal outburst from me. A growl sounds from his throat, and then he sits back again, looking down at my body. "I want to watch you come again. I'm going to need you wet."

He grips my hips and pulls my lower half at an angle. His eyes burn into mine, and then I feel the head of his dick hovering back over my entrance. "I dare you," I say boldly.

"Double or nothing." He smirks, and begins circling it in my wetness, before rubbing it through my folds and then presses it into my clit, exerting pressure against it. I glance down, looking at his large hand gripped around his own dick as he uses the head like the tip of his tongue last time. Only this time feels better.

My hands rise above my head and press against the wall, serving as leverage so that the amount of pressure between the two of us increases. My head rolls back into the mattress, my eyes closing, and my legs spreading further as he rubs my clit with the head of his dick. My mouth opens, pausing before an elongated moan exits. "That feels so good."

My hips buck upward without me instructing them to. My hands cup around my boobs, the lengths of my Thumbs and index fingers clamping closed around my nipples to offset the overwhelming feeling down below. My muscles start to constrict and my toes begin to curl as he continues at a hard, fast, and steady rhythm. The skin-to-skin friction is more than I can explain.

I start to come.

My subconscious checks out, evading reality for a moment.

Nothing moves at a normal rate. Everything is in slow motion once again.

Another slight pressure starts to occur at the height of my orgasm, slowly filling the void that I so desperately find myself wanting filled.

When the pleasure begins to subside and a tickling sensation occurs, a mild pain accompanies it, but nothing worth screaming over.

My eyes open to him digging into my hip, his short nails trying to break skin. "Don't fucking move. Holy fucking hell, don't move. Sweet fuck."

My eyes blink as I try to regain my composure. "Did I do something wrong? You can tell me. I'm willing to learn."

"Fuck, I couldn't stand it. I wanted to feel you while you looked like that. I only inched the tip in, but dammit to fucking hell if you milking the head of my cock doesn't have me wanting to blow my load. Do not fucking move your tight pussy one tenth of a centimeter until I can stop myself. Fuck!"

This isn't a reaction I would think would be happening right now. As if he flipped a light switch, everything changes.

He pulls the tip out, and I suddenly realize exactly how out of it I was, because it hurts, a lot worse than I was expecting, and that was just the tip? I want more, but I want to cry. It's a bittersweet desire. I bite my tongue instead, rerouting the focus of the pain.

He crawls up my body a little, stopping at my navel. The palm of his hand rubs along my center, from heel to fingertips, between my legs. I watch him as he grips the head of his dick in the same fist, twists, then slides it down his length, leaving a glistening effect behind as if it's wet. I'm not real experienced with size, and in school measurements were my weak point in math, but I know that he looks long, which is strange considering he's a lean guy. I would have always thought of it being the opposite, although Meredith told me once that in her experience the tall lanky guys are usually the biggest below the belt while this one buff guy that lived in the gym was so small it was laughable. The irony, even though I'm sure there are always exceptions to every rule.

"Grab it," he demands, as his hand remains at the base.

I look back up at him, nervous. I feel like such a moron right now. "You want me to basically use my own bodily fluids?"

He rubs his thumb along my bottom lip. "You didn't seem to have a problem with it earlier." He smirks. Touché. "It's not as scary as it looks, sexy. I'll show you how I like it. Grab it."

I place my hand in a fist loosely around the center, scared to grip it too tight. His eyes visually trace down my body as his hand doubles on the back of mine, molding the fit, as if he's about to stroke himself with my hand. "Fuck, you have a beautiful body. I need a visual to come." He angles the head up slightly and begins pulling our hands toward the head, together, guiding me.

"Grip it firm, but gently. There is such a thing. The key is tight, not hard." He pulls my hand over the head and makes a noise, then back down the length this time. "Start slow, then speed up. The head is sensitive, especially the small triangular area on the underside, where the head and shaft meet."

As if he can sense my nervousness he continues. "I'm letting go. Don't be nervous. Eyes on the prize, beautiful. Make me come. Make me blow all over your stomach."

He releases his hold on my hand, and then replaces his on the bed beside my head, mirroring the other one, to hold his weight off of me. His eyes stare into mine, and for some reason it eases my discomfort that he's not watching me. He leans in to kiss me, and all nerves subside. We kiss, learning each other with every movement, acquainting with every swipe of our tongues as they explore. My mental consciousness is slipping with every introduction to his taste.

I guide my hand up his length just like before, evenly spreading my wetness. I no longer have to think. It becomes second nature as if I've done this before. My hand stops at the top, and my thumb migrates over his head, halting over the hole in the center. There is a drop of moisture at the tip. I rub in a circle, curious, smearing it around with the pad of my thumb.

He moans into my mouth, motivating me. I enclose my hand a little tighter, and then I begin in a rhythm, stroking him without stopping this time. With every repetition, my movements get faster, and more natural. Each time I reach the head I squeeze, exerting a tighter pressure without hurting him.

He sucks my tongue into his mouth and then envelops his lips over mine, before skimming his bottom to trace up both of mine, and then bites my top lip, pulling it out slightly before releasing it. He stares down at me, his eyes not in focus, but heavy.

The pressure point on the mattress at one side of my head releases, signaling the movement of his hand. Moments later I feel his finger enter me, immediately thrusting to match the rhythm of my strokes. My legs open wider for him, my breathing changing. "Fuck, I want this so bad," he says, making me want to give it to him more. He's quite possibly the sexiest guy I've ever seen . . . and he's here, wanting me. I don't care what form.

When my hand reaches the base again, his breathing hitches. "Grip the head or it's going to be on your face. Now . . ."

I do as he says, and just as I do, I can feel a slight pulsating and then the spurts begin, one by one coating the interior of my hand with a warm, sticky substance: his cum. With each new spurt the previous one runs out of my fist, landing on my stomach in droplet sections. When they stop, I release him and look down at my abdomen, then to my hand. I can't explain the feeling inside. I feel like I've won, but what I have no idea. I like it. I like it more than I probably should. I made him come. I should feel bad, dirty, and guilty, but I don't. This only makes me want more.

He removes his finger and presses his lips to mine, not kissing, but allowing them to linger. He removes them and then repeats, almost like a sweet gesture instead of a lustful one. It's a little confusing. "I'll get you a towel."

He stands from the bed and walks out of my room in search of the bathroom, returning no more than a minute later with one in hand. He rubs the soft cotton across my stomach, wiping it clean, and then takes my wrist in his hand and cleans my hand. Taking a new section of towel, he wraps it around his dick and wipes it clean too, before tossing the hand towel on the floor beside the bed.

I push up on my elbows when he begins redressing. "You can stay if you want."

"That's not a good idea."

"Oh, okay."

He looks at me as he fastens his shorts, still shirtless. "Kambry."

"Yeah . . ."

"Will you do something for me before you completely make your decision on this offer?"

Flutters begin in my stomach as I look at him. My heart is racing. My thoughts are running wild. I sit up and turn toward him, throwing my legs over the mattresses, before placing my arms behind me to lean back on my hands. "What is it?"

He bends over and picks up his shirt, quietly sliding his arms through the holes and then grips the collar between his thumb and index fingers, before pulling it over his head and letting it fall down his body. His hands form into fists beside his body and then he leans down toward me, each fist knuckle down to each side of my hips. "Go to a sex store and buy a DVD of me. There's one a few blocks from here. Since I'm guessing you've already seen images, I'm going to assume it won't be a problem. Watch it . . .alone. Study my actions, my body language, and me. I want you to compare the way I am with her versus the way I just was with you, the way I was last week, and the way I looked at you in the club. "

His eyes flitter back and forth between mine, waiting. I skim my bottom lip. "Okay. Why?"

One hand moves to my knee and opens, before molding to my leg and then begins to ascend, moving toward my thigh. My breathing quickens again. His touch leaves me scatterbrained. "If you can tell a difference, read the contract, in its entirety, from the first word to the last. No one will be there to judge you. Then, when you have all the facts laid out in front of you, you can make a reliable decision. Do not skip one single line."

Am I really going to agree to this? I'm really going to walk in a sex store? Are my thoughts really considering the possibilities that lie within a piece of paper? What's worse . . . Could I really possibly agree to do this with him? That decision could alter my entire life.

"Okay," I say, without any thought at all.

"And Kambry . . ."

"Yeah."

"Just because a camera will be there doesn't mean anything that's happened will be different. Some things can't be faked." His fingertips caress along the side of my body until he grips my chin in his fist, gliding the pad of his thumb down my lips starting from the top, pulling the bottom one with him as he does. My eyes briefly close, and then return to his as my bottom lip returns to its position, still smoldering and intense as they rest on me. "The only difference in just now and then will be that others can witness the way we react to one another. Sometimes the way in which you view things can make a big difference in acting on it. Promise me you'll do that for me before you decide."

There's no harm in that promise, right? He lightly presses his lips to mine again, sealing his question with a kiss. My eyes close. The soft skin-to-skin contact is persuasive. He's conning me with his lips. When he lets go and tilts my head up, I look at him. "Promise me," he whispers. "I need you to promise me."

In this very second I know that I'm a goner. I'm not sure if any woman could say no to a soft-spoken masculine plea such as that one, but I'm not sure I can. This may be where my lack of experience could hurt me, but I know as I stare at him, that at the least I will agree to what he's asking, and I'm suddenly questioning if I'm going to hold to my moral upbringing and turn this down, because if I do this, and my parents find out, I will become an orphan.

"I promise I'll think about it. That's the best I can do."

He smiles. My heart swells. "I will change your mind. You'll see."

"You seem sure of yourself," I retort.

He stands upright. "I just have that feeling." He winks. "Goodnight, Kambry."

"Goodnight," I say back, and he turns to head for the door, grabbing his shoes on the way out.

"One more thing," he says, looking at me in what I know is the final time.

"What's that?"

"Leave Liam alone until you make your decision, and any other guy. I'm between contracts. I can assure you I'll give you the same respect. Please."

"I promise."

I watch him as he retreats, my eyes veering to his backside. He has swagger to his walk, and I can't help but to smile. Lord, help me.

He is going to make me reckless. I can feel it.

CHAPTER EIGHT

Kambry

"You dirty little bitch."

My eyes slowly come unglued at the sound of Meredith's voice as it passes through my conscious awareness, disrupting my beautiful sleep pattern. Her face is a blur. Pressing the heels of my palms against my eyes, I rub, trying to wake up. She slowly comes into focus, sitting on the edge of my bed and leaning over my body with a huge grin on her face and a coffee cup in her hand. "What are you doing in here? Why are you even awake?"

My eyes shift around the room, taking in the light shining through the window. It's light, but based on the strength of sunlight it doesn't appear to be super late or anything. "What time is it?"

My eyes begin to close, sleep calling me once more, before she slaps me across the face. "What the hell, Meredith?"

It didn't hurt, just caught me off guard. "Wake up you little tramp. I just saw your secret spank bank. I obviously a need girl talk session. This is some good shit. Give me the gossip. I brought a peace offering."

She extends the coffee cup between her hands as my eyes fully open, suddenly very much awake from the smell of caffeine permeating the air. "You know I'm not really a coffee drinker."

"Yes, why I brought cappuccino . . ."

"Since when do we have a cappuccino maker?"

"Don't worry about it."

I fold the comforter over, baring my upper body except for the sheet, before sitting up and scooting back to put some distance between us. "You went to the coffee shop down the street and trashed the cup, didn't you?"

"A wise girl never reveals her secrets." She smirks. "Now, give me the juice."

She pulls the rim to her lips and takes a sip. "Mmmm. So good. And hot enough I have plenty of time to wait."

"I have no idea what you're even talking about, though I'll take this. Are you still drunk?" I grab the mug and place the rim between my lips, inhaling the precious nectar, before tipping it back and letting a sip of the cocoa colored liquid travel into my mouth, warming me from the inside out.

"Well, because I love you and want the juicy details, I'll tell you. No, for your information I'm not still drunk, but I forgive you for assuming. Since I didn't come home until early this morning I didn't charge my laptop. It was dead as a damn doornail. I needed it for some research on a role I'm auditioning for soon, and I needed a relaxing view to do so, away from an outlet, so I had a brilliant idea. Do you want to know what that idea was?"

She stares at me with a mischievous grin spread across her face, waiting for me to ask. If I don't, she'll sit here until I do. I take another sip. "Please, do tell," I say sarcastically.

"I thought to myself, I'll just use Kambry's, because she's Miss dependable, so I waltzed in here and grabbed it off the floor, since obviously you were watching the back of your eyelids and didn't need it. I didn't think you would mind."

"Are you going anywhere with this conversation?"

"Yes! Don't ruin my moment. Anyways, I walked into the living room, sat on the couch to make sure I could get through the security before going outside, and opened your laptop. As I would any other bright and sunny California day, I put in your password and guess what I fucking found?"

"An apple."

She narrows her eyes. "Good one, Apple addict, but no." I take a bigger swallow since my tongue has become used to the temperature, not paying her any attention at all. She tends to ramble when traveling from point A to point B. Most of the time I grasp onto the key words and I can connect the dots by the time she arrives at her wordy destination. "I found fucking porn . . ."

I spew some of my cappuccino back into the cup, the spray ricocheting off the surface and landing on my face, and a portion of the liquid being sucked down my windpipe. I begin to cough uncontrollably as the reminders of last night begin playing back in my mind. I thought that was a really awesome dream . . .

"Take. The. Poison," I say between coughs, trying to catch my breath as I hand her the cup.

Her grin broadens as she does. "Why did I not get to be here for your first porn search? I feel so left out."

"You're a freak."

"Says the one looking at porn instead of being the one getting the action."

No pun intended? If she only knew . . .

"I was doing research of my own."

"On what?"

My mind suddenly goes blank, all witty comebacks vanishing.

"Okay, so maybe I was teaching myself."

"Kambry Louise Rivers, do not lie to me."

"Ewww. Don't use my middle name. That's gross. You know I hate it."

"Well, you don't hate your poor old granny that it came from, do you?"

"No, but you got a vital word right. Old! Do not associate me with Louise. The end."

She rolls her eyes. "Whatever. Tell me, tell me, tell me! I want to be your porno, cherry popping, wingbitch. I cannot help if I'm out of the loop. This is a mark in history. My baby is growing up."

My lips purse together, becoming tighter with every second that I sit here and watch her squirm. She can't stand it. Her middle name fits her perfectly for the nosey rosey that she is, unlike mine. Rose . . . because she's nosey as all hell.

I allow my head to fall back against the wall, but I continue looking at her. "You aren't going to leave me alone until I tell you everything, are you?"

Her eyes widen. Then her mouth drops. "You fucking slut. There's more? How could you keep secrets from me?" She dramatically waves her hands in front of her face, feigning the act of drying tears before they fall. "I'm the one that stared at your vagina while I taught you how to insert a tampon. You cannot get any closer than that. I feel betrayed."

"Meredith Rose Love. Filter. Now. Some things should never be unburied. You never know when someone could be bugging our apartment, or worse, show up uninvited."

She flips her blonde hair over her shoulder, dropping the act altogether. "Fine, but so help me if you don't start talking, I will drug you to get it out of you." She narrows her eyes and points her finger at my nose. "Try me if you think I'm playing. I've done worse."

I face palm myself, shaking my head. "Fine, but if I hear one word of judgment from you, I'll never tell you anything else; one word, Meredith. Girl code starts now."

She raises her hand at me, stiffly holding it by her shoulder in a stop sign position as if she's about to swear on the bible. "Cross my heart and hope to die, I promise I shall not lie, but if I do I'll fuck you with a dildo. Scouts honor."

I laugh through my closed mouth, unable to hold back any longer. "That was terrible. Did you just come up with that?"

She laughs with me. "Maybe, but it lightened the mood, didn't it? Success at its finest. Now talk."

"Okay . . . Well, it all started when I met this guy."

"Guy! What guy?"

"The guy I met at the bar last weekend. You remember the night you were supposed to find me someone in the bar? Well I beat you to it, kind of." She looks clueless. "The one that I brought back here." Still nothing. The look of confusion only deepens. "Meredith, we basically stood there and watched you screw some guy . . .for a moment or two. Stop playing dumb."

She taps her index finger over her closed lips. "Why am I drawing a blank?"

My mouth falls open, completely in shock. "How do you not remember? Are you for real? That is not okay!"

She shrugs her shoulders. "What? Have you ever had so much Vodka you blacked out? It happens."

"I'm worried about you. I cannot even believe we're having this conv—"

"Oh! Do you mean Bryant?"

"I don't know his name. He was naked, you were naked, and you were touching your toes while he invaded you from behind. I'm sorry I didn't have a chance to catch a name. How rude of me," I say sarcastically.

"Kind of beefy, average height, total hot body, and raspy voice?"

She continues like this is totally acceptable. "I'm pretty sure that was Bryant. Same guy I stayed with last night. The night we met is a little hazy, I'll admit. I met him when you had to go upstairs to work." There's the light bulb I'm looking for. "I just don't remember our first sexual encounter. It's kind of a blur . . ." Her eyes lose focus. "But he is a total sex machine. Good lord his dick is glorious." She sits the coffee cup on the floor.

"I don't even know what to say right now." I would love to see my face.

Her eyes turn into big saucers. She suddenly slaps her hands together and squeals, causing me to jump. "I remember! That was when I came to. It was as if I was totally void from the world for a bit, like I was in a black hole, and then bam! I could suddenly see consciously. That's perhaps the drunkest I've ever been— worse than senior prom. I probably shouldn't drink that much, because there is a gap in time that is missing, but I remember leaving the club, parts of the ride home, and then that moment." She pauses. "Although vague, I somewhat remember a guy with you. How did I miss this?"

"Uh, maybe because you're on the verge of being an alcoholic. Should I be worried?"

She rolls her eyes. "Oh hell, Kambry. One time of irresponsibility does not make me an alcoholic. It makes me a teenager, but only for another year. I'm so glad we have early fall birthdays. Come on nineteen, one year closer to twenty-one. We're in California, alone. We are entitled to have some reckless fun. Your parents aren't here to keep your virginity under lock and key. Relax."

"Does it still make me a virgin if he put the tip in?" I blurt out.

"You got D action! Why would you not tell me? I don't even know you anymore!"

Her eyes gloss over as if she's actually about to cry. "I'm telling you now. Stop being dramatic. This isn't an audition. Although, well played."

She lights up. "I know right! I'm so meant for this."

Then like a light switch being flipped, it's gone.

"Kambry, you knew the second after I touched a dick. It's been a week and I had no idea you were even experimenting with the idea, let alone rounding third base and headed for home plate. Don't you dare tell me to stop being dramatic!

You've never hid things from me."

"Well, technically it was on two different occasions, three if you want to count the drunken disaster of a hookup with Liam at Drake's pool party, but that really was mild and you're the one that told him which apartment was ours, so that one is your fault. The afore mentioned event of tip action being last night, and I was trying to tell you before your memory went hiatus."

"You are digging yourself deeper, my friend."

I growl out in aggravation. "Time out. If you only knew the entire story you would know why I wasn't sure how to respond, think, or bring up the conversation to even tell you. It's quite laughable to be honest."

She breathes out. Her mouth lines. "Okay. I'm going to put my jealous best friend card away. How about you start from the beginning?"

"Okay. I can do that, but I'm going to make it as short as possible and then you just ask filler questions for crap you want explained. I met him in VIP lounge, thought he was hot with no further thought, since I was his server, but then he kissed me in front of a business meeting before he left. I didn't think I would ever see him again, but he pulled a stalker move and ended up being in my cab, forcing me to hang out with him."

"So he thought your beautiful face, sexy body, and perfect rack were too good to pass up and stalked you at closing. Got it. Sounds hot. Continue."

"Well, fast forward to standing there in an awkward position in front of your door, because it was open, and watching some guy have his way with you shamelessly. By the way you looked like you were completely enjoying it. I just thought I'd throw that out there to help your memory." I pause, not sure if I should admit the next part. Oh, what the hell. I've been caught doing far more embarrassing things since I moved here . . .like masturbating to above-mentioned beautifully hot guy. Why not add one more to the list?

"I may have thought it was really hot watching." I slap my hands over my eyes, waiting for her reaction. "He may have caught on."

Hands enclose around my wrists moments later, prying them off my face. She is biting her bottom lip so hard it's turning white around her teeth. Her smile is massive. "Wait just a minute. You got turned on watching some guy fuck me? This is one of those times I need brutal honesty from you."

I stare at her. Then my head falls between my shoulders, ashamed. "Yes. I know. I'm a freak. Go ahead, disown me as a friend, but I can't help it. It was really hot seeing you all . . .I don't know . . .consumed with pleasure without even having to work for it. I may have been slightly jealous even."

She places the tip of her index finger underneath my chin, pushing up for me to look at her. "You're not a freak. You're just a little behind the rest of us in curiosity of your sexual nature. While you were sitting at home on your couch with Kyle on Saturday nights, the rest of us were at house parties when parents were out of town. Put together co-ed teenagers, alcohol, and no chaperones and what do you get?"

I raise my brows, not sure where she is going with this. She acts like I didn't go to the same high school as her. A mischievous grin forms. "Porn and sex. When you're drunk and having sex, in my experience there is usually someone watching. You are just too mentally checked out to care."

My brows scrunch. "What? I've never heard of any parties like that. Not with you or our class anyway; at least not our friends."

"Okay, I'm going to say this, but it's not aimed at you, love, so don't let it hurt your feelings. No one ever told you about those parties, because well, your parents are like evil spies. Part of living in the same small town meant that most of us went to the same church. Our parents were all friends, conjugating for the latest gossip into our lives. We liked our freedom. You don't really have experience with sneaking around your parents, so you aren't the best liar. These weren't the big parties in fields and other remote locations like during homecoming week. These were the parties after the parties; the ones that you sneak out of your house well after curfew to go to with only a handful of people."

I throw off the comforter and stand, walking off to the other side of my room, staring at the wall. I hold my head high, trying not to cry, but the truth is I feel left out. No one ever gave me a chance to be trustworthy. Instead, I find out that all of my friends had secret lives they never told me about. "Who's the one with secrets now?"

"Can you honestly blame me?" she asks directly behind me, catching me off guard. "After that time we got caught smoking behind your house at fourteen, when your mother couldn't wait to run her mouth all over town about how she had to call my mother and then take you to talk to the preacher. It was a fucking cigarette in our mouths, not a dick. All kids try it."

I turn around, remembering how embarrassed I was. All of my friends kept their distance for a few weeks after that. "Or what about that time when we were fifteen and you stayed over at my house. We raided my mom's vodka stash and drank what was left, got drunk—at least I did—and then refilled it with water so she wouldn't notice, before we snuck out and Branson came and picked us up. That night was so much fun; the most we had ever had together. You were completely free, uninhibited, and acted like the rest of us."

She closes in, still staring at me. "Do you remember that night?"

My heart starts pounding. "Yes, because I wasn't drunk. I was too scared my parents would find out. I remember the dare. Branson never forgot it either."

She wraps her arms around my neck, linking her hands. My stomach drops, nervousness consuming me. The look in her eyes is exactly like it was that night, when Branson wanted us to prove just how close of friends we were. I swallow. "You swore you would never tell what happened that night, but somehow they knew."

"I didn't."

"Then how did they know, Kambry?"

"I don't know. I told you this forever ago."

"You never got to stay overnight again after that. They took part of my friend away. Do you know what that's like? You weren't the same after that. That was the last night you ever tried to do anything against the grain of what your parents wanted. That was the last night you did anything for you . . .until you came here with me."

"Well it doesn't sound like you missed out on any fun," I say, the hurt and anger present in my tone. "I was the one that was left out, left behind."

"Then make up for lost time. Do something for you. Pick up where you lost it all. We can pretend that we are starting back from that night. We'll never have secrets from each other again. Go back with me. Give me my friend back, the part of her that died that night. I dare you."

My eyes scan hers. This may seem weird, but it also sounds appealing in so many ways. Maybe it's that my emotions are all mixed up lately, unsure of what I want, torn between who I've been and who I will be, but she's right. After that night I vowed to always be the good girl, the one that never questioned or back-talked her parents. I was the girl that chose every detail of my behavior to please them, in fear of them, because when they found out what we did they threatened to never let me see her again if I ever did something that sinful again. I was grounded for a month. They immediately took away overnight stays, but I wasn't willing to completely lose the only sister I had ever had.

This is step one to saying fuck my parents.

This is step one to being the girl I want to be.

This is step one to doing what I want.

This is step one to finding Kambry instead of conforming to their beliefs.

I place my hands on her hips and pull her closer as I lean against the wall, before tilting my head slightly. She presses inward and her lips hover above mine. Then they meet. Without the slightest attempt the memory of that night surfaces, taking me back.

"How close of friends are y'all?"

I look outside the glass doors at Meredith sitting on the edge of the pool with her feet in the water, sipping on her Vodka and cranberry juice. She said she needed fresh air, but I know secretly what she's doing; giving us space. I've had a crush on Branson since I started high school and we were in the same Chemistry class, but I was always too afraid to act on it.

"Best friends, Branson. Duh. Everyone knows that," I say in my version of a drunken tone, trying to be flirty.

He stands and walks toward me sitting on the arm of the sofa, and looking at me in a way that makes me want to stop breathing. Branson is the star of the football team. He's a senior, he's gorgeous, has a fun personality, and all of the girls love him. It's no secret. His parents treat him like the football god that he is, letting him live in the pool house, and his only rule is that he has to be on the property by 5AM if he's not on football curfew. He can have anyone over that he wants out here. Rumor has it his dad walked in once on a game of strip pool when he had a house full of people over from two surrounding schools and just smiled and walked out.

He stops in front of me and places his hands on my waist, before guiding them around to my backside, and sliding them underneath my butt. He's been flirting with me for a while now, since homecoming, but this is the first time I've been around him almost completely alone. That also makes me nervous.

He lifts me and I wrap my arms and legs around him, before he takes a step toward the sofa cushion and sits down, bringing me to a straddle on top of him. "You're hot, Kambry; possibly one of the hottest girls in school. I want to kiss you."

I begin to shake; even with the little bit of alcohol I consumed making me less shy. "Okay."

I've never kissed a guy before. I just hope and pray I don't suck at it. He places his hand behind my neck and pulls me toward him, pressing his lips to mine. He wastes no time before sliding his tongue into my mouth, forcefully, giving me no time to react. I have no chance to learn, only to do exactly as he's doing to me. It starts out slightly out of rhythm, but we quickly fall into a comfortable pattern, and then I start to like it.

His hand moves up my back, underneath my shirt, pulling the fabric along with it, baring my upper body. He breaks the kiss just as Meredith walks through the door. "I need a cigarette. Ohhhhh. Sorry," she says as she looks at me.

"Meredith, come here," he says, still pulling my shirt off, not even asking me. I'm not sure whether I want him to or not, but he does. I don't object.

"What?" She walks over until he reaches out and grabs the waistband of her cotton shorts, pulling her closer. She holds out her arms to break her fall as he pulls her down to our level.

"Let's have some fun."

She looks at me, clearly confused, before he grabs the back of her head and pulls her in for a kiss. I watch as they kiss, a little jealous and confused that I have to share him. She moans into his mouth, making it worse. Then just like me, he removes her shirt, leaving us both in our bras. I start to get upset, internally, keeping it to myself.

He's hard between my legs, but from which of us I have no idea. "If y'all are really close, then prove it. I want to see the two of you kiss."

My eyes blink repeatedly, trying to understand why he would want us to do that. She looks at me, just as confused as I am. I'm mad that I really like him and then he so freely wants both of us, causing me to speak out of anger. "Okay."

Meredith shrugs, confirming she's in. "It can't be any different than kissing you. Lips are lips." Branson grabs my hips and lifts me to turn around, then sits me back on his lap to face Meredith. She leans in and kisses me, inching her tongue through my lips slowly, unlike him. They touch, and then her pace picks up. She's leading me. Her softness spurs me to continue, so I stand, evening out our height.

The kiss becomes more comfortable, and before I know it she's sitting on the couch and I'm straddling her. Her hands rub across my waist, toward my back, and then up to my bra strap, unclasping it.

My bra falls, baring my breasts, before being covered with her hands. She squeezes as our tongues continue to caress each other's. "Hell yeah. This is better than I thought."

The vision clears, leaving the two of us standing here kissing in my room, as if years haven't passed between that night and today. My hand slides up her shirt and beneath her bra, stopping on her breast. They aren't as big as mine, but they aren't small either, only coming in at a cup size smaller than me, and they're round and firm.

She moans against my lips as my finger rubs across her nipple. I'm getting more turned on, and bolder with going further when the memories of last night begin to surface, reminding me that what I want is a guy, and more specifically, Saxton.

I break the kiss. "I need you to take me to a sex store."

She looks at me like I've grown a third eye. "Why? We could keep going. This is kind of fun. I won't tell if you don't. Toys are great, but overrated."

"It may be fun, but it won't be satisfactory. Unless you magically grow a dick, it's just going to be disappointing in the end." We're both breathing hard, and both quite possibly insane. I'm not even sure how to explain him anymore, not even to myself, let alone her. "Besides, this is something I need to do. I'm not going for a toy. I'm going for a DVD."

"Fine. I guess you're right. There is no greater thing than dick." I take back my hand and adjust my shirt as she puts some distance between us. "Shopping it is then. Can't you just buy that stuff online now days. DVDs are a thing of the past. Why do you need a sex store? You still have not explained this porn thing. Are you really just curious? Because most guys aren't like those guys . . . You may be disappointed if you're teaching yourself from that. Just a little word of advice."

Rip it off like a Band-Aid, Kambry.

I push past her, heading for my closet to find a change of clothes. "Because the guy in those photos you found was the guy from the club, the guy that came back here, and also the guy I hooked up with . . .twice."

I grab the clothes without looking at her, in fear of what her face looks like right now. "I need it for research purposes, like I tried to explain earlier. The rest I'll have to tell you when the initial shock wears off or you may think I'm insane and have me committed."

"You hooked up with a porn star! What the fuck?"

And so it begins . . .

CHAPTER NINE

Kambry

Meredith kills the engine to her car as we pull into the parking lot of a building with the label, *SINcerely Yours*. I stare at the large curly font that hangs on the front of the building, not far above the tinted glass doors, wondering what I'm about to walk into. What would one expect from a sex store? I'm not stupid, but maybe naive when it comes to this sort of thing. Surely there isn't that much involved; yet the building is much larger than I would have imagined.

The silence in the car has my thoughts running wild, unsure of what to think. Meredith is rarely quiet. At the exact moment I reach for the door handle, the locks sound. She's locking me in. A group of friends exit the building with a frosted plastic bag stuffed with pink and black tissue paper, laughing and carrying on as they walk toward a silver Mercedes. I grab the lock and pull it up with my free hand, not removing my eyes from the young, carefree girls as they get in the car and pull out.

I pull the handle and lean into the door, only for it to do nothing. It's locked . . . again. She clears her throat.

My head dramatically rolls toward her. "It's not like I can't open the door. We can have a war, but it's just a matter of timing. Child lock doesn't work on the front passenger door. No need to be melodramatic."

"When are you going to talk to me? You don't just throw out some crazy shit like you hooked up with a *porn* star and then keep me in the dark. That's rude and wrong on so many levels. I'm dying here."

"I'm really not sure you would believe me if I told you. I'm not sure I believe it myself."

"You'd be surprised at the things I would believe . . ."

"This may be the cake topper."

She raises her brow. "Who's the melodramatic one now?"

I grab a section of my blonde hair and begin twisting it around my finger, lost in thought. A certain pair of masculine eyes flashes through my mind, swaying my thoughts. My eyes close, remembering the look on his face when he admitted to slipping the tip inside. Such a strange confession from someone so used to sex. I've never seen a guy look like that before. So . . . I don't know, raw, bare, with that much uninhibited sexual tension visible; though, that's not saying much, but it made me feel sexy.

My thighs inch together on the seat, already wanting to go back to last night. My bottom lip slips between my teeth and my arms cross over my chest, my hands grasping the opposite upper arm as if I'm cold.

Suddenly I feel a backhanded slap across my upper arm, leaving a sting in its wake. "You're totally mind fucking him. Kambry!" My eyes open. I look over at her, looking at me as if she's seriously considering driving me to an asylum.

My thoughts quickly gather. "You want to be an actress right?"

Her face scrunches. "Is that supposed to be a trick question? We are in the movie capital of the country, are we not? I certainly didn't leave home westbound for a dead-end job in the middle of an unknown place hoping to become a trophy wife. We're better than that."

"Would you do anything to get to major motion pictures? Think of it as working your way up from something less appealing. Would it be something you'd consider given the opportunity? Even if you knew it was immoral, going against everything we've ever been taught?"

She turns and leans her back against the driver's side door, staring at me, before combing her fingers through the top of her hair to give it a tousle. "Well, I've never really been one to go with the grain of what we were taught, hence me losing my V-card long ago, but it's go big or go home right? I'd like to think all the ones that made it had to make sacrifices that they aren't proud of to get where they are. But that's really one of those things where you have to step in those shoes and walk in them before you really know if they fit. Why?"

"Even if they asked you to star in a porn reality television show with the guy in those photos?" I pause. "And that same guy is trying to sway you to say yes by giving you a taste of what you could have if you did? Would you still feel the same?"

My hands steeple at the center of my face, waiting for her response. She stares at me, no emotion registering on her face. "Are you shittin' me?"

There is that deep southern drawl she masks so well, unlike the rest of us. Usually it gets worse when she is speaking with lack of thought or when she is emotional. I guess there is no truer statement than, *you can take the girl out of the south but you can't take the south out of the girl.* "I wish I were."

I'm half expecting her to laugh as well as yell, but to my surprise she does neither. Instead, she removes her keys from the ignition and grabs her purse, before exiting the car entirely, leaving me thoroughly confused.

She walks to the front of her car and halts, before turning toward me and waving me on. I grab my purse off the floorboard and pull it over my arm, leaving it at my shoulder. I meet her at the front. Her mouth lines as if trying to find her words, only the right ones. "Now is not the moment to question. I need time to marinate. The time for a rational conversation would be stargazing rooftop over wine; about the only place you'll see stars around here."

She pauses. "I would say trespassing at the Hollywood sign, but I have yet to find someone that is willing to break that law and risk getting caught. I thought that was a for sure bucket list item for most people."

As if just now realizing she is veering off subject she shrugs her shoulders and carries on. "That will come later tonight. I guess it's a good thing you're off. It was meant for us to have this conversation. If it were anyone else I would hardly find this conversation serious, but given that it *is* you, I'm going to introduce you to a sex store, as well as your first toy."

"A toy? Why a toy? Didn't you just say they're overrated?"

She breathes and a nervous laugh escapes. Her cheeks have a rosy shade appearing. Is she blushing? Embarrassment never happens with Meredith. "I saw those photos pulled up on your computer. It was hard to look away once I saw them. He's hot, he's young, and if he's after you to do it when I'm sure he has many options, then there's likely a reason. It may make me a shitty friend not freaking out and trying to steer you clear of this insane idea, but it's worth giving a thought to. Celebrities have notorious *sex tapes* emerge often. I'm still convinced it's a ploy for publicity, but what do I know? Maybe this is your arrow."

She looks at the building only a brief walk away. "But Kambry . . ."

"Yeah."

"I feel I need to warn you of this. If you plan on losing your V-card to him, then you need to practice with a toy. I've seen some peen in my day; probably more than I care to admit aloud at my age, but regardless, I know the difference in big dicks and small ones. I can point out an average bat with ease. They come in all shapes and sizes, but that boy . . . is fucking hung."

Her eyes scan my body, making me more nervous with every second that passes. "If there is even an ounce of you that wants this, then you need to prep your vagina. That shit is going to hurt. I'm nervous for you."

I feel like I'm going to throw up. I never said I was going to do this. Something tells me that I don't really have a choice. My hand immediately finds my mouth, my fingertips slipping through my lips between my teeth. Reflexively, I start to gnaw on my nails; a nervous habit I started long ago to tune my parents' lengthy lectures out over the years. There isn't much to bite; yet when I'm done my nails will be below the quick.

She wraps her arm around mine, leading me toward the building. It's a quick walk, quicker than I probably would have preferred. Meredith grabs the handle of the door and opens it, letting me enter first.

I walk inside as the entryway chimes, signaling our arrival. Meredith follows behind and stops beside me. I look around, my nerves dwindling as I take in all of the lingerie hanging from the racks. The walls are decorated with stilettos of every color and design. Scattered in the corner I even see themed costume wear, but I don't see any sort of toys in here.

A female wearing a short but classy dress walks toward us. Her makeup is perfect and her hair teased to no end. I have no idea how she is walking in those shoes. Those shoes put any of mine to shame. She is likely pushing forty, but doesn't look it. "Welcome to SINcerely Yours. Is there something in particular I can help you find today?"

I start to get embarrassed. I'm not sure what I expected this to be like, but voicing it aloud wasn't one of them. My cheeks are heating, most likely starting to resemble a cartoon character. "We're here to shop in the back," Meredith says.

"I see. I'm going to need to see IDs please."

My eyes blink repeatedly. Why do I feel like I'm in the middle of a drug exchange? This is awkward. Regardless of how I feel at the moment I'm here, so I pry open my purse and fish out my wallet. I open it and show my license to her tucked inside its slot. "You're going to have to take it out, love. I have to hold it until you leave."

Of course she's going to need me to dig it out from behind that damn clear holder that was not invented to be user friendly. Once you slide it in your wallet all is lost, because you all but break your finger trying to get it back out.

I reel in my arm, before starting the inevitable. Mysteriously it comes right out on the first attempt. It has to be rigged. She's already holding Meredith's when I hand her mine, looking them both over once in her hand. "My name is Betsy. Follow me."

She turns on her heels and begins walking, slow but precise, never allowing her weight to become offset from the skinny heel she's walking on. We follow close behind, navigating through the storefront toward the back. A spiral staircase comes into view. My eyes follow it up, halting on a loft overhead. Nothing is immediately visible to the eye that resides up there, but I almost barrel into Meredith from not paying attention when they stop at the bottom of the stairs.

Betsy grabs the hook end of the velvet rope that is blocking the entry to the staircase. It reminds me of something on the red carpet or a movie premier, just a different color. She attaches the hook on the opposite end, opening up the narrow winding staircase for visitors. "If you need any help getting something removed from the display just press the button on the wall and I'll come right up to unlock it. Go ahead. Look around."

Her arm branches out in the direction of the stairs, her hand outstretched, kind of like the girl on *Wheel of Fortune*. That seems a little too proper for a sex store, but that's just me. I shouldn't be so judgmental when I have no idea what I'm in for.

Meredith begins to ascend first, wasting no time. I place my hand on the railing and follow. The frilly curtain at the top—the makeshift door—hangs loosely in the frame. Her hands feel around until she finds the two separate hems and pulls them apart, allowing us to walk through.

My mind becomes overwhelmed as I stop on the other side, taking it all in, releasing the fabric from my fingers behind me. "What the hell?"

A hand laces with mine. I look down and then up at Meredith. "It may be a little scary now, but I promise in no time you'll be up to par. A lot of people never try most of this stuff. Some dabble a little. Then there are those select few that discover a different side of themselves altogether; a guilty pleasure I guess. It's all about learning you and the things you like. If it makes you feel better, we're almost neck and neck in this category. Come. I'll do this with you."

My heart is pounding in my chest. My brain is screaming at the images my eyes are relaying to it. A glass display stretches the entire length of the room, then turns to form a rectangular version of a U, completely full of boxes and pretty packaging with names I haven't even read yet. The wall behind it serves as a support for things I've never even heard of before, let alone seen.

I work to even my breathing before I go into a panic. She steps forward, pulling me toward the display case. My nervous energy is slowly changing to curiosity the closer I get. Pulling my hand out of Meredith's, I place my fingertips on the top of the case and skim them as I walk down the length of it, taking in everything inside, and repeating the names to myself. *Pocket pussy—some made to resemble those of girls I don't know, Dildo, Bullet, Butterfly, Rabbit, Chinese shrinking cream . . . Really? People use that?*

The list goes on of things that look strange to accompany their odd names, locked away in the glass box. I glance up at the back wall. That area only gets stranger. Swings, things that look like horse whips, smaller whip type things with long tassels of sorts–not really sure what that is. Handcuffs in feathers and fuzz . . . Is that a stripper pole?

My eyes continue to pass over, noting each and every thing. Anal beads? What is that used for?

My derriere suddenly becomes tense at the thoughts plaguing my mind. If I get really out there, I can imagine some things, but I have to run out in left field to get there. My nose scrunches. "No thank you," I mumble to myself. "Nothing is going in there."

I continue to pass. I don't think I'm going to find anything there. In the corner of the room there is a doorway. I walk to it, wondering what could possibly be over there. I'm not one hundred percent sure I really want to know. Before entering I take a deep breath, then peek my head through as if something is going to jump out at me. Aha! There they are . . .

I walk inside the movie section, glancing at the front covers. I swallow, and then veer over my shoulder in embarrassment, forgetting that Meredith and I are alone and no one can see me, or what I'm looking at. My breathing starts to become heavy as I glance at each cover. Some of them have titles alone that are blush worthy, let alone the couple or person that graces the front to accompany it. I really should stop looking, but I can't . . .

Naughty schoolgirls part II? That seems a little more worthy of an eye roll than sexy. Even the girl on the front has the whole pigtails and short plaid skirt getup going on, with a midriff baring white button-down, sitting in a W on the floor with knee high socks and Mary Jane shoes . . . And she's sucking on a red blow pop. Even I've heard the whole Catholic schoolgirl fantasy, but I thought it was more for means of Halloween dress up.

I continue to walk, skimming the various covers, nothing catching my eye. I halt when *that* DVD case smacks me in the face, metaphorically speaking. *MILF: Spring break edition.*

The only reason I know that stands for *Mom I'd like to fuck*, is because I've actually heard some of the guys joking around about that at school; usually toward the few guys whose mothers were the hot versions of what typical mothers dress or look like. Friends or not it always pissed them off to hear MILF comments about their own mothers.

My heart starts to race when I see the name across the top. Starring Saxton Maverick.

I look behind me, confirming I'm still alone, before snatching the clear, plastic DVD security box off the wall that holds the DVD case locked inside so it can't be stolen. That's when I notice another right beside it, *Twins Gone Wild*, taking it as well. I look between the two, comparing.

The first female is older, but you can barely tell. She's dark-complected with long, silky black hair; her skin smooth instead of what you would see on someone that lives in a tanning bed. Her boobs look enhanced, her makeup overdone in a precise manner. He's standing behind her, his arms wrapped around, one covering her nipples and the other holding her between the legs, covering all her goods. His lips are barely touching her neck, but even with part of his face tilted toward her you can still tell it's him. Her hands are threaded in his hair as if she's enjoying what he's doing to her.

For some reason that bothers me . . .

Then there is the other one. Twins . . .with platinum blonde hair just like me, only they have chocolate brown eyes, big and round, but if they're older than me you really can't tell. They look more natural except for the spray tan they clearly have going on, giving them a beachy glow. He looks like he's walking, one girl standing on each side with a seductive smile plastered on her face as they both pull at his button-down shirt, clearly trying to remove it. They are gorgeous, and they're identical. So he's had a threesome? That's not intimidating or anything . . .

"I'd go with the twins."

I jump at the sound of Meredith's voice, almost throwing the movies in the air. "Sorry. I didn't expect you to freak out."

"Shit," I whisper. I go to put the movies back on the shelf, but she grabs them. I turn to reach for them, more embarrassed than I originally thought I would be, but she raises them above her head as she stares at the front. "Are you ready? Maybe this was a bad idea."

"Why are you being all weird? I want to see who you've deemed worthy enough to let in your panties."

"You've already seen him. Remember?"

"Not putting the two together."

She turns the boxes around to face me and holds them in front of her, chest high. "Which one bothers you more to see knowing you've had a taste of him yourself?"

"Neither bothers me. Why?"

"Don't lie to me, Kambry. I can see it all over your face. Your cheeks look like you've just come in from running in the hot sun. Tell me. Which one?"

"This is stupid. You're making me uncomfortable. Why bring out my insecurities?"

"Because that's how you overcome them. We haven't even established why you are purchasing one of his films anyway, so I'm just going to assume there is a logical reason and we move on from there until you tell me the details." She shakes them in her hands. "Which one?"

"The twins," I say defeated. "It's hard for me to imagine having to compete with an older woman. Everyone knows they are more experienced, and if it were real life it'd probably be less common, statistically speaking. All the girls we knew wanted older guys."

"Okay, so tell me, why are you purchasing one of his movies? I can't help you if I don't know."

I exhale loudly. I liked this better when I was the only person that knew. "He told me to compare the way he is with a woman in one of his movies to the way he was with me on both occasions. He said if I could tell a difference to at least read the stipulations of the contract before I say no to the offer."

"Wait one damn minute. You've been offered a contract? It's that serious?"

"Yeah, but I haven't read it. The producer came by the club. That's how I found out what kind of film it was. I freaked out and left. My curiosity got the best of me and I searched him on the web."

I think back to what I was doing less than twenty-four hours ago. "Let's just say he showed up, uninvited, and at the worst possible time. His parting words were to come to a sex shop and buy a DVD, so like a pathetic idiot here I am."

Her mouth is gaping. She stares at me. "You lucky bitch. I'm so jealous right now." She places one film back and tucks the other under her arm as she grabs my hand and pulls me out. "Twins it is."

"Where are we going?"

"We are having a girls' night. Nothing sounds better than wine, porn, and reading contracts. I have the perfect blanket and pillows for a rooftop kind of night . . .if it's vacant. If not, it's a pallet party with smelly candles as makeshift starlight."

How bad is it that I kind of wanted to do it alone?

Betsy is standing behind the counter when we exit. In front of her sitting on the glass is a gift bag just like the one I saw earlier. "Will there be anything else or is that all?"

"All?" I ask confused.

"Just this," Meredith says as she lays the DVD on the counter, ignoring my confusion completely.

She looks down at it and picks it up. "He's one of my favorites," Betsy says as she unlocks the box with a strange looking key on the elastic band she wears around her wrist, and then allows the DVD package to fall into her hand. "You girls picked a good one. Pretty close to your age too I would imagine."

I stand here, feeling slightly awkward while she talks about a porn star as if he's the boy next door. I'm officially ready to bail; glad at least that I know no one around here for the most part.

If this embarrasses me is there really any point in looking into this whole situation any further?

"He's definitely a hottie," Meredith retorts. "Someone that's met him personally recommended him."

I swallow at the wrong time, allowing my spit to go into my windpipe, causing me to choke for the second time today.

She places the DVD into the bag, nestling it beneath the paper so that everything is kept private, and then her expression changes. "Oh really?" she asks, as she leans forward over the counter, resting on her forearms. "Do tell me more. I've always wondered what they were like in real life, given the nature of their careers."

"Kambry, what did she say he was like?" Meredith asks with a witty tone. My palms start to sweat when they both look at me, eyes wide as if they're ready for the latest gossip.

My breathing begins heightening in sound. I hate being the center of attention. I stumble on my words and say stupid things. Why does she do this kind of shit to me? What am I supposed to say so that it doesn't sound like I'm her?

I look between them both, straighten my posture, and clear my throat. "Well, she said that he controls his tongue like a singer, uses his fingers like a guitarist, and has rhythm like a drummer. He's sexy, mysterious, and a little bit cocky, so I guess overall he's kind of a rock star. Oh, and he feels bigger than you would imagine seeing him on screen, but that's hearsay. I really have no idea."

Drops mic and walks away.

I turn and walk toward the door, mouthing all kinds of things to myself . . . like what the fuck was that? Was it corny or stupid? Probably. Actually, I'm pretty sure of it. I found an opening to get me out of this extremely uncomfortable situation and took it. At this point we may be leaving without the purchases, because I am not going back in there. I, Kambry Rivers, am going to the car. I have had enough of this sex store for one day.

My head is tilted back against the passenger door of the car, sun beaming down on my creamy skin, when someone grabs my hand and hangs a bag from my palm. I straighten, looking down at the bag that was sitting on that counter only moments ago, and then glance at Meredith standing before me with a massive smirk spread across her face. "Well played, sugar. Well played. I got fifty percent off and she threw in an extra DVD. She said if you can bring it back signed by him then she will give you a piece of lingerie with matching heels on the house. I'm proud of you."

"What? Why?"

"Girl, don't ask me. Maybe it's good promo for her store or something. She said he was a favorite. Maybe her guilty pleasure is watching porn. To some people signed copies are priceless. How the hell should I know? What I do know is that slowly he's pulling you out of that rock hard shell you've lived in all your life. The Kambry Rivers I grew up with would have never said things like that, even if she were the only one left on the planet with no one else to hear it. Get in the car. We're going to figure this out."

She rounds the car, unlocking it by the remote along the way. I turn and grab the handle, before opening the door and getting inside. She starts the engine and looks behind her as she backs out. "Bryant, the guy I've been playing with, just so happens to work at his family-owned wine and liquor store not far away. He said he's working right now since he doesn't have a class today. Perks for me. Wine it'll be. Just don't judge me if I disappear for a quickie in the back. Know that I'm perfectly fine."

I look at her, waiting for her to look back at me as I buckle my seatbelt. "You're such a hornball," I say at just the right moment.

"That may be, but it's always on my terms. Being in control is a beautiful thing, doll. You'll see. Besides, he's the first person in months. You weren't the only celibate one for a while, but I must admit that it sucks. I'm pickier than you think," she says with a wink as she pulls forward.

"So . . .I can't stand it anymore. What's in the bag?"

"There's only one way to find out. Open it."

I look down at the bag in my lap and remove the tissue paper, hesitantly. I take out the two largest items first and look at them, biting my lip as the blushing consumes my cheeks once again. "Why two?"

"Well, it's good that you asked, doll-face. Do you see anything different between the two?"

"Uh . . ." I bite my tongue trying not to laugh. "Size?"

"Look at you! A+ for cooperation. Neither is quite the size of the image I saw, but I figured you could climb that ladder one rung at a time. The first dildo is fairly small, according to Betsy, when it comes to magical pleasure-enforcing toys, but I figured it would be better than starting out with that man's dick. The second is a middle ground between the two in the size category. I just figured that by the time you got yourself used to those two, you'd be more prepared for the big moment, because that boy has quite possibly the biggest dick I've ever seen. I'm pretty sure of it, actually, but I'd have to see it in person to know for sure."

"And what if I don't do this? Have you really even considered what this is?"

She smiles, but continues looking ahead at the road, avoiding an accident in the heavy traffic. "There is always that possibility, because you're the only one that can decide, but I think we both know you probably will, and yes, I have. It's an ethical decision most definitely, especially coming from a small, southern town. Your reputation will likely never be the same if you do it and people find out, but honestly, who cares? The people that judge shouldn't be in your life anyway. We're young, we're learning who we are, and no one says you have to do this more than once. If the contract is too good to turn down, then I don't think you should. It's not like you're going to do it for free. There are women all over the place that do porn, stripping, or escort services to pay their way through school. If you're making it honest, it's honorable, no matter how you do it."

"Well, since you put it that way . . .prostitution sounds so much better," I say sarcastically.

"Kambry, you want to go to college right?"

"I don't know."

"I'm not stupid. I know that acting isn't your dream; it's mine. You only came with me to get away from your parents, but we both know unless you go back you'll remain stuck with me, carless, and short on money after necessities. You'll be merely surviving. You don't want that life and I don't want it for you. I love us being roomies, I'll drive you anywhere, and you'll always be my best friend, but I know you well. Right now we're both in the same predicament, but what if I make it? What if I start getting roles for major motion pictures? What then? You'll move back home for them to give you back your future before you mooch off my parents or me footing the bill. Tell me I'm wrong."

My fingernails go for my mouth after dropping the items back in the bag. I hate conflict. I hate feeling like I have no backbone, proving her to be right. My parents took that from me by never giving me a choice, never giving me room to make my own mistakes. It was their way or no way. It always has been and always will be. "I can't, because you probably aren't."

She pulls into the parking lot of a building with the hanging letters spelling out *Wine and liquor* across the top. It doesn't matter what state you're in they all look the same. I guess those words alone are advertising in themselves.

She kills the engine and looks over at me. I can feel her staring. I can also see her from my peripheral vision. "Let me clarify what I'm saying. I'm not pushing you to do it. Don't ever do something you don't absolutely one hundred percent want. All I'm suggesting is that if you do want it, then look at the big picture instead of worrying what the general public or people back home may think. No one else will have to live your life or pay your bills but you. We do what we have to do to make something of ourselves."

Without saying anything more she grabs her purse and exits, yet again, and I follow behind, walking alongside her until we enter the liquor store. It's quiet, a totally different vibe from a bar or club. The room is filled with rows upon rows of bottles, some on shelves and some in wine racks, as well as coolers lining the walls. I have no idea what we're supposed to be getting. I'm a complete amateur when it comes to wine. Mentally I had prepared to get a backup; something that I know I like.

The only wine I've tasted was at a family wedding that took place on a vineyard—weird I know—and it tasted like rubbing alcohol. Needless to say I refused to try anything else. Come to think of it, that was probably my parents' goal in letting me try some: to find the nastiest one to sway me. I should have known them giving me alcohol as a minor was strange back then.

I squint my eyes. Assholes.

"Hey, sexy. You miss me? I brought eye candy."

"What's up, gorgeous? You come to play?"

I look over at the familiar voice as Meredith makes her way to the counter. He nods at me. "Bryant. You must be the infamous Kambry I hear so much about." At least he's not calling me watcher . . . His tongue runs out of his mouth over his bottom lip, wetting it, and then his top teeth bite down in its place, before skimming back and forth. "How did things work out with that guy?" His eyes narrow slightly as if he's thinking. Then he smiles at me.

"I have no idea what you're talking about," I lie, hoping he doesn't bring up that conversation from the apartment now that we're all sober.

"I wonder if he'd say the same . . ." That mocking grin is driving me nuts.

"It's long forgotten."

He's sitting on a barstool behind the high counter, spinning a pair of scissors around his index finger, obviously to occupy himself with the lack of customers at this time of day. It probably hasn't been but a few hours since opening. Now that I get a look of him in daylight with no mental distractions, I can see his appeal. He's cute, but then again I've never seen Meredith with a guy that I didn't find attractive. I guess we have similar tastes.

"What do you two know that I don't?" Meredith asks.

"Nothing," I say.

"Speaking of guys," he continues, "have you seen him around lately?" His voice is in a teasing manner, making me paranoid. Does he know about Saxton?

"I can't say that I have." I lie, again. "I think I'm going to look around."

He looks out at the store behind me; an unreadable look on his face. "You do that." His attention goes back to Meredith. "So, you come to play?"

"Mayyyyybe," Meredith interrupts in a singsong voice, clearly playing his little game. "Depends on if you feel like hooking a girl up. We need something." She looks at me, and then back at him. "Preferably something sweet, that is capable of altering mental state for a relaxing girls' night in. Work your drink knowledge magic of the perfect concoction and you might get lucky."

A smirk begins to grow from his lips. He stands and leans over the counter, bringing himself closer to her. "I'm not invited to the party?"

The longer he looks at her, the more she smiles, as if she's totally smitten.

That's my cue to leave.

I turn for the first row I come to, placing my fingers along the labels of the bottles as they sit in the wine rack, browsing the different brands, colors, and types, reading each. I reach the end, now facing the coolers. One brand sticks out: Barefoot. The type that catches my attention is the Moscato, but there are two colors: pink and white. Maybe it's the whole *Deliciously sweet* motto on the label that piques my curiosity. I can't be sure. It just calls to me.

A weird feeling encompasses me, like someone's watching me. I look from side to side, seeing if anyone is close in proximity, but nothing. I shrug it off, then reach for the cooler door and open it, removing the white Moscato by the neck of the bottle. "You're a little young to be buying that, aren't you?"

I jump slightly, but not as much as I would have guessed. "What are you doing here?" I ask without turning.

A body presses against my back, causing me to close my eyes. It's hard; his body that is. "I could ask you the same question," he says, placing his lips beneath my ear.

I shiver.

He splays his hands on my hips, pulling me closer. I grip the bottle tighter, trying my best not to drop it on the dang floor. He begins inching them down my cotton dress, traveling toward my thighs. "Have you read the contract yet?"

"No," I say breathlessly.

"Why not?" His hands reach the bottom hem of my dress and slides to my inner thighs. I cannot stop the uncontrollable shaking as he touches me inappropriately in a public place, yet I can't find the words to tell him to stop.

"I've been busy. This is kind of stalkerish . . ." My words get cut off as he slides the fingertips of one hand under the edge of my panties. My breathing hitches. "You know."

I squeeze my eyes shut tight, trying to calm the raging beating of my heart. I can hear it pounding in my ears. *One, two, three, four . . .*

He slips a finger inside of me and all is lost. "I'm just here seeing a friend, but I must admit I'm glad I came." His voice is huskier than it was initially.

I release a choppy exhale. My hand wraps around his wrist as he slides his finger upward to my . . . "Dammit."

Something starts poking me from behind. He rubs for a moment then stops abruptly, removing his hand altogether. My head falls back against his shoulder. He grabs the bottle from my hand and sets it on the floor, before grabbing my waist and spinning me around.

Our eyes meet and he walks me backward, until my back is pressed against the cool glass door. He grabs my thigh from behind and pulls my leg up around his waist, positioning himself between my legs–a denim bulge pressing against my panties as my dress gets shoved upward.

His face inches forward, his lips coming closer to mine. "Fuck, I want you so bad."

He presses his lips to mine and kisses me, deeply, sliding his warm tongue inside my mouth. I welcome it, more easily this time. He hardens his body against mine as his kiss becomes more heated, more frenzied. I place my hands around his waist and dip them underneath his shirt, allowing myself to feel his bare skin. I moan into his mouth, causing him to nip my lip with his teeth.

He breaks the kiss, his eyes boring into mine, his chest heaving up and down. "Have you done anything I've asked?"

My eyes dart left to right, scanning his. I bite the corner of my bottom lip. "Maybe," I admit accidentally.

His eyes veer down to my lips. "Keep doing that and I'll strip you right here."

"We're in public."

"He's not modest." I pull down my leg at the sound of Bryant's voice and clear my throat, trying my best to adjust my dress, and cursing myself inside. I look back and forth between Bryant and Saxton, both wearing smirks across their faces. "I see you found my boy after all. I didn't figure it'd take him long to figure out you were here."

I shove at Saxton, trying to put some distance between us. "You two knew each other this whole time? Why didn't you say something that night?"

"Hey, I tried," Bryant interrupts. "It seems homeboy here was keeping secrets. So unlike him," he says teasingly. "I guess some girls have that effect on guys." He winks. "The rest is not my business."

"That wasn't the time nor the place for that conversation, and obviously Bryant is starting a pattern of being in the wrong place at the worst time," Saxton says aloud, still staring at me.

I release a breath, catching Meredith walking up from the corner of my eye.

"What'd I miss? I go to the bathroom for one second and it looks like juicy drama. Could my luck get any worse?"

Saxton turns toward her and Bryant and she halts. "Hello, hottie." Her eyes rake down his body, dramatically and shamelessly, stopping precisely at his . . . "So much better in person."

She licks her lips. My eyes widen, then squint at exactly the moment following. No shame. No shame at all I tell you. I also kind of want to slap her right now. She's staring at his junk.

I divert my eyes to him as he grabs me by the arm and pulls me in front of him, wrapping himself around me, his mouth just outside my ear. "She knows, doesn't she?"

"Uh, yeah." There is no need to lie.

"And it's kind of hot."

"Meredith, put a cork in it."

"This could work out in my favor," Saxton says loud enough for her to hear.

"It already is," she replies.

"Meredith!"

Bryant grabs her hand and starts tugging her toward a door. "Hey, bro, can you watch the front for a few? I was on my way to the office to . . ." He looks at Meredith and back at Saxton. "Take care of something when I saw you."

He nods, but doesn't really acknowledge Bryant otherwise. "How so," Saxton asks louder as the distance between Meredith and him grows.

I narrow my eyes at her, daring her to say something. "Meredith . . ."

Her grin changes and that's when I know. "Just check the bag labeled *SINcerely Yours* in the car and you'll know."

That bitch.

She disappears through the door and it shuts. Don't ask. Please don't ask.

"So you did go to a sex store."

He asked.

I can feel him smile against my ear as he hugs me into him. I really don't even want to admit this. I just want to lie. I go with sarcasm. It always has a better effect. "What can I say, my curiosity got the best of me."

"Oh yeah," he whispers, then grinds himself against my butt, making me nervous yet again. "What did you find?"

"Awkward things."

"Show me."

"Will you give up if I say no?"

"Nope."

"Figures. Let's go. Your autograph is needed anyway."

I grab his hands and move them off of me, but he only releases his hold to grab my fingertips as if I'm going to try and run off. "My autograph?" He laughs. "Why?"

"Because Meredith has a big mouth, kind of. Long story."

I walk in a hurry to the car, pulling free from his grasp. I get there and pull the handle. It's locked. Turning, I place my hands on my hips. "Well, I guess you won't be seeing it after all. Oh well."

He presents a set of keys. "Looking for these?"

The small glass bottle keychain filled with sand from an Alabama beach that she got to bring a piece of home with us confirms they are Meredith's. "Where did you get those?"

"Off the counter."

He presses the unlock button on the remote, before walking toward me and grabbing the handle of the door, opening it for me. I sit on the passenger seat sideways, my feet remaining on the pavement, and grab the bag, digging through it hurriedly to give him the DVDs and nothing more. He leans into the car, hovering over me as I extend them for him to take. I lean back against the center console. "So, I'm guessing you like blondes?"

We both look down at the one on top, the one about twins. "I don't have a preference," he retorts.

"Oh."

He smirks. "I have to like whatever they cast for me. That's how I get paid. But, I am swaying towards a particular blonde that has piqued my interest, if I can get her to read the damn contract."

I prop one leg on the doorframe, trying to back up some, but that only makes him put his hand on my thigh. Backfire for sure, because now his hand is close to my area and it feels friggin' amazing. "Why do you even want me to do this? It makes absolutely no sense to me. Even if I agreed, there is no way this is going to be interesting with me knowing a camera is there watching my every move, especially if you want me to get naked. I'm nervous enough being naked in front of you."

Oops. I want to crawl in a hole and die now. *Good job, Kambry!*

He grabs the DVDs and tosses them onto the back seat, before leaning closer to me, invading my personal space. He holds his weight with one arm as the other migrates up my thigh, sending my dress north, my panties becoming visible. He lifts my buttocks to work the fabric over it, before setting me back down, my dress sitting at my waist.

My breathing is coming out in short bursts, unable to breathe through my nostrils. "I make you nervous, huh?"

"I didn't mean that. I was just rambling." Lying is starting to get easier.

He places his lips at the point of my V-shaped neckline, on the roundness of my breast cleavage, kissing it. My eyes become heavy, but I fight to keep them open. His hand detours south, tracing the seam between my leg and torso, before inching to the top of my panty line and slipping beneath it. "That's the funny thing about questions. If you would read the instruction manual, most of them get answered."

"Why don't you just tell me what's in it?"

"Because I want you to read it for yourself."

He slips his finger inside, slowly tormenting me. My other leg pulls into the car, also resting on the frame beside the seat. One hand pushes against the back of the seat, the other on the bottom beside my thigh. "Someone is going to see."

"No they won't. My body is blocking you. Even if they did . . . Who cares? This is between me and you." He slides his finger in and out, twisting it each time he's fully inside.

"Stop teasing me."

"Stop denying me."

"I'm not."

"But you are."

"Ugh. You're so frustrating."

"Not having you fully is equally as exasperating. I want your body, Kambry, in the most selfish way."

He runs his finger up my slit and begins rubbing my clit with his middle finger. It feels so good I can't stand it. Reflexively my body wants to buck forward. “I’ve offered it to you.”

“You know the stipulations, Kambry. It has to be this way. Just read the contract.”

“I’ll think about it.”

We stare at each other, but it’s getting harder for me to focus on him while he does that. He squats and changes the position of his hand. “What are you doing?”

“I’m just going to have to persuade you some more.”

His thumb hooks around my panties between my legs and he moves them to the side, before leaning in, and touches the tip of his tongue to my entrance. “Shit,” I say inching upward.

He grabs my waist and pulls me to the edge of the seat. “Be still.”

“It’s not that sim—”

I breathe out as he begins flicking his tongue back and forth over my clit. My hand goes for his hair and my back arches, the top of my head skimming the center console. He’s not letting up, clearly here to work more than play.

My butt muscles tighten, lifting my pelvis slightly. He shoves a finger inside as if he knew that’s what I wanted; pumping in and out as his tongue continues the fast-paced motion over my sensitive place. He hooks his finger up as he slides it inside, pressing deep into me. “Dammit. I think I’m about to . . .” My eyes close and my mouth falls open as I begin to orgasm, my tongue barely moving enough to speak. “Come.”

Everything slows down. My legs try to close, but his shoulders block them. I don’t know where I am, who’s around me, or what I look or sound like, and frankly I don’t care, because it feels so good. I can’t think or focus on anything but the feeling that is consuming my body and mind. For a brief moment, seconds feel like minutes, but then gradually every ounce of pleasure fades away, and then his touch begins to tickle.

My eyes open and I press back on his head, shoving him backward for me to sit up when I see Meredith looking through the windshield with a big-ass grin on her face. He turns toward my line of vision and removes his finger from my body when he sees her standing there, staring at us, and being completely creepy right now. He readjusts my panties back into their original position.

My hands go for the bottom of my dress, quickly working it down as he stands enough to lean in the car, wiping his wet fingers on his jeans. I clear my throat as I gather myself, still completely horrified. Why can I not have a moment without people walking up on me? Her lips purse and her hands go on her hips. "Nothing better than topping off an office quickie with an oral show. That was hot, Kambry," she says, peeking her head between the open car door and the frame.

I cover my face, unable to look at her. My face probably looks like a tomato. "Meredith, can you give us about two minutes?"

His voice is close. He's clearly hovering over me like when we first came out here. "Sure," she says in a singsong voice. "I'll just be getting that wine now. Someone is going to need it."

I can't see, but I can hear her walking away by the sound of her shoe soles shuffling on the pavement, also reminding me of what I just did in a public location! "Oh, God," I mumble against my hands.

Hands wrap around my wrists; big, strong ones. Those same hands pry mine away from my face. I stare into those beautiful eyes; so deep and bold. The corner of his mouth pulls upward, and then he leans in and places his lips over mine. I moan as he slips his tongue into my mouth, just moments after going down on me. I should find this gross, but something about my taste being mixed with his makes this hard to turn away from.

I should make him stop. This is crazy. I'm letting a guy I barely know do totally inappropriate things to me in a parking lot in California at midday. I press my palms into his chest, trying to create some space. "We have to stop this," I mumble against his lips, finally pulling away. "We are going to get arrested for indecency."

"Promise me you'll read the contract."

"We're already back to that?"

"Promise me."

"Give me one reason why I should."

He places his hand on my upper thigh and my skin jumps. "Because of this." He kisses my cheek; that is currently heated. "And because of that." His finger barely grazes beneath the edging of my panties. "But mostly because of the way I leave you here. We want this, Kambry. You don't think I know this is insane?"

His eyes command me to listen, to hear him out.

"Generally, I'm not turned on by a girl. Not anymore. When you've spent hours a day for days on end over the period of years fucking and sucking and doing everything imaginable, it just loses its appeal; so much so that at twenty-five I take a fucking pill made for erectile dysfunction to get up and stay up."

"Why are you telling me this?"

He grabs my hand and wraps it around his jean-covered erection. "Because you're the first girl in years that has done this with no pills, no prep, nothing. I want to see this play out, Kambry, but this is also my job. This is the only way I can ensure I don't have to touch another woman while I do. Sometimes the best things come in the most abnormal of forms, so promise me."

Without a thought . . . "I promise."

He smiles. My heart falters. "Where's your phone?"

I feel around in my purse until it's enclosed in my hand. I hand it to him, unlocked. He starts touching around on the screen for no more than a few moments and hands it back to me, showing his name and number I've stared at almost daily since he put it in there, only this time it's on my favorites list. "If you have any questions call me. I'll explain. Any time of day. I wouldn't have given it to you if I didn't want you to have it."

I nod and he places his lips to mine, lingering until the driver's side door opens. "Am I too early?"

I hear a thud as she places something in the back on the floorboard, but I can't look away. "No, you're just in time."

He winks.

I can't breathe. I can't speak. I just watch as he backs out of the car and grabs the door. I push up, forcing myself to correctly position my body in the car and then he shuts the door, before backing away. My lips tingle. My fingertips instantly touch my lips in the exact location his mouth just was.

"Do I get juicy gossip on what just happened? That boy wants you some kind of bad."

I never look away as he walks backward, toward a truck that I just now notice parked in the lot. Our eyes never part. "Meredith, right now I just need you to drive. I'm going to need that wine, and lots of it, because I have a feeling I'm about to do something that's going to change my entire life."

For good or bad I'm not sure . . .

CHAPTER TEN

Kambry

I stand from the couch and walk toward the refrigerator with my now empty wine glass—the third one at that. The DVDs sitting idle on the counter catch my attention as they have each time I've refilled my glass. The bottom of my glass clinks against the counter as I set it down.

The slightest hint of a buzz is occurring, loosening me up a bit. I drag my gaze away from the cover and turn for the refrigerator. I open it and remove the large bottle of wine, pulling out the cork and pouring yet another glass half full. I return the bottle and place the rim to my lips, before allowing the sweet liquid to pass into my mouth, holding it on my tongue to savor before swallowing in a gulp. It's sweet up front with the mildest bitter bite at the end: the perfect combination to avoid an upset stomach.

I lean forward, resting on my forearms on the counter, my eyes automatically settling back on the DVD cases. "So, are you going to put it in or stare at it all night?"

I work hard not to laugh. "Depends on what *it* you're referring to. That phrase sounded kind of dirty, Mer."

I glance up at her over the counter. She's standing on her knees on the couch cushions, shifting her weight so that it looks like she's bouncing. "Kambry, I thought we were having a drunken porno party. So far all I've gotten is some girl talk, which I love you for, and a few sips of fruity goodness. You've been quite the busy little hooch this past week, and now you've released the hornball with your stories. Bring out the porn and the party?"

I laugh. "Shut up! You have no room to talk. I'm still deciding if I want to watch them. What if I want to keep him all to myself?"

"The hell you are! You get him in real life. A girl can at least dream and add him to her spank bank. He's fair game in fantasy land, you lucky bitch."

My lips begin to tingle again, but not from the wine. My fingertips reflexively brush over them, remembering the way it felt with his lips pressed against mine, especially just after having them pressed between my legs. *This is the only way I can do that and ensure that I don't have to touch another woman . . .*

He actually wants to only hook up with me. Why?

"You have no idea," I mumble, agreeing with her prior statement, zoning out once again. I can't seem to concentrate on anything for very long before my mind wanders to off the wall random things that have no purpose navigating through my thought process.

When the two of us left the liquor store we stopped by the local deli and grabbed lunch, and then came back here. Meredith took a nap while I cleaned, since obviously I was too high-strung to do any sleeping myself. Usually once I'm up I can't go back to sleep anyway. For hours all I've done is clean in circles, repeating the same places without even catching myself, because all I've been able to think about is him, the way he makes me feel, and how much I want to see him again.

If I'm being honest . . .

After cleaning the toilet for the third time and trying to fold dirty clothes, I decided that maybe today wasn't the best day to clean. I haven't even showered, because occasionally I get a whiff of the faintest cologne as if it's stained on my body. Knowing that it's his, I want it to remain, so I tried cooking dinner instead. That didn't work out in my favor either. Let's just say there is a pot soaking in the sink with pasta glued to the bottom and the spaghetti sauce has a scorched flavor.

This is coming from a pretty decent cook. When you have strict conservative parents there isn't a whole lot of other stuff to do than to perfect the role of *Betty Homemaker*, as Meredith so rudely called me on more than one occasion. The nerve. Sometimes I really wonder how we've stayed friends. Not denying that it wasn't said in fair game. Mom did make me take home economics, and she was all too willing to teach me how to cook. No one wanted to take that class, and the people that I hung out with certainly didn't, because the cheerleaders and dancers had a practice period just like the athletes.

Drama was my only somewhat fun class, and that was all for Meredith. I didn't have the heart to tell her acting wasn't my thing . . .and Saxton wants me to be under a camera twenty-four hours a day; the irony. I still have no clue why my mother agreed to that class. Maybe it was because I wasn't any good at it.

My biggest desire and passion was music, but unless it was singing hymns in church or alongside playing the piano, that was just a waste of a class. I wasn't allowed to take it. Let's not forget that participating in the choir was a must though. My voice was too beautiful not to.

Mom's words not mine. The funny thing—not many people know I can sing. She begged me for years to sing a special in church but I never gave in. It's easier to play the stage freight card. I acted like I hated singing just because it was forced on me. I never got to choose the music that I wanted to.

Music is my thing, my love. It's an art that I'm actually pretty good at. Maybe that goes hand in hand with having it surrounding me at all times. Ear buds are a necessity. Music apps are an absolute must. Spending countless hours scouring YouTube and preset channels for the newest hidden gem is my guilty pleasure. I am very much a music junkie. Also, I'm a mood listener when it comes to genre. It calms my brain. It jump-starts my thought process. It is everything to me and I'd be lost without it. Music has gotten me through some pretty down times.

It's no secret with Meredith that I can sing—a lot of people can—but there is one thing *no one* knows about me. For years I've wanted to learn how to play the guitar, and not for the reason most would think. Fame and glory aren't things I strive for. The opposite is true really. I hate to be the center of attention. As much as I love people, I also love time alone with my mind and myself. It never stops. I love words. There are so many different ones to choose from, yet the combination in which they are used is endless. But I've found over the years that standing alone they fall flat.

I've always wanted to be able to strum along to the melodies and words constantly emerging when no one is around. I have notebooks full of words, pages completely filled that I kept hidden between my mattresses, but no music to make them whole. That is the piece that has always been missing to my puzzle, but one day . . .I will find it.

Snaps sound in my ear, pulling me out of this weird reflective trance I'm in. Don't ask me why I'm going back to days of high school when I'm beyond that period. I honestly couldn't answer. "Kambry! Hello. Are you in there?"

I blink. "What?"

"Oh my gosh, girl. You're making my inner spaz rear her ugly head. Pay attention. What is with you today? You've been super weird since homeboy had his tongue all up in your business." She gives me a once-over and motions her tongue in a crude manner. "That good, huh?"

"Shut up!" I shove at her playfully from across the bar, still slightly embarrassed she witnessed me hooking up with a guy in her car, in a parking lot public enough to be seen, but she jumps back before I can reach her. "What were you saying?"

"Are we going to watch the DVD or not?" Her eyes narrow slightly. "Or are you jealous?"

"No!" I pause. "Why would I be jealous? He's not my boyfriend, Meredith. I don't give a crap who he screws. God, sometimes you can be such a bitch."

"Prove it," she retorts.

A wave of anger washes over me. I grab the first DVD off the bar and walk around it, headed for the DVD player. Without any effort, I slide my nail beneath the plastic wrapping and tear it from the case. I squat down and turn on the television, then the DVD player immediately following, waiting on everything to come on. I grab the case in both hands, pulling away from each other until it opens, revealing the round disc inside.

I begin to get nervous, but I ignore it. I can be stubborn when I want to be. This is one of those times I just need to bite the bullet and ignore every feeling I have in my gut, so I position the DVD in the slot of the player when it opens, and then close it.

Meredith pours herself another glass of wine as the player reads the disc. Just as the DVD introduction begins to play, she walks over with both glasses in hand, extending mine toward me. "Here. I have a feeling you're going to need this."

I take it by the stem, pouring a big gulp into my mouth. She has it filled to the brim. Moaning begins almost immediately and it hasn't even been playing a full ten minutes. I don't know what I was expecting, commentary or something. Hell, I don't know, I've never watched porn, but even porn previews obviously are more than I was prepared for. I begin to roll my eyes, but then I see him.

I can't breathe. Setting is in a classroom. Looks like college. Auditorium style. Meredith pulls me backward toward the couch as the professor points at the board, scribbled on with equations. The back of my knees hit the couch, but they don't bend. She tugs until I make myself sit.

A bell sounds just like the ones back in high school. That's weird. I didn't assume they would still have bells in college to signify the end of a class. What the heck do I know? I'm not in college. He begins to gather his things, but a blonde leans over his shoulder from behind, whispering something in his ear. His expression doesn't really change.

The rest of the class is exiting in a rush, but he remains seated. I'm not sure why, until he looks behind him but to the left, at another smiling blonde identical to the one rubbing her boobs on his back. I take a swig of my wine, settling into the couch. The professor gathers his things and they follow suit—all three of them.

Nothing seems abnormal until they make it to the door as the professor walks out. Saxton braces his arms on the frame, a petite set of arms wrapping around his waist seconds later. His shoulder blades are protruding, confirming most of his weight is leaning into his hands.

Her hands disappear beneath his shirt. I veer my eyes toward Meredith, slightly uncomfortable. She's staring straight ahead, engrossed in the movie in front of her. I take another drink of wine, feeling parched suddenly. My eyes attempt to refocus on the screen. Saxton steps backward and shuts the door, locking it. He's no longer being touched. My breathing picks up.

He turns around. That's when I notice both of them, identical twins, standing beside each other and staring into his eyes with seductive smiles spread across their faces. They're beautiful. One may be a carbon copy of the other, but they aren't dressed the same. The one that was just whispering in his ear removes her shirt; the instigator I suppose.

My stomach is in knots. I have no earthly idea why. My legs pull up onto the couch, tucking beneath me. He stalks toward her, both of them. They are standing beside the professor's desk as if they are willing and ready for him to take them, completely unashamed of what they're about to do. Okay, let's be real. It is a porn film: kind of the purpose. Actually . . . Scratch that. Like I have room to talk. Even if this were real life I'm sure the result would be no different. He seems to have that effect on people.

As soon as he stops in front of them, the topless blonde goes for the bottom of his shirt, tugging it up his body until he allows her to remove it. She wastes no time before going for his jeans, unbuttoning them. Slowly she slides down the zipper, never removing her eyes from his.

I glance at him, like he instructed. I'm not sure how long I'll be able to. His expression almost looks bored. The sister closes in on them and he grabs her by the back of the head as the other pulls his jeans down his body, baring him, until she's on her knees. His focus is on the one standing. He pulls her head into his, kissing her. My eyes close briefly, as if I'm not supposed to look at him naked. I feel like an intruder. Then I remember it's a movie, so I open them.

My nerves begin taking on a role of their own, firing off throughout my body. I hate the way I feel right now, almost angry, as the girl on the floor wraps her hand around his extremely hard dick, placing it to her lips while he makes out with her sister. My jaw ticks, before clamping down so tight my teeth feel as though they could break.

His free hand moves down to her head as she suctions him into her mouth, his dick slowly disappearing until she can't take anymore. He clenches his fingers in her hair, stilling her, before his hips start thrusting back and forth in her mouth. She takes him into her mouth as if she's starving.

My eyes move upward, trying to get away from the vision of him having his dick sucked by someone else. His lips are still pressed to the other girl, but her hands move to her waistband, before pushing her yoga pants down her legs until she can take them off completely.

Their lips part, but only long enough for her to remove her shirt and clear a vacant spot on the desk, sitting in the cleared off space. The girl on the floor alters her position, changing direction as if she knows what's next. With every second that I watch I find myself wanting to drown myself further in the sweet liquid that currently occupies space in my glass; what little is left. I'm not far away from being completely carefree, but only about a glass stands in my way.

I'm staring at his backside. A hand splays across his rear and the motion of her at his waistline picks up to a faster pace, the occasional moan sounding from her throat. He bends forward as the girl lying back on the desk spreads her legs for him, placing her feet flat on the edge. His hand makes contact first; his fingers finding the place that makes her feel good. It makes me angry even though I have no right to be, and it only heightens my anger because I'm starting to feel discomfort between my legs.

I'm so confused. I hate what I'm watching; yet I'm turned on.

His other hand gropes her breast as he places his lips to her abdomen, lowering with each separate one, until his mouth reaches her middle. Her cry out and the instant arching of her back as he begins assaulting her most sensitive place with his tongue causes me to lose it. He's doing exactly what he did to me on more than one occasion to her. I can't do this. I can't watch this. I thought I could easily. Looking at the photos didn't even bother me like this does.

My eyes begin glossing over until everything is blurred. I blink hard. I won't do this. This is stupid. Maybe I'm not ready to give myself to someone in that way. I'm obviously not mature enough to handle casual sex. I'm acting like I've already formed an attachment to him and all we've done is hook up a few times. In no form do we have this mock relationship going on. I need to get over myself. If I can't handle this then what can I handle?

I drain my glass and place it on the side table. I stand, but Meredith never looks over at me. "Where are you going?"

"I'll be back," I lie.

"Okay, boo. Hurry back." Her words come out in a slur.

"K."

I disappear into my room and shut the door, quietly locking it to be alone, hoping she doesn't hear me. She's had almost twice as much wine as me, so I don't think she'll notice I'm gone after she forgets that I got up.

I walk over to my bed and fall down onto my back on my mattresses. I should really try to save for a bedroom suit. My phone chimes beside my bed. I reach over and grab it, holding the screen in front of my face. It's a text message from Liam.

Liam: Hey hey, gorgeous girl. Wanna hang out?

Should I or should I not? Maybe it'll help sort out my feelings. I'd be no fun right now. And I promised . . . No guys. I just watched the guy I'm crushing on get a blowjob from another girl and go down on someone else, but somehow I feel guilty at the thought of hanging out with a guy that's not him. I open the message and quickly respond.

Me: Hey you. You should have texted me earlier. I've been drinking. Sorry. :(Maybe another time?

That should be a good enough reason. It's the truth, even if I wouldn't have agreed either way. I still don't want him to think I'm blowing him off. I'm just in a sticky situation right now. Not even a second passes before I get another response.

Liam: I can come pick you up.

Me: I appreciate the offer, but I think I'm just going to chill here. It's kind of supposed to be a girls' night in. That would be rude of me to just leave. Rain check? ;)

Again, it chimes.

Liam: I'm going to break your shell eventually.

My fingers hover over the keyboard, trying to think of a response.

Me: Hoping someone will. See you at work. Goodnight, Liam.

I toss my phone down on the floor. The sound of material rustling causes me to look over. It landed on top of the folder Michael sent with me that supposedly contains this contract Saxton won't shut up about. I take a deep breath before looking up at my fan blades making circles.

For a moment I consider what it would be like to live in a house with Saxton.

I'm sure it would be interesting to say the least. I'm just not sure I could have my most intimate places and experiences plastered all over the place for people to watch for years to come. What if my parents found out? Do I really care? If I'm one hundred percent honest with myself, I think the part that scares me the most is that I'm going to want more from this than what it actually is and in turn get heart broken. There is something about him that I'm drawn to, even knowing what he is and does for a living, and we barely know each other. I'm still undecided if it's a bad or good thing.

I can't do this. Maybe the best thing to do is to just tell him I can't, go on living my life exactly as it was before I worked VIP that night, and work on figuring out what I want to do with my life. Kind of like Drake said, I don't want to work in a club forever.

I grab my phone again and roll over on my stomach, propping myself up on my forearms as I start a new text message and pull up the contacts, searching for Saxton's number. I choose it when the S search brings me to his, as it's one of the first names. I touch it and it takes me back to the message box, the keyboard popping up. Both thumbs go to typing out words as quickly as possible.

Me: Hey Saxton. I just wanted to let you know I'm going to turn down the offer. I'm sorry. It's been fun though. I hope you understand. Take care. -Kambry.

My stomach feels like it does when you're dropped down the hill of a rollercoaster at crazy speeds. My phone falls from my hands onto the bed and I allow my face to plummet on top of it, my nose buried in the comforter as my forehead rests on the screen. "You're a sucky person, Kambry."

The buzzing against my skin causes me to jump and make a screeching noise on accident. Now I'm nervous. Surely he hasn't read that yet. Awesome. My palms become flush with the mattress, boosting me off so that I can see the screen.

Saxton Maverick calling . . .

I quickly grab it and roll back onto my back, staring at the screen and wondering if I should even answer. My thumb swipes right before my brain even has a chance to decide. My hand inches the phone to my ear. I roll my eyes. *You're such a freaking girl.*

"I wasn't baiting for a call, ya know."

He clears his throat. "Kambry."

"Last I checked, yes."

"What was that text about?"

"I didn't think it was unclear."

"Don't PMS."

I scoff. "I'm not."

"Did you read it? I told you to call me if anything was confusing."

"I didn't," I admit.

"Fucking dammit. Why not?"

"Because . . . I don't know, Saxton. I just can't. Lots of reasons."

"Explain."

I stare at the ceiling, listening to the background noise. Sounds like a truck door shutting. "Are you going somewhere?"

"I'm hungry, and I'm waiting."

"Oh. Look, I don't really feel like talking about it right now. I'm about to go shower. Can we talk later?"

Silence.

I wait.

Nothing.

"Hello."

"Yeah, Kambry . . .we can talk later."

"Okay. Night, Saxton."

"Later."

The call disconnects. I look at the screen, now back to my home screen. "Well, okay then."

I stand and head for the bathroom, just ready to take a bubble bath and go to bed. "Crap. Ear buds."

I detour, looking for my purse. It's sitting on the floor by the wall. Squatting, I open it and dig around until I find my ear buds. It doesn't take me long. They are usually sitting right on top. When I have them in hand, I walk toward my door and ease it open quickly. Once cracked, I peek my head out toward the couch. Surprisingly, the television is off and everything is dark. Weird, she must have gone to bed.

I open my door the rest of the way and tiptoe lightly across the floor to the bathroom that is halfway between Meredith's room and mine. At least I don't have to worry about her asking questions. I quietly shut the bathroom door and set my phone on the counter with my ear buds on top so I can run the water.

When the water begins pouring from the faucets, I test it and adjust the knobs until the temperature is to my liking, then stop up the drain to let it fill. My movements are robotic, his voice fresh in my mind. I love his voice. It's the perfect depth, masculine, and sexy when he says certain things that almost give him a scratchy sound from it deepening; like being emotional.

The bucket on the floor draws my attention. Meredith and I keep our emergency girl stress kit, AKA our spa supplies, beside the tub. One thing we agree on is that every girl should have a long, hot bubble bath at least once a week.

I pick up the lavender vanilla bubble bath and pour the perfect amount into the stream of water. Then the bath salts—one scoop dispersed along the length of the tub and my de-stressing officially begins. The aroma starts to fill the room, instantly calming me.

I stand and grab the lighter off the back of the sink, before lighting the three candles scattered throughout the bathroom, then returning it to its location before flipping the light switch to turn off the bathroom light. Nothing beats soaking in a hot bath when you can actually enjoy it in the dark.

The soft flicker of the candles as the water runs into the bathtub relaxes every nerve in my body. I quickly remove my clothes and throw my hair into a messy bun on top of my head, before stepping into the water and grabbing my phone and ear buds off the sink, plugging them in, and then place them in my ears.

The warm water envelops me as I sit down and pull up Spotify, searching for the station I'm in the mood to listen to. *Bedroom Jams* catches my attention. Perfect. That should be mellow enough. When the first song in the shuffle lineup starts to play, I lay my phone down on the floor out of water's reach and lie back, sinking down into the water.

"This is nice."

My feet take residence on the side of the tub below the faucet, the water raining down between my legs. I like the tub almost completely full, covering my body.

Bubbles are everywhere, the white, fluffy, cloud-like substance reproducing and spreading quickly. My hand wades back and forth in the water as they cover me. The water is almost opaque. I slide my bottom toward the front some more, bringing the water level to my collarbone.

My foot moves to the faucet, my toes wrapping around the handle before I turn it to shut the water off now that the tub is full. Just as my body begins to overheat, the air kicks on, blowing through the vent just enough to cool me down. Good, that means I can stay in here longer. A catchy song comes on: *Sex Never Felt Better* by TGT.

Most of the time I catch on to the lyrics pretty quickly, especially when it's a song I like and I'm relaxed and don't try. My eyes close and I begin humming along to the melody as the song plays through. R&B music is my ultimate love when it comes to music, my favorite. It's so sensual, each song telling a story. By the third time the chorus comes on, the tension in my body releases and the humming turns into singing along as I stare at the back of my eyelids, looking at nothing but blackness. "Sex ain't never felt better. I wanna swim in it all night. Girl, your body belongs to me . . ."

I settle into the back of the tub, trying to get comfortable. My hands rest on my thighs beneath the surface of the water and I allow the music to consume my mind. The scent lingers in the room, the air blowing across my face, and my body warm from the water, the combination soothing me. The hot temperature of the water is making my buzz more prominent. I can barely move. I think I may have a new found love: sweet wine.

I slide my feet down into the water, resting them flat against the bottom of the bathtub; my bent knees and the leg area surrounding the only parts emerged from the water aside from my head. My eyes begin to roll into the back of my head, and I let them, slowly drifting off to sleep as I incoherently hum along to the music.

A hand cups my knee, but lightly as if careful not to startle me. A sense of familiarity washes over me, and visions of him begin to surface in my mind, like the way he looked at me on the steps of the pool just prior to kissing me. The scene replicates, but this time the scene plays out slightly different. It moves down my leg, just barely brushing along the surface of my skin.

It's so vivid and real that the vague sound of water movement registers, the gate between realms open, and the two worlds mix. I moan at the feel as his fingers glide down my slick, wet skin and dips below the water. "Saxton," I mumble. "That feels nice."

The back of my head rolls as a finger moves to my center and swipes up the middle. "Please don't stop."

"You like that?"

"Mmmm Hmmm."

He slips a finger inside of me, causing my legs to fall apart as he begins to slide it in and out. The music in the background is only heightening the way it feels, keeping me from focusing on anything else. The pad of a thumb presses against my clit as his finger slides almost completely out, and then a rhythmic rocking begins between the two, never breaking contact with either place. "Just like that," I whisper.

The water creating a film on my skin reminds me of when he had his tongue on me, rubbing up and down just like . . . "That."

"Come for me."

That voice drives me insane. It causes mental instability, temporary paralysis, and unwise decision making without much more than a few words. Another hand grabs ahold of my breast and the skin to skin friction against my nipple adds just enough effect that I'm about to . . .come.

My hands come out of the water; one hitting the wall and the other smacking into something soft molded to something hard. My fist clenches around it—a shirt. I can't think. All I can do is feel, as I orgasm, wanting to enjoy it for as long as possible, because as quickly as it bursts it will dissipate.

It ends. At precisely the same moment that it does, all touch ceases, leaving me with only my music in this warm water, the image of Saxton in my mind as he stares at me in my post orgasmic state, and a feeling so relaxed it's slightly unreal. My head rolls from side to side, my eyes remaining closed. My body is trying to wake up, but my mind doesn't want to. Waking up requires me to leave him, and that I don't want. "No. I don't want it to end."

"It doesn't have to."

My legs begin rubbing together. That cologne. I can smell it as if he's sitting right here. "You smell so good."

My eyes are rolling around behind my lids, trying to open. I don't want them to. My hands move to cover my face, rubbing up and down, paying my eye makeup no attention as water wets my face. "I have to get a grip," I mumble against my palms. "If a dream felt that good, I can't even imagine what real sex with him would feel like. Shit. A wet dream has a new meaning now. Having orgasms while I sleep. That's a first."

My ear bud comes out of my ear and I jump, in a panic that it's going to drop into the water and ruin. Grabbing for it by the cord, my hand wraps around a hand holding it. My eyes pop open when my head turns, now staring into the blue eyes of one sexy guy that keeps showing up in the most awkward places . . .like invading my dreams. "It would feel so much better."

I blink repeatedly, trying to focus my eyes on the silhouette in front of me. "You even sound real. God, I'm well on my way to crazy."

"You ready to go over that contract yet?"

I'm suddenly very much awake and aware of what is going on right now. I slide down into the water, quickly trying to hide, and splashing water as I do. "Saxton."

He smirks, clearly on his knees, and resting on his crossed forearms on the side of the tub. "Kambry."

"What are you doing here?"

"Getting you wet."

"Funny. Seriously. How did you get in?"

"I haven't been in yet, but I'm trying very hard to get there."

I roll my eyes. "Lame lines are not satisfying my mood. You cannot just keep breaking into my apartment. This is creeper status for sure."

"It was pretty easy. I just knocked on the front door. When your roommate opened it and saw who I was she pulled me into her room long enough to make me sign shit and whisper-scream at me about asking you to watch a DVD that fucked up her girls' night. I'm under strict orders not to fuck with your head, and then she said she was going to bed. Here I am. The door was unlocked. I assumed that was an invite."

"You signed the DVD?"

"Yep, both, since she said you wouldn't be keeping them." He smiles and I want to punch myself in the face. "You want to keep me all to yourself, don't you?"

"I hate you right now. Both of you actually."

"Ball is in your court, beautiful. Sign the line and I'm all yours."

I'm not admitting to a damn thing. What happened to girl code? You don't tell guys this kind of embarrassing shit. "Why are you here? I figured you had moved on to another target by now," I say sarcastically.

"Do I sense jealousy in your tone?"

He's still smiling, only broadening with each comeback. "Shut up."

He closes in. "I kind of like the one I've got. Just so you know . . .there is a huge difference in fucking because you *have* to and because you *want* to. You are the only one that shouldn't be jealous."

He's so damn hot. Hell. The face stubble only adds to his appeal. "What do you want? I gave you the answer."

He shrugs. "You are not deciding until you know what's in the contract. Obviously you aren't going to do it alone, so I'm going to read it to you . . .at my house. I'm taking you hostage for the night."

His house.

Stay strong.

"I'm not going to your house."

"Yes you are, even if I have to carry you there myself, so you might as well stop trying to fight me on it, finish up in here, and dress comfortably. We are going to be up a while. You shouldn't be in a mood to deny me."

I can feel the color-change taking place on my face. That was no dream . . . I don't even know what to say right now. "Okay."

That's all I've got. He leans in, lingering just outside of my lips, his eyes boring into mine. "In case you were wondering, you're just as beautiful coming in your sleep. My dick hates me right now."

He kisses me, and then stands, walking toward the door. "Where are you going?"

"Call us in something to eat and wait for you. I'm hungry, and obviously right now I'm going to have to settle for food."

With that, he walks out the door, closing it behind him. He never even asked if I was hungry and I never told him that I was. He just assumed I needed to eat, and I like that about him, as well as his persistence. I'm quickly finding that when he's around, nothing else matters.

CHAPTER ELEVEN

Saxton

I sit down on her mattresses and prop my elbows on my bent knees, my hands overlapped in front of my mouth. I squint my eyes, trying to erase the previous vision from my mind before I nut on myself or end up with blue-balls. I don't think I've ever wanted to fuck a girl so bad in my life. I don't even know why. Sure, she's hot. Her accent sends my dick into overdrive. When you get her fired up about something her personality comes out and I like it, but honestly, I barely know anything about her. I do know that she intrigues me. I also know that she's innocent, so she doesn't belong anywhere near this world that I've been in for some time now.

With that knowledge, I know that I shouldn't be pushing her to do this, because in doing this it's a win/lose situation for me. I win because I get to publicly claim her for everyone to see, her first time at that. My dick alone is nearly salivating over the fact that nothing has been inside of her, but I lose because in doing just that everyone else gets a front row seat to seeing every part of her body from close up angles, just as I do. Her most intimate places will never be my secret, but there is a method behind the madness.

This is my job. Until I find something that appeals to me more this is how I make a living. Yes, I do have some wiggle room when I want to take a breather from it all as well as contract negotiations, like this one, because I worked my ass off when I was at the bottom and listened to my mentors, but in the end there is always another big dick to replace me if I get too cocky. It may be films, but it's also porn. Fucking has a way of appealing to more people than you would think.

I haven't even entertained the idea of casual dating since . . .well, *her*—the bitch that doesn't deserve to be called by a name, and for good reason. But since I laid eyes on Kambry in the club my mind has had a field day throwing out thoughts and possibilities. Some are hot, some interesting, and others just plain ludicrous, but I'm not a fucking idiot. When I give something this much thought I believe there is some underlying reason, so here I am, trying to get her to agree to this crazy as hell project they are on my ass about.

The truth is I want to toy with the idea of having it all with her, whether mock or not. Like I told her, this is the way I can do this. No harm no foul right? Once the initial trial filming period is up it's a waiting game before they continue out the terms of the contract, so if it turns out horrible it's only for a short period of time. If it turns out well . . .

The door opens and I look up at the exact moment Kambry walks in wrapped in a towel that hits mid-thigh, clenching the edges on her chest in her fist, her phone in the other hand. She has legs for days; smooth, slender, long legs . . .that I really need to stop looking at, because I'm not coming on to her anymore tonight. At least, I'm telling myself that now, hoping my limbs believe it. I may need a shot of whiskey to calm the raging hormones in my bloodstream, because I'm determined to sway her to take this seriously, and I'm never going to do that if I continue to feel what it's like inside her fucking pussy every time I'm around her. It's only a matter of time until my willpower is gone.

"You hungry?"

She shuts the door and walks forward, eying me up and down. "Yeah. Supper didn't turn out too well."

She glances over at a stack of folded clothes by the wall and back at me. I still don't like that she has no furniture. I get that she has a closet and a set of mattresses sitting on the floor, but it really bothers me. I hold up my hands. "You can get dressed. I promise to keep my hands to myself."

She smiles at me for the first time since she walked in. "Oh, now you want to keep your hands to yourself? Now that I'm conscious."

"What? I heard my name. I just figured I better make sure the dream was accurate."

She bites her lip mid smile. "If I remember correctly you touched me before I voiced anything aloud."

"How do you know? You were asleep."

She laughs. "Touché. How do you know my dream was sexual? I could have been imagining something as innocent as a back massage. Besides, you haven't kept your hands to yourself since we met. Do you really expect me to believe that you can keep all eyes and hands off of me now?"

There's that personality. She hides it a good bit, almost as if it's just a defense mechanism, reserving herself. I smirk and lean back on my elbows. "I said I wouldn't touch. I didn't say I wouldn't look though. Go ahead. I'm going to sit right here and enjoy the show."

Light hits her eyes and it gives off a gleam. Just when I think she's about to dart into the closet to change, she drops her towel instead, revealing that beautiful, naked body; only this time it's not covered by bubbles. Not that her wet, soapy body under candlelight wasn't like dangling meat in front of a lion, but damn, it's so much better from this view. My eyes slow their roll, taking in every visible inch. My heart is pounding, my breathing is slightly irregular, and my mouth becomes thick, needing to swallow.

This may be harder than I originally thought.

She turns around and squats to grab something off the floor, giving me a nude view of her ass along the way; that round, beautiful ass . . .that I am visualizing myself opening up as I slide my dick inside.

Stop that shit.

She quickly stands and faces me, her eyes widened. "What?"

Threading her arms through the sleeves of a shirt, she pulls it over her head and it falls to her thighs, her nipples hardened through the fabric. She rubs her lips together, before taking a step in my direction. "Do you like what you see?"

She wraps her hands around my neck as she reaches me and begins playing with the hair at the top of my neck. "What do you think?"

"At first I thought, maybe, but after hearing that growl, I'm fairly certain." She straddles my lap, placing her knees to each side of me on the mattress.

"What growl?"

She smirks. "The one you just did."

I return her expression. "You were baiting me. I guess my subconscious took it before I did."

"Baiting you, huh?"

I thrust my hips up at the same time I press my cock down, toward the center of my legs away from her weight bearing against it. She lowers herself down further, her hot middle pressed against my cotton pants—the thin covering between my dick and her pussy.

"If I was baiting you I wouldn't do this," she says, as she closes in on me, pressing her lips against mine. That willpower is thinning. She begins grinding her wet pussy against the length of my erection.

"Fuck," I whisper, when she nibbles my lip as our mouths change directions. I grab her hips and lie back on the mattress, pressing her down harder against me as I lift my hips to meet her. "I want you so bad."

"Take what you want."

My hands inch up her back, pushing her shirt back up, ready to sheathe my cock and fuck her right here and now. Grabbing her in my arms with our mouths molded together, I flip us over, resting between her legs and rolling my hips to rub my dick against her center. She spreads her legs and arches her back, before grabbing my hand and guiding it up her shirt toward her breast. "Touch me here. I like when you touch me."

"How am I supposed to say no to that?" That is the truth. When she gives me that begging expression it takes everything in me to function properly, let alone deny her. My thumb brushes back and forth over her hard nipple, just before my mouth encloses around it.

She moans and presses her hand on the back of my head, pressing me into her as my tongue flicks over her nipple then swirls around it. "Just like that." Her voice when she is turned on is like nothing I've ever experienced. It's not fake, it's not wild, and it's not over-the-top or over-exaggerated. It's fucking perfect, as if she is experiencing every damn feeling and action being done to her for the first time, even if it's not. I'm nowhere close to letting this go.

The contract.

I stop abruptly, cursing myself on the inside as I release my hold from her body and push off the mattresses, adjusting my pants by the waistband, and work to gather myself in the process. She pushes up on her elbows, her legs still slightly spread and bent at the knees with her feet flat on the bed. Without attempting to I look down, instantly glancing at her bare center. That is one beautiful pussy. "What's wrong?"

"Son of a bitch. Get dressed. We're leaving and I'm cutting myself off before I make very bad decisions and overdose on your body."

Without so much as another damn word I grab a folder off the floor that has Michael's handwriting on it—identical to mine—and walk out the door, for fear that if I look at her one more time I will cave and say fuck it. A healthy man can only turn that down so many times before he's a fucking idiot; exactly what I feel like for even playing along with this whole ordeal. If I give in and she gets her way, then this entire thing will be a bust, and I'll have to take another job and go back to a stale and forced sex life at the hand of pills and producers controlling where I stick my dick. This is one chance I can actually choose who I want to fuck. It likely won't happen again.

I like the choice, the natural sexual attraction, and the fact that she is completely pure. My mind has already factored in that her lack of experience means she has nothing else to compare us to. Anything we do she's never felt with anyone else. That piece of knowledge drives me to places that scare me, because when I enter her she will be formed for me, and only me. I will do whatever I have to do to make her sign that fucking line.

I probably slammed the apartment door a little too hard, but I'm wound tight. My back becomes flush with the wall just outside of her apartment. I shelve the folder underneath my arm and reach into my pocket to pull out a pack of cigarettes, quickly removing one and placing it between my lips before lighting the end.

I inhale the pull off the filter, allowing the poisonous smoke to invade my lungs, reveling in the mild high I get every time I take that first drag. It's a bad habit I picked up about the same time *she* fucked me up. I suppose alcohol, cigarettes, and heartbreak go hand in hand. The heartbreak went away, the alcohol only returns with business or the occasional playful pleasure, but this calls on me when my nerves go haywire. I'm not a regular smoker. I'm more of a mood or anxiety smoker.

The door opens and then closes. I look over, immediately calming as another spike of adrenaline replaces the previous one. She's wearing that same long shirt as earlier, black, but this time I can see the faint outline of a bra, and she's wearing a pair of white, cotton, spandex pants painted on her body that stop at her calves, and a pair of flip-flops with her hair piled on top of her head. The strap of a duffel bag sits on her shoulder, her face free from makeup. I can't take my eyes off of her.

She gives me a small smile. "I'm ready."

Taking one final drag, I throw the butt on the concrete and step on it, rubbing it across the cement with my shoe to put it out. I hold the nicotine in my lungs as long as possible. When it starts to hurt I exhale, blowing the smoke into the night air, never looking away from her. "Good, 'cause I have a feeling you'll need to be."

A feeling overcomes me as we walk down the stairs. It's that pivotal moment when you know in your gut that you're fucked, no matter what the outcome, because either way something drastic is going to happen . . .whether you're ready for it or not.

CHAPTER TWELVE

Saxton

I pull into the garage and park my truck, closing the door behind me. I kill the engine to my Cadillac Escalade EXT truck and look over at her, holding onto her bag as if her life depends on it, looking straight ahead like a timid animal. Things have been fairly quiet the entire drive, from her apartment to picking up takeout to here. My mind is overloaded, making it difficult to hold a normal conversation. I'm not a huge talker anyway. I find myself watching or listening more than talking. I've been that way most of my life, but more so since I left college.

I was an upstanding young adult at one time, full of morals and values, friends constantly around, and stuck between college life and family, even dating. I was, well, normal by most people's standards. I liked to party as much as the next college frat boy, and as a young buck I gave my heart away to that one special girl that caught my eye during rush week; only I didn't know she was going to be Satan's spawn when I laid my eyes on her, with even a name and onyx hair to confirm it. Salem was an evil witch, for better terminology, if you ask me and anyone else that she was able to sink her wicked teeth into, but I'm not even going to go there.

All that matters is that, that girl ruined my trust and me for most people. She's the reason I have such an outstanding work ethic, limited contact with my somewhat conservative family—at least where my career choice is concerned—

and generally keep to myself. I guess it could be worse. I could be an asshole, but given the beautiful blonde sitting in my passenger seat that I've yet to fuck even though given the opportunity, affirms that I'm not. Most would call that hope for a decent human being, but it'll take one hell of a girl to change anything in my life, and I've yet to meet one that would even categorize as a possibility.

She finally looks over at me. "This looks nice."

"It is," I reply, grabbing the bags of takeout and opening the door. She exits just as I do, meeting me at the hood of the truck and following me to the door. "I haven't lived here but about a year. My last place was smaller," I say as I unlock the door and open it. I walk in and hold the door, waiting for her to enter.

She steps in with one foot, placing her toes in first and peeks in, as if she's trespassing, until she sees me looking at her amused, and then straightens her posture and speeds up. "Sorry. I've never seen a house with so many windows. Everything is pretty much solid where I'm from, you know, hurricanes and all. You aren't worried about someone seeing your every move?"

A short-lived laugh escapes as I shut the door. "Uh, have you forgotten what I do for a living? There isn't anything about me that isn't public archive somewhere. The people that know who I am have seen more than what they will see through these windows. To everyone else I'm just a normal, unimportant guy, so they don't care. Plus, I can make them opaque with the touch of a button."

"So I'm guessing the bedroom isn't made of windows?"

"It is. Like in here, each room has at least one wall made of glass, but why do you ask?"

She looks around, taking in the open space of the living room. "Well, you said that they see more in your work than what they would see here. I was assuming they didn't have access to your bedroom then."

I'm intrigued. "And what is in my bedroom that is so X-rated? I don't sleep totally nude believe it or not. Like most men, I don't like my junk cold."

Her face starts to redden. "Well, I mean, like if you and . . .or we . . .were to, you know . . ." She pauses. "If you bring a girl home for recreational purposes outside of work."

"You mean if I want to fuck?"

"Yeah . . .that."

"Then my neighbors or peeping toms, as you're referring to, would probably be surprised since it's never happened or been witnessed."

She passes me, continuing to make her way further inside the house. I follow behind her, curious to see where she's even going, and still holding onto the bags of food. Honestly, I'm trying my best not to laugh. Hell, the food is probably getting cold by now.

". . .Because you black out the windows?" I smirk from behind her. I guess curiosity really does get the best of us. I'm kind of there with her. Which is even surprising with the age difference. I've never been interested in someone this much younger than me. Two years was about as big of an age gap in my personal life that I got. Every few feet she stops, as if giving herself a tour without any help from me. It's mostly open so it isn't really a maze anyway.

"Because I haven't fucked for recreational purposes in a really long time, and I sure as hell don't bring my work home with me. I guess you could say if I'm not on camera I'm pretty much celibate."

That produces a halt as she comes into the kitchen. I place the bags of food on the island, waiting for the moment that she turns around with the deer in headlights look. One foot digs into the tile behind her and she does an about-face. "Seriously?"

"Yep."

"But . . ."

"But what?"

"How long is a long time?"

"A couple years, give or take. Maybe even closer to three. I lost track."

Her eyes cast downward and her forehead bunches. I walk toward her and grab her chin, pulling her gaze to me. "Surprised?"

"Kind of. I mean . . .a porn star that doesn't have sex. That makes no sense."

"I have sex. Just not for fun or behind closed doors. Sex is a job for me. It lost its testosterone-driven appeal when I dove dick first into any film I could get, trying to build my name and bank account." She looks lost. "What's on your mind?"

"If you never just have sex, then what are we doing? I'm just clearly a little confused. Don't laugh, but I thought that was basically what this was; just sex between two people attracted to each other. The whole appeal for you wanting me to do this is because I'm a virgin right?"

The pad of my thumb finds the middle of her bottom lip, pulling downward to graze across the satin feeling skin. "What we're doing doesn't fit into a category yet, and no, that is not what appealed to me. If you want to know the truth, that actually was a turn off."

"Oh, I—"

"At first. In my experience virgins don't really have anything to offer in sex. They just lay there, almost as if you're fucking a corpse. Then there is usually blood. I don't do blood. It's not a pleasant experience to me unless she's been broken in."

"Then what changed?"

My hands become flush with her cheeks, only briefly, before continuing into her hair, grabbing fistfuls. Stepping forward, her backside collides with the island. I press my hips against hers. "Because you do this to me. For the first time in what seems like forever, my dick stands at full attention without the first fucking pill. No Cialis, no Viagra, nothing, and the longer I know you without fucking you the worse it gets. Anytime I'm near you, touching you, looking at you, or thinking about you, it's as hard as a damn steel pipe, ready to be laid."

Our eyes are a direct reflection of each other's. Her hands make a resting place on my waist. "Then why do you want me to do this instead of just having sex with me when I've offered it to you? Sex is just sex right? Doesn't it all feel the same?"

"You really want to go there?"

"Yes. I wouldn't have asked otherwise."

"I've had sex with a lot of women. My dick has been in more orifices than I could begin to count. Over the years I've experienced it all, but no matter what any man ever tells you, sex without raw emotion is stale. Does it feel good? Yeah. If you're just looking to nut. But it's forgettable, and it gets old. In all of the times I've ever gotten aroused, though, no girl has ever turned me on quite like you, and that says something."

I reach over by the bags of food and grab the folder I brought in with them, bringing it between us and holding it out for her. She grabs it. "For the first time since college I want to experience them both simultaneously. That, Kambry, is why I am pushing this project. I've read the contract, and I think you should too."

Kambry

I'm finding it hard to breathe, but with him that really isn't something new. I open the folder for the first time since it was given to me and the word-covered page leaves me feeling anxious; a lot like when I took the ACT exam. It's probably not as scary as it looks, but the jumbled wording and the pressure of choosing the right option is altering my mental capability of actually processing everything here, especially after this beautiful guy standing in front of me just kind of spilled a piece of his heart.

I rub my hand over the left side of my chest. My heart is beating so hard that my chest physically hurts. This isn't some easy decision. This is a moral dilemma. This would be spitting in my parents' faces. There is no hiding something like this for very long. You can't lie when someone asks you about it. This is something I have to live with forever. Ugh. This is stressing me out! I glance at the top of the page.

KISS AND TELL FILMS
EMPLOYMENT OF DAY PERFORMER
FOR ADULT FILM SERIES

PRODUCTION COMPANY (EMPLOYER): <u>KISS AND TELL FILMS</u>
PRODUCTION TITLE: <u>SEX SESSIONS: UNCUT</u>
PERFORMER'S NAME: <u>KAMBRY RIVERS</u>
ADDRESS: <u>413 LUNA COVE APT 3C LOS ANGELES, CA 90014</u>
ROLE: <u>PERFORMER</u>

This agreement covers the employment of <u>Kambry Rivers </u>(Performer) by <u>Michael Prescott</u> (Producer) in an erotic adult film series.

I press it into is chest. I don't even want to know how they got my address. "Can you just paraphrase? I have no idea what any of this means. It's freaking me out a little."

"It's a legal binding contract, Kambry. You need to read it."

"Saxton, I will if I decide to go any further once you basically tell me the stipulations. This is one reason I haven't already looked at it. It's intimidating to someone that's never made her own decisions until a couple of months ago."

The folder gets placed back on the counter. He grabs my face and kisses me, instantly melting away all of the anxiety that's building. I grab his wrists, allowing him to shut my rambling up. I don't understand this whirlwind of emotions going on inside of me. I like him a lot, even though I know I shouldn't. He's admitted to me that he's probably been with more than a hundred women. That alone makes me cringe, but then I look into his blue eyes when he pulls away and I don't give a damn. Stupid right?

Each time his skin brushes against mine I get butterflies. He grabs the bag of food and shakes it at me. "Hungry?"

I shake my head. "Not anymore."

"You need to eat."

"I will later. Go ahead and eat yours."

He turns and opens the refrigerator, placing it inside. "What are you doing? Don't put it up on account of me."

He then pulls out two bottles of water and hands me one. I take it. "It'll still be there later. Chinese food is usually better cold anyway. Sit outside with me? I want to show you something."

Each time he acts like I'm the center of his focus I feel like I grow an inch taller. He gives me choices, no matter how big or small they are. "Okay."

He grabs the folder off the counter and nods his head toward the sliding glass doors I briefly noticed earlier. I follow behind him across the way and wait patiently as he unlocks the door and opens it, but he doesn't turn on a light outside. Instead, he takes my hand and pulls me out the door behind him. I'm not sure how he is supposed to read with it being dark outside. He tosses the water and folder down on the cushion of a fancy lounger. I follow suit. "This is why I bought this place."

"What is?" I ask, bumping into him when he stops, but instead of making an ordeal about me not paying attention, he just pulls me around to his front and molds his body around me, draping his arms over my shoulders and holding me to him in a romantic gesture, like an actual couple; something I have yet to experience since we met.

"This," he says next to my ear, and that's when I notice it—the view.

"Wow. I've never seen anything like it." I grab ahold of his forearms for a hand prop, almost as if I need something to steady me. They are lean, but muscular. I stare out into the distance at the rolling hills speckled with lights from houses tucked inside them. It's like something you would see on a Thomas Kincaid work of art. "I didn't know views like this truly existed in someone's backyard," I whisper, as if we're on sacred grounds. "This most definitely isn't Alabama."

"This is what I do most nights that I'm home. I sit out here, think, and just listen and watch. It kind of became my sanctuary when I needed peace from the madness. It helps on nights when I want to throw in the towel and find something else. I didn't think anything could top this, but I may have thought prematurely."

I wait for more, but nothing comes. He ceased his speech at the exact moment I was hanging off the ledge. "If you don't like it then why don't you quit?"

"Because this industry has a shelf life. Sex appeal dissipates in porn with age. The younger you are the more you succeed. The money is too good to give it up without a cause. Hollywood major motion pictures are too competitive for my interest, so I just stick with this until I find something better."

I remain silent, taking in the sight before me. I like the feel of him holding me. It's nice, and completely unexpected. If I knew it would be like this I could possibly get past the rest of it, but once again, even when they aren't present my parents plague my every thought. I can hear the scolding now, so I force myself to push it back.

His cologne fills the air. "You smell good. What is it?"

"Dolce & Gabbana light blue."

"I like it." Too much actually. As much as I don't want to I turn in his arms to look at him. "I guess we should discuss that contract now. After all, that is why I'm here."

He nods and moves toward the lounger, throwing his leg over it in a straddle, moving the objects out of the way. He pats the seat between his legs. "Let's do business, beautiful."

I hold up my finger. "One sec." I run inside and grab my phone out of my purse where I left it beside the door as I entered, just in case Meredith needs me, and then return outside.

He eyes it grasped in my hand. "Really? You couldn't live without it for a few hours?"

I shrug. "We're here alone with no family. I want to be able to hear it in case she calls."

"Fair enough," he says, grabbing my hand. "Now sit."

I do, but instead of an unladylike position I sit sideways, crossing my legs. He immediately begins shaking his head. "Mirror me."

Defeated, I do as he says, keeping a space between us, but that doesn't stop him from grabbing behind my knees and pulling me closer, only to drape my legs over his thighs. He plants a kiss to the side of my mouth; making me want to grab the back of his head and hold him there. If only he were to move less than an inch to the right. "Now. I like this better. I can see your face and give you motivation when you need it."

I smile. "Motivation? What kind of motivation?"

"The kind that involves my tongue pressed against yours."

"Hmm, I may like that kind; a tool of persuasion."

He opens the folder and removes the stapled papers that could drastically change my life with one signature. "I'm kind of counting on it," he counters. "Okay, I'm going to go over the points that I feel you should probably be aware of. I am going to try to do it quickly. Do you want me to read as written here or paraphrase?"

"Paraphrase please. If I wanted the legal jabber I would read it myself."

"Okay. Just stop me if you have a question. Will that work?"

"Okay." My stomach feels like a massive ball of nerves. If you have ever seen one of those huge rubber band balls that is basically just one overlapping another in the quantity of hundreds, then that's precisely how I feel.

I watch his face as he skims the contents. "Okay, let's start with the length of the contract. Since the company has never done this type of project before they want to introduce it to the public before they expend a large budget for it, basically to ensure they will profit, because let's face it, film industries are never going to lose money for long. They will cut the project if it starts to dip into profit margin, so they've basically broken it up into two parts, with a temporary void in contract terms between the two. The length of part one is one month of filming. During that month of filming, but after enough footage has been recorded to use, it will go into production to get ready for premier on live television. That's when they will cut out small slivers and start marketing through spotlights during other programs on several networks, all adult in this case, but to preview it to the viewers; like a movie trailer."

He pauses. "You know basically what production is, right? The time between filming and premier in theatre or the television air date when you can actually watch it, or the period of mass production for purchase on DVD or digital release."

I might actually be offended if he wasn't so freaking cute sitting there, explaining it to me in great detail like I'm a toddler. "Sounds familiar," I respond, trying not to bring out the witty remark that I really want to use right now. "Go on."

"Okay, well, from the end date of part one to the beginning date of part two this contract becomes void. Dates are listed. During that time, it's basically a waiting game and you're free to commit to other projects, if you wish, that don't overlap this one given they continue filming. Once the first show airs, if it sparks enough attention in the media and numbers show revenue, then we will get a call that the project will resume filming."

Fairly simple to comprehend. "And if it gets cut?"

"Then you are released from the contract altogether."

"Okay."

"Any questions?"

"I don't think. Not right now, at least."

His eyes go back to the paper. "Actor restrictions during filming. I'm just going to name them off. You must be available to live in the house provided by the company. You must be willing to perform on camera all aspects of a couple's relationship, including, but not limited to, explicit sex with the co-star, hereby named, Saxton Maverick. During the terms of your contract you must not participate in any sexual relationship with anyone other than the co-star."

He looks at me, his eyes darkening in color. My pulse begins to race at the mention of sex between the two of us. My skin starts to heat. "When you say all aspects, what exactly does that mean? Clearly, I get the sex part."

He flashes me a boyish grin and I feel like my heart is about to explode. It's one of those smiles that hollow his cheeks to show off those dimples that God gifted him with, even through the stubble. I want to attack him, but I abstain. "It means for all intents and purposes you're basically my girlfriend and vice versa."

I'm his . . .girlfriend. Breathe. Just breathe.

A surge of excitement consumes me. I feel like I used to feel on Christmas morning as a kid when my eyes would pop open only to find out it was still dark outside and my parents were sleeping peacefully . . .and I wasn't supposed to wake them, so I would sit on my bed with my legs crisscrossed rocking back and forth like I was cracked out on candy until they woke up.

I'm having a hard time not smiling. I try so hard, but his expression is contagious, just like when someone yawns, and before long I'm smiling just as big as him. "Okay, so live in a house, pretend to be your girlfriend, and be willing to embark on sexual endeavors with you for people to watch. I get all that, but doesn't it put a damper on things when you know you're being watched?"

He holds up his index finger, stopping me. "I'm getting there."

Pressing my index finger and thumb together, I zip my lips. "Cute," he says. I continue with a thumbs up instead of talking, the ridiculous smile from earlier still plastered on my face. In return he grunts. "They've already thought about that, especially given you'll probably be camera shy, so all of the cameras will be installed in the house prior to arriving. It will be set up just like the way we are right now. The goal is for you not to know where they are. You may be able to find the cameras at some point, but they will decide when filming begins after arrival. You won't know once it starts. It will merely be an add on."

I have a thought. "What are we supposed to do in this house aside from the obvious?"

"Whatever we want. It will be fully set up for anything you need to live, as you would anywhere else. If we want to leave we will have someone following us but you won't know who it is. It will basically be identical to shows that already exist like Jersey Shore, The Real World, and Party Down South. The difference is that instead of roommates it's just the two of us; a couple, and when their cameras only show PG-13 horseplay movement underneath blankets, ours never stop rolling and there are no blankets."

I think about that briefly. It's a fact I've known this entire time; hence it being porn, but hearing it aloud still causes my cheeks to flush and questions to arise. "On those shows don't they have jobs though? Surely, you would want a break from me at some point."

"Nope, the point is to do everything together for the most part; however, you do get to keep your job at the club. Michael has already had a talk with the owner, only I get to join you." He makes this little facial that I can't even begin to explain, and then combs his fingers through his hair. "Do I look like a hot bartender?" Oh, dear lord. I just can't. The end. I want to maul him like a bear.

Reality sets in.

"Hold up. You're telling me Drake knows about this? They were perfectly fine participating in this whole ordeal?"

"I don't know who Drake is. I don't recall that being the owner's name. He was all for it, yes. They get paid because of the filming, and it's traffic for the club. People like to visit places that appear on television. It's human nature." I'm a little embarrassed, because of the nature of this entire situation. Other than hanging out with him I haven't heard of one thing that will benefit me in plastering my entire body and sexual experiences out there for people to watch.

"Am I missing something?"

"Like pay? I was wondering when that one would come up." He's back to smiling. Well, honestly, I'm not sure he ever stopped. I would think his cheeks probably hurt by now.

"Yeah, I guess."

He turns the document around with his fingers clamped in a specific area. I glance at the left side first. The bullet titled in bold is Salary. My eyes trail in a line toward the right following his fingers. They widen when the sum registers. "What the fuck?" I slap my hand over my mouth after my accidental outburst. My eyes meet his. That word doesn't come out often. It's one I've picked up from Meredith. "Is this for real?"

"Yes. It matches mine. You get half upon acceptance of the contract and the other half if they continue the project. They also pay for all STD and HIV testing prior to filming as well as birth control during your contract term to avoid any liability for the company."

"Wait, did you say matches yours? Why? I've never done this before. I mean don't get me wrong, I'm not complaining, but I'm also not stupid. Why wouldn't you make more than me, and if that's the going rate for this type of thing why am I being offered this job instead of another girl when I didn't even do anything to get it?"

"Because I wanted you and they wanted me. Those were my stipulations to accept it, as well as one other."

My pulse is howling in my ear, my heart thumping against my chest. I can only focus on one part of that sentence: *I wanted you.*

My mouth opens to speak, but my phone ringing stops me. It's not Meredith's ringtone. I glance over and my heart plummets to my stomach when I recognize the Alabama number on the screen. There is only one person back home with my new number and that's Meredith's mom, yet my parents' home number is the one calling. My brother doesn't even have it, because we aren't as close since he started college and began kissing my dad's ass to get what he wants.

I pick it up and accept the call. "Hello."

He clears his throat. "Kambry . . .this is your dad, or have you forgotten that you have one of those?"

"Hey, Dad. How are you?" I'm already cringing inside, as my voice is higher than usual and slightly awkward. "Aren't you usually in bed by now?"

"It seems for the last couple of months sleep doesn't come so easily. Funny how that happens when your only daughter takes off in the middle of the night and decides to run away to the other end of the continental U.S. I thought we taught you better than that, Kambry."

I hold up my finger at Saxton and stand. *Are you okay*? he mouths. I nod. I'd rather take this somewhere else. I can hear the aggravation in his tone. Walking to the door, I slip inside.

"Dad, I just wanted to find my own way for a while. I'm fine. Don't worry about me. I'm smart when I want to be."

"Well, I thought that until you pulled this stunt. Do you know what I had to go through to find out you had a number?"

"You cut off my phone!" My voice is rising. I can't help it. They freaking trigger me and it drives me nuts. I've barely been on the phone and he's digging into me more with each line. "What was I supposed to do?"

"Come home. That's what you were supposed to do. No daughter of mine is going to run off to another state like a Gypsy, living here and there." He's screaming into the phone. "Your mother and I have provided for you and in turn you do something like this. It's disrespectful. You wanted to be wild, well, you have. I've held my tongue most of the summer so you can find out what it's like to fail on your own. I'm done. I hope you're happy with yourself. You can come home and we can work through this. You can start to earn your trust back. Things can go back to the way they were. It's not too late to start school. It hasn't started yet."

My head is screaming at me, my heart squeezing, and my eyes glossing over. "I wasn't happy, Dad."

"Happy?" He laughs, mocking me.

"You're treating me like a child, Dad."

"If you want to be treated like an adult then act like one. Life isn't about chasing happiness, Kambry. That's something a floozy would say; like Meredith. It's about doing the right thing, knowing your place, and striving for no regrets. That girl is going to get you in trouble, so stop tormenting and embarrassing your family and come home before you end up pregnant with a bastard child or with a disease that's permanent. People are asking questions."

Tears fall down my face. Nothing I do will ever be good enough for him. He will continue to belittle me and hurt me emotionally to get his way. I'm at a loss for words. I'm heartbroken. Your parents may not always agree with your actions, but regardless they should still support you. How else does one learn? I straighten my posture, finding the backbone that's been buried for most of my life. "She's more like family than my own blood, so don't say those things about her. You have no idea what you're even talking about. You know nothing about her, because you've never cared enough to learn. At least she cares about what I want. You've never asked me what I want. I don't want to go to junior college or meet someone that you and Mom find fresh out of Seminary and become a preacher's wife with five kids by the time I'm thirty. That life is great for those that want it, but I don't."

"What is it that you're going to tell me next? That you met some boy in a bar or that you've fallen madly in love and are going to ride away on the back of his motorcycle? What have you done with my daughter? I don't even know you anymore. You're letting that California sun go to your head."

Saxton opens the door and steps inside, a look of concern present when he notices my face. "Maybe I have. Either way I like it here. I'm staying. This is me growing up. Goodnight, Dad."

I disconnect the call and shut my phone off. I know my dad well and he'll call back. His tactic of persuasion is to drive you insane until you cave. I can feel the anxiety constricting my air, making it hard to breathe. What tears I was holding back fall free. Never do I remember a time that man said he was proud of me for anything. Did I get a congrats for holding onto my virginity through graduation? No. Did I get a pat on the back for avoiding drugs and alcohol? Nope. Did I get a hug and smile at graduation when I was in the top five in my class? Never. I didn't even get rewarded with the option to accept from the college of my choice the fully paid scholarship I was awarded; something most parents can only wish their kids would get to save them college tuition, but not mine.

All of my life I've worried about making them angry, embarrassing them, or betraying their trust. I've fought hard to be the daughter that would make them proud, sacrificing memories in high school that can never be redone, and you know what, it's gotten me nowhere. I'm at my wit's end and I'm done.

"Kambry," he says in a hushed tone, drawing my focus to him. "Are you okay?"

"I'll do it."

His brows scrunch. "What?"

"I'll sign the contract, no questions asked, with one condition."

"I'm listening."

My face is wet from crying. I feel stupid, but I can't stop them. A person can only take so much mental abuse before they break. "Take my virginity . . .tonight."

His pupils constrict. He remains quiet. I continue, not needing an answer. "Regardless of how stupid my dad thinks I am, I can make decisions for myself. If I think about it, long and hard, I know I'll regret losing my virginity in front of the world. I'm not interested in holding onto my virtue until I walk down the aisle, if there ever is one, and I don't require being in love to give it away, but I do want it to be special. I want it to be private. You got your stipulations in the contract; that's mine. Take it or leave it."

He takes a step toward me, and then another. As he becomes within reaching distance he places his hand on my tear-stained cheek and wipes beneath my eye. "I'm not sure I could deny you if I wanted to, Kambry."

My head tilts slightly, readying for his kiss. He follows through as expected, then rubs his hands down my body to the back of my thighs, grips them, and picks me up. I wrap my arms and legs around him, staring down into his eyes. "What was the other thing you were going to tell me about your stipulations in the contract?"

"If we do this it doesn't matter. It was about losing your virginity."

I smile. "Your bedroom is about to become X-rated," I tease, trying to lighten the mood.

"I'll make it better than that," he counters. "We'll make our own movie. Just for us. Will you trust me?"

"If I didn't I wouldn't be here. I have a title."

He smiles up at me. "What's that, beautiful?"

"Sex Sessions: The beginning."

He starts to walk, carrying me. "It's perfect."

In a strange way . . .it is.

CHAPTER THIRTEEN

Saxton

I'm going to be selfish or selfless, depending on what way you look at it. In one way I like this better, but on the other hand I don't really want to have to explain this to Michael. There was no clause in the contract that stated she had to remain a virgin until filming, but that was also the wow factor. He said so himself.

I stood there at war with myself, wanting and pushing myself to say no, but seeing tears pour down her cheeks broke me. I couldn't do it. Maybe it's old habits resurfacing, but in her defense, she did have a point. I got my way, so it's only natural that she should get hers. I really shouldn't complain, because I will get her all to myself just once. After this I have to share her. She will no longer be mine alone.

I walk into my room, holding her by the underside of her thighs, just below her ass. She rubs her fingers through the back of my hair over and over and it brings chills across my skin. Her body is covered in too many clothes for my liking.

My room is dark, the only lighting being the beam of moonlight shining down on the center of my bed through the glass wall. The privacy fence and landscape of tall trees and shrubs keeps the light from the neighboring houses to a minimum. As my tongue glides against hers she pulls it deeper into her mouth, suctioning around it.

An animalistic sound emerges deep from my throat. My shin makes contact with the foot of the bed. I bend my leg, crawling knee first to lay her in the center, holding myself off of her as I continue to take more of her taste. The more I kiss her the harder it becomes to stop. Our mouths align together as if they were made specifically to fit against each other.

My entire house is set up with security cameras, mounted in a corner of each room on a remote controlled, motorized, swivel mount so that I can change the view anytime I'm ready. Over half of my house is on display for anyone on the outside, so I keep it monitored to prevent theft. It's never been utilized for an alternate purpose until now.

She rubs her hands down my sides until they halt on my waist, grabbing onto my shirt and cinching it until she has the shirttail in her fists. Slowly, it inches upward, baring my torso until she has it at my armpits. I pull her top lip between mine as I release her, letting her work it over my head and arms. She tosses it on the edge of the bed.

I upright myself to stand on my knees and then look down at her. Her eyes look a little lazy, most likely from the crying, and her lips are slightly swollen from my unshaved stubble rubbing against them. Even so, she's probably the most beautiful girl I've ever seen hands down, and the fact that the first person to have her is going to be me has my adrenaline pumping like a kid at an amusement park, only Disney has nothing on this.

I grab her ankle in my hand. "You sure you want this?"

"Yes," she says without question.

I lean over her to reach my nightstand, pulling open the drawer to find the T.V. and camera remote. When I reach inside her palms become flush with my abdomen, halting me. She begins at the V of muscle peeking out of my waistband, and then slowly moves upward, almost like a blind person would do, as if she's feeling every contour and ridge, adhering it to memory by touch.

My eyes close briefly. Her hands are soft and small. "I've never touched a body like this before you," she admits, regaining my focus. My dick is so hard it's beginning to hurt from pressing against the stretch material of my boxer-briefs behind my pants.

I pull the remotes out, leaving the drawer open. "Didn't you say you dated someone?"

She is shaking her head. "He didn't look like this. He wasn't really defined at all. Just normal."

"Which do you prefer?" I ask with a slight grin.

"You."

That word has a strange effect on my body. There is a minor pull in the left side of my chest, and my heart is slightly off rhythm, as if it came in brief contact with an electrical current, making it skip a beat. I expected her to say yours since we were discussing a body, as in a thing and not person, because most girls get that look when a guy cares enough to shred his body. If they didn't so many men wouldn't work hard for it. I probably wouldn't care as much if not for my career, but aesthetics goes a long way. What throws me off is her word choice. She didn't say yours, she said you, with no doubt in her voice. I like it more than I care to analyze.

"Even though I'm about to hurt you?" My question has nothing to do with the actual conversation at hand, but more or less the underlying one. I turn on the wall-mounted television but stare down at her, then change remotes when I hear that sound that tells me it's powering on.

Before giving her an option to speak, I twist my body enough to point the remote at the security camera in the corner opposite of the glass wall and begin rotating it as I watch the television screen. It moves slow, showing a trail across the room on screen from its current view to the one I'm aiming for: the bed. When the two of us appear on the television screen, her head peeks to the side, making me smile. Curiosity is a good thing, considering . . .

When it is at the angle I want, I shut off the television and replace the remotes back into the drawer, my attention quickly diverting to her. As if that's what she was waiting for she speaks. "I trust you."

Three little words hold so much power. "Do you feel any different knowing it's there?"

"A little nervous."

I hover my body directly over hers, but not bearing any weight on her. "The secret is to force it out of your mind. It's just you and me. You can only do that by replacing it with something else."

I can see her chest heaving as her breathing changes. "Like what?" she asks in a shortened tone. I push back, my hands gripping her sides, and then raise her shirt up until her stomach is bare. She props up on her elbows, looking at me. "Like letting someone take you to Nirvana?"

"Yes." She sits up so I can remove her shirt, leaving her in a black, cotton bra. It's nothing like lace or satin. It doesn't show major cleavage and isn't padded to falsify what isn't there. It's real, it's natural, it's innocent, and that's what makes it fucking sexy.

I kiss her as I reach behind her to unclasp her bra. It doesn't take long before the elastic pull releases, each side retracting toward her arms. My fingers move to her shoulder, clamping around the strap that rests on top, before pulling it over the edge and letting it fall down her arm. She takes my place with the other side, discarding it completely.

My hand instantly finds her breast. Each time I do I'm surprised, forgetting just how perfect they are, each spilling out of my hand. I release her lips, my mouth roughly moving toward her neck. The tiniest moan escapes her as she extends, letting her head fall to the side. With each inch that I descend, her breathing becomes heavier, until my lips are perfectly molded around one of her nipples, sucking it into my mouth.

My teeth graze a trail down her body, the tip of my tongue lightly brushing as I do. Her stomach quickly rises and falls as I make my way across, before colliding with the waistband of her white, cotton pants. I've never had a problem with going down on a girl, but I've never enjoyed it either; although, with her I actually want to, each time I turn her on.

I grab her pants on her hips, instantly working them over her ass when she lifts, not wasting any time. My lips press against her thigh, just behind the fabric as I peel them down her legs. I sit back on my heels as I pull them over her feet, leaving her completely nude. "Take yours off too," she says.

I look up at her. "You want me naked too?"

"Yes. I want to see you."

I hold out my hand for her to take, and then pull her up on her knees when she does. My hand reaches for her pile of hair, my index finger slipping beneath the elastic band to slide it out, pulling her hair down. The platinum blonde waves cascade over her shoulders, creating a curtain around her smooth, creamy skin. "I like you like this."

Inching backward, I plant my feet on the floor and stand at the foot of the bed, guiding her along with me on her knees until she's at the edge. "You want me naked, then undress me."

She nods as her full bottom lip disappears into her mouth, her hands pressing against my bare sides. She rubs them around to my lower back when I place my hands against her neck and kiss her, deep and a little rough. Her fingers dip beneath the cotton waistband of my trunks and pants, pushing them over my ass in unison, and then swipes her hands around to the front when my pants catch at the base of my dick.

I can feel her shudder as her hand brushes against the length of my cock, trying to work my pants over it. I groan into her mouth, wanting her more than I thought. It already feels like it's been hours since she started removing my pants, when in fact it's been nothing more than a few seconds. The waistband hits my knees and then I step out of my pants when they land at my ankles.

My hand instantly goes for the place between her legs, needing to feel her as we continue to kiss. My fingertips touch to her entrance without entering. She's wet, just as I hoped she would be. I press inward, submerging two of my fingers inside her this time. The moan against my lips and the spreading of her legs confirms I'm leading her in the right direction.

Our lips part as I begin finger fucking her. "I want more," she says. "We've been playing around since we met."

My index finger presses against her lips, continuing to pump in and out of her with my other hand. "We'll get there, beautiful. Let me make love to you."

Don't ask me why I said those words, because I couldn't answer. All I know is that I want to. I've fucked nasty more times than I can even remember. Kink has become second nature. It's been a long time since I've had to try and imagine non-sexual things to keep from coming like most guys. I haven't seen innocence in years. With her, I don't want to rush. I don't want to fuck her hard. I don't want to annihilate her body with my cock.

What I want is to savor her. I want to bring her to orgasm before I cause her pain. When I enter her I want to engrain the way she looks into my mind. I want to change the pain to pleasure. I want to make love to her. She said that she wants this to be special and I want to make it just that. I never want her to regret giving me something so rare. Her eyes stare into mine. "Let me make love to you," I repeat.

My finger falls. "Okay," she whispers.

I pull my fingers from her body and place my hands on her bare ass as I kneel on the bed. "I love your body."

I lift her and continue forward toward the head of the bed, her knees hooked to my sides, and then lay her on her back. She wraps her legs around my waist as I lean in, one hand on the mattress and the other on the outside of her knee as she does. My dick brushes against her middle, causing the slightest moan to escape her.

My lips press against hers as I lightly rub my fingers up her leg, toward her clit. The pad of my thumb quickly finds it and begins to massage in circles. She arches her back into me, her hard nipples rubbing against my chest. Her hand wraps around my wrist next to her head and her kiss becomes heated, her lips quickening their movements against mine, her tongue making its way into my mouth when I pull mine back.

My motion changes from circles to back and forth, picking up in pace. Her moans into my mouth become louder, just before she releases me all together and rolls the back of her head against the pillow, closing her eyes. I press my lips against her extended neck as the lowest erotic squeal comes out of her mouth. If there had been any other noise in the room, it would have been muted. It's the sexiest thing I've ever heard, and I almost missed it.

I know that her orgasm has dwindled when her arch releases and she stops squeezing my wrist. She opens her eyes and looks at me. My hand ascends to her stomach and continues until it's cupped around her breast. "You're beautiful when you come."

"Do you want me to play with you?"

"Not tonight, sexy. Tonight is about making you feel good. We have plenty of time for foreplay. Okay?"

She nods, saying nothing more. I grab her ankle and place her foot flat on the bed. She copies my action with the other one. Hovering over her, I grab my dick in my right hand, pressing the head against her entrance. I rub it through her wetness and stop. It's hot and wet and making me want to press inside of her. "You're not on birth control, are you?"

She bites down on her bottom lip and shakes her head. "Before I moved away from my parents I had no reason for it and they wouldn't have allowed it anyway. I've thought about it since I moved, but I haven't been in a rush because

I haven't met anyone I wanted to go all the way with."

This is that moment when a calm, civilized man wants to pound his fists on his chest like a caveman. I'm forcing myself to stay calm. I kiss her as I shift my weight onto my right forearm, reaching into the drawer with my left. It doesn't take me long to locate my stash. I grab a foil wrapper and place it between my teeth as I change my weight yet again, freeing my right side—my dominant one. Grabbing the bottom half of the package, I tear it open between my teeth, blowing the small piece onto the bed beside us.

I look at her as I remove the condom, tossing the package aside. "Do you have any doubt about this at all? We can still stop."

She wraps her hands around my neck. "No. I want to do this." There is a hitch in her voice. She's nervous. Reaching down between us, I grab my dick and align the opening of the condom on the head, before unrolling it down my length, and then release it. I'm really hard, and that's not going to make this easier. A part of me wishes I were hard enough to get it in, but not fully so there is a period of adjustment.

My lips envelop her nipple and suck the hard center into my mouth as two fingers enter her once again. I spread them, trying to stretch her. She begins to arch again and the inside of her knees press against me as she reflexively tries to close her legs. I pull out and replace them with three, biting down on her nipple at the same moment I thrust three fingers inside of her pussy. A small whine leaves her lips. I stop, giving her a second, before running my tongue over the place I just bit. When she starts to moan, I spread all three fingers, working to stretch her again.

Before she can process the pain, I suck her nipple into my mouth again. My fingers are soaking wet, making taking it slow hard. Fuck, I just want a taste. I run my lips down her front, continuing to slowly thrust in and out of her. When I reach her smooth panty zone, my tongue pushes between my lips, leaving a wet trail on her pussy lips. I harden the tip of my tongue as it passes over her mound and slides between her lips, hitting her clit. I flick my tongue back and forth as my fingers continue in the repetitive, wet motion they've been in for the past several minutes.

"Saxton, it tickles. Too soon." Perfect. That means this won't take long. I suck her clit into my mouth, hard, letting my tongue rub over it as I hold it suctioned to the roof of my mouth. Her hand claws in my hair, pulling hard, her pussy tightening around my fingers. "Fuck."

Her hips buck upward and her hand presses my head further against her, burying my face between her legs more. I love her smell, her taste, and her pussy just got wetter. I can't stop anymore. That's all I can handle.

I release her clit and pull my fingers free, then move up her body until my body is directly over hers, my forearms resting beside her face. "You ready?"

I can hear her breathing. She nods and grabs ahold of my sides with her thighs pressed against me. I take her right hand in my left, placing it on the pillow above her head, and then lace them together. I grab the base of my cock in my right hand and place the head against her pussy, rubbing it back and forth over her entrance, wetting the tip more, and then I press the head inside, but just barely, so that I can free up my hand without my dick coming out.

I grab her hand off my side and mirror the other one, positioning myself between her legs for more control with my hips. "You have my hands. Give me some of your pain."

Before she can respond I thrust inside but stop halfway. It was hard as hell. Immediately her face contorts as if she's about to cry, her hands clenched so hard around my hands that mine are already going numb. "Are you okay?"

A single tear falls from the outer corner of her eye. "No, but I will be."

"Do you want me to stop or keep going?"

"There's more?"

I suddenly feel like the biggest asshole on the planet. Another tear falls. I actually wish I had a small dick right now; the first time that's ever happened. "I'm halfway. I can stop, Kambry." She shakes her head. "What do you want me to do?"

"Kiss me when you do." She chokes on the middle word in the sentence.

I hate myself right now, because even though I know I should stop, I can't. I don't want to. I press my lips against the outer corner of her eye, and then, like she asked me to do I kiss her, slowly at first and then deepen the kiss just before I thrust the rest of the way inside. As I do, I feel something I've never felt before. It felt like the head of my dick pushed through a barrier. Something gave way inside of her as I completely buried my dick. "Shit," I whisper.

Fuck it's so tight.

It's so wet.

Her pussy is mine. Completely one hundred percent mine.

That single thought alone has me wanting to explode. I feel like I'm the one losing my virginity. I've done nothing more than stick it in, yet her pussy is gripping my dick so tight my balls hurt. Fuck, the girl can kiss. Her full tits are pressing into my chest. My dick is warm, even through the condom. A slight tug occurs in my nuts.

Fuck you. I'm not ready.

Her nails are creating impressions in my skin. I can feel it. I pull at her lips with mine, and then release them altogether so that I can look into her eyes. I need to know she's okay. I need something to happen because my mind and dick are working against me. I won't move until I know that she wants me to.

Moonlight is reflecting off of her eyes. They are glossy. Her lips are quivering. Her chest isn't moving. She's staring into my eyes, but they look lifeless. "Kambry?"

Even I can hear the worry in my tone, but as if my voice is all she was waiting for she blinks, coming back to life. "Talk to me, Kambry."

"I've been ripped open." My eyes widen. My jaw slightly falls. My heart stops. That's not really a comment a man wants to hear during sex. Her hands loosen on mine. "It was beautiful."

And then it starts beating. Except this time, it's louder and stronger than before.

"Let me touch you, Saxton. I want to touch you."

I release her hands from mine and replace them fists down outside of her shoulders. Her arms wrap around my sides, her hands becoming flush against my back. My skin tingles beneath her touch. My entire body feels feverish. I continue staring into her eyes, unable to move. "Make love to me," she says. "Make the pain go away."

"This changes things."

Kambry

I'm burning inside. I feel like my body is on fire. On the outside I am calm, but on the inside I'm screaming, wanting to rip my skin off. I was told it would hurt, but nothing could have prepared me for feeling like someone stabbed me in the vagina with a serrated edged knife.

But the moment he tore through me his body language changed. When he looked at me, there was something present that wasn't before. It sounds crazy, but it was as if the air became electric. That was the moment the pain dissipated. That look in his eyes smothered the fire and became the aloe vera I needed for the burn. That look changed everything inside of me. That single look, and my heart knew that there was no way in hell I could walk away from him until I see where this goes.

Then he confirmed what my heart already knew.

This changes things . . .

I'll remember those three little words for the rest of my life.

His back muscles are flexed, every dip and ridge ready for my hands to glide across. He hasn't taken his eyes off of me yet. Since those words exited his mouth it's been the exact same. He slowly pulls out, stops, and pushes himself back inside of me at a slightly quicker pace. Each time he does it feels a little better than it did the time before.

My legs pull back, my bent knees moving toward my chest. I lower my hands to his butt, pulling him closer against me when he thrusts all the way inside. There is only one word to describe the way I feel with him inside of me like this: full. I like it. A lot.

He stops inside of me. I'm slightly worried.

"What's wrong?"

"I just need a minute," he says.

"Why?"

"Just because." He wraps his lips around my nipple and allows his tongue to torment me. I feel like we're backtracking. I endured the pain. Now, I want to keep feeling that beautiful little achy pleasure that it's been replaced with. It feels really good.

"Please, Saxton. I want you to keep going."

"If I do I'm going to come. I'm not ready. I've made myself wait till this point. Now I'm not ready for it to end."

His words motivate me. The bottoms of my feet flatten on the bed and I use them to control the movement of my hips, sliding up and down his dick. I moan.

"Kambry."

His tone is a warning but he doesn't stop me. I increase speed as I get used to it at the current, still using my hands to force him closer. My eyes close. He grabs my hands and pins them above my head like he did earlier. My eyes open as he lowers his body to press against mine. "You want to make me come?"

He sounds irritated, but completely turned on. That's kind of sexy.

"Yes."

"Your pussy is choking my dick it's so tight. You're so wet that I've only held out this long because of the condom. I've tried thinking about sports, nasty shit, anything to sway my thoughts from the way you look right now and when you come. I was trying to last for you. You want me to blow, then I'll nut, but I'm not pulling out." His aggravated tone is turning me on more. His thrusts become deeper, his recoil quicker.

I don't respond. I don't want to. I want to continue feeling him this way. It's a bittersweet turmoil going on inside of me. I want to know that I turn him on so much he can't go all night, or even hours the first time. I want to know that I'm different to someone that's had endless amounts of women and sex, but I also don't want him to stop. I doubt I'm the only girl to feel this way.

My legs wrap around his waist, my heels digging into his butt as I pull him closer. No matter how close he is it's not enough. Our bodies are becoming slick from the sheen of sweat. His right hand moves down to grip my ass and he jerks up, causing me to moan louder.

"Dammit," he grits out and smashes his lips to mine; the best kiss to date. His movements dwindle to a shallow, slow thrust, until he stills completely inside of me, but continues to kiss me as if it's not over. I don't want it to be.

He pulls out and then stops kissing me. Already I want him back in me. I don't like the void that I feel now. "You should have listened to me. I didn't want to come that quick. Fuck, that was like ten minutes." He almost looks . . .embarrassed? "I don't usually . . ." He huffs out. "Shit. I'm sorry. You probably think your first time was—"

"Perfect? Because it was. To me anyway."

He stares at me silently.

What now? Do I go back home now that we've done it? I'm not real sure what is next.

His brows dip slightly as he looks at me. "What?"

He reaches over and turns on the bedside lamp, then props himself up and looks down. "What is it?"

"You're bleeding."

My eyes bug out of my head. At least that's what they feel like right now. I'm a little bit too horrified to look. "I'm sorry. I can clean it up. I know you don't do bl—"

He smirks at me. "I'm fine, surprisingly. We can deal with it later. Let's go take a bath. I like you naked in a tub full of water. This time I can enjoy you from a different view."

He moves off of me, stands, and reaches down for my hand. As I take it and get up the soreness between my legs makes itself known. My knees buckle just a little as the tender skin rubbing together catches me off guard. He scoops me into his arms before I can even balance myself. I notice the circle of blood staining the sheets as I wrap my arms around his neck. My cheeks flush from embarrassment. I can't believe I didn't notice. "You don't have to do that. I can walk," I say, trying to wiggle out of his arms, afraid to get any on him.

"I'm sure you can, but you're not going to."

"You're not weirded out? I thought you couldn't handle blood."

"I can't. I didn't." He shrugs his shoulders. "You're a virgin, or was. That means yours is clean."

I remain quiet, unsure of what to say.

"And before you assume, yes, porn stars think about stuff like that. Disease becomes a very real thing when you're fucking that many people. We probably think about it more than the majority of the population that is sexually active. I wrap my shit up, test always before a new film because of oral and the point one percent that a condom fails, and take all possible precautions to stay clean."

"I wasn't going to," I reply, as he walks us into the bathroom. I won't lie to myself though and say that it doesn't ease my discomfort a little, because if I ever told someone I lost my virginity to a porn star, they'd probably tell me I've lost my mind. I'm not completely sure that I haven't . . .

CHAPTER FOURTEEN

Saxton

I stand her on her feet in the center of the large whirlpool tub, not saying anything as I gather my thoughts, work to at least. She sits down without me having to tell her to, watching me as I look at the wall. I can feel her eyes on me. There are things going on in my mind that are honestly freaking me the fuck out. I can't explain it. I don't even try to understand.

My dick has seemed like a foreign limb that's been dead weight on my body until her, and more importantly moments ago. Now, it's decided to work and work well, considering I've barely softened since I blew my load into the condom still covering me; premature ejaculation at that.

The fuck?

There were aspects of this entire situation that I expected, none of which was that—a man's worst nightmare. I need to stop thinking about it before I do something stupid like attempt to castrate a vital body part that came into this world at the same time I did, and the very one that's been my most prized possession since I found it dangling there.

He worked his way to fame only to betray me the one time I needed him to perform. Figures . . .

I bend forward and turn on the water, waiting for the temperature to warm. It doesn't take long before I'm stopping up the drain to let the tub fill. My thoughts are becoming more scrambled as I push off the tub, still silent. My movements are robotic as I turn down the spotlights above the tub to dim, the only ones on in the room. Then, I turn on the surround sound, letting the iPod that is sitting in the dock play on shuffle mode.

I work hard to keep my eyes off of her for the moment. I need to omit the not so little problem still in effect. The one that is also currently not a result of pharmaceuticals, might I add. Is this normal for the average man immediately after releasing himself? Almost never. You at least have to give it a short period of rest before it's able to stand at attention again. That's just the basics of male dick dynamics.

I place my left hand on the wall as I come to stand at the toilet. Gripping the rim of the condom, I remove it, and then toss it in the garbage can beside me. Water begins to slosh. "Did I upset you somehow?"

That voice. I love her voice. Her accent is quickly becoming my kryptonite. *Head in the game.*

I step closer to the toilet and lean toward the wall, angling myself while holding my dick. I look down and aim into the bowl. This should be fucking fun, trying to piss with a hard-on. "No, why?"

As I begin to relieve myself, I have to engage in a little target practice to avoid a fucking mess I'd have to clean up later. She hasn't said anything back yet. A piss later and I'm still fucking hard. I shake twice, trying not to prolong its uncontrollable behavior.

Before turning I push down my dick and walk over with my hand cupped over it. It's not working out in my favor since it won't lay down.

She's twisted toward me with her arm resting on the side of the tub, her chin lying on top of her forearm. "You kind of look angry."

"I'm fine," I lie, making my way to the tub. The dim spotlights are beaming down on her, creating a glow across her face. She's a beautiful girl. It was what drew me to her that night in the club. There are beautiful girls, and then there are girls like Kambry. Those girls don't fit into any one category.

She sits up and faces the front when I step over into the tub of water behind her. I sit, placing my legs on each side of her, keeping her in the middle. When she starts to scoot forward I place my hands on her hips, stopping her. "I won't bite."

I pull her against me, between my legs. Her back arches slightly when her back becomes flush with my front. "You're still—"

"Yep," I say, cutting her off. "It can't be helped, obviously. I promise I won't touch you again tonight."

"I wouldn't deny you if you wanted to, you know."

"You may retract that statement at some point," I say, just before moving her hair off of her shoulder and kissing the point between her neck and shoulder.

"I'm pretty sure I won't." Her words exit out of rhythm.

"Tonight, I won't touch you. Someone that's held onto her virginity for eighteen years deserves to be cuddled with. That was just an introduction. You, beautiful, have awakened a beast. After tonight, all bets are off."

"So I'm staying?"

"Yes. You aren't leaving until you sign that contract."

"I told you I would. Just give me a pen."

My hand snakes around to her flat stomach. My lips trail up her neck. "No, beautiful. You have to sign it in front of a witness for legal reasons. I'll set up a meeting with Michael tomorrow. We're running out of time."

She breathes out. "When does it start?"

"A week from Monday if there are no hold ups."

The bathtub is almost full, but the water is still running. We must have both noticed at the same time, because she reaches forward and shuts it off. She then turns around, water moving in small waves around us, before straddling me. Fuck my life. She has no idea what kind of torture this is. Looking at her full, perky, large tits is the last thing I need right now. "Will I get to see you between now and then?"

"I don't know," I answer honestly. "I imagine you'll be busy packing."

My eyes keep veering to her chest, unable to help it with them this close to my mouth. "Do you want to touch me now?"

My hands move to her thighs, staying put splayed over the top.

Hell yes I do. Don't do it, you selfish bastard.

"I'll live."

Her lips pull into a slight smirk, almost unnoticeable. She reaches out, grabbing my men's body wash off the side. The cap flips open, before she tips the bottle at chest level and lets the blue gel drizzle out of the hole onto her rounded, fucking beautiful rack. "That wasn't the question. Do you *want* to touch me again?"

"Based on the state of my dick you should know I do."

She may not have been the only one to awaken a sleeping beast . . .

"Bathe me."

Fucking hell.

"You're playing with fire . . ."

"Who said I didn't like a little heat?"

I close my eyes, trying to calm the raging hormones flooding through my bloodstream. I open them. They most likely are deepening in color. "I'm so fucking glad I went to that club."

My palms travel up her body and over her breasts, making contact with the body wash. I begin to hand paint, spreading it into a thin layer all over her front, starting with those perfect tits. Unexpectedly she grabs my dick in her hand, causing me to reflexively scoot backward, closer to the back of the tub. "Easy, handsome. I won't bite," she teases, copying my earlier line.

"You're making being good very hard for me."

"I never said I wanted you to be good."

She leans in and places her lips to mine, drowning out all logical thought. The only thought that will process is the way my dick felt submerged inside of her. Then she begins to stroke me; the moment I became fucked, my good intentions flying out the window.

She pulls free, her lips hovering just in front of mine. "You said virgins are a turn off. I want to change your mind."

"I was just being an asshole. Forget what I said. Nothing about what just happened was a turn off."

"There is always some truth in everything a person says. The subconscious cannot lie."

She sits up and then lifts. I feel her entrance pressed against my head. Even in a tub filled with water I can tell she's wet. It's a different type of wet; something similar to oil versus water.

My hands fall to her hips, gripping onto them as she slowly and meticulously sinks onto my cock. She's a fast learner. I lean back against the back of the tub. "Fuck, your pussy feels amazing."

An intake of air occurs when she reaches the base of my dick. She stops and leans toward me. Her eyes close; her lips so close to my lips that I could reach them by simply extending my tongue. Her bottom lip begins to quiver. "Kambry . . ."

"It feels different this way."

"Do you want me to get on top?"

"No. I just need a second. It doesn't hurt as bad when I lean forward."

My right hand moves inward, hovering just above her clit. The pad of my thumb presses into her folds, searching for it. As I begin to massage she kisses me, moaning against my lips. As if that was the push she needed, she begins to pump herself up and down on my cock.

When she sits back down I hold her there, then change her motion to a rock. I want her to come. I want her to come as quickly as she makes me come. I want her to completely lose it with me inside of her.

She rocks into me as I rub her clit, her movements becoming faster with each rub. She sits upright, continuing in the same motion. I can tell she's becoming more comfortable. Her back arches, her front becoming a beautiful curve as she reclines, and she grabs onto my shins behind her. Her face contorts into something so fucking beautiful I can't explain it, but the pleasure that she's experiencing is drawn out all over her face.

Each time my dick hits against the wall of her pussy I want to lose it, but fuck if I won't do something to stop myself . . .like think of sweaty football players in the locker room. That will give me at least three minutes.

She quickly changes position, leaning toward me again. My hand traces up her back as she does. Her hands grip onto my chest, clenching my skin in her fists. She moans against my lips, and shortly after she clamps around my dick and her movements almost halt. That hot, wet place just became wetter, coating my dick in her orgasm.

Holy fuck.

Her lips leave mine and she sits up, placing her hands on the sides of the bathtub. She uses it as leverage as she begins to experiment. I watch as her beautiful body slowly bounces up and down on my dick. Any upper hand I just had over my balls vanishes and that tug begins. Like a fucking freight train it hits me.

No. Fucking. Condom.

I lift her off of my dick with force, my dick exiting her pussy as the first feel of semen begins to travel through my length. I grip one hand around the head as the initial spurt occurs, allowing my orgasm to release into my fist. My chest is rapidly rising and falling from the panic happening inside. I look at her, holding my semen in my fist; the seed to create something I don't need. "Birth control. ASAP. That was really stupid on my part."

Her cheeks are flushed pink. "It was my fault. It slipped my mind."

I sit up, raking my free hand through her hair. "No, it was mine. You don't know any better. I do. That has never happened in all my years of fucking."

"Never?"

"Never. I do not fuck without condoms, ever. It's a personal preference for me. My dad sat me down and taught me early, so it's followed me. I don't take a job if the studio has a problem with it."

"I'm sorr—"

"But I liked it . . . with you. It felt different, better, which is why I almost didn't catch my mistake. Get on birth control before you do anything else."

"Okay."

I reach out and grab a towel off the bar, wiping my semen off my hand, and then toss it on the floor. Thank fuck my hard-on is going down. I cannot handle this shit anymore tonight. "I'm going to get this off of you and let's go to bed."

Kambry

I've never felt like this before. It's hard to explain. Every second that I'm around him, I like him more. I love everything about him. Those feelings make me want him sexually, more so than I did in the beginning. Before it was merely curiosity. I wanted to dispose of something I've been carrying for a long time, but now, I want him.

That's either a really good thing or a really bad thing. I dated Kyle for two years and never felt like this. Honestly, I'm really not sure how we made it for so long, or why he held onto something that wasn't benefitting him. We never said the L word, we never slept together, and we didn't really grieve when we split. It was almost more of a social relationship. You know, one for show more than anything else.

He really didn't even seem too torn dating that long without sex. Yes, he tried . . . a lot, and yes, he whined every time I said no or backed out when I considered going all the way, but that was as extensive as it got. He never forced himself on me or called me a tease. I wouldn't be surprised if he was cheating on me from time to time. I can't really blame him if he did. But here I am with Saxton, a man I've barely known for any length of time, and I've given myself to him completely for the first time with anyone. The crazier part . . . There isn't a bone in my body that regrets it. It was perfect. The second time even better than the first, but in a different way. There is no part of me that doesn't want him. I have to keep that to myself.

He wraps the fluffy towel around me and leads me into his bedroom. I try to veer into the direction of my clothes, but he pulls me the opposite way. "My clothes are over there."

"You don't need your clothes."

"Why not?"

He opens a drawer and removes what looks to be a folded tee shirt, then closes the drawer and does the same action with the one below; except this time it looks like boxers. He hands them to me. "What you were wearing looks hot. I keep it cold, but body heat will keep you warmer than you think."

"I'm sleeping with you?"

"Where did you think you were sleeping?"

"I can sleep on the couch or something if you prefer to sleep alone."

He smirks. "I want that ass against me and a boob in my hand as I drift off to never-never land." He winks. "You're sleeping with me."

He's so damn cute. Don't smile. Don't smile. Don't smile. I'm smiling. Dang it. "If you insist."

Our towels drop at the same time. I bite my lip and he grunts as we exchange glances. I pull the tee shirt over my head and let it fall to my thighs. He grabs another pair of underwear and we pull them on together. It's oddly intimate.

"So . . .boxers and briefs?"

He gave me the boxers, and he's wearing the briefs, trunk style. I definitely like his choice better.

He glances down and back at me, smirking that sexy smile. "I don't have a preference. When I wanna let the boys hang with a breeze I go boxers; usually at night or if it's really hot. If I wear jeans or fitted clothing it's usually briefs, but always trunks. I don't do the whole man-panty thing. It's just not my style. I may not need my swimmers now, but I may one day."

He steps closer and throws his arms around me, pulling me into his chest. My cheek presses against his hard pec muscle. It's warm. I like it here—in his arms. He's hugging me. I place my hands on his waist, lost in the moment. My eyes even close without meaning for them to. His tone becomes low and deep. "And on rare occasions . . .I even go without."

My eyes pop open. I swallow. I need water, or a fan. I clear my throat; trying to seem like that statement didn't affect me at all. "I bet that is cooler."

What?

He busts out laughing. I shove his body, pushing him back, and laughing in return. "You can be an ass sometimes."

"Never change, Kambry. Innocence can't be faked. That is actually one thing I love about you. It's refreshing. I was laughing with you. It wasn't at you. That I promise."

He grabs my chin and places his lips against mine. Is it possible for a human to physically melt beneath the touch of another human? Each time our mouths meet, I swear I can feel a sizzle. His hands comb through my hair at the sides of my head, just before making a fist and creating a tight pull, deepening the kiss. I pull his body flush with mine.

Without notice he pulls away, leaving me. He has a slightly agitated look on his face. Grabbing my hand, he pulls me out of the bedroom. "Bed before I completely lose control." Then he mumbles something about it being a first under his breath that I can't hear.

"What about the sheets on your bed? Do you want me to wash them?"

"Fuck no. I'll buy more. I have a mattress cover. We'll just use the guest bedroom."

He pulls me along until we walk through the door not far from his bedroom, revealing a simple bedroom set with a king-sized bed, dresser, and two nightstands. It's nothing extravagant and no major décor, but it's pretty nice for a bachelor pad.

I follow behind him and stop when he tosses the few throw pillows on the floor and pulls the comforter down. The white sheets become slightly luminescent under the moonlight shining through the wall of glass. He nods toward the bed for me to get in. "You can sleep with no curtains or anything?"

I throw my leg on the bed and he gives me a boost by placing his palm on my butt. It's higher than a standard bed. "I've never had a reason to hide," he says simply. "It can be relaxing once you get used to it. Isn't that like a big fantasy for some people? To sleep under the stars . . . This is just a modified version."

I move to the opposite side and turn to sit facing toward him. I smirk. "Isn't that kind of a romantic gesture, Saxton?"

He gets in bed, looking me in the eyes, but lacking the same smirk as me. "I never said I couldn't be romantic. I just choose not to be. Someone else ruined that in me."

My smirk falls. A crack runs down the center of my heart. My hands begin playing with my toes, unsure of what to say to that response. My lack of experience hinders me here. He pulls the comforter over him when he lies down, then turns on his side to face me, and props himself up on his arm. "What's wrong?"

I fake a smile. "That's really unfortunate for some lucky girl one day."

He stares at me, not saying a word. His eyes narrow but you almost can't even tell. It's more like someone in deep thought, focusing on something. Not an expression of anger.

I grab the blankets and wiggle beneath them, then mirror his position. Our faces are staring at each other. Both heads hit the pillows at the same time. "People can always change, Kambry. It's just about finding someone that's worth the risk."

His tone is serious and low. My heart is pounding against my chest. I've never felt like I wanted to belt out in song and ugly cry at the same time, but that's precisely how I feel. Sometimes people really suck. Sometimes my mind wanders to that overused expression with Miss America pageant contestants when they wish for world peace. I always think, that's great, but why wish for world peace when so many face war within themselves.

I'm still at a loss for words. "Turn around. I'll hold you until you fall asleep."

I blink a few times, trying to decide if we just had a real moment completely unrelated to anything sexual, and what that could mean. I roll over like he said, facing away from him. He throws his arm over my waist and pulls me close to his front. "Do you want me to move up so you can be in the middle? I have plenty of room."

"No, I like it here."

He molds his body against mine. It's hard for me to breathe, and not because I feel smothered. I've never had this with anyone. "Relax."

"It's just. I've never. I'm not used to this."

"Me either. Now go to sleep."

Inside I'm dying. The slightest flutters are occurring beneath his hand. *One, two, three, four, five, six.*

When my heart starts to calm I place my hand over his as if that's where it was pulled. He spreads his fingers and I lace mine between his. Then I settle into him, and instantly I grow tired, as if our bodies together are meant to meld together at precisely this moment. My mind becomes free, and within a few seconds I slip into sleep faster than I have in a really long time.

CHAPTER FIFTEEN

Saxton

I pull into the studio and park. I look over at Kambry in the passenger seat staring at the company logo and clutching her purse as if her life depends on it. She tends to place a death grip on her innocent bags when she's nervous. This is the true meaning of tainting someone, in the most original form. My selfishness keeps me from caring. I've always been taught you don't pass up a good thing, and well, that girl is like stumbling upon unclaimed gold. You don't just leave it in the open for someone else to grab. You fucking pick it up and run before someone else realizes what you found.

I woke up this morning more refreshed than I have been in years, possibly ever. I'm pretty sure neither one of us moved at all, because when I woke up we were in the exact same position as when we went to sleep. I won't lie. When I woke up and stared into the back of her blonde hair as I held her, I realized that I somewhat miss having that closeness with someone. Maybe that's why I agreed to this project at all.

She was the blinder I needed to see past kinky fuckery and worn out pussy. I was positive that I had moved on from Salem, but if I wasn't truly living then maybe I hadn't moved on as completely as I thought. In reality, moving on isn't just being over someone, but opening up the possibility for a replacement. That I haven't done.

Instead, I went off the deep end and submerged myself so deep in dirty water I don't see a way out, but she's about as clear of a change I can fathom giving myself, so I slipped out of bed and walked outside on my back patio, called Michael, and scheduled the earliest time to do this. I want it permanently recorded on a legal document. I'm going all in.

"You ready?" I ask her.

She looks over at me, her expression a little nervous. "Yeah. It just kind of all hit me, you know?"

I grab her hand. "Tell me what's on your mind. We have a few minutes to spare."

"Is it hard?"

"What?"

"Getting past the judgment from others of what you've done, receiving crazy stares when people know, or the mortification of people you know personally seeing you in the most intimate times of your life."

I nod toward my window. "Come here."

"In your lap?"

"Yeah."

She crosses over the center console and straddles my lap in her denim cropped skirt. I grab her face in my hands and kiss her lips. "Are you having second thoughts?"

She breathes out. "No. I just want to be prepared . . .mentally. Where I come from people are very conservative, judgmental, and harsh of anything outside of their moral bubbles. I just want to be prepared," she whispers, repeating something she's already said.

"It's different," I say honestly. "Those people will probably term you a whore. Most people won't understand how you can do such a thing and live with yourself, even when some of those same people reap the benefits of what you're doing. Then there are those that will become infatuated with you; the extreme thinking they love you. You'll get fan mail that will creep you out. Your life will change."

"Oh."

I hold her stare with mine, running my thumb along her bottom lip to calm her. Then I choose to tell her something about myself. "My parents weren't happy when they found out. They were embarrassed. They still are. I don't come home and they don't come see me. Once a year we go on an undisclosed vacation to spend time together. The rest is left to phone conversation and text messages periodically. I left behind three years of college, a good family, and a life. I left behind heartbreak."

Her lips tremble and a tear falls. "But in all of the films I've done, all of the women I've had sex with, and all of the cameras I've performed in front of, none of them have been as intimate as last night was with you. That was acting. This is real. Originally it was all supposed to be fake, Kambry, but since then it's changed into something more real than I could have imagined. I like you . . .for real. Filming while we have sex may be new to you, but the intimacy of a relationship on camera is new to me. We will do this and experience new things together. Are you in?"

"Yeah," she says low. "I'm in. I think I have been since the beginning."

"Good, because I was prepared to sway you."

"Isn't that what you've been doing?" The expression on her face changes to a playful smirk. The seriousness of this conversation vanishes.

My hands drop to her hips, sneaking beneath her hot pink tee shirt representing her southern roots by logo. I glide my fingertips up her sides, and then inch them around to the hard wiring of her bra, before pushing it up with the front of her shirt, revealing her perfect rack as her breasts fall free; a man's lottery. Give a man three wishes and I guarantee more than ninety percent would wish for the same things: nice tits to grope and suck, pussy for endless dick submerging, and money to do those things in repetition on a near constant basis.

I grab one in each hand and shake, before pressing my mouth to one of her hardened nipples. I look up at her. She's biting her bottom lip with her palm pressed against the window, sure to leave a print. "You haven't seen the best of my persuasion, beautiful," I mumble against her nipple. A set of tits couldn't be more perfect if they were synthetic.

My tongue inches out, swiping from bottom to top. She moans against her clenched teeth. I flick my wet tongue over her taut nipple, then blow, all while rolling the opposite one between my thumb and index finger. "Please. Can we?"

"You want me to fuck you in my truck still wearing clothes like a couple of high school kids?"

Her cheeks flush. "Yes. The windows are tinted. Plus, it's not like I got to do those things in high school."

I grab the hem of her shirt and pull it over her head, her blonde hair immediately falling when it passes through the neck hole. It's a fucked up thing that I would rather be the one she experiences things with most do before junior prom than for her to have had it with someone else, especially considering I have no firsts to give her.

I reach behind her and unclasp her bra, pulling it down her arms until it falls on the floorboard. "If we are going to do this I still want to look at you like this. I want you to be thinking about what we just did when you sign your name to that piece of paper. Get a condom out of the console."

She lifts up on her knees and opens the lid to do as I told her. I unbutton my jeans and slide the zipper down, before lifting off the seat and sliding my briefs and jeans down to my knees in one motion, my hard dick springing free as I do, and then sit back down. I place my hands on her bare thighs as she sits back down on me, handing me the condom after briefly looking down. "You want it in you?"

Her cheeks deepen in color. "Yes," she says in a breathy whisper, the fast pace heaving of her chest confirming before I check her that she's ready.

"Open it."

My hands ascend, pushing up her skirt to her midsection, before rounding to her ass—her bare ass. "Fuck, you're wearing a thong? My favorite in case you didn't know."

She places the corner of the wrapper between her teeth and tears it open. My hands fist the small string disappearing between her cheeks and pull in opposite directions, ripping them at the T shaped seam and removing them from her body. I toss the useless fabric aside. "You just found my fucking weakness."

"I've worn them before."

"I was too distracted by you to really notice. Lift."

Again she does as I ask. My phone starts to vibrate. She looks over at it by the cup holders. "Let it go. There is no fucking way I'm stopping this now. He can wait."

My hand moves between her legs, turning palm up, and my middle finger begins rubbing back and forth over her pussy, transferring some of her wetness to me, before shoving my finger inside. "You're so damn wet. Fuck, I love how wet you get."

I pump in and out of her, watching as her eyes become lazy with each thrust. She whimpers when I add a finger and circle my thumb in her wetness, and then rub it between her lips, separating them as I go, before stopping on her clit. Her head falls back when I begin rocking my hand, alternating between sliding across her clit and my fingers thrusting in and out of her. She looks into my eyes, her blue eyes becoming clearer in color. "Saxton, that feels good, but I want you."

The plea in her voice drives me wild, evoking an animalistic response. "Sheathe me, Kambry. I'm waiting on you, beautiful."

I continue as she pulls the condom from the wrapper and tosses down the unneeded portion. My free hand grabs her breast and squeezes, drawing my mouth toward it as it begins to water from the sight alone. I suck her into my mouth. It takes a few seconds, but then I feel the condom touch down to the head of my dick, causing me to bite down on the hard center of her nipple.

She rolls it in place until her hand is wrapped around the base. I growl against her, before forcing my mouth away from her nipple and vacating her pussy. "Show me you can take control. Make it yours."

"Mine?"

"All yours, baby. It'll soon be in writing."

She looks down as she holds my dick still and positions herself directly over it, and then lowers herself. My head enters first, slowly, and then vanishes as her pussy consumes my cock whole, constricting around it the entire way. My head falls back against the headrest. "Holy hell I love the way you feel."

With my mouth still open she presses hers open against mine. Immediately our tongues push through, meeting in the open space before our mouths close, leading into a kiss. She pumps herself up and down on my dick, using the seat as her push off, and moaning out each time I'm completely buried inside of her. She's going slow, tormenting me, and making me feel every centimeter as I enter her.

My thumb quickly finds her clit and rubs with a pressure I know will quickly bring her to orgasm. Her hands grip my hair and she stops when I'm completely submerged inside her warm, wet place. I still my thumb when she begins rocking against me, fast and hard. Our mouths briefly part. "That feels so good," she whispers. "I like it."

My head is hitting against a hard place that is going to be the end of me if she doesn't come soon. My balls tighten. "Fuck." I can tell she's close, she's just not quite . . .

I thrust up hard, plunging deeper inside of her as she continues to ride my dick. I begin rubbing her clit again, exerting more pressure. She arches until her shoulders are resting on the steering wheel, and at the exact moment her hands cup her own breasts her moan becomes so erotic a shiver runs through my body. Everything slows down for me. Her face seems frozen in time; her eyes closed and her bottom lip pulled into her mouth. "Fuck, you're beautiful."

Her eyes open and she looks at me as I erupt inside of the condom, balls deep inside of her. As if time started again, I lower my hips back down to my previous sitting position on the seat, bringing her with me. I blink a few times, trying to figure out what the hell just happened. I feel like I blacked out without the black vision. "I like seeing you like that."

"What?" I ask.

"When you look like you've lost control. When I can tell you're about to come. My favorite of all is when you say something like you just did. It makes me feel like I'm the only girl on your mind. It's stupid and girly I guess. Don't laugh."

My hands move around to her ass and then rub up her back. She's already sitting up straight. I pull her into me. "What do you mean you feel like you're the only girl on my mind? You are."

"It's nothing. I should have just kept my mouth shut. It's stupid and immature."

She tries to lift and I hold her in place. "Nothing is stupid, Kambry. Tell me what you mean." Moments like these are when the age gap shows a little, but I don't mind having to backtrack if it means experiencing anything close to what I just did. People my age are mostly over that insecure stage, but her statement rubs me the wrong way.

"I don't know. Just . . . I've developed this stupid insecurity since I watched one of your films, or part of it. Those girls are intimidating to girls like me. I don't want to think stupid crap, but I can't help it. Sometimes I worry that sex with me is bland and you may think of a different time with someone else to finish."

I stare at her . . .like a moron, because honestly I'm speechless. Her eyes widen. "You have haven't you? I feel stupid. I would rather not know."

"Wait. Fuck. What? No. Give me a second to process. Are you serious?"

I actually start to soften inside of her at the mention of porn. Wow, talk about cold hard facts confirming themselves. "Well, I was . . .kind of. Just forget I mentioned it. I'm stupid."

She tries to lift off of me again and I grip her waist so hard I'm probably going to leave a handprint. "Have I made you feel that way?"

My brain is still not working correctly. "God, no! I'm going to just shut up before I dig a deeper hole. It's just a thought I've had once or twice . . .or a few times," she whispers on the ending statement. "Before and after we actually did it last night."

A click occurs. My brain is back. "Okay, first off . . ." I scan her body. "Any guy that needs to think of someone else while you're riding his cock clearly needs a mental check: porn star or not, virgin or not, experienced or not, and whether having experienced thirty pussies or one. Secondly, I haven't gotten a natural hard-on before you in so long I can't even remember who the last one was with—

hence synthetic forms readily available at all times—so why the hell would I want to go back to that phase of my life when I just left it. Thirdly, if I needed to think of another girl to blow my load I wouldn't risk ruining your reputation and what you've known your entire life to have you more, because it would be pointless. I'd get them to cast someone else. My dick and me are yours mentally and physically, and you and your pussy are mine in the same way until our relationship is severed in any form. Are we clear?"

Fuck. Is this seriously a conversation I'm having?

She stares at me, saying nothing, and then she leans in and her lips crash against mine so hard it actually kind of hurt. Her kiss is angry, passionate, and emotional. She starts to pump on me once again. Fucking hell she's going to milk me dry. What's insane is that I'm actually hardening again inside the condom I just filled. That never happens.

My phone begins to vibrate again. Dammit. I reach out and feel around until I grab ahold of it. My eyes veer to the screen as I continue to kiss her. I grab the back of her hair in my free hand and pull her back, but she doesn't stop riding my cock. I growl out and place the phone to my ear after swiping right. "Maverick," I say in an uneven breath.

"Not that I don't understand your current position, but are you going to continue to fuck her before I can get footage or are you going to come in and sign the papers so you can actually get paid while you're doing what you're doing in your truck in my parking lot."

"Fuck. We'll be there in a second." She tightens her pussy around my dick. I grunt accidentally. "As soon as I can get free."

"Shut it down, Maverick. My patience has run out and because of the security camera aimed at the perfect angle to see inside your windshield I'm now sexually frustrated with no way to fix it since my day just started. Get your ass in here," he shouts in an aggravated tone, then disconnects the call.

I slap her ass. She yelps. "Our time is up, beautiful. Boss man is pissed and second go around I will go longer before finale, especially with a condom. Rain check until later?"

She lifts off of me so slowly that I actually moan out when my cock exits her. "Okay," she says with a pleased expression on her face and climbs back over the console with her arm spread over her boobs to cover her nipples until she can get her bra and shirt back on.

She sinks down into the seat as she hooks her bra at her front and slides it around, adjusting it in place. When her shirt is being pulled down her stomach and she begins pulling her long hair out of the collar I let the other statement go. "By the way . . .you obviously just had your first performance in front of an audience. See that wasn't so bad."

Her eyes enlarge and she pulls her denim skirt down to cover her ass and smooth front. "What do you mean?"

I remove the condom and tie it at the center, before placing it in the small trash bag I keep in my truck. "Evidently we're right in front of the security camera." My lips line, because I just now actually remembered where the cameras are located. I was distracted before. "Who knew . . ."

I laugh. I couldn't keep it in. Her face is priceless. She reaches over and slaps the top of my arm as I grab her torn panties and clean off my dick, before pulling my jeans back in place. "Asshole. You could have warned me."

"It's not my fault I was distracted. You ask me to fuck you and my brain goes into ADD mode. It's like someone trying to have a serious conversation with you and then you go, oh look . . .squirrel! Well, your pussy is the squirrel."

She laughs, but it's more of a sarcastic one. "Okay then, ADD, what am I supposed to do for underwear now?"

I shrug my shoulders and open the door, stepping out of the truck. "Sit there with your legs crossed and remember why it is that you are going commando right now; a perfect reminder of why you need to sign that line."

She sighs. "If I wasn't living this I don't think I'd even believe it."

I meet her at the front of the truck and wrap my arm around her shoulders, pulling her into the crook of my arm. "Believe it, beautiful." I press my lips close to her ear. "Because when I'm touching you, my goal is to make you forget about cameras."

It's the truth. I don't give a damn about filming. What I want is to be locked away with her for a month. The real fun is about to begin . . .

Kambry

After getting through the receptionist we stand at the door, waiting for the person on the other side to answer it. Every time we come to a halt my legs cross. I cannot believe I'm not wearing panties with a skirt. It's really awkward. I'm not sure I've ever gone without panties to be honest. This would be my luck; that and the one time I make a bold move it's in front of a camera. That's just awesome. Not.

I look over at Saxton as the feet on the other side shuffle across the floor. He has a broad smirk across his face. He seems a little too relaxed for a business meeting.

The door jerks open, causing me to look forward. The same man from the club is standing on the other side, wearing a button-down shirt and a pair of slacks, his tie loosened as if he's been tugging at it, with no jacket. His brown hair is sticking straight out in the front like he's been pulling at it with his fingers. "Saxton," he says clipped. "I'm glad you finally decided to come inside."

Saxton places his palm on my lower back and nudges me forward, toward an extended hand. "Kambry, it's nice to see you again. Please forgive the less than professional attire. Something unexpected happened when I arrived at work this morning."

He's speaking to me, but looking at Saxton with a narrowed expression. Saxton is wearing a smug smile on his face, not seeming affected at all. Instead, he steps forward, lowering his voice. "At least now you know if the chemistry is there."

And I suddenly know exactly what they are talking about. The security camera . . .

Can I crawl under a rock and die now?

He grabs Saxton's shoulder and pulls him forward when I walk through the door. "Son, if I hadn't known you since the start of your career and you didn't make me so much goddamn money I'd retract my offer. Unfortunately, I like you. Get your ass in here and let's do this," he says between gritted teeth. "I swear on my career you have lost it."

I feel like an intruder. The door shuts harder than it should but not quite a slam. Saxton walks to the chairs in front of the desk and sits in one. When I step in front of the opposite I pull my skirt as low as it will go and tuck it as I sit down, trying to keep my normally covered area from touching the seat in any form. "What's wrong, Michael? Bad morning?"

My head quickly turns toward Saxton when I can hear the joking in his tone. He looks at me, and mouths, *what?*

Stop it, I mouth back. Then a folder smacks him upside the head. "What the hell?"

"That's what you get. Fuck up my plans and I fuck up yours," he says, and his eyes veer to me and then back to Saxton.

"Are y'all related?" I interrupt. I can't help my abrupt question. This is the strangest business meeting I've ever been involved in. Well, I haven't been in any, but still, I've seen movies.

"He's just a very good friend where my career is concerned; therefore, I give him hell from time to time to see how lax I can make him, but at the end of the day he's still my boss. I'm just in a really good mood." Saxton winks at me. I can feel the color change occurring on my cheeks.

"And the only reason I'm putting up with him being a pain in my ass is because with this sudden good mood he's bound to give me some good material to work with. Now, back to business. Trailer production will begin as soon as this meeting adjourns." He breathes out deeply. "Did you even bring the contract to follow along or do I have to get another printed?"

Saxton holds his hand out to me. That's my cue. I bend over and open my purse, removing the folder I placed inside, and then hand it to him. "Michael, I may fuck with you from time to time, but don't ever question my professionalism. You should know better."

Michael takes the folder he handed me just a few days ago and lays it flat on his desk. "We will get to this in a minute, since one part that you just had to have in the contract is technically void now. I'm cutting it. I think you'll understand my abrupt change."

He grabs a remote and points it to the television that is mounted to the wall behind him, turning it on. It's a blue screen. He sits down and I cross my legs as he fiddles with something on his laptop in front of him. Then, a picture shows up on the television: a parking lot, Saxton's truck, and . . . The camera zooms. My back as I straddle Saxton. "I got a call from security earlier. Some suspicious behavior in the parking lot since none of the people we compensate for their services would be hiding out in a truck, fucking for fun. At first I thought it was probably just a couple of high school kids trying to gain popularity among peers, but then I realized Saxton here was late, for the first time since I met him."

I want to disappear from the very chair I'm sitting in. I can hear tapping on what I assume is the computer's trackball, before it zooms once again. This time I swear it's like someone is filming just outside the truck. That's one powerful lens—some expensive equipment. I start moving up and down, clearly evident what we're doing. Saxton's hands are all over me.

A few seconds in and the humiliation starts to subside. It's kind of hot; not the getting caught part, but the whole seeing it on video. There is no sound, but the picture is pretty good for it to be from a security camera. I press my legs together, remembering the exact moment in my mind as it appears on screen. I can tell the second Saxton comes, because I get thrust upward and my back falls against the steering wheel, revealing his face. I get to see what he looked like when I was clearly out of it.

My heart starts pounding. I do that to him . . .

When our movements still the television goes black. I look at Saxton and he winks. My cheeks feel hot. "Since the two of you chose not to wait for filming to start sleeping together, for whatever reason, I need an edge; an introduction of sorts. I want to use this video to slice for the beginning of the trailer when we begin promoting, as soon as production can get enough material put together, but I need your written consent since it wasn't actually planned. Maybe this candid camera thing will appeal to people since it's kind of forbidden and indecency is illegal."

I look back at Michael when he stops talking. "Are the two of you okay with that? You'll each get a copy when it's finished."

"Do what you must," Saxton says.

Michael looks at me. "And you, Kambry?"

"Okay," I respond. It'd be kind of stupid to say no, because I'll be doing worse when this actually starts. There you couldn't even see private parts, but I'm really not sure how else this works.

"Good." He grabs something off the printer, placing a sheet of paper in front of each of us. "Sign this release and we'll move on."

A pen gets placed on top. I grab both, staring at the sheet of paper filled with words. Aren't you supposed to have legal counsel for this type of thing? Saxton grabs my left hand, gaining my attention. "Do you trust me?" One look in his eyes and I know I do. I nod. "It's okay to sign the release. It's legit. Michael is my oldest contact in this industry. You heard me call him a friend. He wouldn't screw you over."

"Okay," I say, and place the sheet of paper down on the hard surface of the desk, then sign the line marked with an X.

Michael grabs them both, placing them on a section of his desk. "I take it you are both familiar with the terms of the contract?"

"Yes. I went over it with her," Saxton says.

"Okay. Since we're omitting agents and doing this fairly simple I'm just going to hit high points. No sleeping or sexual contact with anyone else until you're released from the time constraints in this document. The director and the studio will decide when recording starts from time of arrival based on live feed and utilize recorded material as they see fit. You will arrive promptly at noon a week from tomorrow with your bags. Living conditions will be set at one month and then final arrangements will be made during your break once premier occurs. The two of you will retain somewhat normal lives. There are no rules on what you do in the house or out for that matter. If you leave, a crewmember will follow. A camera will be operating somewhere on you at all times. Act no different than you clearly already do. The house will be completely stocked except for what you choose to bring. Each of you will have half of the salary total direct deposited into your accounts the first day you arrive, so Kambry, I'll have to get that information from you. The second half will deposit the first day of filming when the project resumes, given that it does."

He places his palms on the desk and leans toward us. "Bottom line: film, fuck, and have fun. That is adult films in a nutshell. Any questions?"

We both shake our heads and he lays the signature page of the contract before us. A nervous energy floods through my body. I'm really about to do this. With one signature I go from an Alabama good girl to a southern porn star, all because of a guy that turned my head and kept me staring. This can't be undone.

I stare at the line as I hold the pen between my fingers. *I'm sorry, Daddy*. I scribble my name on the line and date the one next to it with today's date, before sliding it toward Michael. He picks it up. "Kambry, I'm going to need your birth certificate, social security card, driver's license, and bank information. I have Saxton's already since he's worked for me before. Then you're free to leave until next week. I'll send the address with you when you go. You still have my number if you have any questions, right?"

I grab my purse off the floor to gather everything he asked for as I nod at him. I should be happy my financial problems are about to disappear, but instead, I'm a nervous wreck, and for so many reasons. I just hope that more good comes out of this than bad . . .

CHAPTER SIXTEEN

Kambry

"So, since this is the last time I'll see you for a week, what do you want to do? Your pick."

We get in the truck and shut the door at almost exactly the same time. Once everything started it moved fairly quickly. After an hour and a half we're free to go. The thought of not seeing him for a week is the part that bothers me the most, but I was given exact instructions on what all I have to do this week in regards to work and preparation. Then Saxton explained it would probably be better when we arrived if we had not seen each other for a while. I don't really think I have much choice in the matter, so I just agreed and moved on.

I'm kind of hungry. We didn't eat breakfast before we left this morning. Actually, we never ended up eating our dinner last night either. My stomach has already complained one too many times. "Do you want to get something to eat?"

He reaches over and places his hand on the back of my neck. "I was already planning on feeding you, Kambry. I meant what is something you want to do; kind of like a date?"

My heart flutters at the sound of that word. I mean, I wasn't really expecting anything in the direction of a real date, since obviously, that's not the point to our relationship. After all, I did give myself away with no real work on his part. I thought that was supposed to be a turn off to a guy in terms of dating material. That's what Dad always said at least. I remember it as if it was yesterday. Sitting on my bed with him in a chair across from me, preparing for the birds and bees speech. It went something like:

"Kambry . . ."

"Yes, Daddy?"

"Do you know what sex is?"

My cheeks are the color of a fire truck I'm sure. I am completely embarrassed at twelve years old. Why it couldn't be my mom I will never know. I respond short in tone. "Yes, Daddy. You don't have to explain."

"Yes, Kambry, I do. Sex isn't something that a boy and girl do as a hobby. It's something that two people do when they love each other enough to get married . . .first. It's something created for a married couple to enjoy; kind of like a reward for good grades. Your body is sacred. It's a temple. You keep it sacred until you get to that point."

"Okay, Daddy," I respond, as I look down at the ground, hoping he will leave me alone.

"Look at me, Kambry." I do as told, but I really don't want to. "Guys want what they have to work for. We're competitive. It's all a game in the beginning. They will try to sway you by telling you things that aren't true. They will try to get you to give them your body, even when it's not meant for them. Don't let them persuade you. You'll think you're trading it for love when they're really just using you. Would you buy the cow if you were getting the milk for free?"

My face has to look horrified, my eyes wide. Did he really just compare me to a cow? "Um . . .depends on how much money I have?"

By the huff of air that exits his mouth and the frustrated eye roll, I can tell that's the wrong answer. "No, Kambry. No man wants to purchase the cow when he can milk it and reap the benefits, then move on. You want a man that wants to marry you. Make him buy the cow first. Until then, sex is bad; very bad."

"Kambry," his voice rings out. "You okay?"

I blink a few times. "Yeah."

"Are you regretting your decision?"

"What? No. Why?"

"You just kind of checked out on me."

Dammit, even when they aren't here they screw with my head. "Yes, sorry.

Was just thinking about something unrelated. What was the question again?"

"I want to take you on a date. Where would you want to go?"

"Oh right. . .a date. That's really not necessary just because I'm new to this. I'm okay, Saxton. I get it. You can't take all your co-stars on dates."

His brows scrunch. "I wouldn't have asked if I didn't want to. Don't compare yourself to them."

His upper body comes over the center console toward me. Looking at him, I lean back, my head hitting against the passenger side window. His hand grips my inner thigh pulled on top of the seat I'm sitting in, inching it upward until his thumb traces the crease of my leg. I shudder from his touch. "The wolf doesn't always want to hurt the lamb. Even when the lamb makes him salivate, there are times when he wants to protect it, to make it his, and to keep it alive and well. This wolf wants to devour his lamb over and over again; not just once."

My heart is being irrational. It's pounding against my chest with every word that leaves his mouth. I think that comparison over: the wolf and the lamb. A wolf is an instinctual killer, a predator. A lamb is soft, innocent, weak, and sometimes used for sacrifice. In some places it's a delicacy. It's always the prey. "What exactly are you asking?"

"To put down your defenses. I want more with you than I do with others. I've never once brought work home. I don't go looking for dating material in my off time. I've never been interested . . .until you. I want to date you. I'm asking the lamb to trust the wolf."

He kisses me. Our mouths move against each other perfectly. It's hypnotic. He places my mind into a trance with something as simple as a kiss. His movement stills within a few seconds. His mouth pulls up into a smile against mine, before traveling to the lobe of my ear. His tongue darts out, tracing the outline. Chill bumps sprout all over my arms. "If I need to I'll persuade you in this parking lot, but I'd rather take you on that date. Don't deny me something I haven't attempted in years."

"Okay, I trust you. I'll be your lamb."

His hand snakes around to my butt, before jerking me forward to press my front to his. "That makes me happy. Tell me something you've been wanting to do, but haven't."

"The Hollywood sign," I blurt out, barely able to control my own words pressed against him like this. He's hard, again, making me forget where we even are.

He sets me back down and pulls away, looking me in the eyes. "That is something I can do. Drive thru and Mount Lee it is."

Reaching in the back seat, he grabs a baseball cap and pulls it on his head. As he adjusts it he looks at me, a huge grin set on his face as he starts the engine to his truck and shifts it into drive. "I'll be your tour guide, Miss Rivers. No client of mine will leave less than satisfied. Get ready for an unforgettable adventure."

"I have no doubt that it will be," I mumble, trying to stay composed. The truth is . . .I can barely contain my nerves when he gets that playful personality. It makes him more real, more down to earth, and that also spurs more emotional outbursts that I'm trying to keep under control. The baseball cap makes him the sugar in my tea. It's not required, but damn if it doesn't make it better.

Not only that for nerves, but also I'm pretty sure I just agreed to be his girlfriend, for real. Kambry Rivers is dating a porn star.

How's that for shits and giggles, Dad . . .

"Are we almost there?" I bend over and place my hands to my kneecaps, trying to catch my breath. I had no idea what I was in for when I asked to do this. Normal girls would have said dinner and a movie or take a walk and get ice cream, possibly even a ballgame or a romantic sail in the Pacific. There's always a walk on the beach, but not Kambry. No . . . Kambry has to say take me to see the Hollywood sign in the California summer heat hiking who knows how many miles.

Movies create a false illusion. They do not show all the little things required to see famous monuments that you actually may benefit from knowing, like that you're going to have to hike up a long freaking trail to see a bunch of letters.

Smart girls would have gotten a clue when he took us both to change into comfortable clothes and sneakers, but of course I had to show the world that some of the blonde stereotype jokes are true by being a ditz to the entire situation. The consequence to my ditziness is that I'm sweating, my lungs hurt from the dry heat, and my legs are aching from the hike. No one around here should judge me. I'm from Alabama. We don't have mountains and our heat is humid. It's different. That's my excuse for being a wuss and I'm sticking to it.

A pair of Nikes comes into view as I stare at the dirt trail. I follow the familiar shoes up the body that is occupying them until I'm staring into the blue eyes of the sexy man that brought me here. He has a grin on his face that I kind of want to smack off. He doesn't even look like he's breathing hard. "Tired already?"

I narrow my eyes. "Don't you dare judge me, Cali boy. Payback is a bitch. When you set foot in Bama and you can't breathe because you feel like you're dying from the humidity, I'm going to say suck it up, buttercup, it's just a little heat."

His jaw locks, his face becoming serious. He pauses. Okay, I was just kidding. I didn't know it would sour the mood. "You'd take me to Alabama?"

"Uh, yes? Is that bad? I thought you kind of asked me to be your girlfriend." My eyes widen. "Oh, God. That's embarrassing. You meant something totally different, didn't you? I'm such an idiot," I mumble.

My hand gets jerked forward, knocking my feet off balance as Saxton runs off the trail into the wooded area. "Where are we going?" I'm having a hard time keeping pace. Height makes a huge difference with stride. "This isn't that point where you become an ax murderer and I disappear in the Hollywood hills is it? I really like living just so you know."

He veers left and shoves me against a tree, the bark scraping the back of my arm. "Ow, you psycho. Slow your roll."

His hands roughly grab my face and his lips crash against mine, all rational thought dissipating. All roughhousing has been forgiven. I moan against his mouth as his tongue locates mine. His hands descend my body, stopping on my hips. One hand grabs the back of my thigh and pulls my leg up to wrap around his waist, then immediately slides under the fabric of my loose, slick, running shorts, until he reaches my bare butt cheek. He squeezes and releases a throaty groan as he realizes I put on another thong when I was able to replace the ones he tore from my body earlier; before I realized I was practically going to be working out or I'd have worn full cover.

He runs his hand over my hip, tracing the crease of my leg, before inching his finger under my panties and sliding it inside me. My knee buckles, but he holds me up. "What are you doing? I'm sweaty and gross and someone may catch us," I whisper, pulling away from his lips.

"Let me in, beautiful. I want to be inside of my girlfriend." That word makes my heart rate speed up.

I look side to side, searching for someone to be around. I hear a female laugh back toward the trail, and then talking, but every few words becomes more distant. "Someone will see."

He adds another finger. My eyes close. "Who? A small, wandering animal?"

"What's gotten into you?" He's tormenting me with his fingers. "Don't you want to wait till we have a bed and shower?"

"You called yourself my girlfriend and you referenced something a real life couple would do. It just hit me. I liked it a hell of a lot more than I thought I would." His thumb presses against my clit and I'm done.

"Okay, boyfriend, okay. Just don't stop making me feel good. If I smell like sweat, I warned you ahead of time."

"Fuck, I love hearing you say that."

He pulls his fingers out of me and sinks to his knees in front of me. I look down at him when he grabs my shorts by the waistband and starts to pull them down, just after my leg returns to the ground. "No, Saxton. I need a shower. I agreed to play. I did not agree to your nose being front row to my sweaty places. Seriously, just put it in before we get caught."

He looks up at me. "I want to try you in every form."

My shorts hit my ankles and he grabs the back of my calf, pulling my foot out of the hole, and then places it on his shoulder. I feel sticky and this is uncomfortable, but as his lips kiss mine over my clit, my worries disappear and the way he feels on me becomes the only thought. My head falls back against the tree as his tongue presses between my lips and then assaults my clit in the most amazing way. "Oh my . . ."

I press my forearm to my mouth to silence myself and grab his hair with the other hand, pulling it. I've come to love when he goes down on me. That feels so good. Perfect spot, the right speed, and his warm tongue rubbing against me sends me into a quick orgasm. The sensitivity replacing the pleasure causes me to drop my leg before I want to.

He pulls me down to his height and turns me around quickly. More voices sound out in the distance, making me nervous. "Hands and knees, baby."

I do as told, positioning myself. I look over my shoulder to him pulling down his shorts to his thighs. He's ready to go. For some reason, that's such a turn on. He removes his shirt, laying it down beside me. He grips my hip with one hand and his dick in the other, placing it at my entrance. He stares into my eyes as he pushes inside of me. "Shit, that feels good."

It still hurts the first time he enters me. It steals my breath for a moment, but I deal with it, because the feeling that comes after makes it worth it. When I feel his pelvis flush with my butt, I bite my tongue to keep quiet. I can feel him in my abdomen. It makes my entire body tense. "I'm sorry, baby. I don't like hurting you."

His hand touches the center of my back, before mirroring the one on my hip. He pulls back slowly, and then pushes all the way inside. My back arches and my hands clench the ground. My head turns straight as he begins to find a rhythm. He bends over and kisses between my shoulder blades.

He runs his hand beneath my tank top and slips it under my bra to cup my breast. I love when he touches my boobs, especially when he rubs my nipple like he's doing now. "Can I go faster," he asks beside my ear.

"Yes," I whisper, preparing myself.

He straightens and grips each hip in his hand, then he thrusts in and out of me harder and faster. I pull forward each time he hits inside of me from the sudden jolt of pain. "Look at me, baby."

I do as he says. "I want to see you when I come." He hits inside again, causing me to bite my bottom lip. He pushes my shirt up my body until it sits crinkled above my breasts. "Just like that."

A slapping sound occurs against my rear and his abs ripple as they contract. When he pulls out again he grips his dick and then I watch as he comes on my lower back, each spurt hitting a different spot, and painting my back in white. "Damn, I wish I didn't have to pull out," he says in a husky tone.

He stands and pulls his shorts back up. I remain in my position, waiting patiently for him to do something. He slides my shorts off the other foot and takes my panties, wiping them across my back, cleaning me. He helps me up and hands me my shorts. Then he picks up his shirt off the ground. "You better be glad my shorts have built in underwear and I just prefer real panties. At this rate I'm not going to have any left."

I step into them and pull them up my legs as he puts his shirt back on. He's smiling at me as he shoves the balled up panties in his shorts pocket. "That's one thing I don't mind spending money on, baby."

I adjust my tank and he pulls me into his arms, laying a brief kiss on my lips. "I'm sorry I practically pounced on you. You evoke that side of me. I feel like I've known you so much longer than I actually have. I promise we're almost to the top."

The mountain. I totally forgot. I look up at him as I wrap my hands around his waist, our fronts pressed together. "It's okay. I like that you want me. It kind of just feels like we lost touch instead of recently met."

"Want is a mild form of what it is. A week might not be that easy."

"Don't remind me. You're the one that made that stupid rule."

"I'm just giving you time to miss me." He winks and then kisses my forehead. "One week and then I'm not letting you out of my sight for a month. Come on. We're so close."

The weird part of that statement is that I already do, and I've not even left him yet. I just hope he misses me, because my heart is falling hard for someone it shouldn't. Deep down I keep reminding myself of what he does. When he's free from this project between us, he goes back to other women. He's only mine for a little while. That's when this modern day fairytale will end. I know it's coming. If I say it over and over again, maybe my heart will fly away before it's caught.

That's what I'm counting on.

Saxton

A girlfriend. It's been a long time since I've said that phrase, even to myself. At first it was just being caught up in the moment. I hardly meant it in terms of a label. It was more of a form of courtship. This mock relationship is becoming more and more real before cameras even begin recording, but the thing is, when she acted so normal about us, a buried part inside of me was recovered.

I've lived for so long now shamed from my family and closest friends that it became normal to me, and in turn I even repelled those things. No one can openly accept what I do. It becomes a moral dilemma, and no matter what shit they are doing in their own lives, they always choose judgment because my sins are more open than theirs. Not her though. She mentioned taking me with her as if my background doesn't bother her at all. In that exact moment her being my real life girlfriend just seemed ideal. I want her. I'd be lying to myself if I said otherwise.

Her embarrassment following was the icing on the cake. For the first time she looked at me like a fan hanging out with a star. Her innocence hooked me, but her beautiful, bold personality in her moments of comfort keeps me interested. She is my lamb. Holding her purity inside of me is one thing that's going to be hard to leave behind when it's time to move on to another project, so for now, I'm taking full advantage of every second I can get to know her.

When I'm gone I want her to remember me. The man I want her to remember is the Saxton I used to be. I want her to think of the man she would introduce as her boyfriend to her friends, and not the guy she keeps a secret because of how loosely I use my dick. She gave me a part of her she can never give to anyone else, and in turn, I want to give her a beautiful memory to go with it. It's the least I can do, since I can never give her what she's given me. In those brief moments that I can feel how I affect her, I really wish I could.

As we near the top of the mountain I stop. She runs into me not paying attention. "Dang it. I'm sorry. My feet got ahead of my brain. I am ready to be at the end."

I turn as she rambles. "Close your eyes."

"What? Why? Nothing can surprise me after earlier."

"Humor me."

Her bare shoulders drop. "Fine," she huffs as she closes her eyes.

I walk around her to stand at her back, and then place my hands over her eyes to make sure she isn't peeking. "Follow my lead."

"Um, it's not like I've never seen the Hollywood sign. If I didn't know any better, I'd think you were trying to woo me so you can get into my pants. You west coast boys are different."

I smile with my mouth pressed into her blonde hair, just outside of her ear. "We aren't as forgettable. By the way, I'll always try to get in your pants. That place is paradise, baby."

I inch forward, guiding her a little further. She grabs ahold of my wrists to keep herself steady. The fence running behind the letters comes into view. As it does my heart starts to accelerate, slamming against my chest. I haven't been here since I was a kid. My parents brought me once. Don't even really remember it. When I moved to LA, coming back here wasn't something I wanted to do. Seemed pointless to do it alone.

I stop when I reach the fence line between two letters so that she has a better view. "Why are you breathing hard?"

"Because you're making me nervous. I can't see."

"I thought you trusted me."

"I do. It's not like I'm used to this sort of thing. Cut me some slack."

I temporarily close my eyes. She doesn't really realize how much her phrases over her lack of experience make me want her more; the total opposite of what I always thought. I guess it's really true about men. We're territorial, animalistic, and once we mark our territory we will fight to keep others out. I suppose that is one thing that really hasn't changed since the Paleolithic period.

"Open your eyes, Kambry."

I drop my hands and replace them around her waist, waiting for a sign to confirm she's done as I've asked. She remains silent, but places her hands on the fence and clenches them through the holes. She pulls toward it and I follow, taking a step forward as she does. I wait, for what seems like forever. "Kambry?"

"I've never seen anything like it," she whispers. "Nothing I say will explain the way I feel."

"It's pretty awesome, isn't it?"

"I'm sure it's not that great to someone that's been here time and time again, but this is really breathtaking, and honestly I've never understood that phrase before now."

"Actually, I've only been here once. I was little, so this is really like the first time, but even if I had, I'm pretty sure this would still top all the rest."

She turns around, her hands moving behind her, waist high, gripping the fence once again. Her face is serious, her lips slightly puckered, the top one sitting over the bottom one. My hands move to the fence over her head like hers just were, gripping onto it with each hand forming a claw. We stare at each other. I'm not sure if anyone else is around, and I don't really care. "Can I ask you something at risk of sounding like an immature girl?"

"Yeah, and I'll answer, at risk of sounding like a cheesy guy."

She bites her bottom lip in a smile. It's contagious, spreading to mine. "Do you think this will change when we're in front of cameras? Will it be forced? The way we are, because I don't want it to change. I like this Saxton. I want to hang out with the guy that gets drunk with me and gropes me in the pool, the guy that catches me in my most embarrassing moments, the guy that does inappropriate things to me in the parking lots of liquor stores, and also the guy that has enough respect for me to take my virginity in a bed when it's just us. But most importantly, I want to hang out with the guy that gets turned on when I'm referred to as his girlfriend and attacks my body in the woods, just before he shows me the world's most beautiful places, making my life more exciting one day at a time."

I say nothing. Instead, my hormones take the lead and I crush my lips to hers, kissing her heatedly. She allows me to. I clench the fence as our tongues tangle, stopping myself. I tighten my closed eyes, leaving my lips pressed against hers.

I grab her hand and press it over the left side of my chest, just before parting our mouths. "I can't promise anything after we're done with filming, but as long as we're together I promise this won't change."

She nods. My heart is pounding. I feel like I've just snorted a line of that fine, white powder. I don't like the open-ended answer, but it's an honest one, and honesty is a good start.

CHAPTER SEVENTEEN

Kambry

I stare at my packed bags sitting in the middle of the floor. It seems surreal it's already been a week since we went to see the Hollywood sign—a long week at that. Saxton texts me twice a day since he dropped me off, after our . . .adventure: once in the morning and once at night, for about twenty minutes. I haven't heard his voice in a full week, and it's killing me slowly. My finger has hovered over the call option of his name so many different times, but I've refrained. It's been hard.

The real summer has ended; at least in my book. Some would still call this summer depending on what part of the country you live in, or the person's preference, but to me August is the beginning of fall, hot or not. It's when a lot of schools begin, the leaves are preparing to start changing in color, and things like football are slowly beginning. Yep, we are entering into Kambry's fall. By October I'm comfortably living in the land of Autumn dreams, where oranges and yellows are at their peaks, and standing just outside the door of winter wonderland.

My life is so different than what I thought it would be. I'm nearing my nineteenth birthday and it's nothing like I always pictured. I thought I'd be moving in dorms, scheduling classes, and starting college, but I guess things aren't as we always imagine they will be. I kind of saw myself as a sorority girl. Something about parties, sisterhood, and four years packed with fun-filled events appealed to me.

Well, you're steering quite far away from that dream, aren't you, Kambry?

Instead, I'm about to find out what it's like to bare my body for the world, ready or not. I'm just hoping that he takes that thought away, because I have a confession. I watched a porno from start to finish; however, it wasn't one of his. I just can't watch him with another girl that way, but I did want to see what I'm about to get myself into; what I'm really about to wake up in the middle of, because I'm not naive. Okay, maybe I am, but I know that the sweet, level one kink we've done is not what I'll have to do, so I kind of surfed the adult channels late Friday night and then hit purchase on the one that appealed to me the most. It's a good thing we pay for the cable bill and utilities instead of Meredith's mom. That would be an embarrassing conversation.

Let's just say I now know what anal beads are used for. I watched with my hand over the channel button, the volume down low, and constantly looking over my shoulder for her to wake up and enter, but no matter how uncomfortable I got I still couldn't change that channel. I was turned on. I fear that the second I hear a moan I will visualize his strong hands pressing them into her anus one bead at a time. My cheeks clench together at the remembrance of her as she took them . . .from behind.

Then there were the famous come moments, like when he blew his load all over her vajayjay, but not in it. It was a little confusing. I'm not sure the point in that. They are swimmers, right? The part that made me blush the most, as well as the most uncomfortable, was when he used her cleavage to encase his dick and came all over her mouth and face. It seemed so demeaning, yet I was still turned on. Cum to the face . . . I don't know. Will that be me?

Maybe I should try not to screw up a blowjob first. He's so big though. With no experience in dick judging I know that. Will I be able to pull it off without embarrassing myself? I want to. I press my legs together. Now is not the time to get turned on.

I've done everything I agreed to do. The entire week I've only worked one shift at the club, which was harder than I thought, because boredom set in really quick. It was a scheduling arrangement that was made by Michael and the owner. I had no control over it; however, the one night I worked I disliked the conversation with Drake. He called me into his office to go over the changes, but when we finished I sat and watched while he stared at me for quite a while, before he finally spoke again.

Then, it became a lecture I would expect from my brother if he knew what I was doing and actually gave a damn, but I haven't spoken to him since I left that night. It saddens me that we aren't as close as we once were, before he went off to college three years ago. If he would remove his head from my dad's ass he would realize we aren't close anymore, but because he's living it up at the school of his dreams he doesn't have a clue what I have to go through with our parents. It's a common story of the boys getting to do whatever with Daddy-O patting them on the backs while the girl in the family is sheltered to no end. To hell with double standards.

Regardless of the awkward educational lecture about my reputation, I put my big girl panties on as I tell myself so often and assured Drake I knew what I was doing. I hope I'm right. No regrets. Life is too short for that. That's the exact reason I threw everything I knew out the window and moved here with Meredith. It's not easy being cut off from your parents financially, but that was a sacrifice I was willing to make to be happy. It's a big one too, because I miss my car more than anything. Mom's hand me down Ford Taurus was better than not having one. I sigh. I have to believe I know what I'm doing.

My mind wanders back to the woods from the dirty memories floating around in my mind; like cum . . . Which leads me to another memory from the many I've made this past week. I saw a gynecologist for the first time in my entire life. Talk about embarrassing. I actually had to put my feet in stirrups. I thought that was a myth. It's not.

As I laid there half naked on that table, my knees were quickly pried open and my bottom pulled to the edge while I had things that were cold and metal shoved inside me, along with dainty glove-covered fingers. My very newly used lady hole was spread wide with the torture device. Scraping of the insides occurred. There was petroleum jelly used. Boob squeezing also took place. My abdomen became a temporary stress ball. Not sure what that was for.

I felt so violated.

Questions were asked that caused my cheeks to change in color. Officially, it was confirmed that I could no longer call myself a virgin. My hymen had been compromised. I had to hold the desire to fist pump the air within myself.

My excitement was quickly nipped in the bud with talk of venereal diseases. See, this doctor was obviously thorough and experienced in the land of Kiss and Tell films, because shortly after the safe sex 101 course, prompted of course by my recent deflowering, a needle was lightly stabbed into the bend of my arm. STD testing is as scary as it sounds. I've been with one man in eighteen years and I trembled with the thought, reminding me how quick I was to trust him. Thank God everything came back negative.

I look down and rub my fingertips over the healing cut in my arm. Knowing a device has been inserted there makes me feel like a science experiment, like I could be tracked. It's to prevent pregnancy they say. Whatever happened to simple pills? Apparently this has less human error and is more effective, as well as preventing pregnancy longer with little upkeep. I personally think it's strange, like an alien has tampered with me, but the doctor seemed to be an Implanon advocate, selling me on the point that it prevents pregnancy for three years; not too short and not too long. Since I have no children this was the logical way to go versus an IUD; so she says.

A knock sounds at my door and then it opens. Meredith walks into my room holding a handful of items. "Tomorrow is the big day, huh?"

She sits down beside me, the items resting on her lap. "Yeah. What's wrong?" She has this saddened expression on her face. It's unlike her. She's usually known for her witty, happy personality.

She looks at me, tears pooling in her eyes. "I'm going to miss you."

I laugh out, and then realize she's serious. "Why? I thought you'd enjoy the burden free month."

"Kambry, you're not a burden. You will never be a fucking burden. You're my best friend. Do not ever think that. I don't care if you're forty, divorced, and need a place to stay. I will always be here for you and your needs."

My lips line. That does not sound appealing at all. "As tempting as that sounds, I'll use you for other purposes. If I end up in that life just put me out of my misery when you open the door. Promise me."

A tear falls down her face at the same time she laughs out. "You're such an innocent bystander and I love you for it." She sucks up her nasal drip from her tears with an inhale. "You need this. I'm going to try not to be selfish because I know how much you need to experience life for once. I'm going to be lonely for an entire month so you can have that."

"When have you ever been lonely in the past? All of those times I was stuck at home you had no problem living without me. I'll still be working at the club, I'll still be around, and I'm sure you can even visit. This isn't goodbye, crazy, this is just see ya later."

She turns toward me and pulls her leg up on the bed, tear trails staining her face. "Okay. I'm being irrational, aren't I?"

"Nah, I've just never had a choice to participate in things like you before, and now I do. This is insane and one day I *may* regret it, but I really like him, Meredith. He makes me feel things that I've never felt before. I want to experience a relationship that makes me crazy, leaves me winded, and becomes a way of life. I want to feel like heated chocolate when he's near. I want to not be able to fathom anyone else because I have blinders for only him. That's the way he makes me feel, and so much more. I never had any of that with Kyle. It was like experimenting on your best friend when you learn that boys and girls kiss, preparing you for the real thing so you don't completely suck at it. I know it may only be temporary with Saxton, but I'm willing to settle for PRN than nothing at all. Fairy tales never start out with perfect conditions, right?"

"Okay. For the record, I should have snuck you out more. That's something I'll have to live with, but I knew when I left Coffee Springs if I left you behind you'd remain their puppet. They may hate me, but planting that seed was the smartest thing I've ever done. Just promise me you'll live for you this time. No one has to live with what you do in your life; only you."

I wrap my arms around her neck and pull her against me, hugging her. "I love you, Mer. I wouldn't be here if it weren't for you."

"I love you too, Kam. Do everything that I would do."

I laugh, a tear trying to arise in my own eye. This is silly. I push her back, trying to stop this madness. I glance back at the boxes in her hand. "What's all that?"

She smirks. "Tools."

"Tools?"

She nods. "Tools. Every woman has a toolset. I'm giving you your first. The biggest one is outside the door. I'll get it in a minute."

"Okay . . .I'm curious."

She hands me the small wrapped present first. It's in pink paper—my favorite color. "You do know you didn't have to get me gifts, right? I still have a month before my birthday."

She rolls her eyes. "You know better. Your birthday present will be epic awesomeness. This is mediocre. Open it."

I smile. If I ever lose her, I'll be lost. I rip it open, tossing the paper on my mattress. I stare at the black box. "Kindle? How is an eReader a tool?"

"Hello . . . Have you never read a romance novel?"

"I tried to read *Wuthering Heights* by Emily Bronte once, since it's a classic. I couldn't really get into it. Not because it wasn't good. People spoke weird back then. It was hard to comprehend. It was really unfortunate because so many love it. I felt dumb."

"Wuthering Heights? Are we in English class? What? Kambry, did your mother not even let you read modern literature?"

"I couldn't read, watch, or listen to anything with sensitive material. She checked my stuff regularly. She said it gave me ideas and was society's way of trying to make conservative people extinct by tainting the minds of youth."

She blinks at me as she shakes her head. "Uh, not everything has sex in it. What about Nicholas Sparks? He's been my favorite romance writer since I entered into teenybopper years. My mom isn't a floozy and didn't condone teenage promiscuity, but she let me fucking read material written for a younger audience until I was a senior. Aren't parents supposed to motivate you to read? We've been told it makes us smarter since we started school."

I shrug my shoulders. "I don't know. I tried to read *Twilight* by Stephanie Meyer when everyone was talking about it and when she found it in my room she threw it away, saying I wasn't reading that fictional garbage. She said God wouldn't be happy with me reading about someone that kills people and drinks blood. I didn't try again because I was heartbroken that I never got to finish it. It was good."

"I swear I fucking hate your mother." She takes a deep breath and closes her eyes. "Meredith, be nice. Be nice. Be fucking nice." She opens them again after giving herself a pep talk. I don't blame her. I dislike my mom at times too. She grabs the Kindle out of my hand and holds the box up for me to see, her other hand introducing it. "Kambry, meet Kindle. Kindle, this is Kambry. You will be responsible for her knowledge of the twenty-first century, because her parents failed her miserably."

I bite my bottom lip, trying not to laugh at her. Really, it's more pathetic than funny. "Kambry, my little innocent bunny, I need you to forget everything you've ever been told aside from church, school, and the news. If your parents said it in regards to the world we live in, there is a fifty percent chance it's all lies."

She pauses. "Let me see how fast I can bring you up to speed. Is it best to remain sex free until you take the oath of marriage? Yes it is; the bible tells us so . . .but given the fact that neither of us did, let's move on. Less sex partners is good. Being nasty is bad. Think before you fuck. Alcohol spurs bad decisions. Condoms serve a purpose. Under normal conditions, glove it until you love it. You should be good now that you've discovered neither of you carry diseases. When sperm meets egg, babies are formed more times than not. Keep that motto and you'll be okay. Birth control works *most* of the time. Dick does not contain a magical elixir to cure the common cold. I don't care what any guy says. In the end he just wants his dick sucked. If he's on top of you when he says he loves you for the first time then he's lying. Sex is not a race. He should at least try to get you off first, even if shit happens. A for effort, but if he doesn't even try he fucking failed and should work harder to bring up his grade. I think that about covers the basics. Any questions before I move on?"

I lick my lips. My eyes are misbehaving even though my mouth is being good. "And this is related to the eReader in your hand how?"

"I'm getting there. Don't you come home and tell me I'm going to be a grandma or you have something incurable. I'm still young. Tell me you understand safe and mature sex. Then we will add the spice."

I grab the collar of my tee shirt and pull it over my mouth. "Yes, mother," I retort, silencing my laughter with the fabric.

She looks at the Kindle. "Now, you get to do your job. Don't disappoint me." She thrusts the box toward me. "This is like the romance version of the Kama Sutra."

"The what?"

She lightly slaps my face. "Don't you dare." I grip my face, shocked. "Even nuns know what the Kama Sutra is. It is the Holy Grail when it comes to sex. I taught you better than that."

I take the stupid Kindle. "You're psycho."

"But I'll never be forgotten."

"Whatever helps you sleep at night."

"Take it out. Introduce yourself. You already have the vibrator packed, right?"

I begin opening the box. "Meredith, why in the hell would I need a vibrator? I'm about to film a series of porn shows! I don't think I'm going to be lacking in the 'O' department."

"It's called teasing, boo. No one wants an overkill of sugar. At some point you have to add the cayenne to heat things up. The things you will find hidden in the words will shock your innocent ass. Now, I have already logged your device in to my kindle account since it will most likely collect dust otherwise. Give it a try one night before bed, but I must warn you . . . Some things are fantasy. Logic, darling, logic. If it sounds a little out there it most likely is. Don't shove your finger in Saxton's ass unless he asks you to. I'm still learning west coast boys, but I think it's safe to say that most heterosexual guys do not like things in their ass. Back home, you may come back one less finger. There is a reason prison is scary."

I crumple my face, my eyes widened. She just continues like none of this is odd to discuss. "It is not a one size fits all with the shit you will read in these books, but your library of knowledge should be vast even if you don't use it all."

My mouth falls. My finger is not doing any such thing. That's just nasty. "Wait, since when do you read? You hated school. Why have I never heard any of this?"

She splays her hand over her chest, her fingers gaping. Prepare for the drama. I can see it on her face. "I, Kambry, am a melting pot. I am filled with different things, likes, and hobbies. I do not discriminate in any culture. I embrace the differences, by choosing the things I like from each, and that makes up me. Do I like to read history books? Hell no. Do I like to read a steamy romance with an epic love story? You bet your fucking ass I do. I may be young, but I am not naive. The stuff I house in my head would shock you. Now, for the love, just read a fucking book. Moving on. I'm aging as we speak."

"By all means."

I place the half opened Kindle beside me as she hands me the larger box. It looks like a clothing box. "This is for Saxton. You will thank me later."

She places it on my lap. It's wrapped in a thick white paper; with a black ribbon wrapped around both ends meeting to form a bow at the center, and stuck just beneath it is a silver, oval tag. The script black wording on the front reads, *SINcerly Yours.*

My fingers brush over the letters, remembering that day in the sex shop; my first time. What followed though was even better. My brows scrunch, and then I look at her. "Please tell me you didn't get a whip or something. Gray always comes between white and black. I'm not quite ready for the dark side yet."

"Oh, hell, just open it. You're such a nut sometimes. Just remember . . .I never forget anything."

I turn the box over and grip the ribbon, pulling until I break the taped seal, freeing the box, and then waste no time unwrapping the beautifully wrapped package. It feels like Christmas in August. I'm not used to being this spoiled. When I pull off the top of the cardboard gift box, a hot pink fabric is nestled in black tissue. The color intrigues me, but I pause, slightly scared to remove it.

"Go ahead, little bunny, earn your Playboy ears," she says with a light, teasing tone.

I grab the satin straps with my fingers, pulling it free from the box. As it falls open, my stomach starts to flutter. "You want me to wear this?"

"Saxton does," she says, without me looking at her.

It's a sexy babydoll. The fabric is a hot pink satin, and short but loose. The triangle portions that cover the breasts are clearly revealing for a busty girl like me, and layered with a black, lace overlay, the pink showing through. Between the two breasts is a small, black bow with a crystal in the center, giving it a little sparkle as the light hits it. It's beautiful, but makes me nervous. When would I wear something like this? You don't just randomly walk out in sexy lingerie. Usually it's for a birthday or anniversary, anything but at random. What am I supposed to do, just be waiting in it when he comes home and opens the door?

The sound of tissue crinkling pulls my attention to Meredith. She's dangling a black, lace thong from her index finger. "Missing something?"

I grab it from her and inspect it. The fabric seems legit. Neither looks cheaply made. This looks like designer. "Meredith, how much did you spend on this?"

"Nothing."

"Don't lie to me or be literal. Fine, how much did your dad's credit card pay for this?"

Meredith's parents aren't hurting for money, but I don't want for her to do anything else for me. I already live here rent-free. Her dad is a pharmacist over his own drugstore in our hometown, so he already does well for himself, but where he made enough to pretty much set their whole family was when they found oil on land that's been in her family for years, handed down from generation to generation. Black gold that stuff is.

As if that isn't enough, her mom owns a small boutique in town. It started over Meredith's love for being one hundred percent girly, developing a fashion obsession early on, and to keep her from boredom during the day since she didn't have to work. But it has actually done quite well being in a small town with a driving distance to the bigger town with all of the shopping malls. People want convenience more times than not. Plus, boutiques have really taken off over the last few years because they have cuter stuff.

"Actually, Daddy didn't pay for that. Don't make me sound like a spoiled, rich princess. I've worked part time at the drug store since I was allowed to get a job. Just because my dad makes good money and allows me to splurge occasionally doesn't mean I take advantage."

"You have a point, but how much do I owe you?"

"I didn't buy that. Saxton did," she says with a shrug.

"What? I'm sorry."

She rolls her eyes as if I'm just playing dumb for attention. "The deal was if we brought back an autographed DVD, she would give you an outfit." She hands me a medium sized gift bag. "This goes with that."

I quickly open it. It's a pair of stilettos in black with the same black lace overlay to match the outfit. "All this for one DVD? I thought she was joking. It can't be worth all that. I'm not buying it."

"Oh girl, that was for just one. There is something else because I brought back both with an autograph and didn't ask for a refund. After seeing you not so casually shimmy away the night we tried to watch it, I knew you weren't going to, so there was no need in keeping it around. Next time just say, 'Meredith, I'm jealous and can't watch the mega hot hunk I'm crushing on lay pipe in another girl's ditch,' and I'll turn it off. You are ridiculously obvious."

"I'm not that ba—"

"Oh, and by the way, his dick must be valuable," she says with a wink. "I took a photo for authenticity while he signed them and had them printed before I went back." She taps her finger to her temple. "Smart, this one. The things that boy will do for your pussy is amazing, considering . . ."

"Oh, god. What's the other one?"

She stands now that her lap is empty. "Be right back."

She disappears temporarily and then comes back inside with a large basket full of things, wrapped in that clear gift-wrap, as well as an oversized tote bag. My eyes enlarge as I take in its size. I shake my head. For an autograph on two DVDs? Maybe if it was an autograph by a player in the NFL, MLB, or NBA, but come on . . .a porn star? That's insane. "What on earth is in that thing?"

She sets it on the bed and we both peek inside. "I'm not completely sure under the top items, but she said it's her ultimate naughty gift pack. She doesn't sell a ton she said, because of the hefty price tag, and that usually it's a bridal gift or uppity customer with the cash to spend. When I gave her the DVDs and the photos with your measurements, she made it up really quick. I know it has like seven bra and panty sets, some toys, and hell I don't know. She said there is a lot of shit in there for play with your man."

"That's awkward." I start to panic. It's all hitting me at the last minute. "Meredith, maybe I didn't think this through. I don't know how to be sexy or seductive. I don't know how to be out there like you. I'm socially awkward. We both know this."

She grabs my face in her hands, shushing me. "Little bunny . . ."

"Is this a new term you've stumbled upon?"

"It's the truth. You're like a little scared bunny, petrified and hiding from the fox. Dig deep within and change your spirit animal."

"You've watched *The couples retreat* way too many times," I interrupt. "I should have never bought that stack of movies from the five-dollar bin at Wal-Mart. It's going to your head."

She scoffs. "Don't make fun because you don't understand. That shit is golden."

I roll my eyes, playing along to move this along. If not we'll be here all night, and still at point A. "And what spirit animal should I become?"

"A pussy."

I choke on my spit as I swallow, coughing uncontrollably, my face most likely turning red from lack of oxygen. That always happens to me when I'm caught off guard. "Wha—" Another cough. "Ta?"

"Be a pussycat. I would say a peacock, but the males are prettier. Fuck that. Ain't no man going to be prettier than me. On top of that, he can strut all he wants, but he's going to be the one chasin' not the other way around. Never chase the man . . .ever. You will be left outside watching like a stalker, days after gifting him your V-card while he flirts with the next twitterpated tramp, crushing your heart."

My brows dip as I lower the outfit back into the box. "Meredith, what the hell are you talking about? You lost your virginity to Chris Ainsworth on Homecoming night freshman year in the backseat of his truck. Hottest soccer player at school and he was obsessed with you for like a year after that while you strung him along with sex so you didn't have to ride the bus home and had an insta-invite to all the good parties, at fifteen! You're a man-eater. I secretly called you a praying mantis until we were juniors."

Her eyes widen suspiciously. "Oh, r-r-right," she says, stuttering. "I just meant rhetorically speaking. Not me. Pffft. Like I would be that girl. Puh-lease. I'm way off track here. I drank coffee after five so I could stay up and practice for this open audition I have coming up. Pussycat. Back to the subject at hand."

"Sometimes you're such a weirdo." I shake my head, completely thrown off now.

"Kambry, guys aren't that hard. Dress pretty, fix yourself up, and flirt. Flirt shamelessly. Not even the hottest one is out of reach; hence Mr. hot as hell sex-god porn star all up in your Kool-Aid. It's all about confidence. Men like pretty things that they can shove their dicks into. Confidence and desire yield seduction and sex appeal. It's a thoughtless skill that gets easier over time. Before long you won't even realize you're doing it, but masculine eyes everywhere notice."

She takes a look at my face. "Let me break this down in simple terms. Picture a pussycat. Isn't it annoying how they—females especially—walk ever so slowly into a room with this arrogant saunter, fluffy tail swaying in the air, with her chin turned up like she owns the fucking place? Picture Miss Pearl, Mom's cat. I swear you'd never know I was an only child. Jealous little bitch. Anyway, moving on. You remember right?"

I laugh, because I know exactly what she's talking about. That cat thinks she's human. I nod. "Yeah, I remember. You pointed it out every time she followed your mom out of the room."

"Ding, ding, ding. Be Miss Pearl. Let your inner pussy reign. Put a little sway in your step, believe you're sexy, and flirt shamelessly. You will have him eating out of your hand."

"Okay, but when am I supposed to wear this or bring out the goodies?" I whirl my finger around at all the new offerings she has brought into my room.

She reaches over and grabs the Kindle. "Read, Kambry. This one little device is filled with so much female—and some male—knowledge, all coded in the words of a story. It's like the bible for romance and erotica, written by so many contributors. Yes, some is fiction within fiction, but also, you will find things added from experience—from one being to another. So much power within one piece of technology. Taint your pure mind a little. You will get ideas, you will get instruction, and the moment will come to you. Men are control freaks in the bed, but they also like a girl that knows and voices what she wants."

I take a deep breath. I long for the day when I don't feel as clueless as I am. "So you're saying just wing it?"

"Precisely."

"Okay, but you act like you're thirty."

"What can I say, I like having a little experience and knowledge under my belt." She winks.

" What's in the duffel bag?"

"More tools." She grabs it off the floor.

"This is overwhelming."

"Awe, you'll get the hang of it in no time."

Opening the bag, she scoots over and sets it between us. There is a thick, white, cardboard postal service envelope labeled priority mail on the top, addressed to me. "What's that?"

I grab it and shake, hearing something moving around inside, before examining the return address section. There is no return sender, only a local address. "It was in the mail. I just shoved it in the bag since I was short of hands with all this stuff." The lack of name makes me think it was from him.

I wonder what he would send me. My heart starts beating wildly, remembering I will finally see him tomorrow. Instead of opening it with her here, I'll wait. I want this to myself. I peek in the bag full of clothes, hand priced tags showing from some of the top items. "What's all this?"

"I got Mom to overnight you a wardrobe. As proud as I am of you for buying a few cute things here and there over the summer, you need to find you, and not Evelyn's Kambry." The mention of my mom's name sends my nerves into a spiral. It always does. "Since you always comment on my clothing, I got her to send things I would wear. Before I take you tomorrow I will help you go back through your things and leave the stuff that looks like you were born a Cleaver kid here."

I want to argue, to throw a tantrum that I will not take any more handouts, but with Meredith it does no good. The girl loves to brighten tarnished gems. It reminds me of that movie, *She's all that,* where the hot jock fixes up the nerd, making her popular and pretty. Even though I know genetics was nice to me, I lack the confidence to make me model material. I feel pretty, not hot.

"Oh, wait, I almost forgot something," she says, running out of the room. "I got you some stuff from work yesterday," she yells from somewhere in the apartment, before coming back with a makeup bag, handing it to me. "This makes a girl go from a hard seven to a ten easily. You know application. I've taught it to you for years. All you need are the right tools. Throw that neutral, Evelyn approved shit away. Color, and even dark, are a beautiful thing when done right."

My nerves are in a huge ball in the pit of my stomach, driving me mad. I'm excited about seeing Saxton again, but knowing everything we say or do will at some point be filmed and watched by other people has me feeling nauseous. I at least want his first reaction to ease my mixed feelings. "Meredith, will you make me hot tomorrow; like scorching, camera ready, I've never seen a girl that hot, hot? Please."

She stands, then grabs my face in her hands and kisses my forehead. "Sweets, I will make you so hot that he will be making every attempt to not swallow his tongue when he lays his eyes on you. I will show you with a little polishing the beauty that's been there all along. It's getting late. Bryant should be closing up the store by now and wants me to come by his place for a bit." She wriggles her eyebrows. "He's going to run lines with me . . .and it's a steamy scene. Will you be okay being a loner for a while?"

I slap her butt and she yelps in passing. "Get out of here, you hornball." She grabs onto the door and turns to blow me a playful kiss. "Oh, Meredith . . ."

"What's up, sweets?"

"I like him. I'm not sure what you're waiting for, but maybe you should give this one a shot at dating."

"Eh, I don't know. The right one will have to come along and sway me. Things change when you add on a title. I like keeping my options open. Night, Kam."

"Night, Mer," I say, watching in confusion as she walks out the door. For the life of me, sometimes I can't figure her out. I have no idea why someone would continue to hang around and sleep with the same person, yet not actually be in a relationship. She's done that since Chris. She will sleep with the same person for an extended period of time, and then one day suddenly move on to someone else. I don't have any solid proof that she's ever had a true one-night stand, even though she plays this super wild girl.

Maybe I'm just living in too much of a traditional mindset. I don't know. It's none of my business. I have other things to worry about.

I stand at the sound of the apartment door closing, eying my room and all the new stuff inside. How am I supposed to be taking all of this crap? He didn't mention a bag limit or anything, not that I have that much. It's not like I could pack my entire room in the middle of the night. I came here with what clothes I could muster in my biggest suitcase, and a few things I couldn't live without. Since we moved here at the end of May I haven't added that much stuff, so with Meredith requesting that I discard some of my more conservative clothing options, I'm sure I'll have room.

The envelope catches my attention, reminding me of the mystery mail sent. What would he send through the mail that he couldn't just bring over himself of give me tomorrow? I guess there is only one way to find out. Snatching it off the bed, I tear it open. When I look inside there is a clear, square case with a disc inside. My brows furrow.

I remove it, glancing at the yellow post-it note on the outside.

Watch me—The words that are scribbled across the front.

CHAPTER EIGHTEEN

Kambry

I remain still, staring at the small case in my hand, slightly nervous. Surely he wouldn't send me one of his films, right? It shouldn't bother me to watch them, since I know this is what he does, but I can't help it. Maybe it's the girl in me. I don't want to see him touch another girl that way now that he's touched me. It doesn't matter whether it's business or pleasure. Touching is touching. I want to keep that part of him for myself, at least for now. Seeing it and knowing that it's there, in the background, are totally different things.

"This is Saxton, Kambry. He hasn't done anything cruel to you so far. Just watch the damn video."

Mind winning out, I grab my laptop from the charger and open it as I sit on my mattress, resting it on my lap. I open the case and remove the round, blank disc, before inserting it into the drive and typing in the passcode to unlock my computer, just as the sounds of the disc being read plays, the movie playback system immediately coming on. I grip the sides of my laptop in my hands, waiting with anticipation.

"Hey, Beautiful."

I yelp and my body jumps as Saxton's voice frightens me, not expecting it. Instantly I glance at the door, half expecting him to be standing there, before realizing that it came from the computer. It wouldn't be far-fetched. It's not like he hasn't barged in my room unannounced before. It's a good thing I was holding onto my computer or it might have gone flying.

The position of my view changes and then his face comes on the screen. Good lord he's beautiful. "Did I scare you?" he asks as he grabs the bill of his ball cap and turns it around backwards, replacing it.

"Yes, actually you did, and ball caps on you should be illegal."

"Sorry." He licks his lips, staring at me. "Do you miss me?"

"Yes, like crazy," I say as a smirk pulls up on his lips. "And you have me talking back to a screen like a crazy person, sexy man."

"Say it again."

"What the?" My eyes widen and I pick up the computer, inspecting it. There is no way he can hear me. Silence is the only thing in the room.

As I place it back on my lap, he has the back of his hand covering his mouth, clearly laughing underneath. "Asshole. I'm not that predictable."

He drops it and leans closer to the screen, his stubble becoming more noticeable. *I want to kiss you . . .* "No, I can't really hear you. I was just hoping that would be your response and that I wasn't the only one stuck in this boat. Come tomorrow—you are mine."

"Promise?" My voice comes out in a whisper. "Still talking to a computer, Kambry."

"Okay, I just wanted to tell you personally that I'm kind of going stir crazy right now. This was the only way to stop me from driving over, because I've already gotten halfway there once and turned around. You're making me crazy, beautiful." The last line comes out with reverence behind it.

"Also," he continues, now speaking in a louder tone, "I forgot to give you something last weekend. I was distracted until I got home. As soon as I stop recording this feed it'll start. I left out a lag time between the videos. I watched it after I dropped you off." Pausing, he takes a deep breath, and crosses his forearms on the table in front of him. His entire voice deepens and becomes just above a whisper. "I need you to see what I saw, Kambry. Nothing I say will be able to describe it accurately. It was supposed to be more of a porn film icebreaker, but this . . . I'm still kind of fucked up over it to be perfectly honest. I've kept it in as long as I can. It's just . . .real, unlike anything else in my life. Starting tomorrow, it's just us. The rest is merely background noise. Good night, beautiful."

My heart falters at his minor confession in relation to us, as he reaches forward, and then the video goes blank, another following immediately after. I grab my computer and roll over, placing it on the bed as I lay on my stomach, watching the dark room. Nothing is on the camera at first, aside from the floor, but before long, the angle is perfectly positioned on us. I can barely breathe, but I can't focus on something as silly as oxygen, because it's us, on the night that we took from each other for the first time.

It's so different watching it after experiencing it, but still, I can't take my eyes off of us, so I don't. I watch it from a third person point of view as we undress, kiss, and touch, just like others will see us. He never got under the covers that night, so I'm able to see as he pushes inside me. The difference in what I was thinking is that it's not dirty, it's not ugly, but the total opposite. There is nothing demeaning about it, because it's natural. It's erotic but in an artistic way.

The sounds are leave me feeling wet between my legs as I watch, listening to the two of us find pleasure in one another. I thought I would be ashamed, but if this is a piece of what it'll be like, then I'm not anymore. Maybe to most people that makes me a slut, or maybe a piece of trash, but there is something beautiful about two people naturally participating in erotic art. Sex is a natural thing, and for the first time I see it as a good thing instead of an evil—what I was always taught.

I grow extremely uncomfortable downtown as I watch the moment that he comes. It leaves a sense of pride completely consuming me, because it means that not only do I want him, but also that he wants me the same. When the video ends I roll over, bumping into the large basket in the place Meredith left it. I'm growing more frustrated by the minute, and the increasing lubrication between my legs from my girly bits confirms it wants exactly what my mind does, but thinking of him while I touch myself doesn't even compare.

My hand rests on my tank, slowly beginning to descend toward my shorts, but then stops as it reaches the waistband, retreating for my hair instead. I pull, growing irritated at the fact that it wasn't a rule that we couldn't see each other, but he made it one. This is stupid, but it's also stupid that it's barely been over a week since I finally had sex for the first time and now I think of it often. I'm horny, but I always feel filthy touching myself. "It's just a few more hours. I can wait."

The memories from that night resurface, playing in my mind as if it just happened. My legs press together as my eyes close. My body gets a prickling sensation in the very place that he's touching me in my head, driving me mad. My hands begin to travel downward again, brushing over my breasts. My nipples are hard through the fabric since I'm not wearing a bra. I pinch them, before continuing toward my lower half, pretending that it's him and not me.

"Kambry, always remember that you should never entertain sexual thoughts. Lust is a sin. In marriage it is good, but outside it is bad. When you get married you want to be completely untarnished and pure. The only person allowed to touch you in any way aside from something platonic is your husband. Do you understand?"

I look at my mother as she pulls into our high school, preparing to drop me off for my first day of freshman year. "Why are you telling me this, Mother?"

"Because I know how high school boys are. They become sinful creatures, only thinking of ways to take your goodness from you. They don't care about your reputation. Do not be tempted by the serpent like Eve. Stay away. Do you understand?"

The carline is long, waiting for the cars in front of us to drop off and move along. I wish it would go faster. I still don't understand why she won't let me ride with Ben. It's stupid to bring me to school when he drives. This is making me uncomfortable. "Okay, Mother," I say as I place my hand on the door handle, preparing to get out.

"Kambry."

"Ma'am . . ."

"I know what you did last night. You should be ashamed of yourself. Years ago, it would have been wise to remove your hand after such an act, and even your eyes. That's the devil at work, tempting you to fall."

I start breathing heavily, terrified. "What are you talking about, Mother?"

My voice is uneven, showing my fear. She tosses the magazine at me, into my lap. I look down at it, my cheeks blazing as I stare at the half naked couple on the front. I want to cry from embarrassment inside. "I found this in your room this morning. I looked after I heard you in your room last night when I did bedtime checks on you and your brother. I can't believe you would touch yourself after sitting in church yesterday, or where you would even get such filth. I'm disappointed in you, Kambry. You need to spend the day thinking about what you did and praying that you will be forgiven. If I catch you doing something like this again, I will tell your father. Are we clear?"

I nod. The magazine is Ben's, but I'm not bringing him into this. He's been moody the past few weeks, but he won't talk to me about it. He just keeps brushing me off. Maybe he's just in that pre-college mindset and this being his last year of high school is sinking in. After all, he's had to listen to Dad harp on this year his whole life. This is the year he becomes a man, so I won't get him in trouble when I'm already getting reprimanded for it.

I found it between his mattresses when I was looking for my iPod that he borrowed to work out with the other day after his went dead. It made me curious when I opened it and saw them doing what they were doing, so I took it, unsure as to why he even had it in the house knowing how our parents are. I was only going to look at it, but when everyone went to bed I just wanted to see if touching that place made my face look like the girls on the pages.

It felt better than I thought it would, making me feel foreign things in my body, but then I felt guilty when it was over. Now I know why. "I'm sorry, Mom, it'll never happen again."

She snatches the magazine and places it between the seat and the console as we ease up to the drop off area, all of my friends standing around in the courtyard. Today should be awesome—not—because even as embarrassed as I feel, I want to feel that amazing vibration even more.

My hand moves away just as my fingertips slide beneath the waistband of my shorts. My eyes fill with tears. I stand and begin pacing the room. I hate the war going on inside me when this happens, when I want so badly to fix the aggravating pressure down below. Five minutes with my finger and it would be over, but the shame that consumes me every time I succumb to the desire eats my soul alive. If only he were here to take away the guilt, like when he caught me.

My eyes sting as I press my back against the wall, hating myself for wanting it, but wanting it so bad that I don't care. All of my life I've tried not to touch, to imagine, or to give in to wanting to be bad, even as strong as the desire was in my core. I've been good, except for the few times that I failed, letting myself have five minutes of pleasure before having to deal with the remorse and scrubbing myself clean for feeling like I've been in filth. This is the result of years of them driving into my head that only dirty, sinful people want those things. I've never discussed these feelings with anyone, not even Meredith. What's weird is I really don't even feel that guilty about having premarital sex, but the sheer thought of the way I feel from touching myself until orgasm sends me into a sweat. Maybe that's why I've wanted to lose my virginity so bad: to escape these feelings when a sexual urge occurs.

I cross my legs as a tear falls from my eye. My phone sitting by my bed catches my attention. It's lit up from a text message coming through. The muscles between my legs contract, angering me more. I don't understand what's wrong with me. Most people can just turn it off. When I get the least bit turned on, it consumes me, making it hard to focus on anything else. The blood flow pounds in my head as I try to fight caving, trying not to give in to myself, or my urges. Sex was never an option, because it's hard to keep a secret with two people involved, so it really was easy to avoid, but the knowledge of knowing I can give myself the same result without anyone knowing was the hardest to run from, because also, there wasn't a single night or day that went by that my mother missed saying, *he's always watching, even when no one else is.*

My body is tense. I grab my phone to three text messages, the first one sent about an hour ago. I haven't even looked at it. I can't smile when his name appears like I usually would because of the guilt washing through me. I can't even enjoy the beauty of his gesture and our video. How many people have a hard copy of the most perfect first time that they can watch any time they want? I've pictured how it would be in my head so many times, and none of them even came close to what I got.

I unlock my phone and open the message box.

Saxton Maverick (9:09 PM): Hey, beautiful. How was your day?

Saxton Maverick (10:12 PM): You okay?

Saxton Maverick (10:48PM): Uh, I really don't like being this guy, but I'm kind of getting worried since you're not working. A simple 'I'm alive' will suffice.

I bite my bottom lip, a few more tears falling free. He somehow always has a perfect balance of funny, sweet, and stern. I respond, suddenly in the mood to play.

Me (10:51 PM): I'm alive.

Saxton Maverick would like to FaceTime . . .

Shit. I most likely look like crap. Do I ignore it or answer? With my thumb hovering over the green circle, I quickly wipe my eyes and inhale the cry snot that's trying to hinder my normal breathing, before lightly slapping my cheeks. "One, two, three . . ."

I press the button, waiting for the video call to connect, staying out of camera shot while I run to the mirror to give myself a once-over. Yep, I look horrible, just as I thought. "Hello."

Dammit, my voice sounds scratchy. I clear my throat. "What's up?"

When he doesn't respond I tilt the screen toward me until I can see myself in the small square in the corner, confirming he can now see me. "Kambry."

As quickly as my eyes veer to the right where I can see him, they stick, because he is clearly lying down in bed, one arm behind his head, and he's shirtless, every lean muscle carved to perfection. He's not totally relaxed or flexed, but a little of both. This, I'm sure, is how babies are created, because this makes girls stupid. "What are you doing?"

I blink a few times repeatedly. "What?"

He smirks. "Had I known this would get your complete attention I would have called you an hour ago."

The stupid finally wears off.

"Oh, sorry. Meredith was here giving me a few things before she went to Bryant's for a booty call. Then I watched the DVD you sent. I didn't have my phone on me."

He stares for a moment. "What's wrong?"

"Nothing, why?"

"Seriously? If we're going to be a couple, we should probably act like a couple. Couples talk about shit. That's how you get to know each other. The tear tracks down your cheeks and the red splotches tell me you've been crying, so *nothing* is an inappropriate response. Plus, on top of that you're in a daze. Most people aren't in a daze when referencing a sex tape."

I take a deep breath. "I guess you're right. Hold on," I say, and place the phone down so I can clear off the bed. When it's free from debris, I pull down my comforter and slide in bed, pulling it over me. I grab the phone after turning on my side, looking at him once again. He hasn't moved and his abs are screaming at me to lick them, the sun kissed color of his skin giving them more definition. It's really unfair for a man to be so hot.

"So you watched our video?" He interrupts the silence. "And it made you cry? Should I be worried? I'm not an expert on the emotions of a female, but that doesn't look like a happy cry."

"The video was great. Thank you for sending it to me. It makes it more special."

"But?"

"It turned me on."

"And that's the wrong effect because?"

"Because you're not here."

"That didn't stop you last time." He winks as the smile pulls his mouth up into a curve. Tears begin to fall again. "Whoa. What the hell? Tell me what's wrong."

"I decided against it. I shouldn't want it so bad. It's only been a week since I've seen you. Before I started having sex I tried hard not to, but occasionally it happened when I couldn't stand the way I felt. I'll see you tomorrow. I shouldn't have to touch myself after that short amount of time, but I wanted to." I lick the tear that has fallen to my lip and continue. "Because you weren't here to make it go away. I made myself stop."

He sits up, his abs becoming more pronounced. It's now that I notice the band of his briefs, showing he isn't wearing pants. His face is displaying a look of confusion. "What's wrong with masturbating occasionally, Kambry? That's partly how you learn what you like. Plus, how are you going to tell a guy what you like if you don't even know? We aren't mind readers, you know, just good guessers sometimes. It doesn't matter how good a guy is at sex or oral or using his hands, because each girl is slightly different when it comes to being turned on and pleasured. The way in which a woman likes to be touched, fucked, and made to come, is as specific to her as her fingerprints. I have to take what I know and learn how you specifically like it, and vice versa. No guy likes his dick sucked or stroked the same as another. It's not like it's going to make me mad, no matter how often we have sex. I think it's hot watching you, but you know that. I mean I would prefer it if you're thinking about me while you do it, but it's a part of life. Everyone pretty much does it. You're human. Sexual desires are a part of humanity."

"It makes me feel dirty."

"Why?"

I'm scared to tell him. What if he thinks I'm a freak or something? What if he thinks I have some weird addiction? I remember Mom making a comment about that once too. If you need to touch yourself because you want sex more than you're getting it she said it shows an addiction problem, and addictions keep us from living a whole life.

"Kambry, talk to me."

"Because my mom caught me once. Freshman year. Ever since then she has made comments as often as she can that it's a sin and I shouldn't want to do things like that to myself. She said only unclean people have those desires, but occasionally something turns me on and it doesn't just go away unless I touch myself. It consumes me."

He stares at me, running his hand through his dirty-blonde hair. At least I can see his face this way. This would be a lot harder if I couldn't. His face softens. "You have those parents?"

"What do you mean?"

"Instead of explaining to you what your body was going through they made you think it was wrong."

"I guess. They're very conservative. I'm basically an orphan until I go home and beg for them to take me back. They have this mentality that a girl shouldn't move out of her parents' house until she gets married."

"I don't care. Even I have conservative parents. They aren't okay with what I do. They don't brag to their friends that I'm in porn. My dad certainly didn't buy me condoms as a young colt and tell me to chase tail, but he explained the best decision morally and the most appropriate behavior if I was out of their supervision and things happened, because that's what kids do. They do the opposite of what their parents tell them to do. They're hardheaded. They think they're ten-foot-tall and bulletproof. They think about sex in the most immature form. Still, there is a fine line between teaching right from wrong and brainwashing. That's brainwashing, Kambry. There is an entire part of Psychology devoted to sexual curiosity and behavior in kids: multiple theories and Psychologists that formed them. It doesn't make you dirty because you become curious over parts of your body and how they work, it makes you human."

"Yeah, but we're having sex now. Shouldn't I just be happy with what I get?"

His hand slides down his face. "That is so fucked up," he mumbles. My heart falls into the pit of my stomach, unsure of what that means. "Holy shit . . .total opposite from her."

That comment came out so low I could barely make out the words. I wish I really knew who her is. "Baby, listen to me."

My heart flutters back to the place it belongs. I love the way that sounds. What makes it better is the way his eyes line a little when he says it. He's being sincere. "I'm listening," I whisper, still in the exact same position I've been in since I got in bed.

He pauses and adjusts a pillow, before mirroring my position on his side, but his hands become free. One goes beneath him to prop up his head. "There are benefits. Let's say we were a couple without the cameras. When I was in college it was for business, marketing to be exact, but I was minoring in film. I had this absurd dream that I was going to be a talent agent, but even if it didn't work out I knew I could still find a job. With jobs like that there is always a possibility of travel, right?"

"I guess so. I've never really had to think about it."

"Okay, so let's pretend we live together just like we will be starting tomorrow. I find you insanely hot, you rev up my engine with one sultry look, and our sex is explosive. We have sex a minimum of four times a week because we haven't been living together all that long, since I'm fresh into my career. I have to go out of town for work on an extended stay. Role-play with me. Are you with me?"

"Yeah."

He starts to smile but then erases it, continuing. "I've been gone for two weeks at this point. I was supposed to be home the week before, but got held up in negotiations—the more clients the more income. You miss me, and you're getting lonely because I haven't had a whole lot of talk time over the past few days. The last time we talked on the phone I kind of blew you off when you were telling me something exciting about your day because I had an important call come through that I couldn't miss. I'm already ready to come home to you, so interruptions have me on edge. We can't seem to get more than a few minutes at a time. When we hang up, Meredith calls. She got the call she was waiting for and she wants to celebrate, so while I'm gone the two of you go out for a few drinks, do your girl thing, so you're not sitting around the house. Are you picturing it?"

"Oddly, yes."

"So while you're sitting in the bar catching up, completely innocent, I'm also sitting in a bar across the country with one of my clients, just like the night we met. You trust me and I trust you, yeah?"

"I would hope so."

"A hot guy walks up to you, offers to buy you a drink, starts small talk, and has the personality to never quit. He flirts with you and gives you attention when I can't. There's no ring on your finger and he wants to fuck you. It's clear when he asks what you're doing later. What do you do?"

"I would tell him I'm not interested and that I'm seeing someone. Isn't that what everyone in a serious relationship would do? I mean if we live together it's pretty serious I would think."

He stares at me for a moment, as if he's truly thinking back on something. "God, I love that about you, but no, beautiful, not everyone would say that. Keep picturing it. He's a guy that doesn't like to hear no. Meredith slipped off to the restroom, leaving the two of you there, amongst the mass of the crowd. He gets closer to you, starts to brush and caress you, and even whispers things you want to hear into your ear. For a moment I don't exist. Out of sight out of mind."

"I don't really like where this is going. I would nev—"

"Stay with me, beautiful. You're human. You start to get turned on from the contact, and the frustration with me being gone already has your mind in a haze. Not to mention you've been drinking. No one likes being sexually frustrated. It clouds your judgment. You have two options. One, you take him up on his offer to leave with the thought that I'll never know, or two, you call it a night, go home, and masturbate to thoughts of me filling you until I can. Which do you choose?"

The look on his face with the final question has my veins on fire. I'm not even sure he's aware of the way he looks right now, but it has become the blurb to the story that is currently untold. More times than not our subconscious has ways of revealing itself. He looks terrified of my answer. Internally he hates that he spoke the question aloud.

Generally speaking, I'm a pretty ditzy person. Sure, I'm smart when it comes to school and things, but my lack of experience keeps me in the dark. Having blonde hair doesn't help my case either. Stereotypes will never die, but in this exact moment, I'd be willing to bet my life that he's been cheated on. It's just a feeling I have in my gut. It breaks my heart in two and it makes me angry. That's something I've never understood: cheating. We've always been taught that grass isn't always greener on the other side of the fence, in the other pasture, whatever. Why cheat on someone?

I'm not sure I could lie next to someone knowing I betrayed him that way. I don't think I could look into his eyes knowing I gave something that's his to another man. Trust is something that can't be fixed once it's broken, because the paranoia that the act that broke it in the first place is being repeated, would lie forever in the back of the mind. I do know that I couldn't whisper the words I love you knowing that it was a lie, because if you love someone, really and truly love them, if you give them your heart, or even if you promise them exclusive rights, then you shouldn't want to break the terms of the contract until both of you agree that it's void.

When I don't know the right thing to say I ask questions to understand, but I don't think now is the time to bring it up though. I'm not one that is great with wordy expressions, so I'll just say the first thing that comes to mind. "You really want the honest answer?"

"Yes. Without honesty you have nothing."

"There is nothing dirtier than a lying heart. I'll deal with the shame of knowing I need to get off without you there before I'll let another man have something that isn't even mine to give away."

He blinks slowly, cautiously choosing his words. "If you want it you want it,

Kambry. It's nothing to be ashamed of, but if you do want it, I'd rather you get yourself off than get it from somewhere else . . .any fucking day of the week."

"I'd leave you before I'd cheat on you," I say honestly.

"Good, because cheating is my only hard limit. I have no shame. You want something I'll give it to you; I don't care how dirty or raunchy it is. I'll fuck you anywhere, place, or time, but I won't share you. I'm not ready to divulge further into whys, but when I say it's a hard limit, I mean I don't care what the stipulations are for the act, I'll walk away. It doesn't matter what girl propositions me, I'll never step out on you if we're together. There are two reasons I haven't attempted a relationship in four years: only two. One is because I know that I have to fuck other women for a living, and that's something I can't do with someone laying in my bed at home. The second we'll get to later."

My heart is pounding in my chest; so hard that I'm having a problem catching my breath. The more I talk to him and hang out with him, the more I like him. Before I met him I felt off balance. I was stumbling along, clueless as to where I was going or how, and terrified of the fact that I felt so lost, but even with knowing that at some point this will end and he will have to go back to the guy he was before this all started, it still gives me hope that the ending will be better than the beginning, and the middle will be juicy enough to ride on the hangover for a long time to come.

"I have a confession," I say with my serious face rapidly changing as the feelings on the inside are trying to expel.

"What's that, beautiful? I'm interested."

"That scenario. If it were real life, I think I'd rather go home, take a cold shower, and tell my body to fuck off, because you touching me, talking dirty to me, and looking at me, are so much better in real life than in my head."

"Fuck that made me hard."

My cheeks flush. Boldness spreads through my mind that I've never had. "Can I see?"

He smiles. "You want to see my dick? You want to see what happens when you say things like that?"

I nod, unable to speak. Inside, I'm a nervous wreck, even post sex. I mean, I've seen it, but it wasn't really premeditated. It was more so in the moment and that makes a huge difference.

He shifts onto his back and his fingers dip beneath the band of his briefs. He lifts, before pushing them down his body until he's dangling them from his finger, showing me he's now naked. "So, since you had a confession, do you want to hear one of mine?" he asks as he rolls back onto his side. I can't see past his belly button yet, and the anticipation is killing me.

As if someone thumped me in the ear I stop staring at his torso. "Yes."

"When you stare at me like that, all innocent and turned on, I get so hard I hurt, like fucking blue balls without even getting my dick wet first to make it worth the pain." My mouth parts. "And then that is the frosting. When your lips are in that exact position, open and full, all I can fucking think about are them wrapped around my dick. It's maddening."

That wetness between my legs has returned with vengeance, as he suddenly switches the camera of the phone to the back one, no longer showing his face or upper half. The angle is directed at the lower half of his body, stopping on the white sheet that rests at his hips. He pushes it down at a snail's pace, making me more nervous, until he's completely bare for me. Immediately he grabs his shaft in his hand and begins to stroke himself. He's hard and thick, the veins visible from the close up angle and the light.

My legs clamp together beneath the covers as I watch him. His length makes the travel from base to tip longer. I know I don't have much experience with dicks, but I'm just going to guess that his is a five-star rating. It's straight, thick, long, and smooth. It's appetizing. My mouth begins to salivate, surprising me, considering I've always been a little freaked out over the thought of oral sex. "See how hard you make me, Kambry? Does it turn you on? Does it make you wet to watch me stroke my cock while I think about you?"

His voice is deeper when he talks like that, but it's so damn hot. He switches cameras again, and then adjusts the angle to an aerial view so that I can see his face while he strokes himself. "Yes," I say, petrified of how to respond. I'm not sure what to do or say.

"Then meet me in the middle, beautiful. Strip. We'll do it together. You watch me and I'll watch you."

Just like that, all of the tension leaves my body. The shame goes away. The guilt dissipates. The only thing left is desire. I want him. I want this. Together I can do.

"Okay," I whisper, and sit up with my phone in hand. I stand on my knees and turn toward my pillow, angling the phone at a tilt against my pillow so he can see me. The look on his face as he strokes himself makes me feel sexy; giving me a boost of confidence I've never felt. His entire stomach becomes defined, as if he's flexing his abs.

I grab the bottom of my tank and slowly pull it up my body, removing it. Not wearing a bra saves a step. "Fuck I love your tits. Touch them for me."

My hormones are raging. I do as told, grabbing one in each hand, and pressing them together. "Like this?"

"Fuck yeah. One of these days I'm going to fuck those tits. Rub your nipples."

My thumbs begin brushing back and forth, making them completely erect. The muscles between my legs start to clench as I can feel the wetness soaking into the fabric of my panties. His hand strokes pick up in pace. "You need to be touched, beautiful?" I nod, unsure how he can tell. "Take your bottoms off. Watch me and I'll touch you while you stroke my cock."

My hands slide down my stomach until my thumbs hook onto my shorts. I take a deep breath, and then push them down to my thighs. "Sit for me. I want to see your pussy." Shifting to my butt, I finish removing my shorts. "Yeah, just like that. Spread your legs."

I feel so open, so bare. "Should I turn the light off?"

"No. I want to see you; all of you."

I fight the urge to cover myself, and spread my legs, my knees slightly bent to allow my feet to rest flat on the mattress. "Damn, I can see how wet you are. I want to feel it. Hold on."

He sits up and drops the phone, only the ceiling in view. I hear a drawer open and then shut, before the camera starts to move again, bringing him back into view. He turns over, standing on his knees like I just was, freeing up both of his hands. His dick is fully erect, staring at me, and all I can imagine is how it feels when he slides it inside of me. With me in this position and him on his knees, it makes it easier to picture in my head, as if it were completely real and cyberspace didn't separate us. He's standing between my legs.

He flips a cap open on a small container. "What's that?"

"Warming lube. Your pussy feels better, but it'll get me closer to you than lotion." He squeezes a decent sized amount into the palm of his hand, before tossing the bottle and wrapping it around his dick again. He begins stroking himself again; spreading it all over him, and making it look wet. His eyes travel down my body heatedly, stopping between my legs. That much is clear. "Fuck, I want in. Your pussy is beautiful. Slide your fingers inside. I rest one hand on the mattress behind me, reclining me slightly to hold my weight, and place my hand over the smooth surface, easing my fingertips toward my entrance.

As I hover over it, I can feel the wetness coating my fingertips. I circle the tips, before sliding my middle and ring fingers inside. "You feel me, baby?"

I look down at his hand and I get jealous. I want to be his hand, so I imagine that I am, as I begin to thrust my fingers in and out of me. My eyes move to his as I moan out, completely soaked from imagining my fingers being his dick. "If I were there right now, I'd suck on your tits while I drive my cock into your pussy. Would you like that?"

"Yes," I say in more of a pant than actual words, the thrusts of my fingers speeding up. "I love having you inside of me."

"Fuck, I'm not going to last long, baby. Your beautiful pussy is making it hard to control. Rub your clit. I want to watch you come. Make me come, sexy."

His motivation is making me bolder. I spread wider, before rocking my hand up until my fingers slide out, trailing up my slit to my clit. When my wet fingers press against it my head falls back, unable to focus on anything but the feeling of every nerve sparking against my skin. My movements are swift, accurate, and full of cause. Orgasm is the destination. A whimper escapes. "That's it, baby. Are you going to come for me?"

"Yeah," I whine, completely lost mentally. I can feel the orgasm building in my bottom. My feet lift off the bed, my knees pulling back toward me. "I'm about to."

"I want to come in your pussy so bad. I want to know you can still feel me even after I'm done."

I moan out, completely high right now with him talking filthy. I never knew I would like that sort of thing, but dammit it's pushing me over the edge.

"Look at me, baby. Let me come with you."

I do as he says, trying to hold my focus on him. "I can't hold off any—" I squeal softly as my orgasm begins, surging through my body. My legs fall open and my back arches as everything quickly spins in slow motion. "Sax," I whisper, unable to finish a whole thought as the pleasure mutes me.

When the high starts to fall I watch as his last stroke ends at the head of his dick, and I can see the slightest pulsing through his shaft, or maybe it was just him barely thrusting into his hand that I saw. I can't be sure. "Fuck, I can't get enough," he says through a constricted voice as his hand grips the tip of his dick. His breathing becomes labored as he stares at me heatedly. My fingers leave my body and mirror my other hand, before I fall back to rest on my forearms. "I wish I could keep that image forever."

Me too . . .

I bite my bottom lip, my eyes lazy. He's still holding onto his dick. "Did you come?"

He releases it slowly and turns his palm to me, opening his fist. The white, sticky substance coats his hand. He smirks. "It's time to go get rid of the boys and girls. How was it? You still good?"

The fact that he cares makes my heart flutter. "Yeah, I'm still good. Can we do that again sometime?"

"You bet, beautiful. You want it I'm your man, whether cyberspace or not. Worst case scenario I'm a phone call away, but starting tomorrow I'm breaking you in." He winks. "You will never be the same."

Nervousness washes through my belly, followed by excitement. "I'm hoping for that."

"What are you about to do?"

I sit up and grab my phone before I stand to get a closer view. He grabs his at the same time, before movement starts to occur, and then water running sounds. He's not looking at me, but he's looking down at something. "Probably lay in bed. I have a big day tomorrow. I may read a little or something. I don't know. What are you doing?"

"Dropping off the kiddos for a swim." I laugh out loud accidentally. I love his personality. You wouldn't find a better mix if you were able to pick out the perfect guy from a list of qualities. "Nah, I guess I'm going to take a quick shower and probably watch a little TV before crashing.

"Okay, handsome. I guess I'll see you tomorrow?"

The water shuts off. "Your beautiful ass better be there early or on time. I have connections around this city and I'm not ashamed to use them for kidnapping."

"I'll be there," I whisper. "There are no other options at this point."

That's the truth. Even if I wanted to back out of this, I don't think I could. Him being in my day has become a part of my life that I desperately need. I've noticed lately that when he's near, in any form, I just want time to stand still. I never want it to end. "Okay, baby, well I guess I'm going to shower and get some sleep. Message me before you fall asleep?"

"If you want me to."

"I do."

My heart starts to race. "Okay. Goodnight."

"Goodnight, sexy."

I press the end button before the awkward lingering has a chance to occur. I toss my phone on my bed, at a loss for actual words. My hand moves over my heart as my breathing becomes uneven. My heart feels like it's suffering from the effects of too much caffeine. Even the most inexperienced person would know what's happening. With him, I forget everything else. I hope I'm wrong. If I'm not, I know I'm going to get hurt, because I'm almost positive that my heart is trying its damnedest to fall in love with him.

I need sleep, and I need to forget that thought, because it's crazy enough to send me into an asylum . . .

CHAPTER NINETEEN

Saxton

As I walk into the house my phone starts to vibrate. Closing the door with my foot, I set down my large rolling suitcase as I fish it out of my pocket. I glance at the front of the screen: Michael. Upon the third ring I swipe right and hold it up to my ear. "What's up?"

"You in?"

"Not yet, but I plan to be soon."

"Funny. Save your porn star humor for when you're on camera."

I laugh aloud. "If you knew then why'd you ask?"

"Glutton for punishment, I guess. Never hurts to have a side of smartass with your coffee. Here's the deal. We decided we want to slice material from the arrival to add for the trailer to begin marketing to the public. You're experienced, and this isn't like the other projects you've done. This is reality television. Tone the porn shit down until she's comfortable. We get that this isn't typical porn and we are marketing her innocence. I like the idea of escalating heat levels, like *normal* couples, so let's use her lack of experience to our advantage. Break her in slowly. It's fine if it takes a day or so to become as close as the two of you have been. We can always cut later, but we can't add."

He clears his throat, as if remembering our little show at the studio. "Don't tell her we're filming, be charming, and save the raunchy shit for later on. I think I got it. Anything else?"

"I think that about covers it. Your charm is what landed you here. The average female in a relationship is against her partner watching porn. We are trying to change that. Let things happen at a natural pace. This is why we are doing a trial period before we commit to anything long-term."

"Got it, boss."

"Did funds deposit?"

"Yeah. I checked it this morning."

"Good."

"I guess I should be going if there is nothing else. She should be here soon."

"Alright. If you need anything at all give me a call. Got it?"

"Yep."

I'm about to hang up the phone when his voice comes through the speaker. "Oh, Saxton."

"Yeah."

"I'm going off the record here, because this would not be wise for my career, so this is coming from your friend."

"I'm listening."

"If you want out, this could be your shot."

"Who said I wanted out?"

"Don't offend me. I'm the one that brought you into this remember? I wouldn't get paid what I do if I wasn't damn good at my job. I know talent when I see it. It's why I picked you out of a bar and brought you into this with no experience, but along the way I've also become your friend. I know you're tired of porn. Everyone knows this job has a shelf life. Even if the viewer wanted older couples, the average porn star is just over it at some point and ready to move on. This could be your bridge to better things. She could be your reason to cross it. Don't blow it."

Without saying anything more, he disconnects the call. The fuck? Where the hell did all that come from? His ego is getting too big. I can't quit. What the hell else would I do? This is just my vacation; my break from kinky fuckery between the thighs of girls that could give head and provide anal sex in their sleep.

A car door shuts, drawing me out of my thoughts. A smile inches across my face. I walk a few steps over to one of the columns providing support in the middle of the large, open floor plan, separating the living area from the kitchen and dining room. Turning around I lean against it and cross one leg over the other, digging the toe of my front foot into the hardwood floor as I cross my arms in front of my chest. Shit, I almost forgot.

Reaching into my back pocket, I grab my baby blue ball cap and slide it on my head, before resuming my position. There is something about the way she looks at me when I'm wearing a baseball cap that wakes the sleeping beast, making him want to come out and play.

The doorknob begins to turn and then the door opens slowly. "Hello? Is anyone in here?"

Her voice is slightly irregular, confirming she's nervous. I've yet to see her. "Kambry, would you go already?" The whisper yell behind her could only be Meredith. I fight to hold in my laugh, trying to keep my element of surprise. "This shit is getting heavy!"

"Shut up! How am I supposed to know this is the right house? It's huge!"

"Oh, you know, the address wouldn't be a big fat clue or anything. If you don't walk through that door, bitch, I'm going to find a belt and lick you a few times with it. Saxton will thank me when your ass is pink and swollen."

"You're such a freak."

"Yet I'm the only freak you want as a bestie. Now move."

"Fine! You're so bossy."

I feel a gray hair coming through. I have forgotten how ridiculously slow girls are. One thing I'll confess that I haven't missed in the least. At least when I'm ready to go somewhere I know I'll be on time. She walks through the door with a rolling suitcase and all thought ceases. "Don't you fucking get hard right now," I mumble to my cock in hopes that it's actually listening for once.

My eyes skim down her floral, button-down dress that stops just below her ass, color pops of pink, purple, turquoise, and lime catching the eye. The top three buttons are undone, introducing the full, round globes that are her fucking beautiful tits.

Thank God it's hot most of the year here.

Her skin isn't dark, but it isn't pale either, giving her the perfect sun kissed color. There's no possible way it's completely natural, but it makes the colors in her dress stand out, especially against the blonde of her hair.

Those legs . . .fuck, her legs. She's wearing wedges, a shoe that was created by the sex gods as praise for a man's good deeds, because to most men, they probably appeal more than heels. It's a more innocent sex appeal, but damn if it isn't still sexy. They show off the contours of her legs, allowing the muscles and tendons to flex just slightly from the position of her feet. Fuck, even her toenails are painted the same color pink that's in her dress. I like a woman that takes care of her feet.

"Score," Meredith says. "We have a boner. My job is done."

I suddenly come out of my little comatose, realizing that I'm staring at her body like a fucking stalker, and of course the dick decides once again to do whatever the fuck it wants. It never works on command. *Not the element of surprise I was going for, buddy.*

My eyes lock with Kambry's. She's biting the corner of her bottom lip perfectly, creating a disturbance in the fullness. Her cheeks have small circles of pink. She combs her fingers through the top of her hair, tousling it nervously, the large curls bouncing as they move to a new resting place. Fucking damn. Memories of last night and her naked body expressing pleasure rolls through my mind at the absolute worst time.

"Okay porn boy, put that thing away. You have plenty of time to contaminate her goodness later, but right now I want a tour. Here. Happy housewarming," she says in a witty tone as she shoves a basket full of shit at my chest.

"What's this?"

"Love shack supplies. Don't say I never did anything for you. You'll thank me later. You're welcome in advance. Explore together . . .when I'm *gone*. Kay? Thanks."

I shake my head as I grab it from her, before walking it over to the bar and setting it on top. How those two became friends I have no idea. It's like oil and vinegar. The two don't mix, yet you find them together often.

I shove my dick down, hoping it will go back into hiding. I should cut him off for that shit, and see how he responds when he isn't getting any. I walk toward Kambry and take the suitcase handle from her, pulling it into the house next to mine, before shutting the door. "No turning back now."

She smiles and shakes her head, her eyes twinkling, telling me that she's in a good mood. She's yet to speak, which is a little odd. Meredith is already walking up the stairs by the sound of the clomping against the wood. "Are you guys coming? I really don't want to have to give myself a tour!" she yells.

"Be right there," I respond, taking a step closer to Kambry. Leaning in, my lips brush along the lobe of her ear. Her neck muscles tense, bringing her shoulders up. "By the way," I whisper. "You look fucking phenomenal. Congratulations, you've successfully rendered me speechless for the first and only time in my life."

She sucks in air, mixed with a light sound of pleasure upon inhale. I walk forward, causing her to step back until she becomes flush with the door. One palm connects with the wood, while the other runs down her hip and around to the back of her thigh. "Thank you," she says breathless, just before my hand becomes mobile without my command, trailing up the back of her dress.

I grip her bare ass. "Fuck, Kambry, you're wearing a thong too." I press my hips into her, allowing her to feel me against her. "You have no idea how bad I want to fuck you against this door. Get rid of her soon or I will anyway, and then she can watch while I eat your pussy until you come on my tongue, because once I start, this door is blocked from entry or exit. If you think I'm bluffing, call me on it. No. Shame. Baby."

My hand inches down her ass and slips between her legs, before two fingers slide beneath her panties and thrust inside of her, hard, causing her to moan out loud, before she slaps her hand over her mouth. It's fairly easy since her legs are already shoulder width apart. I pull out and shove them back inside, harder than before, sending her body into a slight jump upward. Her pussy clenches around my finger. "That feels so good," she says muffled against her hand.

"Yeah?"

She nods.

I continue, never letting up, before moving my hand from the door to her front, between us. I grab the bottom of her dress and tow it upward, just enough to grab the front of her panties, where my hand disappears inside of them. When my fingers back out of her to the tips, I change hands, shoving the dry ones deep into her pussy, while the wet ones trail along the seam of her ass, underneath the string of her panties. "What are you doing?"

"Mapping out my territory."

My left thumb presses against her clit and starts to circle, as my right middle finger presses between her ass cheeks, finding her puckered hole. When it touches against it, she tenses; looking slightly confused, and her knees buckle, causing me to press into her deeper. My eyes never leave hers as I find a steady rhythm with both hands, one rubbing her clit and the other her asshole.

I clench my fingers inside of her toward my thumb, creating a claw. She moans so deep my balls tighten. Her hand turns sideways until she begins to bite the edge, trying to mute herself. Catching me off guard, she grabs my dick through my jeans and grips it hard. Her legs start to clamp around my hand at the same time her pussy begins squeezing my fingers. Her eyes start to close and her head falls back. "I fucking love to watch you come."

"Hornballs! Damn, can't y'all do that later?"

Her eyes widen and her body straightens at the sound of Meredith's voice in the distance, but she's not far. I slide my fingers out of her pussy when she stops squeezing around my fingers, just after my other hand leaves her ass, her dress falling back into place. I spread the fingers between us that were just recently nestled in her pussy, showing her the result of her orgasm. "You should go wash your hands."

I place them in my mouth, and then close my lips around them, before sucking them clean. Her mouth falls open as she watches. "I don't waste anything that tastes that good. Go pick out your room. I'll bring the bags up."

"Two rooms?"

"For now." I smirk. "But I can't promise for long."

She passes me and walks away, adding pep in her step when I slap her ass. "Keep biting that lip and you're going to get it."

I watch her sway toward the stairs as I make my way toward the sink to wash my hands. I'm one lucky bastard. I don't even feel guilty.

Sex Sessions: Uncut . . . So it begins.

Kambry

I shut the door after saying goodbye to Meredith. I kind of have mixed emotions about not being with her for so long. She's been my lifeline all summer, and now we have to part for a month at least. The thought of being with Saxton on a near constant basis, though, is enough for me to suck it up and stop my internal whining. I just hope nothing changes between us and I end up stuck here in an awkward situation.

We took a tour together while Saxton hung back, giving us our space. The house is huge, filled with more stuff than I could ever imagine someone stuffing in a house. It's a little intimidating to be honest, at least for it to only be two people living here. Maybe it's just that I'm from such a small town. I don't know. I'm still getting used to California, even almost three months later.

The plan is for her to come to the club as much as possible. I'm supposed to be moved back downstairs to the main club so that it's more normal scale, but that's fine by me, because I like it down there better anyway. The only good thing I got out of the celebrity realm was him.

I place my palms on the heavy wooden door and stare out the window as she drives away, waving until all I see are the fading taillights. I never thought I'd say this, but I miss her already. She may be a loon, but she's my loon, my best friend. I'll never admit that, though, because that ego of hers cannot stand to get any bigger.

"You're not going to get all sappy on me are you?"

I jump at the feel of his breath as it tickles my skin, just below my ear. His palm comes to rest on my belly, pulling me against him. "You have got to stop doing crap like that."

"Doing what?" he asks with laughter in his voice.

"Sneaking up on me. Showing up when I'm not looking for you. It's kind of freaky that I rarely hear you walking." I turn around in his arms, leaning against the door . . .again. Maybe we need to stay away from this door.

He's smiling. "We're not going to reach a crucial moment in this relationship and then you drop a bomb on me that you're really dead and I'm the only one that can see or talk to you and the rest is just a figment of my imagination, are you?"

His hands grab ahold of my buttons and he starts to unbutton them, beginning with the top. "Why? Would it change things?"

My eyes widen. I begin blinking rapidly. Then he laughs, causing me to shove at his chest. "You're such an asshole."

"That face, though, was priceless. I didn't take you for a girl that believes in ghosts."

"That's so mean, Sax. I don't, but that doesn't mean freaky things don't happen." He growls, already at belly level unbuttoning my dress. "What's wrong?"

"Say it again."

"I'm sorry?"

"Call me that again."

I'm so confused. "Sax?"

"That."

"It just came out. I didn't mean to upset you."

"Say it again."

"Sax," I say nervously, treading on thin ice. The last button slips through the slit and the two pieces of fabric separate, revealing my matching, hot pink, lacy underwear set.

He grips my thighs and pulls me up his body, my legs instantly wrapping around his waist. "No one's ever called me that before. I like it."

"Oh," I say, my breath hitching as he roughly slams my back into the door. I can feel the wetness between my legs already. I have no idea what is happening, but I like that he pretends that I do. I like that he doesn't treat me like a doll or that girl that only gets bed sex in missionary position. I like exploring different things, places, and times.

His hand runs up my body and cups my bra-covered breast. "Is this where you want it?" I ask, tilting my head to the side to give him access to my neck. His lips are in close range anyways.

As if that was the biggest turn off, he slowly inches me back down to the ground, setting me to my feet, my dress still wide open. I'm now more confused than ever. "No, it's not."

"Did I say something wrong?"

The heat in his stare burns me inside. I'm so nervous, unsure of what just happened. I wish I knew, so I wouldn't do that again. I definitely don't like the hot and cold flush with hormones. It kind of sucks. "No, beautiful, you said everything right, but we just got here. Fuck, I shouldn't even want you as much as I do. It's not like I've been lacking in the sex department."

My insides wilt from the anger in his tone during the last two sentences. My face fell I'm sure. I'm not the greatest person at masking the way I feel. "I kind of like that you do," I whisper, depleted. "I'm sorry."

He grabs my face with quickness and looks down at me from the difference in height even with my wedges, pressing his lips on mine, his trapezius muscles heightening from the stance he takes; those perfect little muscles that rise next to the neck when flexed. He's tense. "No, Kambry, fuck, that's not what I meant. I don't know how to do this. You're so different. Grab my dick." I'm starting to get whiplash. He can tell. "Just do it."

I do as he says, grabbing ahold of it. Even covered with his jeans it isn't hard to find. It makes a statement in size, and there isn't an ounce of softness present. It's weighted from the blood flow. "Do you remember what I said? This isn't my norm. I didn't just randomly get hard at the sight of a woman before you; at least not since my first couple of films when it was just hormones raging and the knowledge was fresh that what I was doing was morally forbidden. For the past couple of years, at minimum, I know I've had to demand it with drugs prescribed by a doctor for the same problem older men all over the world experience. Erectile Dysfunction isn't supposed to happen in a fucking twenty-three-year-old. It's embarrassing, but I dealt with it, and I still did until recently, because my dick paid the bills, but every time I'm near you I'm reminded that you're different. With you this happens naturally, and without thinking I act on it. Sometimes I just have to remind myself a little late that you're more than a porn star, Kambry. You're someone that deserves the shit that goes with sex; the other and most important part of a relationship."

I feel like I'm going to have a damn heart attack. If he does that look I'm gone. His eyes narrow as he pushes himself an inch closer. I'm gone. "I simply meant that we just arrived. It's early afternoon. I haven't seen you in a week. My dick can wait. Spending time with you can't. You got me?"

I nod, avoiding speech like an unwanted airborne disease. If any words came out of my mouth, I'd probably sound like a love-struck teenager; one of those girls that screams I love you after a first kiss. I won't be a stage five clinger, as Meredith calls it, but I fear with everything that I am I've already attempted to keep my heart to myself and failed, because that single look has it racing out of rhythm, my mind in a haze, and my body being pulled toward him like gravity. Somehow, some way, I have to lock down this tidal wave of feelings inside of me, before it takes out everything.

"Yes," I respond, and without hesitation he softly kisses me. For a moment I literally feel oxygen deprived. Our tongues reunite in a union as if no amount of time has passed since their last encounter. Everything inside me shifts and pulls as if it's being forced from my body. My insides begin to hurt, but not a hurt of pain. Instead, it's a hurt from the thought of everything returning to its previous state when released.

His lips part from mine, and my lungs expand, as if I can finally breathe. I mentally count to three before I speak, trying to calm myself. "What do you want to do?"

He looks down at my body. "What I started a minute ago."

"Oh my gosh. You're so confusing. What now?"

"Swimming," he says with a crooked grin.

My brows dip. "Swimming?"

"I'm going to personally introduce you to that awesome pool. That's why I started undressing you."

I look down at myself. "Oh. I see."

He pushes my dress over my shoulders until it falls to the floor. "We're going to relax. When it's nightfall, I'm hiding you behind the waterfall, on many occasions I'm sure. Naughty things will happen back there."

My cheeks feel hot. "I'll go look for a swim suit."

"You could wear that."

"Uh, too early in the day for a full moon. I'll get a suit."

"Fine, hurry up. I'll be waiting outside."

He starts walking away, and I finally find my words. "Wait, aren't you going to change?"

"Where we are, beautiful, clothing is optional. Don't keep me waiting."

"Oh, dear lord, help my soul," I mumble as the French doors shut, leaving me alone in this house. "I'm not ready for this."

Saxton

I walk outside, shaking my head at myself. "Well boys, I hope you're ready to get breezy, because I didn't leave the two of you much of an option," I mumble to myself as I grab the back collar of my shirt and pull it over my head, the rest of the fabric following.

I look around, the privacy fence and the large palms blocking the outdoors area from onlookers. The sun is beaming down in my eyes, causing me to squint. Why the hell did I take that cap off? My hands go for the button on my jeans, popping it through the slit as I pull off my shoes with my feet. My eyes are starting to piss me off. I need that hat. Better yet, where are my shades?

I release my pants as the zipper reaches the bottom, leaving the two sides hanging opposite ends of each other, then jog inside, and take the stairs two at a time to find my suitcase. As I pass Kambry's room, I notice a jiggle in passing, stopping me mid step. I barge in the room, not caring enough to announce my entry. My mouth falls open when my eyes feast on her cleavage as she adjusts her breasts in her bikini top the color of sea foam green. I only notice the color because it does something amazing to her skin. "Are you okay? There's no way it's been more than ten minutes."

"How the hell did you get a big rack with such a small waist and long, skinny legs? You kind of defy genetics. Most girls with tits that big, perky, and full are curvier or went and bought them like a pair of jeans. On the other hand, most girls as small as you with natural tits are carting around small anthills. Nothing wrong with it; just how it is. Men love tits in all shapes and sizes. I've seen a lot of tits, and yours still baffle me."

"Because that wasn't random as hell."

"I saw tits, I stopped, then stared at said tits, and now I've had time to think. Call me a tit man, but your rack drew me instantly, and when I found out they were real, well, let's just say it's equivalent to giving a little boy his first puppy. There's lots of internal excitement; some leaks through in embarrassing ways, and then comes the foolish behavior followed by a massive smile before he's ready to hold the prize."

"You like these, huh?" I growl. She has the underside of each one sitting perfectly in her cupped hands, bouncing them up and down in a juggling motion. Her bikini top covers each nipple and the lower half, but the motion alone has my imagination running wild.

"You're about to be missing a swimsuit top if you keep that up. What part of, *I'm a tit man*, did you not understand?"

She rolls her eyes, releasing them, and then slides her hands beneath the string of her panties and pushes them down her legs, never taking her eyes off of me as she reveals that beautiful, smooth, pelvic area. I work hard to keep my eyes on hers, only peeking from my peripheral vision.

She steps out of her thong, a smile on her face, as she grabs the bottoms and holds them open to step in. "I guess it's a good thing they're yours then. Play away, and to answer your question, I guess genetics knew I could be entrusted with a set of D cups, since I obviously didn't get to reap the benefits of having such an awesome squeezable man-toy."

She works the bottoms up her legs and adjusts them as the sides hit her hips. "I'd be lying if I said that sucked. I kind of like being in a no man's land."

She walks toward me, stopping when she's just a few inches away. Her expression is blank, but then her arms come up and she grabs the opposite strap with each hand, pulling them down her arms, before flipping the cups to her top down, revealing her fucking full breasts. I swallow, trying to moisten my mouth as I stare at her hard, pink nipples; each area balanced in size ratio. "Then touch me," she says. "I like when you show me how you feel."

"We should go downstairs. Maybe there's some beer in the fridge, or something." What the fuck am I saying? I have tits staring at me.

She grabs the front of my briefs in her hand, pulling them toward her, creating a gap between the band and my skin. She looks down. "Someone says you want to stay."

I clear my throat. "He doesn't always get what he wants. He'll survive."

She closes the distance, wrapping her arms around my waist, and then presses her chest to my ribs. Her hard nipples brush over my skin, creating a sensitized effect. Fucking hell . . .

"Touch them," she whispers, looking into my eyes with this fucking look that has me feeling like I'm standing on the side of a cliff, about to fall. My adrenaline is heightening. My willpower is dwindling. I'm really trying to refrain here, and slowly I've been headed toward failure since she arrived. I should have stayed my ass outside. Nothing good ever came from being in a woman's bedroom.

My hand begins to move, traveling upward until it latches onto her breast, squeezing into the soft skin. She moans when my thumb finds the hard center of her nipple, lightly rubbing over it. Her hand quickly finds my dick, wrapping around it, and then lightly squeezes. "Didn't you say you wanted to fuck my tits?"

I snap. What the hell kind of man turns down an offer like that? Not any with a pair of balls swinging between his legs. I'm trying to be good, but I only have so much self-control, especially when my fingers have already gotten a feel for that warm, wet paradise she holds between her legs. Plus, listening to her speak so filthy is my breaking point, no matter how strong I am. "You want my dick between your tits?"

I lean forward, replacing my thumb with my lips, before sucking her hard center into my mouth, and not gently. Her free hand grabs ahold of my hair and pulls it hard, hurting me as I've hurt her, and accompanying the pain filled moan that escapes her. "Yes," she says, drawing out the S.

Her hand starts to stroke my cock slowly inside my briefs, pulling upward toward my waistband. "Say it," I demand against her nipple, my tongue lightly sweeping over it to wet it.

"I want you to titty-fuck me."

My hands slide down the sides of her body, traveling to her thighs, before lifting her. She instantly releases me from her hand and wraps her legs around my waist. The way she said it makes it obvious that filthy line is probably a first for her, but it makes it sexier for me. "Why? You most likely won't get anything out of it."

"Because I had my orgasm, so it's only fair you get yours. I want to try it."

"A sexy woman that isn't selfish. Where have you been all my life, beautiful?"

"Waiting for you," she says, and then bites her bottom lip as her cheeks redden, proving she didn't mean to say it aloud. It was a verbal slip. My heart stops in my chest, swelling as I look into her big, blue eyes, and then I grab the back of her head with one hand and pull her lips to mine, dismissing it altogether, before walking out the door, toward my room.

Our lips meld together, making it hard to tell where mine ends and hers begin. I can't get enough of her flavor, driving me to take more of her every time her tongue backs away. She sucks on my top lip, before changing directions. I kick the bottom of my door to push it open all the way from the crack it's in, barging into my room, and then roughly toppling us both on the bed, but holding my weight off of her.

I continue to kiss her, before finally pulling free. Her lips are slightly red, most likely from my stubble scraping against her smooth skin that I didn't feel like shaving off. I stand, leaving her lying in front of me.

She pushes herself up on her elbows and licks her lips as she watches me: an innocent gesture and not a seductive one. "Remove your top," I command, as I hook my thumbs beneath my brief band.

She fully sits up and reaches behind her back, movement occurring before her top straps fall free. She pulls it over her head and tosses it beside her on the bed, leaving her in only bikini bottoms.

In one swift motion I shuck my jeans and briefs, leaving them in a heap on the floor as I step out of them. Grabbing my cock, I begin to stroke it slowly as I stare down at her beautiful rack. She notices, and in turn grabs one in each hand, before pushing them together to create a tight crease. "Like this?"

"Hell yeah."

Lube. I didn't bring any lube. I sure as hell am not wasting a ton of time to go downstairs and dig through that basket. I look around the room, taking in the warm colors of navy and khaki it's done in—definitely the more masculine of the two. I grab the drawer to the dark colored nightstand next to the bed, opening it. Surprisingly, it's stocked with condoms, lube, a few small toys, and edible sex goods like a syrupy, colored liquid.

Of course he did . . .

I grab the bottle of clear lubricant and shut the drawer back, quickly flipping the cap and dispensing a generous amount into my palm, before grabbing my cock like last night and smearing it with slow, long strokes. I watch her, watching me, making this so much better than over a video call.

"Are you going to come on my face?" she asks, while kneading her breasts in her hands, her bottom lip slipping between her teeth. She's uncomfortable with the question. "No, beautiful, I'm not going to come on your face, unless you ask me to. Not too many women are into that sort of thing. Some even find it demeaning. Trust me to respect you, yeah?"

"Okay," she whispers. "I watched it recently. I was just preparing myself mentally."

I walk forward, still stroking my cock to the sight of her. "You watched porn?"

"Yes," she admits.

"But not mine?"

"No. I can't. It messes with my head."

"Did you like it?" I straddle her lap on the bed, atop the navy comforter, causing her to lie back into a flat position. "Did it turn you on?"

"Yes, but I like this better. Experiencing is better than watching."

I nod, because I agree. I feel like I'm experiencing things that I've done hundreds of times for the first time, because with her it's so much different. "Hands down."

She blinks, and then does as I ask, letting go and placing her hands on the bed. I release my dick and place my wet palm between her breasts, transferring the warming wetness to her chest in a horizontal swiping motion, leaving a glossy shine behind.

"Tits together, baby."

Resuming her previous position—the heels of her hands pressed to the outside of her breasts—she pushes her tits together, creating a tight space. I lean forward on my left fist, grabbing the base of my dick again with the right; just long enough to align the head at the center, below her breasts, at the entry of the crevice she's creating. My knees push down the bed, lowering my body to hers so I'm able to thrust through the makeshift channel, and then I mirror the left fist with my right, giving me control.

She looks up at me; her lips slightly puckered, and her thick, bold lashes lining her beautiful blue eyes. I thrust forward, my dick sliding between her tits; slick and warm from the lubricant and the body heat mixing. They part to make room for me, but she pushes in harder to tighten the gap, giving me that tight squeeze that I need. "Pinch your nipples, baby."

My thrusts become faster as her fingers find her nipples and clamp around them, making the sight before me even better. "I love your fucking body; every last inch of it. I want to kiss those lips so bad right now."

Her lips part, revealing a small opening, as her head slides back in a tilt to get a better angle of my face as I fuck her tits, sliding in and out in a quick and repeated motion.

That familiar tug begins in my balls, confirming it's not going to take me long from already being hyped up since she walked in the door earlier. I can't handle the way she's looking at me right now. "I'm about to, baby."

"Make it yours."

"What?" I ask, short of breath.

"I want you to come on me and not in your hand. Make my body yours . . .for every purpose."

I grit my teeth and slow my thrusts, trying to hold out a few seconds longer.

Shifting my weight onto my right fist, I slide my left hand under her ass and grab the top of her bottoms, pulling them down so fast you can hear a stretch of the fabric from being pulled too hard. She wiggles her legs, working them the rest of the way down when I've extended them at max reach. "Birth control?"

"Yes."

"Pill?"

"No."

"Good."

I yank her body upward so that our waists are level, and drive my cock inside of her. One thrust enveloped in her wet heat and I'm done. I can't hold it back anymore. My fist moves closer to her neck and I kiss her. My left hand grips her ass, pulling her at a tilt against me, as I push myself as deep as I can go and empty my load inside of her. A throaty groan pushes through my lips at the seal between us, my short nails digging into her bare ass.

I didn't realize how good that was going to feel. I may have just fucked myself, because I don't think I can go back to a condom with her after that. You can't miss what you don't know, and now I've experienced pure and utter fucking bliss.

My arm wraps under her and I flip us over, never pulling out of her as I move her on top of me. "What are you doing?"

"I want to look at you."

"You were."

"You on top of me is better. I like seeing your legs sprawled over me. It does things to me I can't explain." My hands travel up her sides to her breasts. "I like looking at these, sitting perfectly, your nipples erect for me, and knowing I just made them mine."

The head of my dick is tingling, the sensitivity making it hard to focus, but I can't bring myself to leave her body just yet. "Was it good for you?"

"Good? Come here."

She leans forward as I attempt to ignore my racing heart. My hands slide to her back, my fingertips gently trailing down her spine as my lips press against the front of her neck. She leans her head back, giving me better access. Her nipples are brushing against my chest. I grab an ass cheek in each hand, squeezing so hard it pulls them apart, my fingertips dipping into her crack.

My lips move along her neck, toward her ear. "There is no word in the English dictionary to properly define what that felt like. You're very quickly becoming a drug to me. I told myself no for today, and look where my cock is nestled anyway, and also not ready to leave."

She starts grinding her pelvis against me, my semi-soft cock hardening once again, ready for round two. "Then don't."

"If you don't stop we won't be leaving this room for a while."

"It feels too good to stop. Just let it happen. It's been a week since the woods." She sits up; placing her palms on my chest, and slows her previous increasing speed. "Ow."

"What's wrong?"

"It hurts to sit straight up; more so than the other times."

"It's because I'm lying flat. My dick is deeper and at a completely straight angle. Lean in if it bothers you, or we could stop and pick this up later. I do want to hang out with you, believe it or not."

She shakes her head, continuing to grind her wet pussy against me. There is no way I'm going to be able to come again this soon. The only way to get us out of this bedroom and doing something else is to make her come. I bring one hand around to her front, placing my palm against her pelvic region, and slip the pad of my thumb between her lips until it's pressing against her clit. Quickly I begin rubbing up and down, exerting a slight pressure, with only the goal of making her come. This isn't practice this is playing the game.

She rocks into me with force, still sitting straight up, but going slow instead of fast. "Oh . . .right there," she breathes out, and then moves her hands behind her to grip onto my thighs, creating a curve in the center of her body, tightening her breasts. "It hurts, but it feels so good. I . . .love . . .your dick. Mmmm."

Her nails dig into my skin, and most likely will result in indentions later. She is arching so hard that her hair is sweeping through the air with each thrust she drives against my hand. The head of my dick is hitting against something hard. I can even hear it. It feels good. My toes curl into my feet a little when I realize just how good it feels.

I continue my pace, watching her facials, and I can already tell she's approaching orgasm. With each moan that escapes her lips, her thrusts drive faster and harder into my hand. "That feels . . .so good," she draws out, and then unexpectedly her hand finds my balls and lightly squeezes as my dick starts to get wetter, her tight pussy squeezing my dick, hard. Her moan gets deeper as her rocking on my dick begins to subside. "I'm coming," she whispers, her eyes barely open.

"Fuck, fuck, fuck. There's no way in hell. Bounce on me, beautiful."

Her eyes open and she scoots her legs in, bringing them flush with my body. She repositions her feet as I move my hands to her hips, and then she starts, slowly at first to find a rhythm, but then she gets faster, her hands gripping my wrists for support.

Her titties are bouncing, her stomach muscles are contracting, and her pussy is so damn tight. "Holy shit, baby, just like that. Fuck." I thrust my hips up to hit deeper as that first spurt occurs. She doesn't stop. Instead, she slows her pace and clenches her pussy muscles as she pumps up. "Fuck yeah. Milk my cock, baby," I grit out, my breathing scattered.

I ease my hips back down, my chest heaving up and down to match hers. Her cheeks are splotched with red circles, her eyes slightly downcast. She's thinking. She's sexy when she's thinking, because she's unaware that she looks any different. I smile, sitting up and combing my fingers into her hair. "What's on your mind?"

I kiss her. As I pull away she bites her lip, her hands rubbing up and down my arms. "I just really like it when you talk dirty to me. I don't know why. I can't explain it. It makes me come alive. You know, like when I'm nervous or self-conscious." She releases a breath. "It relaxes me and gives me an adrenaline boost. I really like it."

"Hmmm . . ."

"What?"

"My good girl is slowly finding her naughty side. At this rate we could be testing kinky fuckery by the month's end." I snap my teeth together playfully close to her lips.

"Shut up," she teases, placing her hand on my face and giving me a light shove. "Don't make fun!"

She lifts off my dick and throws her leg over, but I grab her ass, stopping her. "Hey."

She looks back at me. "What?"

"I would never make fun of your innocence. It's a rare find, beautiful, and I'm one lucky bastard to get to experience it." I slap her ass. "Now put that suit on. We're going to go relax if I have to put a lock on it. Grilling and rubbing you down with suntan lotion sounds fun."

She stands, her eyes widening as her legs clamp together. I smile, already knowing what she's figuring out. "Uh, I have to go to the bathroom." She grabs her swimsuit and begins walking backward, leaving the tops of her legs touching each other.

"What goes up must come down, baby. Blame it on gravity. Go dispose of my sperm. You may be a while." I wink. "I'll be waiting downstairs."

"Uh, right." She backs out of the room, and I laugh when I hear running footsteps take off down the hall. I'm assuming she went to her bathroom for more privacy.

I fall back, giving myself a minute. My head is spinning, and I'm not even drunk. I rub my hand over my face—the one that isn't coated in lube. "What the hell."

I grip my hair, pulling in different directions. Dammit, I like her . . . a lot. This wasn't really supposed to happen, and this is only day one. Well, of living together. I didn't even feel this way about Salem until we had been together for over a year, and even then it was just different somehow. The need to be around her wasn't this strong. It was more of a comfort thing than anything else, and I was stupid enough to propose; not a moment I'm proud of.

That tells me one of two things: I'm either going to hurt her out of self-preservation, or I'm going to walk out of here a man in love. I'm not stupid enough to think that it'll never happen again. Human nature wants to feel and to love. It's part of the way we were wired. When in constant company of a woman you're either going to fall or get tired of her, and if the second happens, the only option is to walk away. Fear of it happening again is why I've chosen not to date up to this point, because you can't miss what you don't have.

I can be around that girl and tell she's the kind that doesn't ask you to love her; you just do. That's why option two has to be taken out of the equation, because if it happens, then I would have to give up everything, and with no backup plan, that isn't an option.

I'll just be careful. Yeah, that's it—a fall fling, and nothing more.

CHAPTER TWENTY

Kambry

I walk inside, towel drying my hair with a still damp body. From the moment I went downstairs I was a nervous wreck, but I quickly realized how comfortable I am with him. Each time I'm around him I find conversation easy, flowing pretty naturally within minutes after I begin to relax. He works me up, yet he calms me. It's definitely a contradictory action, but somehow it makes sense.

I stop just inside the door, squeezing out the dripping locks of hair to avoid wetting my body more. It's freezing in here, causing chill bumps to sprout along my body as the air blows over my wet skin. I can't believe it's already nightfall. Needless to say the day has gone by in a bit of a blur. Time literally has flown.

The second I walked outside in my swimsuit, Saxton caught me off guard by grabbing me from behind and sent us both free falling into the deep end. I zone out, thinking back to the specific phrase he used as we broke the surface of the water coming back up for air. *I just wanted to get you wet.*

The way his voice got deeper and his eyes honed in on mine had me barely able to breathe. It definitely wasn't silent, as breathing should be. I was shaking, but trying my hardest to keep it hidden by swimming away, teasing him, and feigning anger, anything to get away from him so that he couldn't blatantly see exactly how he affected me.

Then, with a slight smirk, as if he knew exactly what he was doing, he grabbed a ball and his entire demeanor changed. It was then I realized that I was the amateur in this and he the pro. He wasn't even trying, yet I was a mess inside. He was cool and collected, clearly not affected in any sense by me at all. If only I were that lucky, but no, I was the college freshman about to play in their first away football game inside a massive stadium with lots of noise, terrified of messing up, while he was the starting senior that had done the same thing hundreds of times. We were playing the same game, but in no form were we one in the same.

What started out as an innocent game of water volleyball led to making out in the cave behind the waterfall when I went to get the ball that just so happened to float back there as I missed and he scored. I never had any clue that making out could be so much fun.

He makes me feel like a sex-crazed woman, ready with the slightest touch of his lips to beg him to take me no matter where we are. The second he inserts his tongue I'm royally screwed and totally out of my mind. Add in his one-of-a-kind personality and I have no chance at emotional independence. He can completely manipulate my mood in a matter of seconds. The man is a magician, and my heart is sinking in the quicksand that is Saxton Maverick.

The irony of this all is that if I explained any of this to a normal person they would most likely think I was mentally unstable. I can see the headline of the conversation disclaimer now: innocent, socially awkward, southern girl falls for sexy, made for a model, porn star. Like most Hollywood couples it's only a matter of time before they crash and burn.

I might as well just enjoy my seven minutes in heaven with him and try my best to fireproof myself, so when that day comes I have some increment of a chance at picking myself up and carrying on post Saxton.

"What are you thinking about?"

I scream at the exact moment my body jars, sending my towel into the air. His arms wrap around my waist, crossing at my front and pulling me against his chest. My heart begins pounding in my chest from the scare. "Nothing really. Was just waiting on you. I didn't hear you walk in."

"What do you want to do?"

"I don't know. What do you want to do? I'm kind of tired now that my stomach is full. You're sort of awesome at manning the grill. I'm not sure I've ever devoured a steak that fast."

His lips touch at the junction of my neck and body, leaving enough of a space for him to speak. "Is that so?"

"Yeah," I say breathy, my body betraying me. "I'm not really a steak person. I don't dislike it, but I don't crave it either. It's a mood food for me."

His mouth travels up the seam of my neck. I tilt my head slightly, tightening the path. "I couldn't tell, but I definitely like a girl that can put away a steak here and there. A woman that eats is sexy."

"Because that was one hell of a steak." My voice is monotone now, merely answering his questions to prolong the brush stroke movement he's doing up and down the side of my neck with his soft lips. "I like food. I make no apologies."

He nips my neck. "Good, because so do I. Exploring new places to eat is a guilty pleasure of mine. I've done it alone for years, but I'd rather not continue to. I would imagine bragging about the food found at a hole-in-the-wall restaurant is so much better when there is someone who actually experienced it too. I've gone on travel ventures just to eat at places I've seen on TV before."

I turn in his arms, a smile inching across my face. "You watch Diners, Drive-ins, and Dives, don't you?"

He tries to hide a smile. "And if I said yes?"

"I would say you're a man after my own heart."

He laughs out loud. "Then I guess it's okay to reveal that I'm secretly a nerd at heart. I'm also guessing it's safe to assume you have watched it too."

I bite my bottom lip, my heart going wild with excitement that we actually have something completely normal in common. "I'm a total nerd at heart."

His eyes quickly scan my body. "Hmm. I don't think so. You'll have to prove it. You could be just trying to make me feel more manly over the fact that I admitted to watching the *Food Network* channel."

"What if I told you I used to have a huge crush on Guy Fieri? I even watched Guy's Big Bite for a while." I close my eyes at the memory of me looking over my shoulder with the remote ready to change the channel as if I was watching something totally inappropriate; to avoid being made fun of by Ben, before opening them again. "I used to get so hungry, but that didn't stop me from watching it. There is just something about a man that can cook."

His cheeks become round under his eyes, but his mouth remains closed.

"What?"

He bursts out laughing, as if he's been holding it in this whole time. "Too much info?" I ask with a hint of laughter in my tone.

He wraps his arms around me and pulls me to his chest, my warm cheek pressing against his bare skin as I wrap my arms around his waist, my hands resting just above his swim trunks. I try to discretely snuggle against him, because he feels amazing: just the right amount of muscle tone, a smooth chest, and his heartbeat is slightly erratic, but I wouldn't dare bring it up, from fear that he may pull away. "I don't know that I would admit that to too many people," he teases. "Most girls would say Channing Tatum or Justin Timberlake, but you, beautiful, are the first that I've ever heard a response like that from. Definitely a nerd at heart."

I laugh against his chest. "Are you trying to tell me you never had a weird childhood crush?"

"Nope. I was hiding my sister's Victoria's Secret catalogues under my pillow and spying on her friends when she had them over."

I pull away to look him in the eyes. My heart flutters. "So you aren't an only child either?"

"Nope. I have an older sister. I don't usually refer to her in front of just anyone. She writes articles for a pretty big—" He stops and briefly looks around, then back at me. "A conversation for another time. Okay?" My shoulders drop a little. I like when he gives me bits and pieces of his back history, offering me a peek into who he is. Suddenly it hits me that we most likely are being filmed. Dang. I really had forgotten up until now. He's trying to protect his family's privacy.

I nod. "I just figured out what we're doing until bed," he says, completely changing the mood back into something light from the direction it was heading.

"What's that?"

He grabs my hand and pulls me through the house, toward the stairs. "Showers and then a night in with Food Network. What do you think?"

I think I love you . . . That's what I think.

Did I really just think that? Gah, I'm such a girl. I shrug it off nonchalantly. "Sounds good to me. Meet you on the couch in fifteen?"

"It's a date," he says, melting my heart just a little. "Go ahead. I'm just going to lock the doors and then I'll be up."

"Okay." I bite my bottom lip as I glance at his mouth, wishing he would kiss me, but then take off up the stairs before I have a chance to look pathetic. As soon as I rush into my room and barge through the bathroom door, I slam it and press my back against the closed door.

A date . . .

I squeal, just before slapping my hand over my mouth. I don't care if it's a date in the living room. It's a date nonetheless; maybe not the first, but the intimacy of TV watching and cuddles feels like it. Hiking up a mountain trail is, well, work. Thank goodness I shaved everything this morning. A shower shouldn't take me very long.

Only ten minutes of my normal fifteen and I emerge from the bathroom wrapped in a towel, steam following closely behind. Now would be the perfect time for him to barge in my room like earlier, but I have a feeling he won't. Making my way over to the suitcase and duffel on my bed, I begin digging through the clothes, looking for something to put on.

I wonder if it's weird that I want to look cute even though we're not doing anything. I mean, I guess it'd be stupid to put on actual clothes, but I don't want to do the whole mismatched Pajamas either. I'm standing here, staring into the bag, and running out of time before it becomes noticeable that I'm up here primping.

Something that looks like thick cotton in a baby pink catches my attention. I grab it and let it fall open. It's a nightie, but it's a more casual piece of lingerie—something you could actually sleep in. The straps are wide and the neckline is round instead of V cut, giving a little more coverage. It's completely solid in color except for the breast area, which is done in a floral that reminds me of that Simply Shabby Chic pattern. I kind of like it, and it feels comfortable.

What the hell . . . Might as well.

I let the towel drop to the floor and pull it on. The snug fit around the breasts and the tight band that runs underneath to act as support confirms that it's comfy. I run my hands down it, until they reach the ending of the fabric at my thighs. Am I trying too hard? Isn't sexy kind of the point of being here?

I glance in the mirror to look at myself. To my surprise it actually looks kind of classy. I take a deep breath. "Just do it. Quit being such a wuss," I whisper.

"It's time to move into another level of play."

I quickly dig through my small bag of beauty supplies, until I find a ponytail holder to throw my hair up into a wet, messy bun on my head before I can change my mind. Once secure, I start to walk toward the door when I remember I haven't put on underwear. Okay that I'm not leaving.

I grab the first matching color I can find and pull them on, adjusting them into place. My phone catches my attention, lying on the nightstand. When I light up the lock screen there is a missed call from Meredith and a text from Saxton. I'll call her back later. I'm more interested in reading a text from the person living in the same house.

As the sound of the television comes on downstairs I open the message box.

Saxton: I have to be careful what I say in relation to my family since we are being filmed. Getting to know you I may cut myself off a few times, because I don't feel like I'm working as I normally would, so it's not because I'm hiding things. For their privacy and the sensitivity of my career I have to be careful what true details of my life I reveal to other people . . .like my real last name. What I was trying to say was my sister writes articles for a big women's magazine in New York City, where she also lives.

My shoulders drop slightly. I get it, but just when I think I'm getting to know him I'm brought back to the reality that I really don't know him at all.

Me: I get it . . .

Almost instantly another message comes through.

Saxton: Do you?

Me: Yeah, I do. This is just a little harder than I imagined. I want to know you. I'm just not sure how.

Saxton: I have an idea.

Me: I'm listening. Well, reading.

Saxton: If you want to know me personally, as in things outside of my life in LA, then just send me a text at random times and I'll answer. I'll do the same. We'll just make it a game. In this business you don't want people knowing your most intimate details like family and address or phone information. There are crazies out there. When you become part of the public eye, protecting your privacy becomes your number one goal. On here, ask me anything.

Me: Anything?

Saxton: Anything.

Me: Maverick isn't your last name?

Saxton: No, it's my middle.

I pause, wondering if I should really ask. I never even thought of a pen name. No one asked me. It's not like I would have known it was an option. Maybe they make it up for me, like assign me one.

Me: Will people know my real last name?

Saxton: No. I already spoke with Michael about that last week when it occurred to me. He's in the process of giving you a pen so your private life can remain private. It will probably be something simple like a last name switch for merchandise labeling like me, since I already refer to you by your first name.

Me: Okay.

My phone dings again.

Saxton: It's Cambridge by the way.

Me: What?

Saxton: My last name.

I stare at the phone, unsure of what to say back. First thing that pops into the mind can't be the worst.

Me: Thank you for trusting me enough to know you—the real you. I would never betray that trust. It means a lot to me.

Saxton: Get down here.

Me: Yes, sir.

I smile, tossing my phone down on the bed. It's showtime.

Saxton

I've never told anyone here my birth last name aside from legal binding documents that required it. That's a huge ordeal for me, and to be honest I'm not even sure why I felt the need to tell her. There was one thing I promised my family and that was that I wouldn't drag them into this world. I gave them my word that I wouldn't tarnish the last name I was given by running it through the mud, making a mockery of my family. Still, my family is everything to me, even though I don't see them but a couple times a year. That was a sacrifice that I made by doing what I do. That's not on them.

I hear her footsteps coming down the stairs, turning my head just in time for her to come into view. Oh my god . . .

I quickly stand, a little taken back. My brain is completely frozen, unable to process what I'm seeing. She looks incredible. "You okay?"

I clear my throat. "Wow."

It's all I can muster at the moment. My eyes veer to her full rack, completely covered aside from a little cleavage, and showing a faint outline of her hard nipples. Sex appeal amplified is what that is. This is innocence wrapped with a pretty bow. Fuck, she's hot, and that color on her . . .

"Saxton?"

My brain finally decides to work, my eyes returning to hers. "Huh?"

"Is something wrong?" She looks nervous.

"No, why?"

"You aren't speaking."

"I wasn't expecting this view."

I grab her hand and pull her toward me roughly, until her body becomes flush with mine. "What were you expecting?"

"A ratty oversized tee shirt and a pair of faded pajama bottoms."

"Oh. Disappointed?"

"Are you kidding? Sometimes you stun me. This, I have no words for."

"You aren't wearing a shirt," she says, making an observation.

I smile, placing my palms on the small of her back, holding her against me. "I don't wear a shirt at night. When I go to bed the sweats will come off too, and I'll look exactly like I did when I called you last night." She wraps her arms around me, placing her hands flat on my back, just below my shoulder blades.

Her lips part. "I like you without a shirt better anyway." She's staring at my mouth. I can tell she wants me to kiss her, and as hard as it is I'm not going to, because if I start I won't stop. That's what she does to me. She brings out the animal in me. I've been sucked, fucked, and stroked more times than I could ever remember, but I've never felt more like a teenager than I do with her.

"So, we're in luck," I say, trying to sway my thoughts, pulling her toward the couch. With her looking at me like that, I'm very likely to cave. I already have so many times it's embarrassing, to be quite honest. "It's in the middle of an episode right now, but it's a marathon."

She glances around and smiles. It's one of those breath-taking smiles: one that can't be faked. She's happy, and it shows. That does something unexplainable to me. I like seeing her happy. "You really went all out, didn't you?"

I smirk. "What kind of man would I be if we had a movie date without popcorn and pillows?"

She laughs. "I guess you're right. TV just isn't the same without popcorn, especially watching them eat delicious concoctions, sometimes made from the most random things. Actually, I'm not sure I could go on another date with a man that doesn't bring the popcorn to movie night."

"See. Nailed it. You have no excuse now."

"God, you're so cute. You even have bottles of water and everything."

"Cute is not manly, beautiful. Baby pandas and polar bears are cute. Not men. Rule number one: a man's ego is sensitive. You can call me handsome, hot, sexy, hung, or hell, even a beast as long as one of those other words precedes it, but not cute. That's something a girl says when she's being asked out and trying to let him down easily. Think caveman, not puppy."

She laughs again, but this time a small snort escapes. Her eyes widen as she slaps a hand over her mouth. Her cheeks start to change color. I think my version of like just went a little further . . .

I pull her hand away from her face and shake my head. "Imperfections make a person more attractive. Quirks make you different from any other girl. You just gave me a piece of you. I like it. Always be you."

She stares at me, obviously unsure. Her flushed cheeks still show her embarrassment. "Guys don't come with instruction manuals. We all have different likes and dislikes, so if you think something as simple as that would turn me off, then you're wrong."

Now would be the appropriate time to kiss her.

I place my hand on the side of her neck and lean in to kiss her, soft and brief. I look her in the eyes. "Popcorn is going to get stale."

She starts to close her eyes, but stops herself. "Okay."

I sit, patting the couch beside me for her to do the same. She does, just as I grab the remote and the large bowl of popcorn and place it in my lap. She tenses as I put my arm around her on the back of the couch, making it really hard for me not to laugh. "Does this make you uncomfortable? I have seen you naked, you know."

"No. It's just . . .old habits die hard I guess."

"Did your boyfriend never do this?"

"He wasn't allowed to touch me. It was a rule in my parents' house."

I place my hand on her shoulder and pull her closer. "Well, this isn't your parents' house and there is nothing wrong with innocent intimacy anyway. This is called dating, unless you want me to stop, of course."

After a brief pause she reaches into the bowl and pulls out a handful of popcorn, shaking her head, and then she shoves a few into her mouth. "Good, because I was willing to start a debate to avoid it."

With that phrase she finally relaxes in my arm. I dim the lights with the remote and then un-mute the TV, just as a new episode is starting, that red convertible driving down the stretch of roadway as it always does at the beginning and end of every episode.

She pulls her feet up on the couch and snuggles into my body. "Are you cold? I have a blanket."

"No. You're warm."

I can feel her breathing against my chest. My heart rate begins to accelerate. I could get used to this. I like it; too much, in fact. She fits perfectly, as if she was kind of made to go there. "I can't believe you really watch this. Most guys would think it is stupid."

"I'm not like most guys, Kambry."

"I know. I can tell," she whispers. "And I'm glad."

I stare at the television, wanting to tell her everything about me for some crazy reason. She makes me want to talk, to open up, and to actually attempt to trust a woman again, but why, I have no idea. There is nothing completely out of the ordinary about her. She just makes me want to. She makes me want to be the old me, but circumstances buried that part of me long ago.

I wake up, my back a little stiff and my arm numb. A fruity smell wafts through my nose: her. I look down at the top of a headful of blonde. I have no idea how we ended up like this: her head on my chest as if I'm her pillow, her arm thrown over my waist and her leg draped over mine, and my arm around her. I'm not sure how we both even fit on this couch in a lying position; we just do.

The tingling needlelike sensations in my arm tells me I need to get up, but I don't want to wake her, and worse, I don't want to move. I breathe out. I may have to give in to my sexual want for her on a regular basis, but the rest, I kind of want to take slow. Call me crazy because that makes no sense, but it's just a feeling I can't ignore.

Maneuvering my body slowly, I slip my arm from behind her and inch her head to the cushion, before easing over her body and standing. "Sax . . ."

Damn, I love when she calls me that. I don't know why. Maybe because no woman has ever called me that before, and when she says it, it comes out as if she's called me that her whole life. It's natural.

Grabbing the remote I turn off the television, leaving the spotlights on dim so I can see. The half-eaten popcorn and almost empty water bottles are sitting on the coffee table. I slip my arms under her body and lift her off the couch, cradling her to my chest. "My pillow," she mumbles, as she snuggles her face back against my chest.

"I can be your pillow," I whisper, before walking toward the stairs, climbing them slowly and one by one until I reach her bedroom. The room is lit, but only by the bedside table lamp. She must have turned it on before she came downstairs.

Placing my knee on the bed, I lay her in the middle and pull the white down cover and satin sheet down beneath her, before pulling it over her body. Her eyes crack open, but just barely. "Sleep with me."

I lean down and kiss her forehead, already hating myself for being a damn pussy. "Not tonight, beautiful, but soon. Get some sleep."

"Okay," she says groggily, and turns away from me, making it so much more tempting to crawl in behind her.

I rub my face in my hands as I stand. "Dammit, just go to your room."

Before I can change my mind, I turn and walk out, making myself walk to my room. My eyes land on the crumpled bedding, reminding me of earlier. "Hell . . . "

With one swift push my sweats fall down my legs, before I step out, leaving them in a heap on the floor. I inch forward, falling face first on the bed, and then robotically pull the blanket loosely on top of me, drawing the corner on top of the bed. I don't even care that I'm lying on the bed the wrong way. Either way it's probably going to be a shitty sleep, because with her right down the hall, that's all I'm going to think about.

I'm making myself a promise though. Michael already gave me the go ahead to take things slow if I want. They can cut and dice what they want for a weekly episode. Everyone knows that reality TV really isn't but only so much reality. I'm going to try and make this is as realistic as I can, because I actually want her—all of her. I want to show her a real, intimate relationship, sex and all, but I want the next time we have sex to be fucking explosive, from a small buildup at least. Most of all, I want her to discover her seductive side, because that girl already drives me wild.

Come tomorrow, I am becoming an abstinent porn star; just until she shows me that I make her half as crazy as she makes me, because every time I'm around her I want to strip her clothes off. Her body is all I can think about, so for now I'm going to close my eyes and pretend that I'm sleeping, when in reality I'll be visualizing the way she looked riding my cock in this very bed.

Yep, I can kiss sleep goodbye . . .

CHAPTER TWENTY-ONE

Kambry

The music is blaring throughout the club. It's a full house tonight. It always is on Friday, so that's nothing new. It feels good to be back to a sense of normalcy I have to admit. It's already been five days since we moved into the house. It's been nothing short of amazing getting to know Saxton, but at the same time I'm annoyed. Just when I get used to the fact that my entire sex life is going to be plastered on television for the world to watch, he barely touches me.

In what kind of porn do the leads not have sex? Every morning I wake up to a text from him telling me to come downstairs. I get down there and he has coffee brewed and some sort of breakfast made. I'm not a coffee drinker, but he drinks while I eat, because usually he's already scarfed his down, since he's obviously an early riser.

For the past four days, we have spent the entire day together. It's usually laying by the pool and enjoying a dip for most of the morning, followed by lunch out, and then we play games–yes board games–since he hasn't attempted to teach me pool in the game room, or we just hang out and do something to ourselves within the confinements of the same space. Recently it's been me trying out this Kindle that Meredith got me, and he playing the game system on the television in the living room. I never took him for a gamer, but he can be quite animated when he's playing one of those shooting games like *Call of Duty*.

It's kind of nice, sitting at opposite ends of the couch as if we've been doing it for years. I like watching him. I like being with him in general. He's quickly taking on a role of being one of my best friends. I like it. There is no soap opera drama, no crazy roommate fights, and no absurd partying, but it's still fun just hanging out.

Nights are devoted to cooking dinner together and cleaning up after, before watching television or a movie and then going to bed . . .separately. We've made out a few times; a few times at my bedroom door as if he's returning me from a night out, but he always shuts things down before it goes any further. Like . . .what the hell? I have no idea if I've done something wrong or if there is something I'm not getting. Don't get me wrong. I wouldn't want to give the wrong opinion of myself to others. I love that I'm not just a sex object for him to get off, but porn with no porn kind of defeats the whole purpose of me signing up for this . . .thing.

Well, I've had enough. It's making me paranoid. Tonight, I'm going to do something about it. I've been reading this book and, well, I had no idea books got that steamy. They give me ideas. They make me want to try things; like oral sex for one. I want to go down on him. He's never asked me to, but I want to. Before bed my plans are to just lay it on him and then go to bed. If he doesn't want to have sex right now, then fine, but I'll be damned if I'm going to just sit back and wait on him and his good behavior to change back to the Saxton he was. He's the one that made me this way anyway, so it's his fault entirely.

"Do you guys need a drink?" I yell over the music at the couple sitting at one of the tables by the wall. They've been ordering for the last hour and he's a good tipper.

The girl is bumping her body to the beat of the music, tipping back her drink every few seconds. "Vodka tonic for me."

"You got it." I turn to the guy beating his hands on the table to the music. I'm going to take a guess that he's probably a drummer. "Another Bud Light?"

He smiles, nodding his head, and then hands me a small stack of cash folded down the middle. "Double the order on both, beautiful. We're waiting on people, and it's her birthday." He winks.

"Sure thing. Be right back." I jot the order down with the table number and stop by a few more people I've been waiting on most of the night, checking to ensure no one runs dry. I've learned as a server in a bar, that is the ultimate sin. You never let a drinking paying customer run out of alcohol, unless you're cutting them off or they decline.

I make my way to the sexy bartender behind the bar, my head and shoulders swaying to the music. He smiles and extends a red rose as I approach him. I set down my tray atop the bar and slide the drink order across so that he can start filling the order, taking it from his hand. "I see you've been with the rose girl since I've been gone," I tease, taking it from him.

He smiles, one of those teeth-showing white smiles, and leans over the bar, the sleeves of his black button-down rolled up to his elbows; one of the few choice uniform colors the male staff members can wear if the club isn't hosting a theme party. "She may have stopped by, but then I bought a rose off of her for my girl."

I bring the bloom to my nose, smelling it, my heart racing in my chest each time he looks at me like that. I'm so screwed here. He makes me feel things that I've never felt, and the problem is I like it. He makes me feel like the only girl in the room, even at work. "You look kind of hot tonight."

He stands, grabbing a glass with a smirk on his face. "I would say you look kind of hot tonight too, but I'd be lying. There is no *kind of* to it."

I try to contain the grin that I know wants to form right now, but it's hard. Second by second it's broadening, until I'm gleaming at him. I freaking love that he's my bartender. It makes working so much better. I bend forward. "So . . .Sax. You never told me how you learned to bartend. I kind of expected this to be something you had to wing, but you're pretty experienced."

"College. I actually did work in college, unlike some people. I was a server at a restaurant with a bar. Restaurants do a lot of in-house moving around when it comes available. The regular weekend bartender quit." One by one he places the drinks on the tray, as if it's no effort at all. "I volunteered. Trained for a bit with the day bartender and then did it for a couple of years. Now, here I am."

Finally, he grabs two bottles of Bud Light from the cooler with one hand and quickly removes the caps with the bottle opener in his free hand, placing them on my tray to finalize the order. "Ah, so you have layers."

"And slowly you're peeling them back."

I squeal and stand with the feel of a hand on my inner thigh, dipping beneath my dress. A body hovers over mine, a mouth just outside of my ear, holding me in a position to look at the bar. "It's good to have you back, Kambry. The eye candy just hasn't been as good since you left."

His thumb grazes my panty line between my legs and my reflex takes over, pressing into him and shoving him back. "Watch it, Liam. You're invading my personal space. Damn, that's not okay. I explained things to you."

He holds up his hands, laughing. "Easy. You met someone. I get it. I'm just messing around."

I turn and glance at Saxton. He's starring daggers at Liam. I'm guessing it didn't take a scholar to notice he was being inappropriate. Liam holds his hand out to Saxton. "You must be the new guy that took my girl."

Saxton disregards his hand completely. "I don't remember her belonging to anyone before I got here. And you are?"

"Liam. I'm another bartender, just at the south side bar tonight, and was assigned to Kambry here until they hired you. Management issues I guess. We'll most likely be working together at some point."

"Liam, we won't have any problems unless you touch her like that again without her giving you permission first. Then, I'll just break your fingers and you won't be doing any bartending for a while. Got me?"

They stare at each other briefly, before Liam starts to back away. "Find me later, Kambry."

"Not going to happen," I mumble under my breath.

"Were you two ever a thing?"

"What?" I ask, caught off guard. "Me and him? Uh no. I mean we hung out that once . . ." I breathe out, that awkward feeling settling in, trying to explain things. "He's the one that texted me the night you came over unexpected, when I was freaking out about the conversation with Michael. I explained it."

His smile returns, dismissing the conversation as if he knows it's making me uncomfortable. "That was a good night."

I grab my tray, balancing the weight of it so that I don't spill anything. "Yes, sir, it was. I'm due for a break soon. Want to find somewhere private and be highly inappropriate?"

He looks at me, and then clears his throat. "As tempting as that sounds, we can't get caught on our first night working together."

I roll my eyes. "Chicken. Keep playing hard to get."

"Kambry," he says, as I turn and walk away, ignoring him completely. I head back the way that I came, delivering drinks and collecting tips, until finally I arrive at the table with the couple, only now a few more people are with them.

Setting down the drinks I immediately recognize one. "Meredith?"

She turns toward me and throws up her arms, screaming over the music. "There's my favorite bitch!" She wraps her arms around me, pulling me into a hug. "I miss you."

"I miss you too, but what are you doing here? You didn't tell me you were coming."

"Well, I met Trinity here at an open audition. We got to talking, and then she said it was her birthday and wanted to celebrate, so I told her there was only one place worthy of a birthday celebration because my BFF works there. They just moved here from Ohio!" she screams. Her veins are protruding from her neck each time she speaks, because the music is so loud. "This is her boyfriend Dane. I think Bryant went to the bar."

I grin at her. "You're here with Bryant? Are things getting serious?"

She shrugs her shoulders. "Who knows. Doubt it, though. Things are fun, so why mess them up. Don't get any crazy ideas in your head, girlie. It's not like you think."

"Here. I got your Vodka and cranberry with extra Vodka." Bryant appears, kissing her on the temple as he hands the pink cup to her. My brows rise at the intimate gesture.

She narrows her eyes at me, knowing exactly what I'm referring to. "Bryant, you remember Kambry, right?"

He wraps his arm around me and pulls me into a side hug. "Of course I do. What kind of question is that?" He leans next to my ear. "I will never forget the girl that caught a star."

I laugh. "You're exaggerating. I was just in the right place at the right time. That kind of star can't be caught."

"No, love. You hooked that one. I've already been to the bar."

"What'd he say?" I ask nervously.

"It's not about what he said, but about what he didn't say."

I'm not even sure what that means, but it does bring me back to a question that I need to ask Meredith. "Hey, Mer. I need to take a restroom break before I circulate again. Wanna go with?"

"Hell yeah." She walks toward Bryant. "Watch my drink? I may even save the next bathroom break for you."

Bryant releases me and pulls her toward him, whispering something in her ear, before she blatantly grabs his crotch. Whoa. I really didn't need to witness that. What am I even thinking? I've seen them have sex. Not one of my prouder moments.

I start to walk off, before she runs up to me and grabs my arm. "Not serious, my ass. You two have it bad."

"Maybe, maybe not, but things can always change."

I shake my head as we navigate through the crowd for the hallway to the bathrooms. "Sometimes I don't understand you at all, Mer."

"You don't have to, babe. Some things aren't meant to be dissected."

We walk into the bathroom and I hand her my tray before walking into the bathroom stall. "So, I have to ask you something," I say, as I quickly pee.

"Oh yeah. What's that?"

"Well . . ." I flush and adjust my dress, before making my way to the sink where she's standing to wash my hands. I look around to ensure no one else is listening. It is the girls' restroom. I've heard weirder conversations in here than I can remember, so it doesn't really matter. "I want to know how to properly give a guy a blow job."

She looks at me puzzled. "You haven't yet?"

"No. I could probably figure it out, but I'd rather just kind of know up front so I don't mess up the whole thing. Ya know? I don't want to be that girl that the guy tells funny stories about to his friends. I want to be good at it."

"Okay. This may take a few. How is your gag reflex?"

"What? How is that relevant?"

"It just is. He's big."

"It's fine I guess. I've never really tested it out."

"Do you gag a lot brushing your teeth? Like when you brush your tongue?"

"No."

"Okay, then you should be good. The key is breathing through your nose anyway." She grabs some paper towels to hand me as I shut off the water.

"I want it to be an element of surprise, so walk me through it from start to finish in a way that is sexy. I don't want the result to be clumsy and a turn off."

"Okay, have a seat in my office, my precious." She leads me to the set of chairs and sits in one, me shaking my head the entire way.

"You can be so weird sometimes."

"Yet I'm still the one you come to for all your questions . . ."

"Touché. Let's get this over with before I get fired."

"Okay, so guys really aren't that complicated. As long as you remember the term, handle with care, then you should be good. Tell me how you want to start."

"Uh, isn't that what I'm asking you?"

She rolls her eyes. "Do you want him standing, sitting, or lying?"

"I don't know. What's the easiest way to just do it without him stopping me?"

"Standing if clothed and lying if he's in something with easier access than buttons. Either way, you need to end up on your knees. Guys like to see girls on their knees. Don't ask me why. Maybe it's a power thing."

"Okay, so let's just pretend lying. I think I can work from that angle. I have a vague game plan."

Her brows arch as she grins. "Are you going to wake him to a little sucky-sucky action?"

"I don't suppose I considered him being completely asleep, but if that would work I can wait. Tell me what to do."

"I'm so buying this to watch when it comes out. That's hot."

My nose scrunches. I shove at her arm. "You freak. Focus."

"What?" She scoffs. "You watched me. I'm entitled. Anyway, we're getting off track. This is good, because he'll be soft unless you wait too long. Morning wood . . . I wouldn't go there. That's like coming face-to-face with a loaded gun. Not a good idea."

"You're telling me that story later." I try not to laugh or we'll be in here all night. "Moving on."

"Yeah." She stares off. "Not a good memory. There was just . . .never mind. Only the vagina is hostile enough to endure that. So, if you want to do this, you should kind of do the sexy creeper crawl from the foot of the bed if you really want a sensual element of surprise. You don't want to just hop on top of him and he jump up and give you a black eye. That's not good for the camera."

"Oh my god, Meredith, you're making me have second thoughts."

"What? Do you want honesty? I need to give you the alternate ending so you can make your choice wisely. When he starts to stir, he'll probably say your name in question, rub his eyes, and ask what you're doing. Don't answer. Less is more. Instead, just grab the waist of his trunks and work them down."

"How do I get it over his butt?"

"Note this somewhere: a guy will always lift when his dick is being summoned, no matter what state of mind he's in. It's like a reflex action. That thing wants to be touched, sucked, submerged, whatever it can get inside of a warm, wet, orifice. Watch and see."

"And then?"

"Getting there, sweets. Grab it by the base. Hold it like you would a microphone. Don't freak out. It may be slightly hard just from him seeing you pull his briefs down, but most likely not fully erect. It will not be in an attractive state. Think limp noodle, hanging elephant trunk, or fold up storage capability. It must be stowed, especially a guy carrying around that size snake. You need to prepare it for use, so the basics of a blowjob are to suck, lick, flick, and swirl. Remember those words and you're golden. Give it a little TLC and watch it grow. Sensitive parts are the head and the underside. You'll feel it. It's kind of like a small dip. Play with the little hole at the end. It will give you candy." She winks.

I repeat every word in my head, trying to burn it to memory. I'm determined to do this. I am competing with someone experienced. I really don't want to embarrass myself. "I think I got it."

"I'm going to wrap this up in a few seconds. Swirl the head, flick the tip and the sweet spot, suck the length like you would a Popsicle that's melting, but only to the depth that you can handle. In the end a guy would rather you stay shallow and make him come than to gag all over his dick and leave him with blue balls because you can't finish the job." She uses her pointer finger as a guide to finish. "Breathe through the nose, and remember, saliva is your friend not your enemy. Find a steady rhythm as you suck, even if you have to sing silently in your head. If you really want to go all out then suck or massage his balls, but for the love of all that is holy do not use your teeth. Pucker. You have perfect dick-sucking lips. Use them to your advantage. Some of us have to work a little harder there."

She taps her chin. "Am I leaving anything out? A verbal man is a good sign, but if he isn't that doesn't mean you're doing a bad job. Some are just internal reactors—the silent type. A hand in your hair is your goal. Oh, fuck, how could I forget? For the finale, uh, relax your throat more than it already should be and move your tongue to the back, closing it off. Some guys will tell you when it's time, but not all are that gentlemanly, so if you pay attention you'll know. It starts to spasm just before he blows, and you need to decide whether you spit or swallow beforehand so it's not awkward in the moment. It's salty in taste and creamy in texture. It sounds gross, but that's the cold hard facts. It's easy to hold, but swallowing is a mental thing mostly. Some can handle it and some can't. There is no right or wrong answer in disposal. It's strictly preference. The important thing is to be able to take it during orgasm. The less he has to stop the better for him."

She stands and pretends she's dusting off her hands, being dramatic as Meredith usually is. "Any questions?"

"And after?"

"Replace his trunks, stand, and walk away without saying a word. He won't know what hit him, and I can almost guarantee he'll be in your bed by morning."

She turns toward the bathroom stalls. I follow her line of vision to a couple of girls standing at the sinks staring and listening. This is awkward. "I'm so trying that when I get home," one girl wearing a white sash with the word *bride* across it says, breaking the silence. The short veil on her head confirms this must be her bachelorette party.

"No shit," another retorts. "Hubs would love that. You should explain that to more women. That explanation makes it actually seem fun. Being asked turns me off."

"Want to keep your men interested girls, then blow him once in a while. He'll be wrapped around your damn finger." She looks at me. "You ready, sweets?"

I grab my tray where she laid it and adjust my dress to ensure everything is covered. "Yeah, I've been in here way longer than I should anyway. Drake would be pissed."

I follow her back out into the club. Ironically, I have more confidence now. Now, I need to execute. Excitement builds in my core. My goal is to take him by surprise, in technique and action. I just need to repeat that conversation in my head until it's stuck, and actually make it through the entire night without giving myself away, which may be easier said than done, because when he looks at me and flirts, I go completely blank.

We pull into the drive and he shuts off his truck, both of us exiting at the same time. It's already 3AM. Maybe it won't take him long to go to sleep. I'd rather do this while darkness is still on my side. The truck sounds as he presses the button on the remote, locking it. "Want to go around back for a few before bed?"

"Sure," I say, following him to the gate.

He opens it for me and allows me to enter first. I walk through and instantly head toward one of the seats that surround the fire pit. He sits beside me, reaching in his pocket and pulling out a pack of cigarettes. "I haven't seen you do that since the night outside of my apartment."

He places it between his lips and lights the end, inhaling as he sets the lighter and pack beside him. He smiles at me, and instantly my heart begins to race. He releases the cloud of smoke into the night air, holding the filter between his thumb and index fingers. "That's because I don't smoke from need. I smoke when I want to. It's a bad habit that I indulge in occasionally, because I like it; usually when I'm tense or uptight about something."

I turn in my chair, pulling my leg up along the way so that I can face him; probably not a very ladylike gesture given I'm wearing a dress. "Oh yeah? What are you uptight about? I'm curious."

He eyes me quickly, and then shrugs as he takes another hit, the paper burning down each time he sucks on the filter. I've always thought smoking was gross, but he kind of makes it sexy. Gah, that sounds so dumb, but when we kissed on the last night I witnessed him doing it, I didn't even notice the taste of it, because he's all I can think about. It probably wouldn't have the same effect if he did it regularly. It kind of gives him that bad boy edge. "That guy touching you for one, watching guys eye you in the club as you walked away from the bar. I didn't like it . . .at all. Another—seeing how beautiful you look when you're in a comfortable state, unlike the night I met you. You fit in there. I didn't realize it until tonight. You do well in big crowds. I don't think you've figured it out yet."

Each time he comments about me being beautiful, my heart feels like it's going to burst through my chest. I feel like I'm walking on clouds: weightless and happy. "Guy? What guy? Oh, you mean Liam?"

He breathes out again, this time tilting his head back. "That would be the one. If we were in a normal situation, with no cameras, no one watching our every move, I would have pummeled him right in the face. It pissed me off to say the least."

"Why? He was just being stupid. I kind of blew him off a few times—all for you. He's nice when he's not trying too hard. That's when he gets annoying."

He takes the final drag off the cigarette, leaving nothing but the filter, and then tosses what's left into the pit and stands. His eyes never leave mine as he walks toward me, before leaning down and placing his hands on the arms of my chair, forming a barricade. "Because you never assume someone is single for starters. Even if we were just talking, feeling each other out, you're still unavailable. The way he touched you is the way only I should touch you. That's how someone gets fucked over."

"But didn't you kind of do that when you kissed me that night in the club?"

I don't know where that question came from. Maybe I'm just curious to know why he did it in the first place.

"I did. It was wrong. I should have asked you before I kissed you, but the way you reacted to me I knew you couldn't possibly have a boyfriend, especially being used to men in bars. The problem is I don't think with you. I act. Regardless, I still assumed until the moment I did ask—too late."

He's so close I can smell the cigarette on his breath. "For the record, I'm glad you did, and just so you know, I would never have *let* him touch me now," I whisper, treading around his agitated tone. "I told him I had met someone after you asked me not to see anyone until we knew where this was going."

"It doesn't matter. That's the way everyone feels at first. All it takes is the right person to come along and fuck up everything for someone else. Some people even get off on getting someone that is taken to cross that line; like it's a game."

"I didn't do anything wrong, Saxton."

"I never said you did. You don't get it do you? Why I'm so aggravated. He saw me standing there with you and he still touched you in a way that only your boyfriend touches you, with no regard for your relationship status, because he didn't care. No one cares about commitment anymore, or preserving it for that matter. What if I hadn't been standing there? How far would he have gone to get you to give in? Then, after you give in once, it gets so much easier to do it over and over; all while lying beside someone else at night whose heart is breaking one piece at a time, because he's in love with her, and she's in love with lust, even though she wants to play house."

His mouth shuts and his jaw locks, as he stares at me. I literally cannot breathe. Oh my god. He's vulnerable. He's scared. He's scarred. He's broken. I'm outside of my element. I don't know what to do or say. I can't feel or think. Instead, anger washes over me. I'm mad that I'm taking the heat for what someone else obviously did with no cause. I'm mad that the decent ones always get screwed over; making it harder for the people that would never do someone that way to find a good person. I'm mad that someone else would hurt him, but more than that I'm sad. I'm sad that he's obviously been hurt before.

My heart begins to beat, stronger and louder. I grab his shirt, pulling him toward me so that I can only whisper. "But I'm not her, Saxton. I'm not her," I repeat. He closes his eyes, refusing to look at me. "Sax . . ."

He finally looks at me, regret all over his face. He clearly didn't mean for it to go this way, but the way it looks he's had things locked inside for a while, building and aging. "I don't need anyone else, because you're enough for me."

He scans my eyes, but then stands upright, pulling a mask over his face with a small smile. "Let's go to bed, beautiful. It's late."

I breathe out, defeated, because he's obviously done with this conversation for tonight. I nod, standing when he holds out his hand for mine and walk past him, toward the door. I want him to talk to me, but I will not beg him. I don't stop until I get to my room. I can hear his footsteps not far behind me the entire way. Bracing myself on the doorframe, I don't look back. "Goodnight, Saxton."

"Kambry . . ."

I walk inside and shut the door, making sure I'm quiet as a mouse on the other side. A few moments later I hear his door shut, and as if on cue a tear falls from the corner of my eye. As I walk to my bed I shuck my shoes, before grabbing the bottom of my dress and pulling it over my body, dropping it on the floor. I pull the small, folded stash of cash from the corner of my bra and lay it on the table with my phone—the place it never left—and then remove my bra. Fumbling around in the dark, I reach in the top drawer of the nightstand and grab a tank to put on, before turning down my blanket and getting into bed.

My phone vibrates and lights up a small section of the room. I grab it and open the message.

Saxton: You'll never be her. You're better. Goodnight, Kambry.

I lock the phone and replace it on the table without answering, and then roll over. I'm filled with sorrow and I'm really confused as to why. I feel hurt, but no one's hurt me. I feel betrayed, yet there is no betrayer. I feel heartbroken without remembering what it was like to experience the love that precedes it.

More tears fall down my nose. I close my eyes to try and sleep, but all I can see is Saxton lying in bed beside a girl whose face is blurred. She's lying on her back and he's on his side, holding her; all while in her heart she knows she's committed the ultimate betrayal. She gave her body to a man while it belonged to someone else, and then she did it again . . .and again, while his heart remained faithful to hers.

Now his heart is closed off, because it hasn't forgiven the one that caused it so much pain, and that's what makes me saddest of all.

I tighten my eyes as my heart fills my head in on a secret. "Of course. I feel what he felt, because I'm falling in love with him . . .for real. Please don't hurt me," I whisper. "Don't hurt me."

My eyes pop open, still heavy, but I feel panicked as if I fell asleep cramming for an exam. I roll over and grab my phone, checking the time. 4:03. I sit up, having an epiphany. No more of this bullshit. If I want him, I have to step up my game by a lot. I have to be someone he can't walk away from so easily. I signed up for porn, well a porn star is what he's going to get. I wanted to be someone else. I wanted to find myself. I wanted to be my own person. Now is my chance.

I throw the covers off of me and quietly get out of bed, grabbing my phone and turning on the flashlight. Where is that nightie from the sex shop? Game on. I'm finally ready to play hardball.

After quietly stumbling around a few times, I find it, before quickly putting it on and adjusting it into place. I grab the matching panties that accompany it and change into them, ready to go. I'm forgoing the heels. I don't need them. I turn off the flashlight on my phone when everything is on properly, and quickly look down at my cleavage the best that I can see. There is a small beam of light coming through the crack of the curtains. It's not much, but it's enough to make sure I'm not hanging out but revealing just enough.

When I get to the door I stop, taking a deep breath to calm my nerves. "You can do this," I whisper. "Every girl goes through this brief moment of second guessing, surely. How hard could it be?" I recall every moment that Meredith made a comment about his size, surely knowing the difference from seeing a few, since I can't really compare. "It's just a dick. It's just a dick."

I place my hand in front of my mouth for a breath check. No immediate foul odors register, so I think I'm good. Pushing my shoulders back, I turn the door handle and open it slowly, trying not to make any noise. With my first step forward, I push up on my tiptoes and quietly make my way down the short stretch of the hall to his door.

I stop, continuing to breathe evenly in hopes the slight convulsions my body is making without my consent will cease. There is no better motto right now than Nike's: *Just do it.*

I turn the handle of the door as I exhale, hoping to keep it slow and steady. When the handle's end is pointing toward the floor, I place my palm against the wood and push the door open, but only enough for me to slip through.

I shouldn't feel like the psycho in a thriller or scary movie right now, but standing here watching him sleep, I kind of do. It's a little creepy even for me, but he's beautiful. He never pulled his curtains or closed his blinds, so the moonlight is beaming through the crevices, creating shadow lines across his face. He's lying on his back on top of the comforter, one arm outstretched across the bed holding his phone, and the other bent and resting across his forehead.

My hand immediately finds my chest. Was he waiting on me to text him back? That makes me feel like total crap. I don't know why a man in nothing but boxer briefs is so sexy, but it is. Why am I still standing here?

I tiptoe across the room, freezing when he begins to stir. He releases his phone from his hand and it immediately goes for his crotch, dipping beneath his trunks, creating a mound. My lips purse together. Is he afraid it's going to disappear? How am I supposed to not laugh right now?

I close my eyes and count, calming myself. When his hand leaves his trunks and stops on his stomach, I start to walk the rest of the way, until I'm standing at the foot of the bed.

No turning back now.

I place my knee on the bed and allow my weight to shift, pulling the other on just after. His legs are slightly spread already, leaving enough space for me to crawl between, so I do. When I touch his thighs he jumps, his head jerking forward, a sound of startle escaping from his mouth. No words just sounds.

His eyes blink repeatedly as he stares at me standing on my knees, as if he's trying to get them to focus. "Kambry? Is everything okay? What's wrong?"

Instead of answering, I bend forward and grip my hands around the waistband of his briefs, exactly as Meredith told me to, and start to pull them down his hips. As she said he starts to lift off the bed, allowing me to work them over his butt. "What are you doing?"

"Shhh."

I release them once they hit his thighs, glancing at what I came in here for. It does look a little . . .different, lying in a more relaxed fit over his balls. Still, even soft he doesn't look small like I would have imagined. It's definitely not as big, but it's not small either.

I lean down and kiss the inside of his thigh as I grab his dick, running my lips over the layer of hair. The closer I get to the center of his legs, the more he spreads them. He's already hardened some since I grabbed it in my hand, making it harder, thankfully, because in this state I want to squeeze it, like a stress toy. When my eyes set on it, positioned upright, every worry and self-conscious thought leaves, and is replaced with desire and want. I want to do this, and that's when my mouth navigates toward it, my tongue inching out as I reach the head, swiping across the top.

By the time I wrap my mouth around the top, it's already completely hard; the way I remember it. I didn't even really notice the transition. I swirl my tongue around the head, wetting it, before pushing my mouth down the length, trying to keep my teeth back. I can hear his breathing pick up, but I don't look at him. Instead, I focus on what I'm doing, which is taking him into my mouth as far as I can, breathing through my nose the entire way.

My saliva immediately begins to increase. I stop when I know I can't go any further and change directions, suctioning as I go, and allowing my tongue to caress the underside until it reaches the dip, flick my tongue a few times, and then I start the process over. Each time I get faster than the one before. He's so hard, so thick, and I can even feel the ridges where veins are.

He hasn't said anything, but I try to put it in the back of my mind. He fills my mouth completely, and I can only go down his length about halfway before the tip is at the back of my throat, and I'm scared to go any further.

I wonder . . .

When my mouth is at the head, I place my hand at the center and twist, before spreading my saliva down his length with my hand. I take him into my mouth again as far as I can, and then I mimic the motions of my mouth with my hand, creating a full stroke instead of a half. Instantly I feel him push his pelvis up a little. "Shit," he whispers. One word and I'm motivated for more. A rush surges through me and I increase the speed to a steady, fast pace, holding my weight by my knees and my free hand on the bed.

The more I suck the hornier I become. I feel wet between my legs. I moan around his dick by accident. He fists his hand in my hair and pulls, causing me to suck harder. "Fuck, Kambry. I'm about to nut. Stop."

I disregard his request, continuing. The faintest pulse occurs and then the first spurt hits the back of my tongue. I pull back, leaving only the top portion in as he continues to fill my mouth with his cum. It's warm, salty, and creamy in consistency."

I pull off when he stops, looking at him for the first time, not saying anything: unable to. "Shit. Sorry."

He reaches over the bed and hands me his shirt. "Spit it in here."

I grab it from him and place it over my mouth with both hands; disposing of the substance I can't bring myself to swallow, yet at least. I toss it on the floor. He gives me a lazy grin. "What was that for?"

I pull his briefs back up with his help, leaving them in their original position, and then kiss the area of skin just above the elastic band that represents the brand, before standing on my knees and backing down the bed until I can reach down and touch the floor with my feet. "Goodnight, Saxton."

Without another word I leave his room and return to mine, not stopping until I reach my bed. I turn around, glancing at the now shut door, before falling backward until my back and head hits the mattress. I stare at the ceiling, the biggest grin developing on my face. "That was such a rush," I whisper, unable to contain the words. "Holy crap."

My door swings open and I prop myself up on my elbows. He stalks toward me, all sexy hunk of a man in his underwear, making me nervous, but then catches me off guard when he grabs my head and crushes his lips to mine. My response hums between us in the form of a contented, muffled sigh.

One arm wraps around my back, and then I'm scooted up further on the bed as he straddles me. His tongue has already found mine, and he kisses me so deeply that I can't think. There is need behind it. I can feel his fear. He leans forward, lowering my back to the bed, and then trails his lips along my jaw and down my neck, allowing his tongue to taste my skin. That feels so good.

My legs pull forward into a bend, resting to his sides. I wrap my arms around him. My breathing is heavy. He pushes his pelvis into my center, pressing his erection against my entrance, allowing me to feel him hard. Only thin fabric separates us. I've never wanted anything as bad as I want him inside me.

He nips at my skin and a prickling sensation spreads throughout my body. "Saxton . . ." He shushes me with his lips, but only briefly, causing my feet to relax on the mattress. His hand grabs onto the back of my thigh, before lightly rubbing to my bare butt cheek.

As soon as he withdraws, I open my eyes. His eyes are boring into mine. "Don't cheat on me, Kambry. I can deal with a lot of shit; like knowing other men will see you totally nude, or that anyone can watch our entire sex life with the click of a button. I can even deal with knowing other men are probably jerking off to thoughts of you, as long as I know in reality you're mine and mine alone. If I'm not doing something that you want or need, talk to me. I've said this before and I'll say it again. If you want it multiple times a day come find me. I'm only a car ride away on most days. We can even fuck by plane, train, or video. I don't care. We'll figure it out. Just don't cheat on me. If you want out, say it. I may not like it, but I won't trap you. I gave my heart to a girl once before and it didn't work out in my favor. I may not fall fast, but I fall hard. I forgave her over and over again because I loved her and tried to make it work, but now that's my breaking point. That's the one thing I can't forgive you for if you do. It almost destroyed me before I finally walked away."

I refuse to cry. I know this is something that he fears in a relationship for the simple fact that the subject of cheating has come up in conversation before. I had an idea that he had been cheated on. I just didn't know how badly. "Saxton, if I wanted to be with someone else at any given point during a relationship with you or anyone else then we shouldn't be together at all. I meant what I said outside. You're enough for me. I don't need anyone else. You satisfy any desire for sex that I have."

"You're fucking perfect," he says, before kissing me again. His hand pushes the fabric of my babydoll up my sides, baring my stomach. "Did you wear this just for me?" I nod, trying to calm my breathing. "And you blew me without expecting an orgasm in return?"

"I wanted to try it. You've gone down on me, countless times. I just wanted to, so I did."

"Fuck, I love knowing I'm the only dick you've ever had."

He stands on his knees and tugs the fabric up. I lift my body and arms, allowing him to pull it over my head, before lying back down. His hand inches underneath my thong as his lips wrap around my nipple, his tongue flicking back and forth. I arch into his mouth as his finger presses into me, pumping in and out.

I moan through closed lips, causing him to bite down on my nipple with a slight pressure, before sucking my nipple into a hard point. He switches to the other side, before leaning back enough to look at me. "Because of that you're going to get one. I'm about to suck you till you scream. I want you to sit on my face."

I bite my bottom lip, imagining just that. Nothing turns me on more than him talking dirty and telling me what we're going to do. He uprights himself again, pulling my panties down my legs with force until he has them completely off. "Come here, beautiful."

I sit up, and then stand on my knees just as he is. Placing his hands on the side of my neck, he presses his lips to mine, before rubbing them over my mouth harshly, and taking my top lip between his teeth. He continues to kiss me roughly, one hand trailing down my body until he reaches my butt. He cups the center in his hand, before picking me up and sliding me up his body.

I wrap my legs around his waist as he turns us around and sits. His mouth leaves mine, our eyes meet, and then he lies back in a flat position. "Bring your pussy to me."

Pushing onto my knees, I walk up his body, his hands on my thighs. I'm curious, I'm interested, and I'm nervous. When I reach his chest I stop, but he shakes his head at me. "Don't be scared. Now you get to ride."

"Ride what?" I ask nervously.

"My tongue." My entire core tightens with those two words. "Straddle my face."

I do as he says, continuing forward until each knee is beside his head. "Good girl. Your pussy is beautiful." This is the most self-conscious I've been yet, open and over him like this. "Sit," he commands.

I lower myself, and at that exact moment his tongue presses between my lips; he swipes upward until it hits my clit. A wave of pleasure hits me as his tongue flicks over my clit in a hardened point. My legs weaken, causing me to lower toward him more. He grips a cheek in each hand, squeezing. When he hits a certain spot my hips reflexively begin to move back and forth. I grip his hair in my hand and his tongue stills, the tip hardening even more. "Shit, that feels good."

I can't stop the movements. It feels too good, knowing exactly where I need the pressure and how much, and being able to give it to myself without it actually being me.

My toes curl as the feeling begins in that one targeted spot, before it starts to radiate throughout my entire body. "Sax . . . I'm about to. Oh shit."

He pulls me toward him hard, and sucks my clit into his mouth as my orgasm heightens; then shoves two fingers inside of me and clamps forward as he sucks me harder. "Fuck!" I scream as my fingers tighten in his hair. My body stills, but his doesn't. It would probably have hurt if my entire body wasn't in slow motion, with nothing registering but how good it all feels.

My clit gets sensitive and my mind unfreezes. I try to lift, but he doesn't let up. "Stop. I can't. Oh, fuuuuuck." My entire lower half quakes. "Dammit, Saxton, just fuck me!"

He growls and pulls his fingers out of me, lifting me and flipping us so fast

I can barely even register the action. "Hands and knees."

I turn my head, watching as he pushes his trunks down his legs. "I've wanted to do this again since I took you home from the sign. I think about it all the time."

Grabbing the base of his dick, he presses it to my opening, rubbing the head up and down. "Fuck yeah. You're so damn wet." He inches inside, slowly at first, before he presses all the way in. "So tight. Fuck."

My back arches when he hits something inside. I shove forward slightly. He grips my hips and begins thrusting, each one coming faster than the last. I look down at the sheet, trying to hold still. I can feel it in my stomach. The faster he hits against me; a slapping sound begins. I can feel the soft skin of his balls hitting against my lips from my ass being at an angle.

It keeps rotating between pleasure and pain. Thrusting in feels good until he goes deep. That's when it hurts. The recoil feels so damn amazing, before it starts over. "I'm not going to last much longer staring at your ass while I shove my cock inside you."

I feel his thumb rub close to his dick, before he swipes up my crack and then I feel him press between my butt cheeks. When he hits deep, he slips his thumb into my asshole. I tense from the foreign invasion, until he begins pumping in and out of me. It slows his rhythm just a little, but not too much. I'm not sure how I feel about it, being completely submerged versus just rubbing it, but it takes my focus off the pain of his thrusts.

I moan as a strange feeling takes over. "Sax, fuck."

My hands clench the sheets. "That's it, baby. Come on my dick."

"That feels so good. I think I'm . . ." A different, all consuming feeling takes over my body, but different than before. This one is longer. I press into him, arching my back. He continues to thrust, but after a few times he stills when he hits deep.

He pulls his finger out of me, and leans down, his front to my back, and then cups my breast in one of his hands, pulling me upright with him. I wrap my hands around his neck as he places his lips to my neck and moves just below my ear. "Coming inside of you will never get old. I'm going to use your restroom and then we're going to bed . . .in here."

"You're sleeping with me?"

"There's nowhere else I'd rather be."

"If you want to put panties on because of my cum fine, but nothing else. I'll be right back."

He pulls out of me, and leaves, disappearing into the bathroom. I reach into the drawer and grab a pair of underwear, pulling them on. As I get under the cover he returns, wearing his boxer briefs, and then crawls into bed behind me. His arm wraps over my side and immediately goes for my breast as he scoots closer to me, molding his body around mine. I glance down at his hand holding onto my boob and smile. "Are you comfortable?" I laugh.

"Mmmm Hmmm." He yawns. "Goodnight, beautiful."

"Goodnight, handsome."

I settle into him and instantly I grow tired, my eyes closing almost immediately. I've never been more relaxed and content than I am right now.

CHAPTER TWENTY-TWO

Saxton

She starts to stir in my arms, but doesn't make any immediate effort to move. I've been up for a while. I always am. I've never really been a late sleeper. It doesn't matter how late I go to bed, because I'm still going to be up pretty early. I guess you could blame that on being raised on a farm. The years and the scenery may have changed, but the habits haven't.

When I woke up she was snuggled against me, her back against my front. It felt good, so instead of moving I just laid here and held her. I've thought about things too; like what in the hell is going to happen in a few weeks, especially if we don't continue this project, or even after that if we do, because with each day I only want to be around her more instead of less.

I'm not real sure what happened between us last night, but I think we crossed a barrier. I haven't been that vulnerable around someone in a long time, especially a woman. Every man has a weakness. Every man has something he's insecure about. It doesn't matter whether he's just an average guy or whether he's known and wanted by the world, because there is still something that turns his world upside down when it comes to intimacy, a relationship, or just a part of himself. Mine is infidelity. The chance of it happening again scares the hell out of me.

When someone you love cheats on you, it consumes you, makes you crazy, and every possible scenario plays out in your mind, and a little too vividly at that.

It's all you can think about. Every time I made love to her, all I could think about were things like: did he please her better, is she thinking about him now, or was she wetter for him than me . . . I've never fucked a woman without a condom before Kambry. From the time I started having sex it was about being safe and not screwing up my life. When Salem and I dated we were still in college. I had to make something of myself so that I could eventually provide for a family, and she never questioned me wanting to use one. I loved her, so it was something I was looking forward to at one time, but then I found out she cheated on me. After that I couldn't bring myself to even think of having sex with her without a condom, let alone actually do it.

There is nothing worse than having to endure sharing your woman with another man. It's a toxic poison. Nothing is ever the same after that, whether they keep doing it or stop altogether. The first time you can't reach her on the phone you immediately grow suspicious, wanting to know if she's doing it again.

Every time I would start to try to trust her again, I would find out she spread her legs for another man behind my back. I'd get pissed off, upset, heartbroken, and then she would turn on the water works and I'd cave. She had every excuse in the book as to why she did it, but not once was it just because she wanted to. My friends called me pussy-whipped for staying, but love makes you stupid. I was that guy that actually wanted what my parents had someday, and I thought I found it in her, so I was willing to do whatever I could to make it work, because she said she loved me. I believed her, because my dad believed that a person's word was everything and should be trusted until they prove otherwise.

But people lie. People are selfish. I finally figured that out the night I proposed to her, thinking that was what she needed to grow up. I thought maybe she was just missing that piece that her friends were starting to experience, so I bought a ring with money I had been saving from working through school. We were one year away from graduating and I was preparing to start my life and my family . . .as a man.

Then she fucked my friend's cousin when he came for a weekend visit at UCLA: the same night I slid my ring on her left ring finger. She was supposed to be studying for an exam in her dorm, but instead she ended up at a low-key party I wasn't at, because I had to work. She didn't even have enough decency to take it off, and he didn't care enough to ask any questions about the fucking diamond on her finger. Thank fuck for good friends that don't keep secrets that could hurt you, because when he forced me into a bar late that night to tell me what he walked in on too late over a couple of beers, just after it happened, I realized that you can't have a one-way relationship. It doesn't matter how much you love someone, or how loyal you are to that person, because if it's not reciprocated then it means nothing.

That's what scares the hell out of me with Kambry. That's what set me off when that prick touched her right in front of my face. I like her, but in that very second everything from college that I walked away from slapped me in the face, and aside from the female family members in my life I haven't trusted a woman since then. The insecurity that I'm not enough for a woman to stay faithful steered me into this career, and it's also what keeps me here, because in the end all they want is sex. At least that's what I've thought until now. Now I'm starting to question everything, because I'm really starting to realize that I want more than this with her. I guess I have a little bit of time to figure it out.

She rolls over in my arms, and I let her. She's blinking so quickly that each time her lashes connect they make a fluttering motion as they open and close. She's trying to wake up. Her lips are puckered and she has a sour look on her face. It makes me smile, because she's clearly not a morning person. "Morning."

"Morning," she says, in a hoarse voice. "How long have you been up?"

"A while."

"Mmmm." Her eyes start to close again. "What time is it?"

"Ten."

"How are you not tired?"

A piece of hair falls over her face. I push it behind her ear so that I can see her. "My family owns a farm back home. I used to have to get up early and work before school to help. I guess my body just never got out of it."

Her eyes pop open. "A farm? In California?"

I kiss the tip of her nose as I pull her naked body closer. "It's not all beaches and vineyards here." I laugh. "What, did you think farms only existed in the south?"

"I don't suppose I've ever really thought about it. Don't judge me. I didn't get out a whole lot. This is my first time past Texas to be quite honest. My family really wasn't all for travel. They suck."

"Yet I haven't seen you in a pair of boots yet."

"You'd have to venture off with me to a rodeo for that. I may be southern, but boots are hot. They have a place. If I'm not at a rodeo or somewhere with horses walking around, then they aren't going on my feet. Me–I'm a flip flop kind of girl."

"We could do that. I've been to several back home."

"Rodeos too? Who would have ever thought I could go to a rodeo in Cali. That just sounds so weird."

"You know . . .I'd bet we're actually closer to the king of rodeos than you are Bama. Want to see who's closer to Cheyenne? Distance configuration from point A to Wyoming is just a Google search away."

She laughs. "Just like you? And maybe. I'd like to say I'm geographically challenged without any judgment. If I told you where I thought our great capital was until eighth grade you'd never let me hear the end of it."

"I'm listening."

"Seriously? Why did I open my big mouth?"

"Spill Bama."

"Okay, so I'm Bama now? What happened to Kambry?"

"I like both. Plus, you're deferring. I'm waiting for this answer."

"Fine. Okay, so . . .I kind of thought that the white house was located in the state of Washington, and not the District of Columbia."

I laugh out, completely on accident. What's worse, it's one of those laughs that start small and get out of hand unintentionally before you can stop; the ones where you can't breathe because your stomach muscles are so constricted.

I roll onto my back, my palm coming to rest on my contracted abs, trying to stop. Water builds in the corners of my eyes and my chest expands, trying to get air. "Sax, that's so not funny. Asswipe."

"I'm so-rry." My breaths are short and shallow, trying to stop the laughing that is slowly calming, but not slow enough. "Fuck."

She gets on top of me and the first things I see are tits: beautiful, big tits. That's all it takes and the laughing ceases. Of course now the fact that her pussy is placed just above my dick is registering, and without even processing the thought I already have a chub. "You're so mean. See if I tell any more embarrassing stories."

"I'm sorry. Ditzy is attractive. I haven't laughed that hard in a while." My hands grip her hips, already trying to move north. "What did you think the DC stood for?"

"I don't know. I guess I just never thought about it at all."

"Wait. You didn't tell anyone that, did you?" She purses her lips. My grin grows. "Who did you tell?"

"Maybe my entire eighth grade history class, but my memory could be foggy."

She covers her eyes with her hands. I grab her wrists and pull them away. "How exactly did that even come up?"

"Well . . .my teacher pointed to a map if I remember correctly and said Washington or the capital or something. I don't really remember. What I do remember is that I burst out my question before I could stop myself, because in my mind she was on the wrong side of the United States map."

"And her response was?"

"She was displeased with my answer. There might have been a joke that took place. I handed her a loaded gun, because she had a very dry humor about her already. There were a few laughs around the room. Yeah . . .I felt stupid."

I sit up, ignoring my hard dick, and grip her face in my hands. Her mouth opens when my thumb brushes along her bottom lip. "Had I been there, I would have pretended to think the same thing, beautiful."

She smirks. "Were you that guy?"

I smile. "And what guy is that?"

"The one that always saves the damsel in distress."

My smile broadens. "I was that guy." I laugh. "But in my defense I had an older sister that would have kicked my ass had I been any other way."

"Smart girl."

She looks at my lips. "Yeah, she is. She'd like you. Maybe one day you can meet her."

"I'd like that."

The air around us becomes thick. The mood turns serious. We don't speak or move for what seems like forever. She just looks at me and I stare at her. There are so many unknowns in this situation. Everything about my personal life is a haze; has been for a while, except her.

I pull her toward me until our lips press together. My tongue slips between her lips. I just want to taste her. I pull back. "I know what I want to do today. You can pick tonight. Sound good?"

Rules are pretty simple here. We live normally. That means we come and go like a regular couple. Maybe that's why she doesn't act camera shy, because when you do normal activities, you forget that the cameras are around. We have cameras on us whether we stay here or leave. The goal is to be a real couple and have explosive and explicit sex. That's it. They take care of the rest.

"I want to take you out for a day on the green."

She scrunches her nose. "Uh, you want to play golf? I would most definitely suck at golf. How is that fun?"

"Because it's goofy golf."

She smiles. "That I can do. You should have said that first."

"And miss the look of disappointment on your face? No way."

She pushes me back against the bed and leans over me, her nipples rubbing against my chest. "You haven't seen disappointment. That would come if I lose. I'm warning you. I'm very competitive. And I'll figure out a way to win."

"Oh yeah." I grab her blonde hair in my fist and tug. "I'll play. But I'm warning you that I don't play fair."

She grinds her panty-covered pussy along the length of my dick. "You don't intimidate me anymore."

"No?"

"No."

I roll, rotating our positions. "Nothing?"

Her eyes scan mine. She's unsure, but she's not going to admit it. "Nothing with you."

I push up on my knees and grab her ankle, pulling it to my lips, before crossing it to the other side to flip her over. She gets on her hands and knees and looks back at me. "Then let me fuck you in the ass."

She stares at me with wide eyes. I'm waiting for her to say no, but I can tell she doesn't want to. For a dramatized effect, I grab my dick and stroke it slowly, showing my size. "Okay. I'll try it."

Fuck, my dick just hardened some more, making the skin tight. My heart is racing. I grab her ass cheek in my other hand. "Are you sure?"

"Yes. Will it hurt?"

"Probably, but I'll go slow. If you want to stop, I will."

"Okay."

I lean forward and kiss her back. "Just when I think you can't get any better you surprise me."

Reaching over, I pull the top drawer of her nightstand open, grabbing a condom and the small bottle of lube just like the contents of mine. I upright my body, and then rip the condom open, rolling it on immediately. She watches as I open the bottle of lube and pour a significant amount in my hand, before rubbing it up and down my dick, spreading it all over the condom.

I place the bottle upside down, holding it above the crack of her ass, and then squeeze. It pours out on the top of her ass and drizzles between her cheeks. I close the bottle and toss it aside. My thumb follows the trail, smearing it over her skin, and then I massage it over her asshole. She tenses at first touch, but then relaxes. "Do you like this?"

"Yes. Most guys do."

"Why?"

"It just feels different. It's forbidden territory. For some it's even a way to dominate over his partner. I won't lie. I love your ass, and I want to fuck it. I think about it often, but most of all it appeals to me because no one else has been in there. Have you changed your mind?"

"No. I just wanted to know. I want to try things you like."

"Does it make you uncomfortable?"

"A little."

"I'll make you forget, baby. Push back and spread for me."

She does as I ask, pressing against my thumb. I push at the same time, allowing it to break the seal. She makes a low noise as my thumb enters her completely. "Relax, baby. You've had my finger in there once already. It's a mental thing. It's made to stretch."

With my opposite hand I reach around her and find her clit. She presses into me further when I start to rub up and down over it. "That's it, baby."

I pump my finger in and out, letting her get used to the fill back there. She moans. I pull out and stop touching her. She looks back at me again. "I need both hands for a minute, baby. I'll go slow and explain. Okay?"

She nods her head. "Okay."

I grab my dick in one hand and her shoulder in the other to hold her body still. Pressing the head of my dick between her cheeks, I find her hole, and then rub my head over it. She moans, confirming it feels good. "You like that, baby?"

"Yeah," she says breathy.

"I'm going in. Relax. For me."

Pulling her toward me by the shoulder, I thrust against her ass slowly, allowing my dick to penetrate her. It tries to slip a couple times from the muscle being so tight, but I increase pressure and slowly enter, not stopping until the head is in. She whimpers. "Relax baby. You okay?"

She nods again. "Just different."

"Just don't tense and work against me. I'll make it feel good in just a minute." She arches more and I thrust inside slowly as she does. "Fuck, that feels so good."

She clenches the comforter in her fists, not looking at me as I continue to ease inside all the way. I stop once I'm all the way in, trying to get a grip before I fucking nut from how hard my dick is being squeezed right now. I lean over her, grabbing her breast in one hand, squeezing, and quickly rubbing her hard nipple as I start to thrust. "Shit," she screams out. "It hurts."

I slap her ass hard enough to get her attention, but don't stop, and then follow through with a light rub. I kiss beside her spine. "Do that again."

I kiss again. "This?"

"All of it."

I slap her ass again, causing her to yell a cutoff moan. "You like when I slap your ass?"

I speed up my thrusts a little, squeezing her tit harder to change the point of pain. She whimpers again, but lower this time. I upright myself. "Hands on the headboard, baby."

She grabs onto it. I move my hands to her hips and grip them hard, as I softly pound into her, but taken down a few notches from what I want to do. "I love your fucking body. Shit. You feel so good." My head falls back. For the first time she moans and I fucking lose it, my nuts tightening and my dick starting to throb. "I'm about to come all in that beautiful ass."

I thrust inside and stop as I come into the condom. "Holy shit."

My eyes close. When I open them she's shaking. Fuck. I pull out slowly and pull the condom off, tossing it in the trashcan beside the bed. "Turn over, baby."

I help her turn over onto her back. Tears are streaming down her beautiful face. I feel like shit. I lean over her between her legs; our chests touching, and then kiss her tears, before wiping them with my hands. "Fuck, Kambry. I'm sorry. I'm so fucking sorry. Baby, I'm sorry."

"It's fine. I wanted to." Pain is evident in her voice.

"No, it's not fine. I shouldn't have asked. I'm just used to . . .fuck, never mind." I scoot her head to the edge of the bed, changing our direction. "Let me make you feel good. Let me make you forget." I kiss her. Her mouth is salty and wet from her tears. She kisses me back. My tongue inches out, and I create a wet trail down her body, stopping at her breasts with a kiss on each, then her navel, until I reach the place I'm aiming for.

Grabbing the back of her thighs, I push them back toward her head, spreading her as much as I can. I slowly lean into her, kissing her lips, before lightly licking along them with the point of my tongue. "Mmmm."

I look up at her from beneath my lashes. Her head is lifted, looking at me. I push up on her thighs, just enough to see her. "Lay back, baby. Relax. Don't watch. Just feel. You may have started with pain, but you're going to end with pleasure."

Leaning down, I swipe my tongue between her folds, and then harden the tip just as it hits her clit. Her head falls back, slightly hanging over the edge. My hands move to spread her lips open, holding her legs with my forearms as I flick my tongue back and forth in quick, short strokes. She lets out a deep, long moan. My dick hardens again. It does every fucking time she sounds like that.

I swear on my life no woman has ever turned me on so much naturally that I could get up right after I blew my load. I slide a finger inside of her, just because I want to feel how wet I make her, and she doesn't disappoint. I can feel her arch off the bed. I suck her clit into my mouth as I pump in and out of her. I love the way she tastes.

Her pussy starts to clamp around my finger and her moans become louder. Her hand grips in my hair and she pulls. I go back to flicking back and forth, but faster. She moves her hand to the back of my head and pulls me into her, smashing my mouth against her lips, so I suck again, letting her feel every second of her orgasm, not stopping until she tugs at my hair.

I move up her body, wiping my mouth on my shoulder. When her eyes meet mine, it feels like someone put an electric current to my heart, giving it a jump-start. The rhythm changes. "Feel better?"

"Yeah. You didn't have to, though."

"Yeah I did. I'm your man. That means I do whatever is necessary to leave you happy."

I align the head of my dick at her entrance, and then pull her down the bed a couple of inches. "What are you doing?"

"Now, I'm going to make love to you; slow."

I push into her as slow as I can. She wraps her arms around my waist, putting her hands on my ass. "I'm content even if you don't."

"Content is not good enough. Intoxicated is the goal. I'm going to finish what I started."

And then I lay my mouth on hers and kiss her, the way she deserves to be kissed . . .

CHAPTER TWENTY-THREE

Kambry

He rounds the truck a few moments after he kills the engine, and opens my door, extending his hand for me. "You ready to loosen up those shoulders, beautiful? I want to stare at your butt while you show me your golfer's stance."

I try not to laugh, but really, who says stuff like that without sounding totally corny or like a douche bag? Oh right . . .Saxton does, that's who. "I hardly think I'll be loosening anything. We won't even be hitting the ball very hard unless you know of some form of miniature golf I've never heard of."

I slide out of the truck, before he pulls me against his front. He smells so good. It's a clean, manly smell; not to mention he looks hot as hell in that pair of white cargo shorts and that tee shirt the color of coral. Lying next to his bare skin it creates a dark bronze skin tone. He has stubble, like he does pretty often, and it just makes it so much better. I don't know why, but I like him better with a little bit of a rough edge.

"Maybe. You never know what tricks I have up my sleeve. This is the king of goofy golf courses. You haven't played goofy golf until you've played here." He grabs my butt in his hands, squeezing over the white cotton fabric. "I like these shorts. They remind me of lace." He places a kiss on my bare shoulder. "This is sensual, and sexy; hanging off your shoulder like this. You look good in black and white."

"Yeah. Kind of. The lace thing I mean. Not that I look good. They're comfortable. Nothing spectacular about the top; it's just black. I'm rambling. Are you ready to go start?" I breathe out, trying to stay calm with him touching me like this. I still haven't figured out why in the world my body reacts the way it does to him with just a simple touch or kiss.

I haven't said a whole lot since we got out of bed a couple of hours ago. I was a little unsure of how to feel after . . .earlier. I've never had even a remote turned on thought when it came to my hindquarters. I'm not going to pretend it was all flowers and sunshine. Truthfully it hurt like hell. It was an uncomfortable pressure, like when you need to use the bathroom and have held it too long, making me paranoid.

At first I felt a little degraded, unsure as to why a straight man would want to do something that is so frowned upon and a consequence of things like prison. It's still not clear, but I don't want to miss out on any moment or activity for fear that it's abnormal. I've missed out on too much of my life already. I was nervous, but I trust him. What probably confused me the most was that there was a point at the end, once I finally started to get used to the invasion in my ass, that I liked it. It should have felt dirty and forbidden, and it did, but that's the part that made me like it more.

When it was over, and he saw me crying, it was more of the result from the beginning. I just didn't know how to explain. I was already past the pain. I also have a confession. Once it was over, I was sort of glad that I remained silent, because the way he took care of me, so flawlessly and gentle, was something I'll never forget. He was tender. I felt every part of it. As he looked into my eyes, thrusting in and out of me, I wanted so badly to whisper I love you, but I kept that a secret in fear of ruining it.

I know it's stupid to love a porn star, because I'm only destined to get hurt. At some point he's going to be inside of another woman the way he's been inside of me. My heart will probably crumble, but I don't know how to shut these feelings off. I've never felt this way. I never wanted to tell Kyle those words. They felt like a lie, so when he told me, I just said, I know.

Now that we're here, all of those insecure feelings from earlier are vanishing. I suppose I just needed to move past the shock of what I allowed him to do to my body. I look at him as he inches me to my right, leaving an opening to the truck.

"I kind of like when you ramble and when you get all nervous. It reminds me of high school; a much simpler time."

"Oh yeah?" I lightly shove at him, teasing. "Were you a ladies' man? Making all the girls nervous . . ."

"Damn right." He winks, playing along, with that damn smile that makes butterflies flutter in my stomach. "I worked on a farm." He grabs my hand and lightly rubs it beneath his shirt, over his tightened abs. "They wanted me for my body. Plus, I was a sweetheart and made them laugh. What was there not to love?"

"Pffft. That body does nothing for me, Maverick. You must be getting rusty."

He places his free hand flush against the truck and changes the direction from north to south as he leans toward me, pushing my hand back down toward his waistband. "You sure about that, Bama? Those cheeks sure do resemble the color of crimson instead of peach."

My fingertips break the seal, slipping under his shorts and boxer briefs. I feel the beginning of very short stubble. From the corner of my eye I notice a family walking through the parking lot with a couple of kids. I pull my hand away. "Okay, okay, fine. You win. I love your body, I love your personality, I love y—" I clear my throat. "Everything about you." I'm such an idiot.

The grin on his face looks exactly like *The Grinch Who Stole Christmas*. "Roll tide, baby." His lips stop just an inch from mine, his eyes locked on mine. He's still smiling and I'm pretty sure I'm not breathing. "I've never been much of an SEC fan, but I think you just recruited me, because crimson is now my favorite color." He lightly kisses me and pushes off, grabbing a cap from the truck and shutting the door, before turning to walk toward the building. "Come get your balls."

I watch as he walks away with a swagger in his step. He places the ball cap on his head and adjusts it into place. I slap my hands over my face and shake my head, mumbling to myself. "There is no hope for me."

When I catch up to him he's already at the payment counter, waiting with a golf club in his hand, swung over his shoulder, and a short pencil behind his ear. He's propped on the counter with his other forearm. "I was about to come looking for you."

"Oh, shut up, loser," I laugh. "It has not been that long and you know it." I spot the club rack to my left, grabbing one, and then point it at him. "I thought you were supposed to be sweet. Since when does a gentleman leave his date at the truck?"

"The kind that's giving his girlfriend a view of his ass so she'll want it later. Balls?"

"I should have known. What about your balls?"

"I think he means these balls."

My eyes widen and turn toward the female voice laced with humor. She doesn't look but maybe a year or so older than me, pointing to the bucket full of multicolored golf balls. "Oh. Right."

I grab the pink one and turn toward Saxton. "Welcome back, Crimson. At least I know your mind is in the right place."

I kind of want to die right now. "Are you ready to start?"

"I'm waiting on you to grab my ball."

"Funny. I'm not grabbing your ball."

"No really." He laughs. "I swear I was just fucking around with you earlier. Pick my color."

I grab the green one and extend it toward him. "Here, have a lime, because you're leaving a sour taste in my mouth."

His club swings down to the ground like a cane, and instead of grabbing the ball from my palm he bends down and drives into me like a football player, only soft, before wrapping his arm around the back of my thighs and standing, taking me with him, hanging over his shoulder. "Sax . . . What are you doing?"

"Taking you to hole one."

"My legs work."

"Yes, but so does your mouth, and between the two of us we're never going to start."

"It's your fault. I've asked like twice already. Put me down. I can walk. We are in a family environment."

"What are you trying to say? I can't fuck you against the wall of the cave mid-course. That was supposed to be the plot twist. You're messing up my plans, beautiful."

I swat his butt with my club as the sidewalk continues to pass us by. "No you cannot! I see little people everywhere. I've never been to jail and I don't intend to pop that cherry. I have boundaries."

He laughs. "Bummer. The back of a cop car could actually be fun."

"We shall never find out," I retort, as he finally puts me down on a patch of green.

"Too bad. Could've popped my cop car cherry too. Oh well."

My brows arch. "You've never been arrested? Isn't that kind of a goal with guys? You know, something you can brag about to all your friends."

"Nope. Well, just that time I told you about in the cab at the parking lot of the club, but I didn't actually go to jail. The cop kindly drove my drunk ass back home. Long story. I won't lie. I wanted to beat the shit out of several guys in my life, but two wrongs don't make a right and it doesn't change the outcome of why I wanted to beat their asses in the first place. And two, I like my freedom. I want my pants to stay around my waist unless a female is pulling them off, and nothing is going up my ass."

"Yet you'll put something up mine?"

"Two very different things, sexy. No one, not even female, is shoving something in my ass. Not my preference. I'd rather do the pitching, not catching. I don't judge those that like that sort of thing, but I prefer curves and a nice rack to accompany the ass I'm fucking." He turns to glance behind him. "Before we create a line . . .ladies first. You're up, beautiful."

"Okay, but don't laugh." I look around me, trying to figure out a discrete way to wing this. There are lots of small patches of green as far as the eyes can see. Each one a little different shape and size. Some end with houses, some have caves, and some have moving objects. I see bridges and small ponds and pools.

"I can make no such promise."

I take a deep breath. "So, is that why you called this the king of goofy golf? The whole Cinderella castle they have going on?"

"Maybe. They also have rides and other stuff to do besides golf, like bumper boats." He wriggles his brows.

Bumper boats . . . I really should get out more.

I set the ball down at the start of the green in the center of the lane and stand behind it with my club in hand. I should have gone on that youth night mini golfing trip my church went on when I was in the seventh grade. I'm starting to regret my decision to stay home, because the first thing that pops in my head is the part where the queen and Alice on *Alice in Wonderland* are playing croquet with the flamingos and the little rats—I don't remember what those things are called. Oh yes . . .hedgehogs.

It has to be pretty similar to that. I glance at the rounded lane and spot the hole at the end, trying to figure out how I'm supposed to make that. How many chances do I get? Is it kind of like baseball—three strikes you're out? I grip the club with both hands; each hand holding a portion of the club. I move to the side of the ball and rare back the club, preparing to hit it. "You've never played before . . .have you?"

Dammit.

My head hangs, and I bring the club back down, not making a move to look at him. "Is it that obvious?"

"You could have just said so," he says lowly into my ear, wrapping his body around mine from behind.

"That sounds ridiculous. Who hasn't played miniature golf before?"

"There may not be many, but you're experiencing it now, with me. That's all that really matters." My eyes close as his hands take place on top of mine. "Hands on the grip not the metal."

He slides my hands into the proper place. "You're right handed, right?"

"Yes."

"Dominant hand goes on top of the other. It gives you more control over your swing. Feet shoulder width apart, just behind the ball." His body is molded to mine, making sure I'm aligned correctly. "We aren't playing regular golf with that much distance from the hole, so you don't need that high of a swing. We're sending the ball ten yards at most. See the brick at the curve?"

"Yes," I whisper, trying to prolong this for as long as possible.

"Best bet is to aim at the center and let the ball bounce off of it to send it up the incline toward the hole."

"What if I miss?"

"Then you try again from the point that the ball stops."

"How many chances do I get?"

"As many as it takes to make the hole. Each hit is a stroke. The winner is the player at the end of the last hole with the least amount of strokes."

"That will most likely be you."

"You might be surprised." He kisses my cheek and backs up, leaving me standing alone, gripping this club. My shoulders fall. I want him back over here. I glance between the brick that he told me to aim at and the pink ball, pulling my club back a few inches, and then hitting the ball, driving it forward toward the curve.

It hits, bouncing off and rolling up the hill, but stops just as it reaches the flat green, a few feet from the hole. "Not bad. It should be easy now."

I look at him with a proud smile, before walking up the green to my pink ball, and then repeat the motion, watching as it rolls into the hole. I jump up and down before I can stop myself. "I got it in two!"

"You did. Not bad at all for a beginner."

"What now?"

"Get your ball and get out of the way." He laughs, placing his into position, before making a dramatic warm up with his club.

Just as I move out of the way he hits, sending his ball rolling in the same place I did, only his continues up the hill and rolls until it falls into the hole. I look at him. "Way to crush a girl's dreams. You could have at least given me the first hole."

He laughs, making his way toward the hole to grab his ball, then places his arm around my shoulders as he leads me to the next one. Most of the other families are several holes ahead of us. "I could have, but where is the fun in that? If it makes you feel better, I've had lots of practice. What most people do for fun I do for a living. When you don't date or hang in crowds of couples or go clubbing to look for pussy like most guys, you have to find shit to do. When I'm off, I don't even want to hear the word sex or pussy. I come here a lot. I just figured a place full of kids is a safe zone."

The more I get to know him the further I fall . . .

"So that night at my apartment when I practically begged you to hook up with me, you were probably cringing then, huh?"

"No, baby. You are the exception. That's what got me to your apartment in the first place. It was only those exact circumstances that I even thought twice. I knew you were better than that. That's all."

He stops at the beginning of a lane that leads to a large house resembling a Gingerbread house. "Goal is to make it up the ramp and through the house first.

Then we'll walk around."

"Oh geez. Are they just going to get harder and crazier as the course goes on?"

"That's the goal; the goofier the more fun. Getting it in isn't the hard part."

"Said the guy who has experience with balls and holes."

He looks up at me from writing something on a small square of paper and grins, and then slides it into his back pocket. He watches me, as he grabs the bill of his cap and pulls it off his head, turning it around. *Don't put it back on. Don't put it back on.*

He's putting it back on . . .

"We turning the game up a few notches?"

He walks toward me. I back up, toward the place I'm supposed to be putting, and put my hand out in a stop sign to make him halt. His chest presses against it. "Nope. No, we are not."

"Are you sure? There is no such thing as too much practice."

"For the preservation of innocent minds, would you please cut that crap out? I cannot handle the level of sexiness that you know you're emitting with that damn hat on like that. There, I said it. That is my favorite view. Now step away."

He rests his club handle between his closed legs, holds his hands up, surrendering, and then radiates a huge grin. "You think I'm hot," he teases.

"Oh my god. Are we in middle school?"

"Middle schoolers don't do the things that I do to you, baby, and I'm not through with you yet. Now hit the ball."

I blush, and then turn to continue the game that is going to take us all day at this rate. Taking my stance, I glance between the ball and the ramp, then decide the ball isn't where I want it, so I move it, and then start over. I pull back, and just as I go to hit the ball Saxton smacks my ass, causing me to hit it from an angle, sending it off to the left where it bounces off the corner and rolls just an inch before stopping. "I'm going to kill you. I swear it. You ass!"

I turn to look at him and he's laughing. "It's all about concentration, baby."

"I'm going to show you concentration when I shove this club up your ass. That was a dick move. Now I have to add a stroke just to get it back in front of the damn ramp." I growl.

“So much hostility from such a small body.” He continues to laugh, not fazed by my anger at all. I narrow my eyes at him, and then walk down the sidewalk beside the green, toward my ball. When I get my club into position, I tap it just hard enough to send it to the center. Surprisingly the angle is on my side and it stops right in front of the ramp.

I reposition, but this time hit it harder, giving it enough drive to push it up the ramp. My arms fly into the air, forming a V for victory, then I spin around to look at him. “HA! How you like that?”

“Getting better already. You might even beat me,” he teases, and then winks at me as he prepares to putt.

I walk toward him, on top of the green, making him wait, with my heart still racing from the sight of him.

Using my club like a jousting lance, I hook it with his and continue around him. He stares down at the two connected, and then up at me. “You know, Maverick . . .you may be unaffected by me, but I am determined to find immunity to your sexiness; soon, very soon. I’m challenging myself. Before long, I’m going to be on your level. Mark my words.”

He releases his club, letting it fall to the ground. His hands snake around my waist, underneath my arms, and then he lifts me off the ground. My legs grip around his waist and my hands around his neck. “What are you doing?”

He looks up at me. “That would be a nightmare for me, Kambry. Just because I’m good at pretending, doesn’t mean I’m immune to you. I may pick and play, tease you and give you hell, but that’s just my personality. I’ve been that way all of my life. The guy you met in the club was the unhappy version of me. I was worn down. Sure, it hasn’t been all that long since I first laid eyes on you, but the day that I look at you and see no emotion, I’ll know the fun between us is long gone and it’s time to move on. I don’t want to ever get to that point. You really don’t get it, do you?”

“Get what?” I ask, confused.

“This is the happiest I’ve been in my life in a really long time, maybe ever. There is only one thing that’s been incorporated that is different from any other time, and that’s you.”

My stomach is twisted in knots. My heart is racing. When I’m around him I can’t control how I feel. Every feeling is amplified. It’s addictive. I never want it to end. "I don't know what's real and what's for the cameras anymore . . ."

"You think I would just tell you that for fucking cameras?"

"No, that's not what I mean."

"Then what?"

"Nothing. It's stupid. I'm probably just confused and should keep it to myself. This is where my lack of experience is annoying."

"Tell me."

"It's just, when you say things like that, the way we are together, the way I feel when I'm around you . . . It all feels real. I know it's supposed to be an adaptation or a portrayal, but you kind of feel like my best friend now, except you're that friend that I like to kiss and hook up with. None of it feels fake. The lines are blurred for me. To be honest, most of the time I forget that we actually live under cameras. Weird right? Barely any time has passed, but I feel like—"

"I'm falling in love with you . . ."

Surely I heard that wrong. I blink, continuously. Did I?

"You didn't."

"Didn't what?"

"Hear me wrong."

"How did you?"

"I don't know. I just had a hunch, so I went with it."

"It's not just me?"

"No, it's not." He gives me a small smile. "I'm not sure what to do about it, or how to feel; if I should be happy or not. I have a lot to figure out, but time will tell."

"So it's bad, right?"

"No. That's not what I mean. It's just . . . Kambry, I've loved someone before, like really, full heart in, loved someone. I gave her my all. I thought we wanted the same things. I thought we both wanted each other forever, and one day even a family. I didn't go to college looking for that, but it sort of just appeared, so I jumped on board with no ticket and wound up somewhere that I didn't sign up for. I wasn't stupid enough to think that I would never meet another girl that made me want to try again, but what scares the hell out of me is that my feelings for you are developing faster and harder than they did with her, and it kind of came at the worst fucking time. I'm a porn star. I don't really have a plan mapped out for my life like I did back then. Plus, I know you say you'd never hurt me like that, or do what she did, but even if you didn't I'm still unsure if the benefit is worth the risk. You know?"

My chest hurts. This isn't exactly the way I pictured discovering I was in love with a guy for the first time and basically admitting it out loud turning out. This kind of sucks, but even though it does I still feel the same. "Okay. I'm sorry. I don't really have anything to compare it to. I dated someone for two years, and even though it wasn't, it felt more like an arranged relationship than anything." I pause, thinking. "Yeah, you're probably right. I don't really know what I want to do with my life either. I'm so much younger than you anyway. I probably have way more wild oats left to sow . . ."

"This is not coming out right," he whispers.

I feel like such a downer now. I'm not even really sure how we got on this topic of conversation. I should have kept my big mouth shut. I really should just quit my internal whining, take one for the team, and have a good time and enjoy the pay when this is all over; maybe go back to school, or something.

No, not yet.

I'm not done.

I'm going to whine to myself a little while longer.

Sometimes life really fucking sucks. Right now I feel like curling into the fetal position on my bed and crying. I feel like I did when I found out Santa wasn't real. I've been lied to. I want to burn the storybooks and erase the fairytales that all tell you that when you find your prince you live happily ever after. No you don't.In fairytales good guys fall for good girls and the evil end up in misery, but in real life, the good guy falls for the wicked witch, the evil stepsister, Ursula, or gets eaten by the dragon before he kisses his true love, while Belle ends up with the conceited buff guy that won't shut up, Cinderella dies a lonely maiden, Ariel is sentenced to a life pining after a man that was stolen from her, and Aurora and Snow White die without ever knowing what love feels like.

In real life, love is unfair. It's cruel. The sheltered southern girl falls for the heartbroken porn star and then has to watch their love over and over again on media because he's too scared he's going to be fucked over again, even though hurting him for me is equivalent to stabbing myself in the heart with a knife.

Love. Fucking. Sucks.

I totally get why people end up becoming nuns. Okay, that may be a bit dramatic. I actually like sex and the intimacy of someone touching me, and kissing me, so maybe instead, I'm starting to see the appeal of this being a porn star. You get the intimacy without the bullshit.

My legs release and slide down his body. "Kambry . . ."

I pull myself out of my sappy, love-struck, pity party. He sounds upset; his voice that is. His face is still just as beautiful as it has been even in the most playful mood. "No, it's fine. I get it. I'd probably be the same way too. Actually, you know what? What do you say we finish the game and then get out of here? We're actually off tonight. Surprising for a weekend night. I just kind of want to dance. Let's get dressed and go out. I haven't been to the club off the clock since the beginning of summer. I can actually get away with drinking now. Sounds fun, right?"

"Kambry, talk to me."

"Are you guys done with this hole?"

I look at the couple standing with two young children. "I'm sorry. Yes, we're done. Give us just a second and we'll get our stuff out of the way."

"Kambry," he barks, as I reach down and pick up the clubs.

I smile at him. "Come on. I'm ready to play. I have a pro to beat."

I wink, trying to show playfulness, even though I don't feel it. I walk away, following the sidewalk to the next hole, crossing the wooden bridge along the way, and trying to pull my mood together. Tonight, I'm going to be wild. I'm leaving all reservations behind. Tonight, I'm going to be drunk, without getting sick. I'm going to try my hand at living free, uninhibited, and completely out of my mind. Tonight is the Neon Glow paint party at the club. That huge warehouse out back that was built for theme party nights and blow out bands is finally getting put to use.

CHAPTER TWENTY-FOUR

Kambry

I walk into the house with Saxton's footsteps on my heels. When I release the door to close it, he stops it with his palms and shoves it back open, causing it to bounce off the wall. Instead of looking back at him I continue toward the stairs. The ride has been quiet. I'm just not feeling the chirpy behavior at the moment. Everyone is entitled to a bad mood every now and then. Well, this is mine.

Miniature golf was still fun. Don't get me wrong. Everything I do with Saxton is. I'm just in a bummed out mood I guess, so I want to have fun. The club has been hyping up this Glow party for a while. The fact that I'm actually off is my sign that I need to just go and have fun. Completely letting go is something I've still never let myself do, in fear that I'll get myself into a permanent bad decision by accident or association, but the fact that I will have cameras on me the entire time hidden somewhere amongst the crowd, makes me want it now more than ever.

What better way to get into character mode than a little alcohol and a body covered in paint? Who knows what other shenanigans the night may hold. "Kambry," he calls out in a clipped tone, demanding my attention as I place my foot on the first step.

"Yeah?" I look at him as I respond, waiting for whatever he has to say.

"What did I say that upset you? Don't fucking shut me out like this. I don't like it."

"You didn't say anything that you didn't feel, Saxton. I'm fine. I just want to go and have fun. Can we do that? You said yourself you have a lot of stuff with your feelings to figure out, well, so do I. Can we just drop what happened at the course and go back to before? It will make things a lot easier for me."

"No," he responds. "But we can prolong that discussion if you want. Regardless, it's going to happen. Things have been said. I can't just ignore them. Whatever I said that upset you, I'm sorry. I can almost guarantee it wasn't meant how you took it, but a lack of communication won't fix it. Maybe I was thinking out loud when I should have been thinking to myself. Cut me some slack, Kambry. I'm probably more fucked up over my feelings for you than you are."

"You don't get it!" My hand clenches in my blonde hair. "Fuck, Saxton. I get that a girl screwed you over. I get that I don't know how that feels. I get that you're wigging out because this was all supposed to just be fun, and then you go back to fucking whoever is assigned to you; while I go back to being the runaway from Alabama that had a fling with a porn star, and then went back to being a nobody—the server in a club with no plans or aspirations to be something better."

A tear falls from my eye, but I quickly force it away. "But what you don't get is that I'm just an ordinary girl, standing here with the realization that I've fallen in love with a normal guy for the first time. Like you, I hopped on the train too, speeding along the tracks to an unknown destination, but when two people usually admit that they're falling for each other, the results are exciting and happy. At least that's what I always imagined. You don't want this and you didn't bargain for it. I get it. Neither did I. But here we are. I can't change the fact that I love you. I accidentally fell for you along the way. If I could turn it off I would. I can't reverse time so that you were never hurt. Believe me, I would if I could. You are an amazing guy. I'd bet everything I have that there aren't a big percentage of guys like you left. You deserve happiness. If it were up to me, you'd be living with her in a cookie-cutter house with a white picket fence and babies running around in the yard, because I really want that for you. I really don't understand what was wrong with her, because I'm going to say that I'm probably not the only person that would feel like the luckiest girl in the world to have been in her shoes given the chance. I just need time in my head and we can go back to the basics. It's about the sex. We still have about three weeks left; so let's give them what they're paying us for. I'll be ready in an hour."

I ignore the fact that he's standing there, speechless, and staring at me with his hands in the pockets of his shorts, and run up the stairs as fast as my legs will allow. I can feel the burn in my thighs and calves, but I don't stop until I'm in the safe confinements of my room. I grab my phone to call Meredith. When it starts to ring I place the phone to my ear.

The call connects and giggles sound in the background. "Mer. Are you there?"

"Kambry? What's wrong? I swear on everything I'm going to beat his ass. What did he do?"

"What is it?" A male whisper sounds in the background, but he must be close to the phone, because I can hear everything he's saying.

"Shhh," she says. "Kambry, what happened?"

"It's not anything like that. I just need a night out. Do you feel like going to a Neon Glow paint party at the club? I can get you a band to drink."

"Hell yeah. You know you don't have to ask me if you want to hang with your BFF. I'm always here, no questions asked. One sec." A muffling sound occurs, before she starts to talk, but I can barely hear her, like she pulled away from the phone. "We're going to a paint party at the club. Go get in the shower. I'll be there in a few, K?" She pauses. "Grab the door, will ya?"

The faint sound of a closing door occurs, before her breathing returns in the phone. "Tell me what's up, sweets. Why do you sound like you're upset? I promise it's between me and you."

Another tear sneaks from my tear duct and streams down my face. "I love him, Meredith, and I admitted it out loud, but it was kind of in an argument, sort of. I feel stupid. I just need to forget."

"Shit, babe. This soon? Are you sure?"

"Almost positive."

"When the end occurs, what is your first thought?"

"Tragedy, heartbreak, jealousy, sadness . . ."

"Damn. Okay. Does he feel the same?"

"Yes . . .no . . .I don't know. He said he did, but then he said he didn't know how to feel about it, or if it was worth it. He doesn't have a good track record with serious relationships, so he doesn't really like them. I kind of shut down emotionally, because I didn't really know what else to do. That's why we were fussing if that's what you want to call it. He wanted to talk about the talk and I didn't. At that point, if the previous conversation about us starting to fall was vague or unsure, it isn't anymore. I pretty much belted out that I love him."

"Geez. Are you one hundred percent sure that you want him, even when this is over? This isn't some fly by night relationship, Kambry. If y'all take this further than that house, he pretty much has to give up everything for you. No relationship would survive with him still having sex with other women, career or not. Have you thought of that?"

"Not really. I don't want him to feel like he has to give up anything. I would never ask that of him."

"That's not the point. There isn't a way around that. Are you sure you want him? Only him for possibly forever? You're only eighteen."

"About to be nineteen."

"Same difference."

"It doesn't matter, Meredith. I'm not going to live my life that way. I'm not going to pretend that I'm too young to actually find the person I want to enjoy spending my life with and then he slip away because I did. If it happens there is nothing you can do about it. I just look at it like, if I find the one that I'm meant to be with at a young age then I have more time to enjoy him. I don't see that outlook ever changing."

"Yeah, it totally sucks when that happens."

"What?"

"Uh . . .nothing."

"Meredith Rose Love, you better explain what you mean right now! If you don't, I swear on my damn life this friendship is over. I've never been a liar."

"Fuck. Me and my big mouth." She takes a deep breath. "Kambry, I've loved someone before, okay. He was my first everything. Guys—they get squirrely when things happen they aren't expecting. They're fairly predictable creatures if you just watch and pay attention. Each one may look different, but their behavior is pretty much the same. You just have to prove that you are what you say you are and don't give up until he believes you. I didn't do that. I've regretted it ever since."

"Squirrely? Is that even a word?"

"Yes, Urban Dictionary even confirms so."

"You loved Chris Ainsworth?"

She face-palms herself. I'm assuming that's what she did by the slapping sound that occurred. "The snowball effect begins . . ."

"You're just confusing me more."

"I didn't lose my virginity to Chris! There, I said it. I can finally live in peace."

I narrow my eyes, forgetting that she can't see me. "Oh, do tell. I can't wait to hear this. Backstabbing, secret-keeping hussy."

"I deserve that. I need to go shower. We don't have time to get into this and this is not a phone conversation anyway."

"So help me, Meredith, if you hang up this phone I will tell every embarrassing secret I have on you, especially that one."

"You wouldn't dare. He wouldn't even care anymore."

"Oh, but I would. Are you sure about that? I saw the way he was looking at you on graduation . . .still, after all this time."

I caught her once, hooking up with someone else when her and Chris were pretty hot and heavy. I don't think they were ever a real couple by title, but he was in love with her and she was good at playing the part. No one else messed with them, because to everyone else they were the couple. One thing Meredith hates is to look like the crappy one in a fight or circumstance, even if she should. I never found out who the guy was. I just overheard them in the locker room when I was looking for Ben after a game. He was after curfew and his phone was going to voicemail. My parents being the psychos they were had to go looking. His truck was there, along with a few others. My guess—him and his friends rode together somewhere and lost track of time, because he wasn't there. Mom didn't want to get out of the car, so she sent me.

"It was Ben! Please don't hate me. Please don't say anything. He would be so mad at me. I swore I would never tell."

"Ben? Ben who?"

"Oh my god, Kambry. Let your mind think naughty for five seconds. Think the worst in someone every once in a while. You'd be surprised at how much your eyes would open."

"You fucked my brother! And didn't say anything! I thought he lost his virginity to Molly McCall!"

"It's all lies. Please don't hate me. It was just a cover up. Kambry, no one fucking knows. No one! I'm begging you to please keep this a secret. If you're mad at me, then I deserve it, but I swore on my life I would never let that secret slip. Please. To Chris, I was a virgin. To Molly, Ben was a virgin. I'm begging you to take this to your grave. I was only fourteen. He was seventeen. Please don't fuck up his reputation."

I stand still. Everything around me is spinning. My ears are ringing. Nothing makes sense. I didn't even think Ben liked Meredith. He always made shitty comments about her, saying she's just a girl with looks, living with stars in her eyes. He made it sound like she'd never amount to anything. Furthermore, I've never seen Meredith flirt with Ben. She used to stay at the house all the time when we were younger. They barely even spoke when around each other. Plus, he is older. He didn't hang out with us. When would he have even been around just her for that to happen?

"Kambry, shout at me . . .something! I need to hear you say you hate me, call me a slut, anything is better than silence." She pauses. "Not now, Bryant. I'm dealing with a female emergency. It's gory and gross and you don't want to know. Just like ten more minutes."

I shake my head, listening to her whisper shout at him. The girl is nuts. I'm not sure if I should be more concerned with the fact that she can spin a web of lies faster than a spider could, that she kept an atomic bomb of a secret from me for four years and I never could tell, or that she loves . . . I swallow. Ben. Meredith slept with Ben. Ben slept with Meredith.

Gross.

What in the hell could she see in Ben? He's been an asshole for . . . well . . . four years, if I remember correctly. "Oh my god."

"I'm ready. Get mad at me. I can take it."

"Where did this happen?"

"Which time?"

"Which time?!?"

"Uh, oh . . .you mean the first? Upstairs on the couch in the game room. It was that night you got sick from that pizza and went to bed early after you threw up for like twenty minutes. I was bored and I went up there to watch a movie so I wouldn't wake you. Well, when Ben came home he must have had the same idea. I offered to give him the room, but he told me to stay. It was fun. We talked and goofed off, and then he kissed me. He was so hot. I couldn't believe he was still a virgin. It just happened. When we were redressing post hormones, we realized exactly what we did, so we vowed to just pretend it didn't happen . . .as well as the other four or so times it happened until he graduated, like that night in the locker room."

"That was Ben! Why aren't y'all together if this was some big secret affair? Do you know what kind of person I had to live with until he went to college? He was in a permanent bad mood. I actually thought he was on steroids once."

"Because, Kambry, you know how your parents are, and Ben. He's expected to make something of himself, and he's expected to date a respectable girl that doesn't back talk or have her own ideals. Little miss preacher's daughter was exactly what your parents wanted him with, even though she was no better than me. They had sex just like we did. You know your parents never really liked me."

"But you said you loved him. They can fuck off."

"Kambry, sometimes falling for the guy doesn't keep him around. Sometimes you experience the best too young, before he's ready to be serious. I once heard some men settle down like hailing a cab. He may not be ready for a while, but when he is, the one that shows up ends up being the one he takes. He didn't want me that way. He made it perfectly clear. I didn't question him either, so I moved on and I'll forever hold that regret in my heart. I haven't spoken to or seen him since he left for college."

"I definitely need alcohol tonight."

"Word of advice, from girl to girl, with no bullshit jokes. Love him like you're going to lose him. That way, you'll love harder and with no restrictions. When you reach the end, if he lets you go then it really wasn't meant to be to begin with. It takes two people to love, boo. If he leaves you, you'll still be left with an unforgettable memory and more experience for the next one. At some point, you'll find one that can't walk away."

"So you're saying embrace it?"

"Absolutely. Never ever change who you are or hide how you feel. Just be you . . .like me. You can't hide this kind of crazy, so get up and make yourself hot. You remember the tips and tricks I taught you, right?"

"I think so."

"You still have that neon green underwear set?"

"Yeah."

"Wear that, and . . . Let me think." I walk to the dresser, as she's remaining silent, looking through my underwear for the one she's talking about. I find it almost immediately, tossing it on the bed. "Oh, I got it. Can you find the neon green, low neck shirt that looks like lace?"

I walk to the closet. "Yeah, it's here."

"Get that. Put it with the white, denim, cut-off skirt and the neon pink bandeau. Wear comfortable shoes. Heels serve no purpose with paint flying everywhere."

"Skirt? Are you sure? The flyer looked like tee shirts, tanks, and cotton shorts."

"Yep, you'll thank me later. I'll bring the rest. Make sure you cab it. We'll be too fucked up to drive. See you in about an hour and a half. Love you, chick."

"Okay. Love you too."

I toss down the phone and run for the shower. My mood is already improving. I have a feeling this night is going to go down in the memory book.

Saxton

I stand under the water with my hands firmly against the wall, letting it rain on my head, running down my face in a steady curtain. I was done showering fifteen minutes ago, yet here I stand, still sulking over my own bullshit.

I feel like hitting something, but I refrain. Instead, I tap my fist against it, making a light thumping sound. The constant rhythm calms me. I'm going to fuck this up somehow. I know it. I already am. Sometimes I want to kill her: Salem. She ruined my life. Maybe it wouldn't be so bad had I left at the first sign of bullshit instead of staying, giving her chance after chance to change.

You could hang me off a cliff and I'd be fine, steadily searching for a way to survive, climbing it one groove at a time, yet throw a woman in front of me that my heart is wanting so desperately to love and I freak the fuck out, paranoid I'll be that guy again; the one keeping my dick zipped up while my girl is out giving away what's mine, spreading her legs for every-fucking-body. Sex with her was cut back after that. I just didn't want it as much.

She said she loved me . . .standing right there on the stairs. Do I believe her? God, I want to. I've always believed a person's true feelings come out when they're upset, because you don't have time to think or lie. Watching her cry and yell her anger was killing me. Every organ I had inside was constricted. All I could do was stand there and listen. There was nothing I could do or say at that point to fix upsetting her. The knife in my heart, though, was her wishing she could change my past, giving me a forever in love with someone else. The fuck? Who genuinely feels that way? What I wanted to say was that I wanted that with her. There isn't a single part of me that wants Salem back or wished things had turned out differently, because things always happen exactly like they're supposed to, no matter how much it hurt at the time.

My head is so fucked up. I wouldn't even begin to know how to give her a normal life. What the hell would I even do? Go back to school at twenty-five? Sure, I have the money for it, but do I even want to go back? I'm not a teenager anymore. I sure as hell wouldn't want my girl working in a bar while I'm spending my days finishing up junior and senior year. LA is competitive though. I have no shot at bringing in the kind of income to support a family with my taste without it.

I growl out. I'm never going to make myself see reason.

I'm whining like a little bitch. I don't deserve to carry around the set of balls that's swinging between my legs. You know what . . . Fuck it. Fuck it all. I've never been a fucking pussy and I'm not going to start being one now. I want her. Just about the sex, my ass. Three weeks isn't good enough. That's not enough time to learn everything there is about a person. There is no way I can figure out the path for my future in that short amount of time.

I refuse to let her shut me out. If the studio wants a couple in love with explosive sex, then that's what they're going to get. The only way to get over your fears is to fucking face them head on.

I shut off the water and shake my head, ridding of any excess. Stepping out, I grab the towel from the bar and wrap it around my waist as I wipe my feet on the rug, before taking off for her room without even drying off. When I enter, she looks up at me through the mirror with a straightening iron in her hand.

I halt, taking her in, but I seem to be having trouble figuring out simple motor skills . . .like speaking. Her top is see through, bright green and accentuating her skin, showing off a pink-banded bra of some sort. Barely any material is left once her ass is covered in that skirt.

She places the straightener down on the dresser and turns around, propping her hands against it. "You're wet."

"You're hot," I say honestly. "And isn't that a phrase I should be saying to you?"

A grin starts to appear, but then she destroys it. "What do you want?"

The cold demeanor sends a tingle down my spine. I don't like it. "To see you. I don't like the way you left things downstairs."

"I'm fine. You can go get ready now. I need to finish my hair and makeup."

"You don't need makeup."

"Yeah right. Nice try though."

"Calling me a liar?"

"You don't have to say things like that. I'll let you in my pants regardless."

"That's what you think?"

"Isn't it though?"

My teeth clench together. "Kneeing me in the balls would hurt less than that statement."

I walk forward, our eyes locked on one another. "Words hurt sometimes."

I narrow my eyes at her. "This attitude doesn't look good on you, Kambry. Why don't you just save it and tell me what's really bothering you."

"I. Said. I'm. Fine," she says through gritted teeth. "Just let me get ready, please."

"No. I'm not going anywhere until you tell me which part of what I said upset you. We can stay here all night if you want, but we're not going anywhere until you let it out."

I grab her face, holding her from turning away. "Please don't do this to me. Just let me be mad. Just let me fester in my own hurt and get over it. It's way less painful than the alternative. I'm just being a brat any—"

Leaning in, I kiss her, unable to stand any more of this tension. It's only been a little while, but already I can't stand it. I like that we joke and have a good time constantly. This, I don't like, because the thought of actually fighting with her makes me crazy. When the warmth of our tongues tangle, she moans against my mouth and I reach down and grip her ass firmly in my hands, sliding her up my body.

I shove the items on the dresser back and set her down, her head bumping against the mirror when I press between her legs. I can feel heat on my pelvis, just above my tucked towel, coming from her center. My lips run over her chin and down her neck. She tilts her head to elongate it more. "You always do this to me. The mood swings are driving me nuts."

"Me too," I whisper against her skin.

As if I just slapped her, she places her palms on my chest and shoves me back. "Don't say that shit to me."

"What?"

She hops off the dresser, but I block her in, placing my palms to each side of her on the wood. "What the fuck is it, Kambry?"

"Stop saying things like that; pretending you feel things. Those things don't make you happy. You don't want that stuff. You said yourself you didn't know if the benefits of a couple were worth the risk; so don't take it. Don't confuse me, Saxton. It's not fair."

"That's what this is about, isn't it?"

She looks away from me, and then swipes underneath her eye. Fuck! I keep forgetting she is so much more sheltered and innocent than most girls. Everything is going to be taken to heart with her. Damn. I didn't even mean it like that. "Kambry, look at me, baby."

"Will you please just go get ready? I'm being stupid. I'm confused. Just forget I said anything. Please."

I lift her and place her back on the dresser, then force her to look at me. Her eyes are glossy. Her face is lacking the glow and smile she normally has. I feel like I'm dying inside, knowing she's upset. "Kambry . . ." I rub her bottom lip with my thumb, trying to calm her, like I often do. "Sometimes communication is different between guys and girls. Guys are simple and straight to the point, not thinking of what exactly is coming out of their mouths. It's like tossing something out of a window without a screen. There is no filter to keep it inside when it has no business being outside. Girls . . . Well, they wear their feelings on their sleeves more times than not. They dissect body language, every word spoken, and every silent gesture, usually making a big problem out of nothing at all. It's not a bad thing. It's just how you were made. Does that make sense?"

"I just wasn't expecting the first time I told a guy I was falling for him and he actually feel the same, to then have him turn it into a horrible thing. These feelings are all new to me. I feel like I'm crazy. I'm probably just a stage five clinger."

She breaks into tears. I blink. Then, the inevitable happens. I laugh, that dreadful laugh at the wrong damn time, the worst time. The one you can't smother on command. Like a virus it has to run its course. She cries harder. "Why are you laughing at me? Get out."

"Kambry," I cough, trying hard to stop my uncontrollable laughing. "I'm not laughing at you."

"Yes you are! Don't lie to my face. You're such an ass," she says in a crying whine.

"No I'm not. I'm laughing because you could never be classified as a stage five clinger. Do you know what those girls are like?"

Her face becomes smooth. New tears cease, abandoning the ones that have already fallen. "Not like this?"

"No, baby. Not like this. Those girls imagine an entire relationship in their heads and actually believe it, chasing after the guy, stalking, doing irrational things. Those girls are hard to escape. If you actually sleep with her, you're screwed. I had a friend in high school actually wake up in the middle of the night to his ex-girlfriend standing in his room beside his bed. Her excuse–she was getting a necklace she left at his house–his parents' house. In the middle of the night, just standing over him next to his bed, watching him sleep. Bullshit. She was just crazy. She had snuck through his window because he left it unlocked. She also faked several pregnancies. She . . .was a stage five clinger."

"Oh."

"Kambry, I need you to listen. Okay?"

"Okay."

"When I said those things, I was mostly thinking out loud. Let me try to explain. You know how to cook, right?"

"Yeah. I didn't really have a choice in the matter."

"Okay, so, imagine cooking for years, but then one night while cooking one of your favorite meals, something you've done hundreds of times, something goes wrong. Halfway through you burn yourself by laying your palm down on the wrong eye of the cooktop. It burns through layers of skin, down to the tissue. You suffer weeks or months of pain waiting on it to heal, depending on how deep the burn is, and deal with the misery of only having one usable hand. You've been eating takeout the entire time. You've gotten used to the convenience, you walked away from the source of pain alive, you've eliminated the cause of the misery, and you found an alternate way to survive while you healed. You've become accustomed to the new way, but one day you see an advertisement for your favorite food, and then all of the cravings come back. You think about it often and no one else makes it quite like you, but being scared of getting burned again keeps you away from the stove. In your head you try every possible way to rationalize your insecurity and paranoia, but the seed has already been planted and is starting to grow. You want to enjoy the meal, but you're terrified of letting yourself try again. At some point the desire drives you to face your fears. The burn is gone, Kambry, but the scar left behind reminds me of what it felt like. I may turn the stove on a few times before I go all in, but once I do I'll never look back. The love is there, baby. You make me want to give it another try. Just give me time to lay down my fears."

"When you put it that way I feel so stupid."

"Why? How could you have known? I'm glad you've never been hurt. I wouldn't wish that kind of pain and betrayal on my worst enemy."

"I'm so glad I met you. You're a great guy, Saxton."

"I guess you bring it out in me. I've been living under a dark cloud for a long time now."

She wraps her arms around my neck and smiles. "You know, you look hot too. This look is deadly."

I return her expression. "Where did that come from?"

"I've been holding it in since you walked through my door."

"Nice poker face. I never saw your hand."

"Yet I felt so exposed. I'm exhausted from trying to keep my composure. Wanna know my kryptonite?"

"Hmm. My dimples?"

"No, those are panty droppers."

I laugh. "I'll have to remember that."

"Go on. Guess again."

"My eyes."

"Nope. Although, they can make me tell you anything."

She pauses. I'm guessing she's making this a game. "Okay, abs?"

"Nope, just pretty to look at and fun to touch."

"Ass."

"I do love your ass, but no."

"I give up. I have muscle, but no bulk, so I'm going to skip over major areas like arms, chest, and back. I'm defined, but lean. I have no desire to portray the hulk. I respect those that do, but if I want a damn milkshake I'm going to drink it without having to schedule an extra session in the gym. Spill, beautiful. I'm actually curious."

She grabs my towel and tugs, pulling it loose until it falls to the floor. I swallow, my hands instantly finding her thighs and moving north, pushing her skirt up as they do.

She grabs my hips, her thumbs pulling toward each other at my navel, before descending south. "This. I never thought hair could be a turn on, but every time I see this trail of dark blonde hair that fades into nothingness the lower it goes, I imagine rubbing my fingers through it as I ride. Then, when I remember the way this V muscle flexes each time you thrust inside me, my panties become wet. I get uncomfortable, and no matter what we're doing all I can think about is having this . . ."

She grabs my dick and my head falls back a couple of inches. I pull her toward me to the edge of the dresser, slipping my middle finger beneath her panties. When it passes the barrier that her lips create, wetness saturates my fingertip. I growl out as I push it inside. She pulls her feet up on the dresser, widening her spread. When I start pumping my finger in and out she begins to stroke my dick, rubbing her thumb in a circle over the tip each time her hand passes over the head. "You want it?"

She nods, biting her bottom lip as I slowly finger her. I reach further up her thigh and grab the string on her hip with my free hand, pulling it down as she pushes herself up with her feet.

The door flies open and I jerk my head around to Meredith coming in the room. "Hell no. Put that shit up you two."

"What the fuck do you want, Meredith?" I push closer to Kambry to cover us.

"Y'all called me to go to a paint party, so that's where we're going."

"What y'all? I didn't call you."

"Maybe not, but your other half did, so here I am, ready to party."

I look at Kambry. She's pursing her lips as she shrugs her shoulders, then mouths, *sorry*. She squeezes my dick. "Give us ten minutes," I say, not looking back.

"Nope. You took me away from sex, so here I am. Karma is a bitch, handsome. Love youuuuu."

"Use another room."

"Fuck that. I'm not getting paid. I don't give my shit away for free."

I close my eyes, irritated. "Please, Meredith. Go away for like two seconds."

"Or what? You're going to fuck in front of me?" She falls onto her stomach on the bed. "Go ahead. It might be hot."

"Fuck. Seriously?"

"Oh . . .porn star got stage freight? Can't be good for business."

"Meredith."

"Saxton, you're the one standing there with a full moon. Don't Meredith me. You'll thank me later . . .when you're painting a wall with her tits as you drive your cock forward for a home run. That's the kind of shit we want to pay money to watch. I can do this crap at home."

I pull my finger out of Kambry and lace my fingers behind my head. She's hiding a laugh behind her hand. "You think this is funny?"

She lowers her hand. "I'm sorry, but kind of. I mean, who else does this but her. You're getting angry and that's like feeding a tame lion raw meat from your hand. Tame or not she's still a hungry lion. She may take off your arm too. She has no shame."

I look over, grabbing my junk to cover myself, as much as I can. Meredith is flipping me off with both hands, a victory smirk on her face. She rolls over onto her back as I squat down and grab my towel. Fucking stage freight. She has no idea who she's playing with.

I stand and kiss Kambry on the lips, before moving just outside of her ear. "This means nothing. I'm hard for you. Trust me."

I drop my hand and walk toward the door, passing the foot of the bed, before suddenly veering toward the side and placing each fist to the side of Meredith's body, leaning toward her face. She lifts her head and yells. "Saxton, put that shit away. There is a huge difference in film and right in front of my face. Fuck, that's a snake."

I place my knee on the bed and bring myself closer, until my dick brushes against her leg. She slaps my arm. "Get it off me! Nowhere did I order tube steak today. I was joking, kind of." She squeals. "Kambry, call off your man meat!"

"I am staying out of it. You started it," she says with laughter in her voice.

"Next time you may want to make sure your accusations are accurate before throwing them out. You want to watch us fuck then go right ahead. I won't stop you, but we were in a moment. I was about to make love to her. That's private. There is a difference."

Without another word I stand and wink at Kambry, just as she blows me a kiss, before removing myself from this estrogen overrun room. Thanks to Meredith, I'm thinking about Kambry's tits glowing with neon paint, bent over and painting things as I fuck her from behind. Good luck to me getting rid of this hard-on anytime soon.

CHAPTER TWENTY-FIVE

Kambry

I walk through the entrance and head straight for the counter, handing Lindsey my license, turned sideways to create a diversion from the obvious fact that I'm not twenty-one. Saxton walks up beside me and leans his forearms on the bar, bending forward. He tosses his ID down in front of her, his wallet in his cupped hand. Hip-hop music is playing loud enough that it sounds all over the building, even in here where there are no speakers.

She glances down at my license and places it face down on the counter, sliding it back to me. Lindsey is only a year older than me. I haven't really gotten a chance to talk to her much, but she seems nice. She kind of hangs around Drake a lot. I haven't figured out if she's just uncomfortable completely on her own serving since she's one of the new hires or if he prefers to have her close.

She grabs a wristband and holds it out, underside up. "Left wrist." Holding out my arm, she places the band on my wrist and secures it. "Not supposed to be any posers tonight," she says in a low tone. "But don't get stung. I don't need any bees my way either. Kay?"

I nod, knowing exactly what she's referring to. On occasion, mostly nights that allow eighteen and up entry, the police department sends on-duty officers undercover and dressed like customers for sting operations, to catch underage drinking or people of age contributing to minors. Most of the time at least Drake knows, and we usually figure out nights they are circulating the club pretty quickly, but occasionally one slips by unnoticed. Underage customers will always stick out like sore thumbs, because they get a stamp on the back of their hands that shows up under the club's black lights.

"They're with me," I shout over the music, pointing at the three of them.

"Drake said even employees pay cover since the club isn't the one putting on the event, but drinks are half price. Just tell Liam or Candice to start you a tab. Those two can just purchase under you or Saxton and at closeout they can split the tab. Liam won't say shit. Candice may be a little harder to deal with. They're in charge of employee tabs tonight for the few off if they show. It's supposed to be a full house, so he had to assign two to keep the rest free. It'll be eighty even."

"I got it," Saxton says, throwing down a hundred-dollar bill as I open my purse to get my bankcard. I look at him, but instead of saying something he just winks and waits for his change. She hands it to him as he holds out his other arm for the band, sliding the twenty into my pocket while she puts on his band.

"What are you doing? I don't want that."

"Take it in case you need a drink and I'm not with you."

"Saxton, I can pay for my own drinks when I close my tab. I have my card."

"Don't argue. Just take it. That's what boyfriends do. Ask Bryant if you don't believe me."

I narrow my eyes at him as he grabs his license and scoots me to the side. "It's true. A man takes care of his girl. Always. If he doesn't, you shouldn't be with him." I feel a pair of hands grip my shoulders: manly hands. "Aren't you supposed to know this? I thought the south was known for their hospitality. I figured men down there were automatically held to a higher standard than the rest of us."

I laugh, pulling away from Bryant as Meredith walks up beside me. "Maybe some, but there are always duds, no matter where you are. Even so, I don't expect to never have to pay for anything. It's not a big deal to split."

Saxton grabs my hand, pulling me toward the doorway that leads into the main area. "Not as long as you're with me you're not. Have I let you pay for anything we've done together since we met?"

"I'm going to lose this one, aren't I?"

"Yep. My parents raised me better than that. We will stay home before you pay for anything. Regardless, I like doing it, so just enjoy it and move on."

We walk in, the room already packed with people, some dressed normal and some dressed in casual clothes like shorts and tee shirts. White and neon fabric are the dominant colors. The floors are made of stained concrete, the walls a wavy metal. There are two large bars, one in each corner of the back, to my left and right. Dim spotlights are turned on over the stage that runs from wall to wall at the front. Everything else is dark, only lit up by black lights.

I glance around, taking in the camera crews labeled with production shirts that promote the event. It's a little different here than the main club. It's more relaxed, and resembling more like a concert than a nightclub. Some are dancing to the DJ playing a playlist on stage and some are standing around in cliques, waiting on it to start. I've only been here once: Fourth of July. I also had to work, so it was definitely different than being involved in the fun.

"Blue or yellow?" His voice catches me off guard, pulling my attention to the voice in my ear. His hand is at the small of my back.

"What?"

"Drink. The ones at the bar glowing. The bartender is handing them to that guy. Which do you want? The highlighter yellow or the aquamarine blue one. We have about thirty minutes before the paint starts."

Glow in the dark drink? What . . .

I follow the direction of his pointer finger to the bar. I feel like I'm seeing things. They really are glowing. "How? Is that healthy?"

"Yeah. It's just certain ingredients under the black light. Pretty cool, huh?"

"What's in it?"

"The yellow one is an energy drink like Rockstar or Redbull with Rum, Whiskey, Vodka, or Jagermeister. Which ever you prefer. The blue one is a little simpler: tonic water, vodka, and a sweet drink like Roses Mojito Passion."

I feel like such an inexperienced kid. "Just pick one for me."

"Okay. I'll be right back." He looks at Bryant "You going or staying?"

"I'll walk. I have to get ours anyway."

He begins to walk. "Saxton." He glances back at Meredith. "She won't like the yellow starting off. It's too distinct of a flavor, especially if Jager is in it. That's got a cough syrup flavor kind of. Just get her the blue. Bryant can get me the yellow and she can taste mine first."

Cough medicine? That's disgusting. He nods and they both take off for the bar. Meredith loops her arm around mine. "How intoxicated are you wanting to get?"

"Irresponsible. Free. Uninhibited. I want to be fun, but not sick. Sick did not go over well, even though it probably stopped me from making a bad decision. Don't let me get sick, okay?"

"I got your back, babe. Why I'm not letting you down the yellow first. Most either like energy drinks or they don't. There isn't a whole lot of in between. Vodka is easy to mask with the right combinations. Whiskey will grow hair on your chest. You aren't ready to go there. Rum is pretty much made for mixing. And Jager . . .well, you haven't really lived until you've had a Jager bomb, but it's not the yummiest drink out there. Anything with such a destructive title never is."

"Geez, that really helps. I feel so much smarter now. Not."

"Okay, here are alcohol dos and don'ts in a nutshell, since you've mostly drank weaker drinks to this point or smaller quantities and you're still learning. Beer is a slower build; think slow and steady. It goes buzz, drunk, sick, like when you played beer pong, but you can feel every step as it begins. It gives you more room to slow down or stop. Wine hits you all at once, so you drink it slow. It's made to savor. Liquor is your middle ground. It can be your friend or your enemy. It's less filling, so you can get a buzz out of less, but if your body isn't used to it, you're most likely going to be a lightweight and you need to sip until you've built a tolerance, because less is more. You don't want to be in the war zone if you drink too fast when that bomb hits. That's usually when very bad decisions are made. Blackouts can occur. It's just not a good place to be."

"English, Meredith, English! I feel like I'm cramming for the ACT exam. You're stressing me out."

"You kind of are! Don't get mad at me. It's not easy to explain the levels of drunk. It's a very broad category and takes years of practice to accrue that kind of knowledge. I'm doing the best I can with what I have to work with." She turns to me, taking me by the shoulders. "Okay, if you stop thinking about everything but how hot he looks, wanting more alcohol, dancing, and sex, then stop drinking because you're in the end zone. Any further and you're at the point of no return. Wild is sexy. Sloppy is unattractive. Plus, you really don't want to miss out on drunk sex. It's an experience in itself." She pauses. "Better?"

"Much. I think I can handle that set of instructions."

The boys return with two glow in the dark drinks and each a small tray full of tube shots that reminds me of chemistry class; has since I started here. Saxton hands me the glass full of blue neon. I stare at it, still completely blown away that I'm about to consume something that is glowing in the glass. Even working at this very nightclub I've never seen these before. It's possible it's because they don't usually use much glassware in the main club. Intoxication, bar fights, and glass don't mix well. "What shots did you get?"

"Two of everything. What you don't want I'll drink. Bryant and I already took two shots of tequila at the bar in case they are weak. I don't usually do sweet stuff, so I got her to make half of them a double and mix them up. We can play roulette," he says with a smirk on his face, wriggling his eyebrows.

I laugh. "You're so cute."

"Way to deflate my ego, beautiful."

"Oh . . .right. You're fucking hot and I'd love nothing more than for you to take me in the bathroom and bend me over the sink as I watch you pound me through the mirror. Is that better?" I place my lips to the rim of the glass and sip to get a taste, trying not to laugh.

"Damn, Kambry. Way to leave your inhibitions at the fucking door, shortcake. Drink that shit. We're about to paint soon. That means lots of wet colors flying through the air, glowing in the dark, and dancing as our bodies gyrating makes a masterpiece."

I never look at Meredith. Instead, I continue staring into Saxton's heated eyes as my sips turn into gulps. The drink is good. It's not too strong and not too weak. If it is strong it's so well blended I can't tell. Out of nowhere a smile spreads across his face. I'm guessing his ego isn't suffering. "When the clock strikes twelve, you're mine. I'll share you until then."

On that note I down the rest of my drink, setting the glass down on a server's tray as she walks past us. Meredith hands me her glass, still half full, allowing me to taste it, so I do. It's not horrible, but it's not as good as mine. I hand it back to her and grab a shot from the tray: the pink one. It looks like the pink panty dropper.

As I relax, my body starts swaying along to the beat of the music. I hold my shot out. "So roulette, huh? What's your version? Drink at random until they're gone?"

"As long as they match. One gets the stronger and one the weak." He winks. "One will be drunker than the other or it will end up balanced, but you never know until the end. You want to play? You can't back out until they're gone."

I grin at him, standing there waving the matching tube to mine through the air, before quickly glancing at Meredith, who's already grabbing one out of the tray in Bryant's hand. "Hell yeah. This sounds like so much fun."

I look back at Saxton just as I tap the tube to his and then throw it back, quickly swallowing the burn to accept his little challenge. I cough, just as he shoots his. He replaces it in the tray, so I follow suit. "How was it?"

"Stout," I admit.

"Ready for another?"

I grab the yellow, showing him the next one I want. "Ready."

We tilt back at the same time, emptying the tubes. This one wasn't so bad. He replaces the empty with the blue, so I grab the match. This time, instead of words, we just shoot. The bite of tequila stands out. My face sours. "Damn. Walk me down double."

I grab the green one, instantly consuming it, hoping it's weak. It's not. Vodka and green apple; Martini I'm guessing. We continue to replace empty with full. This time he pulls the red. He laughs at my face as I get a third strong one in a row. I recognize the Crown. I basically tried everything here, but most never went beyond a sip. I can feel my face pucker. I look at Saxton. His face hasn't changed at all. "I'm not fond of the Red Snapper."

"One left, beautiful. How you holding up?"

"Just peachy," I say, noticing a slight slur to my words.

"Only one left. Can you do it?"

I grab the last one; filled with a champagne colored liquid and floating gold flakes. Pulling it to my face, I let my eyes take in the floating pieces. I should know this one. "What's this?"

"Drink up, beautiful, and you'll find out."

He shoots his, so I shrug my shoulders and pour it into my mouth, swallowing. I cough again, but this time multiple times as my throat feels like it's on fire. Cinnamon. I take a deep breath, the cool air running into my mouth and adding a cool burn to it. "Well, what'd you think?"

"That one confirms that you should never judge something on appearance. It was so pretty in the tube. Lies. It's all lies. That was awful."

"You don't like stuff like Red Hotz or Big Red Gum? You know, cinnamon flavored stuff."

"Uh, hell no. What was that?"

"Goldschlager."

"Well that is one form of gold I'll never go after. Gross."

One of the servers walks up next to him with a tray full of drinks. "You still want your shots?"

He places the tray of empty tubes in the open space. She's a little too close to him for my liking. I never get that close to guys when I'm serving. I stare at her, watching. She's staring at him, biting her damn lip, and completely disregarding everyone else. Slut. That was kind of harsh. I'm being irrational. Come to think of it, she's usually the rose girl; the same one he bought the rose from . . . Rebecca is her name I think. "Of course I do."

She giggles. She actually fucking giggles. He didn't even say anything funny. I blink a few times, trying to clear the slight haze, but it does nothing. My body feels relaxed, but my mind wants to pummel her right in the face and scream for her to back away from my man. "Just making sure. Are you staying till close?"

I must be invisible. That is the only logical explanation for her to act like they are the only two standing here. "I'm staying until Kambry wants to leave. The second she does, I'm gone."

"Oh. Are you two a couple?"

"Oh my god. Are you serious? I can't listen to any more," Meredith says. "Whether they're fuck buddies or a couple, it's none of your business. They are here together. The end. That's your sign to serve and walk away. You're being completely disrespectful right now."

I kind of love her right now. I love her hard.

Rebecca stammers. "They're both employees. I was just trying not to assume."

"Okay, well, he's with me. To you or anyone else that may be confused. Yes, we're both employees, which means absolutely nothing. When we leave, we leave together."

I bite my bottom lip as I glance at Saxton, hoping he doesn't get mad. I have no idea where that came from. It just kind of flew out of my mouth. I blame it on the alcohol. Never would I have been that bold. I can't really describe this feeling—I like it—completely coherent, yet not a care in the world. I keep forgetting that the employees don't know about the filming. Who am I kidding? Half the time I forget we are filming. "I'm sorry, Kambry. No one told me."

"It's fine."

He lays cash on the tray and hands me a small frosted cup, filled with a pink colored liquid. "What's this?"

"Sex on the beach. I didn't think you'd want anything stronger at this point."

I will never understand how they came up with the names of drinks, like this one. What I do know is that it's definitely making me think of sex, and beaches. I kind of want to try it.

"What are you having?"

"Tequila," he says with a smirk on his face.

"Can I have one?"

"You sure?"

"Yeah."

I hand the cup to Meredith. She takes it. Saxton passes me a small glass, filled to the brim with amber liquid. "You don't have to do this, Kambry. Tequila isn't sweet . . .at all. It's my sister's favorite. I acquired the taste from her over the years."

"I'm fine. Just tell me when."

He hands me a lime slice, then takes one for himself. He picks up two small packs, but I can't tell what it is. Rebecca walks away, leaving us alone. "Kambry, we're going to go find a spot in the crowd. Come find me in a few. Okay?"

"Okay," I say to Meredith. "Save me a spot."

She walks away. It's just the two of us. Finally. "Did it bother you?"

"What?"

"Seeing her flirt with me."

"Yes. I know it's stu—"

"I liked it. Jealousy looks good on you." He steps closer. "Especially when it's over me. I need to know you're territorial. I need to know it bothers you to think of me with someone else. Only then will you understand how I would feel in the same situation." He pauses. Dammit, I want him right now. "Put the lime in your mouth, peel back."

I do as he says, gripping the peel between my teeth. He grips my hip and pulls my body against his, before tearing something between his teeth. His hand moves to my hair at the center of my back, pulling it toward the floor. My head tilts. He wastes no time before he swipes his tongue up the side of my neck, wetting it. I don't move, even though it feels amazing, trying not to spill what's in my glass.

Tiny granules coat my skin, before he licks along my neck again, removing them. Then, he leans back and downs what was in the small glass. His fist changes, moving closer to my scalp, before holding the back of my head while he bites into the lime I'm holding with my mouth. Holy hell, I want him some kind of bad.

I release my bite on the small slice, staring at him as he removes it from his mouth and places it in the shot glass. "Ready for yours?"

I quiver inside. "Like you just did?"

"Yep. Where you want it?" he asks with a smirk spread across his face.

I pull on his collar, baring a small portion of his chest. "Right here is fine, since you're taller than me."

He grabs the lime and hands me the small packet. "Salt. Lick it, stick it, remove it, shoot it, and then finish with the citrus. Questions?"

I shake my head, just as I watch him shove the lime slice into his mouth. My stomach is twisted in knots. It doesn't matter how long I'm around him, because the affect he has on my body never changes. Either way, I'm completely turned on right now. I'm intrigued. This is something I want really badly, so I tear open the salt just as he did before me.

His hands wrap around my waist, pulling me closer. "Lick me, baby."

My body shudders at his command, but I ignore it, and then lick in a diagonal swipe up his chest. He squats about an inch, allowing me to pour the packet of salt on the wet space. Once the granules are forming a trail, I lick his skin again, picking up the salt with my tongue and holding it in a layer across the top, before quickly taking the shot, swallowing before the taste can really register.

I gag a little, but smother it, trying to breathe through the nausea that is beginning to church my stomach. He grabs the back of my head, pulling me toward him. I open my mouth and bite down as the flesh of the lime touches my lips, allowing the acidic liquid to fill my mouth, washing back some of the dry, bitter aftertaste of the tequila.

When I release the lime, so does he, and our mouths meld together without missing a beat. Suddenly, the bad taste in my mouth becomes one I will never forget. My body heats. I moan into his mouth as our tongues embrace, but then he pulls away. "Where are you going?"

He smiles at me. He grabs my glass and places them both on a tray, as if he knew she was about to walk by with it. "To get filthy with you, and then hopefully make my dream come true, but first, wait here."

He walks off, leaving me standing here in the back crowd alone. The music switches to a different beat: a pop song instead of a mild techno rhythm. My eyes close without me willing them to, and before I can even think, my body starts swaying to the music. My shoulders and hips begin choreographing their own dance, pulling my arms and legs into it mid song, when my body and mind are completely relaxed and lost in the instrumentals of the music.

The air shifts, and my body feels like it's electric, creating a current, before a hand finds my hip, pulling me closer. I don't have to open my eyes to know who it is. I sway my hips, rubbing my ass as close into him as I can without bending. "Just wait till I get you wet," he whispers into my ear.

I smile, before slowly turning toward him, but continue moving my body along with the beat. "Who said I'm not already?" I shout over the music. They've turned it up in the last few minutes, since the bodies have quadrupled in number. I'm guessing it's getting close to starting.

The song switches again to another techno hit. He starts moving his body against mine, only noticeable if you're watching. "I may like you intoxicated."

I close in, bringing my mouth close to his ear. "So why doesn't everyone here know who you are?"

His hand wraps around the back of my neck. I look down and notice two bottles of neon paint in his other: one yellow and one pink. "The one perk of being a porn star . . . Not everyone watches it. It makes living a normal life a lot easier than a Hollywood celebrity. When I want to go out, most of the time I blend in with the crowd, even with the most minute items of clothing for disguise."

He grabs my hand and starts pulling me through the crowd, weaving through the dancing bodies. I glance around as I allow him to lead the way. One set of girl friends are posing for a selfie; one holding up a peace sign with her fingers, the other wearing a pair of sunglasses that look like they're from the eighties.

Various couples are grinding on each other, while others dance alone. One section of girls dancing to the techno music looks like they've been sampling more than the alcohol. As we squeeze through the packed room, the outfits get crazier but more intriguing. One girl is wearing a white tank that looks like it lost a fight to a pair of scissors, a lime green bandeau beneath showing through, similar to mine.

"Kambry, Sax! Over here," Meredith shouts.

I scan a few rows before I spot her and Bryant, standing close to the barricades that are keeping people away from the stage. We finally reach them, squeezing ourselves into a small opening. Lasers begin circling around the room, starting a show that goes to the beat of the music playing. It doesn't take long before the strobe lights accompany them.

The crowd starts going wild, the people in the front screaming into the camera as the member of staff for the event tour walks between the barricades and the stage, documenting the event. That couldn't have worked out more perfectly. Being in the middle of this environment, without a care in the world, has me on some kind of unexplainable high. "What's up, Los Angeles?" The DJ yells into his microphone.

I join in as the crowd screams, jumping up and down to the music and trying to get a better view. The guys in the front row ahead of us are taller.

"Who's ready to get messy?"

His tone goes with the techno bumps within the song as he spins the record. When he quickly starts going over the thank you speech, naming off the event host, Saxton nudges me and hands me the bottles of paint, then squats down to the floor. I bend down. "What are you doing?"

"Get on my shoulders."

"I'm fine."

"Just get on."

I throw my leg over his shoulder, and then follow behind with the other, until his hands are gripping my thighs, standing slowly. I wrap my arms around his neck since my hands are full, scared I'm going to tumble down to the hard floor, and leaning toward him so I don't offset my balance.

I feel like I'm level with the stage this way. A group of guys walk out from backstage in white suits, each holding what looks like a water hose with a cylinder attached to the end. Walking closely behind them are three girls, each dressed in white shorties and what looks like a sports bra, also in white, with a pair of sneakers and a flat bill cap. Each girl is holding a cylinder with a hand pump. I'm not sure what that's for.

A cap is placed on my head. I look over at Meredith, now also on Bryant's shoulders. I free up one hand by holding one bottle of paint against my body with my arm so that I can grab the bill and pull it off to look at it. It's a white, *Rockstar*, flat bill cap with the logo on a large, canary yellow star offset to the front, right side. "Where'd this come from?"

"Don't worry about it. Just accept the gift and put it on. Here." I replace the hat tilted on my head so that I can see without having to look up. She breaks a glow necklace and puts it on me, then puts the extra on herself. "Bryant, paint. Hurry up."

She quickly grabs two bottles resembling mine, but hers are purple and lime green. She pops the cap on both bottles and I do the same to mine, leaving one bottle per hand. A break in the beat hits. "Let's paint," the DJ says, the beat resuming as if he timed it at the exact moment, holding his earphone to his ear with his shoulder while his hands are tied up with his equipment.

The entire stage is emitting a massive cloud. The Go-Go dancers squirt a line of colored paint with each pump of the cylinder, walking and dancing the length of the stage. A line of pink strikes against my chest and body. I can feel the mist from the paint clouds against my skin, and my entire mind goes numb. I raise my arms above my head as I scream with the crowd, getting completely lost in the alcohol, in the music, in the paint, and in the party.

I no longer have to glance around to follow along with the crowd. I'm now a part of it, doing my own thing. Paint flies everywhere around the room in the crowd. I sling my arms around, squeezing the bottles in my hands, as I become part of creating the art. It's not like most art I've ever heard of. It's not classy, it's not beautiful, and it won't be worth any sum of money, but creating it is an experience just as any other form of art. It's an interpretation of fun, and I'll remember this for the rest of my life.

Saxton and Bryant turn, mirroring Meredith and I. I sling paint on her, adding to the dots and streaks that are already covering her body, completely oblivious to anything or anyone around me. I laugh when she squeezes and it coats my face, trying to get her back even though I can't see.

I wipe my face with my hand, smearing it everywhere. I smile, getting an idea. I free up one hand and squirt a dollop in the other, then bend over enough I can see Saxton, as I form a fist and spread the paint all over my palm. "Sax," I yell.

He angles his head to look at me, and just as he does I plant my hand on the front of his face, then rub in a circle. I laugh as he grabs my wrist and pulls me down, causing me to squeal at the feeling of falling, but he grabs me behind the legs as I come forward, cradling me. His pink, half handprint half circle on the center of his face has me laughing uncontrollably, his lips a shade reminding me of what eighties lipstick would look like. "You think it's funny, huh?"

I raise both hands in the air at full extension, each gripping a bottle again, and then circle them over his head, squeezing as hard as I can to get what's left in the bottle out, drizzling it on his hair and forehead, catching him off guard. I laugh harder at what looks like a highlighter explosion occurred all over his skin.

He maneuvers his hand to grip the back of my neck. I tense at the tickling sensation as he squeezes, and then he pulls my face to his and rubs the two together, the tips of our noses circling each other's.

I release the bottles, letting them drop to the floor, before gripping his hair and arching my back to try to get away, so that I can catch my breath from laughing. He tightens his grip, and instead of letting up, he kisses me, through paint and all. That feeling of electricity is back, and my lips are tingling with each brushing against his. My heart is racing beneath my chest. The single-most thought playing on repeat: I want him. I don't care where or in front of whom. I want to be a slave to his touch. I want him to hold me captive with his kiss, but most of all, I want him to possess my body. I want him to own me. I want to be his, and only his.

He releases my legs, and then sets my feet down on the floor, but places his hands on each side of my face, pulling me against him. I wrap mine around his waist, inching them underneath his white shirt until I can feel skin. "I love you, Kambry. I love everything about you. It's insane and scary as hell, but I do. It doesn't eliminate my fears, but recognition is a good first step. I love you, and I can't undo it, not even if I wanted to."

My cheeks hurt from grinning so big. "Will you remember or regret saying this tomorrow?"

"I may be drunk, but I'm never out of my mind. I'll tell you again in the morning if you want me to prove it."

"I love you too, Sax. What do you say we go find a vacant place? Then you can put paint in all the right places."

He smirks. I can feel the outline of his growing erection against the top of my thigh. I bite my bottom lip, wanting so bad for him to eliminate this craving and annoying void between my legs, but then the music changes from techno to a slower hip-hop, and the alcohol becomes more consuming, like it did earlier when I was dancing by myself. I've never danced with a man to this type of music, but suddenly I want to. Instead of freaking out that I'll be horrible at it, the alcohol is taking away my ability to think, to worry. "You aren't going to be sick? You took those shots like a champ, baby."

I shake my head. I recognize the song instantly: *Booty Wurk* by T-Pain. I grab his hands in mine, lacing our fingers, my body already bumping along to the beat, starting with my head. I raise our hands into the air with the instruction of the song, and like a domino effect, my body syncs, each part following the rhythm until my hips are rolling and skimming against his front. "Fuck, you're hot when you let loose."

His praise motivates me, each time more than the previous. I use the lyrics to guide me, turning around as the hook comes on. "Let me see that booty wurk. Go 'head. Left cheek right cheek left cheek right."

He steps closer to my back, his front clinging to my backside. I close my eyes, getting lost in the flashing strobe lights, the lasers, and the beat of the music, allowing my ass to become my greatest asset and my shoulders to become the steering wheel. His erection presses against me, and then his fingertips and hands trail down my palms, then my forearms, before skimming over my underarms in the lightest caress, ending gripped onto my hipbones.

My head tilts to the side when I feel his lips brushing against my neck. His breath tickles my ear. "You started something, sexy. You've officially awoken the party animal; something I haven't been in quite a while. You ready?"

"Mmmm," is the only thing that sounds from my lips, and then he starts.

Oh my dayum . . .

His hips thrust into mine; rolling in ways I didn't even know a guy could move. He follows my rhythm for a minute, before he presses my ass firmly against his pelvis and forces me to move in ways I didn't know I was even capable of moving. I moan aloud when he scrunches my skirt, pulling it up my thighs so that the denim is out of the way and I can move more freely.

My head falls against his shoulder, following his side-to-side circular motion, forming an imaginary infinity symbol over and over again as our legs bend, dropping us lower to the floor. My thighs are burning, but our bodies plastered together and his dick pressing against my ass keeps it from registering very long. My skin becomes glossy from the sheen of sweat forming. "Fuuuuck, where did you learn how to do that?"

"Some of it high school experience, some of it college, and the rest of it from a stripper role I had to play at a bachelorette party and long hours with a choreographer prior to filming."

He presses on the center of my back, bending me forward, and then grinds his pelvis and dick against my ass to the point that my panties are soaked and cold between my legs.

The heels of my hands rest on the top of my knees, and then without even thinking I begin driving my ass in an up and down roll against him, as if I just figured out what the phrases booty wurk and twerking means.

This is so much fun.

"Come on baby keep on doing what you're doing . . ." The lyrics flow through my ears, completely lost, all except for me gyrating against him.

He glides his hands to my stomach and chest, pulling me back upright until my back is completely flush with his front, his cheek just to the side of mine. His hands rub down my body sexually as the song comes to an end. "Damn, girl, you got an ass. If I had known you could work it like that we would have done this sooner."

The song switches and I continue, but at a slightly slower pace, using my whole body again, and rolling against him. I'm burning up. The mist and wet paint spraying and flying through the air aren't even cooling me down anymore. "Fuck this. I want to hand paint your tits while I drive my cock inside you. Let's get out of here."

He laces his fingers with mine and jerks me forward, almost running, as he pushes through the crowd of dancing, wet, glowing bodies, layered against each other from wall to wall in this building, trying to push closer to the front.

I chase behind him, keeping his pace. This is living. This is making memories. This is the reason I came here. This is what blocks out even the slightest possibility of regret. I love him. This relationship isn't at all contemporary. As a matter of fact, it's probably unheard of, but that's what makes it phenomenal.

CHAPTER TWENTY-SIX

Saxton

I notice a set of stairs on one of the sidewalls. I don't know what's up there, but I really don't care. When I reach the bottom, I glance around. Everyone is worried about what's coming from the stage and finding someone to take home when this is over. Me—I'm worried about getting inside the girl at my heels.

I stop at the bottom of the stairs and turn, grabbing her by the neck and pulling her in to kiss me. She's warm, tastes sweet, and smells amazing. Her clothes are wet and coated in paint. My cock is already hard and ready to go, compliments of her grinding her ass into it for several minutes.

I step backward on the first step as my tongue glides against hers. I pull away. "Do you think we'll get in trouble?"

"I don't give a fuck. Tonight, we own this bitch."

I hold out my hand for hers. She takes it. Then we sprint up the wooden stairs, making too much noise, but not giving a damn at the same time. There are a few perks of being involved in filming. You have advantages to places that most people don't.

We reach the top, looking down a short hall with three doors: two on one side and one on the opposite. I grab the doorknob of the first one I come to, but it's locked; an office I'm guessing. I move to the one on the same side at the end of the hall. It's unlocked. I push the door open to a small conference room—a table . . .fucking perfect.

Stepping inside, and pulling her with me, I shut the door once she's in far enough. The lock sounds as I press it into the knob. She looks around, then back at me. "You want to in here?"

"Where is not what's important." I walk toward her, guiding her toward the end of the table, before pulling the rolling chair out and pushing it out of the way as I do. "I could fuck you in a bathroom and be happy."

"Oh. Where do you want me?"

I love her innocence. Her lack of sexual experience is such a fucking turn on. Most wouldn't understand. There is never a dull moment when you have to teach. It makes things more interesting. The fact that she's hot as hell and wants me just as bad as I want her is the fucking icing on the cake.

I lean in and kiss her. She moans against my mouth as my tongue enters between her lips. I grab her ass, squeezing hard before moving to her thighs to pick her up, just before sitting her on the edge of the table. Her fingers are already threaded into my hair.

I grab the bottom hem of her shirt, lifting it slowly up her body. "You drunk?"

She smirks. "Maybe. Are you?"

"Little bit."

She wraps around me, pulling me into the center of her legs. "Good, then this should be fun."

I remove her shirt, tossing it to the side. Before I can grab anything else she unbuttons my pants, and then unzips them. "Someone's in a hurry."

She pushes my pants and boxer briefs over the curve of my ass, working them down my legs until they fall without any help. "I want you. No sense in beating around the bush."

I smile, grabbing her bra in the process. "This have anything to do with what I said?"

"Possibly . . . What made you change your mind?"

"Change my mind?" I remove the cover, revealing another form of bra beneath. "Fuck, does the material end?"

I reach behind her and unhook her bra, extracting it from her body. "You know . . .since what you said at the miniature golf course."

I grab her breast in my hand. I can't help it. They are big and round and tempting me. "It's not about changing my mind. It's about admitting to something that's already there."

I step out of my pants, and then remove my shirt, before grabbing her behind the knees and pulling her ass to the edge of the table. "Lay back, baby."

She does as I say, lying flat on the table. I unbutton her skirt and grab it by the waist to her sides. She pulls her feet onto the table and lifts, allowing me to pull it down her legs. "You're beautiful, Kambry. Your body still leaves me thoughtless."

She sits up. "Kiss me. Please."

I wrap my arms around her waist, pressing her front against mine. "Anything you want, baby."

Her hands go for the back of my neck as I grant her request. My hand disappears between her legs, locating her pussy. She's wet; thankfully, no surprise there. As I press inside of her with two fingers, her kiss becomes more heated. She moans against my mouth when I hook my fingers up to rub against her G-spot, her heels digging into my ass. A pleasure-filled whine escapes her, the sound that drives me nuts.

My mouth veers to her nipple, sucking it hard. She leans back on her hands, arching into my mouth. "Sax. More."

Dammit, I love when she calls me that.

I continue south, streaking through spots of paint along the way, before reaching her smooth bottom half, completely free of any colorful markings . . .for now. Spreading her open, my tongue slides out and swipes up her clit. Her reflex sends her ass back, veering her pussy facing down.

I grab it in my mouth and suck, hard. "Fuck," she yells, slamming back against the table. I grab her hips and pull her toward me more, her bottom now hanging off the edge. The arches of her feet become flush with my shoulders. Her legs begin to clamp on the sides of my head. I flick my tongue over her clit as I shove two fingers back inside of her. She bucks upward, her legs squeezing my fucking head to the point that it hurts.

I look up, underneath my lashes, to a view so beautiful that I could stroke my cock to it right this second, but that would require my attention drifting to something else, and right now, I want her to fucking come. She grabs those beautiful tits in her hands, clenching her fists around them. Fuck she has me so hard right now.

I hook my fingers up in a hurry, finding that soft, squishy spot inside, and then apply a slight pressure as I rub across it, never removing my tongue from her clit no matter how cramped it begins to feel.

She clamps around me. "Sax, I want you to put it in."

I ignore her, wanting to make sure she comes in case I can't last once I finally get in. Removing my fingers, I switch with my tongue before I can offset my current rhythm, continuing to rub her clit in a quick up and down motion with my middle finger as I shove my tongue inside of her pussy as far as I can go. She grabs my hair, pulling my head closer to her. "Shit. Don't stop. That feels amazing."

I thrust my tongue in and out of her as I rub her clit, until she claws into my scalp and arches off the table. At the point that she moans aloud my tongue becomes wetter, the taste of her orgasm coating it as her pussy squeezes around me. I stop, allowing myself to take all of it.

She pushes at my head, trying to move me away from her as she sits up. "Stop. It tickles."

I pull out, swallowing the prize she left behind, and grab her off the table, as I stand upright. I kiss her, letting the moan she makes against my mouth sound through my ears. Her legs fall down mine, signifying she wants down. I let her. She smiles as her feet hit the floor, and then she sinks to her knees and grabs my dick. I can already see the confidence difference from the last time, and it's fucking sexy as hell.

Holding it by the base, she places her opposite hand on the back of my thigh, as she licks around the head, never taking her eyes off of me. Damn. This view . . . I swallow as she wraps her mouth around it, slowly adjusting her jaw to take my size without her teeth skimming my skin. Her tongue brushes the underside, as she takes my cock into her mouth as far as she can, leaving her jaw relaxed while she coats me with her saliva.

Based on the wetness of my cock she isn't swallowing. Instead, she's allowing it to run out of her mouth, catching it beneath her hand grip, but continuously running her mouth up and down the top half of my dick . . .slowly. Fuck. Her hand twists, working it down my length. She's lubricating the bottom half.

"Fuck. You have no idea how hot this is."

I clench my fists, trying hard not to grab the back of her head as she finds her rhythm. I want to fuck that sexy little mouth so bad. I'm drunk. I need faster. It feels good, but could be so much better.

"Fucking shit."

My jaw drops as she suctions around me at the junction where her lips meet her fist, connecting as if she's forming one unit, and then she begins a quick stroke up and down my length. One of my hands immediately grabs a handful of her hair. "Damn," I whisper. "Just like that, baby."

My head falls back, losing focus on her. "Holy shit." She's matching her strokes to the beat of the hip-hop song blaring downstairs, bumping throughout the club. *Sweet mother of . . .*

My balls clench when her suction becomes harder, her tongue flicking lightly over the hole in the center of the head, before swirling and continuing in a pattern. Her hand moves from my thigh, and swipes around my leg, grabbing my balls without warning, and then she gently massages them. The strokes against her wet saliva are making a light slurping sound. She reaches the head again and massages her tongue against the underside of my head in a deep suction. My nuts constrict. "Fuck, Kambry, stop!"

I pull her head back, probably too hard, forcing my dick out of her mouth before I blow into the back of her throat. She looks up at me, that innocent look present. "What's wrong?"

I wipe the beaded sweat off my forehead that formed the second my muscles clamped throughout my dick trying to stop from coming. My nuts are already starting to hurt. My chest is tight from holding my breath. "Up."

That single word is all I can muster. I grab my cock in my hand and squeeze, attempting to evoke pain. "What's wrong, Saxton?"

Eyes on chest.

"I need you to turn around, baby. Questions later. Please."

My stomach is tight. I need to come. The pain is starting to spread throughout my abdomen. She does as I ask. "Bend over."

She follows instruction with no questions, her top half completely lying on the table, her arms spread out to the sides of her, gripping the sides. Grabbing her hip, I align the head of my cock at her pussy, swiping it up and down in her wetness a few times, before thrusting inside of her, wasting no time. Her breathing amplifies in sound. As I bury myself completely, I take hold of her other hip. "A blow job has never felt so fucking good. This is me returning the favor."

I pull out and ram my cock inside of her as deep as I can go, hitting against that mysterious hard spot that I love. She bucks forward, as a painful cry sounds. I pull back. "Want me to stop?"

"No."

"Good. I want you sore."

Sliding my hands over her round ass until my thumbs are pressed firmly below her cheeks, I push up, creating an arch in her back as she is forced to her toes. Then, I pound into her over and over, no pause before recoil. Her pelvis presses further against the table with each hit. "Fuck. I can feel your dick in my back and stomach. Shit."

I never let up, continuing at a fast pace. My pelvis is making slapping sounds against her ass, my balls swinging against her skin with each thrust. Our bodies are coated with a wet sheen of sweat. I slam against her again, closing any gap between us, and then grind up and down against her backside, my abs tightening as I grind up, my head rubbing against something.

Fuck. Fuck. Fuck. I can't hold on anymore. Her back is completely tensed up, her shoulder blades fully extended from gripping hard onto the edges of the table. She's wet, hot, and the sounds she's making alongside our bodies are too much. Each time I glance down and watch my cock drive inside of her beautiful pussy, I'm ready to nut. I can't explain how much I like watching it. Best option is to blow my fucking load and continue through the sensitivity until she comes.

The tug pulls through my balls, and shortly after, the first spurt occurs inside of her. I clamp my jaw shut as a deep throaty groan starts to occur, trying to hide the fact that I just nutted before I could be sure that she was able to orgasm, a muted grunt occurring. My fingertips dig into her skin. Fuck, that feels so good.

I pump my arms at a short pulse, my biceps taking all of the strain as I gyrate her ass roughly against my pelvis. "Fuck, Sax. Don't stop. I'm about to come. Damn. Right . . .there."

She moans and her pussy squeezes me so tight I can't continue. I hold her to me and watch as her beautiful back curves, her chest lifting off the table and her head falling back. I grab a handful of tit when her body starts to relax, pulling her back against my chest without pulling out of her. We don't say anything at first; just stand here and breathe erratically, sweaty and emotionally high.

She reaches up and grabs the back of my neck, combing her fingers through the bottom of my hairline. I kiss her shoulder, trailing my lips up the seam of her neck. I'll be fucking damned. It just gets better each time. I find myself wanting more of her each time since the first time. All of my senses are heightened. I can hear the pounding of my heartbeat. I'm completely fucking drunk on her. Right now, any love I've ever experienced is multiplied by ten at minimum.

My heart has made a decision for me. Until I become bad for her, and until I know there is something better for her than me, I can't let her go. I want to love her. I want to give this a try again for her. I want to be the best man for her. I want to be the only man for her, because my desire and growing love for her outweighs the fear, and that's something I never thought I'd experience. I just hope like hell I don't get burned again. "Say it again," I whisper as I reach her ear. "I'm ready to hear it first this time."

She doesn't immediately say anything. My arm starts to fall from her breast, but she stops me. "I love you, Saxton."

I pull out and turn her around. She wraps her arms around my neck as I enclose mine around her waist. "Promise me you mean it. Make me believe it's not just words, Kambry. I need you to guarantee that I'll always be enough for you. My heart is on the line."

"Saxton . . .there has been something about you since the night I met you that piqued my interest when no one else here has. Refusing to throw those words around is why you're the first guy I've said them to. That's not easy being in a long-term relationship. You don't think I have fears too? My fear of this thing between us ending too soon is why I agreed to this. I couldn't walk away yet, regardless of the consequences or what I become to everyone else. I'm scared that in a short time this whole thing will flop and I'll be heartbroken, picking up the pieces while you move on to the next project, the next girl, just to become a fun memory during your career. You're all I think about, Sax. You've become my best friend. You've been enough for me since the beginning. For me, it doesn't get any more serious than this. I can't even fathom being with someone else. That's the scariest part of all, because you're my first, my only, and it breaks my heart to think there is any possibility you won't be my last. As humiliating as it was to admit it first, I love you, and I don't see that changing . . .ever."

My jaw ticks as we stare into each other's eyes. There is no description to explain how much I want her. My hands brush up her spine, until I reach her cheeks. "The thought of touching another woman after you disgusts me. I don't know what that means if this thing doesn't work out, but we'll figure it out as we go, okay? Together . . . I don't know how you broke down my walls so easily, but it's done. Let me love you, and I promise I'll do it right."

She pulls her bottom lip between her teeth. "You want to get out of here? We could shower and watch movies all night while we pig out on ice cream."

I smile. She makes me feel things I haven't experienced in so long, if ever. I kiss her, craving that internal sizzle that occurs each time our lips touch for an extended period of time. "I know just the place to grab a couple pints of Ben and Jerry's and Red Box on the way. I love you."

Her smile reaches her eyes. "Not that I'm complaining, but now that you've said it, you don't have to feel obligated to all the time." She laughs. "I'll survive on occasional."

"I can't really help it. It just comes out," I admit. "So I think I'll roll with it."

I reach down and squeeze her ass. "Hurry up and get dressed. Now I'm thinking about being naked in a small enclosed shower." Small. Enclosed. Shower . . .and now I'm starting to harden. Damn.

CHAPTER TWENTY-SEVEN

Kambry

He forces me through the door as he walks me backward, our lips locked together, and only separating as he pulls my shirt over my head, stripping me once again. He tosses the paint-covered clothes onto the tile floor. My bare back touches against the cold shower door. I grab for his shirt, inching my hands up his rippled abs trying to remove it.

He breaks the lock he has on my lips, raising his arms and pulling the back collar as he does to pull it off, before dropping it and kissing me once again. I swear it's like he's a starved man. Even for a girl with limited experience I can see that. It makes me feel so wanted, knowing that he could have any girl he wanted at his feet, or in his bed, whether in contract or not. He's that special. His personality is golden and he's so damn hot. I'm not even going to touch on his need for loyalty and trust. Those two qualities in a man right there are worth securing and never setting free. You can't put value on having a partner that is fully committed in a relationship.

His mouth traces down my chin, toward my neck. My eyes close. It feels incredible. I roll my head back, giving him more space. His tongue flutters across my skin as he lightly places kisses along my neck. His body veers to the side, just before the sound of the water comes on. I open my eyes when his touch on me disappears. I didn't even hear the door on the shower open.

He drops his jeans down his legs, completely baring his body. He steps out, not even attempting to cover himself. I love the fact that he's not modest in the least. "You're hard again?"

I bite my lip; uncontrollably gawking at his rather large companion he's holstering front and center. "I seem to stay in this state when in the presence of you. I feel like a deer in rut, constantly chasing after you. You give off some kind of fucking pheromone that drives me crazy."

I hold in my laugh, feeling as if I'm seconds away from choking on my saliva. "Oh yeah?" My hands go for the button on my white denim skirt, undoing it. I hook my thumbs on the sides and slowly work the waist over my hips and down my legs, never letting go until I'm releasing them at the floor, even though they could fall on their own.

I step out and kick it to the side with my foot extended. "What do you know about a deer in rut?"

I remove my bandeau and bra. He's staring at my breasts like he does on a regular basis. I never liked having a big chest size . . .until him. To me it made buying cute tops a pain in the butt, especially having conservative parents. Small waists and large boobs do not go well together in the world of fashion, still. "Are you going to tell me you've hunted as well now too, farm boy?"

His eyes finally rise to meet mine. "Farm boy, huh?"

"I'm sorry, I'm still having a hard time picturing this."

He takes a few steps toward me, and then guides me through the shower door until we're both standing under the water. I wipe my hands over my face and through my hair, trying to clear the excess. Multicolored water is traveling down our bodies and washing down the drain from the paint becoming wet again, transforming into a diluted liquid.

He presses me against the wall, moving me out from under the water until it's raining down on his back. "And why is that?"

"Because when I think of a farm I imagine tight jeans, hats of some form, and boots. You, for some reason strike me as a Sam Hunt, or Brody Jenner from Laguna Beach kind of guy in the area of dress."

His thumb brushes across my bottom lip as he hides his grin beneath a mask. "Never judge a man's character by the clothes you meet him in, beautiful. LA changes people. It's about blending into Hollywood. Don't be simple minded. I can fucking rock a pair of Carhardts and a baseball cap."

A huge grin spreads across his face. Good lord he's beautiful. I must have done *something* right in my life. That smile is blinding. "I've shoveled more piles of cow shit and worn out more pairs of boots than you've probably seen in your lifetime, Bama. Country isn't location, it's lifestyle." He winks. "And by the way, I'm a deadly predator when I want to be." He cups one hand on the bottom of my left breast, just over my heart. "When I aim, I never miss the kill shot."

No you don't . . .

My body feels like spaghetti. "Why do you have to put those images in my mind: sweaty, shirtless, shoveling piles of stinky cow crap in working pants or tight jeans, and a ball cap. Definitely a ball cap. I would probably let you defile me in a pile of hay. What's next . . .mounting lessons? Will you just bend me over now?"

I'm teasing, partially. We've probably exceeded the normal limit for sex in one day today. But who wants to be normal?

Really, I'm just turning into a hornball. An accurate tagline would be: virgin to slut in two point five seconds. That's exactly what has happened. I'm a total Saxton slut. "No defiling until we're clean again; although tempting, I kind of just want to touch you and makeout."

He reaches behind him and grabs a loofa and his body wash. I really haven't even noticed that we're in his bathroom—the nautical one done in navy blues and bight reds. He tends to make me forget things or my surroundings. That's probably a good thing considering . . .

The mesh sponge comes in contact with my shoulder, as he grabs my hand and extends my arm out, before he begins to scrub, forming a foamy lather. "Hey, where do you suppose the cameras are?"

He shrugs, continuing to bathe me. It's a little strange. It feels childlike. Honestly, this entire night has gone in a totally different direction than I was expecting. "I don't know. Everywhere. They are probably in places you would never imagine. Technology makes cameras almost microscopic now. It's actually better this way. You really don't even remember they're here. Imagine us fucking with a camera guy angling a camera a few inches from your groin. It's not the sexiest or most romantic way to have sex, and it takes the word cock block to a whole new meaning, but I guess raunchy and erotic is really the goal. Is it starting to bother you?"

"No actually. That's what's weird. Shouldn't my conscience be screaming at me?" He's rubbing my chest in the direction of my boobs. "Are you really going to bathe me? I can do it myself."

He smiles but doesn't immediately look at me. "I like doing it. Oddly, I like taking care of you. To answer your first question, your conscience will probably get a little louder when it's out in the public. I imagine it won't be long now, if it hasn't spotlighted already."

My stomach flutters from nervousness. I breathe evenly. I should prepare to be an orphan, not that it's really any different than now, since I haven't heard anything from my dad since that night at Saxton's, but this will be a permanent write off from my family. "Hey . . ."

I look up. He's no longer rubbing the loofa over my skin, but pulling me against him in his arms, our bodies slipping together from the water running down and mixing with the soap between us. The shower is full of steam and it smells good, manly. "No regrets okay? Promise me. Originally I was selfish, but now I actually love you, so maybe it really was meant to be."

My heart skips a beat. I'm absolutely crazy about him. If me being here doesn't prove it, then nothing will. "No regrets as long as I'm with you." I grab his hand and place it back over my heart like earlier, inching my breast up slightly and out of the way. "I've already taken the bullet. If you remove it, I'll most likely bleed to death. That's how much I love you, Saxton, and it gets stronger every day. Crazy right?"

The loofa falls to the floor and he grabs my face. "I may have to take back the thing about no defiling." Then he presses his body into me against the wall and kisses me, with so much heat my body temperature is elevating from his kiss alone.

My hands rest over the bends of his arms. So this is what it feels like to makeout with the man you're completely and one hundred percent head over heels in love with. He's also my best friend. I enjoy spending time with him. I want to tell him things. I love our conversation. The best part of being together is learning more about him, even though it's slower with us than in comparison to normal couples, for privacy reasons. He won't ever replace Meredith, but it's a different kind of friendship. This kind is the one where you stumble into someone as if you're lost, and then your soul recognizes his, and it's like coming home . . .

I waltz into the living room shaking a bottle of pink polish. I have this one really weird obsession, and that's keeping my nails painted. At the first sign of a chip I remove the current polish and redo. I've tried to ignore it before but it never works. I can't stand it. Pretty nails make me feel pretty, like makeup for Meredith. Over the years I've collected hundreds of colors and still going strong. Actually going and getting my nails done by someone else makes me feel like I'm on cloud nine, but that's not all that often. Come to think of it, I haven't been to a nail shop since I moved here.

When we finished showering, or kissing under the water for what felt like forever I guess is a more accurate description, I went straight to my room to put on my pajamas. Even though I took my time because I had to remove my polish, I obviously still beat him, because he's not in here yet. Weird. I figured he would be waiting on me.

The sound of glass clinking together comes from the kitchen as I sit on the couch and prop my foot up on the coffee table, preparing to paint. "Sax?" More sounds occur just after my calling out. It sounds like something falling from a cabinet into a metal sink.

"Yeah."

"What are you doing? Are you okay?"

"Everything is under control. I got this. You just relax."

"Okay. Whatever you say, handsome."

Removing the brush, I swipe it on the inside of the bottle's neck, removing the excess polish from the brush. I run my thumb over my big toenail, ensuring there is nothing to stick into the paint like cotton from the cotton ball. "The question is, what are you doing?"

I jump, almost dropping the bottle of polish, not expecting his voice to be so close. I turn my head, almost smacking him in the mouth with my cheek. "Didn't anyone ever tell you it's rude to look over someone's shoulder? Hmmm?"

"Nope. I was too busy helping my parents or being coaxed into being a woman-slave by my sister and her friends. Here . . ." He hands me the bowl filled with two different flavors of ice cream. I instantly notice there is only one spoon . . .

My heart starts to race at the idea of sharing. It's so romantic. I set the bottle of polish down on the table and quickly shove the brush inside, grasping the bowl from his hand as he walks around the couch toward the television, grabbing the DVDs off of it as he stands to face me. "Chick flick or man marvel?"

He wriggles his eyebrows as he presents one movie in each hand. Gah, he's flipping adorable. Keep that thought silent with use of my girly words. A grin begins to appear on my face. I can feel it as my cheeks push back, so I grab a large spoonful of whatever flavor the spoon is already scooped under and shove it into my mouth, trying to get rid of the hopeless in love look I'm sure I'm marketing right now. "Speak now or forever hold your peace."

I quickly squint my eyes and lock my jaw. Oh my gah . . .brain freeze.

I point my head toward the romantic comedy instead of the action movie, trying to wait out the pain in my head. He laughs. "Figures. By the way, that's what you get for starting without me."

I grab a throw pillow and toss it at him. He dodges. "You're the one that handed it to me without a disclaimer!"

He opens the DVD case. "When this is over, I may need you to help me find my balls, because they're probably going to disappear the second I start hearing mushy stuff and girl talk."

"You're being a bit melodramatic, don't you think? That one is supposed to be funny. She acts like a man in her promiscuous ways. You should be able to relate."

He places the disc in the player. "I'm pretty sure I've never been classified as a trainwreck."

He grabs the remote and walks toward the couch, falling down onto it until he's lying diagonal with his head at my shoulder. "Why do you assume I can relate to promiscuity of any ki—"

I shove a spoonful of ice cream in his mouth, cutting him off. "Oh, shut it, sex boy. I've moved past the fact that you have way more experience than me. Don't try to finagle your way out of it."

I try to hand him the bowl as he sits up. "Keep it. My hands will be busy."

"Doing?"

"Your toes."

He grabs the bottle of polish off of the table as the previews begin to play on the screen, then pulls his leg into a flat bend on the couch, as he turns to face me. He grabs my ankle, bringing the arch of my foot to rest on the inside of his knee.

I sarcastically laugh. "Oh, yeah right. It's fine. I'll just wait until after the movie or something. Here, give it to me."

I reach out for it and he just stares at my open hand. "What's wrong? Do you not think I possess the necessary skill to paint a woman's toes just because I'm an attractive, very manly, man?"

"Exactly. Manly—I definitely love that about you—and the art of nail painting just doesn't go together. It has to be done smoothly and with finesse to it. I'm not really going for abstract."

His hand goes for his heart. "I'm a little offended. I never took you to be a sexist person."

"HA-HA! It's nothing personal. I'm just picky. Now give me." I gesture for him to place it in my hand. He grabs my hand instead of placing the glass bottle in it and flips it over, kissing the back.

"You can have that back now. Press play, relax, and pig out on that bowl of sugary goodness while I paint my woman's toes." He extends his arms as if he's loosening them up, then moves the bottle, placing the bottom in the center of his palm and the neck between his middle and ring fingers, before grabbing the top and removing the brush. "It's best that you learn now I don't back down just because I'm told to."

Panic starts to arise as he brings the brush close to my big toe. All I can picture is having polish all over my toe and barely any on the nail, like a toddler trying to color but just can't seem to stay inside the lines. "Ugh." I slam my head down on the arm of the couch and shove another dollop of ice cream into my mouth. "Why on earth would you want to paint my toenails? I've never heard of a guy painting his girlfriend's nails. It's weird."

"Because I haven't done this in years and I am curious to see if I've still got it . . .and even though you won't admit it, you like it. Most guys wouldn't do this. Only the real men are secure enough in their sexuality to dabble in things that makes their women happy. I'm a jack-of-all-trades, baby. You don't need a woman to have a sleep over. You have me. I'm about to rock your world."

I dip the spoon into the untouched flavor as he hunches over and grabs the tip of my toe, touching the brush at the back of my nail. The *Tonight Dough* is one I've never had. Upon spreading it over my tongue a moan escapes. "Oh my gosh," I say with a full mouth, trying to swallow and wanting to savor it at the same time. "This is so good."

He looks up and opens his mouth, waiting for it. I have an idea. I direct a fresh spoonful toward his open mouth, but just before entry I pull back and plunge it into my mouth, swallowing only part of it. "That was dirty," he says laughing, and then goes back to what he was doing. I can feel him on my small toe already.

When the brush leaves my foot, I lean forward and grab him by the back of the neck, pulling him into a kiss, and then share the ice cream my way. When nothing is left but the aftertaste of caramel, chocolate, and peanut butter cookie dough mixture, I release him and grab the remote, going back to my original position, and then turn my head to the television with a slight smile.

I press play to start the movie, trying not to think too hard with my stomach in knots. He makes me want to be bold and lively. He makes me want to live as if I'm dying. He makes me want to experience life with no restrictions. There isn't a single day that I'm with him that I feel like something is missing. He's changing me into the person I want to be. He makes me be the person I'm supposed to be: me, the girl different from everyone else. He probably doesn't even realize he's doing it. That's exactly why I'm in love with him.

He clears his throat and mumbles. "Damn."

My opposite foot inches toward the inside of his thigh, my toes wiggling against the bottom hem of his nylon shorts, dipping beneath the material. Slowly they ascend, sneaking along the length of his leg as if trying not to get caught, and I'm surprised when no boxer briefs stop me in my path.

The pads of my toes collide with one very hard piece of man meat. The round head is soft, but hard—such a contradiction. I skim the length with my foot, softly, trying to handle with care. "You keep that up and polish is going to be all over this couch, because I'm seconds away from shoving your legs back and fucking you without even removing your clothes or mine.

I turn my head away from the alcohol induced coma the girl is in, just after watching her sarcastically stroke his ego by telling the poor guy in front of her how endowed he is as he shucked his clothes. I'm pretty sure he didn't even notice the lies that were coming out of her mouth. It's going to be a long night for him . . .

Saxton is staring at me, a heated look on his face. I rub against it again. "I'm game if you are." I grin, but his face doesn't change. Instead, he grabs my foot and backs it away from his dick.

"Later. I want to spend time with you for a bit instead of fucking you into a coma."

"Such a mood killer, and buzz for that matter," I say in a witty sarcasm. The pop of pink catches my attention. I look down. "Hmm . . . Not bad. I was expecting a massacre and instead got a pretty damn good paint job. The only plausible thing to follow is a story. Spill, sexy."

"Well, it's fairly simple. My sister is a little older. She had hot friends. My dick wanted to be close to the hot friends, so she basically made me her bitch boy in the process. I've painted a lot of toes in my days and massaged many feet. I like feet because of it. Well, cute and dainty feet. I suppose I need to clarify, because some feet just make you want to run. Yours I like."

I bust out laughing and sit up, handing him the bowl of half melted ice cream. "Wait just one second. So you're telling me you hung out at girls' sleepovers on a regular basis? Just so you could be close to older girls? You are such a guy or totally opposite. I can't be sure which." I laugh all over again. "Did it even pay off? Did you ever get some cougar action toward your innocence?"

He places the polish on the table and takes a bite of ice cream. "Cougar? Oh, come on now. They weren't that much older." He winks. "But I will never tell," he says with laughter in his tone.

I shove his arm. "You just did! You sound like you were a total womanizer. My brother would never let me hang out with him and his friends. He turned into a complete jerk if I got anywhere close to his friends, so I stayed away."

"I'm only going to say that girls in general like to be taken care of. I womanized nothing. I simply wanted to admire and was forced to work to do so. What happened when I left those girls was not my fault. My room was on the opposite end of the hall and I went to bed like a good teenage boy. If someone wanted a bed mate, well, who was I to decline?"

He pauses to take another bite of ice cream. "Had you been there, though, I'm pretty sure I wouldn't be the innocent of the two involved. That's why your brother was a jerk, baby. Smart guy. I would bet a large sum of money that they made comments about you. You're beautiful and your body is the type guys go home and jerk off to. I would have done the same thing if I were him. My friends wouldn't be allowed to even touch you with a ten-foot pole. That means he cares. Where is he? You never talk about him."

Thoughts plague me. "Had I known you back in high school, I'm pretty sure the word innocence would not have existed with either party. Just sayin'. He goes to Alabama. He got to go to the college he chose, even though it requires for him to live on campus. Should only have about a year left before he graduates with a business degree unless he goes to grad school. He's smart, and driven to make something of himself, so I'd be surprised if he didn't. I'm sure my stupid dad will pay for that too, yet me, I get nothing that doesn't exist under his little umbrella he has for me."

"Do you ever talk to him?"

"Not really. We kind of just distanced our relationship when he left for college. I think he was going through some things that now make sense as to why he wouldn't want to be BFFs with his little sister, but that's for a different day. I don't know. Maybe some of it is because I'm jealous he gets to follow his own chosen path and am holding a grudge against him when it's not really his fault. Plus, I just feel like he kisses my dad's ass instead of doing what he wants, because he used to talk about wanting to go for engineering, but when he mentioned it Dad kind of shot that down like it wasn't a good enough choice or something. Why? Who knows, because they make really good money and I think he's smart enough to do it, but my dad is extremely cut and dry, stuck in his ways, and very much like old, southern money type men. I'm really not even sure how to explain it myself, because it's ridiculous and stupid."

"Tell me more. I want to know more about you. What made you move to California?"

"You really want to talk about my stupid family?"

"Yes. They are a part of you, and I'm interested in knowing what makes you, so family is just part of it, good or bad. Clearly, you can leave out personal details, but generalize."

"Okay, so my dad has this warped idea that women belong in the home. That's their place in this world. They don't work to put food on the table, and they don't contribute to the family income. If they do anything it's more of a hobby, and it's to be done in a way that doesn't interfere with home life. He just always believed that things worked best how they were back in biblical times, back when women took care of the house and children. To him, it was necessary for kids to have a parent that was there one hundred percent of the time, to teach and mold throughout life. My brother is a boy, and it's been drilled in his head that one day a family will rely on him for guidance, for financial support, and to be the head of the household, so for him to go to college was fine. He was even told once that if he was going to sow any wild oats it better be done there and left behind when he graduated, because then it was time to be a man, but me, I'm expected to find a worthy husband and follow in my mother's footsteps. Since that doesn't happen overnight, I was allowed to go to junior college and live at home until I met someone that my parents felt was an honorable man."

"Well, I put a damper on that plan, didn't I?"

I laugh. "You joke, but it's a miserable life. It leaves no room to be your own person, make your own mistakes, and decide what you want to do. It's a double standard. Why is it that Ben gets a ticket to go party for a few years and experience girls while I'm being held hostage in my own home and hometown? What's sad is that I might be more apt to agree with some of his ideals had I been given the same bargain: to leave it at college and grow up. At least then I would never have any regrets, but he wasn't willing to bend and my mother would never in a million years disagree with him, so when Meredith gave me an offer I couldn't refuse, I ran away. That may have been the coward way, but it was the only way."

He grabs me and pulls me onto his lap in a straddle, as he moves into the correct position with his back against the back of the couch. He runs his hands into the sides of my hair and rubs his thumbs over my ears. "It's like he had a good vision and let it go too far, you know? All of that part about the family is great, and I agree with it in some ways, but the missing key is that it's only great if that's what the woman wants. My mom was a stay-at-home mom. With a farm it's pretty much an all hands on deck thing, but she chose that. My dad would have gladly hired an extra hand to take her place had she wanted to work. If we were married and had kids, I would much rather you raise them than someone at a daycare or a sitter, especially in the first several years of their lives, but I would never force you to stay at home, and I would also never leave all of the weight of the home on you just because I brought home the income. That's fucked up if we're supposed to be partners. Not only that, but I don't want to look back when our kids are teenagers and realize I missed out on all that stuff when they were little."

I can't even find air right now. He just spoke of marriage and kids. I feel like someone opened a jar of butterflies in my stomach and they're fluttering around. I do want those things, I just want them with the person I choose to have them with and not someone that my dad basically hand picks for me. "That's not even a drunk thing to say."

"That's because I'm not drunk anymore. I don't need to be drunk to say those things, because I mean them. I'm not that kind of guy. I never have been. I may not be one of those guys that walks around screwing everything that walks, minus the career ordeal, or blaming the world for my pain by being an asshole manwhore to every girl that I come in contact with, but I'm still a guy that is just as capable of having those things when I'm ready and find the one worth taking that plunge with."

The air is getting thick in here. "So one day you want marriage and kids?"

"I did. It's why I proposed."

"Oh. I understand."

"But then for a while I didn't, because those things didn't work out on my side; although, I'm starting to realize they weren't supposed to, because I had the wrong girl and the timing was off. Gravity was pulling me in a different direction, and nature was making me bide my time, because the girl I was meant to have those things with was still growing up."

"Did she finally grow up?" My face is a reflection of what my heart is trying to say. It's screaming and dancing inside. That is the most romantic thing I've ever heard.

"Yes. It's about damn time. She turned out beautiful."

"You're a total womanizer," I whisper. "Because I'm completely in love with you."

"You're the only girl I'm interested in womanizing, Kambry, because I'm completely in love with you too, and one day I'm going to marry you."

"You're sure?"

Please say yes.

"As long as you don't say no. It doesn't take a year for my heart to know that I am, because when I met you, it just kind of went, 'there you are', and it's only gotten stronger since."

I place my forehead on his and close my eyes. "It did, didn't it? I couldn't have said it better, and I would never tell you no."

He kisses me and then slaps my ass. "Good, because that would be detrimental to more than my ego. Now get back over there and let me paint the other foot. Plus, it's two coats—no more, no less."

I roll my eyes with a massive grin on my face. He's right. He knows exactly what a girl wants; at least me. He's the perfect balance between manly and sweet. And he's funny. He's perfect for me. "Remind me to thank your sister when I meet her."

He smiles when I get back in position to hand him the unpainted foot. "I think she and I would both like that, very soon." He bites his lip. "What about in a few weeks?"

"Are you serious? No pressure or anything."

"I never joke about introducing someone to my family. Plus, why wait? I know I want you to meet them and that's possibly the only opportunity for a while."

"Okay." The nervous flutters return. "What if they don't like me?"

His grin broadens. "Baby, I know my family, and they'll probably talk to you more than me. September in the city? Have you ever been?"

New York City. I feel like that little smiley emoticon with the hearts for eyes. I've always wanted to go. I watched the ball drop every year on New Year's Eve and lived for the Macy's Thanksgiving Day parade. I just read this funny romantic comedy book that described the tiny apartments, quaint little restaurants, and subways that smelt of urine. For something that partially sounds so bad, nothing has ever appealed to me more. I've always wanted to experience shopping and cab rides and Times Square. I guess I'm a country girl by birth and a city girl by heart, because I love LA and never want to leave just in the short time I've been here.

I shake my head. "No, but I've always wanted to."

My voice broke halfway through my sentence. "Well, I guess it's settled then. I'll set it up. I really like being your first experience with all things, not just sexual things. It's like experiencing it for the first time myself, because experiencing it with you gives me a totally different perspective on things."

"Well, you really shouldn't ever run out of those. There's more that I haven't done than have."

"I'm hoping for that."

He grabs my foot and positions it to go back to painting. No date could ever get more perfect than this. It's just the two of us with no need to restrict our emotions. There is no one to judge us or ruin it, and that's what makes it special. Who would have thought that porn would introduce me to the man of my dreams?

I wouldn't have.

CHAPTER TWENTY-EIGHT

Saxton

My phone starts vibrating on the bedside table, waking me. I was pretty much awake anyway because the sunlight was starting to come through the windows. I prop myself up to slide my arm out from under Kambry's neck without waking her. There are only two sets of people that would call me this early: my parents or Tynleigh, my sister. I tried calling her last night and it went to voicemail, so it could be her.

Kambry stirs as I free my arm, but she settles back into her pillow and stills. I love to watch her sleep in my arms. It's pretty much become part of my morning routine, because I'm always up before her. I find myself not able to get up for at least thirty minutes after I awaken. It reminds me that life isn't always shitty, even for those like me that's endured a stretch of loneliness, because I sure as hell missed this way more than I thought I would.

We only have two weeks left. The days fly by faster than I want them to, but at the same time I actually want time with just her. No cameras and no outside viewers. It's crazy because no matter how much time in a twenty-four-hour period we spend together, I can't get enough, so last night I decided it was time to talk to my sister. I kiss Kambry's cheek and slip out of bed as my phone stops vibrating. I grab it and ease out of her room.

We pretty much just sleep in whichever bed we end up in—sometimes hers and sometimes mine—but always together. Even in this short two weeks, I've gotten used to having a bed partner. I'd hate to have to go back to sleeping alone now.

I unlock my phone as I descend the stairs. One missed call from Tynleigh and a text.

Tynleigh: Hey little bro. I was out cold by nine last night, so I put my phone on sleep mode. Call me as soon as you get this or I won't be able to talk until this evening. I have our regular meeting with the editor in chief for the upcoming month's issue article. Usually the worst day of the month for me. She's a real bitch. Pray for me. Love you, T.

I smile, missing her more than I want to admit. As I come into the kitchen, I dial her back, waiting for her to answer. "What's up, little brother? I'm pissed at you for waiting this long to call me. Just an FYI. Tiffany, you have to actually have sex to write an article on different positions that lead to orgasm. She's not going to let you write that. You're dressed like a fucking school teacher."

I laugh, filling the filter of the coffee pot with a few scoops of coffee grounds. "Do I even want to know?"

"Ugh. Sometimes I wonder how in the hell people end up working here—a bunch of damn prudes trying to fill the women of the world in on sex appeal, seduction, and how-tos. No damn sense. Enough of that, though. I haven't talked to you in like a month or some shit. What's up with that?"

"That's my fuck up. Sorry. How you been? How's the city life? Dating anyone?"

I turn on the coffee pot, waiting for it to start brewing. "Oh you know, same ole, just working and trying to have a little fun here and there. And dating . . . Ugh, no. I don't have time for that. My job is going really good right now. I'm killin' it with my articles lately. Relationship writing and fun, single, exploratory writing are totally different. Frame of mind is everything. I'm not ready for my writing to become a snore bore to read and my career to go to shit. Hell, I'm only twenty-eight. I'm still fresh meat. Plus, I kind of like playing the streets of New York for now. Starbucks! Candice, I love you hard right now. Thank you! I need this. I'll come find you in a few. I'm on the phone with my brother. He's three hours behind."

I grab a mug from the cabinet while she has multiple conversations. It doesn't surprise me. Usually I try to wait until she's off to call her. She stays pretty busy since she moved there for college. I knew she wouldn't stay in Cali forever. I'm proud of her. She's done well for herself. "Speaking of. Why are you up so early? Did you not work last night?"

"I'm kind of on a twenty-four-hour work clock right now. New project. Long story. I'm usually still up early anyway."

"Well as long as you're happy and that works for you. I'm proud of you, Sprout."

"T, I'm a grown man. Sprout is a little outdated."

"You will always be my sprout. I don't care if you're sixty. I miss you. When are you coming to see me? Give those girls a rest and take a vacation. You can take a red-eye flight and be here by morning. It's Friday so it'd be perfect. New York is never quite the same without you, no matter how much I love it here. I could introduce you to some friends, maybe a few girls. I bet you'd fall in love and move here before you know it."

"That's actually why I called. I met someone."

The phone is silent for a few seconds. I pour a cup of freshly brewed coffee and take a small sip of the black liquid equivalent to crack for most people. "What kind of someone? Like a co-worker? Or like a normal someone?"

"Think the best of both worlds. She started off as a normal someone and now she's a co-star for this project."

"Look at you. Ahh. So you really like this one then? Thinking of actually giving the whole dating thing another shot?"

"I'm already there, T. I can't explain it. I didn't mean for it to happen. It just sort of did. You know I haven't shown interest in a girl in a long time. It was only supposed to be a project pitch that night, because I needed a break. I was over sex, girls, the lack of emotional intimacy, everything. I was days away from coming to stay with you or going somewhere alone, but then I laid my eyes on her and she hooked me. She's quirky, beautiful, and I just couldn't let her go, so I went back for her, and I haven't completely left since. You'd like her. Sometimes she reminds me a little of you. She has this spitfire side to her that she lets out sometimes. I knew I had to make her mine one way or another, so I did. I love her, T. I have to figure all of this shit out. It's the only option. I want to see where this goes. She's the one. I can feel it in my soul. Don't laugh."

"What the fuck? For real? Wow, sprout. That's great. But why would I laugh?"

"Because it's fucking crazy, that's why. The more I think about it, the more I feel like a jackass. No one falls in love this fast, right?"

Phones are ringing in the background and I can hear people talking in a muted volume. Her silence is short lived. I can tell by the way she breathes out. "Saxton, I'm going to pull my wise older sister card for a second. And no, it may not be from experience, it's common sense. No two love stories are the same. Some are epic, some are ordinary, and some are just downright accidental. You've always been a levelheaded guy. You know what you want quickly and you go after it without much doubt or thought. Look at you now. You've done well for yourself. Is it an orthodox career you want to brag about to your kids one day? Well no, but you love hard, always have, and this was your way to cope through a broken heart instead of finding a rebound like some people do; not caring if they hurt someone else like they were hurt. Women everywhere are thankful that you were the guy that took the time to let yourself heal before you dove into the pool of love again."

She pauses, and I remain silent. "And personally, I think if you really love someone you know pretty quickly. If it takes you a year to fall for someone then it just seems like it's more of a comfort level romance than actual love. Just remember that your heart can love several times. That's pretty much what it was created to do, but the part that no one gets is that it only begins as a feeling. Circumstances can cause that to burn out."

"Like Salem . . ."

"Yes. Once the new settles, if the love is still there, then it becomes an act that you continue over and over without question. That's the part you didn't have before, and that's the part that I believe is reserved for one person. *The one* isn't some magical firework show that goes off in your head and heart around one particular person. It's finding the one person that you want to love no matter how hard it gets or who tries to stand in your way. Loving them starts as a want and becomes a need. At least that's my two cents."

"And you've never been serious with anyone because . . ."

"Because my expectations for forever are too damn high. I'm a bitch that cares more about my career than giving my time and myself to someone else. Love takes time and commitment that I'm not willing to give. You're not like me, Saxton. You're a lot like Dad. More so than I think even you know. Look . . . Here's the million-dollar key piece of information you need. There will be temptation in the world . . .on both parties' sides. We live among people with no conscience, no morals, and no regard for other people, but *real love* that's worth entering into a marriage for is two sided. When two people are in love, it doesn't matter what temptations arise, because the love they share will withstand it and turn away from it. Every. Fucking. Time."

I wish I hadn't waited so long to call her. She's always been the person I wanted to talk things out with. She has always been able to make things clear when they seem hazy, or when my mind tries to go back and forth. "Why aren't you writing these types of articles? You need to be bottling that shit up and selling it."

She laughs. "Would you read love advice from someone that's never been in love?"

"You have a point."

"That's only part of it. The rest is because there is this statutory position called an editor in chief that controls the finances, the staff, the issues and what they are filled with. Sex sells to a broader audience. You know how heartbroken people are. They want to drown in their hate music, alcohol, and sex. No one wants to hear things like that until they're ready, which is why I've never spoke of it to you until now. Pity parties are the most common and longest-lived. People just want to submerge in heartache for a while."

She stops, assumingly to take a breath, and then she sighs. "And . . . because Tiffany gets the sappy assignments. The girl would probably consider making out and boob squeezes being rode hard and put up wet. The chick makes me look like a whore."

The laughter building escapes me. I almost spew my coffee as I take another sip. "Does Dad know you have such a filthy mouth?"

"Little brother, there is a gate that separates what parents think their kids do or say and how they actually behave. I'm pretty sure you busted it wide open long ago. You paved the way for me to follow in sainthood, porn boy."

"Asshole."

She continues on with laughter in her tone. "I love you, though, regardless of your indiscretions. Just answer one question. Is she different than Salem?"

"Not one similarity. She's it for me. You were right all along. I wish I could thank her for giving me an out. I just have to figure out what to do about my career when this whole thing is over, because I haven't the slightest idea of what else to do."

"I'm so damn happy for you, Sprout. You deserve this. When can I meet her? If she swayed you away from your world I'm sure I'll love her."

"A little over two weeks? Can you take some time off? Maybe a day or so around the weekend? We'll probably come for a week and catch Mom and Dad when we get back."

"For anyone else, no. But for you, hell yeah. You know I wouldn't miss seeing you. I never ask for time off. Consider it done. Can you text me the details tonight? We can work out the airport when you have flight details."

I look up over my coffee mug when I catch something blue from the corner of my eye. Kambry is standing in the doorway in my navy tee shirt with messy hair and squinty eyes. I love seeing her like that. To me this is when she's the most beautiful. She rubs one eye and waves at me. I set my mug on the countertop. "Sure, I can do that. Kambry, come here."

"Sleep overs? You really weren't kidding. You never do that."

"That's part of the long story I was telling you about, but yeah, what you said too."

"Can I talk to her?"

"If you promise not to scare her."

"Scare her? It's nice to know I'm thought so highly of. I love you too, brother."

"You're kind of scary when you're excited. That doesn't mean I love you less. I'm just used to it."

"I just want to say hello. I'm about to have to go anyway. Duty calls. I promise I'll be good and I won't tell any embarrassing stories . . .yet."

"Okay." I grab Kambry's tee shirt between my two fingers and pull her toward me from the place she stopped. I kiss her. "Morning."

"Morning."

"You're up early."

She shrugs. "The bed was empty. I couldn't sleep."

"My sister called me back. Can you talk for a second? She wants to say hi."

Her eyes widen, as expected. A look of terror graces her face. She nods and I hand her the phone. "Hello . . ."

Her voice is a mix between groggy and nervous. She begins rubbing the bottom hem of her shirt between her thumb and index finger. I can't hear what Tynleigh is saying, but I can hear her voice pitching every few words. Suddenly, Kambry smiles, and then it turns into a grin. "That sounds amazing. Thank you. I can't wait."

I grab another mug from the cabinet and remove the milk and white chocolate creamer from the refrigerator—the ingredients to basically make her a White Chocolate Mocha Olay. I listen to her talk more as the seconds pass, while I warm her milk in the microwave since I clearly don't have a steamer. I don't know what they're talking about, but I like the light interaction between them. Family is important to me. They would be crazy not to like Kambry, but I still want them to.

"Okay. Talk soon. Bye."

I pour the coffee and white chocolate liquid into the half cup of hot milk, forming a mixture until the cup is full, and then replace the cold stuff and put the coffee pot back. "What are you making? I thought you liked it black."

I grab a spoon to stir and look at her, her butt now propped against the counter with her hands on top of it. "This isn't mine. It's yours." I hand it to her. "How'd it go? Did she behave?"

She stares down at the brown mixture. "She seems great, and easy going. I bet she's a lot of fun." Returning her eyes on me, she looks like she wants to say something. "You do know I don't like coffee right? I hate you went through all of this trouble."

I carefully lift her to sit on the bar. "Ever tried it?"

"Coffee? When I was younger. It didn't matter how much sugar and cream I added; it still tasted horrible. Something about that flavor I don't like."

"Well, this is different. I have one rule that you have to abide by."

"Rule? What rule?"

"You can't knock something until you try it. If you try it and hate it, I'll never ask you to try it again, but you can't assume you dislike something based off an old experience with a beverage in the same family as the one at hand."

"Fine." She places the rim of the mug to her lips and blows, before taking a sip. Never before has such an innocent act been a turn on. "There. Are you—"

Her mouth begins to move but then clamps shut and her jaw rocks back and forth, as if her tongue is gliding against her palate. She takes another sip.

"Good, huh?"

She nods, barely leaving any pause between sips. "Are you sure you want me to meet your family? That's a huge step. I don't want you to feel pressured."

I place my hands on her thighs, slowly rubbing upward. "I've never been more sure of anything. I now have two girls important in my life aside from my mom. It's only natural you two know each other."

"Okay. I just wanted to be sure."

She takes another sip. I let my thoughts run for a bit. For the most part we stay here during the day, at least during the week. Some nights we work and some weekend days we do something fun, but aside from that we chill here. I want to start the weekend early. I want to do something with her. "What do you say we go to the beach today? Someone I know has a house with a stretch of privately owned beachfront. I could give him a call. What do you think? Just me and you, sand and sun?"

She sets the mug down and wraps her hands around my neck. "I thought you would never ask. I was starting to think it was weird that you haven't brought up the beach when you have lived here all of your life."

I enclose my arms around her waist, before pulling her toward me. "There have been places that I've avoided for years. Places consumed with couples and places that have memories attached have been off limits for the most part. It was just easier to live that way, but it's time to make new memories and to experience actual life again. I want lots of memories with you."

"Just when I think I can't fall any more you go and prove me wrong."

"I hope you never stop."

"I'm really glad you came into the club that night. I'm even gladder that I was moved upstairs to VIP and actually accepted it. That night changed my life. That kiss was the start of something beautiful. Since then my life has never been the same."

"I couldn't agree with you more."

CHAPTER TWENTY-NINE

Saxton

The sound of the window being let down pulls my attention to Kambry from the road in front of me. She's not paying me any attention. She's singing along to the country music she has playing on the radio. She knows every word and I'm not even sure I've ever heard this song.

My heart swells at the sight of her. I have never felt this full before, or this satisfied with another person. She's facing the door and has her chin propped on her bent arm that's resting on top of the door frame over the window housing, as the other extends outside of the window, waving up and down against the pressure of the air. It's a surreal visual, watching her exist.

She's beautiful. I really can't say that enough. I feel like the luckiest guy in the world. It's hard to even pull my eyes away long enough to ensure I'm not swerving and veering into another lane. I know deep down I'll never forget seeing her like this. Our eyes lock in the side view mirror as I reposition it just a little. The way the strands of her wavy, blonde hair blows across her face is hypnotic. "I love it here."

"I love you."

She smiles. "That too. What are you thinking? You've been looking at me for a while."

"Just how crazy I am about you. Things can change so fast. You have no idea what you do to me."

"I'm just an average girl, Sax; no special powers, just a smothered runaway you rescued and recovered. I'm not rare, I'm just in love, and that makes you see me in a different light than everyone else. That's all."

She stands in the seat on her knees and sticks her head further out the window, resting her stomach against the door. Instinctively I glance to be sure the doors are locked, and then grab the back waistband of her cutoff shorts when she extends both arms to her sides like an airplane. "Hey! Easy. I'm carrying precious cargo."

My foot automatically releases from the gas pedal. The vision of her falling out of the truck is enough to kill this view of her clearly enjoying herself. I pull back, trying to get her back in the truck, glancing back and forth between her and the road. She finally retracts back inside. "That was so much fun. I've never gotten to do that before. I've seen it in movies."

"What? Didn't you live in the country? Where abandoned back roads are as common as urban development is here?"

"Yep, but my life experiences are very underdeveloped. Dirt road livin', parties at the falls, and creek swimmin' are things I never got to do. For a country girl I never got to experience much country."

I grab her hand and kiss the back. "Not for long, baby. Not for long."

"Girls back home would love you," she says.

I laugh, readying to pull into the drive. "But the only one I hope actually does is you." I come to a stop and kill the engine. "Here it is."

She opens the truck door and hops out, pulling her beach bag along with her. I follow behind and grab the small, handheld ice chest out of the back. "This isn't at all what I expected when you said a private beach. I was thinking mansion tucked away from society and this is cute: not too big and not too small. I love it. Whose it is?"

"Just a friend I met filming. He's been trying to get me to buy it for a while, but he doesn't want to sell it to just anyone. California real estate is expensive for a lot less, and places like this are hard to find. People tend to hang onto them. He wants to invest somewhere else, though, since he already has a permanent home here; east coast I think. New York City isn't cheap, even for those with good paying careers."

I place my arm around her and lead her toward the side of the house to the small drop off where it turns to sand. "Are you thinking about it? At least it's not all windows."

I slide down first and reach out for her hand. She's obviously not fond of the windows. I guess some people just don't see the appeal in living in the open. "I hadn't much. I didn't really have a use for it being this far out alone. I don't know, maybe."

She grabs my hand to keep a balance as she comes down the slope, and then lets go to remove her flip-flops. She stares out at the water. It's mostly calm with a mild breeze out today. "Oh okay. Well, might as well enjoy it while we're here." She takes off running, the words trailing behind her. "Last one there is a rotten egg."

Sand sprays from her heels, both hands full with something. Instead of running behind her like I should, I remove my shoes, grab them with my hand, and walk at a steady pace with the cooler in the other. I watch her; because it's so much better than letting the image go as I run after her.

She stops midway; dropping her bag and shoes, then quickly discards her shorts, leaving her in only a bikini. Already I'm not far behind because of my wider stride. Before I reach her she takes off again, running full force into the water, screaming the entire way. She doesn't stop until she's far enough out the water reaches her waist so she can fall forward to submerge herself.

I stop and set the cooler down next to her bag, before tossing my shoes down beside it. "How is it?" I yell out to ensure she can hear me.

I smile when she does a barrel roll to face me. She starts to backstroke toward deeper water. I can see boats off in the distance. "You'll have to come in to find out! I'm not telling," she yells back.

"So it's like that, huh?"

I toss my cap down and remove my shirt, before walking toward the shoreline. "It could be worse."

My feet hit the water. It's cool, but not cold. The sun is bearing down, keeping it temperate. She's becoming more distant, still swimming away from me. "You're too far. Hold up."

All of those shark attack stories in shallow levels suddenly hit me. I don't like it. Call me crazy, but it can happen. "Or what?"

I trudge through the water as fast as I can without looking like a total douche.

"You really don't want to know."

The distance finally starts closing between us. "Maybe I do."

"Guys and panic usually results in rough sex while firmly grabbing less orthodox places that some may even classify as abuse to the mildest degree."

Her mouth drops. "Really?"

Her hands wade in the water. It's deeper than I thought. Only my head is above water. "Yes."

"And this is supposed to scare me away? Sounds like fun."

I grab at her hip. "Come here."

She grips the back of my neck and I pull her against me. She wraps her legs around my waist. "Someone is protective."

"That's what happens when someone works her way inside your barriers and steals your heart."

"I admit to nothing."

I laugh. "But you didn't deny it either. That's the same thing."

"No, I just call it a tradeoff. We're even."

My arms enclose around her waist, squeezing her against me. "I like that."

She stares at me. The look on her face has me hardening. It's one of those looks like she's trying hard to read all of your thoughts without asking you, to ensure you're thinking of what she's thinking of.

My eyes close when she leans in to kiss me. Her tongue is warm. Her taste is an addiction I've formed. It doesn't matter how many times I experience it, because it never becomes old. She tightens her hold on me and moans against my lips. "Have you ever had sex in the ocean?"

"Surprisingly no. Never seemed sanitary."

"I'm no expert here, but sometimes it's not about all the mental dissection of microbiology. Sometimes you just need to experience living in the moment, doing crazy things, and daring to be different, because those are the times you'll reflect back on for the rest your life and wish you could go back, even when I'm gone."

"I don't want to think about you being gone."

"You never know. I could die tomorrow. That's reality. I want to live my life as if I were to, and ours, so when it's my time to go I have a beautiful story to leave behind. It's hard to understand until you've lived the complete opposite. Right now we have a beautiful canvas ready to make a memory. I want one of your firsts,

Sax. You have so many of mine."

Even being so young she makes perfect sense. My sex life has been planned out down to the phrases I use during the act for so long now that I've somewhat forgotten spontaneity, intimacy, and passion—not that I ever really experienced those things on a deep level anyway. "Even without the spill I wouldn't have told you no. I'm not sure I could; though I'll be honest, the thought of you dying isn't really a turn on. I know I *could* live without you, but I'm to the point, Kambry, that I don't want to."

"I love you so much," she whispers, and then kisses me again, but the power and neediness behind it this time leaves me feeling dizzy and oxygen deprived like when you hold your breath under water for too long. I like it. I like it a lot, so I reach between us and push my swim trunks down low enough in the front to bare myself, then grab the base to position my dick between her legs. With my thumb I swipe her bottoms to the side and enter her, giving her what she wants, because doing that is what I want. She is what I want. At some point I'll make her my wife. I'd be stupid not to. I'm just depending on time to eliminate the fear I have of asking . . .again.

Kambry

"Bring me that bucket."

I point to the large lime green one that came filled with sand toys we stopped and bought at the surf shop along the way. "Do you actually know what you're doing?"

I grab a handful of sand and toss it at his legs as I smooth out a place for the foundation with my lower arm. "Puh-lease. I am a pro at making sand castles. Just wait. I'm confident enough to compete with the best. I've been doing this for years."

"A sand castle pro, huh? Never heard of one of those before. I guess there's a first time for everything." He retrieves the bucket, handing it to me empty. "What next?"

I grab it and stand to my feet. "Every build must start with a stable foundation. I need wet sand."

I squat and begin to fill the bucket with the sand at the shoreline. He mirrors me, doing the same. "I'm pretty sure when I think of the words wet sand and you, as a necessity, it's for totally different reasons than yours."

I laugh and shove him backward, causing him to lose his balance and land on his butt. "You're such a perv."

"That's it. You're going to get it."

My eyes widen and I jump up, before running down the stretch of beach to my right. I look back to see him running after me, already gaining on me. I run faster, my calves burning from my feet pushing through the texture of the sand. I scream when he grabs the strings on the back of my swimsuit top, pulling it loose.

My arms bend upward to cover the triangular fabric over my boobs, trying to avoid falling out of my top. I glance back again, but he's not there. "What the hell?"

I slow down, and just as I stop he knocks me down in the sand. I scream again, louder this time from being caught off guard. His body is lying over me, his eyes searing into mine. "Where did you come from?"

The water washes ashore, wetting us as we lie in the sand. He grips my thigh in one hand. My heart is pounding hard against my chest cavity. Nervousness sets in. It always does with him. My breathing is still hard and uneven from running. "It doesn't matter where I came from. What matters is that I caught you. I'll always catch you."

"Then I'll always let you, as long as you never stop chasing me."

"Never. You're the perfect catch. If I ever forget, though, because being a guy it's highly likely, just take it with a grain of salt. If I ever have a lapse in good judgment or my memory fails me, just keep running and know that I'm not far behind, because my heart will remind me when my brain tries to betray me. That I promise. Don't run to someone else."

"I don't think I physically can. I'm kind of stuck on you."

"Like the song?"

I smile, my insides feeling like they could combust. I've found the complement to my soul. "Perfect song," I respond. "If you like music like Lionel Richie, then we'll be just fine, because to be with you till the end would be a dream come true."

"And here I thought you were too young to know about soul music," he says, still staring at me.

"My body may be young, Sax, but my soul is aged well beyond my years."

"I guess that makes two of us. Maybe they were just searching for each other."

"I'm the luckiest girl in the world."

"Funny, I thought I was the luckiest guy."

He pushes my top toward my neck with the tip of his nose, brushing along my breast. I can't think when he touches me this way. His lips envelop my nipple, before lightly sucking. He pulls the string of my bikini bottom to untie it, and then does the other side, before letting the back half fall to the sand. "What are you doing?"

"It's my turn to ask for a first. I want to make love to you on the beach."

"Yeah?"

"Yeah. It's kind of your fault, you know."

"How is it my fault?"

"You started talking about how you need wet sand, and that was a code to me that meant you needed to be fucked in the sand; naked and wet."

My body begins to shake beneath him. His voice is so low and deep. It always is when he's turned on. I place my hands on his lower back, then slide them beneath the band of his shorts and squeeze his butt with both hands, trying to calm my nerves. Happiness overwhelms me. The need to have him again is consuming. "You've never had sex on the beach either?"

"No. I guess I was holding out for the right girl even though I didn't know it."

I bite my bottom lip as he kisses the round portion of my breast, running his hand up my side, as he licks his way up my neck to my ear. "So sand castles can wait?"

I wrap my wet, sand covered legs around him. The gritty, annoying texture no longer registers. The only thing I can consider is that I'm about to make a memory that I'll never forget. People may not understand our need to have each other so frequently, but unless you have that kind of a relationship with someone, you wouldn't understand. Sometimes the best way to tell someone how you feel is to simply show them how much you want them, in every possible way. We have years to tone down our desire. Right now I'd rather enjoy the fact that he wants me this way, over and over again. I've learned that sex isn't a bad thing. It's a beautiful thing, but the imperative part is to find the one that makes it a beautiful experience.

My hands comb through the back of his hair. "This is so much better than sand castles."

I push his swim trunks down to his thighs, showing him I'm ready. "I was hoping you would say that."

He kisses me. Each time he does it's slightly different. Each kiss becomes more telling of how he feels inside. Every emotion has a kiss specific to it. It's not something I can explain properly with words. It's one of those things you just have to experience. My heart has never felt so content in all of my life. If someone were to ask me what I want right now, given the opportunity to have anything, I would say nothing at all and mean it whole-heartedly, because I've noticed that when we're together everything seems peaceful and my world freezes. Nothing or no one can top him. He's my life altering person.

I've always had this weird take on what being in love is. I guess you can blame it on all of the fairy tales, but I kind of thought it was this magical, glittery, instant, body warming feeling that kept you in this fantasy bubble; like a snow globe, but it's not. Real love is built just like a sand castle: carefully and a little at a time. Creating the foundation is just realizing with each second that you want another, regardless of what you're doing. It's finding someone that piques your interest one night and then seeing him again becomes a consuming thought that never really goes away. It's your heart pushing you to find out where it could go and trusting that it's leading you right where you want to end up.

Once the basic foundation of attraction, lust, giddiness, and flirting have been constructed, over time and with each memory you add, you fall harder, deeper, and before you know it you're looking at the most beautiful castle you've ever seen, because the builder with passion for what he's developing will always put in the hardest work.

Being here with him on this very beach, and being completely inappropriate as he enters me for anyone to catch a glimpse should they arrive doesn't bother me at all, because my heart is falling so hard for him that I don't care about anything else. That's what he does to me. He owns me . . .in every form imaginable.

I'm completely in love with Saxton Maverick Cambridge—the farm boy from Oakdale, California, the sexy heartthrob, the loyal boyfriend, the guy that stole my heart, and the porn star. He isn't any one of those things, but all of them. His career doesn't define who he is. His character does.

CHAPTER THIRTY

Saxton

I grab my black leather jacket off the back of the couch and walk to the bottom of the stairs. “Kambry. You ready? We’re going to be late if you don’t come on.”

“One second. I’ll be right down.”

I pull my jacket on over my bare skin, waiting. It’s the last weekend in the house for a while . . .or ever, depending on which way this turns out. It’s hard to believe it’s gone by this fast. Originally I thought it was going to drag, that I would get bored, and that I would get tired of sex, like I usually do when filming. None of those things have happened once. Not one damn time have I had issues getting up. Amazing. It’s more like miraculous. My boys are back and they showed up with a bang.

Midnight on Sunday the cameras stop for privacy. Monday we leave. The first episode will be available for purchase and viewing next week, and we’ll be New York bound. I’m ready. It doesn’t bother me that the cameras are around, because I’m used to them, but at the same time I want to be around her with no other eyes and ears. I want to have unrestricted conversation. Not Q and A’s here and there over text. I want her all to myself again. I have no idea what the trailer or the first run consists of. Michael hasn’t given us our copy yet. I’m a little curious.

I glance at my watch when I hear her heels tapping against the wooden stairs. My attention diverts to the direction of the sound, just before my jaw falls toward the floor. My eyes slowly move up the length of her legs from the tall, black heels she's wearing. Her skin is glistening with a light shimmer. She's smooth, bare, and legs for fucking days. I finally reach the black, leather fabric, hitting just below her barely covered ass. The waistband rises and stops at the bottom of her navel, and then it returns to bare skin. Her stomach tightens as she descends the stairs.

Two steps away from me and her fucking beautiful tits stare me in the eyes: black bra, mostly sheer, cleavage everywhere, her breasts covered by nothing more than black lace above her nipples. "Fuck. Hottest damn girl I've ever met."

I blink a few times, trying to force my mind to work. Black lacy bra . . . I clear my throat as the words exit. "Hell no, Kambry."

Her bright red stained lips spread upward. "What? It's leather and lace night. I kind of feel like a modern day Sandy from *Grease*."

"We work in a nightclub. There is plenty of other shit you can wear besides that."

"The point. We work in a nightclub. I love theme nights." She holds up a short leather jacket that matches the skirt. From the looks of the length it stops at rib level, serving absolutely no purpose. "I have this to wear until I get there."

I shake my head. "I never tell you what to wear or not to wear, because that's something assholes do and it's your choice, but baby, you cannot wear that. I'm asking you."

"Sax, come on. Are you serious? It covers the same as a bikini. We fuck in front of cameras. Are you really worried about my covered boobs? Everyone is going to see the real things at some point."

"Kambry, it's not about someone seeing your tits. Okay, maybe a little, but I've come to terms with it on a screen; not in the flesh where someone can smell you—damn you smell good—and they can be felt up by one touchy asshole. Those are mine. I'm the only one that can touch. I have to work the bar. I can't stand beside you the entire night to make sure stupid, drunk fucks keep their hands to themselves. All it takes is you dropping one thing on the floor and some arrogant frat boy whipping his dick out to try to be sly. I may be nice, understanding, and forgiving for the most part, but all it takes for me to snap and commit murder is someone tainting what's mine. With her, I didn't do much of fucking anything, but with you, a side no one wants to see will come out. Make sense?"

She takes another step toward me, still grinning, before threading her fingers into the back of my hair: her favorite place I've learned. "Is someone jealous?"

"Extremely."

"Does it make me sound immature if I admit that I liked hearing that you're different with me than her?"

"There is no comparison. You're my person."

"It makes me hot when you talk like that." She drops her jacket. Her fingers lightly descend the folded down collar of mine. "And this bad boy look you have going on is even better. You aren't wearing a shirt. I may be jealous myself."

My hands snake around to the top of her ass. "Not the same thing. There is a huge difference in a beautiful girl with an absolute perfect rack and ass and a man with a set of abs. Men have repulsive minds."

She roughly grabs my hard dick through my black jeans, catching me off guard. "Fuck."

"You like that?" Her voice is thick. Her tone is low. She has adopted the act of being sexy as if she never went without it.

"Yes. Damn. I may like you in leather."

"Ahhh. What if I let you mark me on these stairs before we leave? We have a few minutes. You up for a quickie? Then I'll be a natural male repellant."

She's rubbing my dick. It's been over twenty-four hours since I was inside of her. That's a long time for us. "Your offer is very tempting."

She grabs my jeans and unbuttons them; then slowly slides the zipper down as she speaks. "No underwear?"

I smirk. "Nope."

"You sure know how to make a girl horny. You don't even have to kiss me. Just fuck me from behind and make me smell of you. Then I'll be on you too and neither of us will worry about anyone else."

"You wet?"

"Aren't I always?"

"Fucking shit. There is no way in hell I'm turning that down. Turn around and bend over. Place your hands on the step."

"As you wish, baby."

She slowly turns and seductively bends forward, placing each palm shoulder length apart, and then shakes her ass side to side. How in the hell did I get this fortunate? Maybe my fucking loyalty in the past is finally paying off.

I push my jeans to my thighs. With her bent over, her pussy is fully accessible with a slight displacement of her thong. More reason she should not be fucking wearing what she is. Sadly, I'm going to lose that battle. She spreads her legs. With those heels extending her height . . . What a view.

I hook my index finger under her thong string and pull them over her ass, baring that beautiful pussy, completely molded for me, and only me. That thought still makes me hard as a damn rock when it's already erect. I place the tops of my fingers directly on her pussy and slap her ass next to it with my other hand. It's become one of her and my favorite forms of foreplay. I do it, knowing it makes her wetter, and I get to feel her pussy contract several times as it does. "Shit."

"You want it again?"

"Yes."

I spank her again, harder, as I shove my fingers into her pussy, the sound louder this time. She clamps down. Leaning forward, I unhook her bra and push the straps over her shoulders. When we fuck I want her titties bare. That still hasn't changed. I love her tits. They're one of her best features.

I bring my lips down to the base of her spine, then swipe my tongue all the way up the length, slowly, carefully, in a caress, and then cup her breast in my hand. I've noticed licking her spine makes her horny as hell. "Sax, you're torturing me."

I remove my fingers and grab the base of my dick as I rub my thumb over her nipple. "No, beautiful, you're tormenting me."

I rub the head over her pussy to wet it, and then thrust inside fast and hard. "Shit yes. I needed you."

I pull one foot on the next step up for a better balance, position my opposite hand on her hip, and begin driving into her without stopping. "Yeah. Right there. Fuuuuck."

She squeezes around me. I don't think I'll ever become immune to how good she feels. For a few minutes I can incubate my dick in a warm, moist channel that can tighten on command. She moans out, a gritted cry with each hit as I bury myself deeply inside of her. Fucking hell. I tighten down on all of my muscles to try and not come. It's no easy task, especially when she's this wet.

I pinch her nipple. "Come, Kambry."

"I'm about to. Don't stop. Fuck."

She places her hand over mine on her breast, forcing me to squeeze harder. I pull up on her hip as I thrust as deep as I can. I can't hold it back anymore. She starts contracting around my dick. "Shit, that feels so good."

She threads her fingers with mine. "I love you, Sax," she says, and squeezes harder when her words become short moans. She's coming, and the first spurt inside of her confirms I can't stop myself. I lean forward, my front over her back until I'm closer to her ear. My thrusts become slower and more shallow until I still altogether, feeling through the pulsing of my cock as I release my cum inside of her. "I love you too, Kambry, and don't you ever forget it."

She turns her head to the side and I kiss her briefly. "Promise?"

"With all my heart. Come on, beautiful. We're going to be late."

I pull out of her and replace her panties, before pulling my jeans back up and putting my dick away. "Stand up and I'll fasten your bra."

She does as I ask and holds it in place at the front. I sweep her long, curled hair to the side, hook her bra, and then kiss the meeting point between her shoulder and neck. "So there's no chance in me changing your mind on the outfit?"

"The point is to live with no rules, Saxton. I want to be free to do as I choose, to make my own decisions, and to make my own mistakes. I would never do anything out of line or to hurt you. I'll think before I act if it makes you feel better. My goods are covered."

"Okay, fair enough. I can understand that, but when I can't be near you remember we belong to each other. We're partners. Men are going to look at you in ways that I don't like, but if someone gets out of line come and get me. Okay?"

"Okay, Sax. I will."

"Good. If you're uncomfortable there is probably a reason, so don't stick around."

She turns around in my arms and places hers around my neck. "You know,

I fall in love with you a little more when I see you like this over me, because deep down I know that I base my behavior on the fact that I only do things I would do with you standing beside me. I also know that you trust me, so instead of getting mad I just believe your words a little more. It makes me feel special. Mild jealousy is good for a relationship, because it reminds you that they chose you when they could be with someone else."

"You aren't special, you're rare. People do crazy shit to hold onto rare when they have it. I'm a lucky guy, and I don't know what the hell I did to end up in the right place at the right time, but unless you want out of this I won't question it."

"That's never going to happen."

I'm at the point that I want to give up everything to make this work. I want to alter my entire life to make her a permanent fixture. It's time now that I start taking the necessary steps to do that.

Kambry

I set my tray on the bar and give Saxton the list of what I need. He stands with his palms down on the bar and grins as I lean forward on the bar top. "Back so soon?"

I love that playful, seductive tone. His abs peeking through the open jacket distracts me from looking him in the eyes. "Thirsty customers."

"Or you just wanted to come back and see me."

My eyes rise. "I'm just fast. Deflate your ego a little."

He grabs a glass and begins filling it with draft beer. His body is moving along to the beat of *Cookie* by R. Kelly. It's not noticeable unless you're paying him some attention. It's subtle, and that's what makes it sexy. The man is gifted in all areas. "If that's what you want to keep telling yourself . . ."

I bite down on my tongue, trying to keep a straight face, but my lips always betray me. "So . . ."

"Spit it out."

I have a love/hate relationship with the smirk he has when he knows I'm being shy. "You played a stripper role, right?"

And his grin grows . . . Great! "I did. Why do you ask?"

He's already done with three of the five drinks. *Rip it off like a Band-Aid, Kambry.*

"Can we role-play sometime? Ya know, if it's not weird for you or anything. It's just, Meredith and I watched that Magic Mike XXL movie a while back, and . . ." My fingers go straight for my mouth. "I kind of wondered what it felt like to be one of those girls on stage at the end. It's weird I know."

His top teeth are scraping against his bottom lip as he displays the mildest form of a smile. It actually reminds me of that face that Channing Tatum makes when he's the sexiest; that kind of half pucker, half smile, serious but sexy look. He begins to roll his stomach as he skims his hand down the middle, over his abs. "You want a lap dance?"

Geez-ums. I'm starting to sweat. I will not fan myself in front of him. "And if I said yes?"

He sits the last cup on my tray and leans forward on his forearms, extending his body toward me over the bar. "Then I would say, you shall receive."

The back of his index finger brushes along my bra line over my cleavage. "Maybe even tonight when we get home."

"Shit," I whisper. "I got to go."

I grab my tray and walk off, but not as fast as I want to because of these heels. Good luck getting through tonight with those thoughts.

Saxton

I watch her walk off, her ass swinging as she does. "Yo, Kayden, can you cover me for about five minutes?"

"Smoke break?"

I look at Kayden, one of the other bartenders tonight. "I need to run something by Drake. Can you dance?"

"What kind of dancing?"

"Dance porn." I wink, waiting for him to quickly respond.

"No shit? I'm no male stripper, but I think I could wing it if I had to. Why?"

"Cool. I'll let you know when I get back."

I quickly walk to the hall wall just beside one of the exit doors, where Drake likes to watch the club and stay unnoticed in case some shit goes down. He's there just like I expected he would be. "Can we have a word?"

"What is it?"

"I need your permission for a club takeover."

"For what?"

"Get the crowd turned up a few notches, and I need to borrow Kambry."

"She's working. I don't like pissed off customers. Then I get phone calls from the owner that I don't want to deal with."

"I guarantee your customers will be anything but pissed off when this is over. Plus, I can almost guarantee you a full house tomorrow night. I'll even pretend it's your idea if anyone asks."

He rubs his hand through his hair. "How long, Maverick?"

"Ten, maybe fifteen minutes. I need a mic, a certain playlist from the DJ, and the bar. That's it. I guarantee there will be customer participation."

"Fine. What playlist? Don't make me regret this. The owner doesn't like to be surprised unless it spurs a huge spike in alcohol sales. I don't need him giving me shit."

"Magic Mike XXL soundtrack. Tell him to pick slower and change along with me. I'm using Kayden."

"Give me ten minutes."

I salute him with my index and middle fingers before turning to walk back to the bar. Kayden has money coming at him from several directions. From the looks of it the bartenders on the other side of the bar are just as busy. I come to stand beside him. "I need you to follow my lead when Drake brings me the mic. Pick your girl."

I slap my hand down in front of the brunette. "What'll it be, sweetheart?"

"Surprise me."

"Sweet or bitter?"

"A little of both?"

Typical flirty college girl. Most guys are used to them. Strapless white top that stops just below her first couple of ribs and skintight leather pants—I'm going to assume she isn't looking to go home alone. I grab the plastic cup, fill it with ice, and quickly make her a Long Island. She hands me the money and winks. "Keep the change."

"What you need?" The guy with two girls following behind moves up to the bar as the other girl gets out of the way.

"Two Millers, draft, with a lime, and one Corona."

I grab two cups in one hand and pull back the lever, letting one fill and then switching to the other, before shutting it off and pushing a lime wedge on the rim of each cup. I hand them to him to take as I grab a Corona from the cooler and pop the cap off with my bar key, replacing it in my back pocket, and then grab a lime slice and wedge it down into the opening of the bottle like a cork.

He hands me the money plus tip. Drake walks behind the bar as I'm ringing up the purchases and adding the cash to the drawer. He hands me a microphone. "DJ is ready and waiting for your cue."

I grab it, and just as quickly as he walked back here he leaves. I turn it over and flip the mic switch on. "What's up?" I ask low into the microphone. The DJ turns the music down. "Your fellow bartender here. Anyone game to turn the heat up a few notches? Ladies . . . "

A select few scream. "Oh come on now. I know you can do better than that." More people respond this time, but still not a club full.

I look at Kayden. "I thought tonight was supposed to be about leather and lace. Do I sense females clutching pearls instead? Where are the bad girls?"

That did the job.

I jump up on the bar and stand, raising my outstretched arms in an up and down motion, palm up, requesting more from the crowd. Kayden follows behind. The music slowly turns back up, but not as loud as it was. It's a slower jam. *Freek'n You* by Jodeci. "Who here is a Magic Mike fan?"

The screams pick up and spread throughout the room. The girls closest to the bar start touching our calves and jumping up and down. I glance around the room, looking for Kambry. "Guys . . .who here wants the chance to be Magic Mike?"

A good many testosterone-driven, pussy-craving males speak up. I still don't see Kambry. "I'll tell you what . . . The first guy that can bring me the cute little blonde server wearing a black bra and leather skirt gets the opportunity at a dance off with Kayden and I here on the bar, lap dance style. You even get to pick your girl. You win, I pay your tab at the end of the night and your partner gets a hundred bucks for being a good sport. You have five minutes while Kayden chooses one lucky lady. She goes by Kambry."

I give him the mic and watch the participating males weave back and forth like ants, while the others glance around them. Kayden reminds me of a body builder. He has the bulk up top, the lean waist, and then the thighs—like an hourglass. Every inch of visible skin is smooth and free of hair, no doubt for more definition. It's blatantly obvious with the leather vest he's sporting over nothing but cut muscle. I don't see him having a problem getting a participant. From the screams alone he has plenty of options.

Even without all of that, he has that dirty blonde hair that's longer in the front than everywhere else—a fade—and it's soft enough in texture that if he were to lean over a woman's body the tips would hang and brush along her skin, and most likely drive her crazy.

A redhead in a short, tight, leather dress comes to stand in front of Kayden. She has a slightly nervous grin on her face. "What's your name?" He's looking down at her, his voice deeper than mine.

"Loren," she responds. The crowd separates.

I notice Kambry's ass first, thrown over someone's shoulder as a guy walks toward me. She's pulling the bottom hem of her skirt down in an attempt to cover herself, with not enough material to do so. It's too damn funny to be mad over. That . . .and his arm is holding her behind the knees. He gets bro points.

"This the one?" He points at her as he makes his way to the front of the crowd, stopping just in front of the bar.

"Yep. That's the one." I extend my hand toward Kayden, waiting for him to place the mic in my hand. "Let's get this show on the road."

I hop down as he sets her down, and then walk toward him. "What's your name?"

"Ryan."

His jeans are a little tight for my personal liking and his shirt fitted. He's not as cut as Kayden, but he doesn't appear to have much body fat, most likely the result of exercise from work and not the gym. He's clean cut and has an accent similar to Kambry's. His leather is a little . . .different than the rest of us. Chaps, but who am I to judge. Leather is leather, and clearly he's not from around here. Tourist.

"Ladies, who here wants to be Ryan's partner? Looks like we have a cowboy.

They generally know how to . . .ride." A new set of screaming starts. I stare at Kambry as I continue to speak into the microphone. "Ryan, you hear 'em. Take your place on the bar and choose your woman."

"Are you seriously going to give me a lap dance in front of the entire club?"

"It's a little late to turn back now, beautiful."

"You have no shame, do you?"

I shake my head. "Not even on a molecular level." When I glance to my left Kayden, Loren, Ryan, and a cute blonde are standing in a similar position to Kambry and me, waiting on my lead. The mic touches my lips. "DJ, give me a beat."

I walk around her and turn, then push her toward the bar. Her cheeks are pink, but her eyes are locked on mine. She bumps into the pulled out barstool and reflexively sits. "I'm gon' make you feel it . . ." plays as the music becomes louder. *Feel it* by Jacquees. It's a slower jam: bedroom music. I rid of the microphone, and for the first time since we met I switch to character mode, losing myself in the music, leaving no one in the room but her and me.

Popping my jacket over my shoulders, I grab her hand and place it to my sternum, before slowly guiding it down, letting her fingers slip into each ridge of my abs as I roll my stomach and hips, and then allow it to settle over my hard dick, atop my jeans. I pop my pelvis forward.

Her mouth parts. My hands free, I slowly allow my jacket to fall down my arms until it drops to the floor. My hands leisurely slip the button through the slit of my jeans as I roll my shoulders in the opposite direction of my hips, and then fold them over in the front, revealing only the base of my dick. The loosened fit causes the back waist of my jeans to slip over the top of my ass, leaving it bare and peeking out. I can feel the draft.

I grip her thighs and pull her to the edge of the stool. "Baby tell me that you want it deep-er." With the last word of the line I pop my hips forward and thrust up, grinding my dick against her center. She places her hands behind her on the seat of the stool and arches her back.

My hand moves to her ass and I grab onto the bar with the other, before stepping on the first prong of the stool for height and pull her body against me as I do. I can feel her heat radiating through the pores of my jeans.

The song changes to *Pony* by Genuine. I grip onto her hips and lift her to the top of the bar, stepping up the barstool as if it were stairs, and then throw my leg over her as I turn her and push her back into a lying position. “If you’re horny, let’s do it, ride it, my pony.” I buck forward and fall to my knees on the bar, straddled over her. “My saddle’s waiting, come and jump on it.”

My hands lace behind my head as my waist takes over. She presses her palms to my rolling abdomen, her bottom lip tightly wedged between her teeth. My movements become one with the beat, and at the peak of the rhythm, I fall forward and land on my palms to each side of her head in a push up position, my face just above hers. “Fuck,” she whispers.

It gets easier the longer my body rolls and sways. She spreads her legs some, letting me closer.

A mock fuck. That’s my goal. I shall strive to make her feel as good fucking her clothed as I do when I’m inside of her. With each rock forward, my body scrapes against hers; sweat mixing, and only parting for recoil, before ascending up her body like a worm. She presses her lips to my sternum and extends her tongue, then allows the tip to swipe down the center of my body as I climb her.

Chanting vaguely sounds through my ears as my pelvis reaches her face. I feel wet from sweat, but I won’t stop before the finale. I lower toward her face, allowing her nose to brush along the skin just above my dick . . .and I begin riding her fucking face, alternating between fast, slow, and rotating motions.

Screaming sounds. I know the end of the song is coming. Pushing off my hands, I pull my knees up to straddle her face. I grip my fist into her hair and pull her face into my crotch as I continue to dance. When the beat starts to wind down, I alter my weight away from her face toward my feet, so that I can pull my knees up and stand.

I smirk at her as I extend my hands to help her up. Her mouth is literally almost spread from ear to ear. Her cheeks are flushed and red. Her eye makeup is even starting to smudge a little underneath. “Damn, that was so hot. You did all of that and you weren’t even drunk.”

I grab her face in my hands, sliding them back into her hair, before pressing my forehead and lower body to hers as we stand on the bar. She wraps her arms around my waist. The song that just started playing I finally recognize. It’s the song *Heaven* that Matt Bomer sings in the movie.

Well this is a change of pace . . .

I begin to slow dance against her, bar top, in front of God knows who, but I don't give a damn. "I don't need alcohol to make you happy, Kambry."

I can't help but to listen to the words of this song. I'm not sure that I ever have before, and even though I'm not much of a singer, I can't help but to start singing along right as one of the lines plays. "Love is all that I need."

She moves her arms around my neck and stares at me as we dance against each other. Then a tear falls. "And you think you're the lucky one. I can barely breathe, let alone think of words right now. Who would have ever thought a lap dance could turn into something romantic . . ." She laughs in the midst of a few tears falling from the corner of her eyes. "God, I love you . . . So dang much, Saxton. I've never felt this way about someone. Please don't hurt me, kay?"

"I can't make a promise like that, Kambry, just like you can't. Humans do stupid shit, all the time, but I would never do anything that wasn't best for you, because a girl like you deserves the best, and I'd give up my beating heart to give it to you."

She nods against my forehead. "Just remember so would I. This is our song now."

"And it's perfect . . ."

CHAPTER THIRTY-ONE

Ben

I sit up in my bed, glancing around the darkness of my room. I must have dozed off. It didn't help anything, because the room is still spinning as the liquor continues to flood my system. I toss the comforter off of me and throw my legs over the edge of the bed. My foot rubs across the floor, looking for my boxer briefs. An arm wraps around my waist and then lips become flush with my skin, just beside my spine. "Where are you going?"

I find my shorts first and stand, pulling away from her. "Downstairs. You need me to drive you back to the sorority dorms?"

She sits up, holding the sheet over her chest. "It's only midnight, Ben. The party is still in full swing. Are you ever going to let me stay with you? We fuck all the time."

The music is blaring throughout the house. Sleeping on a Friday night before daylight here isn't a possibility. I can hear people talking in the hall and an occasional body hit the wall next to my door. I step into my shorts and fasten them, before passing Rowdy's unmade bed to get a clean shirt, since mine was used to wipe my dick after pulling the condom off. He'll be in here to get his sucked and fucked around three. We have a system and it's worked since we became roommates.

"Probably not, Kristin. I don't do sleepovers, fucking or otherwise."

"Why not? It's not like I'm a tramp making my rounds with your brothers.

I'm not asking you to make me your girlfriend, but a little more than a hit and run would be nice."

"If you don't like how things are you can always say no. I've never forced you to fuck."

"I'm just trying to understand. It's just sleeping. Are you honestly telling me you've never stayed the night with a girl before?"

"Only one."

"Well, what happened to her? Did she do some kind of crazy shit to you while y'all were sleeping or something?"

"It's never just sleeping. Not to me anyway. It's intimate."

"So an ex-girlfriend then?"

I exhale, already done talking about this. I don't have to explain my reasons to anyone. It's no one's business. Still, I feel like an ass because in some ways she's right, but I can't. I don't want to.

I grab a shirt and pull it over my head, letting it fall down my body. My fingers rub through my dark brown hair. "I guess some people just never get over their first, Kristin. I don't share my bed with another girl because I don't want to. That's the best answer I can give you."

"First love or . . ."

"Both. Look, I'm going to see what the guys are doing. You good or do you need a ride?"

"I think I'm going to stay for a while. It's early. My friends are somewhere around here. I'll just go back with them. Go ahead. I'll be down shortly. I have to get dressed."

I look between her and the door, spotting my sneakers where I shucked them earlier. The alarm clock by my bed and the electric neon pinup girl Rowdy has hung on the wall over his are the only forms of light. I grab my shoes and pull them on, not even bothering with socks. "Alright. I'll see you later then."

I grab the door and walk out in the hall, closing it behind me. Red Solo cups are already littering the floors and lining the walls of the hall. Doors open and close in no particular order, being used like a hotel. I glance across the hall into Blake's open room. I step across to see what he's doing since no one leaves their doors open with this many people in and out. "Yo, Blake. You in here?"

I glance toward his bed and a set of tits greets me, bouncing slightly as she rides him, her head tilted back. "What's up?" His voice is flat.

She never even glances at me. She just continues riding his cock like no one's in here. Even after everything I see being in a fraternity, I still can never get used to the lack of modesty some girls have. "Never mind."

I walk out and shut the door, before jogging down the stairs for the kitchen. People are everywhere. I grab a cup and fill it with beer from the keg, then walk toward the party room in search of someone with a familiar face. I weave through bodies. The lights mostly turned off makes it harder to see. Strung party lights and the DJ's black light are the only on aside from the kitchen.

I pass through and notice some people out back on the patio. I walk outside. A few of the guys are sitting on the furniture with the television on and a couple of girls hanging around. Andrew pulls the pipe out of his mouth and glances at me. "Ri-vers," he says, smoke exiting from his mouth. "Where you been, dog? Want a hit?"

"You know I don't smoke weed." I take a sip of my beer. "If my parents found out they'd pull me out of school. I'm not going home."

He sits back. "Missin' out, man. This shit is good."

He places it back between his lips and lights the bowl, burning the grass. I notice the other two with girls in their laps, all engrossed in the wall-mounted television. "What y'all watching?"

"Porn."

"Why?"

"Because it's hot," David responds.

"Makes sex better," the girl sitting in his lap adds.

I drink more of my beer and finally veer my eyes to the screen. My brows dip. "In a truck? Porn is supposed to be nasty. That's kind of the point."

"We just ordered it. I think this is just an advertisement or some shit."

It switches to a different scene but the couple looks the same. She's arched back on top of him. "Damn, she's got a nice body. Look at that rack."

"Fuck yeah she does," Andrew says. "They don't even look fake."

It changes again, this time showing a slideshow of sliced videos with text attached, advertising an available purchase date and the network. My blood runs cold. "What the fuck?" My voice comes out loud and hard. My heart starts pumping rapidly.

"Look Rivers, she has the same last name as you. It's just spelt weird."

Starring Saxton Maverick and Kambry Ryvers . . .

Two people.

One house.

Sin at an all-time high.

And filming never stops.

Can you handle it?

Let the sessions begin . . .

My jaw steels, and without any thought I grab up the remote and shut the television off.

"What the fuck, Rivers? Turn that back on."

"No," I grit out.

"Don't make me beat your ass. We paid for that."

"That's my sister on there, asshole. Come try."

I throw the remote at the wall as hard as I can. Every fucking one of them is staring at me. "That was your sister? Fuck dude, why didn't you say she was that hot? She's a porn star? Damn Rivers . . ."

"Taylor, would you shut the hell up . . . You're digging your grave and if he lays you out, you deserve it. You don't talk about a guy's sister—at least not in front of his face. That's bro code, dude," Andrew says. High as fuck probably and still the only one with brains.

I feel sick to my stomach. I just saw my sister naked and I said she was hot, out loud. I gag. Then down the rest of my beer. I crush the cup and throw it down. I'm going to beat her ass. I'm shaking. I'm mad. I can't think. How the hell did she end up doing something so low and degrading? Oh my god. If my parents find out . . .

I lace my hands over my head. "Which one of you fuckers can drive me to the airport? I can't drive. I'm drunk as hell still."

"Airport? Where are you going?"

I glance at David. "California."

"I haven't drank anything tonight. I have somewhere I have to be early. What the hell are you going to California for? That's halfway across the country."

"To talk some fucking sense into my sister and bring her ass back home before she destroys her entire reputation, or her life."

"I'm assuming you didn't know of her recent activities?"

"She's on there, is she not? Had I known, she wouldn't be. If it were your sister . . ."

"Noted. Let me go get my keys."

"Give me thirty minutes to pack a bag." I turn and walk away but stop. "So help me if any of you turn that back on you won't have to watch another one, because your dicks will be temporarily disabled."

I walk off without waiting for a response. I knew she wanted freedom, so when Dad called me to tell me she ran off to California, asking if I would talk to her to come back home, I kept putting it off, trying to give it to her. I know my parents have always been unfair with her, keeping her under lock and key. I didn't blame her for leaving. Hell, I was happy for her, but I wasn't letting her have space to do shit like this. I've seen documentaries on what female porn stars go through, and Kambry fucking Rivers is not going to be one of them. I don't care who I piss off.

I walk in my room and turn on the light. My bed catches my attention, bringing my mind back to the conversation with Kristin. One person flashes in my mind: Meredith. She's the single most reason I've distanced myself from my own sister. Some days I regret us not being close the past several years. She hasn't done anything wrong. I have times where I hate myself for not calling her once since she ran off. I should have, to at least make sure she was okay, but Kambry can't breathe without Meredith, and I can't be around Meredith. I knew she was fine as long as they were together, but maybe I've trusted Meredith too much. It's been years and still I can't speak to her. I can't even think about her. Now I have no choice. I have to see her to get to Kambry. I haven't laid eyes on her in a few years, and for a damn good reason.

I'm still in love with her.

CHAPTER THIRTY-TWO

Meredith

"He left your house to come to mine. I have proof. See . . ." I extend my empty hand toward the full body mirror in the corner of the room that will have a cell phone in it during filming. Got to start somewhere. I walk a line back and forth in front of it in my living room. "That's not good enough. The first job you got and you only have a few lines. Own that bitch. Make an impression. Again."

I clear my throat, slightly altering my tone to be bitchier. "He left your house to come to mine." I practice my bitch grin in the mirror. "I have proof. See." Extend again. "Ugh. I feel like this is the worst line ever. Maybe I need to find a RomCom. Seems more my style." I take a deep breath. "Start from the filthy bottom, Mer."

A knock sounds at the door. I roll my eyes and huff in the mirror. Must be Bryant trying to fuck up my plans. I told him no sex today. I toss my script pages in the air when the knock gets louder and walk across my apartment to the door. "What, Bry—" I smother my own words upon opening it. "Ben . . ."

"Meredith. Expecting someone?"

My heart is beating erratically. I feel faint. Are my fucking cheeks flushed? Dammit. *Do not touch your face.* It's hot in here. Did I forget to turn the air down? This has to be a mirage. I'm having a slight out of body experience. I can't move from my current position. Good lord, he's just as sexy as ever. Time has been good to him. And he's staring at you, standing in the doorway, while you drool . . . Snap out of it, bitch.

"Is it about that time already, Benny? I'm sorry. I've moved on from you—r dick." Fuck, that was a close call.

"Still just as bitchy as ever I see."

I squint my eyes. "What are you doing here? Kambry isn't here. How did you even know where I live?"

"I called your mother. How else would I find out?"

Tonya Love, you fucking traitor. See if I confess to anything else.

"And she just willingly handed over that information with no questions?"

He grabs the door just above where I'm holding it and pushes it open enough he can get through, before stepping forward. I don't budge nor do I let go, even with my arm fully extended. I did not give him permission to enter. "Of course not." His body becomes flush with mine. Dammit, he smells so good. He always did. He smells clean, like male body wash mixed with cologne. "I told her I wanted to surprise Kambry—because *someone* let her run off and plaster her body all over a film while some guy has his way with her. Of course, I may have left the last part out, but she always has liked me."

"Which is why I question her judgment . . .and Kambry is a grown ass woman. If she wants to be in a film, regardless of the type, it's her business. I will not ever tell her what to do, and neither should you."

"We will open Kambry up for discussion shortly, since she's . . .absent at the moment, but first, back to the topic at hand. You did at one time."

His lips are so close to mine. I can feel his minty breath as it kisses my lips. It's been like three fucking years since I've seen him, and he just waltzes to my door and has me a damn wreck. He makes me weak. I hate him for it. No other man does this shit to me.

He takes a step closer and grabs my hand from the door, forcing it away. I take a step back and he swings it shut. "What can I say? I was a tween and you were aged meat. I was just in it for the rush. I grew up and came to my senses. It was just a mistake, remember."

"A lot of them."

"Oh, who's counting? It meant nothing."

"Then why is your heart racing?"

Asshole. "The same reason yours is."

"Then this is only fair," he says, just before crushing his lips against mine. Like a favorite song you haven't heard in over a decade, when it plays, you instantly remember all of the words while the memories from the last time you heard it hits you full force, leaving you in a state of déjà vu.

His hands become rampant all over my body. He grips my thighs and lifts me. I wrap myself around him as he walks further inside of my apartment. I shouldn't let this happen again. I shouldn't do this with him, because I know that when it's over and he leaves I'll hate him again, but only because I love him so fucking much and I want him. I have since that beautiful night we spent together while everyone else was sleeping and we experienced sex for the first time . . .together.

He pulls free. "Where is your bedroom?"

"The door by the mirror."

He walks inside and falls forward on my bed, laying me down, but pulls himself back up and grabs the waist of my shorts, before pulling them down my legs, baring my lower half. "I was with someone last night," he says as he rubs his hands up my legs.

"So was I."

His chest is noticeably rising and falling. "Is he your boyfriend?"

"No, but you should know that. Have I ever had a boyfriend? He's just a friend with benefits. He gives me what I need when I want it. Do you have a girlfriend?"

"Good, because I didn't want to stop. It's been a long time." He then shakes his head and reaches for my tank top. I sit up, letting him remove it. "She's just a stand in."

"Did you wear a condom?"

"Yes, always, did he?"

"Yes. I've only had sex with you without one."

"That always was our thing, wasn't it?" His eyes search mine, and then he removes his shirt. "I still want you."

"Welcome to the club."

He quickly removes the rest of his clothes, as if he can't get them off fast enough, and then crawls over me. "Why are you still single, Meredith?"

"I guess I'm just leaving the door open for something better to walk through. Why are you?"

"Because I haven't had the balls to come after the one I want and filler just isn't good enough."

"And now?"

"Circumstances left me no choice. I grew a pair. After this I need you to take me to her. Then I'm staying with you for a few days."

"Aren't you supposed to ask?"

I smile, unable to contain it. He removes my bra and places a kiss on the globe of my breast. "You aren't the kind of girl that wants me to ask. You'd get bored. Besides, stop trying to overlook the elephant that's been in the room for years."

"Oh yeah? What elephant is that?"

"The one where this has never just been sex and we both know it. You're just legal now."

I roll us over, straddling him. I lean forward as I grab his dick in my hand, aligning it to slowly sit down, taking all of him inside of me. "Then I guess it's time to show you what you've been missing."

He briefly closes his eyes and then opens them when he's all the way inside of me. "You always do."

My heart is going crazy. I can't breathe. I'll never want anyone the way I want him. Sex is never the same with anyone else. I hope he's serious this time. Admitting things is a first step we've never taken, but I know better than to get my hopes up about anything, because at the end of the day he's in school across the country and I'm building my life here. One of us will have to sacrifice a lifestyle, or just go right back to the way things were, and it won't be me, because I have stars in my eyes, and that's enough to keep me here, regardless of what I have to live without.

I slowly begin to pump up and down, reveling in the way it feels to be on top of him again. It's an unexplainable desire that never goes away; one that no one else can fill. He's been my addiction since the day he took my virginity. It doesn't matter how many days I stay sober, because all he has to do is offer me a little hit and I relapse all over again. "And it keeps you coming back after all these years . . .”

He grabs my face and turns us again, taking control. “That most likely will never change.”

And that’s because we’re two wild hearts that can only be tamed by each other. He’s the boy next door that caught a falling star, and I’ve been his ever since.

CHAPTER THIRTY-THREE

Saxton

I walk in the living room after my shower and sit at the opposite end of the couch from Kambry. "What are you reading?"

I pull my leg onto the couch and turn toward her, grabbing her small foot in the process, and then begin pressing my thumbs against the arch as she looks up at me from the small, square device she's holding in her hand. Her hair is up in a whirlwind of a mess she calls a bun. It doesn't look like any bun I've ever seen. The shit girl's come up with I'll never understand.

She smiles at me, but it's a shy smile, and she has the slightest hint of a blush. She looks beautiful like this: no makeup, a gray, cropped off sweater-jersey that hangs off her shoulders, and tight, spandex pants that stop at her calves. "It's just a romance. Meredith kind of got me into them. You know, male gag material."

I smirk at her. "Now, Rivers, how would you know if it's gag material? That's a little stereotypical. Just because I'm a guy doesn't mean I don't respect the arts, even romance. Read to me."

Her eyes widen in surprise. "I'm sure there is something on television you would rather watch. Some of these guys are a little far-fetched from real guys, but I guess that's why fictional boyfriends create such a hype."

I try to smother the laugh inside. "Fictional boyfriends, huh . . . Should I be jealous?"

"No! It's just a book, you know."

"I love you for that, but I'm curious. Read to me. I want to know what I'm up against."

"Saxton, you really don't want me to read to you. I'm likely a horrible narrator. Sometimes when I read aloud I stumble on my words. Plus, isn't that weird? You know, especially in an intimate scene."

I raise a brow. "How intimate?"

"Almost like an instruction manual in some cases. Some are quite detailed."

I keep a straight face. "So, you're reading porn?"

Her cheeks deepen in color. "There is a huge difference in porn and erotic literature, I must say, even being an amateur reader. Only those uneducated in the world of books would call it that. However, that doesn't make it any less embarrassing having to read it aloud."

"It's not weird. I call it homemade couple's therapy." I rub along the bottom of her foot with pressure. "Come on. Read me some lady-porn. I may even like it. We're way past embarrassment, baby." I circle my index finger in the air. "Don't you think?"

She huffs and crinkles her nose. "I cannot believe you're going to make me do this."

"Hey, I need to have a full deck if I'm going to play a game. I swear not to judge or make fun of said fictional man. It's just for boyfriend research purposes."

She scoots toward me on the couch and props her neck on the arm of the couch. "That feels really nice."

"Good. It should relax you. Now read."

"Fine. Here goes. Let me just back up to the beginning of the chapter." I study her as she starts moving her fingers on the front of the screen. I like this—casualness between us. It always feels so natural and like we've been doing it for years.

"Chapter 3: Lacy . . ."

My eyes settle on her full lips as she begins the excerpt.

"I can feel him watching me again. One might think I'm crazy if I revealed my thoughts, but I know he watches me. Each time I look down at my notebook to take notes on the PowerPoint presentation, I can feel his eyes set on me. I have no way to prove it with an auditorium full of students—several surrounding my seat—but it doesn't change the way I feel in these very moments."

"My body burns from a fire I can't see. Feelings I've never had begin down in the bottom of my belly. The hand that holds the pen I'm writing with shakes uncontrollably, making my notes look like something of a serial killer. I find it hard to breathe until I look up at the projected image, and then all of those feelings cease. I can't explain it, but I think he wants me. Even more, I think I want him too."

"He looks at me as he dismisses the Biology 101 class. 'Lacy, can I see you for a moment?' My nerves become haywire as I gather my notebook and close my textbook, inserting both into my backpack for my next college class. I nod, unable to speak among the rustling of feet darting for the door. He meets me at the door with his brief case in hand. 'Follow me to my office.' What could he possibly want with me? We're halfway through fall semester and he's never once called on me."

"Regardless of my reservations I follow him down the third floor hall of the science building until we reach the end, next to the emergency stairwell. As he slides the key into the lock my insides feel like they are being pulled into a tight knot. 'Did I do something wrong, Mr. Lambert?'"

"He opens the door and walks inside, not saying a word until he closes it. 'We're not in class right now, Lacy. You can call me Jason.' I look around the office, stacks of paper piled high and models of organs and humans scattered around, among other molecular graphs and diagrams."

Kambry glances at me in a pause. "Keep going."

She looks back down at her Kindle. "He places his briefcase on the chair facing his desk. 'Come here and leave your backpack.' I do as he asks. As I walk toward him he catches me off guard. 'Are you attracted to me, Lacy?'"

"Is he serious? Is this a real life situation? I feel like I'm living in the dream of a forbidden romance novel. He can't be more than thirty in age, but still. Teachers don't hit on their students. It's like a law in the teacher's contract, not to be broken. Still, that doesn't make him any less desirable. He's muscular, unlike the typical stereotypical type you would imagine as a teacher. His brown hair is short, but gelled up in the front as if he's trying to rebel against the classic business appearance. His button-down is rolled up to the elbows, revealing his bronze skin. He reminds me of what I would mentally visualize as a Greek god. And his voice—so deep, making you want to adhere to his every command. Who on earth would not find this hunk of a teacher attractive? I may be a freshman but I'm not blind. 'Yes,' I state."

"He grips my waist. 'Do you ever think about me touching you? Because I want to touch you . . . It's becoming all I can think about. I can't concentrate on my classes because I want you so bad. I can't avoid it any longer.' I'm almost positive my heart is a few beats away from self-detonating."

"I stare into his deep chocolate eyes, deciding if I should admit my naughty thoughts to him, or the dreams that have affected my sleep pattern for the past couple of months. What if this is a test? Cops set up prostitutes all the time. That sounds stupid."

"His hands move around to my ass and stop. I can no longer hold my tongue, because I want this. I don't care how wrong it is. 'Yes,' I admit."

"He grips my cotton dress and pulls it up my body, leaving me in only my underwear and flip flops. 'Can you keep a secret?' I think on that question. Can I keep a secret? When he begins unbuttoning his shirt after tossing my dress on his desk and the muscles underneath appear section by section, I know that I can, because any girl that would turn this down has lost her mind."

"I step out of my flip flops. 'Yes. I'll never tell a soul.' He reaches over and locks the door after unbuttoning his pants and folding them down, giving me a glimpse of the black briefs underneath. My now damp underwear is creating a bit of discomfort."

"He reaches behind me and unhooks my bra with little effort. Most guys that I've experienced sexually have problems with a bra, even looking at it, but he does it with ease. 'Good, because I'm about to eat your pussy like I'm starving.' And that's when he grabs me roughly, kissing me as he maneuvers me to his desk and lays me across it. I feel like I'm fulfilling a fantasy; satiating a dark desire."

"He rips my panties from my body and I find it hard to breathe. My body craves his tongue there even before he touches me. I moan out as he swipes his tongue up my center, between my lips. He smothers my sounds with his hand, and then he keeps his word. It seems so wrong, but it feels so right . . ."

I blink when I don't hear her read anymore, pulling myself out of this weird trance I'm in. "Why'd you stop?" Damn, that was kind of hot. Even without the pictures to accompany the words. It was so vivid in my mind, as if I was watching it. That's weird as hell. I've always hated to read. Is that what Michael was referring to with this whole project that night at the club?

"Because it's hard to concentrate with you massaging my foot like that and I'm not reading their entire sex scene to you."

"Why not? I'm intrigued. I feel like I'm getting a peek into a woman's mind. Is this the kind of shit women get off on?" I think for a second. "Wait a minute. Do you picture yourself being the girl? I don't know if I like that."

She shrugs. "Some girls may, but not me."

"Explain. Don't lie."

"I mean, I do, sometimes, but I imagine you as the guy, so I basically just replace the characters with us in dirty scenes, and the scene still plays out in my head. I like when we do role-playing stuff, like at the bar last night. That was hot. Other times, I just sit back and enjoy someone else's love story."

She slides her other leg across my lap and smiles. "Are you hard?"

I glance down, still rubbing her foot, and then switch it to rub the other one. "It's not my fault. Your word porn took me as its victim and mind fucked me. Plus, I am a guy. We think about sex most days every two and a half seconds on average. Far less can make guys horny. My dick has a mind of its own. I've learned not to try to control it. It usually does the opposite anyway. Recently, I've discovered it generally makes better decisions than I do, hence you. Are you trying to tell me reading stuff like that doesn't make you horny?"

She swallows. "I'm not horny."

Her voice proves she's lying. "Are you sure?"

"Yes."

I shift onto my knees, bringing her foot closer to my face. "What are you doing?"

I brush my hand up the bottom of her foot and between her toes. "Battling the book boyfriend. Let's see if you've read this in any of your books."

I place my lips around the base of her big toe, lightly, and not exerting any pressure so that my lips remain soft. I swirl the tip of my tongue around it, and then slowly pull back, letting my tongue brush alongside the bottom until it reaches the pad. "Oh. My. Shit." Her whole lower half arches off the couch as she pushes off her other foot. "It tickles."

I open my mouth and return to the base, my eyes never leaving hers, before repeating the motion again, never speeding up. Her entire body tenses and bucks upward until I release my mouth. On the fourth time her hand grabs my dick through my athletic shorts. "I lied! Fuck, I'm so horny."

When my mouth releases she pulls her foot free, then mirrors my stance, wasting no time in pulling my shorts down to my thighs. She stands and pushes her pants down her legs, stepping out of them as they reach her ankles. Placing her hands on my bare chest, she pushes me backward, barely giving me time to get my legs out from under me before she straddles me. "Damn, Kambry, where has this girl been hiding?"

She strips her shirt off, baring her completely—no bra. "Maybe that needs to come with a damn warning label: possible combustion upon wetting." She sits down on my dick before I even realize she was holding it. "Because when I think about what you just did it's disgusting, but holy shit that felt amazing."

"Fuck, you're wet."

She grabs my hands when I place them on her hips and moves them to her tits as she rocks back and forth on my cock. "Right there."

Her head falls back and she arches, placing her hands behind her on my thighs. All I can think about is the fact that she just took control of my dick as if she owns it, and she does, but fuck. This has me in a complete and utter mind fuck; watching her use me like this. Her movements are fast and hard. She's riding to come and it feels too good. I can't concentrate from the wet warmth alone, let alone the sounds coming from that beautiful mouth. I squeeze her tits and nipples, hard, trying to distract myself, but her nipples harden further and it backfires. "Fuck yeah. Hurt me, baby." Oh my fucking hell. I close my eyes and begin mentally chanting the plays from the ballgame I watched this past week.

My eyes open when she begins clamping down around my dick. She's looking at me. "I'm about to come."

"Thank fuck."

She leans forward and kisses me, moaning against my mouth. Her movements slow, so I move my hands to grip her hips and ass, taking over. I can feel my balls preparing for release, so I pull my knees up to place my feet flat on the couch, and then thrust up as I start to nut, driving as deep inside of her as I can. She claws into my chest and I suck her tongue as she inches it into my mouth again.

I slowly ease back down on the couch. My hands glide up her back into her hair. "You're perfect for me. We're good together."

"The best balance," she whispers.

"I realized something."

"Oh yeah? What's that?"

"That sometimes a person has to experience bad to embrace good at the maximum level possible. I may not have loved you first, but I love you the most."

Her lips quiver. Then they part. I can tell she wants to speak, but doesn't know what to say. A knock sounds at the door, saving her. We both sit up together and turn our heads toward the door. "Are you expecting someone? Like Meredith . . ."

"No, but knowing her it's a possibility. She doesn't need an invitation to barge in on someone. Crap."

The knock gets louder. She pushes herself off of me in a hurry, searching for her clothes. "I'll get it. Just get dressed."

She pulls her shirt back over her head first, while I pull my shorts up to my waist. I walk to the door, hearing hobbling from behind me, and a whisper-shout curse word every few steps. The annoying knocks now sound like banging. I reach the door and open it. "Chill out, Mer—"

"Hi," she says in a tone that is definitely un-Meredith-like. She's currently not the center of my focus, though. The guy standing in front of me that I don't recognize is.

"Who are you?"

"Maybe that's what I should be asking you," he responds in a tone of sarcasm.

"You're on my doorstep, bro. Watch your tone."

"Where's Kambry?"

"What's it to you?"

"Saxton, this is—"

He holds his hand up to silence her. His eyes settle on my chest, and then out of nowhere a fist flies into the side of my face, causing me to stumble into the door. Reflex takes over just as I hear a scream; from whom I don't know. I spit and wiggle my jaw, then shove him outside to give me some room, before throwing a hit right back at him, nailing him in the side of his nose.

He touches the side of his index finger under his nose and checks for blood, then comes running at me, but before he reaches me a blonde blur runs by me into him, slapping him on the cheek and shoving at his chest. It's like watching a hot Tasmanian devil on roids. "What the fuck is your problem, Ben? Huh?" She shoves at him again, but he just stands straight, letting her push at him. I don't blame him. I would too.

He looks at her and when his face changes, it dawns on me who he is. They don't really look that much alike or I would have caught it sooner. Relatives yeah, but siblings aren't obvious. "What the hell are you doing, Kam? You're a porn star now? Is this your way of getting back and Mom and Dad?" His tone is elevated, angry. "What are you thinking?"

"It's none of your business, Ben. You don't even speak to me anymore."

"It is my business when I see you on television and I have to explain my angry outburst to my friends. I saw you naked, Kambry! I watched you riding some guy's cock. You're my sister. I can't fucking un-see that. Then I fly across the country and show up to try and figure out what's going on in your head and there are claw marks all over his chest. Look at you. Your hair is disheveled and your lips are pink and puffy. You aren't a dog's play toy. You're a girl—a good girl. I haven't spoken to you because I thought you needed your space, but not like this. Come home with me."

"Fuck you! I'm not going back to that hellhole with them. You don't get to show up here and act like a protective older brother now. You forfeited that right. I'm not going anywhere. If that's all you came here for you can go back home, *empty handed.*"

"Do you really want to be another notch on his bedpost of many? You aren't special to him. You're a piece of meat. You're the bull in a bullfight. He gets all the glory while you end up hurt in the end. I know you, Kambry. This isn't who you are. This lifestyle is for broken girls with daddy issues. You're too good for this."

He's pissing me off, brother or not. Meredith slips beside me. I inch forward, about to say something, but she holds out her arm. "Let it go. This has been coming for a long time."

"You don't know anything about me," she says in a . . .cry? Is she crying? I step forward again.

Meredith faces me. "Let it go, Saxton. Let her get it out. Trust me."

"Why don't I? Tell me how you feel, Kambry. For once yell at me, tell me you hate me. Tell me how sucky of a brother I am. Vent. Fuck, do something. Stop internalizing everything. You've done it all your life. It's not healthy. It leads you here. You rebel in the wrong ways."

She shoves him back. "I hate you!"

"I love you."

"You left me out. Why didn't you ever let me hang around you and your friends?"

"To protect you from ending up like Meredith did with me."

I look at her. "Don't ask. Another day."

"Why didn't you stick up for me with them?"

"Because I didn't know how."

"You left me there all alone, with them!"

"I'm sorry."

"Why did you get to experience it all? Don't I deserve to go to college and live? I want to experience new friends. I want to go to frat parties and make stupid decisions. I want to flunk a test and then beat myself up because I stayed out too late instead of studying. I want to experience the smell of the library, walking two miles to my class, dorm rooms, cafeteria food, football games, and college love. Why do you get those things and not me?"

"I went for us both, Kambry. Why do you think I've studied my ass off with a double major: one to please dad and one for myself behind his back? I skipped a lot of parties to study. I know the library and its smells like the back of my hand. I skipped meals in the cafeteria on several occasions so I could sleep from pulling an all-night cram session. I haven't flunked a single test, because that isn't an option for me. I didn't experience college love because I was in love with someone out of reach. The only thing I did for *me* was joining a fraternity, and I pay the dues myself. College is some of those things, but not all of them for most people. I've been working my ass off so when I graduate I can get a high paying job and pass the torch to you, parents be damned. I know how they are. I know they aren't fair. They're sexist bastards. I get it. I know what you went through. Some of it, I even went through too. I just hid it from you."

"Then why did you forget me when you left?"

"Because of her." He points at Meredith but continues looking at Kambry. "I couldn't stand to be around her if I was going to do any of those things . . .for *you*, but that doesn't mean I forgot you. Just because I had to grow up doesn't mean I care about you any less. I'll never forget you, Kam. You're my sister, my family."

He actually starts shedding a few tears. His jaw is setting into a lock. "Don't ever think I don't want those things for you. If you want to be wild then be wild, but not like this. You're going to ruin your reputation. You're going to regret this one day."

"It's not like that, Ben. We love each other. You act like I'm a prostitute."

He sneers, shaking his head. "Nah, this isn't love, Kambry. No real man wants the woman he loves plastered all over the place for men to gawk at and use as a spank bank. Real love is the thought of forever. Real love is preparing for the future. Real love is a man figuring out how to get you to marry him so that no other man can be given the chance to replace him. No man in love wants to share his girl with the world in the most intimate way there is. Love is selfless, not selfish. If he really loved you, he wouldn't have conned you into doing this to yourself."

I zone out, his words starting to set in my head, and hers. He glances at me, his face red and splotchy from the anger. "Would you? Be a man and take responsibility for what you've brought her into. Meredith filled me in on how this started. You pursued her. You know what they do to girls in this. And girls like her that need the money can't stop. It's nothing more than a legal and accepted form of a sex slave or prostitute. Am I wrong?"

I glance at Kambry. Things I haven't considered because of my blinded desire for her are coming to a head. "No."

"Don't say that," she whispers, tears still falling down her swollen face.

"It's true."

He cuts in again. "Are you going to marry her? Are you going to give her babies? Are you going to be able to support her in a way that doesn't involve your dick? If so, what would you tell your kids when someone finds out and brings that shit to school one day? It may not be an embarrassment now, but one day it will be . . .for her anyway. You'll get the status of a sex god and she will be labeled as a whore. Her value as a woman will cease and she'll be nothing more to people than a sex object. We live in a world that will always have double standards. It's fucked up but that's the way it is. Do you care, or have you not even thought about it? You chose this, while she chose you, and this was the circumstance to have you. You didn't give her another option. And that right there tells me you don't really love her."

"Maybe not at first, but I do now."

"Then do what's best for her. You're a grown man. She's still eighteen: maybe not for long but for a little while longer. The age gap is too wide right now. You'll be ready to settle down right about the time she should be enjoying her life. If she trades that in, it makes her running away from her entire life and what they wanted for her to be done in vain."

Kambry shoves at him. "Leave. Stop planting stuff in his head, Ben. You talk all of that smack but if you loved me you would want me to be happy. He makes me happy. That's why I'm here. I made this decision. It's on no one but myself."

He doesn't look at her. Meredith grabs his arm, trying to pull him toward where her car is parked. "Think about it, before you ruin everything. Everyone in my family will disown her."

He finally glances at her as he starts to leave. "I'll be at Meredith's until Monday afternoon. Then I have to fly back for Tuesday classes. Call me if you need me. We'll figure this out."

"Bye Ben," she says, and then runs up to give him a quick hug. I walk inside to give them a minute, and to clear my head from the shitstorm that just brewed. I don't stop until I make it to my room, quickly grabbing a pair of jeans and a shirt to change into.

The door sounds downstairs as I pull my sneakers on my feet. I grab my wallet and shove it into my back pocket, then pick up my keys. "Where are you going?"

I glance at the door where she's now standing. She crosses her arms over her chest. A worried expression appears on her face as she takes in my outfit. "Out."

"What do you mean out? Where? Do you want me to change?"

"I mean out, alone, to clear my head."

"Is this about that stuff Ben said? He was just being a dick."

"He's right, Kambry, about everything. I was just too blind to admit it until he pointed it all out."

She walks toward me, wrapping her arms around my waist. "Please don't do this. Don't shut me out. Talk to me. Isn't that what you told me once?"

My chest hurts because I wish he were wrong, my ego is wounded because I don't want to let her go, and my brain is screaming at me to leave her alone, just like all of those times it kept telling me not to let this turn into anything.

I brush my thumb along her bottom lip. "Maybe we should use the film break to break from each other, and to take a few steps back from this."

"What? Why? You said you loved me. Why would you want to do something like that? Was it just a lie?"

"I do love you, Kambry, but sometimes that's not enough. I promised you I would always do what's best for you, even if that requires removing myself from the picture."

"That's not what's best for me, Saxton. You're what's best for me. We're a team remember. We do everything together."

"No. I'm not what's best for you. I would have been, had I met you years back. I was just fooling myself into thinking this would work. Heartbreak sent me over the edge. I made decisions that are costing me now. This is all I've got."

"Stop saying those things. This doesn't even sound like you. All we need is each other. That's it. The rest we just figure out as we go. That's how we've done it since we met."

"Oh, come on, Kambry. You know that's not true. You want different things. You said it yourself."

"What things?"

"University life, parties, college love. That's not me, Kambry—none of it. You're looking at a minimum of four years. I can't fucking start over. I can't give you all of that on a damn minimum wage job. Even if not for a while, at some point money I've made runs out without something to replace it. My twenties are halfway over. Marriage and kids—I'm not saying that I'm ready for that. Maybe I don't need kids. You know, I never thought of any of that before when

I agreed to do this. It was just something I did in anger and pain. It seemed like a good idea at the time. I didn't have anything to lose, because I had already lost it all. I didn't consider what consequences it would have on a family later down the road. I was convinced I was over that phase of my life until you came along. I wouldn't want my son or daughter to do this, and I shouldn't have brought you into it either."

A tear falls down her cheek, rewetting her barely dry face. "So you regret us?"

"I'll never regret you, Kambry. You're the girl that changed me. You're the girl that made me realize there is a difference in loving someone deeply and being submerged deeply in love with someone. That's why I think it's best if I let you go before I drown you."

"Don't do this. Please. I wouldn't want those things without you."

"I'll talk to Michael and see what options we have for breaking the second half of the contract. I can't do anything about this past month, but I doubt it'll harm anything. Most people will never see this. For the most part it'll be like it never happened. You can take the money and go to school, meet more people closer to your age, and get what you came here for."

"Saxton, stop." She growls out angrily. "I don't want to pretend this never happened. I want you. I can't just turn you off."

"I know. That's why I am."

She drops her hands from my waist. "What are you going to do instead?"

"What I'm taught to do—fuck, film, and forget. That's the life of a porn star."

"How could I forget? It's so easy for you."

"On the contrary. Things are never as they seem; not even sex. Fucking another woman after you will be the hardest thing I'll ever do, but that's life. People do it all the time. Ben and Meredith know all about that apparently. I don't like it, but it's something I'm willing to sacrifice to give you the best life."

I kiss her on the forehead. "Don't wait up for me."

I walk out and leave her alone, slamming the door behind me. A bar is where I'm heading. An odd sense of Deja vu is consuming me; only this time, I'm hurting myself while the one that's good is standing on the other side of that door. Sometimes a man just needs to fucking cry, even if only on the inside. The best way to do that is to get lost in music and alcohol . . .

CHAPTER THIRTY-FOUR (BONUS)

Saxton

The bar music is loud, the room hazy from the smoke clouding the small bar. Even better. Easier way to blend and be forgotten amongst the mass of people. I drown myself in the Southern Comfort shots I've had coming in steady for a while now, trying to force myself to forget every place on my body that her lips have touched. The harder I try the more those very places tingle, reminding me it's impossible to forget a girl like that.

I grab my pack of cigarettes off the bar, removing one. Drinking and smoking have been the only forms of nutrition I've had since I left that house hours ago. Nutrition for a broken heart is what they are: a savior for the lost. When I left I drove around for hours, trying to think about what I've done. The same face kept replaying in my mind like a song stuck on repeat. The tears running down her face completely broke me—any part of me that had finally mended from the first time.

I wanted to turn that fucking truck around so many times, and once I did, only to go a different direction once again. Sometimes it takes someone to put us in our place when we're fucking up. I hate myself for what I've done to her, but I still don't regret it, selfish or not. I've never felt like more of a man than I do with her. I'm the guy I like, instead of the guy I force myself to be.

Finally, I ended up here. I guess it's really true that when you let your heart lead it seems to always find home, like a compass pointing north. The memories assaulted me the second I walked in the door. It's been a long time since I've sat at this bar. It's not even my style. The Johnny Cash playing on the jukebox proves it, but it was a familiar need. It's the happy medium between the place I've known as home my entire life and where I thought home was going to be.

Joel always liked this place; from the moment I brought him here freshman year. Tynleigh found it in high school. It was a little off the radar from the nightclubs that drew the bigger crowds. It's low-key, and that's all that matters to underage drinkers. The dude was your typical California guy: straight bill hats, Adidas track pants, and chucks. There was nothing country about Joel, but he always had this thing for *country girls,* and this was the best place to find them. He bragged about fucking girls in their boots on more than one occasion. I thought he was fucking nuts, but maybe now I understand the appeal. Most didn't have the southern accent like Kambry, but the getup they did. This was the closest place to her without being with her. This is also where he met Karleigh.

We were both business majors, so from the first semester we seemed to keep ending up in the same classes. When the only available seat open was beside him in Macro Economics spring semester, we just sort of ended up being friends, and he was my best friend until I walked away. I'm not even sure whose fault it is at this point that we became distant. I think I've always just assumed it was him, but maybe it's been me all along. Things seemed harder with him after that night, considering his blood was the one that drove me into this shithole in the first place. Our friendship was never hard . . .until then.

I light the cigarette, waiting for the poison to invade my lungs, and enjoying every second as I release the cloud of gray when I can't hold it in any longer. "Adele, will you bring me another?"

"Sure." She places two shots in front of me, filling them to the brim. "These are on the house. You look like you need them."

I shoot one, wanting the bite in the back of my throat, needing something to hurt me in a way that doesn't stab another hole through my heart. My phone starts to vibrate on the bar top. I glance down at the beautiful blonde on the screen. She's been calling off and on since I left. I haven't answered it, for fear I may fucking cave at the sound of her voice. "Girlfriend troubles?"

I glance at the female giving herself permission to sit on the stool beside me. I power my phone off, because each time it's getting harder not to answer. "Just ex problems," I respond in the most robotic tone there is.

She smiles and orders white wine. It makes me cringe inside. That's the shit Salem used to drink, like it made her look more important than she actually was. It was always about looks with her. Status was everything to her. "Those problems I can deal with," she says, taking a sip from her glass. She flips her hair from one side to the other, letting her sweet perfume fill the air. It's too sweet. "I'm Roxanne. What's your name, sexy?"

"Ben," I lie, giving out the name that ruined my day.

"I like that name. You don't look like a local."

"I'm not," I respond, bored. I inhale again, not paying her any attention. I haven't even looked at her.

Her hand settles on my upper thigh. "That could work out in your favor . . .if you want."

I glance at her: dark hair, bronze skin, caked on makeup, and overdressed. I take the other shot, her hand slowly migrating toward my dick. "How so?"

Her elbow is propped on the table, the top of her hand under her chin. Her eyes are filled with lust. It's obvious. Maybe I should just go ahead and get the inevitable out of the way. Breaking the ice is always the hardest part. And I'm drunk enough that maybe I'll be numb to the whole damn thing. "Someone I know is out of town for a few days. It could be fun."

She's rubbing my crotch. I glance down at her hand covered with a large diamond. The fucking irony. Being on the other side of that table for the first time. In some ways, some place deep down in that dark space at my center, I wonder how that would feel—to fuck someone's girl like he and so many before him did mine. I've often assumed some indescribable high must come of that—the power to make someone cross that line with their own free will.

Is this how she did it? Every time she made it sound like she was pushed into it. She would cry, scream, and beg, promising it would never happen again. She played the victim—like a rape without the force, or date rape without the drug. More times than not I was more pissed off at him than her. With her it was heartbreak that someone else had trespassed on my fucking property. But is this how it was all along? Was she a fucking siren? Luring them into her web to the point they don't even consider what they're actually doing because their dicks have already taken advantage of the situation? Fuck, I was pussy stupid and blinded by the idea of love. Poor fucking schmuck is probably working his ass off somewhere, thinking his faithful fiancé or wife is lying in their bed, alone, when she's trying to stain it instead.

One revelation stands.

My dick is soft. It hasn't hardened in the least since she sat down. It hasn't hardened since the girl that fixed it to begin with pulled her pussy off of it this morning. I remove her hand, placing it on the bar. "I'll pass. You aren't going to get me up, sweetheart. Only one woman seems to be able to do that."

"That's easily fixable," she says, trying to go back for my crotch. Been there and earned a fucking degree in pills.

"Like I said. Not interested. Maybe it's you, or maybe it's the fucking promise on your finger, but either way, I have no desire to plant my dick between your legs. You're wasting your time."

I raise my hand at Adele, signaling for another round, and peacefully finish my cigarette that's steadily burning—wasting. "Asshole," she whispers, standing and positioning her purse on her arm.

"I've been called worse. Good luck with the next one though."

She huffs and walks off, taking her glass with her. Adele places another shot in front of me and walks away, keeping all of the customers at the bar happy. "And here I thought you were supposed to be a ladies man."

"You thought wrong." Michael sits down beside me, placing a tumbler on the bar. Obviously he's already made his way to the bar. "How'd you find me?"

"Studio called about some visitors that showed up at the house. Red tape, you know, since we have to get releases signed to use the footage. I watched it. When you stormed off I figured I'd give you some time to cool off. I was in the middle of some shit I couldn't just walk away from. Once I was free, I made an educated guess. This is where I found you the last time . . ."

"You mean the first time?" I turn up the shot, quickly consuming it.

"Same difference. What the hell are you doing, Saxton?"

"I'm doing her a favor."

"Is that what they're calling it these days?"

"What?"

"Being a coward."

"That's funny. I thought it was called being selfless."

He turns a little on the barstool, facing me. "I've known you for a while now, but not once have I ever thought you were stupid . . .until now."

"Fuck you, Michael. What do you know?"

"Cut the shit, Saxton. Put the broken, arrogant porn star aside long enough to realize what you're doing. I hand you an out on a damn silver platter and you're fucking it up. Just because you decide that she is better off without you, doesn't mean she is. Love doesn't work like that, dumbass."

He's pissing me off. I can take a lot, but he's driving me over the edge at speeds that are unstoppable. "Oh yeah? A platter, huh? How exactly is that? Because unless I'm missing something things don't seem to be any easier. No questions have been answered for me. If anything, they're more confusing than ever, so tell me, Michael. How in the fuck have I been offered any way out? And by the way, unless you've walked in my fucking shoes, you don't have any room to talk. You watched it. You heard what he said. He's right."

He finishes off his glass, his jaw working back and forth moments after he swallows. "Alright. You want to get real for a minute? Man to man? Fine, I'll go off the record in ways I've never done before, because I saw something in you the last time we were here. I saw someone like me years ago—driven, destined for success, and humble. I saw the way you were looking at her that night in the club. I've seen the way you are with her on screen. We all fucking know that reality T.V. really isn't reality at all. Reality doesn't drive up numbers. Drama does. What the two of you have is real. I put my fucking job on the line to give you a chance to man up, to get over this broken heart shit and finally move on. You think we all haven't been hurt at one point or another in life? You've let heartache brainwash you over the years. You don't belong in porn, Saxton; at least not on that side of the camera. The second I ran salary by them for Kambry they wanted to cut you for getting cocky, just to prove a point. The men with the money don't like to be backed into a corner when it comes to their wallets. I vouched for you. Ultimately, I deal with the numbers. I made it work to give you a push in the direction you needed. I have connections, Saxton, but in order for me to help you, you have to help me, and right now you're fucking it up. I can't show you my hand before I'm ready to call. There are only so many hints I can drop to you. I know more about your background than you think I do. This shit you're pulling isn't the guy with a 4.0 GPA his junior year in college."

My hand anxiously runs through my hair. "She's too good for me. I can't give her the life she deserves without embarrassing her."

"And what does that make my wife? A cleaned up whore?"

"I never said that."

"Most of us have families, Saxton. It's a job just like anything else. The only embarrassing career is no career at all. You didn't finish school. You can't just come in and wear a suit, but you can work your way up until I feel you're ready. You want a mind fuck? I'm going to tell you something I've never told anyone, so that I can make you understand. My wife is a reverend's daughter. She was born and raised a preacher's kid. From the time she had her eyes on me I thought she was too good for me. I partied all through high school and most of college; had a different girl in my bed at least a few nights a week. Graduating was a struggle for me. Finding a job was harder, and it was a wake up call. She made the dean's list every semester, had never been wild, and stayed away from trouble. Why on God's green earth she wanted me I'll never know. I was her first and I wish to God I could say I was her only, but like you I tried to walk away. Six months after graduation I had no job prospects and a girl that deserved a family, a man that could support her, and it sure as hell didn't look like it was going to be me at that point, so I did what I thought I had to. I let her go."

I rub my hands down my face, my hair standing all over my head. I'm drunk and at this point I need a bed, but there is no way I can sleep. "Yeah? So what happened?"

"Kiss N Tell films had a paid intern spot open a couple months later. I applied, they called, and I worked my ass off until I became a valuable asset."

"So you just waltzed back and now you two live happily ever after?"

"I tried. I didn't even recognize the woman she was by then. She was reckless, creating a path of destruction to attempt mending the damage I had done to her heart. Just because you force a woman into a life you think she should live doesn't mean she's going to. More times than not she actually gets worse, because love isn't something we can control. You can't just take your love away and expect her to be okay with it. I went from first in line to last. By the time I finally got her back she didn't give a damn who signed my paychecks. The only thing she cared about was that I loved her enough to walk the line with her instead of without her."

"And kids? How do you expect me to explain this kind of lifestyle—porn?"

"The same way I do."

"You have kids?"

"Three of them."

"And the magical answer is?"

"You keep your home life separate from your work life. You show them a father that works hard to provide for them and their mother. At the end of the day you come home and then you're just 'Daddy'. The small details don't matter. By the time they're old enough to figure out the rest they won't care, because they had a good childhood and parents that loved them. That's what's important."

"If I asked you to let her out of the contract?"

He stands, preparing to leave. "Tonight I'm your friend. Tomorrow I'm your boss. In the end we all have families at home that depend on us. They are my first priority, not you and your guilty conscience. Word of advice: if it's closure you're looking for to move on, then go get it. You have a heartbroken girl at that house and a narrow window before you lose her. Don't make the same mistake I did. I think we both know where heartbreak leads." He places his hand on my shoulder. "Consider this your warning."

He leaves, and suddenly this bar becomes so much smaller than what it was when I got here. My head is spinning. I need to lay down, and based on my blood alcohol levels it's probably going to be the hotel across the street. I turn my phone on and a voicemail pops up. I listen to it, against my better judgment.

"Hey, Sax."

She pauses, clearly crying.

"It's late and I'm worried. I know you said not to wait up for you, but I can't sleep. It's too quiet here without you. I just want to know you're okay. I hope you're alone," she whispers. "The thought of you with someone else is destroying me. Please, don't do this. I'm begging you. If I could rewind today I

would. We can get past this. I just need you to try. I'll do whatever, as long as I have you. Please call me. We can talk this out. I love you. Goodnight."

Fuck. I can't do this shit. The first place she thinks I'd go is another woman's bed. If only she knew. This isn't going to get solved tonight. I have too much on my mind and too many open-ended questions. I power my phone off again, because if I don't I'll call her. If I hear her voice I'll end up driving my drunk ass back home, risking killing myself or someone else. Right now, I need that fucking hotel room, and I need it now.

CHAPTER THIRTY-FIVE

Kambry

I stare out at the pool from behind my sunglasses. My face is still wet from the constant trail of tears that hasn't stopped since he walked out yesterday. I am still unsure how everything went so wrong. One second it's perfect and the next, utter and complete disaster. I've been lying in my bikini on this lounge chair with my ear buds in since I pried myself out of bed this morning. I didn't get much sleep anyway.

The calls started around midnight, when I realized he wasn't coming back. I called every fifteen minutes on the dot, worried. Each time after the first time it went straight to voicemail. I shouldn't have left that message, but I couldn't help it. I had to say something. I finally dozed off around three, but then woke up at four-thirty and went and crawled in his bed, hoping I'd hear him when he finally came home this morning, but when I woke up the house was empty.

I stayed, because well, I had no other place to go. I didn't want to go home to face Ben and Meredith and the smile on Ben's face when I told him he got to Saxton, so here I sit, in this chair, cooking my skin. It's already pink across the top from the hours under the blazing sun.

Another tear runs down my face, as I listen to these damn lyrics for about the fortieth time. For the first time in my life I have a break up playlist. As if that matters, because for the last hour I've had one on repeat that I can't bring myself to change: *Stilettos* by Kelsea Ballerini. I found it through a key word search in my numb pity party state I was having when I first came out here. There is one line I can't get past: *I wear my pain like stilettos. As bad as it may hurt, no you'll never know . . .*

It reminds me of what Ben said yesterday—about me internalizing everything. I've never really noticed that I do, but I guess he's right. I've never been one to whine about my problems aloud. It doesn't solve anything to. Right now, though, for a little while, I'm that pathetic girl wallowing in my sorrow and living through the sad lyrics of a song.

I pull up my call log as the song ends and try to call him for the first time today. It doesn't ring. His voicemail comes on. "It's Saxton. You know what to do."

It beeps. "Hey, Sax. It's me again. I just want to make sure you're okay. I'm worried. Call me, or at least text when you get this so I'll know. Please."

As I hang up a call comes through from an unsaved local cell phone number. I answer it. Maybe it's him. "Hello."

"Kambry, it's Michael."

Crap.

"Hey. I suppose this is about yesterday? I'm sorr—"

"I just talked to Saxton."

"He called you?"

"Yeah. Can you come into the office? I'll send a car."

Interesting . . . So he's basically just ignoring me and no one else. That's more hurtful than him walking out.

"Okay. I'll get ready now."

"See you in a bit."

He disconnects the call, leaving a nervous feeling in the pit of my stomach. I feel like I'm being sent to the principal's office. This should be awesome . . .

I knock on the opened door when I see Michael sitting at his desk hunched over a pile of papers. He looks up. "Kambry. Come in and have a seat."

I walk inside as he stands and rounds the desk, then shuts the door, before returning to my side of the desk and standing against it, facing me. "Am I in some kind of trouble?"

"Well, no, but this isn't exactly a congratulatory—you did an awesome job—meeting either."

"Is he coming back?"

I couldn't help myself. I had to ask. It's killing me.

"To the house? No."

"What does this mean?"

"He wants me to find a way out of the contract. That's what it means. That gets costly, pisses people off, and makes me look bad."

"I'm really sorry. I didn't know my brother was going to show up. This is such a mess. What can I do?"

"You each continue together, or you continue on separate projects under the same contract stipulations in accordance to all but co-star, place, and time. You'll have to sign the revised contract if you choose option two."

"What did he say?" My heart is beating fast.

He stares at me for a moment, as if he's thinking. "He's convinced I find a way to relieve you of your contract. He'll do whatever project I put him on. He's obviously lost his mind. This is a business. I have investors, budgets, higher ups to answer to, and since a continuation wouldn't be a short, simple project that doesn't require emotion, I can't force it, so what we are going to do is this: we will run the stuff we have over a few weeks releasing one segment at a time, as planned, and if the two of you choose to move on separately to finish out the terms of your contracts should we get a good response, we'll go forward on that with another couple kind of like a second season in reality television. Otherwise, you two get over this love hump you're having and continue if we decide to go forward. The only way completely out of this is if it totally bombs and we lose money, forcing the studio to discontinue it. According to the terms in your contract it will then be null and void. What's it going to be?"

I breathe out, trying not to cry again. One issue arises and he's done. How can you say you love someone and then forget them within twenty-four hours? I didn't even do anything. He's obviously made up his mind. He doesn't want me anymore. He's moving on. He won't even answer my calls. That just means it will be awkward if we continue in force. Another line in that song repeats in my head: *When you get burned you learn to be strong*.

I need to build a life for myself. I need to go to school. School costs money and I'm already here. This is what I'm faced with. I made a decision and I need to follow through. This is growing up. Part of growing up is experience, mistakes, regret, love, heartache, and responsibility. He may let other people's opinions and words get to him, but I still have the same stance as I did before: a career doesn't define a person, character does. If someone wants to judge me for surviving on more than club tips then so be it.

I look up at him again. "I'll do a different project. The other is a burnt bridge that can't be crossed. Just tell me what to do."

"Very well then. I've cut cameras. You're free to get your things from the house in private. I'll call you sometime after we release the first segment, when I have a decision and the revised contract for you to sign should you need to. I'll let Saxton know as well. Just stay available."

"Meaning don't go out of town?" I cringe at myself. That was a stupid question. That trip is cancelled.

"Not until I know the schedule."

I stand and place my purse on my shoulder. "Okay. I'm really sorry."

"I saw what happened, Kambry. It isn't your fault. Things happen. It's called curveballs. You just have to learn to watch for them and adjust your swing when they're thrown. I'll be in touch."

I nod and walk out, able to hold it together until I reach the parking lot. Then I lose it, rushing to the nearest spot outside of the walking area as the tears pour down my face, before ridding of everything in my stomach, because the thought of having sex with another man physically makes me sick. In this moment, I feel like everything Ben accused me of: a sex slave and prostitute. Before, it was what I wanted. There was a method to the madness. There was a reason for the rhyme. I wanted him and I still do. I miss his smile and his jokes. I miss his personality. I miss his hard and his soft. I miss the closeness between us. I just miss him, and it's only been a day. When I told him I loved him I meant it. I've never cared what anyone else thought of me, of him, or of us, because we had each other. That's all that is supposed to matter.

Instead of helping me, Saxton's hurting me, whether he knows it or not.

In what seems like the shortest relationship in existence, I've experienced all of the emotions possible, including heartbreak. I didn't ask for the love but I embraced it. This heartache can go to hell. It's not welcome. It hurts. Now, I don't know where to go from here.

CHAPTER THIRTY-SIX

Kambry

I walk in the apartment blinded by my crying. I don't think I've ever cried so long in my entire life. It's been a repetitive pattern off and on all day. I'll cry and lose myself in the tears, and then I'll pull myself out of it long enough to gather my breathing and it starts all over again as soon a thought of him or us pops into the forefront of my mind. I've avoided this place as long as I can, but I've spent enough on cab fare today to classify me as insane. There was nowhere left for me to go but here.

Ben is standing at the bar, talking to Meredith as she cooks. I rush forward and shove at him, mad as hell. He stumbles a little before he stabilizes himself. "Are you happy now?"

"Kambry, what's wrong?"

I shove at him again. "Because of you he left me! You got what you wanted. I finally found someone that truly makes me happy and because of you I'm miserable all over again."

He tries to hug me, but the shoves are coming without warning now. I'm angry, and I have every right to be. "Kambry, this is for the best. You'll see when this is all over. You want a guy that respects you. One that will do anything to take care of you. Why don't you see that?"

My fists clench against his shirt and I scream. "No, Ben, that's where you're wrong. You had to come butt into something that was actually real; something you know nothing about. He loved me and I love him. You waltz in, screw my friend, and then mess everything up for me. Not once have I meddled in your life. I wish every damn person would stop treating me like a child! Did it ever occur to you that I'm an adult? I can make my own fucking choices! He was the guy for me. I want him with every part of me. Do you not understand loving someone fiercely and without question? Oh, of course you don't, because you just let yours go with no remorse for her feelings just like you're doing to me. You will go back to Alabama and I still have to pick up the pieces of what you've done in this tornado of destruction you've become. Not every relationship operates the way you see fit. You're thinking like Dad. This was us. It was our thing. Why can't for one damn second you let me be happy? Can you not understand loving someone so much that you'll do things you wouldn't normally do to see where it goes?"

He looks at Meredith, making me even angrier. "Yes, Kambry, but that's why I just want the best for you. After all these years you deserve it."

"Then butt out. When I need your advice or your help I'll ask you for it. All you've done is make things worse, because now, I have to actually be a porn star. He doesn't want to continue this project with me anymore. I'm in a contract. I hope you're happy, because instead of someone that actually does respect me and cares about me and what I want, you can feel better sleeping at night to know that I'll wear giz on my face and possibly be double teamed or some shit; maybe even worse. That's as good as I can come up with because I don't know of what could be worse yet, but I'm sure I'll find out. Now I really get to be the girl you didn't want me to be. Not once has he done something degrading to me. He allowed me to explore sexually with one person that I care about. I guess it never occurred to you that we spent time together before I signed that contract. I knew what I was doing when I agreed to it. Now, I have no choices. You've taken that away from me. Congratulations, you fucked that up."

His jaw locks together. "I'm not going to let you be that girl."

"What part of this do you not understand? I signed a contract—a legal binding document. This was my decision, just like it was yours to have sex in Mom and Dad's house with my best friend. You can't just get out of a legal contract your way." My voice lowers to a whisper. "I was in love with him, and now I'm heartbroken . . .because of you."

"Kambry . . .I'm sorry."

The tears are streaming down my face. "Hey, this is what you wanted, right? I applaud you. You took a *good* guy away from me. I guess the good girl doesn't deserve everything. Not once did you ask me questions about his character. You never thought that maybe there was an underlying reason he was a porn star in the first place. But you know what? I did question things. I learned about him. I'm smarter than any of you give me credit for. I'd rather live my life knowing I was in an adult film for a short period of my life with a good man that loves me than to end up with a guy that beats me behind closed doors but is a respectable guy to everyone else. We all have issues, Ben. I've never known you to be so judgmental until today, because I'm not going to find a better guy than him."

"You will, but maybe in some ways you're right. I was angry. I should have talked to you first, but you're my sister, Kambry. We've always been in this together. You're all I have. You're my family. I care about you, regardless of what you think. Fuck. Do you want me to talk to him?"

"No. Leave it alone. You've done enough. I love you even when you do me wrong. You're my brother. But I don't have to like you right now. I hope you enjoy California, and I wish this visit had been under different circumstances."

"Kambry, wait." I walk past him. He tries to grab my arm but I yank it out of his hand, walking straight to my door. "If he really loves you he'll come back."

I stop, my hand gripped on the door handle, my eyes burning from the constant crying. "No, he won't, because he has a conscience, and he actually thinks in his warped mind that this is better for me. That will keep him away. Goodnight. I just want to be alone."

I walk inside my room and shut the door, locking it. A few minutes later Meredith's door slams. Every place my eyes look around the room, a memory follows. I can't escape them. My own mind and heart are trapping me. My body slides down my door, until I'm sitting on my floor, and the only thing that I can will myself to do . . .is cry.

CHAPTER THIRTY-SEVEN

Saxton

The cab pulls in the parking lot of the apartment complex located in the hills. My suitcase is in the trunk and my airline ticket is ready. I wasn't supposed to leave for New York until we officially left the house tomorrow with Kambry, but I need to get away from here for a little while. I've been drinking since I stormed out of the house yesterday in an attempt to calm my thoughts of her. It was failure at the highest degree.

Drinking and thinking don't often go together, hence me being here. I take a deep breath and hand the cabby a wad of cash. "Wait here and I'll double that when I get back, plus fare to get to the airport." When he nods, confirming, I exit the vehicle, allowing the alcohol to rush throughout my body.

I grab the cigarette from behind my ear—where I stuck it in my brazen decision to do this—and place it between my lips. I pull the lighter from my pocket and light it, taking a long drag to calm the fuck down. I've got to be one stupid fuck, but I'll never move forward otherwise.

I blow the smoke into the night air, and then start walking down the sidewalk toward the exterior stairs, climbing them slowly as I filter down this cigarette. When I get to the fourth floor, I pass the doors, reading the numbers in the center until I reach the one I'm searching for.

I spin, slamming my back against the wall beside the door to finish my smoke. My phone vibrates, but only once. I just turned it back on in the cab ride to check the voicemails, but I guess I forgot to turn it back off. I haven't listened to her last message from earlier, because I know if I hear her voice one more time I'll cave and go running back like a fucking pussy. It took every last ounce of strength and willpower to walk out that door, and more to actually stay away. I didn't want to, but I never considered the fact that I was bringing someone else down with me. Michael can talk, but he's still on the other side of that camera. He remains hidden. His dick isn't on display in God knows how many women.

I seem to have forgotten my lifestyle isn't normal. Maybe because my parents stopped commenting about it when they realized it wasn't just going to go away. I guess it's an out of sight, out of mind thing. I really can't argue with anything her brother said. He put things in perspective for me. If someone had asked me to do this with the girl I love four years ago, I would have told them to fuck off.

I've pulled her into a world she has no business being in, because Kambry is the girl you take home to Mama and the one you marry without a second thought. She's the girl you make the mother of your children. She's the girl your heart and soul captures and never lets go. And she's the girl you love forever, travel the world with, experience life with, and die within a heartbreak apart because you can't bear to live without her. She's unforgettable and she's rare. She sure as hell isn't a porn star.

I pull my phone from my pocket and look at the screen—a new voicemail, but not from Kambry this time. It's from Michael. Opening the mailbox, I put the phone to my ear, almost at the end of the only cigarette I brought, because I've already smoked the entire pack. I feel like I need a box of them. It takes a second, but then it starts to play.

"Saxton, it's Michael. I laid out the terms for Kambry earlier today. If we go forward, it's you and her or you both and someone else. I'm not releasing her completely. I need revenue. This is what you both agreed to. She's who you wanted. I told you last night; today I'm your boss. I'm not willing to ruin my career because you started having a conscience. Remember what I said before I continue—I warned you. She agreed to go forward with someone else. What you need to decide is if you want to let her or get your shit together and go after her, because we're already getting a response from the trailer run online. Putting her with another porn star is like putting a lamb in a lion's den. I've

told you multiple times. You're a little different than most. You aren't here for the same reasons most are. They will eat her alive."

He pauses. Son of a fucking bitch. I suck down the rest of my cigarette and toss the filter down, smearing it into the concrete with my shoe. *"Remember what I told you the day filming started, and reminded you of last night. She could be your out once this is over. You've only proven me right since, and you've never cared what anyone else thought, so why now? You may be pissed about my decision until you come to your senses, but I don't really fucking care. One of these days you'll thank me if I'm right about this. Consider it a gift. I could see the look on her face today when I presented her with everything. All she wanted to know was what you wanted."*

He breathes. *"I'm just going to say this and then it's on you, because I've vested more time in this than I should have to and I feel like I'm rambling on a fucking machine. I took time to explain things last night when I could have been with my family. When you find a girl that can accept this kind of world if need be, you don't let her go you marry her, because that shows strength, and also that in the midst of controversy and fire she'll never leave you. That's what I did at least, and had I known it earlier I'd have no regrets. Anyway, you may not be much on country, but listen to this song: Don't Leave Her (If You Can't Let Her Go) by Chris Young. It may put things in perspective, because no smart man will pass her by. Talk soon."*

The voicemail stops playing. Dammit, I'm so torn. I slide my phone in my pocket and rub my hands up and down my face. There's no question in wanting her. The fact is I don't want anyone else. I sure as hell don't want her with someone else, even if he's better than me, but for once I was really just trying to think of someone else first. Well, I guess I'll see how this goes and then I'll know.

I extend my arm and knock on the door with the exterior of my balled up fist. I wait, knowing it's late. No more than a few seconds pass and I hear footsteps across the floor. "Who is it?"

Chills run down my body. That voice is like nails on a chalkboard. It's funny how you can go so long without hearing something, but the second you do it's as if no time has lapsed. I turn to face the door so she can see me through the peephole. "It's Saxton."

Locks turning sound immediately, and then the door opens. She looks exactly the same, just a little aged, standing in her cotton shorts and tee shirt just like she used to wear to bed, her long black hair piled high on top of her head. She's still wearing makeup. I'm not sure I remember ever seeing her without it honestly. At one time I thought she was beautiful, but now, she's a little above average at best. A shocked expression resides on her face. "I never thought I'd see you again. How'd you find me?"

"Joel."

She nods and steps aside. "The asshole that ruined everything for me. Come in."

I walk over the threshold into her apartment. Joel was my best friend from college, and the only one that had the decency to tell me when she was cheating on me. "You live alone?"

She shuts the door. "Yeah. After graduation I got a job at the news station as an intern. I've worked my way up to feature stories since then."

I place one hand in my jean pocket and the other behind my head, rubbing up and down in my hair uncomfortably. "So you stuck with journalism then?"

"Yeah. I've wanted it since I was a kid, but you knew that. Some things never change."

"You with anyone?" I hate myself for asking, because I really don't give a shit, but I think my ego just really wants to know.

"No. I haven't been with anyone serious since you. It just never felt the same." She passes me and sits down on the couch, pulling her legs up to rest her heels in front of her butt. "Not that I'm not happy to see you, because I am, but what are you doing here? You said some pretty nasty things to me the last time we spoke. Then you left, changed your phone number, and just kind of fell off the map. You left me, Saxton . . .hours after you proposed."

I walk toward her and sit down next to her. "Because you couldn't keep your fucking legs closed, Salem."

"I was a different person then. College is about figuring out who you are and making stupid decisions. I regret that now."

Okay hold up. My comfort zone just got warm. "About figuring out who you are? What the fuck is wrong with you? Normal people break up with the person they're with if they want to fuck someone else. It's called decency, not stupid decisions."

"Oh come on, Saxton. I was scared back then. You were so intense in the way you loved someone. It was like being the heroine in an epic love story, only this isn't an epic love story. It's the twenty-first century. It freaked me out that young. People don't love that hard. We live in an age where people want what they can never completely obtain, so that's how I lived. I was scared to lose you. I was also scared of getting hurt, so I kept you at arm's reach, and for three years it worked. It kept you mine. It got you to propose to me. When you left is when I realized that maybe I had a warped view on what I wanted, but then it was too late."

I stare at her, completely astounded. I'm sure a look of disgust is written all over my face. I finally remember exactly why I'm here: closure. I wanted to know why she did it. I wanted to know my worth to her back then, and I just got it. "Thank you."

"For what?"

"For showing me what a horrible mistake I was about to make back then." I stand, unable to sit any longer. "You want to know why I fell off the map? I'm a porn star, Salem, and a fucking good one at that. You drove me to that. You made me realize that it didn't matter how big your dick was, how much you aimed to please, or how hard you loved someone, because in the end greed takes over. All a woman wants is more, never satisfied with what she has. She says she wants someone to love her and only her, but then the next attractive guy walks along and gives her attention, and then just like that, everything you've done to make her feel loved and important means nothing. For the past several years I've lived under that notion. I felt like I was inadequate somewhere because of you. You were always so smart until it came to relationships. I loved you with intensity because I loved you. It's simple. There are no formulas or theorems involved. When you love someone you treat them like royalty. That's how I was raised."

"I'm sorry. I wish I could take it back."

"But you can't. Life doesn't work that way. So many people live irresponsibly, when they should be living with the constant thought that they don't get a do-over. I loved you, Salem. When we were together you never had to question it, because I showed you. I loved you a lot; I did, and to some extent I always will.

You were the first girl I ever really loved, but you prepped me for the real thing. That's why I'm here. I just wanted some answers, because without getting them I can't love her and give her what she deserves. And she deserves the fucking best, because when she loves, she doesn't love me like she may lose me, she loves me like she has another day with me, and that's the difference. I've hurt over what you did to me for a long time, but finally I understand that it was meant to happen, because you weren't the one I was supposed to be with. It makes me cherish her so much more, because I believe with everything in me that she would never do to me what you did. I guess it was nature's way of changing my course. One day I may be embarrassed for what I've been doing, but at the same time, it led me to her. Maybe that's what life is all about—following your arrow—because if you do you end up exactly where you're supposed to be."

Fuck . . .

I turn and walk toward the door. "Where are you going? You just got here."

I stop and look back at her as I grab the door handle. "To grovel. I'm going to beg her to look past my idiocy and we start back where we left off. I'm going to tell her that I can't live without her, because I don't want to, and I sure as hell don't want someone else to have her. By the way. Just a word of advice, Salem . . . Next time someone loves you for you, love him the way you want to be loved. I honestly hope you never experience what you put me through. I wouldn't wish that kind of betrayal on anyone. It's a mind fuck that can ruin your life, and it almost did mine. If he loves you, go hard or go home. Being faithful to someone is the only way to ensure you never lose them."

I walk out and rush down the stairs. I'm going to get her, and if she'll take me back, I'll do whatever I have to do to keep her . . . forever.

I bang on the door of Meredith and Kambry's apartment in repetition, never letting up. Finally, the door opens, Kambry's brother standing on the other side in his boxer-briefs, rubbing at his half open eyes as if he's trying to wake up. "What, dude? Fuck. It's late."

"I've had time to think. I need a word with you."

"Can't this wait until tomorrow? What time is it?"

"You barged into my house and had your chance, so shut up. I don't give a shit what time it is."

He breathes out and steps aside. "If you must. Come in, but keep your voice down."

I walk through an apartment door for the second time tonight, but this time pacing. He shuts the door and crosses his arms over his chest. "Well, what is so important?"

"I get it. Everything you were saying makes sense. I have a sister. Fuck, I don't want to see her screwing some guy. It's weird, but I can't change it. I was an asshole for bringing her into this. I'm okay with that. I understand that I'm putting her reputation on the line. I'll live with it. If you want to hate me then I can't blame you. You were right about every thing, but one thing."

"What's that?"

"I do love her. I love her with all that I am. From the second I laid eyes on her I knew she was different to me. She entranced me. I can't explain my actions except that I had to have her for myself. I saw an opportunity to make that known to the world and I took it. It was selfish. It was insecure. My subconscious knew it a little while before my heart, mind, and soul, but the second I realized she's the one for me, I've never had a problem showing it. I want her, and only her, in every way possible. If she wants marriage, I'll get down on one knee. If she wants babies, I'll give her a fucking houseful. If she wants me, I'll do whatever I have to do to provide for her, whether it be to finish school at twenty-five or to work at fucking Walmart making just enough to pay bills."

I stop pacing and look him in the eyes. "I need her. I can't promise I can always give her everything she wants, but I'll spend my life trying my best. I can't change anything in my life that has already happened, and I can't get us out of this contract, but I swear on my life I will never let anyone disrespect her in my presence or within earshot for this, and the second that this project is over I'll remove us both from this world, because I can't bring myself to be with another woman after being with her. She's not my first or my second, not even in the first ten, but I want her to be my last. You may not like me, but I'm asking you to trust me. I can be the best for her. I can love her better than anyone else, because I've experienced betrayal and heartache, and I'll never do any of those things to her. I'm in love with her. I'm not asking you to take my word, I'm asking you to give me a shot."

He stares at me for a moment, and then holds out his hand. "Make her happy and I'll have your back. She deserves happiness. She may not have had a hard life like some people, but she hasn't had an easy one either. It takes guts for a man to silence his ego and squander some of his testosterone to come here and say all that shit. Plus, you're going to need it for my fucked up family, because it's only a matter of time before my dad snaps. He can't handle losing control over his kids, and when he finds out about all of this . . . Good luck. We might as well all band together, because he's not going to approve of who either of us want to be with."

I shake his hand. "By the way. This isn't a, *three strikes you're out,* kind of thing. This is your shot. Nice guys don't always finish last. You hurt her I'll break every limb on your body one by one. Are we clear?"

I smirk. "I would expect nothing less."

"Awe! That is so sweet. A bro-mance is forming." I look toward the sarcastic voice I would recognize anywhere.

Meredith has her head pushed through the crack in her door. The dim sconce lighting in the foyer is enough to see throughout the entire apartment. "Why are you spying?"

"Because I'm not company appropriate."

"You don't strike me as a modest girl if I remember correctly," I say in a teasing tone.

Her eyes widen and then she mouths for me to shut up. "Well, I'm not, but Benny boo doesn't like to share, even in looks."

"Damn right. Why I stayed away . . ." He looks at me. "Are we done here, since she's now awake? I have better things I could be doing."

"Kambry in her room, right?"

"Actually no. If she were here she'd be awake by now with us talking. She left not long before dark. Something about needing to go somewhere special she can think openly without a crowd. Don't ask me what that means. She's not happy with me right now. Apparently, I fucked everything up for her. That's what made this conversation easier for you. I hate seeing her like that. The only time she's spoken to me is a mixture or screaming, crying, and using me as a punching bag. She asked to borrow Meredith's car when she finally came out of her room. I didn't ask any questions because she was still crying hours later and I felt like an asshole, but I'm just trying to look out for her. When we fell asleep she hadn't come home yet. Honestly, I kind of figured she was with you." He starts to look a little worried, then walks to her door and opens it, checking inside.

Somewhere special she can think openly without a crowd . . .

As if the thought triggered the memory, it hits me. Would she go there alone? Does she even remember how to get there? Surely not at this time of night. Dammit. "Hey, I think I know where she may be. I'll let you know."

I run for the door, wasting no more time, panicked at the idea she would actually go somewhere by herself at night, but it's no one's fault but my own. I did this shit, and that's not a quick drive. I'm glad I've sobered up enough to drive. I swear on my life if something happens to her I'll never forgive myself. That girl is everything to me.

CHAPTER THIRTY-EIGHT

Kambry

I've been to many places today, but none of them have been as peaceful as this one. When I left the studio I wanted something that would take away everything on my mind, so I went to a movie. I figured if I had something to occupy my eyes then I wouldn't think about him. It was also somewhere that would give me time to myself. I didn't want to keep sulking like I've done since he left. I don't want to be one of those girls that literally lets her life halt at the second she's dumped. I also discovered it's easier said than done.

Instead of watching the movie I found myself watching the couple sitting a few rows in front of me. Something about him having her snuggled in his arm just held my attention. I realized that we never got those moments, not really. We never got to just exist as a couple in a world that was going on around us. It was all part of an act, even though the emotions were very much real.

When it was over and I ran out of places to go I went home. I figured I needed to face Meredith and Ben at some point. That proved worse for me, because the two of them are sickening in their newly found reunion. It seemed to make the crying more extreme. I stayed in my room after screaming at Ben. I only got Meredith alone long enough to ask her if she had told Bryant what was going on when I went to the bathroom. I was a little relieved when she said she called him and explained everything and that she wanted to see where this went for now. I know she made it clear on several occasions they weren't exclusive, but I still kind of feel bad for him. Every time I was around him I could see that it wasn't just a casual hookup for him. Either that or I'm clueless to all of this still. It may not have developed into love yet, but it was more than just lust.

At the point of listening to flirty giggles seep through the walls from the living room into my bedroom, I knew I couldn't stay there. I love my brother and Meredith, but I'm here because of Ben and his big mouth. It just seems so unfair. He came here to screw up my relationship yet he jumps into one almost instantly. It's too much for me. I just found out they had a thing like two seconds ago it seems, but also, it's not that easy to go from being around someone twenty-four hours a day, seven days a week, to not seeing or speaking to them at all. It hurts. It feels like you've been abandoned. It also feels like you've lost your best friend.

The way I found my way back: remembering that day like it was yesterday. When I'm interested in something I have a photographic memory, and that was an amazing day for me, so with both hands on the wheel and the headlights beaming down on the pavement, I came back here.

It's a quiet night. It's peaceful and I love it here. Places like this are hidden gems in such a large, busy state. The sound of the waves slowly rolling into the shoreline has a calming effect. The beach shows its best qualities at night, and while I look out at the body of water caped in starlight, for a few moments at a time my mind is totally free. I feel brave. I feel like I can conquer the world, alone, because even though I'm completely in love with someone that has me on a pedestal, I know that I'm really just a runaway and an adopted west coast girl that's no different than anyone else. I just wish he could see it too.

I lean into my bent legs, my chest pressing against my thighs as I lay my chin between my kneecaps. I wiggle my toes into the sand again and rub my palms side-to-side beside my hips, creating a windshield wiper motion. "You trespassing now? What's next . . .sitting in the backseat of a cop car?"

My heart begins to race and my hands form fists in the sand. "Please don't be a hallucination," I whisper. I turn my upper body toward his hollering voice. "You talking to me now?" I yell, as a smile begins to slowly form. He's standing on top of the slope at the beginning of the beach.

He places his palm over his chest, looking at me in a way I'll never forget. He's missed me as much as I've missed him. I can feel it in my gut. *Heart be still.* My eyes begin to fill. I stand when he slides down the small slope. He then takes off running toward me, picking me up the second he's within arm's reach. "I'm sorry," he whispers. "I'm so sorry. I thought I was doing what was best for you."

"Being with you is what's best for me."

"Okay. If that's what you want."

"How did you find me?"

"I just thought of where I would go if you forced me to be without you. I guess we think alike."

"This was our most memorable day. I wanted to remember."

"Were you really going to film with another man?"

"The thought made me sick, literally, in the parking lot, but I thought you didn't want me. I was only given two options."

"I'll always want you, Kambry. I can't be with another woman after you. That would be equivalent to requesting a cheap wine when you're being offered an expensive one. If we can delete this last day and a half, it'll be just us from here on out. I went to Salem's. I needed closure. I needed to know if it was something I did in the relationship, because I don't want you to ever feel like you need someone else."

My stomach suddenly feels nervous. Jealousy is already trying to consume me. "Did you want her back?"

"No, not even a little."

"So why did she do it? Why did she cheat on you?"

"Because I loved too hard, too intense, and she was acting out of fear I would leave. Some kind of bullshit like that."

I stare at him, trying to decipher that in my head. "And someone would not want that because?"

"Because it's not the right fit I guess, but I'd rather never love someone again than to change the way I love when I do. At some point you'll find the person that is the perfect match for you, and that's what I found in you."

"I'm glad I wasn't the only one to see it, because being without you totally sucks ass."

He smiles at me and sets me down on my feet, before lightly kissing my lips, but never slips his tongue into my mouth. When he leaves me, I open my eyes, and he sits down in the sand, pulling me between his legs. I sit and he scoots me against his chest. "So you like this place?"

He wraps his arms around me, placing his cheek against mine as he eases over my shoulder. "Yes. It's somewhere we experienced together and a day I'll never forget. When I wanted to hold onto you a little longer, this place just seemed appropriate."

"I love you, Kambry."

"I love you too, Saxton."

"There was no way in hell I was letting another man have you."

"So I'm not the only one that was dying inside at the thought? He made it seem like you had already made that decision."

"Fuck no. Michael has ways of pushing people into the most appropriate direction. It's why he's so damn good at his job. When Michael said that you had chosen to film on another project my heart was racing, I was breaking a sweat, and my entire world was caving in. He knew I wouldn't let that happen, so he forced me into it when my stubborn ass wouldn't just run back. I only left because I thought it would give you back a normal life."

I wonder how many people in the world right now are sitting on the beach, staring out at the ocean while they experience life-altering moments. I turn around to face him, standing on my knees in the sand. "I don't want normal if you aren't right there with me to experience it, Saxton. That's what I keep trying to explain to you. You can't just revoke your love and expect someone to live a happy life. You don't choose love; love chooses you. I love you. I'm in love with you. Other options are no longer possible."

"I guess it's a good thing I had a man-to-man talk with your brother then."

"You talked to Ben?" I bite my bottom lip.

His hands take up residence on the back of my thighs. "I did. A friend made me realize that I shouldn't leave you if I can't let you go, so here I am."

I wrap my arms around his neck, running the tips of my fingers into his hairline. "Thank God for good friends."

"So I guess there is only one thing left."

"What's that?"

He reaches into his pocket and pulls out a small, black box, handing it to me. "This is for you."

I stare down at it, my eyes wide. "What is it?"

"Open it."

Taking it from the palm of his hand, my shaky hands pull off the top. Inside is a black, velvet box. My breathing is hard and heavy. I look up at him, scared to open it. He looks at me with no emotion on his face. He's completely blank, making me more nervous.

My thumb rubs across the velvet at the split, before lifting the top. What lies inside is exciting, confusing, as well as a tiny bit disappointing, if I'm being one hundred percent honest with myself. I remove the silver key pushed down into the opening, before being pulled into his lap to straddle him.

He takes the key, staring at it. "I had already been thinking about this. I just wasn't completely sure, but now I am. I want to take the next step in our relationship. I want us to have something that is not mine or yours, but ours. There are a lot of things I'm not quite ready for, and you're still young; still inexperienced, so I'm not going to do that to you either until more time has lapsed, but I want you, Kambry. I want you forever. We've been living together for a month now, and frankly that's nowhere near long enough. This is a promise for a future. This place is going to be ours."

My brain is not physically able to process what he's saying. "What place?"

"Our place." He nods toward the house behind him. "I just thought this was a way to start fresh . . .together."

"You bought us a house! This house? This cute, beautiful, perfect house!" I can't breathe. Physically the air is having difficulty flowing in and out of my lungs.

He places the key back into my hand and closes it up. "It's not legal or anything yet, but I called the owner and he told me where to find the spare key. It's ours for the night. Tomorrow we leave for New York. My sister is expecting us. When we get back I'll get the process started, but it's going to be ours in a matter of time, if you'll say yes."

"Say yes?"

"Kambry Rivers, I no longer want to sleep any nights away from you. I'm willing to do whatever I have to do to work this out. We'll figure out our futures together. I want to begin building a life with you. I need you. I don't want to live without you. Will you move into this house with me?"

Tears instantly flood down my face, unable to stop them or control their production. "Yes! I love you so much. That was the most beautiful thing I've ever experienced."

He grips my waist and stands, before walking toward the dark house. "I can't believe you did this."

"Believe it, baby, because this is only the beginning of our epic love story. You tamed the porn star and I tainted the good girl. I'm sure weirder things have happened."

I laugh as he climbs the steps one by one. "It'll make one unforgettable story that's for sure."

"One for the kids . . .when they're much older than we are."

"You want kids?" The happiness comes through in my tone.

"One day, after we've enjoyed each other for a little while. I didn't really want it for the right reasons until you. Before it was just part of moving along in life, but now, I want it because I love you and want to share that with you. There is nothing more special than combining the two of us into a tiny person, so when we're ready I'm on board. For the next few years we can practice for that performance, starting by breaking in our new house."

I kiss him as he shoves the key into the lock. I will never be able to properly explain the way I feel with him. I've never felt like I fit in before. I've never felt like I knew who I was supposed to be or where I was going to go. I've never felt whole until he walked into my life. In just a couple of months my life has drastically changed.

I no longer have any questions about any of those things, because it's not about who I should be or where I should live, or even that I should fit into a crowd. I'm just me. I don't have to have the answer to every question or have it all together. Having someone you love to walk the journey with you is the only thing that I need and want.

I know there will be people that judge us. There will be people that slur our names and try to trash our reputation because of what he was or what we do together for people to watch, but as long as I know he loves me and only wants me, I don't care, because fifty years from now when our love story has proven that even the craziest of situations can be beautiful, it won't matter what people have said. He's mine and I'm his. That's the only thing that is important, because no two love stories are the same.

CHAPTER THIRTY-NINE

Kambry

"The big apple, huh?"

I hug him tight in the middle of our apartment while Saxton takes my suitcase down to his truck. We spent a beautiful night together, and had an even better morning. Snuggles, showers, and breakfast out at a quaint little pancake place before we came here so I could pack my bags and drop off Meredith's car. Packing was pretty simple, because I never unpacked from the house.

He's warm. I haven't hugged my brother like this in years. It makes me realize how much I've missed him. A tear falls. I finally feel like things are falling into place. "It's my turn to have some experiences. I need this, Ben. I need time alone with just him."

"I know. I'm happy for you. I mean that. Promise me you'll have fun and fill me in on all the details when you get back." His voice is a whisper in my ear, so only I can hear.

"Promise. Cross my heart. What will happen with you and Meredith?" I ask against his tee shirt.

"I'm not letting her go again, but I still have a lot to figure out. I'm not done with school yet."

"Don't hurt her, kay. She puts on this big front but I think deep down she's scared of what you do to her."

"Promise. Cross my heart."

I smile. "Kambry, you ready?"

I pull away at the sound of Saxton's voice. "I'll let you know when I land. I love you, Ben."

"I love you too, Kam."

Meredith is standing in her doorway, giving us space. She walks out and I give her a hug, laughing at the tear streaks down her face. "I'm going to miss you. Everyone is leaving me and it totally sucks."

"I'm sure you'll forget about me in no time. It's only a week. But for the record, I'm going to miss your crazy ass too."

She laughs. "As long as I've left an impression, I can deal with crazy."

"Thank you."

"For what, love?"

"For caring enough to bring me along. I owe my happiness to you. If you hadn't asked me to come that night I wouldn't have any of this. I'll be forever indebted to you, Mer."

"I have a confession," she says.

"What?"

"I did it more for me than you. You're my piece from home I can't leave behind. You're my best friend. I wanted you with me. I'm not sure I could have left without you."

I wipe my eye as she releases me. "Best friends forever?" I ask, trying to dab my face without completely ruining my makeup.

"Nothing less," she says. "You'll always be my BFF. When you get to New York, live for both of us, okay?"

"That I can do."

I grab my purse off the bar and take Saxton's hand, letting him lead me out the door. We walk in silence until we get to his truck. He opens the door for me, allowing me to get in. I watch him round the truck to get in the other side. My heart is light and full. I can't believe I have him back. It makes me feel like I just woke up from a nightmare and everything was the same it was before I went to sleep.

He cranks the truck and leans over the console, kissing me. My eyes close the second his lips touch mine. My emotions have been in a whirlwind this weekend, but I'm glad things are finally back on balance. He's my world, and without him it's off its axis. "I'm so glad you're back."

He rubs my bottom lip. "You'll never have to say that again, baby. I'm yours. I've been yours since the night I met you in the club. It just took me a little while to realize exactly how much."

He kisses me again. "Are you excited?"

"Yes," I whisper, grabbing his hand as he puts the truck in drive. "You have no idea."

"Good, because there was no way I was going without you."

My heart fills a little more. New York here we come. It's going to be unforgettable. I know it . . .

CAMERA TALES BOOK TWO

SEX SESSIONS
After the Cut

CHARISSE SPIERS

CHAPTER ONE

Saxton

"You going to be alright?"

I look over at Kambry with a smirk firmly in place to avoid laughing. She looks somewhat like a zombie sitting beside me in the first class seat, waiting for takeoff. Her eyes finally start to blink again, and then she looks over at me, an expression of terror present. "What if we crash and die?"

"Well, I would imagine that our hearts would beat no more and life as we know it would cease to exist."

She smacks the top of my arm. "Ow," I laugh. "I'm just stating the obvious. There's no need for hostile behavior . . . until later," I wink.

"This is no time for your jokes, Sax. I'm freaking out. I've never in my life been on an airplane."

I grab her hand and lace our fingers together. "There is always that possibility, but you're more likely to die in an automobile accident than on a plane. The odds are not very high."

"But if I have a car accident I have a better chance of living."

"If it's our time to go, beautiful, it doesn't matter where we are or what we're doing. Nothing can stop it. By the way, what happened to living in the moment? I remember something of that nature being said in the middle of the Pacific Ocean not too long ago when the two of us were in possible disease and piss-infested water. I thought you were ready to walk on the wild side."

She takes a deep breath. "Well, when you put it that way . . ." She scoots back in her chair, aligning her back to the seat. The flight instructions ring through my ears. We're about to takeoff. Releasing her hand, I buckle her in, making sure it's tight.

I notice her staring at me from my peripheral vision. "What's on your mind, beautiful?"

"You know . . .if I had to die, though, I'm glad it'd be with you, because then we'd still be together."

A sharp pain registers in the organ that keeps my blood pumping through my body. I look up at her, trying to find my air. I grab the back of her chair in one hand and place my hand on her cheek, tracing the full bottom lip that I was tasting just hours ago. "I go first or we go together, because living a life without you is no longer a possibility."

She smiles. "So you'd miss me?"

"You have no idea."

"I love you."

I smile. "I love you too."

"Sir, we need everyone's seat belts fastened for takeoff." I sit back in my seat and do as instructed by the middle-aged flight attendant. "Is there anything I can get you once we're at cruising altitude?"

I have an idea. "A blanket."

She looks between us for a moment; surely knowing it's not that cold in here, and then nods. "When the pilot gives the okay to remove seat belts I'll bring one." As she walks back toward the cockpit, I can feel Kambry's eyes on me.

I turn my head, no doubt a cheesy grin on my face, especially after the look of confusion gracing hers. In three, two, one . . . "A blanket? Are you cold? We just entered into September."

"Why do you just assume I would be using it for warmth? They are also known for being used as a cover. Maybe I want to join the mile high-club . . . "

"The mile-high club . . ." Her eyes widen as it clicks. "Oh. Erm, how about no."

"Why not? Are you becoming modest after all this time?"

The plane starts to roll down the runway. "No," she says clipped. "Why would I be modest? I just don't want to get in trouble. Plus, you had some last night and this morning. I wouldn't want you to get tired of the goods."

"Impossible. Your pussy is like crack. I only want more with each hit."

"Is that so? Weren't we always taught to just say no to drugs?" She grabs my hand as the plane lifts into the air, squeezing it hard. She looks tense.

"Shit happens. You seduced me with your body and I took the bait. Now, there is no hope."

"I did no such thing."

"You did. In a pool to be exact."

"You were a hot stalker. What do you want me to say? I didn't hold a gun to your head and make you touch me."

"A hot girl asked me if I was gay. That is the same thing."

She laughs and her shoulders drop, all the tension leaving her body. "I did do that, didn't I?"

"Yep, so I only had one option."

"Which was?"

"Show you exactly how much I like lady parts."

"I think you've done a fine job of that. My lady parts went from being covered by invisible cobwebs to *in use* pretty much constantly." She gives me that witty smirk, her eyes settling on mine.

"Don't pretend you don't love my dick just as much. It may have been me last night, but if I recall correctly it was you that was ready to go this morning before our showers."

She bites her bottom lip, most likely remembering the same memory I am. I will never complain of waking up to her lips on mine as she climbs on top of me. Funny part was her breath was minty. She had brushed her teeth, and she never wakes up before me. "This is true. Make-up sex, I suppose. It's scary how much I want you to use it on me."

"Oh, I plan to use it on you all over New York City. I'm taking full advantage of no cameras."

"Not at your sister's you aren't."

"Uh, yes the fuck I am."

"No the hell you aren't. That's rude and disrespectful. I've never met her.

I don't want to come off as a tramp." I truly cannot explain how much I love it when her sassy side comes out—almost enough to pick a fight. I laugh out loud. "What's so funny?" she asks.

I bring the back of her hand to my mouth, softly placing my lips to her skin. "I'm about ninety-nine percent positive that the second I told my sister we were filming porn together, all slutty thoughts were considered null and void, but there is always that one percent chance that I could be wrong."

"So what you're saying is?"

"We aren't living in the twenties. We are in a committed relationship, we are adults, and we want each other. Sex between us is expected, in or outside of her apartment. Respect is easy. It's called a door and muting your screams with my mouth."

"Screams? You sound confident in your performance there, Maverick."

"Maybe, or just wishful thinking, but if not I'll start over until I get it right. Screaming is always a man's goal. Sometimes we just need to have our egos stroked."

"I don't know . . ."

"We will be there a week. Unless you're bleeding down there the gates are open, and maybe even then, depending on my mood. I'm getting in your panties, Rivers. You might as well quit fighting me on it, because I know where your direct-to-fuck buttons are, and I'm not afraid to use them to get what I want."

"Direct-to-fuck buttons, huh?" She purses her lips together with squinty eyes. "Do I even want to know?"

"Probably not. They are my secret weapons. My sister is not like that anyway, and she's known of worse things than me fucking my girlfriend. At least we love each other. One-night-stands are pretty damn common in the world, especially on vacation." I give her my best panty-melting grin.

"Worse? Are we referring to your womanizing, toenail-painting, feet-massaging days with older women?" She wriggles her eyebrows, but she can't get them in a proper sequence to be funny. It just looks awkward. God, I love her.

"Hey," I correct. "I was the victim. You should feel sorry for me."

"Yeah, I bet you were traumatized alright," she says sarcastically.

I pause, letting the tone in her voice linger between us, because it makes me fucking happy. "Is that jealousy I detect in your voice?"

"I'm pleading the fifth."

"Sir, here's your blanket, as requested."

I turn toward the familiar voice from earlier, grabbing it from her. I must have completely missed the cue that seat belts can be removed. "Thanks."

"I'll check to see if you need anything else in a bit."

I peek over into the aisle as she walks off. The good thing about first class—no one fucking bothers you. It may be expensive, but it's worth every damn penny in times like this, when I need space, and no prying eyes. Most of the people on this flight look like they're heading back to Wall Street, big boring offices, and workloads that would piss any normal human being off.

As I pull back into the seat, I remove my seatbelt and unfold the blanket, before helping her undo hers. Draping it over our laps, I lean toward her and the window, close to her ear. "Have I ever told you it makes me hard when you get jealous?"

"No," she says, the nervousness present in her voice.

I grab her hand and place it around my hard dick under the blanket, solidly positioned along the inside of my leg, only the thick cotton of my pants separating them. "It does. It makes me want you so fucking bad. Claim your territory, baby. You know how much it turns me on."

"It's not fair when you talk to me like that." Her voice is a whisper. "I love when you talk dirty." Her fingers climb me until she reaches the waistband, and then crosses the barrier to the other side, before returning to the spot it just was, opposite side. She takes my dick in her hand, slowly stroking full length. My head falls against her seat. "I feel like I'm doing things as an adult that I should have done in high school; like risk getting caught doing inappropriate things in public."

"I'll pretend like we're in high school with you. Better late than never, right?"

"You would do that for me without giving me shit, even though you're way beyond that level of immaturity?"

"Yes. You're the girl I see a future with. I want you to experience life, Kambry, not take it from you. I want you to know that you can do that with one person." Her thumb rubs over the head of my dick, smearing that bead of pre-cum she's so fond of. I fight to keep sounds to a minimum. My body turns slightly, facing her so that I can reach her at a better angle, my shoulder resting against the back of the seat. "Anytime you want to do something, come to me. We're partners. I love you."

She mirrors my position, pulling one foot on the edge of the seat beneath the cover, creating a homemade tent of sorts, and then pulls the blanket up on top of her shoulder with her hand. "You have my attention. Let's play."

She grabs my hand in hers and guides it to the inside of her thigh as she continues to stroke my dick. As if navigating by memory, it continues on its own when she returns her hand to the blanket as it starts to fall, keeping us covered. Her cotton dress is hiked up to her hips. I can feel the satin material between her legs. It's damp. Damn. "You're wet," I whisper.

"I've never been dry with you."

A low growl comes out. I move her panties to the side and rub the tip of my finger over her pussy, wetting it. It slips inside before I can even instruct it to, submerging itself in her hot, wet center. Her breathing becomes ragged . . .with only one finger. I love watching her unravel with the simplest actions.

She squeezes my dick as I pump in and out a few times, before coming out and moving to her clit. I work the tip up and down in a steady rhythm, quickly, but never losing contact. Her hand stops stroking me, and her eyes close. "Shit," she says. "I love when you touch me there."

Her voice is so low I can barely hear her. I grab the lobe of her ear between my teeth, skimming the skin, and then lick along the outline. She quivers. One direct-to-fuck button down. I can feel her fighting to keep her one leg up. She wants to lower it with the other and squeeze them around my hand. Her pelvis presses against my palm. "You going to come for me, baby?"

"Yes," she says in a breathy whisper upon exhale. I move my other hand beneath the blanket and shove two fingers inside of her, just as she whispers. "Right now. Sax."

Her pussy squeezes around my fingers and her hand tightens around my dick. When her slightly arched back relaxes against the seat, I remove my fingers and replace her panties in the appropriate position. Her leg lowers, the back of her thigh aligning with the bottom of the seat, next to the one that's been there this whole time. "Do you need a tissue? I think I have a travel pack in my purse."

She releases my dick and pulls her hand out from under the blanket, already attempting to get her purse. "Ugh uh," I say. She looks at me, slightly confused.

"I don't think I'd use your clothes since we're in public," she says, still whispering. "It won't be clear when it dries."

I smirk. "I don't intend to."

I place both fingers in my mouth completely and wrap my lips around the ends, next to my knuckles, before slowly pulling them back out, sucking them clean. I can taste her, wishing like hell my face was between her legs right now. Her mouth is hanging ajar, her eyes lazy. "That is so damn hot. It still surprises me. I didn't think guys would be into that sort of thing."

"I'm only into it with you."

"Still, it's hot."

"You coming is what's hot."

"Tell me how to get you off."

"You really up for it?"

"Of course. An O for an O, right? I don't like you being selfless all the time."

"It doesn't bother me. I'd rather you get one."

"And that's what makes me want to more."

"Alright then. Get up and go to the bathroom. Act like you feel a little sick. I'll wait a couple of minutes and come *check on you*. I'll knock once. Whatever I say, just go with it and let me in."

She bites the corner of her bottom lip. If only she knew how much I love her lips . . . But if she did, she probably wouldn't bite them so damn much. "Okay," she says, and hands me the blanket, before standing and making sure her dress is covering everything as she does. I turn back toward the front and watch as she passes over me for the aisle, staring at her ass that I'm about to be gripping.

When she disappears I toss the blanket in her seat and glance at my watch. "It's not fucking normal to be this horny over a woman all the damn time." I know this, yet in about a minute and a half I'm going back there with no shame. I look up and down the aisle again. Everything is quiet, most likely because it's still early in the day.

Easing out of my seat, I walk toward the small restroom and knock once, just as I said I would. "Kambry, you okay?"

"I feel sick to my stomach. I'll be fine."

"Let me in."

The door starts to open and I push my way inside of the small space. She has a mischievous grin on her face, standing in front of the sink. "How did I do?" she asks as I shut the door.

I press my pelvis against hers, gripping onto the back of her thighs. "Good, but we need to finish before someone comes knocking on the door."

"Oh, right." She wraps her hands around my neck and leans toward me. I meet her halfway, driving my tongue between her lips as they connect with mine. My hands ascend, pushing up the bottom of her dress, contouring to her body as I trace along her ass: her fucking bare ass. She always does this shit to me.

I break the kiss. "You wore a thong?"

"Yes," she says cautiously.

"You know what that does to me." I grab her hips and turn her around. "If I didn't have to be quiet right now I'd slap that ass so hard." She moans as she grips the edges of the sink. "You'd like that, wouldn't you?"

"Yes."

I grab the triangular section of fabric just above her ass, pulling it down until it sits below her cheeks, baring her lower half. I quickly push my pants down to my thighs, grabbing my dick just after. "Give me that ass."

She bends forward, pressing her ass toward me, the head of my dick ready and waiting. One hand returns to her hip to stabilize her, as I rub the head up and down in her wetness. I waste no time before thrusting inside, filling her completely. As my pelvis meets her ass and my hand returns to her opposite hip, mirroring the other one, she squeezes her pussy around my dick. Still to this day it's a tight fit.

I rub up her body, dipping my fingertips beneath the wiring of her bra until her tits are firmly in my hands. Her nipples are hard. I pull back and begin thrusting at a quick and steady pace. "Fuck," she whispers. "That feels so good."

I lean toward her, minimizing the distance between us. "You feel good. I don't want to stop."

"Me either."

I pinch her nipples between my thumbs and index fingers. "But I have to before we get caught.

I skim the lobe of her ear again with my teeth. "Dammit, that shouldn't be allowed. Come inside of me. I want to feel you."

Her hand wraps around and grabs my ass, pulling me closer to her. "You want me to come on command . . .you know what to do."

I thrust harder, using her breasts to keep steady. She inches up on her toes when I hit deep. "I love you. Only you. Always."

"Fuck." On the next thrust I start to come, before I even make it completely inside. I stop when my dick makes it all the way, letting myself finish. She turns her head to look at me. Grabbing the underside of her chin with one hand, I force her to look harder, and then kiss her deep and hard. "I love you too, Kambry. Even in my fucking weakness I still want only you. There is no moving on from those types of feelings."

I slowly pull out and jerk my pants back up my legs. She turns around as she does the same with her underwear, and then adjusts her dress back into place. "I'll be your strength when you're weak, just like I did this past weekend. Just don't leave me again. Yesterday was hell. I know we haven't talked it out since we got into the house last night because we were more worried about making up from being apart, but I'm going to risk killing our mood to say this."

She wraps her arms around my waist, pulling me closer. "I love you, Sax. It's not just words to me. The feelings are very real. You hurt me. You walked out on us without even talking to me. I could've been more harsh and made you grovel more, but the fact is that you've been through enough in the past with a girl. I'm not going to add to it just to prove a point. That's not me. In the future, promise me you'll talk to me before you make a decision again that could alter both of our lives. Things are going to get harder at some point. We've been in a honeymoon phase since we met. This is the beginning of real life. This trip. We're bringing family into this now, and I'm sure it's not the end."

"Sometimes men are idiots. That's all I've got. But, the important thing is that when you force yourself into a decision, you're also forced to live as if it were real, and I know for a fact I don't want a life without you. Worst two days of my life. I was a drunk the entire time, so that I promise."

Her demeanor changes, as if we didn't just have a completely serious conversation, and a smile emerges from hiding. "How are we supposed to discretely make our way back to our seats?"

"Do you want the good news first or the bad?"

"There's bad?"

"Okay, well, maybe just not so good."

She breathes out. "Uh, bad."

"There's about a ninety-eight percent chance everyone will know we just fucked in the bathroom. Welcome to the mile-high club, baby." I shine a completely synthetic grin.

Her eyes widen. "And the good news?"

"We'll be in New York by this afternoon and we'll never see any of these people again."

"Nothing good ever comes from our rendezvous in public."

"That's not true," I say as I open the door. "One hell of an orgasm comes from it. I would say that's a damn good outcome."

"Of course you're going to find the simplest response," she retorts as she inches past me.

"Nope, just the most logical."

I follow her out the door, the flight attendant turning her head toward us as we make our way down the aisle to our seats. She just shakes her head and goes back to what she was doing.

I take my seat beside Kambry and wrap my arm around her, pulling her into me, and then spread the blanket over her. "Be thinking of a New York bucket list."

She settles against me. "I'm just thankful to be going. I don't care what we do as long as I'm with you."

"I still want to know at least one thing you've always wanted to do there. It can be anything, big or small. Okay?"

"Okay," she says with a sleepy voice. Can we take a nap?"

"Sure, beautiful. Jet lag will set in before long."

I lay my cheek on top of her head and close my eyes. "Sax?"

"Yeah."

"Thanks for bringing me along. There's so much I've already gotten to experience because of you."

"I'm the one that should be thanking you, Kambry. I promise I'll show you the world before I die, one way or another."

She says nothing more. I'm guessing she's already dozing off.

New York here we come. Be good to her . . . She deserves the best that you have to offer.

CHAPTER TWO

Kambry

Saxton wraps his arm around me as we walk side by side through the terminal: the final one. Thank goodness. I'm just going to throw it out there that layovers suck. I'm tired and excited all rolled into one, and that is not the best combination. I feel like I'm spracked out on shots of espresso, yet my mind is telling me to calm the hell down. Changing time zones twice can be draining.

"You feel okay?"

I look up at him and he kisses me. "Yeah, just a little physically drained, but not sleepy."

"Good, because someone looks excited to meet you," he says with a smile on his face.

I look out in front of me as we make our way into the waiting area. A beautiful girl with long, chocolate brown hair curled into bouncing waves hitting mid center of her back is standing with a purse hanging in the bend of her arm and a grin on her face, waving. All of her features are darker than his, like her skin tone, her eyes, and her hair, but she has the dimples to match Saxton's. She's a little shorter, and has the perfect figure. She's fit, like she works for it, but has curves that would make any girl jealous. My stomach is working overtime. Why am I so nervous?

I glance back at Sax and he has that panty-melting smile on his face that he graces me with every once in a while. It makes my heart skip a beat. He's happy, and that's easy to see. "What if she doesn't like me?" I whisper.

"That's crazy. No one would dislike you."

I clutch the strap of my purse into my fist, trying to calm down. This isn't easy for me . . .meeting someone new. I lack necessary skills to feel comfortable in the presence of unfamiliar people, at least on a personal level. I hate that about myself. I take a deep breath, trying to even out the nerves shooting off like firecrackers in all directions.

Saxton releases me as we close in on her, and then he grabs her in a tight hug, leaving me standing here . . .awkwardly at that. He rocks his body side to side, clearly trying to take his time. I feel like an intruder. I glance to my left and right, taking in all of the people in each direction. "Kambry," he says.

I glance back at him, now looking at me. "This is Tynleigh, my sister."

"Hi," I state, awkwardly. "It's nice to finally meet you."

Her smile continues to grow from the original as she walks toward me, her arms outstretched. She wraps me in a hug, squeezing tight. I return the gesture, trying to be polite. "Thank you," she says in my ear, for only me to hear.

Thank you? "For what?"

"Being someone different, for loving my brother, and for making him happier than I've seen him in a long time. That's clear just by looking at him."

"It's pretty easy, honestly. He's an amazing guy."

"Well, it takes a special girl to pull his attention still, so I think we will be great friends, Kambry. Welcome to New York."

She releases me and looks between the two of us. "What's first on the itinerary?"

Saxton is still gleaming, looking between the two of us. "Me–I don't care. My two best girls are in the same place. We could stare at pigeon shit in silence and I'd still be happy. It's up to Kambry. She's never been here before. I have."

Tynleigh looks at me. "Never?"

I shake my head. "I didn't get out much until I graduated. My parents weren't the traveling kind."

"Well, Kambry, it's a good thing I'm your tour guide, because I rock, and I know all of the best kept New York secrets. Come on, let's get the baggage and then go hail a cab and we'll decide the first course of action."

"Okay."

Saxton grabs my hand as she turns and walks away, leading us. "Well, that wasn't so bad, was it?"

"You didn't say she looked like Miss America. You could have warned me."

He laughs out loud. "I'm sure her ego would love that. If you've ever thought I'm cocky, she's about a hundred times worse. It's actually concerning at times."

"If I looked like that I'd be cocky too."

He stops, pulling on my hand as I keep going. I look at him. "What?"

"You really don't know how beautiful you are, do you?"

I squint my eyes. "I mean, I would say I'm a hard six."

His eyes widen, bigger than I've ever seen them. "A six? Are you fucking kidding?"

"Uh, no. I wasn't. Too high?"

He rubs his hand over his face, and then looks at his sister, that has now stopped, most likely because we have. "T."

"Yeah."

"On a scale from one to ten, what would you classify Kambry?"

"Hard nine. Eh, easy ten. Why?"

"Because Kambry seems to think she's a hard six."

"Six? Oh no, girl. Your rack alone puts you at an eight. Then add in the small figure and model face, and we're looking at a nine." She tilts her head right and then left, before speaking again. "That's without factoring in your lips—what we call dick-sucking lips. The blonde hair and blue eyes give you a bonus, because it makes guys think of Barbie. Easy ten."

I glance at Saxton, whom now has a heated gaze as he stares back at me, his eyes directed at my lips. Of course, all he heard of that was dick-sucking lips. Are we really having this conversation? He shrugs his shoulders when his eyes finally set on mine. "What? You weren't going to believe me. I'm fucking you."

I smack his arm. "Would you be a little quieter?"

"Uh, no. When you're fucking the hottest girl on the planet, you don't strive for privacy, because there are most likely already handfuls of guys in this airport that have thought about it upon glancing at you, so as your boyfriend, I make that shit known. You're off the market."

"You're ridiculous. Y'all are related. It's a biased answer."

"If you were a hard six she would have told you. She doesn't give a shit about feelings . . .most of the time. She's blunt. How the hell do you think she has the job she has? You don't make it in New York being nice. People here are a different breed than what you're used to."

"You're freaking me out."

"It's the truth. It's a different world here. It's fast paced. People have no choice but to be that way. There are too many people and it's constant competition."

"We need to get to baggage claim if the two of you want to have your clothes."

He grabs my hand and pulls me along behind her. I can't believe I'm in New York. My parents would be livid if they knew what all I was doing; yet still, I don't care.

We stop at a rolling belt, spitting out pieces of luggage one after another. I watch each one, waiting on the bright pink one to emerge. Saxton's black rolling suitcase comes out and he grabs it off the belt. Several more come out after his, but not mine. I'm beginning to get concerned when it finally does. As it circles around Saxton grabs it, setting it upright for me.

"Thank you."

He kisses my lips and then grabs my hand. "Be thinking about that bucket list."

We walk through the airport that resembles an ant colony to me: everyone running in different directions, passing each other by. We follow behind his sister. "There is this one thing."

He smiles at me. "It's about time. Tell me."

"Okay, promise not to laugh?"

"I promise not to laugh in a cruel manner. Tell me."

"Okay, so, when I was in fifth grade, I had this teacher. I remember she took a trip here, and when she came back she spent a small period of class telling us about it. The way she described it was so vivid and colorful. It was almost like being there. The thing that stood out the most, though, was when she spoke of this toy store—FAO Schwarz I think was the name. The details just made it seem like something you couldn't pass up. She brought back these candy bubbles. They were edible. I remember thinking that was the coolest thing I'd ever seen. I've wanted to go there since."

His hand moves to my shoulders, wrapping around me. He kisses my temple. "That may be one bucket list wish I can't give you."

I look at him, and the look on his face shatters my soul. I didn't even know there was such a feeling. "Why the sad look? It was just a thought."

"Because I want you to be able to do everything, and something like that is such a simple request. I hate to be the bearer of bad news, but it shut down, baby; just last year at that. I went once. It was pretty cool. It had this huge floor piano that you could step on the keys. Cool as hell. Massive place full of high-end toys, but mostly just a tourist attraction. It's a shame it shut down. I'm sorry. I'll make it up to you, though, with something better. I promise."

"It's no big deal. Just an idea, like I said. Probably wasn't what I expected anyway."

We finally make it outside the main doors, stopping curbside next to a yellow cab. Tynleigh opens the door and pokes her head inside, and then the cab driver steps out as the trunk opens. Saxton grabs my bag from me and lowers the handle, before putting both inside the trunk and guiding me to the door.

I scoot along the leather seat, stopping in the middle next to Tynleigh, and Saxton gets in beside me, shutting the door. "Why don't we go to my apartment and the two of you can relax while I go finish some stuff at work, and then tonight I'll take you both somewhere. Plus, I know you guys will want some alone time anyway to explore while you're here. I've managed to get some time off, but I still have to be in and out of the office a little bit each day. Will that work?"

Saxton wraps his arm around me and tugs on Tynleigh's brown hair. "I'm good. What about you, beautiful?"

I look up at him. "Sure. That's fine."

Tynleigh rattles off an address to the cab driver that doesn't mean a hill of beans to me, given the fact that I don't know where anything in this city is. The cab pulls out into the street. The further we get into city traffic, the more things start catching my attention. It's like nothing I've ever seen before.

Incidentally my body starts drifting toward Saxton, my face headed for the window. My hand perches on his thigh as I glance out, building after building passing us by. Okay, well, I guess technically we're the ones doing the passing, but I've never physically seen buildings this tall and close together. Sure, Los Angeles is huge and has similarities, but this is just . . .different somehow. They go on and up for miles, most full of glass windows from bottom to top. I feel like an Emoji right now: a happy one with a gaping mouth.

An arm loops around my waist. "Come here, baby. Sit in my lap."

I glance at Saxton, just now realizing I'm completely invading his personal space. "I'm sorry. This is rude."

When I try to back up to my space on the bench seat, he pulls me toward him. "Don't be crazy. I should have offered you the window seat. Come here."

He forces me into his lap, wrapping his arms around my waist to hold me here. "This is awkward. I'm sure your sister doesn't want to see me sitting on top of you."

She glances up from her cell phone as the words exit my mouth. "Nope, not bothering me." She winks. "I like seeing him like this. Gives me blackmail material for later. Hell, who knows . . .I may even get a little inspiration for an article."

I laugh. "Well, we probably won't be that entertaining."

I look back out the window, traffic moving slower now. Saxton sits up and aligns our bodies together. "I love seeing you like this," he whispers into my ear.

Chills travel down my body, my eyes closing, but only for a moment. "Like what?"

"When you fall in love with something for the first time."

I stop breathing. My throat feels closed off, and my attempt to swallow is unsuccessful. The way he says it is with so much reverence it's terrifying. "You say that like you've witnessed it before."

The words came out before I instructed them, but he doesn't seem bothered by them. "I have. I just didn't recognize the action then, because the blinders were in the way. I'll never forget it, though, and each time I witness it again, it makes the memory of the first time so much stronger."

"And the first time was when?" I continue looking out the window, the two of us speaking in hushed tones back and forth, no longer paying much attention to our surroundings. My heart is no longer beating in a steady rhythm. He does this to me. It never dulls from the last time either. I feel completely out of control in his grasp. His chin is pressed forward over my shoulder so that we can talk without everyone hearing us.

"When you fell in love with me."

"You could tell?"

"Yeah, it just took me a little while to understand what I was seeing. You have this look about you when your heart is falling for something. It's indescribable. I knew it was different at first, but like I said it took me some time to catch on. I don't know. It sounds fucking corny unless you see it I guess."

I will not cry like a damn sappy girl. My god, who says stuff like that and looks like him? He puts most guys to shame. In moments like these, I feel like a writer sat down and wrote out a list of the perfect guy to capture the hearts of women all over the world, and then like the fairy godmother on Cinderella, Bibbidi Bobbidi booed him to life.

I want to kiss him so bad right now; because I'm the one lucky girl that gets to kiss him anytime she wants. I want to commit his lips to memory over and over again, so that he never forgets how much I love him. "It's not corny. Not to me. At least you know that I am . . .in love with you."

"Our stop," Tynleigh says, reminding me that it's not just the two of us in this cab. He nibbles on the lobe of my ear and runs his lips down the length of my neck. My body jerks to the point I feel like someone about to have a seizure. I slide off of him and he lets me. My body is reacting to him. Instead of exiting on his side, I follow Tynleigh, leaving Saxton where he is. I hear a deep-throated laugh behind me, causing me to flip him the bird over my shoulder. Asshole.

Standing on the curb, I look up at the tall building before me. Wow. Vertigo starts to set in from looking up too long, causing me to sway. Tynleigh loops her arm around mine. "Come on. I'll show you to the place you'll call home when the two of you come to visit. On the mental count of three, add some sway in your step. It's clear you're fresh meat. You're hanging with the big girls now, so you'll play like one."

She starts walking and I adjust my purse on my shoulder. "Oh, Saxton, you can get the bags," she calls out without stopping to ensure he even heard her. I can't concentrate on anything for trying to enhance my walk as instructed. I'm not real sure what was wrong with mine in the first place.

I pretty much drool the entire way to her apartment door, stopping only long enough for her to open it. Twenty-fifth floor: what that view must look like. I follow her inside, stopping in the center of the room. Everything is tidy and decorated to resemble a magazine photo. Large framed posters of a magazine issue with a name I recognize hang on the exposed brick behind the couch. "Is that where you work?"

"Yeah," she says. "Each time my article made front page header I had the issue cover framed. Pretty cool, huh?"

"Amazing. Must be awesome to have that kind of accomplishment under your belt."

"It is. I've worked my ass off to get here: endless hours, not much of a social life for a while, and a relationship status that is non-existent, but it's paying off. What do you plan to do, Kambry? After your current career path, of course . . . Don't take this the wrong way, but you hardly look like a porn star. Eighteen, right?"

"I'll be nineteen this Friday actually. Don't mention it to Sax. We've never discussed actual birthdays, as strange as that sounds. I guess it just never came up, and I don't want him to feel obligated to go all out or anything. He's already brought me here. That's more than enough."

"Eighteen, nineteen, same difference . . ."

"I haven't thought about it, honestly. The only thing I'm interested in is music, but I'm not sure what I could do with it. Anything would be pretty cool, though, if I could make a career out of something I love."

"When you say music . . .do you mean singing, songwriting, or living through it from behind the scenes?"

"Any of the above. I love singing, and I have tons of word scribblings, but if I'm honest with myself, I don't think I have what it takes to make a career out of that. I don't like being the center of attention. I like so many different kinds of music and I've found that my favorite pastime is finding hidden gems that no one knows about. Sounds weird I know."

She tosses her purse on the couch and turns toward me. "Actually, it sounds like you need to look into being a talent agent for a record label. You know, getting to listen to tons of cool bands and artists in places like bars, traveling all over to do so, judging music all day and getting paid for it. Imagine being the name behind the next big hit. I'm sure it's a competitive industry, but if it's something you have a passion for it's always possible. Look at me. I found a love for writing and here I am."

"I've never thought about that before. Thanks. It's definitely something to think about soon. I know I need to be thinking about what I want to do with my life aside from this . . .thing we're doing."

"Porn." She raises her brow and laughs. "It's okay. You can say it. I'm used to the term. I've watched enough of it that it doesn't make me blush."

"Yeah, it still makes me slightly uncomfortable to say. Blame it on being sheltered all of my life." She walks to the small kitchen and opens the refrigerator, bringing back two bottles of water, and hands me one. "Thanks."

Twisting off the top she takes a sip. "Yeah, which is my next question. How did a girl like you get pulled into porn? I get why my brother ended up there, but I'm going to guess that's not the case for you."

"He hasn't told you?"

"I haven't asked. If I want to know something I go to the source. Otherwise it's gossip and that's not my thing."

"Well, I work, or worked at a nightclub." I point to myself. "Insert VIP fill-in at Saxton's table with some other people. Gosh, when I saw him I was scared to death I was going to spill a drink or trip on my heel. He kept looking at me and my entire body would shake. I was a nervous wreck. I'm sure it showed too. When he kissed me I was sure I'd never see him again. I figured I was just part of a joke since I probably looked like a total fan-girl, when really I was just uncomfortable. Then he came back at closing."

I stop talking, remembering that first night . . .in the pool. I take a gulp of my water, trying to wet my now dry mouth. "He lured you a little at a time, didn't he?"

She has a huge smirk set in place. "Yeah," I admit, defeated. "Did I get caught in a web that traps many?"

"No, that's why it's so funny. I honestly don't remember Saxton having a single girlfriend until he went to college. It just didn't seem to interest him. Maybe that's why he fell so hard for that cheating tramp."

A twinge of jealousy arises every time his ex-girlfriend is mentioned. It's stupid. She was before me, but she'll always be in the background in a way. "Just so you know, he never looked at her the way he looks at you, even after all that time. I didn't bring her up to upset you. Sometimes my mouth says things before my brain filters them."

"No, it's okay. I never had that thought. I wasn't really upset anyway. I just don't have much experience period, so I wear expressions that I don't even know I have."

She stares at me. I'm a little uncomfortable with the direction this encounter is going. I want her to like me. Our age difference makes it hard to read her. I don't know what's even taking Saxton so long. He keeps things light. "You really do love him, don't you?"

"To the point I'd clearly do immoral things to have him."

"Good. He deserves that. Don't hurt him, Kambry. I'm begging you. I'm not saying you would, but as his sister I feel I need to say this. If you ever change your mind, which let's face it, can happen, we're human, but please leave instead of doing what she did. I don't want to ever see him go through that kind of heartache again. This whole porn thing is fine for now, but he's getting older. It's not the filmed sex I'm referring to; it's the constant change of scenery if you get my drift. The two of you are entitled to do whatever you want for people to watch and that's your business, as long as it's a couple thing. I know deep down he wants what our parents have. The two of us have always been close. His loyalty to a woman is rare, and maybe why he didn't date much, but the fact that it still exists within him after being taken advantage of is almost unheard of."

"I know, and that's one reason I fell so hard. He'd be the one to leave. That I can promise." I shrug my shoulders. "He already has once. It was on its way to destroying me."

She walks up to me and grabs me in her small arms, pulling me into a hug. "I guess it's a good thing he came to his senses then. Oh, and I'm glad you both are here."

"Thank you for having me tag along. I'm sure you wanted some time alone with your brother."

"Oh, please. Don't even think about it. I love him and all, but he can be a bit of a bore in the fun stuff. We can do manis and pedis tomorrow. You like getting your nails done?" She backs up, looking at me. A burst of laughter escapes my mouth. "What's funny? Did I miss the punch line?"

What I thought was a short burst becomes a laughing fit, stealing my air from my lungs. In my attempt to stop laughing a sound escapes that sounds something of a hyena. It's something that only happens when I laugh really hard, which isn't very often. After several tries at inhaling, I finally calm myself down. "Can we just talk about your brother's foot fetish and the fact that he can paint toenails as good as a woman?"

She returns a laugh of her own. "Surprised you, didn't it? You. Are. Welcome."

Banging occurs on the door, drawing my attention. Tynleigh walks over and opens it. Saxton walks in with the suitcase handles hanging from his arms and two hotdogs in one hand with stacked sodas in the other. The two bags of chips are being held between his teeth. I meet him halfway in my effort to take some of the load from him. I grab the chip bags and he releases his grip on them. "Hungry?" My attempt to be serious fails miserably.

He bends to set the suitcases down on their wheels and bottoms, fishing his arms out of the pull-up handles, careful not to spill what's in his hands. "Next time you two run off at least offer to feed a man. Pre-wifey lesson number one: a man is always hungry, especially in times following travel, sleep, and sex. Since all three have occurred today, I'm fucking starving."

"Pre-wifey lesson. God, you're adorable."

Before I can say anything more—like that I'm sure his sister doesn't want to know our sex schedule—he cuts me off. "No, beautiful. We've discussed terms that involve cute, adorable, and those of feminine nature. They do not belong in the same sentence when referring to your man. I'm a fucking beast. I'm sexy as hell, or even funny and sweet I can deal with, but nothing on my body is adorable. I'm not a puppy. Adorable does not come with an eight pack, a big pecker, and is not responsible for making your eyes roll back in your head. I am fucking iron man. If you need me to remind you I will."

My eyes are bugging out of my head. I can feel it. The man that can paint toenails with no shame, talk about fictional boyfriends and listen to me read romance, has a problem with the word adorable. It makes absolutely no damn sense. I'm a little mortified he speaks so openly about our sex life in front of his sister. I keep waiting for her to scream gross any second now, like any normal human being would do when someone mentions parents having sex.

I say nothing as he extends a hotdog toward me. I take it, my lips pursed tightly together in fear that I may do something I'll regret . . .like ruin his testosterone-packed moment. "Well, sprout, I'm glad we established you do in fact have balls . . .in case any of us were confused. Is there anything else we should cover before I leave the two of you to your wieners?"

I'm so glad she broke the ice. He shoves the end of the hotdog in his mouth. I can see the slightest hint of a smile on his face as he chews. I shake my head at him, waiting for him to swallow. "Nope. I think I covered all bases. Just show us where we're sleeping since you've moved since the last time I came to stay."

"Oh, right," she says.

He looks at me. "Eat up. We haven't had lunch and you don't come to New York without trying a street hotdog."

"A street hotdog?"

"Yeah, you know, the ones they sell out of the carts. Here, give me a bag of chips and take a drink."

We exchange as Tynleigh grabs her purse and walks to the first closed door, opening it. "Here is where the two of you will be staying. It's not anything fancy, but you have your own room. I moved enough times to get a two bedroom at a decent price. Do what you want, but if it requires acrobatics and vocal training then give me a heads up so I can put in ear buds or go downstairs."

She looks at her watch. "I need to go before my boss calls me. I'm supposed to be checking in. You guys fine? I'm pretty organized so nothing should be hard to find."

Saxton shoves the last half of his hotdog in his mouth and gives her a thumbs up. "Okay, good. I'll be back later this evening."

She starts to walk toward the door. "Oh." She looks back. "There is a spare key on the nightstand in case you need to leave. Don't do anything I wouldn't do, sprout."

He looks at me and winks. "I don't think you'll have to worry about that," he says. "See you in a bit."

"Oh, Kambry, we'll let Saxton tag along with us tomorrow. He may even enjoy it."

She winks and walks out, leaving the two of us alone. Manis and pedis with Saxton. That should be an experience. I follow Saxton to the small table and sit down as he pulls out the chair for me. "So, what have the two of you been doing while I was gone?"

"Just chatting."

"About?"

"How much of a sexy stud you are."

"Funny."

"Hey, it wasn't a banned word at least."

"You been thinking about that bucket list?" he asks as he pops the top on the Coke, followed by the sound of the bag crinkling as he opens the chips, tossing one in his mouth.

"I don't know what to choose. I've never been here before. We could just wander around and make a game out of getting lost."

He smiles. "I may like being lost with you."

We eat in silence. This is one thing I love about him. We can talk for hours and then sit here and just enjoy each other's company with no words at all. Some of what Tynleigh said earlier replays in my mind, now that I can actually think clearly. "I thought of something."

He straightens his posture from the relaxed position he's in, and crumbles the now empty bag of chips. "Oh yeah?"

"Yeah. It may be a little corny and outdated, but it's something I've always wanted to do."

"What is it?"

"Do any of those old, secondhand vinyl record stores still exist? You know, the ones you walk in and it's crates or bins filled with various records in no particular order, and the only way you can find the good stuff is by digging through every one?"

The movement of his eyebrows proves he's a little surprised by my request. "I would have never taken you for a vinyl kind of girl. That's a little ahead of your time. I'm curious . . ."

I shrug. "I don't know. I've just always been into music of any kind really, but I have this aunt that I rarely see—my mom's sister. She's a good bit younger than my parents and lives in Atlantic City now. She rarely comes home and my parents definitely don't go to see her. Maybe because she's cool as shit, unlike my parents, and doesn't fit into their way of life. Anyway, when I was younger she used to live close by, so occasionally my mom would let me go stay with her for a few hours at a time. I remember she was into vintage stuff. You know, like old cameras, record players, stuff that you find at flea markets and secondhand stores or pawnshops. It was her hobby, but the thing that always intrigued me, even before I realized how much I love music, was this built-in shelf she had on one wall."

I pause long enough to try and remember what it looked like. "It kind of looked like cubbies, but the shelves covered the entire wall, left to right and top to bottom, and were slam full of vinyl records. Most were, of course, people I had never heard of back then, but it was really cool; like a real library of music. She liked to travel. She said every time she went somewhere new she would go exploring for old stuff, and never came back home without at least one new record to add to her collection. There was a few times she even played one for me. That may have been what hooked me with music. Since then, I've always wanted to start a collection of my own."

He stands and holds out his hand for mine. "I'll talk to my sister and see if she knows of any. Surely there is one somewhere close by. For now, let's go lay down. I want to hold you in my arms and squeeze your boobs."

I smile and take his hand. "Of course. Let's not leave out boob squeezes in there. How romantic."

"That's because those are my kryptonite. I'm not ashamed to say, if you ever want your way, just show me a boob or place it in my hand. Better yet, just shove your nipple in my mouth. Like a Jolly Rancher, one suck will never be enough."

He grins at me, pulling me toward the bedroom Tynleigh told us was ours. "The things that come out of your mouth will never cease to amaze me."

"It's all your fault."

"How is it my fault?" I ask walking through the doorway and past him so he can shut the door. He turns the lock, and then without warning comes at me in full attack mode, quickly grabbing the bottom hem of my dress and pulling it up my body until it's laying on the floor in a pile.

"Because you hypnotized me with your body and drowned me in your love. Now I'm a perv." He shucks his shoes and falls on the bed, fully clothed. "I'm love-drunk on you, woman. Bring your fine ass here."

"Oh yeah? Well, why do I have to be in underwear while you have all your clothes on? That's kind of unfair, you know."

I straddle him, creeping up his body from legs to waist. His hands go straight for my cheeks, and not the ones on my face. "I never said you couldn't undress me," he says.

"Hmm." I reach behind me and unhook my bra, letting it fall from my body. "I guess you must not want these too bad . . .or you would already be naked."

His eyes widen and he sits up in a hurry, pulling off his shirt as if he has fire ants crawling all over him. He grips them in his hands, pulling his mouth toward my nipple. "Tits are the magic word."

My head falls back, my back arching. I begin grinding my middle along his hardened dick. He sucks hard, biting down as he pulls his mouth free. "You want it?"

"Don't I always?"

"Show me."

He lays back and laces his fingers together behind his head. My hands clench around the elastic waistband of his cotton pants; the ones I love so much. There is just something about a man in a pair of loose, cotton pants that is sexy, or maybe it's just him.

I pull them over his hips, scooting down his body as I bring them down, and then pull them over his feet when I get to the bottom. He's fully hard, like he always is when we play, and that's one reason that I'm always ready to go with little effort on his part. It's a turn-on to know I turn him on. I lift his ankle, kissing just above the top of his no-show sock as we stare at each other. "This is sexy. No showing off, no preparation, and no premeditated thought. It's real."

Sliding my finger under the edging of the thick, white cotton, I inch the fabric over his heel, removing his sock from his foot, and then do the other one, leaving him wearing nothing but the skin he lives in. "You amaze me more and more every day," he says.

"Shhh," I say. "No talking. Just enjoy." I grab his dick in my hand, holding it at the perfect angle for me to utilize, and then lower myself until I inch it in my mouth, slowly.

I circle my tongue around the head as I look at him, and then take him in my mouth as far as I can. His head hits the back of my throat, causing me to gag, and triggering my glands to release more saliva. I use it as lubrication, letting it run down his length, meeting the top of my hand. I loosen my grip just enough for it to slide beneath it, and then I use my hand to smear it down the rest of his length since I can't take all of him in my mouth. He's too big. I already have to coax my jaw to stay open so my teeth don't skim his width.

He groans when my hand becomes one with the rhythm of my mouth. "Fuck. I love watching you suck my dick." When I reach as far as I can go, I suction all the way back up until his head exits my mouth.

I smile at him, and then begin jacking him off with full strokes instead of half as I was, lowering my mouth toward his balls. My tongue inches out, touching the soft skin. I run my tongue up the line that separates his balls. "Holy shit. Baby."

Before he can say anything more, I wrap my mouth around one side, lightly suckling the soft skin in my mouth, allowing my tongue to rub the underside, easily exerting enough pressure that I can feel the ball inside. It reminds me of one of those water toys that have objects on the inside, like to relieve stress. I switch sides each time I get done sucking one, to give the other attention, all while stroking his dick.

He grabs my hair in his hand and pulls, hard, until I'm staring at him. "Fucking turn around. If you're going to suck me, then I'm going to suck you."

I crawl up his body and turn around when I reach his waist. He instantly grabs my thighs and pulls me toward his face until I'm staring down at his dick, my ass in his face. It's slightly uncomfortable knowing my ass is not far from his mouth, nose, and eyes, but one thing I've learned with Saxton is that he even loves nasty with me, and I love him more for it. It's a way for me to tap into a forbidden territory without feeling judgment from anyone.

He pulls my panties over my ass, lowering them until they end just above my bent knees. "Damn, I love staring at your pussy," he says, just before his tongue enters me.

I reflexively back into him, wanting him deeper. He slaps my ass, causing me to scream out, not expecting it. "Suck me, baby."

I grab his dick again, putting it in my mouth. His tongue moves to my clit, rubbing up and down on it, making it hard to concentrate on anything but sucking what's in my mouth harder and faster, so I do, grabbing his balls in my free hand. Our pace matches each other's.

I love sucking his dick. I can't explain it. I never thought I would necessarily like this, indifferent sure, but like, no. It may be the way he reacts when I do it that makes me like it, because he never asks for it, but when I do I can tell how much he loves it.

He presses his thumb inside of me, and then moves toward my asshole, before gently pressing inside. I'll never get used to that, but it never fails, that after I get used to the initial shock, I like it. It feels good. When he begins to back out of me, I moan around his dick. His finger begins rubbing my clit when he removes his tongue. "That's right, baby. Show me how much you like my finger in your ass."

I suck harder, massaging his balls in my hand. As he presses back inside, a feeling I don't particularly recognize begins. "Oh, fuck me. You're oozing fucking cum." His tongue licks over my pussy, one finger still rubbing my clit as the other pumps in and out of my ass. It's too much. It feels too good.

My pace picks up, changing from thought to thoughtless motion. Out of nowhere I start to come, completely not expecting it. His head ends at the middle of my tongue, moaning being the only physical action at the moment. His dick starts to pulse on my tongue, warning me that he's about to explode in my mouth. I can't move from the feelings overcoming me.

The first spurt of salty, warm, creamy liquid hits my tongue. After a few I swallow, not even thinking, continuing about three times before he finishes. My body feels sticky and hot. I lick over the slit on his head, making sure he's clean before removing my mouth. He shoves his tongue inside of me one more time, before swiping over it, leaving me clean.

I sit up and pull my panties back in place, then move off him and toss his underwear at him to put on, before lying on the bed beside him. He quickly slips them on and turns over, grabbing my hip. "You swallowed my cum."

I stare into his eyes. "Yes."

"You didn't have to."

"I know."

"Fuck it was hot, though. I could feel your throat close each time you did."

"What can I say . . .I was short on my protein quota today," I wink, trying hard to hold in my laughter from the sudden shocked expression on his face. "What? I can't make dirty jokes?"

"Pure minds aren't good at cracking dirty jokes on the spot. It takes practice to obtain that kind of skill."

I shrug. "I guess you've polluted my brain. I like it."

He smiles. "As long as it's me doing the polluting I can live with that."

"Hmm. Are you sure you're not going to miss the Goody Two-Shoes version of me?"

"Oh, you still hold plenty of goodness. You're just slightly tarnished now."

He squeezes my boob. I raise a brow. "Miss them already?"

"They're mine. I can grope them whenever I want without judgment."

I grab his balls. "As long as these are mine. I like them."

He grunts. "Forever."

"I like the sound of that."

We stare at each other. "What's on your mind?"

"If I told you, you'd think I was a whore."

"Doubtful, unless you cheat on me. Then, well, you title yourself."

"I should slap you for that."

"What?"

"I would never cheat on you."

"Okay, then you have nothing to worry about. Talk to me."

I take a deep breath, preparing for the worst feeling in the world. "I kind of miss filming with you."

He bites his bottom lip, the mildest smile showing through. "I've created a monster, haven't I?"

"That bad, huh?"

"No. I remember the hype in the beginning."

My brows scrunch. "That's not what I mean, Sax, but thanks. Now I feel awesome. Not."

He rolls over me, pushing me on my back, and then gently kisses me. "Don't do that."

"Do what?"

"Make it seem like I'm comparing you to every other girl. All I meant was that I remember the excitement of filming in the beginning. Then it got old. With you, it doesn't matter what I'm doing, because I'm happy, filming or not."

"I miss filming with you, not filming. There is a huge difference. It's weird. I don't miss the house. I don't miss knowing everything we did was being monitored. What I miss is knowing that the two of us are doing something so intimate together without caring what anyone else thinks; showing our love to the world. It made me feel like you were really mine."

He laces his fingers in mine, looking into my eyes. “Baby, I’m always yours. Always. No girl can ever take me away from you. I promise.”

“It’s stupid. Just forget I mentioned it.”

He kisses me again. “No. I want to give you the experiences you want.”

“I don’t want it twenty-four seven like we were. That’s the strange part. I like our privacy during conversation and being together. It’s just the sex. I liked the idea of being an example couple for other couples. Does that sound stupid?”

“Nothing that comes out of your mouth could ever be stupid, Kambry. You want to share some of our experiences while we’re here, then that’s what you’ll get.”

I wrap my legs around his waist, my heart beating wildly. “Really? How?”

“Well, if it’s just posting moments during sex you want or being able to pick and choose what you want to share in general, we could create a couples’ blog on Tumblr. It’s known for homemade porn posted by couples. It’s the one blog host that is completely unrestricted in what kind of content you can post.”

I wrap my arms around his waist. “So, just sign up, and then we can post short videos and stuff as we want to?”

“Yep. It’s that simple. We can have our privacy when we want and be public when we want. I guess it’s the best of both worlds, only you aren’t getting paid. We would basically be volunteer porn stars.”

I laugh. “It sounds . . .fun.” I pause. “You know I would never in a million years want this if it were anyone else, right?”

“You know you have ruined me from any other girl, right?”

I bite my bottom lip. “So what you said in your room after my brother left?”

“All lies. My heart hated me for it. Seeing you like that is something I never want to see again, baby. I know I’ve said it already, but I’m sorry.”

“I shouldn’t have brought it up again. I just wanted to hear it. The part that hurt the most was thinking that you could so easily go back to someone else after what we shared together. I never doubted that you loved me.”

“I’d rather sever my dick from my body myself before shoving it into the crotch of another woman, or anywhere else for that matter. You are it for me, Kambry. I hope you’re as serious as you say you are, because there is no moving on from this for me. You’re my forever.”

I close my eyes, trying to remember how to breathe. “And always. I may not have known where I was going, but the destination is worth putting down roots. I'm not going anywhere, Sax. The heart wants what it wants, and mine wants you."

He uprights his upper half and grabs the comforter beneath me, pulling it down my body. I lift, removing my weight from the bedding. He gets beneath the covers and pulls it over us, before grabbing ahold of me and pulling me into his body as he molds himself around me. "Good, because I've already claimed it."

I lay my head on the pillow, my eyes becoming heavy. "I love you, Sax."

"I love you too, Kam."

I smile at the use of a nickname he's never called me—only Meredith—my body completely at rest. I'm content. I always am with him, no matter what we're doing. As I drift out of consciousness, a few words embed themselves into my mind. "I'm going to take you on a real date."

I lace my fingers with his on my belly, squeezing to show that I heard him. "I'd like that. I'd like it a lot," I whisper. Our breathing evens out at the same time, and the jet lag kicks in.

CHAPTER THREE

Saxton

A constant bouncing begins to occur, coinciding with the image before me. "Fuck yeah. Ride my cock, beautiful."

Something soft smacks me in the face and laughter occurs. "I know what someone with a filthy mouth is dreaming about."

The image disappears. Come back. My hand takes a direct shot for my dick, pushing it down, or attempting to anyway. The front of my boxer-briefs are damp in a circular area about the size of a quarter, maybe more. Fuck. I groan, my eyelids trying to pry themselves open from the glued state they're in.

The bouncing starts again, directly above my waist, the weight rotating from left to right. "Is someone excited to see me?" Kambry says in a singsong voice.

My eyelids finally part. A blurry body with a mess of blonde holding a big, white, rectangle is the only thing that registers. I attempt to rub my eyes so that I can focus; now recognizing the fluffy pillow in her hands. "I don't know. Why don't you find out for yourself?"

Before the command can even register her hand grips around my dick. "Saxton . . ."

I blink a few times, taking in her fully clothed body and face painted with makeup. Her hair is straight; too straight for just a blow dryer. "Where are you going? How long have you been up?"

"Why are your briefs damp? And directly over your head . . ."

"Because that is one limb that has a mind of its fucking own. That's why."

She has one shit-eating grin on her face if I've ever seen one. "You had a wet dream, didn't you? When I was bouncing, you came." I look at her, now fully awake and becoming aware of the situation at hand. "Don't you dare lie to me right now." Silence. "God, this is great."

"I'm glad you find this amusing. It's your fault. You were the one bouncing up and down on top of me."

"Just like the night in the bathtub was your fault? Funny how the slightest touch or motion can bring a dream to life isn't it? I'm finally playing in the same league as you. Hell yes."

"Hey, that was a memorable night for me."

"Awe." She places her hand over her heart. "Baby, that is so sweet."

"Yeah, yeah. What time is it? Why are you dressed? You never wake up before me and now all of a sudden the roles are reversing."

"Six in the morning. I was too excited to sleep. Get up sleepy head. I'm ready to explore and I think our first stop is already planned: breakfast. Tynleigh just started getting ready. She's the one who is an early bird. She was brewing coffee when I got up an hour ago."

I'm so confused. "Wait. Six in the morning? I thought we were going somewhere last night. How long have we even been asleep?"

"Tynleigh said when she came home we were sound asleep and wouldn't answer the door, so she figured we were tired. I'm not sure I want to evaluate how long we've been asleep. I guess it's from all that staying up late at the beach house and the lack of sleep prior." She pauses, a smile spreading across the lower half of her face as her cheeks become a light shade of pink. "I love that house . . . And also having to be up early to get all of our stuff ready to catch the plane in time, plus crossing time zones. I suppose it just caught up with us."

I'm having a hard time processing the number of hours I just slept, especially since I'm not sure if it's ever happened before. "What are we doing today?"

"Tynleigh said it's all a surprise. She did tell me of a record store a few blocks from her office. We could go while she checks in at work, so get up, sexy. You need a shower."

She kisses me, her minty breath blowing across my mouth. "Why didn't you wake me up? I could have showered with you."

"Because I knew bathing would not have occurred. Instead of cleaning we would have been dirtying. I've never been on the east coast. I want to have fun. Come on, come on, come on."

She starts bouncing again. "Keep on doing that and we aren't going anywhere." I stare at her, finally realizing just how good she looks . . .and smells. "You look beautiful. I like that outfit on you."

She grabs my hands and laces them together with hers, before raising them above my head, lowering her body toward my face. "Is it the low cut shirt?"

Her cleavage is peeking out of her top, staring me in the face. I try to free my hands, but she puts more body weight into me. It would take me little effort to move her, but I'm curious about her next course of action. "Nice compliments yield rewards, but no touching with hands. Mouth only. Then you're getting ready."

"Kind of bossy, aren't you?"

"You know you like it."

"Hell yeah I do." I buck my hips upward, pushing her into the air. "Every. Fucking. Time."

She shoves her chest against my nose, allowing the tip to dip between her tits. My eyes roll back in my head, taking in the sweet smell of her. It smells like dessert. Like red velvet cupcakes, but it's not sickly sweet; just enough to make me feel like I'm starving. Fuck, my mouth is salivating. Now I'm thinking of cupcakes. Red Velvet is my favorite. I turn my head slightly, and bite down on the large, round globe. "You remember when you made these yours?"

"Yes. I'll never forget it either. Fuck, they're perfect, and all mine." Without thought, I lift us into a sitting position, then push my face between her breasts and motorboat them.

She begins to laugh at the vibration of my voice against her skin, fighting to get her hand free from mine. "That tickles!" she screams in a fit of laughter. "Oh my gah."

She finally grabs ahold of my hair at the front and pulls my head back, freeing her tits from my assault on her jugular region, and I don't mean the one that is responsible for blood flow. I can see the sly smile trying to stay hidden. "Did you just *motorboat* me, Maverick?"

"I have no idea what you're talking about. I must have blacked out. If there was the slightest chance I remembered committing such an act, I would say it was definitely worth it; although, I'm just speculating."

"What if I told you it was another first for the girls? They may have even liked it. Would that clear up your memory any?"

"Come to think of it, I may remember something dark, big, and jiggly that smelled phenomenal. I could give it a try; see if something jogs my memory."

She tugs at my hair, pushing my head back in a further tilt as she looks down at me. "You sure do know how to make a girl feel sexy, Sax." She kisses me. "I'll leave you to get ready."

She gets up and scoots off the bed, walking toward the door. I want her to come back. It's kind of depressing that I want to just stay in bed all day with her in our little bubble. "Kambry."

She crosses one foot over the other and turns in an about-face, already at the door, her thumbs dipped into the front pockets of her washed-out, cutoff denim shorts. Her shirt is hanging off of one shoulder, making it bare. She's stunning. "What's up, baby?"

"I just wanted to tell you that I love you."

"Always and forever, right?" She winks.

"At minimum." She turns and grabs for the door. "Wait."

"Yes?" Her eyes are telling. I'm missing something.

"Nothing to say back?"

"You can't say it back when you said it first. Get a shower, baby."

My brows dip into my eyelids as she walks out of the room, closing the door behind her. Okay then . . .

I get out of bed and walk into the bathroom, suddenly realizing what she meant as I glance at the mirror in passing to the shower, causing me to stop. Written in lipstick the color of fire engine red are the words, *I love you.*

My right hand rubs over the left side of my chest, trying to ease the ache that started. You don't leave these kinds of things to be forgotten over time. I run back in the bedroom and grab my phone long enough to snap a photo of the message on the mirror.

This reminds me how fucking lucky I am. Just when you're ready to give up on humanity and the one thing that's as old as time—companionship—someone appears in your life and shows you that she's not there to make you forget the one that broke your heart, but to remind you that she's the one that never will. I'd like to think that she's been looking for me all along and just got lost for a while. She arrived a little late, and even late, she was the one all along. If I think about it, I guess she's right on time.

I close my eyes when they begin to sting. I need to start planning that date . . .because it has to be unforgettable.

CHAPTER FOUR

Kambry

We walk up the steps of the Fulton Street subway station; my nose finally relaxing as the smell of pee slowly fades away. That was a rather interesting experience, but even though Saxton and Tynleigh both tried to warn me that it's not as *cool* as I thought, I still wanted to do it. It's about the experience for me, and living life to the fullest; something I've never done before. I chose to stand in the arms of my man and now I've made a mental note to buy stock in Germ-X. Otherwise, all good.

The streets are busy, and I learned quickly that you don't walk slow or stop suddenly around New York City. You'll get trampled on. There have been a few times that Saxton had to pull me along, because I would get sidetracked by the amazing city that surrounds us. I won't lie; it's a little scary at times, being in a foreign place, but man, it's so cool. Buildings line the streets and go on for miles. I'm almost positive we won't be able to cover everything in this short trip, but I want to try to fit in everything I possibly can.

"What are you thinking about?" I glance at Saxton as we follow closely behind Tynleigh down the sidewalk. I'm not sure where we're going, and I don't care. I am digging the element of surprise. Walking into the Subway station was definitely not at all how I imagined it to be, but much bigger.

"Just how amazing this all is. You were really holding out on me."

"Nah, it just wasn't as cool the times I was here by myself. It's much better experiencing it with you."

A corner diner comes into view. It looks old, versus modern like the buildings full of glass that surround it. Even the neon sign that reads, *Diner,* is only partially lit up. It has character, and I love that in a place that looks so corporate.

Saxton grabs the door and opens it, allowing both of us to enter first. I smile at him as he places his palm at the small of my back. "Such a gentleman."

"My mom knows everything, even when she's not around to see it. She would skin my hide if I walked in before a woman in seriousness." He pauses as we make our way to a booth. "And I agree with ninety-five percent of what I was taught."

"Geez, that's a high percentage. I'm the opposite. I only agree with about five percent. That makes me curious. What is in the small percentage that you don't?"

Tynleigh sits down on one side of the booth and I take the other side, scooting toward the window to make room. Saxton follows. "Well, they're a little more traditional in some things, like being married before you cohabitate with a member of the opposite sex."

He reaches over me for the stack of menus at the back of the booth, handing me one. I glance at Tynleigh reading her menu in silence with a smile etched on her face, before giving my attention back to the sexy guy sitting beside me. "And you don't agree?"

"I never went against it, and I respect their view on the matter, but over time I have learned that you can find out a lot about a person if you live with them first. I wouldn't condone jumping from person to person, but I think if you're serious enough about someone then you should go all in with semi-permanent arrangements before you end up stuck in something that isn't so easy or graceful to get out of."

In my brief lapse of speech the waitress walks up to the table, introducing herself and taking our drink order; a quick and painless encounter and she's gone. "You never went against it? But what about—"

"Nope," he says, cutting me off as he places his arm around me on the back of the booth. "We never lived together. I had roommates and so did she. Stay-overs happened—sometimes more often than others—but more times than not, when it was time to sleep we ended up separately, which was why it was so easy for her to end up in everyone else's bed I imagine."

"Then why are you so quick to want that with me?"

His eyes divert across the table, I'm assuming at his sister. The left corner of his mouth pulls up. "Well, originally I just walked into it with no expectations, and now that I've had that with you, living separate lives isn't an option for me. There will be times our age difference will cause some problems, but I'll just grow with you." He kisses the side of my mouth, lowering his voice. "Because one day, when I know you won't regret it at your age, I'm going to ask you to marry me, and that's a promise. That's the exact reason I'd go against what my parents believe is right. We might as well start now and make sure we can put up with each other's faults."

My heart doesn't care about age, though, is what I want to scream out. We could date for ten years and I'd still know he's the one, but voicing some of those things might spark a sign of insanity or immaturity on my part, because I shouldn't be in a rush with my whole life ahead of me.

It's hard, holding back when you find the person that makes you want to live with absolutely no restrictions. Everything between us has been fast paced, just like this city, but I love it. Maybe speed is our thing. "Wait, does this mean your parents are going to hate me?"

The waitress sets down a large glass of orange juice before me at the same time she also brings theirs. I grab the straw she tossed down and open it, before shoving it into my glass and sucking down some of the pulp free goodness. It's been a while since I've had orange juice. "Do the three of you need any more time or are you ready to order?"

Panic sets in. I haven't even looked at the menu. Tynleigh looks at me. "Go ahead. It won't take me but a second."

I quickly scan the menu as she takes their order. When no sound registers, I know they are waiting on me. "Western omelet," I say, reading off the first thing that stands out. By the time I put up my menu she's already gone again, leaving us alone.

"They'll love you," he says.

"Mom may be a little opinionated about the matter, but she's not the judgmental kind. Dad will keep his thoughts to himself. He's not much of a talker until he has to be." I glance across the table. "They would never assume it was your idea anyway, even if it was."

She looks between us, stealing a sip of her water between sentences. "Saxton has gone against the grain of their version of appropriate behavior for a while. You don't have to worry, though. They are traditional on some things, but not overbearing. They don't force, just teach. When are you taking her to meet them, Saxton? Can you call Mom while you're here and put her on speaker so I can witness her reaction when you tell her you have a girlfriend? Oh," she blurts out. "You can just introduce her over FaceTime. Then I can see it. That's even better."

I sneak a peek at Saxton at the word FaceTime. I'll never think of that the same way again. He smiles at me, obviously having the same thought. "Why? Should I be worried?"

"No," he says. "T just likes to think she'll react differently than she actually will. It's not that big of a deal."

"You are full of crap. You almost had her in tears last time because she kept asking when you were going to settle down and meet a nice girl. What was it you said again? Oh, right, it was: *the chances of me announcing I'm homosexual are greater than the chances of me dating a female again, let alone settling down.* You broke her damn heart."

I smack the top of his arm, like I do often. Not hard enough to classify as abuse, but enough to get his attention. "Ow. What?"

"That's a risqué thing to say coming from someone that is funny about things close to his hind quarters."

"It was to make a point. I was saying it wasn't going to happen."

"Why would you say that to your mom?"

"Because she wouldn't leave me alone. T is older than me and she bugs her half as much as me. I wanted peace. It worked too, because she hasn't asked me since."

"Sprout, she asks me every time she calls, which is about twice a week. I just find an answer to appease her, so yes, this is a massive drama fest about to go down, and I'm getting front row seats. I may even indulge in popcorn with *movie theatre butter*. It could even shock her so much that you actually found a decent girl versus what you could have picked up, like a stray, that you can just slip the— *and we're moving in together*—thing right in there."

"That should be good news compared to what she's used to."

I catch a glance of the waitress about to head our way. "Hey, Sax, can you let me out? I'm going to wash my hands."

He slides out of the booth, letting me out. "You okay?"

"Yeah, just feel slightly less clean after the subway."

He laughs and kisses my temple. "Okay, baby. Hurry back."

Meeting parents is definitely a conversation or venture I'm not quite ready for. I just got away from parents, so I'm not in a rush. What if they hate me, or think I'm not good enough for him? I'm being stupid, but I want them to like me . . .

Saxton

Tynleigh glances around me. "So . . . I have a secret. How much is it worth to you?"

"Depends. What do you want?"

My phone vibrates in my pocket. I fish it out, waiting for her answer. A text message from a number I don't recognize shows across the screen. "I want you to suck it up and go to Coney Island with me."

"You know I hate lines. Furthermore, you know how I feel about amusement parks and rides. It's not my thing. I can pay to stand around somewhere more fun, like a sporting event."

I open the message, instantly recognizing the hostile person on the other end.

Unknown: I better get a massive best friend call about your epic birthday gift since you so rudely took her away during her birthday. This is normally our thing.

Me: Well hello, Meredith. Exactly what day are you speaking of? Don't you dare pull my dick right now.

Unknown: You better be fucking with me, Saxton. If you don't know when her birthday is after knowing your way around her entire heart, mind, body, and soul, I may very well come through this phone and beat you to death.

The sound of plates being set on the table draws my attention. I put my phone up. The waitress leaves no lag time; quickly ensuring we need nothing else and then leaving to tend to another booth inside of this busy and worn diner.

"Well," Tynleigh says. "Are we going to discuss this or are you going to be glued to your phone the one week I get to see you?"

I look up. "What kind of secret? On a scale from one to ten how important? Ten being if you keep it from me it could possibly ruin my life."

"Definitely a ten." She grins. "Feeling Coney Island yet? I bet Kambry would love to go . . ."

She's dangling shit in front of me. She's asked me to take her every time I come to visit and I always say no. I've never been a fan of theme parks. It could have something to do with me getting deathly sick at one when I was a kid. I have few fears, but that is a top one. They're scary as hell.

I place my elbows on the table. "Dammit, Tynleigh, fine. If I get sick you're in for it, and does this have anything to do with Kambry's birthday?"

"So you know when it is?"

"Well, not exactly."

"Do I even want to know why you don't know her birthday, yet you said she's the girl you intend to marry? Isn't that kind of backward? I thought most normal people established elementary questions on the first date."

"Our first date wasn't really a date. I'm working on changing that. Nothing about our relationship has been orthodox. Oddly, birthdays never seemed to come up. Just tell me before she gets back."

"Fine. It's Friday. You didn't hear it from me, because she asked me not to say anything while you were here."

"Why? A person's birthday only comes once a year."

"From what I gathered she's a very humble person and you bringing her here is more than enough."

"That's stupid. This wasn't a gift. This was taking a step forward like normal couples. I wanted her to meet you. This is where you live."

"At least you know she isn't after your money," she says in a low tone, and then clears her throat. "Food is here. Hungry?"

I glance behind me at Kambry stopped at the edge of the booth, waiting for me to let her in. "What'd I miss?"

She scoots in when I move out of her way. "Tynleigh trying to talk me into Coney Island this week."

The excitement on her face makes me feel like an ass for even considering saying no. "Are you serious? Oh my gosh! I've heard of the famous spinning teacups."

I fold my arms and rest on my forearms on top of the table. "So you want to go?"

"Is this a trick question? Of course I want to go!"

A sudden feeling hits me in the gut. "Kambry, have you ever been to an amusement park? A county fair? Anything?"

She shakes her head. "Okay, baby, we'll go." I grab her hand under the table and squeeze, digging into my food with the opposite. "Eat up. It looks like we have a busy week."

I have my work cut out for me, because moments like these break my fucking heart. I never want her to go without experiences again. It'll just be up to me to give them to her.

CHAPTER FIVE

Kambry

As we walk along the sidewalk, a sign reminds me of something Tynleigh said we could do. *Nails*—labels the top of the building just ahead of us, directly above the glass door. "Hey, Tynleigh, didn't you say you wanted to do pedicures?"

She turns toward me, following my head nod to the building that caught my attention. "Oh, that's right." She winks. "Come on, Sprout. I bet those man feet of yours need to be groomed."

"Hell no. I have something I need to do anyway. You two go ahead and I'll catch up with you when you're done."

I pull on his arm as he tries to walk past the nail salon. He stops and glances at me. "What's wrong?"

"I wanted you to be a part of it. If not, we can do something else."

"It's fine, baby. Go do your girl thing. I can wander aimlessly for an hour."

He gives me a smile, no doubt trying to reassure me it's nothing, but to me, it's something. This is our week, and while I don't mind us being apart from time to time, it doesn't mean I like those times. "I just wanted us to do . . .couple things. We had feetsy time back at the house. Why is this different?"

"I'm going to go put our names on the list," Tynleigh says, walking through the door to leave us alone. My eyes never leave Saxton. Instead, I just scoot off to the side outside of walking traffic.

"*I* play with *your* feet and we are in *private*. No one watches me rubbing your feet, painting your toenails, and sucking on your toes. That's our thing. Mine are not part of the equation."

I'm going to be that girl and I don't give a damn who judges me. My bottom lip turns down, my eyelids fall, and I remember all of those drama lessons. Puppy face at its best in three, two, one . . .

His hands grab my face, tilting it up to look at him. "Do you really want me to go in there that bad? I was raised on a farm. If my dad ever found out I got a pedicure, I'd never hear the end of it. He would shamelessly make fun of me."

"I just wanted to spend time with you," I say in the most pitiful voice I can conjure. "While it's just the two of us. You know . . .with no one watching. Is that a bad thing?"

"Dammit to hell. You know if I go in there you're stealing my manhood: full on castration. My dick will not be worthy of pussy anymore. Do you really want to take that from me? Men are supposed to be rough and tough, not soft and pampered."

"Don't be dramatic. You're with two attractive females. No one will think anything."

"I don't want a guy touching my feet. Period. I don't like my feet being touched at all."

"Says the guy with a foot fetish . . ."

"Judge me if you must. It doesn't change things. You'll have more fun without me bitching the entire time and causing a scene."

"I'll let you fuck me in the ass."

Silence.

My eyes slowly creep down his body, stopping on his groin area. The faintest outline of a snake resides there, trying to make itself known. His hands drop from my face and immediately travel to his pockets. This is one of those moments, where as a woman, I want to hold my imaginary gun to my mouth and blow the smoke from the barrel, because this job is done. Nailed it. Being a woman comes with some pretty awesome super powers when you learn how to use them. He looks at me with so much heat in his stare that I have to work really hard to keep my lips from turning up into a smile. Oh yeah . . . He wants me. Suddenly, I feel parched.

He leans in toward me, his lips inching just outside of my ear. "I think you just decided on our first Tumblr post, baby. Wet for wet, you can suck my dick just before I go in."

I shiver as the tip of his tongue swipes along my ear. "Remember last time? Don't make offers you can't uphold."

"Have I yet?" My eyes close as the words escape on a whisper.

"No, and that's why you have my balls in your hand. Let's do this."

He stands upright and opens the door, again letting me enter first. "Love you," I say in a singsong voice, as if nothing abnormal just happened.

"Love you too, baby. Always will."

And then he smacks my ass as I walk in, catching me off guard, in true Saxton style. My man . . .

Saxton

I glance up at the sky as I hold the door open. "Dear God, help my soul. That girl is going to be the death of me."

I enter, dropping my head in shame that I'm walking into a nail salon. Porn star to pretty boy. I'm shaming all masculine men across the world. If my dad knew I was about to soak my feet in feminine, smelly water, he'd probably bury my face in cow shit just to kick my ass and remind me that I was born a man. I'm going against the grain of nature, all because I can't stand the thought of upsetting her. There should be classes for this: lessons on how to fight pussy-whipped-itis. Yes, I've diagnosed myself.

"Sprout, over here."

I look up at the sound of the familiar voice I've heard over the last twenty-five years, my hands back in my pockets, and working hard not to make eye contact with anyone else in this damn building. Fucking embarrassed, that's what I am. Kambry is placing her purse on the floor beside the middle chair, next to Tynleigh. There is a vacant chair on her other side with a male sitting on a stool in front of it, adding various shit that looks like sea salt as the water runs. I begin to sweat. Kambry nods me over from where I've obviously stopped not far inside the door, as if my subconscious is preparing me to make a run for it without informing my brain.

I finally begin to move, each step becoming slower than the first as I near the area of doom. I take a step onto the platform that acts as a housing unit for the lengthy row of pedicure chairs and just as I do Kambry pulls me toward her chair, and then pushes me into a sitting position beside Tynleigh. Before I can even think her lips connect with mine, just before her tongue enters my mouth, relaxing me . . .and turning me on at the same time. It's heated, but brief.

"What was that for?" I whisper against her cheek as she leans her lips toward my ear.

"I'm switching chairs with you . . .for you. You didn't look like you were breathing when you saw the guy that would have been doing your pedicure. This is the one and only time I'm going to willingly allow a hot girl to touch my man. Enjoy it, and then you can take your frustration out on me later."

She stands upright and takes a seat in the empty chair. I can't take my eyes off of her. She has the hint of a smile, even noticeable only looking at her profile as she removes her shoes. "God, I love you," I say when she dips her feet in the water. I obviously verbalized what was passing through my mind, and now I can feel eyes on me, but I no longer care. The world around us ceases to exist so many times when we're together, having some kind of weird moment. That girl makes me come alive, even after walking dead for so long.

She looks over at me, unable to hide the smile that is taking up half of her face. "I know. Even if you never said it, you prove it over and over."

"Sir. Shoes. Can you remove them?"

I glance down in the direction of the soft voice, just now noticing the beautiful Asian girl around my age sitting on the rolling stool in front of me, her hands covered in latex gloves. "Oh, right. My bad."

I remove my shoes, toe to heel, and then my socks, before placing them in the warm water. Kambry grabs what looks like a remote connected to the chair's arm and then lowers the arm into place. My back arches when two hard balls start rolling against my shoulder blades. "You have to have the back massage or it's not the same."

When the initial shock goes away, it feels pretty damn good, instantly taking my mind off of the fact I'm partaking in girly activities. "This, I might actually like," I say in a low tone as my head falls against the headrest and I close my eyes.

The amazing relaxation of the back massage is short lived, though, when she lifts my foot out of the water, sending my hands to the sides of the chair, clenching in a fist. I hate people touching my feet; always have. It's probably something to do with the fact that I have the most sensitive feet when it comes to being ticklish.

My grip becomes tighter when she begins rubbing some kind of salty scrub all over my feet, but that's not the worst part. She begins scrubbing the heel with some kind of textured square, tickling the fuck out of me. My toes curl. I can't concentrate. It's taking all of my focus to not tell her to cut that shit out.

A finger begins sliding in and out of my clenched fist, ever so slowly, swaying my attention elsewhere, like to my hardening dick, caused by the in and out motion of her finger in the tight opening, reminding me of something else. She's not looking at me, as if trying not to draw attention, but she never stops; at least not before my head is completely polluted with filthy thoughts of what I'm going to do to her later. I have an idea, now that my mind isn't focused on the tickling sensation still occurring on the bottom of my feet.

I pull away, reaching into my pocket for my phone, quickly unlocking it and pulling up the message box. Hers is second from the top, only because of Meredith's earlier message. I type out the first thing that comes to mind.

Me: You trying to make me hard for you?

I press send and almost immediately hear the buzzing of a vibration. I lay my phone face down in my lap, not looking at her even though I can feel her eyes on me. I hear her digging around in her purse, and it doesn't take long before my phone vibrates, signaling a text coming through. I open it.

Kambry: Maybe . . . Is it working?

Nail shop sexting? I think so . . .

Me: I'm hard enough that I could take you in that fucking chair if there weren't so many people in here . . . Then again, I'd consider it regardless.

This time I wait; knowing from here on out they won't take long. The vibration occurs. And so it begins.

Kambry: I love when you become territorial and aggressive about our sex life. I like that you want to show the world I'm yours, and that's why I'd let you, why I do. I'm so wet right now.

Me: Let's fuck.

Kambry: That's kind of hard right now. How?

Me: Just think about it, and it will happen. The mind is a powerful tool. Anything I say, imagine it, and you'll feel it.

Kambry: I'm listening . . . or waiting.

Me: We disappear out the back door instead of the front, into the vacant alley. I've watched your long legs that are barely covered by those tiny shorts and your beautiful feet beside me as long as I could. I want you . . .now. I'm so turned on that I can't keep my hands off of you. Currently they're on your ass, roughly pulling you toward me as I suck your bottom lip into my mouth and guide you pelvis to pelvis into the wall. You taste good, sweet, making me want more.

A few seconds of silence occur, before my phone vibrates again.

Kambry: My hands fall to your waistband, instinctively unbuttoning your jeans. I fall to a squat, bringing myself eye level with your waist. The trail of hair is the first to pull my attention. I place my mouth over it, and then sweep my tongue up it as I work your pants and briefs down just a little, needing to taste you.

Fuck, this is so hot . . .

Me: Looking down at you like this has my heart racing. You have no idea how much looking into your eyes, as you look up at me, makes me want to place your hands on the wall and slide inside of you.

Kambry: Not yet. I want to show you how much I want you too.

Me: Show me, baby. I'm all yours.

Kambry: I grab your dick and pull what remains inside your pants free, slowly stroking my hand up and down. Damn, you're so big, even after all this time, and I love that you're always hard for me. It only makes me wetter. I'm salivating for you.

Me: Put me in your mouth, beautiful.

Kambry: I touch the head to my tongue. It's warm and smooth. My tongue passes over the opening, swiping the small bead of cum at the end. You taste good, but it's not enough. My lips close around it, before I slowly work my mouth on your dick, wetting the underside with my tongue along the way. It always takes me a few strokes to get my jaw just right, but you're always patient with me, never forcing me.

Me: The heat from your mouth feels so good that I briefly lose my train of thought. With each stroke you make my dick wetter. It feels almost as good as your pussy. My hand grips in your hair. I can't help it. Each time you suction and increase your speed I want to lose it, right here in your mouth. And when you use your hand with it. Fuck.

Kambry: You never let me go very long, though, before you pull out of me. Rarely do you let me suck you off.

Me: Damn, woman, I love when filthy things come out of your mouth, but you're right. I can think of somewhere else I'd rather be. Stand for me.

Kambry: Where do you want me, sexy?

Me: Stand in front of the wall, hands against the brick. Give me your ass.

Kambry: What if someone sees us? I didn't wear a dress.

Me: Oh, baby, this won't take long. I love your ass. Just like that.

Kambry: I'm throbbing for you. Take me. I need you inside of me.

Me: Fuck, you feel so good. Hot. Wet. Tight.

Kambry: You're so hard. Shit, I love your dick. Your hand . . .yeah, right there. Hell yes. Harder. Faster.

Me: You like that, baby?

Kambry: Fuck. That feels so good. Don't move. That's the perfect spot. I'm going to come.

Me: I want you to. Come for me, baby.

Kambry: Not till you're ready.

Me: I'm waiting on you, beautiful. I was ready the second you said harder. Yeah, push that ass closer to me.

Kambry: Shit. I'm coming.

Me: Fuck yeah. I can feel you. Now you're going to feel me.

"Not cool, you two," Tynleigh whisper yells next to my ear.

I clear my throat, attempting to cover my hard-on. "What's wrong?"

Tynleigh rolls her eyes. "I wasn't born yesterday. Can you save that for a more appropriate time? Her cheeks are the color of a tomato, and unless you have a flashlight in your pocket, people are going to notice why the nail salon sounds like a vibrator between the text exchanges. Knock it off, hornballs."

I take the opportunity to see just how red her cheeks are. Yep, tomatoes would be an accurate description. Makes me damn proud. I wink at her. *Later,* I mouth, then glance down at her thighs pressed together. *All mine.*

She bites her bottom lip as my feet are being dried, cluing me in on the fact that I'm almost done with this torture. I grab my shoes, putting them on starting with my socks. "Where are you going?"

The guy is still working on her toes. I stand when my shoes are on, and then lean in to kiss her. "There is something I need to go do for a bit, and it's something you can't go with me to do. Don't ask what, because I don't want to have to lie. Just trust that it's for a good reason and you'll thank me later."

Her face falls a little. "Okay. For how long?"

I grab her hand and lace it with mine. "Maybe an hour." She's glancing at our hands connected. "Hey, look at me."

She does as I say. "I remember not all that long ago you mentioned not being able to get your nails done for a long time now and it was something you enjoyed. Right?"

She scans my eyes with hers. "You remember that?"

"I remember everything you tell me. You're important to me. It's okay to do things for you sometimes, Kambry. We aren't filming. There are no rules here. Furthermore, this trip isn't a gift to you. This trip is stepping forward for us and making our own memories as a couple. I know you, because I've paid attention. You don't have to feel like you have to stay up my ass and not have a little bit of time to yourself just because I brought you here. As much as I love that about you, it's not fair to you. Sometimes I want to do things for you or plan things. I want you to have fun. Right now, we have no schedule. If you want to stay two weeks then you'll get it. Let's enjoy it. There are things I want to experience before having to go back on camera. Okay?"

"I love you so much."

I smile. "I'm glad you see it my way . . ."

I kiss her briefly and stand upright, before glancing at Tynleigh. "Don't rush. There's something I need to do. Just call me when you're done and we'll meet up."

She nods. The girl that was tickling my feet is standing as if she's waiting on me to pay before moving on. I point to Kambry and then Tynleigh. "I'm getting theirs too. Ring me up for the works—feet and nails. Just give them the best you got and give me a total so I can get out of here."

She leads me to the register. As she writes up a ticket I drop my credit card on the counter, sliding it to her when she reads off the total. The only thing on my mind as I sign the slip and fill in the tip line and the total is one question: what in the hell am I going to get her for her birthday?

I can't fuck this up. It's been a long time since I've done this kind of stuff, and with this one, I want it to be unforgettable, because she's one of the few people that deserve it . . .

CHAPTER SIX

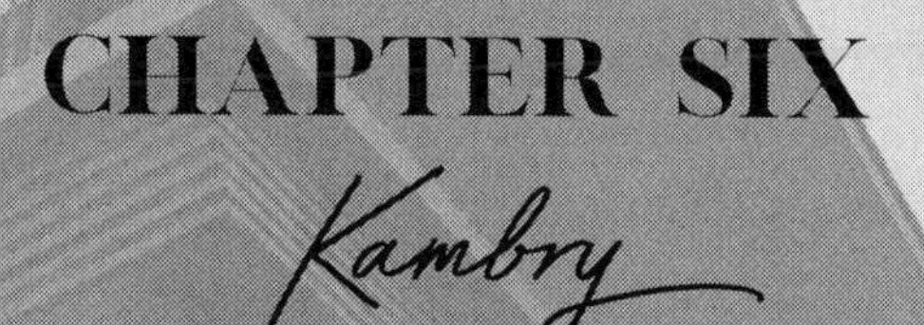

"Where are you? I think I'm where you said to meet you."

"Are you sure? I don't see you."

I look around, trying to find him among all the people. One would think it'd be easy to pick out the sexiest man in the city, since the building he instructed me to use as a marker a few blocks from Tynleigh's office building now stands before me. "Yeah, well, I can't be sure; however, your sister went into her place of employment, so I'm navigating myself from the small set of instructions she gave me just after you. You know it's never wise to leave a blonde wandering around a foreign place, especially when it's a big city. Dangerous things could happen."

"What are you trying to say? Someone could come along and steal my woman?"

"No worries. They'd bring me back. At least that's what my dad always said." I internally laugh at all the times I remember him saying that as a kid when I joked about getting kidnapped on my way to a restaurant bathroom, just after pleading with Mom to go with me.

The line is silent. "Hey, you still there?"

"Even criminals are smart," he says just outside of the ear that's not being covered with an electronic device, making me jump. "No man able to grab ahold of you would be stupid enough to let you go."

My eyes close, focusing on the pounding of my heart inside my chest. "You almost did."

I internally curse myself for still not completely letting that go, but I can't help it. It just comes out at the worst possible times, ruining such an amazingly sweet moment, but in the end I'm just a girl, that's hopelessly in love with this man, and it scares the hell out of me to remember what that very short period without him felt like. It's reassuring to know it was a mistake for him.

He places his hands on my waist and slowly turns me around. I instantly regret my stupid outburst when I see the look in his eyes. Immediately, though, he covers it, revealing one of those panty-dropping smirks as if I said nothing stupid at all. "Yeah, I did that, but I realized the error of my ways and turned the fuck around before you were too far gone. I can promise you this, though. It'll never happen again."

I wrap my arms around his neck as the smile spreads across my face. "Good, because I might even be crazy enough to chase after you next time, pulling on your shirttail as I plead for you to stay."

He kisses the tip of my nose. "I like that kind of crazy."

"So . . ." I say, dragging out the word a little. "Where did you go?"

"That's for me to know and you to find out. It's a surprise. Let me see those digits."

He grabs my hands, inspecting the newly done nails. "Not much longer than natural length and hot pink? I thought girls were more into the long, fancy looking shit."

I glance at them. "I like bold and colorful. I change it up depending on my mood. And I have to have them short. I'm too clumsy for the long. I wouldn't be able to do anything without ripping one off."

"I like it. It's hot. Do your toes look like this too?" He wriggles his eyebrows, making me laugh out.

"With the exception of the length, yes. They are the same color."

"Noted for later."

"Why?" I lower my voice. "Is there toe sucking somewhere in the vicinity of that dirty mind?"

There's that smirk. "Only when I'm ready to seal the deal." He winks. Dang it, he's fine, and he's all mine. "Admit it, though, you loved it. You dream about me sucking your toes, don't you?"

"You may never know . . ." I bite my bottom lip, knowing he will look, and give him a wink in return.

His head falls back. "This is not the ideal place. Shut it down," he says to . . .himself? He looks back at me, a new expression carefully and quickly slid into place on his face. "Now, where were we before this conversation went way off track?"

"Thank you by the way, for the nails, but yes, back to the subject at hand. What if I don't like surprises?" I reach down and pat his pockets. They feel empty, except for the slight outline of his phone in one. "The mystery drives me nuts: no bags, nothing in pockets, so I'm guessing you didn't buy anything?" The hitch in my voice gives away what I'm trying not to admit to, even deep down inside. I refuse to bring up my birthday, or pretend to myself that I want a birthday present, even though secretly I think I do, just to see what that feels like. I want to experience giving with someone that has your heart, but I know Saxton, and he'll go out and buy me something when he's done more than I could ever imagine already.

"I guess I'll just have to keep your mind off of it. I found a place along the way, though." He wraps his arm around me and pulls me alongside him. "I think you'll like it."

"Oh yeah? What kind of place?"

"You'll see."

I roll my eyes. He's not going to tell me hardly anything this entire trip. It's going to lead me to my grave one surprise at a time. He kept his word too; the entire six blocks we walked, side by side.

He opens the door to a rustic blue building, the front decorated with large square windows to each side of the door, and each reflecting a window display behind it. The one that catches my attention is holding an acoustic guitar inside of a case. My mouth starts to salivate. I stop, glancing at it, before moving closer to get a better look. It's beautiful, starting with the gorgeous inlay pattern on the front. It looks used, played, and that's one thing that has me staring. "There are things I don't know about you, aren't there?"

I glance over at him, caught off guard. "Well I'm sure there are things we both don't know yet, as learning a person inside and out comes with time, but nothing that comes to mind. Why?"

He nods toward the window. "You know how to play?"

I shake my head.

"It's something you want, though, isn't it?"

I shrug my shoulders.

"Is this one of those things you get shy about? I've noticed you like music, but I just thought it was a love for listening like most people."

"It's nothing really. Just something I've always kind of kept to myself."

"Does Meredith know?"

I shake my head again.

His face lights up like a kid seeing Christmas lights for the first time. The door slowly closes to the building as he lets it go. "Let me know a part of you that no one else does. Please."

"It's silly."

"No it's not. Tell me."

This is one of those things that make you feel like you're baring your soul when telling someone. It's a scary feeling, because deep down it's always been your thing, and with telling someone you risk feeling stupid, but regardless, he makes me want to tell him things. "I've just always wanted to learn to play. I want to be able to put the music to the pages of words I have written, or will write. I don't know. I just feel like it would be easier if I had a sound to the lyrics."

He looks at me with a curious expression. "You write songs?"

"It's just words on a piece of paper. A song without music is like a body without a soul. It may be able to stand alone, but its reason for existence isn't complete in that state."

He's still looking at me. "You know, like a soul without a mate. Nothing is ever right until they find each other." I'm getting frustrated in his silence. This is why I don't explain my love for music to people. Most don't understand. "It's stupid."

"No, it makes sense. What I'm trying to figure out is why I didn't know this about you."

"Like I said, it's stupid."

"Why is it stupid?"

"I don't know, because unless you make it big there is no purpose behind it, but I don't really want to sing my songs for the world. I just want to sing them for me, but my mother always told me that kind of singing was selfish and self-centered, so I just kept it to myself. I was only allowed to sing in choir or for a Sunday special in church, so it took that passion out of it for me."

"You can sing too?"

"Yeah. Everyone can sing." I play it off, not wanting him to ask me for a sample. Singing along to a loud radio is all I let people hear. It masks your voice, because most people are paying more attention to the artist singing it.

"When did you start writing songs?"

"I picked it up when I was a kid. They kept floating around in my head and I would sing little jingles to myself, so I started writing them down to pass time when I was bored."

"Amazing."

"What is?"

"You. You amaze me more and more every day."

"You're the amazing one, Saxton. You have a heart of gold and I get to exist in its presence. That's what is amazing."

"I'm buying you this guitar."

"What? No you aren't."

He shrugs. "Yes, I am. I'm buying you your first guitar. I can buy it with you or without you, but regardless of which, I'm buying it, so you might as well get a good look at it and make sure it's the one you want."

My shoulders drop. "I never wanted to tell you. I can't even play it. It'd be a waste of money."

He takes a step over and grabs the handle of the red door again, opening it. Hmm, I never thought I'd like a red door. It's almost calming: the red and blue. "I guess we'll just have to sign you up for lessons when we get back home, you know, so I don't waste my money." He winks. "I have a feeling it's a good investment anyway."

I take a deep breath, defeated, and then walk through the door as he holds it open. When I walk inside, I realize exactly what kind of store this is: a music store. In the center is a massive wooden table made to hold plastic crates filled with vinyl records, the outside walls lined with CDs. Toward the back is a counter, guitars of different makes and models hanging on the wall behind the guy occupying the area. I've died and gone to music heaven. I can barely contain my excitement.

I stop just inside the door. "Can I help you?"

I can't speak. I'm still in awe of actually being in here. I haven't seen vinyls in a long time. My mouth opens, but still no words exit. "We're just looking for now. I'll let you know if we need anything," Saxton returns to the man at the counter.

His body wraps around me from behind, his arms crossing at my chest. "Well, what do you think? Was this the kind of record store you wanted to see?"

"It's so much more."

"It won't do us any good to just admire. Come on. Let's look at the guitar."

When he grabs my hand and pulls me toward the window display, I get a closer look than when I was outside. I halt. He looks back at me. "What is it?"

"I can't touch that guitar. You aren't buying that guitar."

"What? I thought we already established this."

"Saxton . . ." My tone lowers, bringing it to a level of reverence. "That isn't just any guitar. That's a Martin D-45."

"Okay . . .what's that mean? I'm not a music junkie. Speak dumb farm boy lingo."

"Think King Ranch edition in terms of the basic Ford. This is like a top of the line guitar. You don't just run to the store and purchase a Martin D-45 when wanting to learn to play. You buy like the D-28, or maybe even just a cheap beginner. This is what the pros use. This is for the people that use it as a tool to make a living. I can't let you buy that guitar. I'm talking like seventy-five hundred dollars at minimum, and that's a standard D-45 base price, not specialized, heavily dressed out, or any kind of customization."

"You know, you're sexy when you start spewing off facts about shit that most people probably don't know. How do you know all of that?"

"I had a huge love for music and a lot of spare time growing up. I guess I was even a little bit of a dreamer."

He pulls me toward it, yet again. "Pick it up."

"No, Saxton, if you want to buy me a guitar you can get something else. This is too much."

He grabs my face, before softly placing his lips against mine. "How serious are you about wanting to learn to play?"

"I want it more than anything, but that's not the point."

"Look, I learned a long time ago that if you keep buying cheaper brands of the best or what you actually want, over time of replacing it you end up spending about the same, so you might as well just get what you want upfront. If it's a crazy number like forty thousand then we'll move on to a different one until you know the route of your career, but if it's like ten grand I can swing it. Without details, I've been saving my money for a while, Kambry. I'm not a spender. I'm a saver, but I'm also kind of enjoying spoiling you a little, so let me. If you want to look at it as a promise of forever like a ring then so be it, but let it go. We can't take our money with us when we die. We'll figure out a budget when we need it, and that's not this week or next week. Okay?"

I don't see winning this argument. "Only if you let me buy you something."

His eyes scan mine, then he smiles, and I know he's going to formulate a plan to appease us both. "Pick us out some vinyls for our collection and you have a deal."

My brows bunch. "Our collection? What collection?"

"The one that will be in our music room at the new house, alongside your guitar."

"I get an entire music room?"

"Might as well have a place to go for lessons. We don't have kids yet."

My mouth falls a little. "Are you sure there isn't something I can help the two of you with?"

Saxton's hand falls from my face as we both look over at the guy that was previously at the counter. A few seconds later a credit card becomes visible between Saxton's index and middle fingers, the front facing the man. "How much for the guitar?"

He takes one look at it and nods for the counter. "Meet me at the back. I'll bring it and we can work out a deal."

He folds up his wallet and kisses my temple. "Go start looking through the records. I'll meet you there in a minute. Okay?"

"Okay," I say, before nervously migrating toward the treasure hunt in the middle of the store. I'm at that point where I'm not sure if I should be excited by this purchase or terrified. If he does this I can never back out. I can never be scared to go for something I've wanted almost my entire life. This is about to be real, and that's scary as hell.

Saxton

"She the one?"

I look back at the man ringing up the guitar. He's looking at me over the top of his glasses as he lays the credit card slip on the counter for me to sign. "Yes, sir. I believe with every cell in my body that she is. Why do you ask?"

"Because this is an awfully big purchase for a man that's not in love. Just figured she must have been special."

"Special is putting it mildly," I say, turning back to look at her after signing the slip of paper. My eyes have been on her almost the entire time she's been looking through the crates of vinyls. She has an animated expression every few shuffles through the stack at hand, as if she found a nugget of gold at the edge of a riverbank. "She's worth every penny."

I tap the counter with my hand without looking back. "Hold on to the guitar for a few, will ya? We'll be back in a few minutes when she's done looking."

"Sure thing. Take your time. I'm not going anywhere."

I walk over to her, wanting to be a part of the moment she's in. I want to share her excitement. "Find anything good?" I grab the front of the stack in the next crate over, beginning to shuffle through each one.

She glances at me with a huge grin on her face. "I found a few, but one is hidden treasure."

The mildest ache in my chest occurs when she looks at me like that, proving without words that she's happy. "Well, let's see it."

She grabs a small stack already pulled out and shuffles through until she makes her choice, placing it on top. When she turns toward me she slides the one on top over, revealing two. I instantly smile when I glance at the one on the left. *Bryan Adams—Heaven,* single in vinyl. The one on the right is *Lionel Richie—Stuck on You,* single with another song of his on side B.

Those two songs hold some very important memories for me. One, being the night we danced on the bar after I gave her a lap dance, and two, was the day on the beach at the house that I will make ours as soon as we get back. I've already contacted my banker and realtor to go ahead and start the process. As soon as it's possible, she'll put my house on the market. I don't need it anymore. What I need is a home, not a house. I know what kind of girl Kambry is, and she wouldn't be happy there. She's a simple girl, and that's one thing that fascinates me about her.

"I'd say you found the winners, baby."

She starts bouncing up and down in excitement. "I thought the same thing!"

I wrap my arms around her and pull her to my chest. "This can be our thing, Kambry. You're the girl I want to travel the world with and find random music shops for technology that is no longer in style. This—seeing you happy— makes me happy."

She looks up at me, hugging the vinyls to her chest between us. "I like when we have *things* that are just ours."

"Why don't we grab a record player and get out of here. I have plans that involve you being naked, and that requires privacy at the present time. If you don't want Tynleigh to hear you, then I advise we get a move on it before she gets home."

Her cheeks start to change in color, showing off the perfect shade of pink. She pulls away, making a run toward the counter, her blonde hair swaying back and forth. "I guess I'll get the player," I yell, but only loud enough for myself to hear.

My right hand unconsciously finds my heart. "She's my person. Please don't let anything happen to her," I whisper in prayer, my eyes briefly closing as I do. "I know it's been a while, but I'll do anything you want to keep her."

And I meant it. I'd give my own life to preserve hers, because that's what happens when you fall in love with someone. Your heart becomes a sacrifice whenever one is needed. I just hope I never have to, because together forever is how it's supposed to be . . .

CHAPTER SEVEN

Saxton

I unlock the apartment door and pull her in quickly, wasting no time before slamming the door with my foot. Setting the guitar case down in the foyer, I grab the handful of items she's currently holding, placing them on the small table. "What?" she asks as she places her hands in her back pockets. My smile grows, but I remain quiet. For what I'm wanting I don't need many words.

Grabbing ahold of her waist, I roughly pull her against me, mildly swaying the two of us as I slip my hands beneath her shirt. I push her against the door, lightly gyrating my pelvis against hers, showing her instead of telling her. Her cheeks begin to flush. "Oh," she says, her voice never rising above a whisper.

"I have plans for you, and for your body. Those plans involve taking my time." I pull her phone out of her purse before taking it off her arm and placing it too on the table. I can feel her watching me as I quickly put it on a Spotify preset playlist, before inserting it into the dock connected to the surround sound. The R&B music begins to play from the *Bedroom Jams* channel, exactly what I need: something soft and sensual, but sexy.

"You still make me nervous," she says when my eyes return to hers.

My thumb brushes down her bottom lip when my palm rests against the side of her neck. "You still make me crazy, and that's why I need you all the damn time."

I mold my lips to hers, slowly tasting and touching them in a way I haven't in a while. My hands grip around her waist again as I kiss her, slowly ascending her sides. Chill bumps begin to develop all over her skin along the way, until finally, I reach the point that we must part.

I toss her top on the floor and lock the door. "We have hours to ourselves. I want to worship your body."

She grabs the back of my head and pulls it toward her, crushing her lips to mine. I dispose of her bra and grip her tits in my hands. They fit perfectly, not leaving an inch of open space in my hands, and just the right amount of overspill. Her nipples are hard, making me salivate to suck them. My mouth travels over her chin and down the center of her neck, before reaching the destination.

Her tiny hands grip around the front waistband of my pants as I slowly and torturously flicker my tongue in a point over her nipple. I switch sides, before continuing downward. Before I make it to her navel, she pulls my phone from my pocket. I smile against her skin, but don't stop until I'm on my knees before her. I glance up at her as I pop the button through the slit of her shorts. Her back is against the door, my phone in hand. Her chest is heaving up and down. "You're so damn hot."

"Funny, I was thinking the same thing about you," I return, as I slide her shorts and panties down her legs until they are in a heap on the floor at her feet. I grip her ankle and pull her foot in front of me, gently removing her shoe, and then set it on my shoulder, giving me better access to the place I want to be. My hand glides up her leg, making its way to her ass for control. Her lips become flush with mine with little effort at all: one slight pull in my direction. I extend my tongue and flatten it against the base of her pink, swollen lips, before lightly swiping over them fully until I reach the top.

She shivers beneath my touch. I repeat, familiarizing myself with her soft skin. On the third time I slip two fingers in, dying to feel how wet she is inside. It's like discovering the prize inside a fucking Cracker Jack box. You know it'll be waiting, but never quite sure what you'll get and just how good it'll be, no matter how many times you've done it before. Even though I know I could go straight to the reward, I still sit here and eat the whole damn box waiting to get to the center—every time.

She never disappoints my ego, always wet and ready to go when I want her.

I spread her lips with my free hand, meeting her clit with the tip of my tongue. She breathes out, verbally confirming I've hit her sweet spot. My fingers pump in and out of her in a slow motion, intentionally drawing it out, matching my tongue to the rhythm. I pull my tongue back inside, long enough to moisten it, but grip the skin that covers her clit between my teeth, tugging lightly. "Shit. Harder. Do it faster."

I glance up at her and the camera to my phone is facing me, her shaking hand working hard to hold it steady. I smirk. "As you wish, beautiful." She screams out as I jab my fingers deep inside, sending her on her toes.

"Like that?"

"Yes. Fuck."

I grip the back of her thigh, lifting her higher on the door to throw her standing leg over my shoulder, spreading her. She grabs the door handle for some support as the back of her thighs rest on my shoulders. I don't want this to take long, because I want her to record until she comes, keeping it short. The tip of my tongue meets her clit again, but this time to work, using the sound coming from her mouth as a guide.

I change the position of my hand as I quickly flick my tongue back and forth over her clit, submerging my thumb inside instead of my fingers, moving my middle finger back until the tight hole between her ass cheeks becomes flush with the pad of my wet finger. I begin massaging her asshole just as I suck her clit in my mouth, hard, allowing it to rub between my tongue and the roof of my mouth. "Shit," she screams. "I'm coming. Fuck."

Her hand grips in my hair, pulling as her pussy begins to contract, lubricating a way for my dick. I always have to watch her face when she comes, no matter what position she's in. It's an expression that will forever haunt you in the best of ways, and even knowing I'll never forget it, I still have to watch it over and over. "Stop. I want you to fuck me. Now."

I lick her pussy, tasting her wetness along the edges of her skin, before setting her down on the floor. "Not yet. I'm not finished, which means you're not ready yet."

I stand, taking my phone from her hand. "You film it?"

"Yes. Probably too long. I was temporarily paralyzed and unable to touch buttons or process that I should stop recording."

"I can clip it, and speed it up if I need to. Short clips are better for what we need. Free only grants a person a sample in most cases." I wink, pulling her toward the bedroom. "We'll upload it tonight."

"Don't we have to create an account?"

"I've already done it. I had a lot of free time when you were getting pampered. I'll put it on your phone later."

"Okay," she says, as she follows along behind me.

I turn toward her to shut the door, again locking it. "You still plan on keeping your word?"

She skims her bottom lip with her top teeth. "A promise is a promise. Just go easy on me."

"Good, because I'm changing the game."

"What do you mean?"

She watches my smile as I walk backward, leading her to the bed. "A beautiful compromise."

"Should I be scared?"

Her expression proves she isn't nervous, not in the least. "You should be prepared."

The blush on her cheeks deepens in color. I lean over her until she falls back first on the bed, but stop myself with my hands. "Prepared for?"

"An explosion. I told you I'm going to worship your body and I meant it." I stand upright and remove my shirt, then begin unbuckling my belt. "It's my job to show you new things, explore with you, and keep our sex life from becoming stale. That's my promise to you."

Her eyes never leave mine, as they usually do when I begin discarding the lower items of clothing, baring my dick. She likes to watch me undress; staring at the goods like she's dying to suck my cock, and it leaves me hard as a rock. But this time she keeps her eyes on mine. "Well it's my job to always meet your needs, to never turn you down, to always love you unconditionally, and to be the best lover I can be. That's my promise to you."

"Why do I feel like we just recited our wedding vows?"

She smiles. "Maybe we did."

"That's not fair. I didn't even get to present a ring first."

"I don't need a ring to promise my heart to you."

I lean in to study her. "So you'd marry me right now, at the drop of a hat, and never regret it?"

"Yes."

"No lag time in your answer. I'm impressed."

"When you let your heart answer instead of your head, there generally isn't."

"You're eighteen, and you've only known me a couple of months at best."

"It doesn't change my answer."

"I'm not sure what to say right now."

"You don't have to say anything. Just know that when you're ready, so am I."

"Kambry, don't fuck with my heart. I have a few years on you. My time and your time could be totally different."

"I don't think you really understand. I just figured it out myself. It first occurred to me when you presented me with a key in a ring box on the beach. As excited as I was to move forward, I was also slightly disappointed it wasn't a ring. I just never had the balls to say anything from the fear of sounding crazy. I'm not sure why I do all of a sudden, but I can't really stop now. We're plotting our lives with the outline of forever. You've asked me to move in with you, to meet your family. We've both proven the thought of being with someone else isn't what we want, let alone the act. You even said I could view the guitar as a promise of forever. I love you, Sax. That's never going to change. Where I come from, even though I never found it there, people in love do crazy things, like get married after only a couple of months of knowing each other if that's what they want. My point is there are no rules in love. If we grow together in our lives, married or not is no difference to me. It's just the world's marker that we're untouchable to other people. If it means no other girl can touch you, then bring it on. I'll marry you before we board the plane to go home. Time is just a bookmark."

I lace my hands on top of my head, staring into her eyes with my heart pounding against my chest. I'm dizzy, not even registering that we're having this conversation butt ass naked. I don't care. "The average person lives what, eighty years, give or take? There is no such thing as divorce in my world, Kambry. We make it or die trying. That's the only option. I won't give you a divorce. Think about it. Can you be with me and me only for sixty years and never once wish you had lived your life more?"

She crosses one leg over the other, resting her elbow on her knee. "The day you walked out of that house and didn't come back I was forced with the option you're trying to entice me with. I didn't want it then and I don't want it now. Having my will to make a life for myself taken away has me very in tune with what I want. Every facet of life is always optional but you. You, I need, with every part of me, forever and ever, until I take my last breath. If I can't live it up with you, then I don't need it in my life."

I pull my fingers through my hair, trying to decide if I'm going to own up to this insanity on my part. I never want her to regret me. I never want her to feel like I loved her too hard. I never want her to feel smothered, or pressured. I also never want to let her go. "Fuck it."

"Uh, not exactly the kind of answer that belongs here. Do you feel like I'm pressuring you into this? That's not what I meant by this conversation. Shit, Sax, I forget. I'm sorry."

"What? Kambry, shut up. This has nothing to do with her. Shit, hold on. I just need to process."

I walk to my suitcase and open the front, before unzipping the inner pocket and removing the contents, holding it in front of my dick. "Aren't we past modesty at this point," she says as she glances at the fabric covering my groin.

"Whatever you do or say, just don't judge me too hard. I'm aware this is fucking insane. Okay?"

She looks confused. My head falls back. "This is where you have my back," I mumble.

"Sax—"

"Kambry, when I left the nail salon I went wandering for a while. I walked in a few shops and made a few purchases, before heading back here to hide those purchases until I was ready to show you, but along the way this one particular store caught my eye. I felt compelled to walk in because there was one more thing I lacked before I met back up with you. I knew they would probably have it. When the lady started asking what I was looking for I told her, so she took me to the appropriate section to show me what they had. I thought it was going to be a quick in and out. It wasn't. For the fucking life of me I have no idea why, but before I could stop myself I went in a direction totally opposite of what I went in there for."

I close in on her. "Then I saw it. The one. I knew in my heart I couldn't leave that fucking store without it, whether I had to hold onto it for eighteen months or ten years. Everything was a guess. My heart was throbbing, I was sweating and scared to death, but I knew it was yours. I knew you were the person that would always complete me, and I was willing to spend the rest of my life proving it to you."

I take a deep breath. "This conversation now is weird as hell. I never in a million years thought I'd actually need it today. My intentions were to lock it in the safe and forget about it. Fuck, I'm rambling. I'm not a rambler."

She straightens her posture when I hit my knee and pull the rubber band off the rolled up shirt, revealing the small, square box nestled inside. I toss the shirt aside. "Baby, I love you. I may have been slow to realize it, or slower than you, but I do. There isn't a day that goes by that I don't think about you. I want to be around you every second that I can. I want to make you happy, whether it's living poor and in love or filming porn together to get by. I'll stay up all hours of the day and night to make your dreams come true, but there's one thing I can't do, and that's lose you."

I open the box, revealing the ring inside. "Kambry, will you spend the rest of your life with me?"

Tears roll down her face instantaneously as she stares at it. My stomach is in fucking knots. I wish I could say this is the first time I've done this. Hell, the first time was at least planned out. This, well, this isn't something for the storybooks or Facebook approved to share with family and friends, but my entire life thus far with her has been one big surprise after another. This one is more from the heart, though. She's the one that deserves the fairytale. Maybe I should have forced myself to wait until her birthday that I was already planning for. Her silence is weakening. Dammit, maybe it's too much.

When I'm about to close it, she comes off the bed in a hurry, mauling me like a bear. The sudden weight shift offsets my balance causing me to fall backward. "Yes. Dammit, yes. That's what I meant to say. I'd be honored to spend forever with you."

The speed effect disappears, giving my racing heart a break. I can finally breathe. "Thank fuck. I felt like I was going to die."

She transitions into a straddle on top of me. "Did you really think I was going to say no?"

"Yes. This wasn't really epic like it should be. It was completely fucking random."

"So, it was perfect and totally us. This is better than epic, but I would have said yes without a ring."

I remove it from the box and slide it on her left ring finger. It travels over her knuckle with ease, stopping in just the place it's supposed to. It fits. My sign it's meant to be. This one is bigger and better than the last one, giving off more light and covering more finger with the overall setting. I had to. I know she doesn't know what it looked like, but I wouldn't have been able to live with myself knowing the one that didn't deserve it got the better cut, clarity, and carat. "That is one tradition I would never allow you to miss."

"I can't imagine a more beautiful ring if I tried. It's perfect."

She leans down and kisses my chest. "It was meant to be yours." She begins to descend until her mouth makes its way onto my dick, sucking in a way she's never sucked me before. "Fuck. I'm a lucky bastard."

CHAPTER EIGHT

Kambry

I swallow as he comes in my mouth, his abs tense as he does. When the spurts stop, I lick my flattened tongue over the head of his dick, leaving no more. At first, the thought of swallowing grossed me out, but now, knowing I'm taking a part of him, no matter what part that is, appeals to me. For some reason he also tastes good to me. "Fuck, woman, that was the best head ever."

"I'm glad you approve," I respond, as I move up his body, wanting more. "Fuck me, Sax. I want you."

He grabs my face and pulls me to him, kissing me. I love his lips. It's always astounded me how perfectly they fit together with mine, and now, they're mine . . .forever. *Forever.* I love the way that sounds. He's my fiancé. For once in my life I wasn't afraid to say what I wanted and it paid off. My heart already feels fuller, bigger, as if it grew in a matter of seconds.

He rolls us over, positioning himself between my legs on this floor. I can feel his dick resting over the place it needs to be, only in the wrong position to actually penetrate like I need it to. "No matter how much you want me, I'll always want you more, Kambry. It's been that way since the beginning."

"That's a matter of opinion."

"You'll get my dick soon enough. I'll make love to you slow and steady or fuck you fast and hard, but first, there is something I want to do. I'm gonna make you feel it; every fucking inch of it."

I clench between my legs. "The last time I heard similar words I was close to orgasm on a bar as you went through the *Magic Mike XXL* soundtrack. I will never hear *Feel it* by Jacquees and think the same again, or any of those songs for that matter."

He reaches over and pulls out the drawer to the nightstand by the bed, removing a small box. "That's great, but the goal is for something to remind you of me or us at least every thirty minutes of the day for the rest of your life."

"What's that?"

"This, beautiful, is something that is about to rock your world, also known as the Marc Dorcel *Geisha Ball.*"

"It looks kind of like one of those torpedo toys you use in a swimming pool."

His massive grin confirms I'm very much wrong in my comparison. "Well I assure you it will cause much more commotion than that would."

"Wait. What do you do with that? Is it like a vibrator or something?"

"It's a plug," he so bluntly says.

"I'm not sure I understand. A plug for what?"

"Your beautiful ass."

My mouth drops. I can feel it gaping. I prop up on my elbows. "But why? I thought you were putting your dick in there. What's the point in that?"

He rubs down the length of his face with his hands. "I can see I have my work cut out for me, which I like, by the way. The rectum is actually known for causing intense sexual pleasure. Like your pussy, it has nerve endings that can cause orgasm. You know how you like when I rub it?"

I nod, my cheeks on fire. "Well, that's why. The rectum and the vagina share a thin wall, hence some women getting double-teamed by men, which will not be you. No other dick is going in there."

I roll my eyes. "I'm just reminding you in case there was ever an increment of confusion. Last time we went down this road we had no privacy, so I couldn't talk you through it as much as I should have. This time it'll be different. I should have started this way anyway. I got carried away with the thought of going in there and lost my train of thought. Are you up for it?"

I glance between the box and him. I'm a little nervous, but I want this. I want to be the person he can experience things he likes with. I want him to be the person I try things with, and we're completely alone. No one is watching, there are no cameras, and we have the intimacy of doing something together. "Yes. Tell me what to do."

"Get on all fours, baby."

I do as he says while the sounds of the box being torn open registers in my ears. I glance over my shoulder when it stops. He's grabbing lubricant from the drawer. "Have you used the bathroom today?"

"Uh, not sexy conversation, Saxton."

"It'll make things more enjoyable for you. I'm your fiancé. Days of awkwardness will soon be gone, so we might as well start now."

I cannot believe I'm having this conversation with a guy, fiancé or not. "Yes. Before my shower."

"Good. Relax."

I turn my head and look down at the floor, between my hands, trying to breathe evenly. He begins massaging my thighs in a circular motion, slowly moving upward until his thumbs are pressing into the center of my butt cheeks. Some of the tension in my body leaves in the weirdest way. "Pressure points," he says.

I love him. He loves me. This isn't dirty . . .

I can hear the cap open and then his thumb begins rubbing wetness over my butthole. My toes curl from the sensation and I can feel throbbing between my legs. I will never understand why that feels so good, but it does.

He begins pressing the tip of his thumb inside, slowly, stretching the small muscle a little at a time. "Fuck," I whisper.

"You okay? Talk to me. Communication is key here, baby."

If I curl my toes anymore, I'm liable to get a calf cramp. "It just feels weird, like I have to use the bathroom really bad. It's a pressure that makes me uncomfortable and paranoid."

He slips his thumb in and out at a steady pace. "I need you to relax your mind, baby. You're over processing it. Don't think. Just feel."

His breath hits my lower back just before his lips touch, causing chills to run up my spine. Then comes his tongue, quickly tracing the vertical contour of my back. I reflexively arch, no longer processing what is going on down below, except that I feel wet.

I moan out when he rubs the head of his dick up and down in the natural lubrication that is awaiting use. In one swift motion he thrusts inside, filling me entirely. A sound of fulfillment escapes my barely open mouth and my fingers claw into the carpet. It still takes some getting used to when he first enters me in positions like this. It's a bite at first, but it's a pain that feels so good it's unexplainable.

Slowly, he pulls out and thrusts back inside, not getting in a hurry. My eyes close, unable to hold them open any longer. He slaps my ass, hard, causing a deep guttural moan to occur. When his fingers trail along the freshly stinging skin is when my mind goes completely blank. I hear nothing. I see nothing. But I feel everything.

His hands disappear from my body, both of them. His dick, however, continues to penetrate me in the slowest torture. I clench around him as he pulls out, using his hips only as a control source. "Shit, I love your dick, Sax."

"That's it, baby. Take it. Claim it."

Something smooth makes contact with my butthole, but this time it doesn't faze me like the first time. Slowly it presses inside, opening me once again. One hand starts softly rubbing up and down my back. He doesn't stop, just slowly inches it in every few thrusts inside of me. The more my back instinctively arches, the wider my ass opens for him, and the deeper it enters, until finally, he pushes it in all the way. It's a noticeable change. "Fucking shit," I scream.

His thrusts halt when he pushes completely inside again. His hands become flush with my sides, before slowly moving upward until he is hovered over me and grabbing ahold of my boobs. I can't explain this feeling: full maybe. I can't breathe. Everything feels like it's sitting at my throat. "You okay?"

He pinches my nipples. "Yes."

"Good." He grabs my chin, turning my head toward him, before he kisses me. "Now enjoy the ride."

Before I can think, he's already upright, grabbing onto my hips. His thrusts begin again, slowly at first, and then the pace picks up, not giving me time to prepare for the transition. "Holy . . .fuuuuck."

"Feel it, baby."

As my body rocks back and forth from his thrusts, something starts moving inside of me, rolling around. "Sax. I can't. Too much. Shit."

He pulls me back until my ass is sitting in his tilted lap. He's sitting on his heels. "You have no idea how good your pussy feels right now," he grits into my ear. One hand scrapes down my torso, traveling over my belly button, and stops at my lips, pressing inside. "You're squeezing me so tight it hurts. Fuck, it feels good."

He thrusts upward, holding me on his lap. My hand immediately goes over my head, behind me, gripping his hair. I can't stand this feeling, being filled from two different places, yet I don't want to stop. I can't stop.

I moan when he bites my neck muscle: the one connecting my neck to my shoulder. My body is covered in a light sheen of sweat. My core feels like it's cooking. He closes his fist tightly around my breast as he begins rubbing my clit. "Damn, Sax. No."

His thrusts are so slow that I can barely feel him moving. "Fuck. I want to come so bad right now, yet I don't."

He holds me to him, no longer moving, but still rubbing my clit at a quick pace. My body begins to lift, unable to handle the mixture of sensations, before automatically rocking back and forth. He forces me off of him. I look over my shoulder. "What's wrong?"

"Turn around. If you're going to do that I want to see your face."

Standing up on my knees, I turn around, facing him. He alters his position into a full sit, leaning against the side of the bed. His eyes briefly close, still glued to me when they open, as I walk toward him on my knees. "You're so beautiful."

"It's because I'm in love with you," I say, as I straddle him. His hands snake around my waist and brush up my back, pulling me closer to him.

"Put it in," he commands, just before his mouth sucks hard on my nipple. I grab the base of his dick and hold it in place, before lowering myself on him. "Godd—"

I moan against his mouth, silencing the word that I know was about to come from his lips, and the only one I can't bring myself to say and still cringe when I hear. I kiss him, deeply, getting lost emotionally and mentally. Every action goes from being controlled to reflexive. I grind myself against him. I can feel both simultaneously: the plug and his dick. The ability to stop disappears and the need to orgasm becomes necessary.

He grabs a cheek in each hand and pulls my ass apart. The balls inside of the plug are rolling, driving me insane. Our tongues tangle. I need his kiss, his taste, like I need water. My hands grip in his hair as the orgasm begins, erupting as soon as it starts. My eyelids clench shut and the moans won't stop. It's like nothing I've experienced thus far. Everything is pounding in my head, and the sensations throughout my body have me tingling and feeling like I'm on fire. I'm so wet we're starting to slip against each other.

When the feelings start to fade and the world as I know it to be comes back into focus, I open my eyes. Saxton has sweat beads on his forehead, his chest glistening from the moisture and heaving up and down rapidly. "Are you hot?"

"Between wondering if you were going to break my dick off and trying to keep from coming until I knew you were, I'm exhausted. There was a time or two I didn't think I'd make it till the end, but as always you timed it perfectly, because I couldn't hold out any longer. That was fucking hot. I love you. Dammit, I love you with all of my heart."

"I love you too, Sax," I say, as I press my forehead to his. "Always and forever."

"Till death do us part . . ."

"And even after."

Pounding on the bedroom door causes me to jump. "What?" Saxton calls out as if it's not embarrassing at all, doing this in someone else's apartment.

"I can't deal with this shit anymore, Saxton. You two are hornballs to be in porn. I need some ass."

"Not what I want to know, Tynleigh."

"Shut up, you little prick! I have clothes scattered from door to door in my apartment and after what I just listened to, you deserve to hear a lot worse. It's been months, and I may possibly be a bitch if I don't get some or you two put a lock on it until you get back home."

"Probably not going to happen."

I smack him and try to get up, but he holds me to him. "What? Do you want me to lie?"

"What I thought, so we're going out tonight. I did an article involving this hit nightclub, basically giving them free promo, so the owner owes me. I'll get Kambry in. Be ready to walk out this door at nine sharp. Cab will be here."

"Fine. We're taking a nap then."

"I don't care what you do as long as you're ready on time."

"Someone is bitchy today."

"Can you blame her? We did just have sex in her apartment. That's kind of rude," I say.

"She's family. She'll get over it. I had to do plenty of shit for her growing up." He releases me, letting me up. An awkward expression appears on my face. I can feel it. One look and he knows. He always knows everything. It's like playing a hand of poker against the one who invented the game. I have no chance in hell. "Need me to remove that for you? Or do you want to try it out for an extended period?" The sarcasm in his tone accompanying a large smirk makes me want to shove something up his ass . . .

"If you ever want to use it again I would say yes. There is no way in hell I'm wearing this outside of the apartment."

I turn and walk toward the bathroom across the room, not looking back. I don't need to with the clomping sounds against the floor as I place my hands on the sink palms down, bending forward.

I look in the mirror when I feel him behind me, his fingers grazing my ass. "Ready to discard all feelings of awkwardness?"

"Rip it off like a Band-Aid."

"At least you know when we're old and gray I can take shit like a champ."

A look of horror graces my face. He laughs, confirming he knows I got his double-edged sword of a joke. "I'm just shitting with you, baby, kind of."

"Would you stop with the shit jokes right now? Fuck. Baby steps. This is equivalent to accidentally farting in front of a guy you've been crushing on forever. I'm mortified of this entire situation now that I'm mentally aware of what we're dealing with. If I knew how to take it out myself I would just to avoid this."

"Girls really fart?"

I can feel all of the color slowly drain from my face. A tear of embarrassment slips from my eye and trails down my cheek. His laugh evolves over time, as if he's trying his damnedest to hold it in and failed. "Fuck, baby, I'm sorry. Seriously, I'm joking. You know nothing you do could ever turn me off, right? I know what you're thinking and I shouldn't have brought it up till after, but even if it did, I would never look at you any different, especially over something that I wanted to do. I'm completely aware of how all of that works back there. You're perfect to me."

He grabs me by the throat from behind and holds my face steady and straight. We stare at each other in the mirror as he removes the plug from my ass. Me—I'm just hoping and praying that damn plug comes out as clean as when it went in. This will definitely go down in the memory book as one of the most embarrassing couple moments. It's a good thing I've already hooked him for life, because this . . .is not sexy.

Saxton

I place my hands laced behind my head, staring at the ceiling, thinking. I'm fucking engaged. I'm getting married. I'm going to have a wife in possibly a few days. Holy shit. How the hell do things change so drastically over the course of hours? I got the girl. *The girl.* The girl of my dreams and then some. Am I prepared to get married and give her everything she deserves?

I won't lie. I don't feel like a deserving man when it comes to her. I'm always going to feel like I come up short because of what she's given me that I can't give her back. Never could. She gave me something that she can never give someone else, even if things hadn't turned out the way they did. She gave me her first, a part of herself. She's never been wild or careless with her heart or her body. What's more . . .is she loves me despite the fact that I've been all of those things. The proof is as simple as purchasing it off the Internet or the shelf of an adult store. Those decisions, those mistakes, those regrets—that part of my past can never be erased like a normal person's can.

That's exactly what they are to me now; for the first time since I became what I am. Now that I've found the person I actually want a forever with, I wish I could erase some of the stupid decisions I made over a girl that didn't deserve it. There's another part of me, though, that is glad I did it, because for one, even though I believe that every person walks into your life for a reason, I'm not sure I would have met her given any other situation. Secondly, I know for sure now that I'll never wake up wanting something outside of my own backyard. I'm absolutely sure that the grass isn't greener in another pasture. I've been there, I've done it, and I've fucked them all. I somehow struck gold with her, and I'll spend every day of my life putting in overtime to ensure that she knows it.

The door to the bathroom opens. I tilt my head to catch her as she walks out, wearing my shirt. "That looks good on you."

"It was the only thing in there."

"I like seeing you in my shirt, but you know that. You can wear them whenever you want."

I turn on my side and get under the covers as she pulls the edge back to climb in. Before she has a chance to settle, I pull her closer to me. "Hand me my cell, will you? I put it on the nightstand waiting on you."

She follows instructions. I pull up the newly recorded video and watch it play through. She snuggles against me when she hears the sound, her eyes glued to the screen with her head on my chest. I smile, trying not to draw attention that I know she's engrossed in our little oral session earlier. I can feel her swallow against me. I force myself to keep my eyes on the screen so I know where to clip it when she begins rubbing her fingers through my happy trail. It's a hypnotic feeling, and she dips her fingers beneath the waistband of my briefs just enough to tease me, before starting the process over again.

When I find the perfect spot I clip it down to make it short, then open the Tumblr app, handing her the phone. "I created the account, but I didn't personalize it. Do that how you want to while we're together and then later I'll add the app to your phone and log you in."

"How does this work exactly? I don't really have any kind of online account."

"It's kind of like your Facebook without all the bullshit restrictions or childish prudes reporting the stupidest shit ever. You can post whatever you want. It's just blogging, but with no rules. We can post dirty or clean. We can blog together or separate, because it'll post to the same account. It doesn't have to be one or the other. This is our couple blog. It's all about us. If people want to follow, then they can, but it's mostly for us."

"I don't have a Facebook, but I think I get what you're saying."

"You don't have a Facebook? Isn't it unheard of for someone over the age of sixteen to *not* have a Facebook? I haven't had time to verify this for myself. We're always together, so I haven't had a reason to get on. Don't get me wrong, I don't really get on mine a lot anyway because I get some random shit on there, but I still have an account."

"Parents." One word is all she says. It's all she really has to say to explain anything peculiar about herself. She's told me enough. It's no surprise anymore.

"Should have known," I say flatly.

She glances at the phone, familiarizing herself with what's on the screen. "Okay, so cover photo. What do you want it to be?"

"Your tits."

"Original."

"You asked. I answered. I like your tits. That's original enough."

She rolls her eyes—or at least that's what I envision her doing based on the silence—and hands me the phone. I stand on my knees as she pulls up her shirt, baring them for me. Her nipples are semi hard, but not all the way. I bend over and suck each one in my mouth, making them fully erect, and then get the phone ready to take the photo. Once the still image is staring back at me, I lay back down beside her and show her the final product to ensure she approves, since after all, the page is both of ours and that would make me an asshole to just assume.

She glances at it as she pulls her shirt back down. "Why do you like my boobs so much? There is nothing really spectacular about boobs."

"Well, to be honest, no man is ever going to turn away a set of tits, because let's face it, tits are amazing, squeezable, suckable man-toys. That's just the way we were wired—visual stimulation and all—but with that said, some tits are sexier than others, and yours are aesthetically perfect in every way."

A curious grin quickly becomes displayed on her face. "Just out of morbid curiosity, what would you do if we had a kid and they became a meal ticket in place of man fun-bags?"

"Uh . . .I will share, not give up. We'll be under a mutual understanding. Meal times they're his or hers, but between, they're mine. End of story."

She laughs. "Well, in that case, post away. I'll just take your word for it."

I save it to the cover photo and hand it back to her. "What about Profile?"

"You decide."

She crawls over me into a straddle, and then starts grinding her middle along the length of my dick. One look at her tits and I'm already sporting a chub. A groan escapes. "What are you doing?"

"Getting you hard."

"Not that I'm complaining, but why? I thought we were in the middle of something."

"We are."

She slides herself down my legs, taking my underwear with her until they hit my thighs. "You want it again?"

"No," she says, as she grabs it in her hand, slowly stroking up and down. Burn. She sets the phone on my chest. "You get the cover photo. I get the profile." She wiggles up my legs until her body is directly behind my cock as she holds it, her black, lace panties peeking through as the shirt sits at her hips. "Take the photo."

"You want the world to see my cock?"

"I want the world to see *my* cock," she retorts. "When a girl is proud of something she shows it off, and you've always had a beautiful dick to me, experience or not. It should be admired from time to time. It's still mine, forever, and I want the world to know every inch of it, and that it's off limits to anyone but me."

I stare at her for a moment, completely surprised and shocked to hell and back. "You aren't jealous? Most girls would be jealous."

"Well, I kind of was forced past that point with the filming porn thing, but as time went on I changed. I learned. Jealousy is something that cannot be controlled completely, but then it can. Yes, there are times that I get jealous, but it would be more in a situation when a girl is within touching distance. When you told me you went to Salem's I had a tinge of jealousy. Okay, a tinge might be putting it mildly. I was terrified."

"I told you, I needed closure, for us. Nothing more. That I swear on my life."

She continues stroking my cock, keeping me hard, and making it fucking difficult to concentrate even though I hear every damn word she says. "I know. The difference is that most girls are jealous over someone else even seeing the goods, I would imagine out of paranoia that what they have they could lose easily, but I know your heart. I can feel and sense how much you actually love me in comparison to what you tell me. I'm not paranoid at all. I know you would never cheat on me, because you know how that feels, and in return I would never do that to you. We're happy with what we have. It doesn't matter if someone else looks, because they'd never actually get it. We each guard what's close to our heart. That's just how much we love each other, so they can look all they want, because at the end of the day it's still mine to touch and have."

We stare at each other. I'm a little baffled sometimes at the things that come from her mouth when I'm not expecting it. Without saying a word, I pick up my phone and position the camera, capturing the image she wants and saving it without even looking at it in a still image. I don't need to. Her reasons are good enough for me. The fact that she's so territorial over me is actually comforting. "What now?"

"We finish what we started," she says, and gets off of me, pulling my boxer-briefs back into place. Not really the route I was thinking with that phrase, but if we fuck this entire trip we'll get nothing accomplished and she'll regret it.

She settles under the covers and I turn on my side to face her, watching calmly as she scrolls through the page. My arm snakes over her abdomen and I pull her toward me so that I can see the screen. She's pressing the different buttons to see what they do, changing colors and fonts here and there. I enjoy this: lying here together with no rush to do anything or go anywhere. Companionship—that's one thing I love about our relationship. It comes naturally.

In the edit section, she begins typing in the space for a bio or whatever a person wants there. I mold her body into mine, reading as she types.

Just a fun-loving, adventurous, sex-crazed couple that decided to blog about anything and everything directly related to us. We love our lives and each other. Follow if you dare, but enter at your own risk. Things may get a little heated from time to time. Clothing optional, love required . . .

She pauses. "What's it called if they share stuff? Isn't that a thing?"

"For Tumblr . . .reblogging I think."

. . . And reblogging welcome. XOXO, Sax and Kam <3

"I love you, Kambry."

"I love you too, baby. Will you upload the video now? How do people see it?"

I grab the phone from her and extend my arms, holding it out before us so we can both see it. "You sure you want to upload this? You can still change your mind."

"I'm sure. This is who we are, Sax. I know it doesn't make sense, but I like this part of our relationship for now: maybe not forever, but right now I do. I want to experience getting to be wild and free, but I only want to do it with one person. You're my person."

"Yes. I am and will always be your person. I just wanted to make sure." I rise and kiss her cheek, before concentrating back on the screen. "Well, the biggest key to being seen is a public profile, which we are, and hash tags. It extends your reach to use common, everyday hash tags that are category appropriate. For example, we don't want to hash tag a porn video on something unrelated to sex or mature content. If it doesn't already exist it will be created, and if it does the post will be added along with everyone else that has used it before. Once you use a hash tag, related posts will be recommended if they also use the same hash tags. There are also other ways users can browse. Think of it as finding your audience. Let me show you."

I go through the steps to show her how to publish a post, starting with the pencil icon. Once the bubbles appear, speaking is not necessary since it's self-explanatory. I choose video and add the clip, saving it. "Here is the caption box where you can write anything you want. Like this . . ."

#Sexting with my fiancé ends very well for me. #Tasty #pussy door side covered in cream. Never too early for dessert. #SexSessions #Afterthecut #SaxtonandKambry #NewYorkRendevous #Coupleblog #Iloveher #Fuckinghotgirl #IEatPussy #OralSessions #PornStarRomance #PornNeverEndsInLove #bigtits #mydickishard #SoTight #dontyouwishyouweremerightnow #sex is next. See you on the flip side. —Sax.

I choose the publish option and wait. It's done. "No going back now, baby."

"Sax?"

"Having second thoughts?"

"I changed my mind."

"I can delete it."

She grabs the phone before I can do anything and rolls over. "Not about that. I want it."

A cheesy grin spreads as she pats my ego without trying. I roll over on top of her. "You want my dick?" I tease.

"That was by far hotter than any book I've read. You have a filthy mind and I love it. I think I'm going to like this blogging and hash tag thing. It gives me a rush."

"I didn't know I was marrying an adrenaline junkie," I state.

She slips her hands under the waistband of my underwear and pushes them over my ass, before grabbing it and pulling me into her center as she spreads her legs. "The high is too good to quit."

"I thought we were supposed to be napping for tonight."

"I'm good with a quickie. We still have a few hours before we have to get ready. We have plenty of time to nap.

She pulls my dick out and aligns it correctly for entry. I lean in and kiss her as I push inside with ease. This is my life. This is where we're headed. We aren't a normal couple. We're an exceptional one. Do we have a lot of sex? Hell yeah. Most would probably think we shoot up with testosterone, but this is us. This is our couple therapy to each other. We each need it for two different reasons, yet still a complement. We don't have to make sense to everyone else. We're moving forward at the speed of a freight train, and I fucking welcome it.

CHAPTER NINE

Kambry

Saxton rubs his thumb over the knuckles on my right hand as we ride in the cab in silence. The city looks even better at night. I can't believe I'm really here, sitting in this cab as we ride through New York City. This is like a dream come true. I keep looking around, waiting for the clock to strike twelve and me go back to the girl I was just as Cinderella did, but it's yet to happen. I hope it doesn't. I love my life right now.

Tynleigh grabs my left hand, pulling it toward the window as she inspects it. "What the fuck, Sprout? When were you planning to tell me you're fucking getting married? After you get the marriage license? When did this even happen?"

I blink at her like an idiot, remaining quiet. I'm not sure what to say even if she didn't direct her question at him. "It was random to be honest."

"Fuck you. A rock this size isn't random. Don't be an asshole. I'm your sister, your family. You're supposed to *tell* me these things at least, *before* you pop the question. I always thought you'd take me with you to purchase the next—"

She silences her own statement. He squeezes my hand. I can tell it's a reflex action. I won't lie and pretend that the mention of his ex doesn't hurt a little, but that's a part of his past that I accepted with him. It doesn't make me love him or want to marry him any less. This I want wholeheartedly. I don't give a damn about my age. Still, it puts a damper on things to know it's your first and not his, but I'd never admit that aloud. At least he didn't actually go through with marriage.

"Tynleigh, everything just happened. It wasn't planned. I saw the ring and knew it was hers, so I bought it. I was prepared to store it for a few years. Then, one thing led to another. If this is what she wants then I sure as hell have no reason to wait. She's the one I want to spend my life with. End of story. No one else knows yet, so you're the first anyway."

I glance side to side between the two of them, staring at each other, and neither cracking a smile. This doesn't seem like the happiest way to tell someone you're getting married. Isn't it supposed to consist of champagne and giggly girls jumping up and down in excitement?

Out of nowhere a high-pitched scream occurs, causing my ears to ring, before I'm pulled into a hug so tight I can barely breathe. "Welcome to the family! This is great. Beautiful ring by the way. Good job, Sprout. When's the big day?"

I clear my throat, trying to breathe evenly. "I—" My voice comes out in a strained whisper. She releases me, giving me air.

"That's up to her," he finishes for me.

She looks at me. "Well?"

My mind is running a million miles a minute, trying to process the simple question at hand. The words come out before I will them to. "How's a New York wedding sound? Is it easy to get married on short notice?"

Her grin starts small and spreads rapidly, covering half of her face. "Holy shit. Seriously? The most logical would likely be to go to the Justice of Peace and let the court marry you, but we can still get you a dress. No girl should get married without a dress. I can take you."

"I can take her, Tynleigh," Saxton says.

She gives him the most disgusted look I've seen on her yet. "You aren't supposed to see the dress until it's time. Just because you are going the route of a modern day shotgun wedding doesn't mean we have to bypass all traditions."

Her smile falls. "Wait. The two of you aren't going to drop the—*we're pregnant*—bomb on me, right? That's not the reason for this sudden engagement is it?"

I try to hide my smile. She catches it. "Oh God, seriously? Why are we going out then?"

"I'm not pregnant," I interrupt. "It does kind of seem that way, though, doesn't it?" I laugh, unable to help myself. "I just decided that if we love each other, why wait. I guess I'm more of a simple southern girl than I thought."

A sigh of relief from her noticeably occurs. "Shit, that was a close call. Not that I don't want beautiful baby nieces or nephews someday, but I was planning a party night with my brother and his newfound soul mate. That would have hindered the plans a little." She becomes quiet for a moment. "Damn. No wonder the two of you have been humping like rabbits. This makes me feel better. At least now I know there is a reason. This makes that behavior totally normal."

"Today is no different than any other day," he says, matter of fact.

"Shhh." She puts her hand up. "I can pretend I'm not in a dry spell and you are just celebrating your love. Leave me to be in peace."

The cabby keeps glancing in the mirror at her, making it hard to contain my grin. My nose crinkles. Eww. I'd choose the dry spell over that any day, but based on the way she looks I'm going to say he's dreaming in color when he should stick to black and white. Any dry spell that girl is going through is self-induced. She's gorgeous.

The car stops curbside, drawing my attention from my thoughts since we stopped moving. I look out the window at the large neon blue lettering labeling the building, giving it a name. The line is long, people waiting behind the poles and rope that keep them pretty much single file at the door. Saxton's arm reaches in front of me, handing cash to the driver.

A nudge occurs on my shoulder. Tynleigh hands me an ID, upping my age quite a few years. The girl's features at first glance are similar to mine, but we really don't look related. I glance at Tynleigh, confused as to how this is supposed to work. "She's a coworker that had no plans tonight and it will get you in. He knows we're coming, but he has to glance at an ID."

I nod my understanding as Saxton reaches for my hand, already standing on the outside of the door. I'm nervous. I'm in a foreign place, unlike the club back home. I really don't want to go to jail. What the hell am I thinking? I wanted to live. This is living. This is elementary stuff to Meredith. She was getting in clubs at seventeen.

I slide across the now vacant seat, letting him help me out on my feet. As I stand, he pulls me against his front so he can whisper in my ear. "I didn't tell you earlier, because I couldn't, but you look stunning. I'm not sure whether I love or hate this dress. Why have I never seen it before?"

The short, satin, black number he's referring to is narrow on the shoulders and deep cut V-neck in the front and back equally, stopping just above my navel in the front. Cleavage is not scarce and a bra is not an option. Nothing in this dress is left to the imagination between the lack of fabric and the thinness of the material.

It took me quite a while to get enough guts to walk out of Tynleigh's room from the floor length mirror I was standing in front of. She said it would make me look older, so after a pep talk here I am. Dressed like this in my small town, it wouldn't take but one glance to classify a girl as a harlot. Stores didn't carry pieces such as this around home. Even the night I wore the leather bra and skirt with the short jacket looked more appropriate than this, but why I'm not sure; maybe because this is ultimate sex appeal wrapped in a skimpy bow. I think it was totally worth it, though, seeing the look on Saxton's face when I walked out of her room standing tall in the dark pink, bootie heels that accompany it. I had to scoop his jaw off the floor, and he's been quiet about it since.

"It's your sister's. She suggested it to help with the age I'm supposed to be, clubbing in New York City." His hand skims my bare back, his fingertips causing my skin to feel like it's being zapped by electricity.

"This may be one thing she isn't getting back. Black is your color, baby."

"I'm glad you approve," I say, nervously, barely able to function with him rubbing me the way he is. "I thought you'd be upset with how revealing it is."

"I'd be lying if I said I didn't want to say something upon first glance, which is why I've remained quiet this long, but the longer I see you in it, the more I remember that conversation earlier. That dress belongs on your body, and you're mine, so I may as well show you off and enjoy the looks when they realize you aren't here alone."

I wrap my arms around his waist, clenching onto the back of his shirt, not wanting to move. "Let's roll," Tynleigh says in passing, keeping her voice clipped.

Saxton places his arm around me as Tynleigh makes her way to the doorman, giving him our names. She instantly flashes her ID, and the two of us follow suit behind her when he moves the rope to let us through.

The door closes behind us as we walk inside the mostly dark room, only lit by the white twinkle lights spread all over the ceiling and the blue and pink lights dimmed and alternating above each seating area, keeping it to an elegant feel throughout the entire building. Now I understand why she wanted to dress the way she did. No one is dressed simply here.

I'm frozen as I take everything in. The music is loud, drowning out the voices of the bodies packed inside. The bar is in the middle, reflecting the theme of the rest of the bar, elegance to no end, the bartenders dressed in white button-downs and black pants, each with a long black tie versus a bowtie. My head falls back when the balcony surrounding the building catches my attention. It reminds me of a huge loft taking up the entire upper half of the building structure.

White catches my attention. Sheets, or curtains, are hanging from canopy style beds and secured in each of the four corners, revealing the white linens covering the bed. My body rotates in a three hundred and sixty degree turn, taking in the entire floor. Replicas of the bed are scattered as far as you can see, all currently exposed except for the two that the sheets have been pulled, closing it off.

I find Saxton and tug on his shirt. He lowers to my height, his ear next to my mouth. "What are those?" I ask, pointing to one of the beds.

"The beds? Those are private reserves, kind of like cabanas on the beach."

"What do you do up there?" I don't know why I'm so curious, but I can't look away from the one in use.

"Whatever you want."

I turn to look at him, my bottom lip lost between my teeth. "Anything?"

He shrugs. "Yeah. This is New York, baby. You aren't in Alabama anymore. You're way beyond *The Bible Belt*."

I stare into his eyes and remain silent, trying to figure out what I want to say. He smiles, already reading me like an open book. "You want one later?"

I nod, shamelessly. "It looks fun."

He winks at me. "Anything you want, beautiful. Go to the bar with Tynleigh. She knows what I want. I'll go reserve it for the night before they fill up."

Again I nod, glancing at it once again. He grabs my cheeks and lays a kiss on me—a hot and wet one—taking my breath away. "What was that for?" I ask, my lips tingling and raw.

"For being mine."

He releases me and walks away, leaving me standing here watching him as he does. It's hard to function when he's not near, and that's a scary feeling. The longer we're together, the more I need him. I'd do anything for him, including drain my own body of blood if I knew it'd save his. "He really is different with you. It gives me a little bit of hope for a future."

I glance at her as she hands me a champagne flute. "Celebratory drinks first. How are you liking New York so far?"

I take it and sip the rim, letting the bubbly liquid enter. "It's amazing. Seriously. I can see why you live here. Is it always so . . . I don't know, alive?"

"Always," she says. "There is always something to get into. People love to party, to be vivacious and free. You guys really should come back for New Year's Eve. You'll never forget it as long as you live."

"That would be a dream come true. I used to stay up and watch the ball drop on T.V., wishing I was there."

"Girl, you're family now. Come anytime you want, with or without him. My place is always open for you."

"I'll keep that in mind. Thank you." My mind begins to wander, as it does so often. It's a weird quirk I have, because it happens so frequently. "Can I ask you a question? What did you mean earlier? When you said it gives you hope."

"Nothing really. Just that him and I are a lot alike in some ways. We fall hard and love unconditionally. When you have a heart like that, getting hurt is more like becoming a live sacrifice than a simple break. We both grew up wanting that kind of fierce love that our parents have, but the world has ways of showing you it's rare." She tips back her glass, her throat contracting as she swallows. She shrugs her shoulders. "I don't know. I guess we both had become content with letting the possibility of it pass us by, no longer seeking a stopping point in our current lives, but you've restored that in him, Kambry, and in turn restored it in me."

"Have you ever been in love, Tynleigh?"

I'm not sure where my nosy outburst came from. It just kind of slipped out.

She downs the rest of her champagne. "Love hasn't found me yet, Kambry. It has to be two-sided to work. I'm still having fun. You want another?"

I look down at my half empty glass, and then I glance at the busy bar. "Sure. Might as well if you're going."

I glance around after she slips away, people watching: the flirting, the looks between them, and the bodies grinding against each other appeals to me. There is something I've loved about clubbing since I moved out on my own. I'm not sure what it is. I suppose maybe it's the freedom in the night to do whatever you want, be who you want to be, and act the way you want without anyone telling you otherwise, or judging you. To most involved you're just a body in a room they'll never see again.

As I stand alone, I pull out my phone from the clutch in my hand, unlocking it. Quickly I snap a photo of the gorgeous diamond on my left ring finger, before preparing my first Tumblr post. I still am clueless, but here goes.

First night out as an engaged woman! I can't believe I'm marrying the man of my dreams. #LuckyLady #DiamondsAreAGirlsBestFriend #HeDidGood #LovingNewYork #Hopelesslyinlove #ILoveHim #ShowOff #ClubSexLater #BeJealous —XOXO, Kam

I post and quickly look through the notifications. The video from earlier today has three reblogs and six notes. A few catch my attention.

BigAl35: *Wishing I were you right now, bro.*
Marriedcouple15: *Nice video! Following . . .*
Sinisterslave: *Classy women don't allow men to demoralize their bodies for the world to see. Any good man doesn't want a woman that acts like a whore; at least not for life. Don't be a slut and you'll find a real man.*

"Wow, what an asshole."

"What's the matter?"

I jump from the soft words spoken into my ear. "Shit, you scared me. Read this," I say as I turn around, showing him the post. His eyes scan back and forth quickly, before he looks back at me.

"Just a jealous douchebag. I'm sure it won't be the last. Don't worry about it, baby. If it bothers you we don't have to post. I told you we don't have to do this."

"What? No, fuck him. I don't give a shit what some asshole thinks. I have a real man. I've never questioned that. It just took me by surprise that some people are so blunt about their opinions."

"When you become a public emblem for sex, or whatever type you are, you also become a target for the haters. That's just the way it is."

I lock my phone and place it back inside of my clutch, returning my focus on Saxton. I grab his waist and pull him against me. "How did I get so lucky?"

He wraps his arms around my shoulders. "Shit, girl. You aren't the lucky one. You just got stuck with someone that wouldn't let go."

"Not true."

"You two are sickening. God, I feel like I signed up for a couple's tour. I'm about to catch a ride to singles' island. It's cute for about two seconds and then I want to gag even though I love you both." Tynleigh shoves a drink at me, forcing me to grab it, and does the same with Saxton. All three match. It doesn't go without notice. "Don't ask me what it is. Just drink it. Whether the two of you like it or not I'm getting you wasted. I need something besides all of this sappy shit reminding me a million times a day just how single I am. I need you two to be wild for just one night. This can be your bachelor . . .and 'ette party of sorts. We can even pretend we're in Vegas if you want."

"Okay," I say, shrugging my shoulders and pulling the cup toward my mouth. She places her hand over the top just as I bring the rim to my lips. "What?"

"Just one question so I don't regret this later. Do you have any underlying medical conditions?"

My brows scrunch. "Not to my knowledge. Why?"

"Just checking. Drink up." She moves her hand and I again try to drink but Saxton pulls my wrist, moving the cup toward him, causing it to slosh inside of the cup and almost spilling some of the drink.

"Fuck no. What's in the drink, Tynleigh?" Saxton's voice is razor sharp and laced with venom.

She rolls her eyes, as if she isn't scared of him at all. Funny, because that tone has my hair standing all over my body. I've never heard it from him before. "The same thing that's in yours." She stares into his eyes; boring into each other so hard I feel it. "Just *trust me.* It'll be fun. I would never hurt her or you. I vow with my life."

They continue to stare, questions being asked and answered leaving me out, moments passing as she sips her own drink, before he finally breaks the silence. "What about your damn job? You're telling me they don't periodically check?"

"Oh, don't be stupid. I'm not going to, although, I wish I could. I miss those days of occasional carelessness, but I have to somewhat adult tonight. You know . . .grown-up career and all. It's better this way. I can keep my eyes on the two of you." She winks, my curiosity about to kill me, before she carries on. "Neither of you do, though, with your cool-ass jobs, so I'm going to live vicariously through each of you. Please," she begs. "I saw you reserve a bed. Call it an early wedding present. You'll thank me later."

"She's never done this shit before, Tynleigh."

"If I recall correctly, neither have you . . ." The pitch of her voice is different, intrigued, and ready to play a game. She's instigating. "It's sad. I tried so hard."

"Not the point I'm trying to make. You don't just experiment on my wife to be for an hour or so of fun. You don't know how a person's body reacts to that shit. It's all fun and games until someone gets hurt."

"All things are fine in moderation, Saxton. Isn't that what we were always taught?" She winks dramatically. "And I only buy from trustworthy people. You, little brother, are being a drama queen."

"Is it drugs?" I interrupt, unable to stay quiet any longer.

They both look at me at the same time. Finally, I'm no longer the invisible girl. I raise my hand—the free one that is. "Hello, I'm Kambry, remember, party of *three*. Why don't you just explain and let me decide. Y'all are kind of treating me like a child and I don't like it."

Saxton's eyes soften. He releases my wrist from his clenched hand. "Yeah, okay. I just don't want anything to happen to you. Can you understand that?"

I nod, urging him to continue. "Tynleigh used to have this thing back in college. She liked to party with E from time to time, along with a vast majority of teenagers and young adults, high school and college age. It's kind of known for its enhancing effects and heightening party mode."

"Like you would know," she interrupts. "You wouldn't ever try it. You were a little bit of a golden boy back then.

"Shut up, Tynleigh. I just didn't roll with that kind of crowd, or *roll* for that matter. Don't piss me off just because I didn't party your style."

"What's E?"

"Ecstasy," he responds. "You aren't missing anything."

"Like hell she isn't! Don't put ideas in her head just because she's in love with you and you're a little conservative in some areas while liberal in others. Let her discover the world her way, Saxton. Your job is to be by her side as she does. Everyone should try it once."

I'm surprised I'm not even mentally fazed by this conversation. I'm more interested than shocked. His head snaps toward her. He's clearly mad she's egging this on, but only one portion of this conversation is really registering in my head. "You've never done it?"

He looks at me, his eyes locked with mine. I have him now. It's that connection we form occasionally where his soul can communicate with mine. I know that's what it is with every cell in my body. Things become very different when we're like this. I open up in ways I've never thought possible. He's totally disregarding her now. "No, I've never rolled."

"Rolled?"

"Yeah, a term when you party on E; like a discrete code. The ones that are very aware of what it means take it just like when you say you're getting drunk."

"No girl besides your sister has ever asked?"

"Yes. It's known for enhancing certain . . .activities."

"Why didn't you . . ." I swallow. "Do it?"

"I never wanted to."

Adrenaline begins pumping through my veins, strengthening every vessel in its path. A high is already beginning to form. "Do you want to with me?"

His jaw tightens. He's nervous, a little angry, and there is fear present. I can feel it. His head twitches to the right, as if he's about to tell me no. "Don't lie to me. Don't try to protect me from things I may possibly want."

The heel of his hand goes for his forehead, rubbing circles just under the gelled front. "Just think of every sense or emotion being heightened to the most sensitive degree: touch, sight, desire, happiness. Sex as you know it becomes foreign, and you get to explore each other's bodies in ways you've never explored before; every sensation is new, *enhanced,*" she chimes in.

My entire throat feels dry. "Do you want to with me?" I ask again, wanting an answer.

"Yes," he says, with finality in his tone that has me shaking.

"Me too," I say, relieved. I really wanted him to want to experience something with me he's never experienced with someone else. These moments are few and far between. Sure, it's not honorable to most people to try drugs, but to me it's no different than trying a glass of wine. I guess when someone tells you that you can't for so long, you just want to finally say you can. As long as I don't make a habit out of it, it's fine.

We raise our glasses at the same time, each taking a sip in unison. "Hell yes," Tynleigh says. "This is going to be fun."

The flavor is fruity. It tastes good: just the right amount of sweet with a balance of bitter thrown in. After a large sip, I toast my glass with his. "Here's to forever, baby."

He smiles. "Nothing less."

Saxton

My body feels hot. I want to take my clothes off. Fuck. The music is pounding in my head, clearer than it's ever been before. Either they have a badass sound system or it's me. I don't know what time it is, or how long it's been, but what I do know is that I want her to fucking touch me, and I need more than the sliding of her hands across the back of my jean-covered thighs as she dances to the music in front of me.

Grinding against her to the beat of the music, my front aligns to her back as it has in a repetitive motion since we started. Her ass rubs against my crotch for the umpteenth fucking time, making me want to whip my dick out right here. I could so fucking easily, without a care in the world.

Her head falls back on top of my shoulder, her arms rising above her head.

My hands slide down the sides of her body, gripping ahold of her inner thighs. "Mmm. Touch me," she says.

My face tilts to get a look at hers. She's grinning from ear to ear, before her hand grips the top of my hair, pulling roughly to where she wants me. "I said touch me. I just want you to *touch* me."

"I am touching you, baby," I say, as I swipe my tongue up the side of her neck, a salty taste remaining. Her dress is short; especially with her in this squatting position, opening her legs up more. I can feel her heat; so close to where my hands are perched on her thighs, holding her against me.

She willfully turns in my arms, that beautiful smile still plastered on her face. It's been there for a while. If I had to guess it started growing about thirty minutes after we trashed our empty cups. I was a little worried when I agreed to this, my mind focusing heavily on overdose, but Tynleigh is right. I shouldn't ever assume what's best for her. Instead, I should remain by her side, like this—equally fucked up. I can see she's happy. Most may be the drugs, but anyone that knows a thing or two about drugs knows that E only enhances the emotions that are already there. If she were depressed, she'd most likely be sad.

Her fingers begin brushing against the bare spot at the bottom of my hairline, spurring chill bumps. Her body grinds against mine, pelvis to pelvis before she sways, rolling and moving in that uninhibited way I've only witnessed a few times at most. It's hypnotic, watching her like this.

Her face is flushed, her chest glistening and wet. Her hair is starting to get a wavy texture from the sweat. She moves a little to her left, bringing one of my thighs between her legs. I thrust my hips from right to left; plunging my thigh between her legs further. She uses it as a cue to rub harder against my jeans. I want to fucking strip her bare and watch her do this. She alters position a little again, but this time not by direct choice.

My eyes dart over her head to the male now moving up behind her, his hands taking residence at her waist above mine. My jaw steels, knowing he's touching her and dancing on her. He's clearly fucked up and just wanting to dance, because he's not even looking at her directly, but more so at the floor. It's the only thing that is keeping me from decking him right now. That and the fact that I just want to fuck her brains out as I rub my body on hers inside of a happy, naughty bubble with nothing but skin. The urge to touch her body with every damn limb is becoming immense.

He moves in closer to her when I don't stop him, his crotch touching her ass. My eyes never leave his head, until finally, she forces me to look at her. "Does this bother you? If it does, just tell him to move. I didn't ask for this."

"No," I lie. "It doesn't fucking bother me at all. At least he has the decency to do it in front of my face."

Her leg hooks around my waist and one hand moves to my hip, pulling us closer together. I clench her sides, before moving up her back, due to her ass being blocked by another man's jean-covered dick. "I can tell you're lying, you know."

"Maybe I am. I'll never admit it one way or another. He's not disrespecting me. More importantly, I'm not that guy."

"Yes you are, and that's one thing I love about you. You're jealous and paranoid, even when you don't want to admit it, but it's what keeps me from those same emotions a lot."

Hip-hop songs change one after the other. I stare at her, now remaining still as my fiancé gets dry humped from behind along to the beat of the music. My heart doesn't know whether to beat or stop, even being fucked up; no doubt a side effect of my past. I trust her, and I'm standing here watching, but the fucking past will never completely leave me alone. The last night I was in this exact position, newly engaged, my entire world came crashing down in the matter of hours.

A female walks up behind him, forming a train, and begins grinding on his backside as he grinds on Kambry's. My face is tilted down to look at one beautiful woman that I've called mine for a while now. Her leg drops from my waist and moves between mine again, before her body begins to move in a sensual way. She's doing more of the movement this time. She grabs my hand and places my fingertips at her collarbone, slipping it beneath the satin fabric, and guiding it along the seam toward the middle of her chest.

My eyes briefly close as the tips of my fingers pass over the globe of her breast. Electricity existing between two conveyors: that's what it feels like. When they open, the lights begin pulsing with the beat of the music around us. Our eyes meet and something snaps inside. Something I've never felt before washes over me: peace, relief, and all-consuming happiness. But the crazy part—it's coming from her. She made me feel it before the words exit her mouth. "I'm not her, Sax. I'll never be her. I'll never do to you what she did to you, whether in front of your gosh damn face or behind your fucking back. I love you with every single part of me. I can't even fathom someone else touching me the way you touch me."

"It's not fair to you. I'm trying."

Her index finger crashes against my lips. "Shhh. You were hurt. Wounds take time to heal, even when you're nowhere near the cause of it. I'll remind you every day for the rest of our lives if that's what it takes."

I don't fucking deserve her. That's the God's honest truth. I will never really deserve her, but she still wants me, even in all of my fucked up paranoia. I grip the back of her thigh in my hand, pulling it back to my waist, hiking her dress up, her middle pressed firmly against my crotch, and then I start to dance, joining in.

At some point you meet someone that doesn't question your trust. She's the once in my lifetime person that I could share her with another man on the dance floor and not worry about what could happen after. Because I know deep within my bones that even if I was fucked out of my mind worse than I am, I would wake up the next morning with her right by my side where she started. And that's the one and only reason I'm putting all of my insecurities aside and taking the plunge to make her my wife, because losing her would be the greatest catastrophe I've ever known.

CHAPTER TEN

Kambry

My body is loose and my mind is free. I love music, have all of my life, but no music has ever blasted my soul the way it has tonight. The lyrics openly flow through and embed within me, and some part of every song reminds me of us: Sax and me. I think tonight I finally got through to him—how serious I am about us. I'm not going to go as far as to say I liked another man dancing on me, but I think it was a step taken for us, and something we desperately needed.

I knew deep down he still worried that I'll betray him. I'd probably be in the same position if I were him, but the one thing I want is to earn his trust. When he looked at me, I bared my soul without words; hoping deep down it would work. I've never really understood the whole *soul mate* thing. It just made no sense to me, sounding far-fetched that one person could be your chosen one for all of eternity. I'm a home-grown church-goer, a believer in the unseen, and am a supporter of spending a life with one person at a time, but the whole concept of one person actually being made for you specifically was a little of a stretch even for me. But now, I don't know, maybe it's real.

His hand begins to migrate up my thigh, underneath my dress. We've been dancing for a while, our bodies covered in sweat. I'm a little relieved ole boy finally turned around to take advantage of the short skirt at his tail, because even though I didn't admit it, it made me uncomfortable to have him so intimately close.

Saxton's fingers wrap around the small strip of fabric that makes up the waist of my thong, trying to pull it down. "I want you so bad right now. Why do I want you so fucking bad all of the time? Kambry, this can't be normal, going from the inability to get up naturally to a near constant hard-on and thinking about sex around the clock."

"Who wants to be normal when we have this?" I ask in a whisper, our lips merely an inch apart.

"This is better than normal," he says, and kisses me suddenly without warning. I moan into his mouth when he digs his fingers into my skin as he holds the underside of my thigh. His free hand wraps around my lower back and he picks me up, my legs reflexively wrapping around him.

Our lips part, even though I don't want them to. He begins to walk through the dark crowd, the only bright light being the strobe light making a show around the dance floor; the rest of the club still dark like when we arrived. He glances around me every few seconds. "Where are we going?"

"That bed I paid all that money for is calling. I'm either going there to be discreet or I'm about to fuck you in front of whoever is standing near. I figured this was the most appropriate option."

"But I'm not even tired . . ."

"Neither am I, but these beds aren't for sleeping. I guess that can only mean one thing."

"What's that? Marathon until we end up in a sleep-induced coma after sex?" I ask, intrigued as he sets me down on the floor.

"Not tonight. There is no race, but I am going for distance. Tomorrow your pussy is going to be sore."

I finally notice the large man guarding the entry to the bottom of the stairwell, where we're currently standing. Saxton reaches in his pocket and hands him a small plastic oval with a number branded on the front. The man takes it and hands him a key with the matching number on the same type of plastic attached, and then moves out of the way of the steps.

Saxton takes my hand and begins climbing them one at a time. "What's the key for? I thought it was just a bunch of beds . . ."

He smiles at me, flashing those gorgeous white teeth. "I suspect you're going to be loud. I reserved the private one. Soundproof walls sounded enticing."

My heart begins to race, clenching onto my clutch as I follow him up. I'll be glad to rid of it. Now I understand the need for women to stash things in the band or cups of their bras.

"That does sound a little . . .exciting." My voice comes out in a way that makes me sound winded. I mentally roll my eyes at myself, leaving my muscles out of the equation. I'm such a pathetic girl when it comes to him, and I don't even care anymore. As we take a step onto the top floor—the loft I was glancing at earlier—I notice that more of the beds have the curtains pulled down, the soft silhouette of bodies behind each one.

I glance at one to my right, noticing three shadows instead of the usual two in passing, my cheeks feeling hot. I don't think I could share my man with another woman; in fact, I know I couldn't, and I already know I have enough of a man that I don't need two.

I bump into his backside, unprepared for a stop due to my wandering eyes. "Sorry," I say, as my eyes come in contact with clear glass. The bed matches the others, only enclosed inside of a box of glass. "So this is it?" I ask, noticing that the walls are very much translucent. "Won't people . . ." I swallow. "See us?"

He slides the key inside of the small lock under the handle and turns it, before pulling the door open. "Only if you want them to," he says, pulling me inside. "It wouldn't be out of the ordinary here. This club is known for its extracurricular activities and in-house shows for the bold. It's a very narrow entryway into a world you have no idea exists; and one I hope you don't want to know more about. It's why Tynleigh was able to get the drugs so easily, because I know her well enough to know she didn't travel with them on her."

"What kind of world?" My curiosity always gets the best of me.

"I was afraid you'd ask that. Sex clubs. And it's every bit of how it sounds. Cameras I can deal with without thinking twice, but live performance even goes a little far for me." He takes a deep breath. "But, if that's an area you want to explore once in your life I would make an exception."

"Have you been?"

"Yes."

"Oh."

"But not as a participant. I'm a porn star. I've pretty much explored everything that deals with public sex."

Surprisingly, I'm relieved at his answer. "Someday I may, want to do that I mean, ya know a sex club, because I like doing things with you that you've never done, but I don't think I'm ready for *that* just yet. This, I think I can do."

He smirks. "Are you getting modest on me?"

"No. I just . . . Well, it's a little more intimidating in a live setting with an audience I would think; having everyone watch your every move as you make them."

He shuts the door and locks it back, placing the key into his pocket, before instantly reaching for the bottom hem of my dress, pulling it slowly up my body. I breathe in and out, waiting for him to get it over my head, only focusing on him. I can do this. We film and we have a Tumblr account now. How much different could this version of a sex life be? My peripheral vision is filled with bodies that resemble ants from up here, but if I can see them then they can see me.

He removes my dress completely, leaving me in only booties and a thong. My entire stomach is sitting in a tangled knot as I stare at him. He outstretches his arm, and seconds later a light sound occurs, pulling my attention away. Every piece of glass is now frosted and opaque, confusing me. I look back at him. "Wasn't that just—"

"Yes," he interrupts, a heated expression on his face. "I don't think either of us are quite ready for that honestly. I haven't had you to myself long enough to share you again yet."

"Well that's cool," I say in awe as he closes in on me, each palm gripping a cheek of my ass. Before I can try to amend my childish remark, he drops to his knees before me, placing a kiss beside my belly button.

My breathing becomes erratic. I glance down as his hands clench around the strings of my underwear at my hips, before rolling them down my body, his lips gliding across my skin as he bares me. When I lift my leg to leave them on the floor, his mouth presses over my lips. "Shit," I whisper, dropping my clutch on the floor, my hands going for my long hair, pulling hard on the ends to offset the way it feels with him touching me. I can't explain it. Every sensation is maximized to the most sensitive degree. Even the occasional blow from his mouth as he disperses kisses against my skin drives me nuts.

His tongue swipes between my lips, making my entire lower half tense up, and just when he reaches my clit his tongue creates a point, flicking back and forth in a fast motion. "Ugh uh."

I grab his hair and push his head back until he's not touching me. He looks up at me. "Let me eat it."

"Not until you let me suck you. I want your dick."

He doesn't argue like I know he wants to, standing at the end of my sentence. "You want my dick, baby, then pull it out," he says, his voice deeper than before. I love when he gets bossy. It just makes me want him that much more. I grab the bottom of his shirt and remove it, showing the body I love so much, before dropping to my knees. We stare at each other as I slowly unbuckle his belt. His stomach muscles contract the entire time I unbutton his jeans, following through with the zipper. I can see the hard outline, waiting on me to expose the most perfect dick there ever could be, at least to me.

Saliva is coating the inside of my mouth in excess as I lower his jeans, his dick springing slightly off his balls from the denim no longer confining it. I stare at it, his jeans landing in a crumbled pile at his feet. "Fucking sit. Now," I demand, being bold with my language.

For once he does exactly as I say, backing up far enough he can sit on the edge of the bed. He leans back a little, holding his upper body weight with his arms. I quickly remove everything left that is covering any part of skin, followed by my heels. He hasn't stopped staring at me.

I grab his dick in my small hand, sizing him up like I always do, preparing myself, and more importantly my jaw. Sucking Saxton's dick is no easy task. It takes concentration, muscle training, and breathing skill. I would imagine if a girl could master sucking a dick this size, since I have yet to, she could suck one smaller like an expert.

I sit back on my heels and stroke the tight but smooth skin at a slow pace, allowing the inside of my mouth to become evenly coated with my saliva. He remains quiet, still staring down at me. His jaw is clenched shut. I can see the muscle locked into place. My breathing is even, forcing each breath in and out of my nose.

I stand on my knees and he catches me off guard. "Suck my balls, baby."

That's a strange request coming from Saxton. I've played with them here and there, even with my mouth as he's requesting, but he's never bluntly asked it of me any time that I can recall. My memory is hazy at the moment, though. "Why?"

He can tell my question isn't directed in a way that implies I don't want to or feel pressured. I'm just honestly curious. "Because I want your hot, wet mouth wrapped around them. Just handle with care," he says, a grin appearing on the last word.

Adrenaline rushes through my veins, causing me to stand to my feet. I like knowing what he likes. My palms make contact with his chest, forcing him backward. He complies, even though he could easily overtake my strength. This time when I grab his dick, I grab it with a goal in mind: to suck the porn star better than he's ever had before. I know I can do it, because I've done it a few times before. There is no greater high than doing something better than any other woman, especially when you came into the relationship with little to no experience.

I bend forward, holding his dick out of the way, before placing a light kiss on the soft skin. My lips part, just before my bottom lip drags upward to reunite with the top, leaving a trail of wetness behind. I can hear his breathing get more pronounced. I repeat the action, but this time allowing the edging of my bottom teeth to scrape along the skin very lightly.

My mouth opens and I suction, pulling one side into my mouth, but only briefly, before releasing again. My tongue exits, creating a point, and touches at the bottom center, then traces up the textured line that separates the two sides like I did last time. They still fascinate me. I move to the other side, giving it the same attention: a marble inside of a small bag of water. Playing with them becomes addictive. They're fun. I like playing with his balls like he likes playing with my boobs. Female fun bags.

His hand wraps in my hair as I continue back and forth between the two, savoring and suckling on each one for a few moments before the switch. He pulls my hair hard, lifting me from his groin. His heels lock around my thighs, pulling my waist closer to the bed until our lips roughly find each other's. His hand grips the front of my thigh to the point that could lead to a bruise, before my body is lifted enough that he turns me around, his lips leaving mine just as he does.

When my eyes open and focus, I'm staring down at his dick from a different direction than before. I've discovered in play he likes this position: 69. I push up on my hands and knees, straddling over his body. Instead of looking back at him, I continue as if nothing just happened, only this time placing the head of his dick against my lips, and like a *Blow pop,* I suck.

He slaps my ass hard, leaving a stinging burn in its wake, and then clamps his thumb and index fingers on the skin covering my clit, pulling back until I back my ass up. It hurts, but I like when he gets a little rough. I can feel the point of his nose skimming between my closed lips, and then slowly he presses his tongue inside of me. All of the muscles between my legs tighten, but I'm completely turned on. I grip my hands on his thighs, his dick only stabilized by my mouth, and find a rhythm as he begins tongue fucking me, making it hard to concentrate.

His thumb presses between my lips and immediately touches my clit. He begins rubbing back and forth, causing me to moan around his dick. His hips thrust upward, his dick driving forward. The head hits against the back of my throat, causing me to gag, but I control myself before it gets out of hand.

He exerts more pressure against my clit, and within a few strokes back and forth I'm ready to come. My nails dig into his thighs, but I force myself to keep sucking, his dick drenched in my saliva. I'm not ready to come yet. I suck harder, faster, trying desperately to only focus on what's in front of me.

Then I feel it; the fingertip trailing from my pussy along my backside until it's pressed against my asshole. Dammit, no. He presses it inside as he continues assaulting my clit in the best possible way, his wet tongue matching the rhythm with trusts in and out. Shit.

Before I can stop it I'm coming, moaning around his dick, his tongue entering completely at the perfect time, as if he knew I was about to come. His finger continues to slide in and out of my ass, making my orgasm deeper, harder, and longer. As my body relaxes he bites into the skin beside my lip, just beneath my ass.

I feel like a failure. I wanted him to come or at least for us to go a while before I did. "Come here," he demands, just as I was trying to suck some more. I turn around, knowing that the tone in his voice means he wants sex. I glance at him, his eyes heavy as he looks at me. He flips us over. "You will never know how much I fucking love you."

"I do, because I love you at least that much." He's standing on his knees between my legs. I love this view. I never realized how beautiful the human body is totally naked until I met him. Now, in a weird way, in which I would never admit aloud, I understand why some people prefer to live nude. I would totally encapsulate myself in a house with him nude twenty-four hours a day, seven days a week. He's beautiful. "At least that much," I repeat, hoping he gets the point without me sounding like a psycho.

He slides off the edge of the bed and bends down, returning back in his original position seconds later, his phone in hand, before lying it down beside my body. "You still want to be my wife?" he asks, rubbing the head of his dick back and forth over my entrance.

My heart begins to race faster at the verbalization of that last word. *Wife.* It's the first time I've heard it since he proposed to me and slid the ring I am wearing on my finger. That word rattles my soul to my very core. "Yes. Forever."

"Push up." When I do as he says, giving my lower body more height, he thrusts inside, his phone already back in hand. My lungs experience temporary paralysis as my body encounters the fill of a void I've been trying to ignore. He holds the back of the phone angled toward me with one hand, grabbing the back of one of my knees in the other; just before he starts controlling his pelvic thrusts, sliding in and out so slowly I can barely hold myself still. I clench my hands on the fabric of the comforter. My lower half lifted off the bed, stretched and creating half of a backbend, allows me to feel his dick deeper, forming a tighter fit within me. "Tell the world you'll never tire of my dick being inside of you; only my dick."

His rhythm is hypnotic, causing my eyes to roll in circles to avoid closing them. My feet push further into the bed, lifting my waist more. I'm so high right now, but I'm not sure it's totally the drugs. As I lay quietly, trying to bypass the level ten sensitivity going on within and all over my body, he turns the phone a little toward the juncture in which our bodies meet, his eyes watching as he thrusts in and out of me. "Fuck, I love watching my dick slide inside of your pussy, coming out wetter than when it went in. It sends me over the edge."

His voice is deep, breathing scattered within the words. I watch him as he watches his dick slide in and out, over and over. It's hot seeing him so turned on that he temporarily forgot he even asked me a question. I feel sexy when he wants me like this. "It feels just as good as it looks," I say, causing him to look back at me, bringing the camera back to my face.

I look into the small lens on the back of the camera and speak as steadily as I can. "I'll never tire of this . . .with you," I say, meaning so much more than just his dick. The complexity of us is indescribable with words. I want him, I need him, and I know already that I cannot live without him. "You're my first, my last, my forever and my always."

He touches the screen of the phone, before tossing it aside, his hips still pumping his dick in and out of me. I love the way his stomach ripples each time he pushes inside.

I place my palms flat against his abdomen to feel them as they contract. He doesn't allow me to keep them there for long, before he grabs them in his hands, lacing our fingers, and bends down to hover his body over mine, forcing my waist to remain elevated by altering his legs into a parallel position under me, his knees pressed into the mattress. He releases his hands from mine long enough to place my legs on his shoulders, before lacing them back together and leaning forward.

His upper body is pressed against mine, pinning me to this bed. My feet are almost touching my ears, but he never stops. His hips stay in constant motion. It fucking hurts, being stretched this far, but holy hell he's so deep. I don't want him to stop. He's clenching my hands so tight his forearms are hard on top of mine. My body heats to the point that I can feel my skin become wet, but I will endure it, because I don't want him to move. He's touching me. I just want him to touch me. I like feeling this close to him. He pulls almost completely out and drives his pelvis against my ass, his dick forging inside me like an army at enemy lines. The force was so brutal that we gained about an inch of height from the bed. "Fucking yes! Oh my god, yes."

His trusts are now shallow, never pulling out more than maybe an inch or so before pushing back inside, his pelvis connecting with my skin once again, our bodies rubbing against each other. He looks into my eyes so fiercely that I can't feel my own heart beat. "In so many ways you're that for me, Kambry. Promise me you won't regret marrying me so young. I can't live knowing I'm your regret, even if not now."

I grab his face and hold him close to me so that I can look him deep into his eyes without them straying. He stops completely inside of me, his hand rubbing up and down the outside of my shaking leg. "I solemnly swear on my life that there will never be a day I regret marrying you, period, age or otherwise. You're my soul mate, Saxton. Now I know why I left that night. I went back and forth in my head for hours, scared to go against everything I've ever known, but now it all makes sense. I was supposed to find you, to save you from the path you were on. It wasn't meant to last. I was all grown up and my heart was ready. It was time."

He stares at me, not blinking, and for the first time since I met him his eyes look glazed over, watery, as if one blink would release an actual tear, but then he starts blinking rapidly and nothing falls, the slightest disappointment trying to brew. "I definitely needed saving. It just took the right girl."

"I'm your girl, Sax. Always." My legs fall down his arms into the bend of his and he starts to move again, this time in silence. The night's end may have started out in party mode, fucking on a high I've never experienced before, but it turns out that sometimes drugs enhance more than just the state of mind. It is possible that when life hacks don't get in the way, parts of the way you feel for someone can come out so easily. That phrase that he just used will stick with me forever . . .

Saxton

I carry her limp body snuggled against me inside of Tynleigh's apartment, shutting the door behind me. I work to lock it holding her in my arms. It's 5AM. It seems we lost track of time being in that soundproof room, showing with our bodies the way our hearts feel. Hours of foreplay, sex and sweating, and I'm pretty sure my nuts have been drained of cum. There cannot physically be anything left, not even an ounce.

Between rounds we talked, more as the drugs started to wear off, getting to know each other a little better than before. And with every word from her mouth I wanted her more. I've never craved to be physically connected to another woman like I do with her. It's the only form in which I feel truly complete. It's not even about the orgasm anymore, but about the intimacy.

On the final round of her straddling my dick and attempting to sit down on it, I realized all that remained was the sticky remnants of my earlier cum wars. She was dry and I was semisoft; and her eyes were close to closing, so I called it quits. It was only a couple hours shy of the club's closing down time anyway, so I pulled her beside me to lay her head on my chest. Then I rubbed her arm draped over my stomach until she fell asleep. It didn't take long and she was out, as if she was just waiting for my cue.

I laid there longer than I had planned, thinking and watching her sleep. In some ways I feel like I'm being an asshole; taking her life away by making her a wife before she starts college or has her twenty-first birthday, but then I remember the smile on her face when she was over the shock and agreed to marry me, or even simply when I'm around. She makes me a whole man. I just hope I'm not being selfish here.

The sound of a bouncing mattress registers as I make my way to our room, moaning sounds in a patterned rhythm. My eyes squint, my feet picking up speed. Fucking hell. I don't want to hear that shit. I had a voicemail from Tynleigh after Kambry went to sleep. She said she was easing home early, with someone. She knew I'd be coherent by closing. From that point I tried to take my time, hoping they'd be done and asleep by the time we returned. Obviously, I'm not the only one in this family with a late night drive, or morning.

Once I walk in the bedroom and lay Kambry on the bed, I return to shut the bedroom door and turn on the television on my way back, leaving it on the channel it was already on—an infomercial—just turning up the volume a little to drown out the close proximity of the bedrooms. "What are you doing?"

The groggy voice behind me causes me to turn around as I put the remote down. "Just turning the television on. Go back to sleep, baby."

"Not until you come to bed."

"I'm coming. You want some water?"

She shakes her head. "I just want you to hold me."

The organ behind the left chest cavity feels constricted, as it does so often with the smallest phrases from her. Shoving off my shoes, I remove my shirt and jeans, just before climbing in beside her. She raises her arms, waiting on me to take her dress off. I do, and then she wiggles under the covers in only her panties, grabbing my hand and draping my arm over her body.

I snuggle up behind her. "Sax," she says in a whisper.

"What, baby?"

"Please don't leave me, okay? Please grow old with me."

I kiss her shoulder, barely able to breathe. "Why would I leave the best thing that's ever happened to me?"

She turns over, her eyes still heavy as she blinks. "I don't know. People get bored. They want change. That honeymoon phase I've always heard about fades and like with drugs people go looking for that relationship high in someone new. I don't really have much to compare us to since I fell in love with the second guy I dated and the first I slept with, so I never feel like I'm missing anything. I guess I just started thinking tonight about how much I love you and the fact that I can experience new things with the man I want to be with forever. Tonight was fun, really fun. I know you have more experience and all. Just tell me if you want any of those things and we can fix it. I'll try to change. I can be as adventurous as you want me to be. Just don't leave. I'm pretty sure it would destroy me."

A tear falls from the corner of her eye, running down the side of her nose. I can see it with the light flickering from the television. I swipe it with my finger. "Fuck, baby, why are you crying? Seriously? I can't walk away from you, Kambry. I've already tried and only lasted like a day. Remember?"

"Now you can't, but what about later? What if someone better comes along?" I have no idea where all of this is suddenly coming from. It's hurting my damn heart. The only thing I can figure is she's coming down still; her body smaller and her tolerance overall lower, so the effects probably last longer on her. My lids are getting heavy, but I fight to keep my eyes open. This would be the worst possible time to fall asleep.

I yawn, my eyes blinking rapidly, immediately following. My hand slides down her side, stopping on her ass in a tight grip. I pull her toward me, kissing her forehead, the tip of her nose, and her lips. "Can I be honest?"

She stares at me for a minute, her eyes going back and forth between my eyes and lips. "Okay."

"Now that I've met you, I wish I had waited for sex prior. What I have with you can't be had with anyone else. I'm smarter now. Back then I was stupid. Teenagers don't think about the consequences or the future when creating a *fucked* list. After so long most can't even remember who's on it. It's all about living in the moment and nothing more. Teenage boys have one thought in mind: getting laid so you don't have to go to college a virgin, because that's what losers do. Then, heartbreak makes you just want to fuck everything, with no standards. If it's a woman, interested, with a pussy between her legs you'll screw her; mostly hoping in some alternate universe it proves something to the one that did you wrong. I only avoided some of that because of the career I chose shortly after. I was speeding down the highway to Hell until I found you. Now, my regret is that I didn't have enough respect for you—the girl created to be my wife—back then to make you my first, so I sure as hell am not going to make someone else my last."

"You didn't know me back then. How could you?"

"It doesn't matter. Deep down I knew I'd find *the girl* one day. That should have been enough. You didn't know me either, but you still saved yourself for me whether consciously or not, and Kambry, nothing will ever be comparable to that feeling. I just wish you could have experienced it too. I'm sorry."

"You shouldn't be. Had my parents not been the way they are I may not have, if we're being honest."

"I know you really believe that, and thankfully we'll never know one way or the other, but I think deep down you knew it wasn't time or you would have, just like your brother. Most kids don't give two shits about what their parents think or want. We all think we're ten-foot-tall and bulletproof at that age. We're cocky little bastards that think we know it all. You didn't rebel, though, like most would have given your strict upbringing. Most would simply sneak around. In fact, you're a little peculiar at times, but it's one thing that drew me to you."

Her brows dip and her bottom lip puffs out in a pout. "Peculiar? What do you mean?"

"I never told you about that night we met?"

"I was there. You didn't have to."

"No, like from my point of view."

"Oh. No. I don't think."

"Well, I had just finished a—never mind. Anyway, the single, only reason I went was because I never turned down a meeting with Michael. I always felt like I owed him too much, so I went, expecting to turn down whatever offer he had.

I was tired of everything. Two seconds after I sat down your tits were in my face. It really didn't surprise me, given the high-profile section of the club we were in. Most girls with a rack like yours would have done more than bend over in a place like that. I've seen it. They just play it off well enough they don't get fired if the outcome doesn't end up how they expected. You, on the other hand, had no idea what was even happening. I was fucking hard, confused as hell, and staring at you like a lamb dangling in front of a lion, and you were concentrating on the damn drinks, not even looking at me."

"What's wrong with that? I didn't want to spill them on some rich-ass celebrity."

"See what I mean? The average girl in that kind of setting, waiting tables for a fucking living, would have intentionally had an accident as close to a man's crotch as possible, just so she could try to clean it up by getting him hard for a social insurance policy at the end of the night. It's not hard for a girl to figure out how a man works. We're territorial, wanting to claim and mark every damn thing until we settle somewhere we don't want to leave. None of that even crossed your mind. When you walked off you moved like you were scared to death of tripping in your own heels while still trying to hold it together and be the sex object you were trained to be. It wasn't you. It didn't work, or it did in my case. The whole thing was an accident waiting to happen."

"Well, fuck, I—"

"Yes, I wanted to fuck you and all of your awkwardness. I even went home and watched porn to try to forget you and the insane deal that Michael was trying to make; the one I knew he would fail at because you weren't that girl. I knew it like I know my name and date of birth."

"And the porn didn't suffice?" she asks sarcastically.

"Nope," I say, letting the p pop as it comes out. "I wanted to get wet."

She finally smiles. "How'd that go for you?"

"Oh you know, just like any other night; ended up between this hot girl's legs and quenched any thirst I may have had in that moment. You still make me thirsty."

She laughs. "I love you."

"I love you too, and I promise you don't have to worry about me leaving you."

"Good. I can't believe you said I'm peculiar and awkward. That's a little depressing."

"I call 'em as I see 'em, beautiful. It worked out in your favor. Otherwise, you may have ended up with some asshole to leave you at home to go wet his dick in someone else and doesn't have a fetish over your feet. That would have been the worst possible ending. You were everything I didn't know I wanted. Two Food Network weirdos should always stick together."

She peeks up at me from under her lashes, a light laugh invading the room. "I guess this is true."

"You good? Can we sleep now?"

She nods and turns over, placing her back toward me. I snuggle her into my front, molding my body around hers. "Goodnight, handsome."

"Goodnight, beautiful."

CHAPTER ELEVEN

Kambry

"What the fuck are you doing here?"

My eyes pop open just as they would if trying to wake myself up in the middle of an unsatisfactory or scary dream, my hand feeling around on the bed as I work to gain visual focus. It's empty, but the spot beside me is still warm.

My body shoots up into a sitting position and I look around the room. "You fucked my sister, prick!"

"How the hell was I supposed to know? We're on a different coastline."

The deep shouting is getting louder. As if part of reflex, I bolt from the bed when something hits hard against the wall in the other room. The sound of something breaking immediately follows. "Saxton stop! What the fuck is your problem?"

I run into the living room just as Saxton's fist connects with the jaw of a guy I can't see the face of, knocking him to the ground. Deja vu hits me hard, reminding me of the day Ben suddenly turned up at the house, only in reverse.

"Fuck, dude." The guy grabs his face and rolls over into a loose fetal position as Tynleigh runs toward Saxton, grabbing at his arm in only a tank and panties. He jerks his arm out of her grip and looks at me, his chest heaving up and down.

"Are you for real right now? Why the hell did you hit her date?"

"He deserved it. That's why."

"You don't even know him!"

The guy on the ground forcefully swings his leg in a horizontal motion, knocking Saxton's legs out from under him. He stands and turns around. "That's not entirely true."

My mouth falls slightly in confusion as I glance at the red circle above his cheekbone. "Bryant? How did you end up here? Wait, do you know Tynleigh too?"

"Not until last night," he says, his eyes not meeting mine. "But I would say I know her pretty well now."

Saxton kicks the back of Bryant's knee with the arch of his foot, forcing his legs to give out. "Shut the fuck up, asshole."

"You shut up, Saxton! Dammit, I've listened to you and Kambry fuck since you got here pretty much. Karma is a bitch. Now you know how it feels."

I'm so confused, staring into the face of a man that was just recently screwing my best friend, and now my soon to be sister-in-law. "But why are you in New York?"

"I needed a change of *scenery*," he says, drawing out that last word, clearly talking about Meredith. "And I have a few friends here, so I booked a flight." He pauses, and then continues. "I mean they went to school here. Grad school . . ."

His speech is getting slower. What is he looking at? A masculine arm wraps around my front from behind, running along the center of my . . .boobs, creating skin-to-skin contact. Oh my god. The smirk beginning on Bryant's face and spreading at a rapid rate confirms my most embarrassing moment. I want to crawl under a rock and die. How does one not notice she's missing items of clothing? The cold draft should have been a telling sign. Have I really gotten that comfortable with nudity?

"Get your boner in check, bro, and put your eyes back in your head while you can still see," Saxton grits out in an angry tone beside my ear. "Because your fucking dick better be hard for my sister and not my fiancé or else I will rip your heart out."

I finally glance away from his face now that the earlier commotion has calmed down. Bryant is in boxer briefs only, just like Saxton, only he's sporting a decent sized bulge in the front; nothing quite as extreme as the piece Saxton's packing. I'm starting to realize that Saxton is like a Great Dane in terms of dicks.

It's a good thing I fell in love with him, because being broken in with salami and then downsizing to sausage cannot possibly have the same effects. That's radical change to say the least. Oh my god. I am totally comparing their erection sizes in my head. What the hell?

My hands cover my face, making a slapping sound. "I'm so sorry," I mumble against my palms, a little unsure of what exactly I'm apologizing for. It could be the fact I'm almost completely naked, only my thong covering anything on my body, or the fact that I'm sizing up the dicks in the room. Both are equally embarrassing and highly inappropriate.

"There is no need to be sorry with that body," Bryant returns. "Now I know exactly why he put a ring on it. Congrats by the way."

My hands slide down my face. "Thanks," I say, unsure.

"Dude, don't disrespect my sister. You're pissing me off."

"It's nothing personal. Tits create hard-ons, and I was graced with a nice set. You of all people should know about that." He smirks. "It seems you had the same problem when you got a look at them, but it doesn't really matter. I wouldn't *touch*."

Dick to the booty: check. Sax is sporting a semi, and at the stop of Bryant's words starts rubbing it side to side on my backside. I'm trying to hold my breathing at an even pace, but Bryant makes it easier, speaking again. "Besides, your sister has her own perfect boner-making set."

Movement halts and he pulls me against him further.

"Ah fuck. I'm out of here. You may have fucked her. Hell, you may again. That's her business. Have your fun, but I'm warning you, friend or not, don't fuck her over. At some point a plane, California bound, is waiting for you."

My eyes lock with Tynleigh's. Her lips are pursed together. "What's so fucking funny, T?"

She closes in on Bryant and wraps her arms around his waist, staring at Saxton. This is weird. I keep thinking I'm supposed to see Meredith, when in fact she's with my brother. "I'm just trying to decide if this is really my life right now. I just can't. This shit would only happen to us, but just so we're clear, brother, we're just fuck—"

"Uh ugh. Shut up, T. It's not the same as you hearing about my shit. I'm a guy. We brag. You're my sister. Assuming you have sex but never knowing, witnessing or listening is totally different, especially with one of my only friends. No details are preferred."

My hands grab onto Saxton's forearm stretched over my nipples as he begins moving, towing us both toward the bedroom, covering my ass with his body. "I'm taking her dress shopping in two hours, Saxton! That's all the time you have," she yells out just as he slams the door, not stopping as he walks us toward the bed. I can't see his face, but based on the amount of pressure coming from his chest as he breathes, I can tell he's not happy.

"He wanted you. I could see it in his eyes." He's angry. His tone tells me so. He places his hand on my shoulder and pushes me forward, bending me over the bed.

I catch myself with my palms. "I'm sorry. I forgot we slept without clothes. The two of you were yelling. I woke up in a panic. I know this is in the flesh, but men are going to see my body, just as women will yours. We might as well get used to it now."

"Men are always going to want you. You're beautiful, your body is sexy, and you're innocent."

"Hey. Are you mad at me?"

"Do you know how hard it is for me to think of sharing your body with other men? Yet it turns me on to know that I'm the only one that can have you. Such a contradiction . . ."

His hands grip my waist and slide beneath the string at my hips, quickly pushing my panties down to my thighs. My body shudders at his light but rough touch. I turn to look at him and he's already kneeling behind me. "What are you doing?"

Without saying a word, he leans in and swipes his flattened tongue from top to bottom of my center, then stands and grabs his dick. "Ensuring you're wet enough. I figure I have about an hour to remind you what's mine is yours and what's yours is mine."

The head of his dick touches my skin and without even spreading me he shoves it inside, pushing me up on my tiptoes. "Sax."

He roughly pulls out and thrusts back inside, harder this time. "You remember that name next time a man looks at you the way he just did."

I stand upright as much as possible with him inside of me, and wrap one hand around his neck, my head turning to meet his lips. His hands become flush with my hips before I grab one and move it to my breast. "How could I ever forget? Another man may look at me, Sax, but you're the only man I see."

He smiles. I love his smile. His smile can chase away rainy days, even with the darkest of clouds. "You really know how to make a man happy, Kambry. You sure you want to marry me? There's still time to back out."

I arch my back and begin sliding up and down his length, the cheeks of my butt hitting against his skin each time I come down. "I've never been this happy over something so permanent. Nothing is ever really ours until we buy it. It's time to take you off the market."

"You are the most perfect creature ever created," he says in an overworked whisper. "I love being a part of your life."

"You aren't a part of it. You are my life, Saxton."

"Forever and always."

I smile back at him. "Always and forever."

I look down at my phone screen, glancing at the latest post on our Tumblr page; also not posted by me. As a matter of fact the time stamp is way past midnight. My cheeks flush as I watch the GIF version of the video I haven't even seen from last night play through. Over and over it replays, in a much higher speed than I remember as he slid in and out of me without stopping, but even if it didn't I'm pretty sure I'd replay it constantly. All you can see of my body is from my ribs down in a horizontal angle, him the same in lateral. Our bodies connect and then they part, repetitively and hypnotically showing his dick entering me. When my eyes finally unlock themselves from the GIF I read through the entire post.

> *#Clubbing in the city with my bride to be. Thank fuck for bed reserves. Her ass was working me hard. I'm pretty sure a man discovered club dancing, by the way. Dick between the cheeks . . . Yeah, all man. I love that girl. And her ass. #Sexinthecity You can*

look, boys, but you can't touch. This one is all mine.
In and out of that beautiful #pussy for the rest of my life. Still fits like a fucking tight glove. Salivating yet? One happy #dick tonight. Gentlemen, if the room doesn't need to be #soundproofed, you aren't doing your job. ;) #Sextograms #SaxtonStyle #NewYorkRendevous #KinkyAfterDark #Fuckeryatitsfinest #SexSessions #AfterTheCut #TumblrSex #Porncouple #CoupleBlog #PussyWhippedPornStar #PornStarRomance #Fuckinginlove #ForeverHorny And don't forget the #WordPorn of the day—love your woman with all that you are. Fuck hard, love hard, but don't act hard. Trust even when you don't think you can. Until next time, peace out. —Sax.

"Why do you have such a massive grin on your face?" I glance up at the sound of Tynleigh's voice and shove my phone back in my purse without looking at anything else; much like being caught with your hand in the cookie jar by Mom before dinner. "I would say it has something to do with the fact that we're standing in a bridal shop and you're about to pick out your wedding dress, but based on the fact that your eyes haven't moved from your phone screen since we walked in that would be an inaccurate assumption."

"I'm sorry," I say. "He just surprises me at every turn. Right when I think I'm at max capacity in the love I hold for him, it somehow grows deeper and stronger. I'm kind of lucky I get to spend an entire lifetime with him." I sigh. "I miss him now. Pretty pathetic, huh?"

"Maybe a little," she retorts, as the side of her mouth pulls up. "But I wouldn't want anything less for him. He's always been my sprout. I want him to be happy. You make him happy. Now that I've gotten that out, stop being all sappy and let's find your wedding dress so you can actually get to the wedding within this decade."

I scan the room, dresses in every shade of white filling all sides and down the center of the building. My eyes bug out of my head. I can feel them. "Well, where do I start?"

"With that Mimosa waiting at six o'clock. Our reservation is right on schedule."

Confused, I turn around, and sure enough there is a female wearing a dark gray pencil skirt, cream-colored silk blouse tucked in and shoes to match. If I had to guess she's already shucked a jacket that goes with that skirt. Her black hair falls in face-angled layers and stops just above her breasts. She smiles, holding two champagne flutes filled just below the rim with an orange liquid.

"For the bride," she states, extending one glass toward me. "You must be Kambry."

"Yes."

"It's a pleasure to meet you. My name is Melanie. I'll be your consultant today."

I take the glass instead of acting like the eighteen-year-old that I am, and turn back around. "What reservation?"

She grabs the other glass. "The one I made last minute. Thank God for cancellations. Luck on your side is a good start."

I take a sip, forcing myself to have proper etiquette and not gulp even though I want to down the yummy drink. The size of this place and the glass I'm drinking out of versus a cheap plastic version tells me that I should be on my best behavior. I don't recall ever hearing about complimentary fancy beverages at the nearest *David's Bridal* back home, and I thought that place was legit in terms of being upscale. I'm a little afraid to check the price tag on something here.

"Come with me. I already pulled a few things based on my conversation with Miss Cambridge earlier. We can start there." She turns and finds the biggest opening between bars of dresses, leading us down the center. I hold the glass close to me, afraid to spill it on the beautiful fabric. Orange is not the new pink. I'm pretty sure it's not supposed to be worn down the aisle and I don't wish to purchase more than one dress today. I'll forever be thankful I decided on flats before I left.

Tynleigh walks up beside me, looping her arm in mine with the rim of the glass sitting perfectly between her lips. "A sudden cancellation, huh? And on the same day you called?" I whisper, my brain and common sense finally kicking in. "At a place like this? The inventory alone is probably worth more than my parents' house. I don't buy it, Cambridge."

"What's the point of working at a huge women's magazine, busting my ass for a bitch of an editor, if I can't use it to my advantage once in a while?" I squint my eyes. "Okay, fine. I may or may not have also promised to freelance a piece on your wedding with a couple photos of you wearing a gown to go on their advertisement page coming up instead of a staged model they have to pay. They win, we win, and everyone is happy. They're already clients of the magazine, so yes, I had a contact even though I'm not in the marketing department. Summer— June especially—is the favored time for weddings, so this will be a marketing boost."

Screw etiquette. I take a bigger gulp this time. "You want me to be in a magazine? For everyone to see?"

My nerves start firing off. "Now, now, sister. Don't tell me you're getting camera shy with the idea of having all of your clothes on in a still shot image. That would be insane. I just need your pretty little signature on a release form. It may actually be good for you. More to put on that resume for later." She winks. "But don't worry about a thing. I'll take care of all those awesome sisterly duties and do all the preparation for this small ceremony, wherever it ends up being, since your knowledge of New York is limited. All you have to do is show up and say 'I do'."

"Now we're having an actual ceremony? What happened to the courthouse? You're freaking me out a little. Small town girl. Remember?"

"Just something very small. I have to keep in mind the bigger picture and be the voice for the greater good of everyone involved besides you two love birds that have lost all sense of reason. It's quite disturbing actually." She pauses and takes another sip of her mimosa.

As slow as we're walking, we're bound to have people gossiping. "Anyway, I have a few owed favors I can cash in around this city. I'm damn good at what I do and I've neglected everything else in my life to make sure I am. But even with that, it's quite impossible to pull off anything most would consider an actual dream wedding in only a few days. That would take a witch and unfortunately I'm as mortal as they come."

"Whatever makes you happy. I take that back. I've seen your apartment. Whatever simple thing makes you happy. I was always forced to accept the idea of a small church for all marital purposes. We're talking wooden pews and original hardwood floors on a raised foundation white church house, its own cemetery, that still very much loves Sunday hymns and worships promptly from eleven to twelve. Contemporary was not a word used. My parents are as traditional Baptist as you can get. No dancing, no alcohol, and no receptions were ever allowed, so anything else and I feel like I want to hyperventilate. A judge, a room, and us were actually appealing ideas, but I am going to trust you. Weddings or planning of any sort is not my forte."

She stops, stopping me. Her eyes are staring forward, urging mine to follow. "This is step one and every girl's dream: the dress."

A platform made of white and gray swirled marble becomes the strong focus of what I see, and mirrors. It's surrounded by mirrors: a large floor to ceiling one in the back and two matching in size angled toward the platform at each side; no doubt for a twirling effect. The powder blue fabric-covered couch facing the platform before us now makes sense as to why she stopped. "The dress, Kambry, is the most important part of a wedding. It's the first thing he'll see you in and what makes you feel more beautiful than you've ever felt before. No girl feels complete without a pretty dress, no matter how simple or extravagant it is. There is nothing wrong with a little tradition every now and then."

"You ready to get started?" The beautiful woman from earlier, about mid thirties I'd guess, is standing atop the platform, her hands linked in front of her. Her posture is perfect. I wouldn't be surprised if she could balance a stack of books on her head. She's standing with poise. She has class I've never before known.

I nod, glancing at Tynleigh as she grabs the strap of my purse, pulling it off my shoulder and the glass from my hand, leaving me empty handed. "I'll be here when you're ready to come out."

"Okay," I say, a little anxiety slipping out with the word, and then make my way around the couch toward the platform.

Melanie turns and starts to walk toward the edge of one of the side mirrors, leading me. Once we round it, I realize it's a well-lit hall decorated with doors, all shut but the one at the end. She stops at the open door, allowing me to enter. The room is large, the colors again white and light blue, with wedding dresses hanging down the two longest walls, each on its own hook. It would be a beautiful backdrop for a photo that's for sure.

I breathe in, a little overwhelmed as I take it all in. "I'll be standing just outside of the door. When you're ready to fasten each one, just press this button on the wall and it'll turn on the light above the door that'll go off when I open it."

"Where do I start?"

"Always start by the mirror, sweetie. You're pretty busty to accompany that tiny waistline, which I was expecting from the questionnaire I took from your friend."

"Sister-in-law." I'm not sure why I felt the urge to correct her. It just felt right.

"Oh, okay. Well, as I was saying, if it's a little big in the waist or tight in the bust, that's okay. We have some talented seamstresses on staff. Anything consisting of fabric and stitching can be fixed, so don't let that sway your opinion."

"But what if I can't decide?"

She grabs the door as if she's about to pull it closed. "Oh, honey, you'll just know when you find the one; a lot like you probably experienced with the one that is your reason for being here."

She closes the door, leaving me standing in the middle of this huge room all alone. My eyes move through the lineup, scoping each one out. Some are puffy, some are sleek, some have tulle and some have lace. Long sleeve, short sleeve, halters and strapless, trains are present and absent on some. There's beading and ruching, crystals and skirt lines of every sort.

My breathing is becoming heavier, my hands reflexively going for the ends of my hair to twirl. What apparently is every girl's dream come true is my worst nightmare. I don't know how to do this kind of stuff.

You'll just know, she says . . . I guess we'll see.

I make my way toward the tall body length mirror and slide off my shoes, my feet resting bare on the short but soft commercial grade carpet in the perfect shade of gray; almost a silver if that makes any sense at all. I imagine white carpet would have been a very bad idea in a high traffic area.

As I stare at my reflection in the mirror, I unbutton and unzip my white shorts, before sliding them down my legs and stepping out. I lay them on the large, white, round ottoman behind me, and then follow behind with my quarter-length sleeve pink and orange chevron button-down blouse. All that remains is my orange camisole, but not for long.

I stare at the first dress hanging beside me, and then as instructed grab it. It's stark white with a sweetheart neckline, Swarovski crystals lining it, the bodice long and the skirt branching at the thighs into a flowy mermaid bottom. "Do not think about the price. Do not think about the price." My eyes remain closed as I whisper the chant, willing it to help ease the anxiety building inside of me. "This is for Sax. Dammit this is for me. This is for us."

I step inside the top of the dress carefully and pull it up my body, positioning the top of the neckline to cover my boobs. It has built in cups, so I quickly remove my bra and reposition it, never looking at myself in the mirror. As soon as the button is pressed the door opens, just as she said it would, and she walks inside. "Turn around."

I do as she says and stand quietly as she slowly raises the zipper up my back, starting from my tailbone. "This one is on the simple side, but elegant, and it's beautiful on you."

I wonder if she's trained to say that or if she really believes it. "Thank you."

"What size shoe are you?"

"Six."

She grabs a box and squats with her legs closed, grabbing the back of my right heel. "Use me for balance. Lift your foot."

She slides both heels on my feet, one after the other, giving me a few inches of height. "Come on. You have someone waiting to see and we have a lot left. I'm not rushing you, just informing."

I follow her in the direction we originally came until we get to the platform. At her motion, I step up and walk to the center to face Tynleigh. "Well, what do you think?"

The shutter button sounds on her phone and then she looks up with a smile on her face. "Oh, I can't wait till he sees this."

"Who, Saxton? I thought the idea was for him not to see. Isn't that why he's having boy-time with Bryant instead of being here?"

"Only on *the dress*, but this isn't the one. I can feel it in my gut; therefore, I can toy with him."

"You already know what it looks like?"

"No, but this isn't it."

"You don't like it?"

"Oh it's beautiful, and fits your body like it was made for it, but just call it a girl's intuition. This one isn't it." She sets the empty champagne flute on the side table beside the couch, next to mine, and stands, before walking toward me. "But you can still have a little fun.

"What do you mean?"

She holds out her arm toward me, palm up, above her head. "Always test drive before we purchase, love. Take her for a little spin."

I smile. I feel like we're bonding and becoming more comfortable with each other with every hour that passes, and it makes me feel better, like she is okay with me entering into their family.

"Like this?" I place my hand on hers; clamping it lightly, and then turn slowly like the ballerina in a music box, making a full turn.

"Yes. Do it again. But this time I want you to look at yourself in the mirror as you do and not at me."

"Okay." When my eyes connect with the mirror I look at myself for the first time since I put the wedding dress on. It stops me at half turn, stealing the very breath I was about to take before I could inhale the air. "Wow."

"That's all you, girl. Still think you're a hard six?"

She's staring at me through the mirror, our eyes locked. My eyes start to moisten, causing me to blink rapidly to avoid crying like a baby. I like her. She doesn't treat me like I'm ten years younger. She treats me like I'm her sister, whether by blood or law. I really like her. I always wanted a sister; a Meredith that never had to go home. In a sense I feel like that's what Tynleigh is becoming. She's a sister that arrived almost two decades late. "I feel like a princess. Anyone that looks like royalty has to at least be a hard eight, right?" I laugh. "I guess even porn stars can feel pretty and classy in a formal dress."

She moves around the skirt, training it manually on where to lie, and then stands. "Oh, babe, don't talk like that. You're not a porn star. You're just a girl coming into womanhood and living out a dirty fantasy with the man you love. One day this phase will fade and the two of you will leave behind a legacy for others. You won't be the porn stars, you'll be Saxton and Kambry—the two that made it against the odds—just like you are now. Besides, there's nothing wrong with distressing a perfect piece a little. It adds beauty and character that others can enjoy for years. Remember, you set the value for what others see in you and no one else."

She fixes my bust area and tousles my hair in a few places, then moves from in front of me. "Don't think. Just look at the person in the mirror. What do you see?"

"A girl. She's giving off a slight glow. Her eyes are bright. Her body may not be the proportion of most but it's the perfect proportion for her. She's happy. She's beautiful. She's a ten."

She grins at me. "And she's the future Mrs. Saxton Maverick Cambridge. She's my sister. And you're damn right she's beautiful. My brother doesn't pick ugly girls. I'll even tell you a little secret from an unbiased person. You're the prettiest one yet."

My heart is so full it's working overtime not to burst. "I'm kind of liking this dress more now."

"Well, then you're one dress closer to being prepared to adequately handle the one you're meant to stand at that alter in. When you're ready for it is when your heart will instruct your body to put it on. Until then, we will model the runners up. Now shoo. I have a little brother to taunt with pretty pictures." She smiles at me as she does the hand motions along with the instructions for me to get lost, so I do.

Melanie starts walking the second I make it to her, as she's trained to do I'm sure, staying back until I'm ready for her. This is more fun than I originally thought it would be, and we've only tried on one so far. If this is any indication on what a life in this family will be like, then I'm the luckiest girl in the world.

I walk down that hall for about the eighth time in a new dress. My stomach is growling and I still haven't had any new or stronger feelings from dress to dress. I've made it a pattern to not look until I get on the platform, giving Tynleigh her moment to critique her likes and dislikes, just before teasing me with text message responses from Saxton on the dress before. Each one is an unfiltered threat that he's one photo away from coming down here, but then she dishes it right back, threatening to run away with the bride if he does. It's humorous, getting this look inside of their relationship, especially when it's in regards to me. It makes me feel special.

The second I step around the mirror clapping occurs, followed by a fingers-in-the-mouth whistle. My cheeks hurt from grinning so hard. As I close the distance between us, a petite girl with a short blonde bob around her age is standing close enough I can tell they aren't strangers. "This is the one. No picture this time."

"Do I dare ask what makes this one worthy enough to be called *the one*?" I ask sarcastically, stopping when I get to my place on the platform, as I have every other time. She hands her phone to the girl next to her and then comes toward me.

Her eyes begin at my neck and slowly take in the entire dress. I stand impatiently, waiting for her review. "Because I can picture it in my head like a movie and it fits perfectly. That tells me it's the one. It's simple like you wanted, yet classic, nothing overdone or missing. It fits your body like a custom tailored dress, which proves it was waiting for you. It's sexy but elegant at the same time. Lace can go one of two ways: innocent or sexual, the color doing the telling. You may not be a virgin, Kambry—as if that even matters—but you're still a good girl, and you deserve for your dress to be a reflection on the outside of the person on the inside. The nude underlay from breasts to thighs keeps it from making too bright of a white statement, or too much sexuality, giving it a vintage feel. Meg, come here," she says, a little louder than she was just speaking.

The blonde previously standing beside her walks forward, stepping up onto the platform. "Kambry, this is Meg, my best friend." She grins at her. "We met in college and the bitch couldn't live without me. The rest is history. Her parents have a house in the Hamptons that she's going to let us use for the ceremony."

Now I don't know much about New York, or anywhere for that matter, but any normal person with a television has heard of the Hamptons: a place for the rich of New York to go and play. "Wow. Seriously? It's nice to meet you, by the way."

"Of course." Meg smiles. "When Tynleigh says she needs an emergency location for family, my place is all yours. She's saved me on enough college exams that it's really just a payback. I figured it was meant to be anyway. My parents will be out of town for two weeks. They went to Turks and Cacaos for their anniversary. "

"Thank you. Both of you." My eyes well up, filling to the brim with tears that are attempting to break free. I've never experienced this kind of hospitality from someone that barely knows me.

"Uh ugh. Do not get makeup on this dress, Kambry." I glance at Tynleigh.

She's as serious as a heart attack, not cracking an inch of a smile. Meg is holding a laugh back.

I begin to fan my face, clearly emotional. Am I really about to get married? This is amazing, yet insane. I'm about to marry the man of my dreams. I'm about to finally do something for me. I'm about to make one of the biggest decisions of my life, all on my own. This is as real as it gets. I laugh at her non-faltering expression. "Sorry. When is this wedding, if you don't mind me asking?"

"Not at all. It's Sunday. Will that be a problem for you?"

"Let me check my schedule." I open my imaginary planner and turn the pages, stopping on the appropriate day. My finger trails down the time slots in midair. "Nope, looks like I'm free all day."

"Funny," Tynleigh says. "At least someone has a personality about her. You're going to need it to spend an eternity with my brother. Bless your soul."

"Will this one be it?" Melanie returns from her corner, checking out the dress on my body.

I glance at Tynleigh and Meg, both urging me to give it a whirl. I turn around until I'm facing the mirror. I freeze, taking in the person before me, unfamiliar in the current state. The person before me isn't a girl, but not quite a woman; instead, transitioning from one to the other. She's beautiful, confident, and even though she's still finding her way, she' s sure this is what she wants.

A tear falls as I realize I'm about to get married without my parents being a part of it. I always envisioned this day as something happy for everyone, not just me. Even in all of the times I wanted to hate them for making moments of my life hell, I still wanted them to be happy for me, experiencing the special moments in my life with me. I never wanted this alone.

Lyrics from a song I haven't listened to in years surfaces from my mind so easily: *I'm not a girl, not yet a woman* by Britney Spears. *"There is no need to protect me. It's time that I learn to face up to this on my own."*

With or without them, I will find my own way. I'm not a little girl anymore that they can bully. I'm grown, and I'm in love. This is what two people do when they fall in love. They get married. They spend forever together. My parents should be proud of the person I'm becoming. I may not have done things along the way that they would have wanted me to do, but I followed my heart, and that's something worthy of recognition.

Tynleigh places her hands on the outside of my shoulders and rubs up and down, looking at my crying eyes through the mirror. "Are you okay? Is this a good cry, a bad one, or an, I'm not sure? Do you need me to clear the area for a girl chat? Talk to me."

I shake my head. "Just thinking of some unfortunate circumstances, that's all."

"Do we need to talk about it? I'm your sister now. We can talk about it if you want."

I smile, loving her all the more for playing along with my pity party. "It doesn't matter. It's in the past and only adds storm clouds to a sunny day." I rub my hands down the sides of my dress. "This is the one. I love it. How much?"

She shakes her head. "Doesn't matter. Sprout is paying for it."

I shake my head with power behind it. "No. He's not paying for my dress. I'll pay for it."

"I was under strict orders. You aren't paying for it. Trust me, girl. If a guy offers to buy, you so kindly say thank you and continue on your way. He sent his credit card. Keep your money."

I huff. "What is the point in working and showing my body and all of my private moments to the world for money if I'm not going to at least spend some of it? It's stupid for the groom to pay for your wedding dress."

"Let me show you something," she says, and goes for her phone. "Read this."

Sprout: Make sure she gets the best, T. I don't care what it costs. She deserves the best. I want her to have the best. She's my world, and by marrying me she's giving me the world, so make her the happiest girl in this world. Please, T, for me. I know she'll try to get something cheap. Money means nothing on forever. Make it a good one.

My teeth lock together as more tears inch down my face. "Why is he so good to me?"

"Because he loves you, Kambry. Love makes people do *crazy* things," she says sarcastically. "Like buy his girl a wedding dress to walk down the aisle in. The insanity. The madness."

I laugh. "You're being such a bitch right now. I thought we were having a moment."

She smirks. "Someone has to mentor you and lead you into womanhood." She winks. "Tough love, cupcake. Let him buy you the damn dress and enjoy it. Save your money. I'm sure he has his reasons that we don't understand. Besides, you still have to buy his ring."

My eyes widen. "Shit. I totally forgot about that. I don't even know what size he wears. What am I supposed to do, Tynleigh?"

"Well, for starters, I guess it's a good thing he's meeting us at the jewelry store after lunch then, isn't it? *He* probably doesn't even know what size he wears."

"He's meeting us?" Excitement floods my body. My cheeks tighten.

"Oh my god. You two are ridiculous. What's it been? A few hours tops . . . I can't handle this shit."

She walks off. "Hey. Where are you going?"

"To pay. Get dressed and she'll bag it on a hanger for us to take. Don't forget the shoes."

I glance at Meg. "We aren't as bad as she makes us out to be."

"That huge grin tells me that isn't true, but just own it. If you have that kind of relationship with someone, I think it's pretty rare. If I were you, I'd show it off every chance I got." She smiles and grabs her purse from the couch. "I'll catch you guys later. Have to get back to work. Took a long lunch for Tynleigh. It was nice to meet you, Kambry."

She turns and walks away, leaving me all alone. I breathe deeply, studying myself in the mirror once again before I change. She's right. I found my person. That's something worth showing off every chance I can. In a few short days I'll be Mrs. Saxton Maverick Cambridge. I'm leaving behind Kambry Rivers forever. I squeal, and then glance around to ensure no one heard me. I'm in the clear, so I scurry off before I make a fool of myself.

Who would have ever thought running away from my small town in Alabama would lead me here? Already in the short time since I left, I've become a west coast girl, met the guy of my dreams, and I've taken on New York. Best damn decision I've ever made . . .

CHAPTER TWELVE

Kambry

MirandaNLance08: *Love your post! Keep blogging.*

Henry145: *I'm salivating, man . . . Damn that pussy looks tight.*

SexKittenAfterDark: *Reblogging! Follow me back please . . .*

SinisterSlave: *If I were to come to New York, would you give it to me like you're giving it to him? Don't wear it out for the rest of us . . . Look like a whore, smell like a whore, act like a whore, and you pretty much are a . . .*

"Fucking asshole!"

Tynleigh stops and grabs my arm, stopping me too. "What's wrong? Did Saxton say something?"

My eyes gloss over. I feel like someone took a knife and slashed open the top layer of skin just enough to cause pain, kind of like a paper cut. "No, it's this guy."

She looks confused. "What guy?"

"He's commented on our blog post before and he did again. I recognize his username. I don't get why he's still looking at our stuff if he doesn't like it."

"Blog? What blog? Kambry, what are you talking about?"

I look at her, and then breathe out in frustration. I can't start a movie in the middle and expect the other party to know what's going on with the plot. "Sax and I, we created a couples blog on Tumblr . . . Promise me you won't judge me, kay?"

"Just for the record, I can't imagine anything being more extreme than filming porn for a living, and I'm totally okay with that in this circumstance that you two are in, but I promise not to judge regardless. You have my word."

I pause for a moment, taking time to prepare for the lengthy explanation ahead. Okay, here goes . . .

"Well, I kind of missed filming. I can't really explain it. I've tried to reason with my brain on numerous occasions and make myself see that this isn't normal; to want to show our most private moments to whoever is willing to watch it, but each time it does no good. I still want this part of life with him. Maybe it's that I like showing the world he's mine and I'm his. Sex is art just like anything else; at least it is to me. As long as it's respectable then I don't see the wrong in it, and he's the only one I want this with. Then again, it could be that I was sheltered for so long that I just like being a rebel against society and conservatism: the things that kept me locked behind my parents' doors to begin with. I know some people will hide behind their judgments and view me as a whore, but whatever. Those people probably don't know how it feels to never get to really live and make mistakes for yourself. I do. It sucks. And Saxton being the truly amazing man he is, offered this as a middle ground: Tumblr. He explained it to me—couple blogging—and showed me how to use it, and I like it. We can post what we want and keep private what we want. The control is ours. We've made a few posts—sexual and appropriate—and I find that aside from him, the highlight of my day is reading the feedback from our posts and posting new things. But still, even though I don't care about others opinions, words still hurt. I will never understand cruelty. We live in a complex world, mixed with so many cultures and views on right and wrong. Beliefs and morals differ from person to person. Why make someone feel like a horrible person because you don't agree with what they're doing? It's mean. What happened to the phrase—*if you can't say something nice then don't say anything at all*? Just go elsewhere if you don't like our lives or us. Ya know?"

She holds out her hand. "Give me your phone, but prepare it for a comment reply so that I can't actually witness my brother having sex. There are just some lines you don't cross and that is one."

"What are you going to say?"

"Don't worry about it. Just do it. I'm sick of fucking douche bags. They exist everywhere and thrive off of being assholes."

A nervous feeling begins in the pit of my stomach, but I do as she says. I hate controversy. I hate drama. I just want the world to live in peace. I could totally be a Miss America participant and actually be truthful on that question. World peace is what I would wish for.

She takes my phone from my hand and her fingers begin typing at a rapid rate, faster than I can text or type on touch screen, then holds it out for me. "There. If he has any decency at all he'll get off your page and feel like the jerk-wad that he is. Don't sweat the small stuff, babe. Only you and Saxton know what kind of relationship you have, and that's how it's supposed to be. The only opinion that matters is the other person's. A little lesson: when you're in the public eye, whether you be a writer, actor, painter, singer, or pubic figure of whatever kind, people love to tell you how they feel, especially when it's negative. They hide behind their computers like armor and talk shit. If you're going to live this kind of lifestyle you have to toughen up that skin of yours, because you'll have followers but you'll also have haters, and the haters are more verbal than the lovers. They are so unhappy in their own pathetic little lives that they want to try and bring others down instead of grabbing life by the balls and making their own better. You know what I mean?"

I take a deep breath and take my phone back, glancing at the comment reply that was already posted. "Yeah . . ."

Sax-Kam reply to SinisterSlave: *Hey, baby balls. Just because Mrs. #IGetFuckedWithASmallDickDaily is unhappy with your teeny tiny penis and makes you aware of it regularly, doesn't mean you can be an asshole to the rest of the world. Hell, maybe it's the other way around and you're fucking #LooseyGoosey, wishing you had some of this. Whatever the case may be, if you don't like what you're seeing, get THE FUCK off this page. You know what they say . . . #JustSayNo to bullying. #CyberSurfResponsibly. Always use protection so you don't have to worry about nasty shit rolling off the tongue, because if not . . .two can play this game, bitch. Fuck on.*

I glance up at her, trying to lock down the smile from appearing. "You were that girl in high school, weren't you?"

"What girl? I have no idea what you're talking about."

"The mean girl."

"I wasn't mean . . .to innocent people."

"Same difference."

"Whatever. Bullies deserve to endure the same internal pain they wreak on others. My tolerance for them is below zero."

"Regardless of the reasons for your awesome comebacks, I loved it. Thank you. I wish I held that skill like you and Meredith."

"Who's Meredith?"

"My best friend. Her and Bry—never mind. She's dating my brother. I think the two of you would click if you ever met. Your personalities are on point with each other's. It's almost a little scary to imagine the two of you in the same room."

"Ha! Well, I'm always game for new cool people. We're pretty much here. Do you want me to tag along or do you want to do this couple style? I can always go to work for a few hours."

"Either is fine. I'm not picky. We're the guests here, so I wouldn't want to order you to do one or the other."

Her mouth moves from side to side, kind of like when you swish with mouthwash. "I think I'm going to sit this one out. Go on . . . The two of you need some time alone to actually experience an adventure . . .outside of my apartment." She smothers a laugh. "When the hormones settle what remains is life without rose-colored glasses. Learn to love the simple things together just as much as the chemistry."

"Are you sure?"

"Yeah, girl. I would just be in the way. I really need to show my face at work anyway. In the life of New York careers, there is always someone waiting to take your place if you can't step it up and go the extra mile. That's my motto and it's paying off. Getting there is a breeze. Keep walking straight and take a right on the corner of that floral shop up there. You won't miss it once you do. I'll see you guys back home."

"Okay." I start to walk but stop a few steps up from where she's standing and look back. "Hey, Tynleigh."

"What's up?"

Her hand is already held high standing on the curb. "Thanks for taking me today. It was fun."

"You don't need to thank me. No family of mine is getting hitched in New York without some decent threads." She winks, something she does often. "Besides, one of these days I'm counting on payback."

I smile, my heart fluttering in my chest from the constant state of happiness lately. "Absolutely. I'm your girl."

A cab pulls up and she opens the door. She nods her head for me to go. "If I had to bet on it he's already there. Make him a little nervous but not break a sweat."

"Okay. Bye."

She quickly gets in the cab and slams the door shut behind her. I continue in the direction we were already heading, following her instructions. When I take the corner, I notice Saxton sitting on a metal bench outside of the building it's resting against.

I stop. I just want to watch him for a minute. He hasn't noticed me yet. He's bent over, his forearms resting on his thighs, and staring at the ground between his legs. His heels begin tapping up and down against the cement in a steady rhythm, as if he's keeping a beat in his head. In that position his arm muscles are putting on a show. I love that boy. Lord knows I do. I don't even understand it fully myself. There is just something about him that has always entranced me. He grabbed my heart right from the shelf it was on and took it for himself. That right there is my life in one picture. He's my future, my forever.

I pull up the camera on my phone and aim the lens at him, zooming a little to get a better shot. It takes a second to focus, but I touch on his body to speed it up a little. He glances the other way, the back of his head facing me. I wait for the perfect moment without making myself obvious, even with the constant traffic of people bypassing me.

Just before his face is fully facing me I snap the picture, and then pull up Tumblr to make a quick post with the photo.

I found the sexiest man today venturing down the streets of #NewYork. Cute guy, sitting outside of a quaint little shop all alone . . . There has to be a #story there. #APennyForYourThoughts? I wonder if I would look like a total nutcase if I went up and sat beside him. Reckon he has a misses? #FullThrottleLiving #iThinkiMight #AKissForKeeps #GonnaPutARingOnIt #GottaMarket #Hesmine #SorryGirls But you can count on me for #StealingKisses —XOXO, Kam.

I post it and begin walking slowly, making an effort not to draw attention to myself just yet. He glances at his watch, and then laces his fingers together between his knees. I stop a few feet away. "This seat taken?"

He glances at me, sliding in place the smile he keeps reserved for me. "It is now."

I continue forward and sit beside him, resting my purse on my lap. We both sit back at the same time. He grabs my hand in his and we look at each other simultaneously. "How was dress shopping?"

"Good. I think we found a winner."

"I can't wait to see it."

"Oh, speaking of. I have your credit card. You didn't have to do that, Sax."

"I know."

I roll my eyes. "Is that all I get?"

"Keep the credit card for right now."

"Not what I meant."

"I know." He smiles. I smile. This is totally pathetic. I don't know how to step off the cloud I keep walking around on. My stomach feels like that of a new kid in a huge school.

"How was boy time?"

"Eh. Guys are overrated."

"Overrated?" I laugh. "That bad, huh?"

"Well, it would have been less awkward had I not been sporting a boner half of the time we were together."

I laugh out loud. "I don't even want to know." I turn my body toward him. "No, that's a lie. I totally want to hear this story."

"I was set up. Tynleigh kept sending me all those photos of you trying on dresses. I was picturing the afterlife."

"Afterlife?"

"Ya know . . .getting to remove it in our hotel."

"Hotel? What hotel?"

"The one I have reserved for our makeshift honeymoon until we can plan a real one. I'm not staying at my sister's apartment on my wedding night. I plan for things to be completely inappropriate, to have a noise complaint, and it comes with a bar and a Jacuzzi in the room." He flashes a cheesy grin and I laugh. I can't help it. Things can go from completely serious one minute to goofy the next, and vice versa.

"So . . . What are your plans then? Get drunk and make out in the hot tub?"

"Oh, baby, my plans are never that simple . . ."

I think back on the lap dance in the bar, the bed in the nightclub, and the butt plug in his sister's apartment. "Touché, my love. Touché."

There is a brief but happy silence between us. I glance to my side, watching a young guy in a prep school uniform walk out the door of the flower shop as it chimes with a bouquet of roses in hand. It places a smile on my face, knowing some girl is about to get a surprise like that to make her day better.

Contentment—that's what this is. This is a time in my life when I don't want to rewind or fast forward. I just want to sit back and let it play, enjoying every second of it. "I'm sorry, Kambry."

I glance back at Saxton. "What do you mean? For what?"

"I've never done things like that for you."

"What sort of things, Sax?"

"The romantic things. I've never taken you on a proper date. I've never bought you flowers or surprised you at work. I've never done most of the things that normal couples do."

"Stop it. I don't wish for any of that. I'm happy just being with you."

"No, Kambry, let me finish." He places his arm behind me on the back of the bench and turns toward me so that we can face each other. "There are things I've been thinking about that I need to get out in the open."

"Okay," I say nervously.

"It occurred to me that for the most part I've never done things with you that I couldn't do with, say, a female roommate—aside from the sex—but even that can be plausible in a *friends with benefits* situation. I was raised with a sister. I was very observant most of the time. I guess that's just what kind of guy I am. I noticed the little things that girls go through when it comes to dating. I was there—most likely making fun of—when it took my sister two hours and thirty outfits to deem herself fit for her date. I remember us watching a movie once and catching her grinning from ear to ear as she read a text. She slightly squealed, and then looked around to make sure I didn't notice even though I was watching her from the corner of my eye. She got roses on Valentine's Day and a kiss in front of the door of a new relationship when she was being dropped off at curfew. She got the little things—the expected things. I'm sorry I haven't been that man for you."

His voice is something I can't describe. I can feel the emotion spilling through his lips. It's thick, and somewhat dripping with sadness. It's sincere. "Sax."

"I know this relationship has been anything short of normal, and considering the circumstances we've bypassed some of that list and can't go back, but I still want you to have most of those things, Kambry. I want you to get nervous before a date. I want you to light up when I send you flowers just to brighten your day. I want you to have stories to tell your friends. I'm only saying that it may take me some time, and it's most definitely going to be backward, but I'm going to give those things to you. I promise you I'll try every damn day to be the husband you dreamed about when you were a little girl."

Without willing it to, a tear falls from each eye as I blink, followed by others close behind. "I like to eat my dessert first." I wipe my eyes cautiously, trying not to smear my makeup. "Butthole. Why you gotta go and make me cry, you perfect man?"

He kisses my lips. "I just thought you should know."

I lay my head against his shoulder, and like a reflex his arm wraps around me. "Well maybe you should know that I get nervous every time I know I'm going to see you, so you can cross that off the list. I bet I have you beat there."

"Baby, if a nervous stomach were as telling as a heartbeat, then you would have seen long ago that I was yours."

"Oh yeah? Name the first time I made you nervous."

"The night I showed back up at the club and waited for you in the cab."

"What? No way. You were a little bit cocky that night, fiancé; kissing me like you knew I wanted you to. I didn't detect any nervousness whatsoever."

"Let me tell you a little something about men, baby. We live behind a testosterone-driven mask, acting on whims and dares, hoping that it'll end in our favor. That's it. We aren't naturally as bold and abrasive as we seem. We are frauds to be quite honest. I would even go as far as to say that a woman's biggest fear is never finding love, while a man's is finding it, revealing his true feelings, and then losing it and becoming less of a man. I kissed you in hopes that I'd blind you so that you wouldn't see through my macho facade and know just how affected by you I really was. And maybe a little bit to prove to myself that it was just physical attraction and nothing more."

I nestle in closer to him. "Hmm. Well I guess it was a successful plan. What was your final verdict?"

"You're wearing my ring and shopping for wedding dresses, aren't you?"

A surge of excitement blasts through every facet of my body, similar to that of a rocket in take off. I straighten, but his arm doesn't leave me. They only loosen. "It's crazy, though, isn't it?"

"Definitely unexpected, Miss Rivers, but in my experience unexpected is the most rewarding." I lace my hand with the one wrapped around me. "So tell me. Are you ready to be Kambry Cambridge?"

Silence. I let that sink in for a moment. "Oh my god, Sax!" I whine. "That's humorous. I think I've been so hung up on you going by Maverick that I haven't even put those two together. I'm going to be that person."

He laughs. "Like the Kelly Kellys and the John Johnsons of the world that give doctors' offices a laugh."

"Yes! It's not funny."

"It could be worse."

"How could it be any worse than that? Nature hates me. That's so mean."

"I could have the last name Dick. How would you like to go around calling out that last name for the rest of your life? Picture it—Kambry Dick, the doctor will see you now. Think that'd be easy without a few red cheeks and chuckles? Or what about passing it to the kiddos and them being in grade school when that word is a sin."

"Okay, I take it back. I can live with that." I stand and hold out my hand for his. “I say let’s do this. I have a bank card that’s itching to be used and you have a bare finger that needs to be covered. Ring shopping with me?”

He takes my hand and stands. “I see you haven’t backed out yet . . .”

“Nope. I don’t intend to, Maverick. It’ll take more than a funny name to send me packing. You’ve already given me the goods and I liked it. Forever it is.”

I can see it coming—the joke in his expression—making it harder to keep a straight face. “Oh, so it’s about my penis, is it?”

I stare at him blankly. “Yeah . . . That’s not working for me. You’re not allowed to say the word penis anymore, especially following the word dick. I’ve decided. It’s a little too doctoral for me and I’m not your patient. Sexy porn stars should not be allowed to house such an awkward word in their vocabulary. It’s a banned word . . .kind of like adorable and cute in reference to you.”

He pulls me into a hug. “Then which one would you prefer I use?”

I shake my head with a smile present.

“Say it,” he says. “You know what it does to me. No one has to hear your secretly filthy mouth but me.”

He looks into my eyes and grips my face in each hand. “Cock,” I whisper, with a lingering syllable. “I’m marrying you for your cock.”

His hands rake through my hair until it’s tangled within his fists. “If only you knew what I wanted to do to you right now.”

“Make that text message fantasy from the nail shop come true?”

His head falls back. “Rewards. It’s all about rewards.” He looks back at me. “We get this ring and marriage license taken care of and then I’m feasting on your body somewhere. Go inside and be looking around. I’ll be right behind you. I just need a few minutes to take care of something you can’t help with.”

I bite my lip and look down at the wrapped present waiting and wanting to be touched. I’ve always loved that his arousal sticks out like a like a snowman in a place with no snow. There is no hiding it for him. He’s too big and his frame is lean; his clothing always fitted. Discrete boldness is what I strive for. I close in. “You might want to cut that timeframe in half and get it done, because I kind of feel like watching you fish. It’s an ocean down there.”

I turn and walk away, quickly opening the glass door and walking inside. “Fuck,” he whisper-yells, just as the door closes. I’m fighting really hard not to fist pump the air right now, because my forever freaking rocks.

CHAPTER THIRTEEN

Saxton

My alarm starts to sound on my phone, causing me to wake in a hurry so I can grab it and shut it off before she hears it. I get out of bed and stumble quietly to the bathroom to take a piss. My groggy state makes aim a little messy, but my eyes finally gain focus as I flush the toilet.

I stop at the doorframe when she rolls over in her sleep, my hands immediately clamping onto the top above my head. Her face now in my direction catches my attention. A few strands of her blonde hair are draped across her cheek. She's beautiful, especially when she sleeps. I can tell she dreams a lot by watching her sleep. Her face contorts into whatever emotion I'm guessing is present in her dream. She's even muttered things here and there, but I don't dare mention it. That's one of my secret happy places and I don't want it to end or result in paranoia. It's peaceful watching her when I'm not ready to sleep before her, so on many nights I just pretend to be asleep until her breathing evens and I know she beat me to it.

Sometimes it takes her a while and she rambles about random things, and I listen, but then other times the second her head hits my chest she's out. It's hard not to wake her when it looks like a bad dream is occurring, but I can't take my eyes off of her when a smile is present, because in those moments I wish so bad dream walkers were real.

We were able to find a ring in my size in the store that I actually liked. I was willing to take whatever they had, including the traditional gold band. Ordering wasn't an option on a short time frame. It may not have been a first choice pick, but it's a band nonetheless, and that's all that matters. I don't need a fashion statement. I need a symbol.

After we left the jewelry store we went and applied for a marriage license through the state of New York, signing our lives of solitude away on a fancy piece of paper: a step I never got to before. I signed away my bachelorhood in a few short minutes. My right to entertain the thoughts of another woman is forever gone. For some that may be a scary revelation, but for me it's a fucking amazing feeling.

I never have to touch another woman and deal with the stress of disease or fucked up accidental pregnancy due to contraceptive failure ever again. Meaningless paid sex is over. I can finally stop contracting out my dick for a living. I don't care who you are or how brainwashed you've become; pussy rental is not all it's hyped up to be. Nothing behind the scenes is ever how is appears in that short clip for the viewer. My dick was no longer participating without force. Neither of us was happy. He only works for her—volunteered overtime at that. It's sad when your damn dick starts taking a stand for what you want before the rest of you.

In a few short days I'm giving her my last name. Until then, I'm going to do everything I can to court her and to make up for the lost dating time while we were under the nose of a camera constantly. That month was the best month of my life, but I want to give her memories to look back on. I want her to have a story that she's proud of. Sex will fade at some point in our lives. It will become less in frequency. It will also become routine when life gets in the way, because at some point it won't be just the two of us. But in the meantime, I'm going to show her how much she means to me, because every smart man knows that women talk, placing aspects of their relationship out in the open for spectators they call friends. They tell stories, they compare, and it becomes this weird competition that us men will most likely never understand, but I don't want her to sit there embarrassed if those times arise because we never had epic adventures or romantic journeys.

So, with that thought, I have a few short days to come up with mind-blowing things for us to do together and in the midst of all that give her the best fucking birthday she's ever had. My work is cut out for me, but what can I say? I love a challenge.

The apartment door opens and closes. I quietly walk out of the bedroom as Tynleigh is setting her purse on the counter. "What's up, Sprout? Napping?"

"Yeah. How was work?"

"Eventful, but I wouldn't expect anything less. It's damn crazy drama most days but I love my job. I was inspired for a new column idea I'm considering bringing up to my boss. We'll see how things pan out. Where's Kambry?"

"Still sleeping. Did you get them?"

"Depends. How much are they worth to you?"

"I already promised you Coney Island tomorrow. What more do you want, woman?"

"Are you sure you want to walk into this conversation? I can be a hell of a negotiator, because the list of requests can get lengthy."

"Hit me with it. I need them and I don't have much of a choice. Since my alone time is limited, I need you to help me make the rest of this trip unforgettable. You're the local, not me." She gets a gleam in her eye. "Don't get extreme. I know how your crazy ass is."

"Well, you need me, and regardless of what you think I need you in this too. This can easily become a give and take thing. For starters, I need you to call Mom and invite her to the wedding."

"For what, T? It's not a legit wedding. The idea is to just get married. The dress is only to give her that tradition."

"Yes, you're having a *small* wedding. It's nothing fancy and would never be headline worthy, but it's something more special than standing in a courtroom before a judge. She isn't knocked up and this isn't Vegas. There is no reason for you to be against a tiny ceremony. I'm busting my ass to put something together on short notice because I know you'll both thank me in the end, but I swear on my life I'll drop everything and tell you to do it yourself if you don't at least call Mom and Dad and invite them. I would do it myself but it would mean more coming from you. They've done a lot for us over the years, as annoying as they can be at times. It comes with the job. They're our parents. You know I hate to be the levelheaded advocate type and all because that's no fun, but someone has to be in this. They've stood behind us both even when they don't agree with what we're doing. They may not advertise to their friends what you do, but they've never shunned you either. They deserve to be present at the life-changing events in our lives if they want to be, and you know Mom is dying for one of us to settle down. Throw her a fucking bone, Saxton. You already make me look like the golden child with your interesting career choice, but I'll never hear the end of this if you don't."

"There's no chance of you letting this go is there?"

"Nope."

"Fine. What else?"

"You have to stay with Bryant or at a hotel the night before the wedding."

My mouth falls. "What the fuck, T? You're kicking me out? That's bullshit. We film porn and we live together. We've had sex more times than I can count in more ways and places than you want to know. What the fuck is that going to accomplish? No preacher is going to agree to marry us. Technically we're porn stars. That doesn't coincide with the teachings in the Bible and it's not something we can just walk away from right now. You're going to have to just get someone certified by the state to do it."

"Hostile much? Damn, it's like twenty-four hours if that. You're like a junkie. You'll be fine. It'll have a better effect when you see her walking down the aisle. You're going to part ways by mid-afternoon, and Bryant is taking you out for a bachelor thing and Meg and I are taking Kambry."

"Hell no. No, T. I don't give a damn about a bachelor party. She can go where she wants but I'm coming. I'm not turning her loose in New York for her to end up on the news in a missing persons report. Hell to the mother fucking no."

She grins. "I don't remember that being a question. You know what happens when you argue with me."

"I don't care. There's a first time for everything. I'm not backing down on this."

She slides something off the bar and starts fanning herself with the two rectangular tickets. "I can also spend the rest of the time you're here at work."

"That's fucked up."

"It's fucked up for you to insult me. I've been living here since graduation and nothing has ever happened to me. I would never let something happen to her. I know how you feel about her. I can see it. If you don't trust anyone else, you should trust me. And also, I've got three years on you, Sprout, so take that shit to someone else."

"You can be such a fucking bitch sometimes."

"Awe, thank you. That's so sweet."

I slam my elbows on the bar and lean my forehead against my palms. "How late?" My voice comes out reflecting the defeated state I'm in. "I don't really want my fiancé making permanent vows still drunk or hung over."

"Two at the latest. I'll cut her off earlier if she's getting too drunk."

I stand and look at her. "No drugs; not even a fucking Xanax. You promise you'll guard her with your life? I'm not fucking kidding, Tynleigh. Don't rip my heart out."

"Always. She's family. If it makes you feel better I'll go somewhere I know most of the bouncers in the safest areas of New York: we kind of have to. Her age is an inconvenience when seeking alcohol. You just missed robbing the cradle on this one," she teases.

I snatch the tickets out of her hand. "So help me, if you don't have her in this apartment by 2:30 on the dot only God can help you. And she better be able to at least slur an, *I'm okay and I love you or goodnight.* If not, I'm knocking down the fucking door."

"I knew you'd see it my way," she continues, adding fuel to the fire she started.

I grab the phone from where I sat it on the bar and walk toward her bedroom. "Where are you going?"

"To call Mom before I decide this is all a horrible idea and take her to fucking Vegas."

"Tell her I said Hi. Love you," she says in a loud whisper as I pretend to slam the door but catch it before it can actually make noise. Fucking sisters: the one form of female you can legit hate and love at the exact same time.

Kambry

"Mmm. That feels nice."

Soft lips touch just beneath the juncture of my ear and jaw, before lightly descending the length of my neck. His stubble is grazing my skin. My breathing picks up in sound and pace when his hand begins rubbing up the outside of my thigh. The bottom of my foot travels along the sheets of the bed toward my butt, forcing my leg into a full bend. My legs spread the second his tee shirt touches my thighs at the bottom of my shorts, allowing him between them.

A void takes place, and I can feel the air hit against my face and chest, giving me a chill. "Come back."

My butt is lifted off the bed just enough for my shorts and underwear to come down. I arch when his fingers touch me there. A moan escapes when he slowly enters me with two fingers. "You going to sleep while we do this?"

That husky voice lures me out of the mental coma I'm obviously in, my eyes slowly coming unglued. I blink a few times, trying to wake up, and realize he is still fingering me. It, once again, was not a dream. "This is becoming a habit," I say, my mouth a little dry. "You could warn a girl."

He enters harder and hooks his fingers up, looking at me from up on his knees. "My fingers entering your pussy were assumed to be warning enough. It's a restricted zone to everyone else so it shouldn't set off any alarms. Plus, I kind of like pushing myself into your dreams."

His fingers leave my body. "Don't stop."

He removes his shirt and my shorts the rest of the way, then stands from the bed. "Not a chance in Hell. Show me your tits."

I look at him in all of his lean-muscled glory as he pushes the basketball shorts and his boxer briefs down his legs; that's what I call them anyway. When he stands upright his dick is saluting at full attention. "I still can't believe that fits," I mutter aloud, incidentally, instantly wanting to bite my tongue.

My mouth begins to water staring at it. The thickness inches my hand forward, wanting to grip it. Holding it always makes my hand feel so small. I force my eyes to ascend, locking with his. He's not speaking, just standing there, creating this somewhat awkward moment. I avoid the little voice deep down that is telling me to sit here like a corpse and be weird. My first instinct is to shut down, so instead I stand to my knees, facing him, and slowly peel my shirt and camisole up my body, leaving me in nothing but my bra.

His eyes scrape down my body so slowly that I can't breathe, and my skin releases a thin layer of sweat even though I can feel the air circulating in the room. As many times as we've done it and he can still make me feel like it's the first time . . .

I stumble to reach behind me and unlatch my bra, letting it fall from my arms in a peculiar fashion; almost a fumbling act. This is usually second nature, but now, I feel like it's something unfamiliar. My heart is beating out of my chest.

The second my bra falls to the floor he comes at me in full attack mode, pushing me to my back as he positions himself firmly over me. In a matter of seconds—barely enough time to move my legs out from under me—his head is entering me.

He stops when the head is fully inside and grabs behind my thighs, folding them back to my stomach. Without taking his eyes off of me, he leans over me, holding my legs in position, and then he laces our fingers beside my head. With one motion he thrusts inside of me until his pelvis is completely flush with the back tops of my legs and my bent knees are beneath his underarms, my shins to his sides acting as a resting place for some of his weight.

I clench around him, trying to quickly accommodate him and the fully submerged state he's in. He's not usually this aggressive or straightforward with entry considering his size and my small frame, but occasionally, or more so on rare occurrence, he surprises me and treats me like a vixen instead of a kitten.

The look on his face tells me he's all in. He's vested in what he's about to do. He needs this. No foreplay this time. I read once that a guy cares about his woman if he initiates foreplay every time he wants sex, like it's selfish otherwise, but you know what? I don't find that to be true at all. To me, it's quite the opposite really. Every romance book I've read to date is really the same thing over and over, even with them being so drastically different or just mildly. She *always* gets off first. It's the same formula. She comes then he comes, and he's a bad guy otherwise, but from what I've learned about sex and the human body, neither male nor female always work on a controlled timer. Sometimes he lasts longer and sometimes he makes it obvious that he knows he won't be able to by going down on me, or getting me off through clit stimulation. But this, on occasion, is perfectly acceptable and makes me love our sex life even more, because I'm his partner, and I'm his vice when he needs a fix.

I want to be wanted, and sometimes to the point that he can't wait to be inside of me. Foreplay takes time. Orgasm takes concentration. Sometimes I just want to be woken up and attacked. Coming not always necessary. Even if he didn't feel the need to get me off every time, I don't have to. It feels good regardless, and the suddenness of the act itself has me so turned on I don't care how it ends. I believe there should be a thing called a mental orgasm: where you're so turned on you can't think, you can't act except on instinct, and you lose the ability to fully function. And maybe there is. Maybe that's what it truly means to reach nirvana: a state of mental orgasm.

I move my feet over the fronts of his thighs, my heels now resting against the back. Our eyes locked, his face lowers toward me and his hips begin to rock. Not a thrust, but a steady, slow grind inside of me. His entire body is stationary over me, his hips flexing only. "When you fucking look at me like that I'm a goner."

He's so deep it's hard to speak. Words won't come. Still, in the beginning of sex, it hurts, especially when he pushes himself as deep as his length will allow, but it also feels so damn good. The rhythm is hypnotic. My eyes roll toward the back of my head. "I'm already there."

"You'll always be my girl," he says, and just as my eyes return to his, he kisses me, long and hard, followed by short and sweet once his hips stop moving.

"Promise?"

"With a ring and my last name."

He pulls out and looks down briefly. "I'm sorry. I was wound up. Want me to eat it?"

My cheeks heat from his vulgar slip of the tongue. "No. Why fix something if it's not broken. This was perfect."

"Thank you."

He stands. "Where are you going?"

His hand extends and rubs through his hair. "We're going to shower." He turns and starts to walk into the bathroom. "I'm taking you on a casual date. By the way . . ." He sticks his head out of the bathroom, already turned back around. "You're going to meet my parents this weekend. They're coming."

Then, like a turtle disappearing into its shell, he reels his head in and shuts the door, but doesn't lock it. I imagine the look of horror most likely on my face has something to do with that. My hands cover my face. What the actual fuck just happened here? Parents! I'm not ready to meet his parents. Silly I know, considering I'm about to be his wife, but backward looks good on me. It clicks. The light bulb comes on and it shines brightly. "Oh my god. I totally just got buttered up with sex," I mumble against my palms.

I stand and burst through the bathroom door as he's stepping in the shower. "Saxton Maverick Cambridge, you totally just brought me the dick to drop that dynamite on me . . . Didn't you? You just put it on me as a softener. I cannot believe you." The laugh that escapes with the last word gives me away, but I am going to continue anyway, and try my damnedest to be mad at him for ten seconds at least.

"I love you," he says, his voice revealing the hidden laughter his smile has already introduced.

I smack his butt before he pulls the final leg into the shower and then point my index finger of my stinging hand at him. "No, sir. This is not okay. I'm not prepared to meet your parents; for them to know I'm screwing their son for the world to see and to become their daughter-in-law all in one whammy. I need baby steps, or crap just steps, like climbing stairs. I need preparation. What's more: I need a notice. You don't throw someone into an exhibit at a zoo without warning them that the dangerous animal that could be their ruin is in there. Rude. And by the way, just because you came and gave me quite possibly one of the best fuckings of my life, doesn't make this situation okay or give you a free ticket to pass go. You have no idea how scary this is for me. Your hot-boy smile and big dick cannot get you out of everything."

I finally stop my rambling long enough to actually *look* at him. He's leaning on his forearm against the shower wall. He's mostly dry, except for the spray from the water coating his body. His dimples appear. Dammit. Those are like panty-shredder buttons. I need a superpower. This is so unfair.

He says nothing. Literally, he just stands there with a big damn grin on his face, staring at me, completely butt ass naked. "What is so funny?" I shout the question a little too loud. "You're supposed to be in trouble. You're not supposed to look at me like you're about to drag me into the woods and never let me be found. Not the time to be a sexy creeper."

"Did you just . . ." His voice is deep, with a raspy tone behind it. His words come out slowly. ". . . spank me?"

My head rears back, a little caught off guard. "Uh . . . maybe." I straighten my posture; confident I can be a badass in the presence of an alpha of the deadliest degree. A controlling man with the goodness of a golden boy is a weapon. My nose turns up slightly. "I mean, yes. Well, serves you right. You don't just throw a grenade at me and leave me to fend for myself."

Neither his position nor his facial expression has changed. "Oh, stop it with that sexy smile. It's not even that big of a deal. So I slapped your ass. Whoopty-do. You slap mine pretty often. It was there and perky and shouting—*smack that ass*—at me. You have a cute butt. I'm sure weirder things have happened."

"Actually, nope. That would top them all."

"Shut up." I laugh. "You're trying to create a diversion and it's not working. We need to discuss this."

"Okay, fine. Bring me a boob to squeeze and we will discuss."

"You're ridiculous."

"And you're letting the water go to waste. What's your point?"

My shoulders drop and I walk toward the shower. He moves aside to let me step inside. We stand face to face with him under the water, letting it run down his body. I glance down at his dick. I can't help it. The way it looks soft and stowed away amazes me. Dicks are magical. The way they can grow in a matter of seconds to twice their size or more is just nuts.

I wonder what a guy that isn't so blessed downstairs looks like soft. Does it disappear completely? Does peeing become difficult with his balls in the way? Or do they just stretch it out like one of those *as seen on TV* crinkle water hoses? Saxton soft, I wouldn't necessarily call small, even though it isn't a comparison to it fully hard. My hand could wrap around it soft and still have length left over, but according to Meredith he's in the minority. I wouldn't know, but that probably wouldn't look good in your Google search history: dick pics. I would just hope those that are less fortunate have skill to back up where they lack in size, because I kind of gather that there is probably a fine line separating the whole phrase—*size doesn't matter*.

"Does it meet inspection?"

I clear my throat and quickly divert my eyes back to his. "Um. What?"

"My dick. You're just staring at it, inspecting every inch. If I had a dick-do I would think you were counting how many hairs."

I feel like that little blushing emoji with the wide eyes and rosy cheeks. I'm a little embarrassed, until he starts walking toward me, pushing me toward the shower wall with a slight smirk on his face. "For the record, I like that you're clean shaven."

He grabs my boob in one hand, placing the other on the wall behind me. "Every guy should manscape in some form. It's more pleasure for the girl and less of a nasty hassle for him. It doesn't take much effort either. Think of it as a barrier. You can go deeper with nothing in the way."

His words end as his mouth closes around my nipple. That feels amazing. He sucks hard, leaving it erect as he pulls free. "What was it you were wanting to discuss?"

Parents.

My eyes open and I lightly shove him back. My lost train of thought was short lived. I'm not turned on anymore. That word is enough to dry you up even in the midst of water. "Seriously, what happened? Why is this turning into a parental chaperone thing? I thought this was just going to be between us." The stressed thoughts show through my voice. My head falls. "I was good with just us," I say in a whisper.

The curve of his bent index finger lifts my chin, tilting my head back to make eye contact with him. "What's the big deal about meeting my parents? When you marry me they will kind of be your parents too. Talk to me."

I breathe, a little unsteady, and unsure what exactly *is* the issue with meeting his parents. I met his sister and was fine. "I don't know."

"You remember our talk about communication? It's necessary to form a good relationship. It's the foundation of trust. If we're going to be husband and wife I need to know you can confide in me, even if you think it's a hard conversation to have."

The thoughts I've obviously been suppressing instantly float to the surface with one look from him and a few sentences, causing my eyes to well up. It's like he's speaking directly to my soul sometimes, purging my deepest thoughts without me knowing they even exist. That makes him my master in some ways. My soul belongs to him, and everything else just follows. It reacts to only him when he calls upon it. There are no secrets between us—not really. All he has to do is ask and I spill my heart with no effort.

A tear falls. "What if they think I'm a whore? They could hate me. What if they think you deserve better and your mom comes to you about it? Then what? Would you walk away from this? The two of you said she's opinionated about things. Conservative people don't approve of this lifestyle or behavior. I know that, but I wasn't really expecting to find my life partner when I agreed to this. It was supposed to be a little bit of rebellion with a lot of fun. Good parents don't want a porn star for their daughter-in-law. There will always be double standards. Boys will be dismissed of all charges and their indiscretions will be written off as misconduct while girls get stuck in the category they were originally placed in. I would never want us to coexist in a world where only one of us is welcome. It's easier to just pretend no one outside of us exists, because I can't bear the thought of us not being together."

My lashes are wet from my tears. He stares into my eyes, and I swear I see a tear form, but knowing the man of steel that resides beneath that beautiful skin I know it'll never fall if it is. "Fuck, baby."

He runs his hands down my body until they are firmly set on my butt, and then roughly lifts my body against his and plants my back against the shower wall. My legs clamp around his waist, trying to hold on. "I just can't be without you. Pathetic as it may be, but I know exactly how that feels. I do know that I can't be a hindrance either. I'm terrified of meeting them."

He kisses me, smothering the sentences mentally prepared to come next. When our lips are raw and our breathing is ragged, we stare at each other. Water is dripping from his hair, running into his lashes and down his face. Unknown emotion is written all over his face. I wish I could freeze this moment in time so I can look back on it forever. "Are you serious? Was me giving you a ring and looking like an ass after I told you I'd wait years for you to age before doing something like that not proof enough? Kambry, I would never walk away from this now that I know exactly what I have. I don't give a damn what anyone thinks, including my parents, but you really have no idea how my parents are. They've not one single time in mine or Tynleigh's life tried to butt into our personal life."

One hand clenches in my hair at the back of my head and he repositions my weight in the other. My fingers find the hair at the back of his neck. "Baby, they would never think you were a whore, and I swear on my fucking life if that's the way you see things then I will walk away from filming for both of us, contract or not. They can fine me or throw me in jail. I don't care what the consequence of breaking it is. You're my life now. You're what is important to me. You're mine, and anyone that doesn't see you for the girl that I see is dead to me. You're what I want. Most people wouldn't even classify girls that have been around the block a few times a whore, much less someone that's marrying the man she gave her virginity to. As far as the filming, I was doing that way before you came along. Sex isn't a secretive, dirty thing anymore. What we do together is our business. They will not ask those kinds of questions. I promise they don't want to know about our sex life. Even if they knew, I can almost guarantee they'd rather me film porn with my wife than with a variation of women. Stop worrying, okay? They will love you."

"I know I'm being stupid and probably immature. I'm just trying to deal with all of these new feelings. I'm not doing a very good job either. I think I was just expecting for the two of us to stand in front of a judge and that be it. We'd be married and go on our way. This is overwhelming."

"I wasn't thrilled about it either, but after I spoke with Tynleigh she made me realize that she's right. I'd be an ass of a son to not even extend the invite. I've been the other end of extreme for a long time now. They deserve a little bit of family normalcy."

"This was Tynleigh's idea?"

"Yeah, baby, it was, but she's right. It needed to be brought up before years of anger and hurt followed. I didn't see it until I called my mom and heard her voice when I told her."

I close my eyes briefly and open them, still nervous. "Okay. What did she say?"

"She dropped the phone." My heart starts to race. "From covering her mouth with her hands I imagine and forgetting she was holding it. She does that when she's excited."

"And then?"

I feel like I'm waiting on the damn plot twist to be over. I can't stand the suspense. "After much fumbling, she screamed and told me if this was a joke she'd personally make sure I regretted it."

"After that you said . . ."

"That even though it seemed humorous after all this time, it wasn't. I told her I had found the girl that I couldn't live without, so I'm permanently ensuring I don't have to try. Funny, though, isn't it? Most kids would probably get that response if they mentioned filming porn, while I get asked that about getting married. She did ask how we met and what I was planning on doing about my career at present . . ."

"Oh my god. What did you tell her?" I want to chew on my newly done nails.

"I told her not to ask questions she didn't want the answer to . . ."

"I want to bite you so hard right now."

His smile disappears. "That can be arranged."

I pull at his hair as hard as I can. "Focus. I can't even deal with your sexual humor right now. Why did you not just make up something?"

"Lying is not a good habit to have."

"There are times when an exception should be allowed!"

"Why? I gave her enough information to suffice if she feels obligated to tell someone. I then said, 'but if you need a legit answer for marketing purposes I met her in a nightclub and I'm still working out the details.' She was perfectly fine with that answer."

"Okay. That I can live with. When is she coming?"

"Saturday. Mid-morning. She wasn't sure until she looked at flights."

"This is really happening. I was kind of expecting you to say Sunday."

He shakes his head. "I tried. She wanted more time to get to know you. I even told her Tynleigh and Meg were taking you out Saturday night and she said her and Dad would find stuff to do then."

"Wait. What?"

"I'll tell you later. Can we finish here? I'm still thinking of biting . . ."

His teeth immediately dig into the flesh of one boob. My eyes close and my head falls back when his teeth scrape along the surface of my skin. A breathy moan escapes. "Biting what?"

"Your pussy lips."

A shiver overcomes me. He moves to the center of the shower space, wetting us both. "Are we going to be a while?"

"As long as it takes. On your feet. Then ass up."

All the muscles between my legs lock. I can't explain the way my body reacts when he gets this dirty, raw demeanor about him. I guess it's my fetish with us. "Will it hurt?"

My legs slide down his body until they hit the floor. His face is completely serious. He's transitioned into this alpha male that has nothing on his mind but fucking. He's not the boy that just made love to me. He's the man that wants to use and abuse my body in the most beautiful way. "Do you want it to hurt?"

I turn away from him and bend over, placing my hands on the edging of the tub. His thumb and the curve of his bent index finger clamp around the skin that encompasses my clit and he pulls. My body follows; a reflex of the pain. "Kind of like this?"

All I can think about—wanting him to touch me more and longer. The way you feel when you're starving for food and can't do anything but suffer through the salivating occurring in your mouth is exactly the way I feel between my legs. He slaps my ass, still locked onto me. I look over my shoulder at him standing behind me, his feet firmly planted. "Yes," I say, my breathing exiting my mouth in jagged spurts. The words exit without me willing them to. "Bite me."

The water changes from the showerhead to the faucet, and I can hear him stop up the drain. One by one he drops to his knees, but doesn't let go of his hold on me. Instead, he tightens it, and as he does the pad of his thumb grazes my clit still nestled inside. "Bring your pussy to my face."

"Shi—" I whisper, and slowly push off with my hands, sending my lower half toward him. He wiggles his thumb a little, barely touching it again. He knows what he's doing. My body starts to move in the opposite direction from the sensation it caused, but as I do his teeth lock on the skin outside of my entrance, creating a tug-o-war effect. Like a rubber band I retract.

I can barely stay still with him doing that. He inches inward and sucks the surrounding area into his mouth like one would the overspill of soda on the lid of a cup. He jerks on me again and I scream out on accident. Everything down below feels like it's throbbing. He nips my skin again and then pushes a thumb inside of me, thrusting in and out a few times. When he pulls out, he circles the tip and then moves up until it's perfectly aligned over my back entrance.

I want him to push in so bad. I want it in the dirtiest way possible. He never disappoints. I bite down on my bottom lip when he pushes through the puckered muscle slowly, opening it. "Fuck, your pussy is beautiful when it's dripping wet because of me." His tongue swipes along one lip as he begins to thrust in and out with his thumb.

His thumb and index fingers release me, but immediately are replaced with the flush mounted position of his index and middle fingers against the sensitive skin. He exerts a hard pressure against it and swipes back and forth once, parting my lips enough to touch my clit. "Right there. Please right there."

As soon as the last word exits my mouth his pace increases tenfold. My back arches, forcing my bottom harder against him. "Your pussy is contracting so hard. You're so wet. You want my cock in there, baby? You haven't had enough yet?"

If I were aware of the sounds coming from my mouth right now I'd probably be mortified, but I'm at a point of no return in the mental awareness department. All I know is he's coming at me from two different directions and the occasional nibble at the center. It feels glorious and euphoria is knocking at my door. Only a glass window stands in my way but not for long. It's about to shatter in five, four, three . . . "Don't stop. Dammit don't stahhhp."

The words trail off as my entire body stills. For a few moments I'm lost in another world before I'm pulled back. He knows when I'm gone and when I come back, though, because the second my orgasm dwindles he's pulling out of me. I stand upright in the calf deep water and turn around. He's already standing. "I can't believe this is my life. What I did to deserve you, Sax?"

He wraps his arms around me and pulls me to his chest. A very noticeable appendage is driving a space between us. "How much time do we have?"

He looks into my eyes. "We don't have to do anything more. I got off earlier. I'm perfectly satisfied with just showering and getting ready. It'll go down. You deserve couple time that doesn't involve sex or clubs."

I grab his dick and begin stroking it. "How much time do we have?" I ask again, driving my point across.

"Enough."

"How do you want it?"

A smirk appears on his face. "How about a little *Throwback Thursday*?"

"It's not Thursday yet."

"It's close enough."

The water continues to rise. It dawns on me. My expression now matches his. "Bathtub sex?"

He shuts off the water and sits down. "Just like that first night."

"That seems so long ago."

"But nowhere close to being long enough. A lot of firsts happened that night."

"Did I ever tell you how nervous I was that night?"

"No, but some of it was noticeable."

"Not for the reason you think. That actually didn't bother me at all. I was ready for that. I was actually nervous as hell that I would fall in love with you."

He smiles, and with that smile comes the showing of how much love he really has for me. That's one thing I love about his smiles. "And here we are."

"Here we are," I repeat.

"How'd that work out for you?"

"I had every reason to be nervous. You bewitched me, and I failed miserably, because even though I told myself not to, I've fallen hopelessly in love with you."

"Show me."

His phone on the bathroom counter catches my attention. I grab it. "How about a bonus edition?"

"Whatever you want, beautiful."

I straddle him and lower myself onto his thighs. "Sweet is always better with a little heat."

His hands wrap in my wet hair and he pulls me into a kiss. I always love the way his stubble makes my lips feel raw. A tingling effect begins shortly after. Our warm tongues meld together perfectly, every time we kiss.

He grabs the phone from my hand. One hand finds a place to steady the rest of my body. I grab his dick and sit down on it, the water starting to move. I pull away from his lips as I begin to ride him. He places one hand on my thighs and waits for me to look at him before saying anything. "Some of the best scenes come after the cut."

"I like to think of it as deleted scenes."

And with the angle of the camera pointed to where he wants it, he looks back up at me. "Then let's make them good ones. Ride my cock, baby."

So I do. Clip-by-clip and post-by-post we're documenting our porn love story, because in a way I don't want to lose this. After all, it's what brought us together in the first place.

CHAPTER FOURTEEN

Saxton

"Are you going to tell me why I had to dress a little . . .different than my usual taste?"

I glance over at her in the cab. "You'll find out soon enough."

"Aren't you supposed to dress a little classier than Rockstar for a date?"

I look down at the Rolling Stones band tee shirt she's wearing. "You make a mouth look good, baby. I think that tongue between your tits fits the occasion pretty damn well. Just know that if I face-plant your chest later it's totally normal."

She lifts her foot holding each end of the shoe. "Sax, I'm wearing Converse. I've never owned a pair in my life. They make me look like I have clown feet. I would hardly think this is appropriate for any sort of date."

"You could never have clown feet baby," I interrupt.

"Just curious, though. What would you have done if Tynleigh and I wore different sizes?"

"You brought your own jeans; the only part that matters. The shirt looks amazing because your rack is bigger than hers. No man ever said loose is better than tight when referencing a woman in any way. Everything is the way it is for a reason, beautiful. They were just meant to fit. Nothing is random, just maybe temporarily unknown of its existence, but if you must know look out your window and find out for yourself."

She instantly turns her head toward the window as the cab pulls into Madison Square Garden. Her body draws closer to get a better view I suppose. Me—I sit back and watch the expression on her face as it changes, because one thing that makes me happy is seeing her explore new things in life. Every new adventure with her is what makes living life worthwhile.

"Wow." Her voice is reverent, soft. She's in awe, as she is from time to time, and that is what strikes my heart and makes it beat harder and faster. "I've never seen anything like this in real life. It's beautiful. Is this?"

She pauses and looks back at me. "Is this Madison Square Garden? *The* Madison Square Garden . . ."

The cab stops and I jump out to run around it before she can open the door herself. I want to do this right. She looks at me out the window as I grab the handle and open the door. I reach for her hand as the smile begins to break through. She stares at me, waiting for me to speak or do something first. I hand the driver fare plus tip to get him out of here and shut the door.

When he pulls off I wrap my arm around her and rest my hand on her shoulder. "It is. I was trying to decide our first little nighttime journey in the city together that didn't involve sex or partying and I just felt this was right with your love for music. It's a well-known event venue all over the continental U.S. I'm going to put it out there that I'm aware it probably isn't who you would have chosen to see given the option, but I figured we could have a little fun and it was about the only reasonable option. I'm sorry but I can't do Kanye. Rock or girly shit, fine, but him I didn't think you'd want to see either."

"I cannot believe I'm really standing here, staring at Madison Square Garden all lit up. This is amazing, and it's perfect, regardless of who we see. You really do get me. Do you realize that? I don't think that's something that you easily find in someone, but you really think about my likes and my dislikes. You always go the extra mile with us. I love you so much, Sax."

I can't explain the weird as hell feeling I get in my chest every time she makes it known that she loves me. What I do know is that I would spend my last fucking dime or take my last breath to make her happy like this forever. I kiss her temple. "I love you the most. You ready to rock out?"

She glances up at me as we start to walk. "Who's playing?"

"AC/DC."

"No crap?"

"Do you like them?"

"I'm not a huge fan or anything, but I've heard a few songs. I'm actually kind of excited."

"That makes me happy, baby."

When we make it through the gate I hand her the ticket stubs. "What's this for?"

"I was thinking. It might be cool if you made us one of those books. You know, the ones that you fill up with different stuff. It could be something we can take with us when we buy that house; also something we can add to here and there. Like memories and shit. Whatever it is that girls put in there. I don't really know what I'm talking about. I just remember my mom having several of them. I've been noticing you taking pictures here and there and I just thought it was a good idea. Maybe not. You don't have to. Like I said it was just a thought."

She pulls on my hand when I stop at the concession stand line to get my attention. "Are you talking about a scrapbook?"

"Yeah. That's what it was called."

"You would participate in random girly things when it comes to an overabundance of photos and ridiculous ideas to make one?"

"Yeah. I'd rather play along and have a lot of stuff to look back on one day than to be an asshole and then regret it. I've already wasted so much of my life I feel like. I don't want to waste any more. I've found the girl I want to be with. I don't know. It may not be a very masculine idea and I'm not a crafty person so I'll leave the production to you, but I'm a pretty simple guy. I don't want much, but I do want memories."

I move up as the line slowly dwindles. Once we stop again, she walks in front of me and wraps her arms around my waist. I glance down at her and her lips touch against mine. She pulls away from the kiss quickly to avoid a scene. "What was that for?"

"For being the greatest man there is. I think that's a brilliant idea. I've never done one, but I can research and experiment. I'll just put these in my wallet for now."

"You want a beer?"

"They serve alcohol?"

My brows dip. "Most concerts do, especially rock. They just don't carry the glass bottles. It's usually aluminum." I pause, thinking. "I'm going to risk sounding like a jackass. Have you never been to a concert at all?"

"Not secular. I've been to some with my youth group."

I take a deep breath, letting out some of my frustration before the words expel. It angers me every time I realize just how sheltered she was. It's fucking ridiculous. I get a parent wanting to keep your kid out of trouble, but there are plenty of *in-betweens*. I know I shouldn't be surprised anymore, but I am. Living on a farm I had a lot of responsibility that most kids didn't, but I still had time to experience being a teenager.

She's staring at me, and I realize she's worrying. I wrap my arms around her shoulders and pull her in for a mutual hug instead of me standing like a zombie while she hugs me. I need to let all expectations of dating go and just go back to the basics, because with most things, that's what it is with her. "It's no big deal. I guess I was just assuming you had been to something like Nsync or Britney Spears: a family oriented, kid friendly concert."

"Ha! I wish. That would have meant I had normal parents."

We make it to the counter. "What do you want?"

"Whatever you get," she quickly replies.

I hold up my fingers. "Two Bud Lights please."

I grab them and pay to quickly move out of the crowded way, then hand one to her and take her hand as I do. She keeps pace until we make it toward the direction we're supposed to go. A tee-shirt stand selling band gear catches my eye as we move through the sea of people walking in different directions, so I stop. "Which one do you want?" I ask close to her ear so she can hear me.

She points to the one she wants hanging on the metal caging behind the few people working the table. The older man with the staffing badge glances back to see which one it is. "Make it two. A large and a—"

"Large," she says as I look at her.

"Large?"

She smiles. "Sleepshirt. That way I don't have to wear shorts."

Wrong time to think of her in a tee shirt and panties, but I give her a look I know she'll understand and move on. "Whatever the lady wants," I state to the man waiting for us to make up our minds.

He pulls two from the same large cardboard box and hands them to her, rolled up and secured with a rubber band, as I pay. "Add a pair of those too," I say, pointing to the red staring at me from the table. I set my beer down to take them in one hand as I place my wallet back in my pocket, before turning to her. She has the rim of the beer at her lips, taking a sip. Her face sours as she brings it back down.

"Don't like it?"

"It'll just take some getting used to. I haven't quite become accustomed to that taste yet. I still prefer the sweeter stuff."

"It's an acquired taste. Once you get used to it you'll never stray."

My eyes are focused on her hair as I pull the small tag to make them blink, and then place the headband on her head in a way I know it won't mess up her hair too much. "There. I think we're all set. You look kind of cute, but definitely naughty."

As I pick up my beer she tucks the shirts under her arm and grabs my other hand. "Well, this is definitely a change from the angel my parents always forced me to be. Maybe I should take a photo and text it to my mom. That would be a laugh for sure . . .or collateral damage."

We walk toward the stadium seating according to the tickets to find our seats. "Oh, a couple horns here and there never hurt anybody."

The stadium is already mostly packed. I'm actually relieved that somehow we ended up with seats at the end of a row. I let her in, and then take my seat, immediately placing my arm around her. "What do you think?"

Her eyes are all over the place, and the most contented expression resides on her face as she people watches. There are thousands of other people with the same blinking red horns that she has on scattered throughout the arena. "I think this is the coolest thing I've ever done. I owe you for that. Thank you for bringing me here."

I kiss her and pull her into my side. "You're welcome, baby. You do know if there is ever anything you want to do all you have to do is ask, don't you?"

"I guess, but that's just it. I don't think about things usually because I'm so used to not being able to do them. By the way, I don't think I've ever seen this whole rocker grunge look on you. It's kind of hot."

"You think so? This shirt is old. I'm a little surprised it still fits." I take a swig of beer. "Back in college me and a few friends would go to concerts here and there or music festivals. When you're working your way through college the music festivals were the best way to go. One price, all you can drink, multiple bands, and usually food all in the same place. It's a broke kid's dream."

"Oh yeah? Did you take Salem to a lot of concerts?"

That name puts a bitter taste in my mouth, especially where something so pure sitting next to me is concerned in the same place, but I can tell by her tone she's just curious and carrying on conversation. I let Salem go long before she came along, but that doesn't mean I like talking about her either; nonetheless, part of a strong relationship is open discussion, even about things that no longer matter.

"Actually no. She was a bitch even on good days, and that form of entertainment was beneath her. Things that made her happy usually included drama or juicy gossip; even high exposure situations. She would often tell me about faculty dirt and secrets around the school no one should really know. It was annoying honestly, because no one but her cared about that shit. I guess that's why she was a journalism major. She only wanted to do uppity type stuff. She was really kind of a boring person. We weren't friends like you and me. Dating someone like her wasn't my greatest decision in life. We did not go together on any level. I see that with 20/20 vision now. It was usually just me and my roommate Joel and a few others that hung around a lot; our crew I guess."

"That sounds so cool. I like doing this kind of stuff with you. It's fun."

"So, I have to ask since you brought up the ex. What did this douche do for you if he never took you on dates?"

She shrugs her shoulders. "It wasn't his fault really. He wasn't allowed to take me out. He had to come to my house to see me outside of school. My parents knew they could control a lot of things, but having a boyfriend wasn't one of them, so they found ways to still twist it into their fun little game. I can probably count on one hand the amount of times we actually did something away from parental supervision and it wasn't for an extended period of time. Maybe a ride home here and there after a ballgame or something of the like, and if you think my parents didn't calculate the time frame it took me to get from point A to point B then you're wrong. To be honest, I'm not sure what he did in his spare time when he wanted a normal teenage life, or why he even continued to date me. I'd be surprised if he didn't meet his needs elsewhere and just keep me around because I was a goody-goody, AKA, what most would deem parental girlfriend material. Seems like I got wind of a rumor once, but it went quiet quick. I didn't really question it because I wasn't sleeping with him, so in a way I had no right. I had a sucky life."

I turn on cue from the relaxed state I'm in as if someone just blindsided me and hit me in the fucking face, grabbing her chin in my thumb and index fingers, holding her face mirrored to mine. "No, Kambry. Holy fuck. No. Seriously? Cheating is never okay. Ever. Not even to be on the receiving end of it. Whether you're sleeping with someone or not, if you're in a relationship, you are bound under that invisible law of dating to be faithful unless you sever the contract between the two of you in a verbal agreement. Once you're married it becomes a damn sin to even lust after someone else, let alone act on it. My eyes and thoughts are for you only. When you are with someone, you have every right to question their actions or whereabouts. You can't get me on the phone and you want to know why, or where I've been, you better fucking ask me. I'm obligated to keep you informed. If any man or woman in a relationship of any kind has a problem with that then they should take a seat on the singles train, because that's where they belong. God, I could breathe fire. This is something I have zero tolerance for. Don't you dare ever take fault for someone being a pussy when it comes to being committed to his partner. Do you understand?"

"It didn't really bother me . . ." I'm about to open my mouth again. "*Because* I didn't love him. I just didn't care, Sax. He was just filler in my story. If *you* did, though, I'd never be the same. My heart would stop beating and life for me would end. That I know for sure. Not loving him is what led me to you, in a way, because if I did I would have never left."

That somersault effect in my stomach that most humans know begins as I consider that ending: her loving someone else. I can't ever let that happen. I need her like I need my fucking heart. Without her nothing would work the way it's supposed to and survival would be impossible. I relax. "Better for me I guess, but no man with any amount of raising or sense would cheat on you, Kambry. The day I even fathom sticking my dick in another woman is the day you need to just put a gun to my head and end my life, because that would only happen if my soul has been conquered by a dark source that doesn't need to exist. And if I had known you back then . . ."

Her pupils dilate. "You would have . . ."

"Been the boy your parents despised. I would have probably thrown all good sense out the window and you would have ended up pregnant by graduation. All it takes is the front seat of a pickup truck and ten minutes, five in which to remove your bottoms and the other five to come. That's long enough to explain to parents we had to stop for gas. You're the kind of girl that makes a teenage boy stupid."

The words fell from my mouth without thought as to what I was actually saying. She laces my hand with hers. "But either way the ending would have been the same?"

"Ass backward? Yep. Either way I would have permanently made you mine."

She smiles. "Then whatever middle there is I can deal with, two pink lines and all."

I taste her smile. "One day I'm going to enjoy that view, but I'd rather us be trying for those two pink lines together in our own home instead of you finding out in a Wal-Mart bathroom because you couldn't do it at home. And maybe that's why God knew what he was doing, because the two of us together is a form of crazy love that is not normal. First, you have so much more life to experience."

She takes another sip of her beer when I do. The arena is full and the crowd is settling into the place they are supposed to be according to their tickets. "Hey, will you take a picture with me?"

"Sure, baby."

She pulls her phone out of her small purse and holds it out in front of us, the front camera turned on. "Okay on three. One . . . two . . . three." Before she snaps the photo I stick my tongue out to touch her cheek and make a goofy face, causing her to laugh as the photo captures and becomes a still image on the digital screen. When the screen is ready for another photo, she speaks, looking at me through the camera lens, reflecting on the screen like a mirror. "I love you. Be serious."

"I'll do it for a kiss."

"You'll get the kiss after I get my photo."

"Okay, okay." I smile like any good fiancé would do and she takes another photo. "One more. I didn't like that one."

"What are you a girl?"

"I think you know the answer to that question without me having to elaborate. Humor me."

She preps for her position again, but on the three count I quickly pull her chin toward me and lock lips with her. She moans a little when my tongue slips between her lips, entangling for just a brief hello. "Put that in the scrapbook beside the caption—*I love you too*."

Her eyes are lazy, a smile set deep within her cheeks. "You're the best kind of high." She glances down and pulls up the camera roll just as the lights dim throughout the arena. I glance over. The shot stilled at the perfect time, the lighting just right to catch the pink blushing of her cheeks. That's my girl, completely wound up with the simplest things.

Screams begin all around the arena as the sound of the big screens come to life, playing a video, initiating the start of what's to come: the band's introduction. Hands go into the air as asses leave their seats, index and pinky saluting only. We do the same. Her eyes are completely glued to the stage. I wrap my arm around her and pull her close. Her arm circles my lower back and her hand grips onto my waist. "I hope I'm the only high you'll ever need," I say in a whisper as the band comes into spotlight on the stage, their voices sounding all throughout the arena with the first song, but she didn't hear me, as I intended, and her yells into the crowd confirm it.

It doesn't take long and you'd never know she was a virgin rocker or concert newbie. Her head beats to the music, she loudly sings along to the lyrics within a minute at most into each song, and she's jumping up and down with the crowd, throwing screams and yells into the air at random. She's gone wild, she's broken free from all restrictions, and I fucking love it.

She finished her beer off with the start of *Sweet Candy* a couple songs back, and so I handed her what was left of mine. Normally, I would have finished it forever ago, but I'm enjoying the slow and steady. I don't need the altering state of mind watching her, and one is not enough to do the job anyway. She's a lightweight and I'd rather her have the full experience to take home.

I stand here, hands in pockets, watching her body move in an exaggerated form, heightening with each guitar solo as she plays her imaginary guitar strapped to her front.

She turns toward me and puts her arms around my neck, just before jumping onto my body like a bear climbing a tree, latching her legs around my waist. Reflexively my hands pull from my pockets to grab onto her. *"Hot blooded woman just waiting for me."* She begins to sing—or scream rather—along to *Rock The House* as she stares into my eyes. The veins in her neck show how loud she's trying to be. *"Gonna kick up her heels, make you scream."*

Dear God. "Is that a request?"

She leans into my neck, placing her lips at the base, then the tip of her warm tongue breaks through and she licks up the entire length until she pulls my earlobe between her teeth. "Making me scream is always welcome, Maverick. I'll even let you fuck me to this song."

The little Devil horns accompanying her bold behavior in this sea of people are completely throwing me off my game. It's hot. And I'm hard. I loosen her grip at the ankles sitting at my lower back and slide her down to the appropriate height. I want her to feel every damn inch of the massive bulge I'm sporting between her legs that is now viewable for every person that steals a look at my crotch once she moves. "Don't make offers you aren't one hundred percent ready for, because this behavior is making me want to fuck you until you can't stand. Your body is small and my dick is big. I can find ways and positions to beautifully destroy your pussy."

She deadpans me straight and center, completely hiding behind a poker face now in place. With the rock music continuing to invade our ears, she says, "Mutilate me."

My jaw drops from the locked position it's in. And this is our life. It's fun as hell, it's dirty as shit, and it's completely fucking perfect. She completes me in every aspect of the word; even the most perverted parts. Match for match she competes and wins my heart over and over again. In a few days that girl is forever mine in front of God and bound to me by the law of the land.

I'm as happy as a fuckboy in a room full of naked and horny women. So what do I do? I pull her back up my body and shove my face into the open mouth resting nicely on the most beautiful tits I've ever seen and burrow my face rapidly between them until I'm submerged deeply in the middle of boobs.

Her laughter fills my ears and her back arches away from me. She fists my hair; pulling me out of the cozy boob cocoon I was in. "You totally just motor-boated me again, but this time in front of way too many people. What do you have to say for yourself, boy?"

"I like that bra. It's nonrestrictive. What kind is it?"

"Not what I mean, my sexy boob-crazed psycho."

"Hey . . .I forewarned you. It's totally normal. Let it happen." I smirk. "Besides, I'm sure by this point people already know what those beautiful tits look like and those same people will completely understand my addiction to your breasts and the need to nurse said addiction by getting my daily fix. And no one gets to fucking touch them but me!"

The last line came out a little too excited for a grown man that has seen more sets of tits and pussies than I care to admit. Nothing about female sex organs should amaze me or excite me for that matter, yet hers drive me damn near insane. "You're an overgrown child. I hope you know that."

"In my defense, it's not completely my fault. You should not have been graced with the damn finest body possible and the equivalent in hearts to match. I'm not even going to get started on how beautiful you are, because you will never understand what you've got going on. The fact that you don't is a plus for me. You're a damn lethal being. If your heart wasn't so pure I'd be worried you were created by the Devil himself. I ate from the apple long ago."

"Dammit, I love you," she says, and her lips come crashing down on mine; every full, glossy, beer-flavored inch of them. She's kissing me with fight and perseverance, rubbing my lips raw in the process. She climbs my body a few inches between beats. It takes all of my center balance to avoid falling into the surrounding people, but I fight gravity just to stay like this for a little while longer, because I never want times like this to end.

CHAPTER FIFTEEN

Kambry

The sunlight peeking through the white curtains wakes me. I peek over at Saxton, but he doesn't move from the position he's lying in: stomach to the bed, hand on my boob, and the other under his pillow. It's a position that is pretty common when it comes to his sleeping now.

I glance at the ceiling and shake my head. Maybe I should search the web to see if they have a boob model squeeze toy for stress. There has to be a perverted enough person to have thought of it by now. If I could find one, I would order him his own. I can picture it, and every time he panics and needs a cigarette he could just reach for his portable pocket boob if I'm not around and squeeze on it for a while.

A small laugh escapes and I smother it with my hand. The amount of love I have for that goofy ass sex machine is not measurable. I'm pretty sure of it. I sigh in a contented whisper. My heart is so full on most days breathing is difficult.

Slipping from his hold on me, I sneak out of the bed quietly, my bladder full, and grab my phone off the nightstand once I'm out of the danger zone of waking him. I pull up the camera and snap a shot of his face and torso. It's hard not to. When you love a person as much as I love him, there is an extra special appreciation for them when they're sleeping: a person's most peaceful form.

I tiptoe to the bathroom in the AC/DC tee shirt he bought me last night and slowly shut the door. After all that talk he didn't even give me any. Bullshit talking men, I swear. Just because I dozed off on the cab ride home doesn't mean I'm too tired for sex after the fact.

And I was not drunk. I don't care what he says. Who the hell gets drunk off of one and a half beers? He just doesn't think I can hit when he throws me sex-talkin' curveballs, when in reality a comfy shoulder is a booby trap for those of the conscious state of mind. No pun intended. It sucks you into dreamland faster than you can feel sleepy.

I shuck my panties onto the floor and sit on the toilet. I want to expel a sound of relief as my bladder frees itself of the piss burden it carries, but I refrain due to the sleeping giant on the other side of that door that I don't want to wake yet, because no person just pees and gets off the pot when they first wake up. If they do then they're psycho monsters that are bred from another species and not human, because there is something relaxing about just sitting here and not having to do anything for a few moments in time once you wake up.

I unlock my phone and pull up Tumblr. It's been a little while since I've been on, and apparently Saxton has posted twice since I have. I glance through all of the notifications first, and it doesn't go without notice that there is an overabundance of new followers in the last twenty-four hours. I glance at the number again: 745. How does that even happen? Something has to be screwy with the app.

Regardless, I continue to the first post of the two new: bathtub sex in high speed. I watch, remembering that very moment as if no time has passed, but as usual, the hashtags and the post are what get my attention the most.

#AintNothingLikeTheFirstTime #AsCloseOfAViewAsYoullGet #OneNightWonders #Remake #TheStartOfForever #WaterSloshin #PussyWorkin #DickSubmergin following #BedLovin and those are the #BestKindsOfNights . . . Or days. #SexSecrets #MakinMovies #LoveStories #PornStarRomance #XXX #Sex #ReservedMemories #TopSecret #RestrictedAccess #VIPonly #TheFuckingFeels #YoullNeverKnow #SexSessions #AfterTheCut #TheRealMVP goes to this girl right here. Kambry, you make my world go round. You're the only girl I see and I'm happy as fuck that you agreed to marry

me. If you're reading this, I love you, and get your naughty ass back to bed. For everyone else—hate none, love always, and pray to God you find a person like me. See ya on the flip side —Sax.

I read a few of the comments, blurry eyed, before moving to the next.

MaryJane69: *That's hot . . .*
Justin4Pussy: *A girl like that and I possibly would leave the hoe life . . .*
Luke_JennyXXX: *This is great. Love your posts. Naughty notes to come for you both. Reblogging.*
SinisterSlave: *Can't turn a hoe into a housewife. How can you bring God into this filth? A relationship that starts with sex ends with sex. Cheater cheater pumpkin eater? I bet he's a few screws away from finding a replacement, sweetheart. No one wants a used model for long . . .*

"What the actual fuck?" A tear falls down my face. How can someone be so mean? Cruelty is not a skill I'm good at. Being on the receiving end hurts. What do I do? Do I reply back like Tynleigh? Do I ignore it? Do I block him? Or should I just delete this damn account altogether? "What is it with the damn rhymes and riddles with this guy? Why is he still on our page?"

I hover over the post options. He obviously gets off on feedback and getting under my skin. Fuck it. I'm going to leave it right there. He's not going to hurt me. "Grow tough skin," I whisper, trying to make myself grasp onto the very words I need to believe.

I move to the second post. It's the photo of the two of us kissing at the concert. The lighting looks softer, the photo covered in a vintage effect. He's done something to it, but it's beautiful. Our eyes are closed, my cheeks flushed, but even though it's our profiles showing and our lips are locked together, we both look . . .happy.

My first ever #WCW and forever #WCE is this beautiful girl.
The possibility to have everything you want is within your grasp.

#NoSettlingRequired. The sky is the limit. You can have sex and love simultaneously. Monogamy is not a means to an end. One woman can do everything a list of females can and more. If anyone knows, it's me. #PornStars have #Sex but not #Love. At least not with dignity. The only option is to #MakeTheChoice between the two. I was lucky for once not to have to. Take the #Dare if you're #Bold enough. #FindYourPerson.

Kambry Ryvers, I love you. Never let the douchebags of the world make you believe any different. I know your heart and what you're thinking right now as you read this. Shit talkin' is easy when hiding behind a computer. You're my girl just as much today as you will be in thirty years, and the only one. When in doubt, remember, you're the girl that tamed the porn star. #BachelorNoMore #PussyWhippedAndProud #PussyPride #CouplesOnly #MyGirl #CandidMoments #NewYorkNights #MadisonSquareGarden #ACDC #RockandRoll #DateNight #ShesMine #iLoveHer #NoSexRequired #AskHerIfSheGotAnyTonight #DickOnLock #PussyOffLimits #JerkOffSessions #NotAllowed #ProvingPoints #FuckTheHaters #DontJudge #MindYourOwnBusiness #FuckYou #PornStarDiaries

#WordPorn of the day is from one of the greats, #BobMarley, in paraphrase and it fits: 'before you start pointing fingers, make sure your hands are clean.' —See you on the flip, Sax.

P.S. If you're into #porn with meaning, and maybe a little #RealityTV, click here >>> http://www.kissntellfilms.com/movies/directstream/payperview/Saxton_Kambry/SexSessionsUncut/Premier

A laugh escapes. That man . . . I don't even know if I want to browse through the notes. My curiosity, I'm afraid, will always get the best of me.

Buckeye80: *Fuck the haters. Do you, dog.*

Weezy6: *Bob Marley!*

LynnZLou: *People suck. Judgment will never die, hence my backup account for stuff I like. You sound like an amazing guy, and she's lucky to have you. Found this page through a naughty-loving friend that follows your work and wouldn't shut up about the new release. Checking out the link. It'll make the hubby proud . . .*

I continue to scan the many notes; more in number than I would have thought, but don't see the lunatic. He's actually quiet for once. Imagine that . . . My stomach becomes full of fizzling nerves. I want to click the damn link myself, but the amount of time I've spent sitting on this very toilet is a little embarrassing. Where did he get that link? Why didn't I get one?

In my effort to not get off my damn phone I somehow open a message box with a message inside from SinisterSlave, titled: Truce?

"Tired of being a dick finally?"

When the message opens I immediately squeal and toss my phone, making a loud thump as it hits the floor. It hits screen up, staring at me like an alcoholic stares at a bottle of vodka: relentlessly and hypnotic with no chance that either party will remove itself from the situation without help. No matter how sickening it is to you or how much you loathe that it's there, it still puts out some kind of invisible signal for you to look at it.

One eye open and one eye shut, I grab my phone, my lips soured into a pucker. Lying on the screen is a dick—an ugly one at that. I didn't know such a thing existed really, but upon recent confirmation it does. The curly dark hair in a large, grown up patch encompasses the base, covering a good bit of the length, visibly similar to a Brillo pad. It reminds me of a stump, or a mushroom growing wild in a non-landscaped meadow. Why is it purple? Is it bruised? And bent? It looks like it's broken.

My eyes finally take in the entire photo and my phone goes flying once again. "Dicky-do, dicky-do, no, no, no. Who would fuck that? She was so right. I don't want to see. Make it go away."

The door to the bathroom opens in the midst of my dick pic meltdown. "What the hell are you doing?" he asks as he rubs the heels of his hands over his eyes. "It's loud as fuck in here."

My blinders, also known as my hands, go back over my eyes where they came from. "It's dicky-do. I'm blind. It's the damn dicky-do disease in the flesh."

"Disease? What the fuck, Kambry? What the hell is dicky-do disease and why are your feet on the toilet seat?"

"His stomach sticks out further than his dick do!"

The entire room becomes so silent you could hear breathing in the most relaxed state. My hands slowly fall from my face and I chance a glance at him to see if he's still in here, if he's angry, or if I just dreamed up that entire situation.

Yep, he's still here. The look on his face is frightening. "Care to explain?"

His voice sounds pained as each word leaves his mouth. "I was peeing, you know, minding my own business, and I was playing around on Tumblr and reading your posts and some of the nice comments and the not so nice one. I was really emotional one second and smiley the next with little hearts in my eyes. And then I told myself I needed to get off the toilet because I was way past the girl safe zone. But instead somehow ended up in the message box and saw there was a message so I opened it because it was from the lunatic and I thought he wanted a truce. But in reality, it was a photo of a purple-headed mushroom slinger stationed in a bird's nest with a broken arm. I shouldn't have looked twice but it was ugly and then I realized it was a case of dicky-do disease to top it off and for the second time my phone became the hot potato. Then you walked in and the rest is history."

He's standing in the doorway, leaning against the frame with his feet crossed at the ankles and his arms at his bare chest. There is no emotion flag flying. He's just there, staring at me like a damn loon. "Would you say something already? Scream at me! Show anger! Something! I cannot deal with this look of disappointment you're wearing. It's driving me nuts."

He brings his hand up to rub the stubble that I want to lick. Not the time. His face doesn't change. "Just for the record . . .what is the girl safe zone in regards to pissing?"

My frustration appears on my face. "Not the part I was expecting to discuss."

"One thing at a time."

"If you must know, it's that fine line between the time it takes to pee and poo. Never do I want you to think I'm doing number two. Girls must always remain the clean and reserved between the species of male and female. We do not do that."

"I know you take shits, Kambry, just like all girls. It's a part of life. We already discussed that prior to me shoving a plug in your ass, so there is no need to have some ridiculous bathroom code on my account. I'm still going to fuck you, even in that ass, and I'm still going to marry you, whether I'm knowledgeable of the fact that you shit or not."

"Not an argument you're going to win. Moving on."

"Fine. Secondly, can I get first thoughts when you looked at my dick?"

"What? How is this even relevant? I thought you'd be upset that I saw some other man's disabled penile structure."

I search his face long and hard for a crack in the mask he's wearing. Nothing. He's locked up tighter than a damn virgin in a room of hungry teenage wolves, also known as boys. I have no idea what is going on in that head of his. "I think it's completely necessary."

My shoulders drop. My eyes close. And I go back to that night when I saw it for the first time in the flesh. When there is something he wants to know he's not going to let it go. "I thought it was big when I looked at it, but not having any experience I wasn't sure what average, big, and small were in terms of dicks. Then you placed my hand on it and I realized in comparison to my small hands just how big you were. It was beautiful. I knew that even then. There were no scars, no imperfections in the build. It was made from a flawless mold. You really do have the most perfect dick there ever could be. The coloring is the right shade to match your skin, the ratio between your length and how thick you are is proportionate, and it even has a beauty mark that I love."

"A beauty mark?" He's curious from his tone.

"Yeah, the faded brown ring you have as a marker to show how much it's grown from soft to hard. I like it. Now I know how thankful I am that you shave. It's clean, it's manscaped, and it adds to its appeal. I also like running my hands along the veins when you're hard." My eyes open and lock with his. "It reminds me that you're hard for me. The head is soft to the touch and I like the taste of that little bead that comes from the center. Every time I look at it I get . . ." I swallow. "Thirsty."

In one push his white boxer briefs fall to the floor and he grabs his dick in his hand, immediately stroking it. My eyes follow the back and forth motion of his strokes as he walks toward me. "This dick?"

I clear my throat, still watching him jerk off shamelessly. "Yes."

He stops in front of me. "You want it in your mouth?"

My heart starts to race. Even sitting spread eagle on this damn toilet I can feel the sudden onset of wetness down below. Him talking dirty and harsh is so hot. "Yes."

"Open wide."

Oh hell . . .

I do as he says, my tongue inching forward as I do. He lays the underside of his head on the edge of my tongue. "Close."

With his head in my mouth I do, swirling my tongue around it. The excess saliva is already being produced. "Suck," he says, and grabs the back of my head, slowly pushing himself inside of my mouth.

I work to breathe in a way I won't gag as I do what he commanded of me. I like being his little slut sometimes. "Fuck yeah. Wet it, baby."

He knows exactly how deep to go before recoiling. I work hard to relax my jaw to make room for his size. He pulls out just as I was getting comfortable. "Take your shirt off and bend over. Hands on the seat."

The middle of my bottom lip scrapes against my top two front teeth in the midst of my smile. I stand, discarding my shirt onto the floor as I do. One foot in front of the other, I pivot, slowly and seductively until I'm facing the toilet. The toilet seat closes with command of my hands. I bend forward, gripping the edge of each side. My head turns just enough I can see him out of the corner. "Fuck me like you mean it."

I feel his teeth sink into my butt cheek as my eyes fall to the top of the seat. Shit. "Like an animal."

I can't even register he's ready before he shoves forward, submerging himself completely inside of me, hard. My body throttles forward, my hands reflexively positioning on the wall in front of me. His lips end just outside of my ear. "You sure you're ready for this?"

The light pain goes ignored. I'm disregarding the fact that I'm a little terrified of completely letting this tone in his voice go. It's one I can't explain. He doesn't sound upset. He doesn't sound angry. He sounds . . .hungry. We've had reasonably rough sex, even to the point of pain, but a part of me has always thought he held back a little bit because of his size and my lack of experience prior to him. This sounds like he's ready to push his limits, and well, so am I. Even though I'm nervous, I lie. "Give me all you fuckin' got."

I sit down slowly, my hand cupped between my legs as I do. "I completely underestimated you."

"You usually do."

"No. This is different. You fucked it up. My V will never be the same. It hurts. I'm in physical pain. It's probably swollen. I'm not even sure that I can walk. If I do, I'll be walking bowlegged. I'm broken. I think this means it's gone kaput. No more entry." I create the X with my fingers as I stare at him from the bed.

He drops his towel to grab a clean pair of boxer briefs, black this time. My attempt to not look at his groin is unsuccessful. Even as I sit here in pain, I still want him between my legs. I feel like a sex addict: loving something that could kill you. Why is it that we love things that are bad for us? That man's dick is definitely bad for me. "Baby, I'm just now breaking it in."

I lay back, my towel falling open as my wet hair hits the bed. "Oh my god, you're like a sweet tooth. I want you on a near constant basis, even when I feel the pain that you're causing."

Once his jeans are up, he walks forward without zipping and buttoning them. His hands grip behind my knees and spread my legs. My knees try to press together on reflex, but he's stronger than me, holding them spread wide to look between. "There is nothing broken about that pussy. It's just a little overworked. A very brief time to recuperate and it'll be good as new."

I prop up on my elbows. "So, are we going to finish the conversation from the bathroom? You know, the one that we started before you annihilated my girly parts with your warlike fuckery. That thing actually became a weapon for a while."

"Such a dirty mouth." He smirks. Why would I expect anything less? "Are you complaining? Do I need to go easier on you next time?"

"Uh, hell no. Did you see me waving a white flag? It'll take more than a few stab wounds for me to be overcome by your sex assaults. We will take it to the trenches before I surrender. Really, I just want to know . . . Are you upset?"

He looks genuinely confused. "Why would I be upset?"

"For real? Uh, well you really didn't have any expression at all."

"I walked in on your pussy completely uncovered. There was nothing in my way. You kept rubbing on my dick last night and trying not to fuck you was the hardest thing I've ever done. It wasn't fun. I woke up with a one-track mind. I wanted to fuck you. Every few thoughts I heard something about a dick that was fucking up my wood. If you knew how hard I was trying not to laugh, we wouldn't be having this conversation. The pain in my voice—me swallowing back laughter. All I can say is bless the poor bastard that sent you that photo, because if my dick were being cut down like that I'd never want to whip it out again. The weakness to a man's pride is his dick. It's no different than owning guns and knives. No matter what kind of guy you are or how big your current is you always want bigger and badder. You can destroy a guy with a few words."

I lightly kick him. "You ass. I was really distraught. I didn't ask for a dick pic. It was just there. Why did you make me go through all that shit about my first thoughts of your dick? Egotistical, compliment-fishing ass. I should cut you off. Like you didn't already know I'm a total Saxton slut and I'm addicted to your enormous dick."

He leans forward, pushing me flat on the bed as he puts one knee at a time on the mattress. "I already told you. No man wants to hear about another man's dick. You were killing my wood and I was going to fuck you one way or another. I meant what I said. It was necessary." He smiles. "And it worked."

"Fine. I'm not complaining." My legs lock around his waist. "It's better to get it in before your parents get here and we have to do without."

"Who says we have to do without?"

My face, I know, is displaying a look of pure and utter terror. "Sax, no. We aren't talking about your sister but your parents. That's just code. Are they staying here? If so, we are *not* having sex with your parents in the same apartment. Period. I will cut you off. I don't care how damn sexy you are, how much I love you, or how much I want it. I went eighteen years without it, a few days will be easy."

He grinds his groin against my tender center. "You really think you can go without this?"

"Oh god. Stop," I say, with a moan in the middle of the request, completely going against the very action of stop with, *but I really mean continue*. "We have to quit this. Don't make this hard."

"I don't give a shit if my parents are here or not, in this very apartment or in a hotel. You don't think I've heard my parents goin' at it over the years? Payback's a bitch. Daddy may be quiet, but Mama is a screamer."

"Saxton! Gross." I smack his shoulder. "Shut the hell up. Seriously."

He laughs, his face lowering to kiss me. "Hey, the big dick had to come from somewhere."

My face loses all emotion; except for the telling blush I'm sure remains. "I hate you sometimes. I have a love/hate relationship with you right now. How do you expect me to look at your dad after saying something like that? Every time my eyes wander innocently, I'm going to feel like they need to be plucked from the very sockets they sit in. I do not want to have the knowledge in my brain that your dad *may* or may *not* have an enormous dick like you! Shit, man. Not cool!"

"He wears Wranglers too."

"Saxton!"

"And they're tight."

I dramatically close my eyes. "Father, forgive me, for I have sinned. In the case that I kill him, I'm sorry. He provoked me until I had no choice."

I open my eyes to him trying desperately not to laugh. "You know they say those that react defensively are guilty. Do you, Kambry Rivers, have the hots for Allen Cambridge?"

My mouth drops. "I don't even know him!"

"Old man may even like the attention; although, Lori might get a little jealous when she sees you all hot and bothered over her man. Thirty years can bring out the claws, even in the sweetest person."

"Do you feel the sting yet? 'Cause my hand print is about to be etched on the side of your face."

He presses closer, pushing my legs back toward me. There isn't an inch of space between us. He bucks his hips against me, reminding me of the pain that is still very much there. "Oh yeah? You gettin' mad?"

Good lord he's beautiful; every part of him. My heart cannot physically love him more than it does, or at least I don't think it can. On most days it feels completely full, like it's at maximum capacity. It's not often that you find someone that can make you angry and laugh within a millisecond apart, and then you turn around and want to screw his brains out before that pattern starts all over again.

We never fight. Even the few times previously that we've had some kind of spat, it was more us just fighting against what we knew was inevitable: us. Every waking day I want him more than I did the one before. It's a crazy cycle that gives me some kind of nutty high I want more of.

With him I don't care about my future, even though I do, if that makes sense. For the span of my life thus far, I've racked my brain wondering what I'll do, what I'll become, and if I'd be good at what I chose. We're raised with one goal: be somebody. But what if I just want to *be*? To exist in happiness should be an option. Everyone screams at you to choose an amazing career that you'll fill and follow along in the footsteps of people before you. Way back when, it was about life and living simply. Now, it's about a career and what we can acquire.

Right now, technically, I have nothing. I have no ownership of residency, no car, and no plan. I'm a high school graduate with college off my radar at the present time. All I have is the money I've made so far and what I came here with, and you know what? I'm happy. Nothing about my life currently would I change if given the chance.

To be honest, I don't give a damn about a career, and that baffles me when beforehand my parents tried to take that away from me. I had no identity back then and wanted one, but now, I have one and don't need one. I like the simplicity of our life. That's why I don't care what people think about what we do. We film the most intimate parts of our relationship. We create porn. So what. It sounds worse than it is. It gives us the flexibility of being with each other more, and that's worth every damn judgment. For longer, we get to be . . .us, and still survive.

I know I'll figure out my path at some point and create a plan to get there. But truthfully, I don't care what I'm doing in ten years as long as I'm with him, because he's my future, and I'm ready for the ride on an open road with no destination in sight.

For effect I squint my eyes, feigning anger. "I hate that I love you."

"Really? Damn. No chance I could change the way you feel?"

"I don't think so. You've really done it this time."

He leans down into my neck, running his lips along it slowly from bottom to top and back again until he's at my ear. "You sure about that?"

Chill bumps are creating a covering on my entire body. My grip around his waist becomes tighter, trying to pull him closer to me even though there is no physical space left between our bodies. His body lies on top of mine completely, but all of his weight is on his knees and shins below our middles. "I'm determined to change your mind."

"It's not possible."

My eyes close and roll to the back of my head. Within an instant, my body surges into a fit of laughter as his fingers dig into the tops of my ribs on each side, tickling me. My body seizes in every direction like someone having a seizure. I scream. "Stop!"

I would imagine my face has morphed into something ugly. I've never been a pretty girl when it comes to mega laughing fits. All of my awareness drains and the expressions I wear reflect the ticklish pain that I have to endure against my will. I've never figured out why some people are more ticklish than others, or how some can mask it to show that it doesn't affect them at all, even though deep down it's killing them. Me—I can barely be touched in the right spot and I lose it.

"Say mercy."

I try to push him back without giving him access to my armpits, but all strength has left my body. The only thing that remains is the constant need to jerk and tremble from the tickling sensation assaulting my body. I can't breathe from the constant laughing. My stomach hurts from the nonstop contracting of my muscles. And if that's not enough my voice is becoming hoarse from the onset of screaming and laughter. I'm in a state of tormented blissful harmony.

He doesn't let up, but rather, gets worse. A snort that I don't recognize and is completely unladylike exits from a mouth I hope isn't mine, even though I'm sure it is. My vision is blurred from the watering of tear ducts, but I see the silent laughter on his face. He's making no sound. I try to kick but his body is blocking me. "Please . . . Can't . . . Breathe."

"You know what to do to make it stop."

"Mercy! Have mercy."

His fingers fall from my body. My chest and stomach are heaving. My breathing is nowhere close to evening. He grabs my face between his hands and holds my eyes staring into his. "I'm ready for forever with you."

The door flies open. "What are you doing to her? It sounds like a pack of Hyenas in here."

Our heads turn to the door at the same time. Tynleigh is fully dressed in denim shorts and a turquoise and pink tee shirt that really brings out her tan, a pair of matching sneakers, a cup of coffee in her hand, and her long brown hair in a low wavy ponytail that falls over her shoulder. The strings of her swimsuit tied behind her neck are visible just above the collar of her shirt. "Do you really think entry prior to knocking is wise, T?"

"With her sounding like that I knew there was no way in hell you were hittin' it, and if you had been I'm willing to cross that forbidden line to see why, because that shit would be bad for you. Laughter should never be the direct response to sex, Sprout."

I laugh again. "Still, don't come knockin' if the boat is rockin'. Get out."

"No!" I scream. "Help me! My brain is compromised with shit I don't need to know about your dad and I can't get ready with him on top of me. He's holding me hostage."

"Saxton, get off. Coney Island is calling my name. I can hear it. Today is my day to act like a kid with no responsibilities and you're not going to ruin that for me. I took the entire day off for this, so get your ass up. Besides, I know you. You aren't trying or your ass would be bare."

He grabs the back of my legs and presses them forward, turning my ass up toward him, and then starts rocking his crotch against mine, slowly and seductively, while looking at his sister. I'd be embarrassed that I'm completely naked if he wasn't covering all of my goodies. "She's delusional, and my ass doesn't have to be bare to whip it out. You can shut the door now."

I yell between laughs. "Oh my god. No I'm not. Stop it, Saxton! He was totally talking about your parents knockin' boots. I'm scarred. I'll never be the same. If you don't get him off, we'll never make it to Coney Island. I'm calling an S.O.S."

She walks forward like a woman on a mission, setting her mug down on the dresser against the wall. “Leave, T, or I can guaranfuckingtee you’ll see more than a bare ass.”

“I think you’re forgetting I’m older than you, Sprout. I’ve seen the snake you’re packing at points in my life. Whether it was a baby or a mama makes no difference to me. Your terror tactics don’t scare me. Don’t make me break out the spirit fingers. You know, after years of cheerleading, I’m so much better at it than you.”

“Don’t fucking touch me,” he says with bite behind it, catching me off guard. His tone is suddenly less play like and more agitated.

“What are spirit fingers, aside from the obvious?”

“Saxton here can tell you all about it . . .or you can witness it. The choice is his.” She’s almost at his backside and he flinches, but doesn’t let go of me. “You can make this easy on yourself by getting off of her. Things can get ugly when someone stands between me and an amusement park.”

“I can’t. She’s naked. Just leave and I’ll get off of her.”

“He can’t be trusted!” I blurt out before clamping my mouth shut.

His head whips toward me so fast I swear he’s going to have a crick. His eyes narrow at me. “If you knew what was good for you right now you’d keep quiet. The soreness you’re experiencing is about a six. I can still go all fucking ten, baby.”

“I’ve seen all the parts she’s got my entire life. Pick another argument. I’m going to count down from five, Saxton. That’s how long you have to stand up and start walking.”

He leans into me further, smothering my breathing. “Tynleigh, I’m not fucking kidding. Leave or you’ll regret it. I prefer not to hit a woman, but for one that knows she’s pushing my limits I’ll make an exception.”

“Five, four, three . . .”

He scoots us both up the bed as she closes in on him. She’s too close for him to go anywhere else but further up the mattress. I have no idea what is going on right now, but what I do know is I kind of want to find out. That makes me a horrible girlfriend I know, but when a man that is so secure in his manhood on every level starts getting squirrely like a girl it really makes you curious. “My elbow is ready.”

"Two, one." Without a second's lapse she digs her fingers into his skin in a precise location she doesn't have to guess. The sight before me becomes one I'll never forget as long as I live. He's so close to me I can't breathe, bucking and jerking against me with the manliest, sexiest laugh, and one I've never heard from him. It's deep and strained, short of breath.

He tries to elbow her to knock her away from the underarm area, but that just gives her better access it seems. She jumps on top of him, on top of me, to hold him still. All I can do is put my hands over my mouth and try like hell to smother my laughter so I can live; while I watch him toss and scream like a little girl. I'm totally buying her a corn dog or a chicken on a stick when we get there. I figure that's appropriate since we likely won't be around alcohol. Against his command my mouth has a mind of its own. "So you can dish out the tickles but can't take it?"

He looks at me, teeth clenched. He's in physical pain and I'm dying inside. "You're getting it later," he says, in a short, clipped tone. "In more ways than one." The laughter starts to slip through my lips, but I lock my lips tighter as he pushes off my body, standing with her still attached like Spiderman. "Fuck, okay. Enough. I'm off. Stop, Tynleigh."

She stops the tickling motion but doesn't remove herself from his body. Instead, her arms lock together at the front of his neck to match her feet on his stomach. He looks at me, slightly choked I'm guessing with his arms grabbing hers, as I push up on my elbows, hands on my nipples to try and cover myself. One leg crosses over the other to act as a pair of panties of sorts. "Walk away and I'll get off," she says, but not in a quiet manner.

On accident I burst out in laughter. I can't hold it back anymore. "Oh my god. I'm sorry, but she totally just manhandled you. I know your weakness now." One hand immediately covers my mouth, before disappearing once again. "You're so sexy, baby. Stay testosterone strong. I love you."

He walks toward the door, before turning around to face me. "You and me." He does the finger motions to match. "We aren't finished. Now I know whose side you're on. Like I said . . . Payback's a bitch."

He's full of shit, Tynleigh mouths from behind him. My lips line as my eyes widen, waiting for them to leave. Before I can catch myself I find that my head is slightly nodding up and down in agreement. Following my line of vision, he turns his head toward her in a hurry, as if he's trying to catch her talking behind his back, but she begins rubbing the top of his head with her mouth closed. "Good brother. Resist the temptation. Just say no."

He backs away, through the doorway, and just before he closes the door she winks at me. My face luckily doesn't crack throughout the stare down from him. *I know nothing,* I mouth.

The door finally shuts to the bedroom, leaving me alone, everything now silent. "I'm in so much fucking trouble."

"Yes you are," he replies, catching me off guard with a response, but again, the door is shut, and he makes no effort to open it.

Crap . . .

"Love you!"

"You're still in trouble."

I laugh again as I roll over on the bed and stare at my ring. I'm not sure that I like the silence. I want his laughter back in here. I want him back in here. I prefer his presence to his absence any day.

The bad part is . . .I look forward to being in trouble with him. As a kid, when your parents tell you that you're in trouble it makes you nervous. It makes you squirm. I remember a time that Ben and I had teamed up together on something that wasn't good. I don't even remember what it was now, but it was done in vain, only for Dad to find out that we had basically taken up for each other in the error of our ways so we were both in for an ass whooping. We stared out the bedroom window together, layers of pants on, and watched as he picked a switch from the switch tree, shedding the leaves as he made his way toward the house, whipping it side-to-side in the air to make sure it was a good one. It was terrifying. Worse than the actual punishment is the anticipation. It's a constant thought of the pain that will accompany your bad behavior, but with him, I want the pain that I now know he can cause. I want the hours of thought of what he's capable of doing to me later.

He's my one and only. He's the love of my life. He's my owner, my partner, my best friend, and my life mate. Never in a million years would I want that with someone else. I push myself off of the bed; because the faster I get ready the sooner I can be back by his side.

CHAPTER SIXTEEN

Saxton

I glance at her from my peripheral vision, just like I've done this entire ride. Her head jumps from looking out the window to me, and back again. I'm being an ass, remaining silent the whole way and leaned against my window; minding my own business, but it's really more of a joke. The girl has me pussy-whipped ninety-nine percent of the time. I just want to see how long she can hold out before she caves and does something about it. Most people only get to see the sweet exterior she carries around, but only a select few, such as myself, are blessed with the opportunity to see her sassy side; the very side that has me in this exact predicament: pussy-whipped.

She's already casually laid her hand on the seat between us a few times, halfway open, making it near impossible not to laugh; especially when she slowly navigated it toward me after several minutes of waiting empty handed. But with careful focus on the bill of my hat and Bryant's not so sly attempts in the front to touch my sister, it ended a success. I kept all limbs to myself. God as my witness I wanted to grab it, though, and hold it tight for as long as she wanted me to.

I was a little caught off guard that she didn't immediately take my side earlier. Couple code should be well established by now. I thought we were past that, but then again, a person will do surprising things to fit into someone's family.

I should know. Salem's family was completely unlike anyone in mine, for the worst, and some of my not so proud moments as a human happened back then for that exact reason: wanting to be liked by the person you're dating's family. Looking back now, it shouldn't have surprised me at all that she was the way she was. I dodged a lethal bullet there, on all supporting levels.

The real traitor in all of this is Tynleigh, and my form of revenge has yet to be determined. There are two things in life that will make me scream like a little bitch, shaming the big dick swinging between my legs. Hypocritically speaking, I know, I despise being tickled. It puts me in a state of physical pain that I cannot endure more than two seconds. I go into a panicked defense mode and my world enters a state of emergency. My actions become a matter of survival at that point and I cannot be held accountable for my behavior. She's used it against me my entire life. I am deathly afraid of being tickled like some people are over more understandable triggers like snakes, spiders, and needles. I accepted long ago, again, that based upon occurrence and for a temporary lapse in time it makes me a pussy. It's a side I don't let people see; especially hot as fuck females I'm not yet permanently bound to. Right now she can still walk out that door at any given time. No woman wants a pussy of a man. I don't like the way it feels. I don't like the way it makes me act. Nails on a chalkboard effect for me. End of story. Moving on.

Number two—pay close attention—would be sudden spikes in adrenaline caused by the following: heights, speed, and sudden change in motion or direction caused by drops, twists and barrel rolls or loops that make me feel like I'm going to fall. That rapid heartbeat and stomach sinking feeling leaves me sweaty, nauseous, and ready to throw up. Three out of four times that's how it is going to end.

My memory is a little hazy on the cause that started it all, because I've had this fear for as long as I can remember, but I want to say it was the earliest memory I can pull and what I would say is a faulty safety harness, or whatever the hell they're called, that didn't tighten or lock close enough to my body on the seat of the rollercoaster. Or maybe I was just a lanky, skinny fucker that didn't belong on that damn ride even though I was tall enough, but all I remember is flying forward as we descended quickly down the drop and then hitting the top of the loop at seventy miles per hour and holding on for dear life as my body fell way too far from the seat before the bars stopped my narrow shoulders. I didn't think we'd ever make it to the end, but embarrassing screams never stopped, deafening those around me the entire time.

I about shit my pants.

I may have peed a little.

I swore I'd never do it again if I made it off alive.

And when I finally got off that damn roller coaster I threw up everything still in my stomach and then some.

For months I had nightmares of falling; to the point that half a body roll happened during sleep and I jerked in bed to prevent going off the edge, even lying in the middle, nowhere near the drop. On occasion I still do. I do not like fucking amusement parks. I've tried them a few times over the years to try and beat this fucking fear or to impress a girl, with no luck.

So why in the hell am I going to Coney Island?

Because I love that girl more than I can explain to another human being, and when Tynleigh ran her damn mouth openly, knowing I would say no, and I saw the excitement in her eyes, I couldn't do it. The decision was made for me. She owns me. I will face my worst fears and step in front of death to watch her experience things she's never gotten to, so here I am, sitting in this car with a nervous stomach and sweat perspiring on my forehead under my ball cap while I endure raging thoughts. Tynleigh set me up. I deserve to be soured about it for a few minutes, even if just to prove a point.

I grab the bill of my hat and smack Bryant with the back upon removal, the material slinging into the side of his head. "If you don't fucking stop doing that in front of me . . . One more time, asshole. If your hand disappears under her shorts again I'm breaking it. Who invited you anyway?"

He turns around, a cocky ass grin on his face. His hand remains on her bare thigh, sitting just below the bottom hem of her shorts. Backstabbing disloyal bastard. It amazes me I'm still his friend after this shit. I think I was doing pretty damn well knowing, but seeing this fucked up shit is not going to cut it. "The one that likes my hand in her shorts. Looks like I'm crashing your wedding too, bro."

My hat becomes a lethal weapon in my very hand, he the target, and my body surges forward toward the front passenger seat to get around his ducking motions. "Cut it out, Saxton! I'm trying to drive."

The second I get him locked in my sights I'm pulled back with force as my hat is ripped from my grasp, a tiny blonde settling herself straddled on my lap, her index finger centimeters from my face with a large diamond staring at me. There is no ounce of laughter present. For such a little person she packs some heat. "Before God and every witness in this car, if you don't shut the hell up about Bryant and your sister then you won't touch me next time Ben is around!" She's yelling in this small space of the car's interior like we're football fields apart.

She grabs my hands and places them firmly on her tits, only a thin piece of fabric in my way. I squeeze, because, well, I shouldn't need to give an explanation. They are self-explanatory. "See these?"

She waits for my response like a toddler being scolded. The car is deathly silent. This could be a trap. Of course I see her tits. I see them every ten seconds at minimum. Confused as to what my answer is *expected* to be, I stall. But then I take the route of a man that wants to live—without his dick in time out—and nod my head dramatically with my mouth shut. "Restricted area. Access denied. Closed to viewing and hands on usage if you don't get your shit together. If you need a simpler explanation let me know."

"That's blackmail." The words flew out without instruction. And the evil laugh that follows from her is a hint that it should have remained locked inside where it belongs.

"Two can play this damn game. You keep giving them a hard time about having sex when they're two grown adults; well, guess what, you don't get any either. You're being a pompous ass when this situation was in reverse a very short while ago. My brother *saw* us fuck. You only *know* about them. How do you like those apples? Would you want to be in Ben's shoes? Or are you comfy where you're sitting?"

My mouth closes as I stare at her in her very angry state—noticeable by the quivering of her bottom lip—but then opens. Obviously my mouth won't just shut up today. "You couldn't. You wouldn't. This is totally different. I saw what he was doing with his dick before inserting it into my sister. Now, two seconds later, he's making his fucking rounds in our circle."

She clamps that tiny little hand together at each side of my mouth, making me feel like a fish, and presses her chest against mine. Her lips sit right in front of mine. "Oh, but I fucking would, porn boy. Do you want me to bring up your priors? Hmmm . . ."

Holy fucking shit. I lost my train of thought in the midst of her sarcasm. The ability to utilize my brain in a sarcastic or witty manner is malfunctioning. Bryant lets a laugh escape. I kick the back of his damn seat, my face not moving an inch. She lowers her middle onto my current problem from the raised straddle she was in, closing the space between her middle and my lap. "I see you're paying attention. Good. Let me put this in perspective for you, because you were dipping your wick in someone else and it probably wasn't all that long before me. I still gave you my virginity knowing what you were. And don't tell me. I don't want to know the timeline. Not my point. It's so different, huh? Give him a break. He's the damn victim and you know it. Since you brought up the elephant in the room, let's elaborate for all parties to avoid any confusion of his charged manwhore ways that you're accusing him of. He was seeing my best friend, but guess what? She ditched him for my brother when given the opportunity. She's been waiting years for it; an unfortunate circumstance is all it is. It wasn't meant to be like you and me. He's a good guy from what I can tell and she's fun to be around. Does it really surprise you that they ended up bumping into each other?"

I nod my head, but don't speak. I could easily remove her hand from my face, but this dominant role she's playing is really fucking hot, so I'm going to play. "Well it shouldn't. Was it a little awkward at first? Yeah, but move the fuck on. As far as it being different, you bet your ass it is, but not in the way you see it. We are by far worse. *My* brother had to come to terms with the fact that I lost my virginity to a porn star," she bites out. "A well-paid one at that . . . So what does that tell you? And also that we film porn . . .*together*."

Her hand drops from my mouth and she starts the animated waving of each as she speaks. "Sheltered virgin girl insecure in her own body. Scorned porn star that's probably inserted his stick in more women than I want to elaborate on for my well-being and mental sanity. And might I add, the same one that I wrap my lips around and let inside of me unprotected. Sounds like the ingredients to a damn soap opera if you ask me. Oh, but wait! We are actually in the middle of an uncensored television reality series and we fell for each other instead of acting. We are now about to be getting married. Beautiful. Romantic. Out of the ordinary. Also laughable. Stew on that for a while, but in the meantime, Ben got a lick off you for wandering into what he considers a 'no trespassing' zone and you got a hit off him for the same. Lay your sword of testosterone down and shut the hell up with your younger brother bitching, for all of our sakes."

"Baby . . ." My hands tangle in her hair and I pull her closer. My mouth is dry, causing an offset in the way my voice comes out. "My dick hurts so bad right now. That was hot as fuck."

"Saxton!" Tynleigh yells. "We can hear you!"

"Don't listen."

"Kind of hard right now."

Everyone else doesn't matter at the moment. She stares at me. Her eyes are smiling at me even though she hasn't given her lips permission yet. "You say the worst things at the most inappropriate times," she finally says, a broad grin following closely behind.

"But that's why you love me, right?"

"Dude." I inch my head to the right just enough to give him one eye. "You better lock that one up until you have papers to prove she's yours, because that one wouldn't stay on the market long. She just burned your ass," he says, laughter behind it.

"Shut the fuck up, asshole," I laugh. "May you burn alive in the very liquor that makes you money . . ."

"Love you too, bro."

"That's for taunting me with my sister. Next time get a room."

"Noted."

Kambry turns her head toward him and he winks at her. "I owe you a little credit, girl. You got that dick on a leash."

He glances at me at the exact second I flip him the bird. "I don't know about you, but my mom taught me not to bite the hand that feeds me." He laughs, and instead of carrying on with this fucked up conversation, I grab her ass to pull her toward me. The fact that I'm in the very car with my own sister doesn't even faze me anymore. That fine line I've never crossed just got busted to hell and back.

My eyes close as my nose gets close to her hair, the smell of her shampoo making itself known. Everything is peaceful, until her squeal sounds off like a twenty-one-gun salute, making my ears ring. I'm going to assume we made it. Without even opening my eyes the nerves return. It's time to armor up. I'm not the first man to ever walk toward the face of death for a woman, and I'm sure I won't be the last.

Kambry

"Sax, are you alright?"

We chose to come to Deno's Wonder Wheel Amusement park first, and we've barely made it past where he purchased our tickets. Tynleigh and Bryant wandered off to do their own thing once we came through the gates of Coney Island. It was probably the better decision due to the awkward tell-all couples' therapy session in the car, followed by the inappropriate phrases and groping from Saxton that followed. Conversation between them was most likely needed after that.

The wounds of my embarrassment are still fresh and I need time to get past everything blurted from my lips as my frustration took over my brain. Everyone obviously thought my outburst was funnier than me. It took about two and a half seconds after I was finished to realize exactly what had happened. We were not alone like we should have been for that conversation. I'm pleading temporary insanity caused by his bad behavior.

I don't think she was expecting to be more than a third wheel when this trip was planned, but now here we stand, alone. I guess it kind of worked out for the best.

My excitement was tipping into the extreme zone until I got a look at him when we started moving toward the Wonder Wheel. His paling skin is worrying me. He shoves the tickets in his pocket. "Yeah. Why?"

"You look like you're going to throw up."

He shakes his head. "Must have been the car ride. Occasionally I get car sick and left feeling nauseous if I ride backseat. I'm good."

He starts to walk forward, toward the line to get on, but I side step in front of him and turn around, crossing my arms over my chest. He grabs my shoulders as he tries to halt suddenly instead of knocking me over. "What the hell?"

I narrow my eyes at him. "You're lying to me." My shoulders drop as the disappointment settles. "You never lie to me," I say in almost a whisper. "Is this a bad memory for you? Did you bring her here?" He looks like he's seen a ghost. A thought occurs to me when I take in his face again and my eyes flit from one direction to the other. "Did you see her? Is she here right now?"

"Her who?" His voice is casual. Without a second's lapse his eyes widen and the color returns to his face. "No, baby. Oh my god. No. Stop it. Come here."

He pulls me against his chest, my arms instantly wrapping around him. My body begins to melt. It always does when he holds me like this. Like they always do, the words just leave my mouth. I'm not sure that I could ever keep anything from him—not that I would want to. But the way he just draws things out of me is hard for me to understand when I've always been so quiet. "Then why won't you tell me why you look like that? Since we got out of the car you've been acting weird."

The aftermath of my brazen attitude in the car is starting because of the change in his mood. I'm getting paranoid that maybe I embarrassed him or made him angry, or even made him second-guess us. My constantly surfacing insecurities make me feel stupid. This is the part of myself that I will always hate. "Hey. Look at me."

I do as he says, waiting for him to continue. "I need you to trust me. I promise to tell you what's really bothering me later, but for now your enjoyment is more important to me. It's not any of the things you think. That I promise. Hint: you'll discover that men are stubborn. We hate asking for directions, we never need help, and we are always Tarzan. Always. Even on days we feel like Jane."

My cheeks hurt.

My teeth are in full show.

The laugh escapes.

I squeeze him tight.

"You'll always be my Tarzan."

"So what's first?" He lightly pushes me back to separate us and wraps his arm over my shoulders, before he begins to guide us along. "Because right now I feel like I'm living Tarzan's first encounter with civilization: the man's only downfall. Everyone is starting to stare."

"That," I say, pointing to the massive wheel.

"Alright. Well, let's do this."

I take off, grabbing his hand as I do and tugging him along behind me. I can't take the temptation anymore. It's too much; like someone putting a cupcake right in front of your nose when you're dieting and daring you not to eat it. The end result is always the same: failure.

Luckily the line wasn't horrible and we got on the ride in a time frame that wasn't curse worthy. When I sat down on that bench seat and the ride worker lowered the bar, all of my adrenaline started to rush through my veins. I've never gotten to go to a fair or amusement park in my life, at least not since I was old enough to remember. This is great.

It stops a few seats from us being on top—on top of the world. My adrenaline has died down a little since the start, most likely because we're only moving like one mile per hour at a time. Slowly we continue to ascend, one bucket load at a time until we're here. I can see the whole park from this point. The people passing look so small. This view is impeccable.

With each move of my head and shoulders the seat rocks to the slightest degree. "Shit. Fuck." The fear-filled whisper calls me. I turn to look beside me with the recognition of whose voice it was. He's clenching the bar so tight his knuckles are white. His eyes are tightly closed.

He's scared.

My heart plummets to my gut as everything weighs on my brain and finally makes sense. It's a funny thing; in the sense of being weird that is: seeing the strongest person you know at their weakest point. It's heartbreaking, but it's also comforting. It humbles you. I think as females we put too much pressure on men. They are supposed to be brave, have no fears, stand ten-foot-tall and bulletproof, and also be the one that sweeps us off our feet with romance and carry us into the sunset. They are supposed to be the shoulder we cry on and the humor behind our laughs. They are supposed to be perfect.

But to me . . .this is perfect. I can see that his shield of bravery sometimes gets laid down, he gets scared, and sometimes he doesn't stand quite as tall. Bulletproof doesn't mean unbreakable. It means tougher than most. Occasionally they deserve a free break with no judgment that they're less of a man. Men should be entitled to a few days where they need the shoulder and they need the heart that causes them to laugh without any expectations in return. And because he's the man that did sweep me off my feet, I want to be that for him.

This is real.

I place my hands to each side of his face and turn his head toward me. He's stiff as a board. His eyes are still clenched tight to match his hands. "Don't rock it."

My forehead presses against his. "Look at me, baby; only at me."

His eyes slowly start to loosen and open, our eyes barely any distance apart. The slight slip of our skin tells me he's sweating. "Why didn't you just tell me?"

"Pussies don't get the girl, and you're my world."

"But, baby, this version of you is so much better. This is *you*. Real is always the best. I need you to remember forever that every superhero has a kryptonite." I'm not sure why I'm whispering, but I just feel like I need to. "And for your information, you'll always have this girl. Never keep your fears from me."

"Prove it."

Two words.

One meaning.

A single command.

So I do in the only way I know how. I kiss him.

The wheel starts moving in a constant turn, only going fast enough to blow a light breeze against our faces. Without my eyes open I witness something beautiful.

He let go.

His hands settle on me loosely instead of being death-gripped to the safety bar in front of us. A couple minutes worth of go-rounds and we are suddenly back at the top, waiting once again, seat by seat, to unload.

The lips I've come to love so much leave mine. His arm outstretches behind me and he looks out over the park, but only briefly, before his eyes return to mine. "You know, there is no other man that could love a woman as much as I love you."

I try not to smile and fail. "I bet there are a few men out there that would disagree with you. It's a great big world out there, and it's full of women-loving men just like you."

"Maybe, but their women aren't as good as mine, so it's not likely."

"That's a matter of opinion, handsome."

He looks at me for a moment, smirks, and then shakes his head. "No?"

"No," he says. "I have the best. I know it. Years of living and aged wisdom tell me so. Only one can be *the best*. A singular being. The order in which things are labeled: good, better, and best. You never have more than one queen or Miss America because there will always have to be a best. That's life. And when you have the best you love it the most."

I love how he uses his fingers as he counts, like I need help counting one and then to three. "Okay fine. So let's say I'm intrigued by your theory. What is your process of elimination to get you to the answer?"

"That you're the best?"

"Exactly."

"That's easy. You have everything on a man's checklist; not lacking one single thing."

"What checklist?"

Again with the fingers. "You don't bitch. You don't blow money. You don't lie, steal, or cheat. We get along. We have fun. You're funny and sweet but not a doormat. You love me. I can take you home to Mama and I can see you as the mother of my children." Those damn fingers. Not once did he mention . . .

I grab his hand and pull it toward me, opening my mouth at just the right time. His middle finger enters and I close around the base, before lightly sucking with my tongue caressing the underside as it exits. "And you do shit like that," he whispers, before clearing his throat.

It exits with a pop. "*We have mind-blowing sex* should have been at the top of that list."

"And your willingness to explore sexually is a bonus. How could I forget?"

"One freebie is all you get. Better not do it again."

"Yes, ma'am."

"That's such a southern thing to say, farm boy."

"Baby, I converted to the south a while ago. Right after I experienced that mind-blowing sex you speak of. My mind has been fucked ever since."

We finally reach the bottom and the worker releases the safety bar to raise it out of our way. Saxton unbuckles the belt that runs over our laps and we get off.

I bump into him purposely as we begin to walk side by side. "And you haven't even seen me naked in cowboy boots yet."

A few more steps and I realize I'm now walking alone. I turn around and his face is priceless. His mouth hangs ajar, his eyes are wide, and the hypnotic blinking pattern is making me want to laugh. "What's wrong?"

My lips purse as soon as the last word exits, trying desperately not to laugh out loud. His hands robotically slide into his pockets and he scuffs his shoe against the pavement. "Can we do that?"

I lose it. It's like a little boy passing by a sweets shop before dinner with his mother. All of the multicolored candy elegantly tucked into pretty glass is staring at him from the other side of the window. He wants to go in, but he knows there is a possibility she'll say no before he even asks so he doesn't spoil his dinner. He has one shot, so he asks in the sweetest, most innocent tone he can muster, hoping she'll feel guilty enough to give in. And I'll tell you, that dammit, the puppy eyes are more than I can bear.

I grab his shirt in my fist and pull him toward me and out of the way. "This is a little surprising. You wanna fuck me in cowboy boots?" I ask in a taunting manner.

"With every ounce of semen in my body."

"Tell me . . . Has this ever happened before?" I'm enjoying this way too much.

"No," he says, matter of fact. I note this small tidbit of information in the back of my mind, because every human being alive likes to be someone's first at something. I'm a fresh map on an open road. There are no little pushpins for me that marks where I've been prior to him, and with Saxton, the list is short. His map is worn and full of holes, but I accepted that with his love. Internally I sigh just a little, but then remember this is one more to add, and the perkiness returns.

I'm going to be evil for a minute. Not in the sense one would think when hearing that word. I'm just going to have a little fun. As a woman, I've figured out that one of the greatest compliments is not the words from a man's mouth or the amount of times that he makes her feel wanted through sex; for it is knowing of the power she has with her body over the man that holds her heart.

When you openly love and want one person infinitely, it can get frustrating at times, because there is no chase left for him when he has you. You're just . . . his. But when that person that you hold so close stands and looks at you like this, wanting and needing you, no matter how many times you've given him the very thing you're offering, and the degree in which he wants you is higher than you can measure, it makes you feel alive. It makes you feel more beautiful than anyone could ever say with words. It makes you feel like an Audrey Hepburn or Marilyn Monroe. It makes you feel irreplaceable. So I'm going to use my body against him on occasion, because I can. Besides, I know he can do it—face his fears that is—and when you love someone you help them battle their fears at least once. He's done it so many times with me. "I'll tell you what."

I point in the direction of the park I know it's in. "You get your sexy ass on that rollercoaster with me . . ." I pull him as close to me as I can get him, the fabric of his shirt still crumpled in my fist. "And on our wedding night I'll have a pair of fresh cowboy boots for you to break in. The leather will be a little tough. You'll have to grip 'em tight."

He grunts. His breath touches my cheek as he speaks. "That's all I gotta do? Ride that death trap one time and you'll keep your word?"

"That's right, farm boy." I provoke. "Ride it once. That's it. No catch. If you hate it, we'll play games the rest of the time we're here, but if you love it, we'll try another one. Either way, it's a win/win for you. All you gotta do is survive through it. I'll even throw in a cowboy hat for good measure and show you how bareback is done in the south."

He takes off faster than I've ever seen him move, leaving me standing here. He doesn't make it too far before he runs back and grabs my hand, jerking me until my feet catch up to his speed. "Let's do the damn thing."

Saxton

"Are you ready?"

I glance at her in the same seat beside me as the safety device is locked into place. My stomach feels like it's heading in the direction of gastrointestinal upset and my palms are sweaty. The wheel was high at times, but it was slow, and she was able to sway my mind off the fact that one wrong move and I'm watermelon being dropped from a tall building: spatter on cement.

"I'm ready to get this over with," I state honestly. "But I'll tell you this . . . If we die, your pussy is still mine in the afterlife. Don't let some smooth talkin' angel with badass wings steal you away. Flying is not all it's cracked up to be."

She surrenders a laugh and looks at me, before rolling her eyes. "Oh my god. This can't be my life right now. You're so dramatic sometimes. We are not going to die."

"You don't know that. Technical malfunctions happen every day. My feet were made to be planted on the ground. If I wanted my faith to be in humanity I wouldn't be a porn star. It died long ago. All I'm saying is, don't you dare fucking leave me in the after. I will chase down your ass even then."

She raises her brow. "You better. I wouldn't expect anything less, but we aren't going to die. You're sucking all the fun out of it! Even if we did, I hardly think that's appropriate conversation when talking about Heaven."

I stare at her, baffled. "Uh, weren't you a churchgoer?"

"Yes. All of my life. What's your point?"

"Do you not remember that the devil himself was a fallen angel? I hardly expect him to be the only one."

"We are not having this conversation."

"Why not?"

Before she can respond, the train of cars surges forward, and at that exact moment my stomach plummets to my gut. Everything surrounding me is now foreign territory.

I can't breathe.

I can't think.

I can't move.

I feel like I'm going to hurl.

The twisting and turning has my insides sloshing around. Life around me passes like a flash of lightning. I don't like it. And just when you get slightly used to the accelerated speeds and the jerking of your body as the car runs along the track, it changes it all on you.

Rung by rung the damn rickety piece of shit climbs the hill. This is the worst feeling: anticipating the fall downward. As it peaks the top she does something unexpected. She glances at me and grabs my hand, lacing our fingers, and making sure that as we fall, we fall together. "Here we go."

The smile on her face is enough to make a grown man fall to his knees, and the excitement in her voice overthrows my fears. Even though I hate this still, and I'll probably regret agreeing to it when I'm alone within the confinements of a bathroom bent over a toilet, I'll lie. I'll ride every damn ride that sits on this property for her. I can think of nothing else but her happiness.

Her hand squeezes mine as the inevitable happens. I'm not sure where all my head has been, but this is the moment I realize something vital. One truth I know for sure. She will never leave me.

Everything in my world becomes peace. My erratic heartbeat dies down. The sweat stops production. The fear goes away. Nothing in this world is scary when you know someone is standing beside you the entire way. I wish I had known this before. I guess it doesn't really make sense until you find the one. She is my *one* that is vastly different from all others. She is the one I breathe for, and the one I can't live without. She is my hope for a life I didn't see for myself before.

She's my lighthouse. She lit my way out of a darkness I was lost in, she guides me through storms, and she's my beacon to find my way home . . .

CHAPTER SEVENTEEN

Kambry

"Sax."

My voice is groggy. The smell of bacon and coffee invades my nose. He doesn't answer like he usually does, even if he's asleep when I call his name. My arm extends to his side of the bed, searching for him. When it's empty I open my eyes to something red on his pillow, still lying on my stomach. My vision is a little blurry and out of focus, but it doesn't take long to figure out what it is.

My hand wraps around the single, long stem and I bring the bloom of the rose to my nose. As the silk of the petal tickles my skin I smile, reveling in the way it makes me feel. Even though I know it'll soon die and lose its beauty, it doesn't change the way your heart beats unevenly and your stomach becomes nervous at the sight of a man giving you flowers.

The card-stuffed envelope beside where the rose was becomes my next focus. It's white, with my name scribbled across the front in his handwriting. I position on my side to gain use of my other hand and open it, pulling the beautiful card out of the envelope.

It's a birthday card.

Tears expel at the sight of that word. I had actually kind of forgotten about my birthday with everything going on. It's hard to keep the days and dates straight. I certainly didn't tell him.

Tynleigh . . .

I read over the poem in the card, loving every word, but the part that gets my attention the most is the handwritten portion at the bottom.

Good morning, beautiful . . .

I'll never miss out on your birthday, even when you try to keep it from me. This day, nineteen years ago, was the day I was given the mate to my soul. My reason for existence was confirmed. I've been wandering through the years jaded ever since, waiting for the day when you would walk into my life and complete the missing part of me. It's one day that is actually worth celebrating. Happy birthday, baby. I love you. Sit up, enjoy your present, and come find me.

P.S. Don't forget to call Meredith. I kind of owe her this one.

—Your soon to be husband.

Meredith . . .

I should have known. My grin is set firmly on my face, taking up most of the space. I sit up, allowing the blanket to fall to my waist, and my mouth falls as I take it all in. The ceiling is covered in pink, white, and red balloons, silver curly strings as far as I can see. Red rose petals litter the hardwood floor. "He didn't."

A squeaky sound starts. My eyes target the large wrapped box sitting in the middle of the room. It gets louder. What is that? I stand and walk toward it. When my footsteps sound the box moves. A scared yelp exits my mouth. In response to the bark that follows, my heart liquidates.

I rush toward it, tugging the lid off the box. The baby blues that meet me steal my air. The only response I can muster is a blood-curdling scream. The words finally come. "You got me a puppy! Oh my god."

I lift the tiny, shiny, gray baby out of the box and hold her under her front legs out in front of me. Her hot pink collar is beautiful against her fur. "Hi, little one. I'm your mama."

Her tongue slips through her closed mouth and then she yawns, followed by another bark. I cradle her against my lavender tank top and squeeze her as tight as I can without hurting her. Her head turns up toward me and she licks my chin. It's a weird texture; kind of rough like sandpaper. I've never had a pet, aside from the low maintenance goldfish I had for years before it kicked the bucket. It was the only pet my parents would allow. They didn't want the upkeep responsibility to fall back on them from our lack of, as we got older.

I'm a sappy mess. Tears are streaming down my face. The silver plate on the top of her collar becomes visible as I wipe my eyes. It has our information on her, but the top line is unscathed metal, unlike the etching below it. Her name is not listed. *He's letting me name her . . .*

The tears start all over again. This is the best birthday ever. I walk us back to the bed and sit her atop, then grab beneath her mouth to look at her. "What do you want your name to be, little girl?"

She walks to my lap and jumps in, wagging her small Labrador tail along the way, before settling into a little ball with her head on my thigh. I grab my phone off the nightstand when it starts to ring.

Meredith calling . . .

I swipe to answer and put it to my ear. "Happy birthday, love! Another one down for the count."

I laugh. "Thank you. I've missed hearing your voice."

"To be expected. My voice rocks."

"Your ass is conceited." I laugh again, my good mood holding.

"You wouldn't love me the same if I wasn't. It's part of my charm. So . . .good birthday or bad? Just tell me if I need to get my ball-busting supplies ready. I can be there in a few hours."

"He got me a puppy!" There is no way I can stop the excitement as it barrels from my lips. It feels like champagne finally being released from the confinements of the cork it sits behind.

"Asshole."

"What?"

"That's a total asshole move. Damn porn stars. They aren't supposed to be good with romance and sex. It's unfair. How do you think small dick men land a woman forever? Hmm . . . They are hopeless romantics; that's how. Do you see Ben doing sweet shit? He's an asshole. Your boyfriend cannot top my birthday presents on the first one. It's unnatural. It's insulting. He needs to work for that shit like the rest of us. The first one should suck ass and you smile nicely like it's the best damn thing you've ever gotten. Do you know how long I plan what I'm getting you for your birthday?"

"Isn't it great? He's totally getting laid later."

"No, don't condone bad behavior."

"You're being a jealous hag right now."

"Growing up with your ass and being the best damn friend ever earned me the privilege of that behavior. Deal with it."

"Fine. I really miss you and your bitchiness."

"Miss you too, Kam. California is a bit smaller without you and porno boy around. Don't you dare tell him I said that either. His ego doesn't need to get any bigger. But for reals . . .it's depressing. Ben is long gone back to school, so I don't have the amazing sex boy toy to occupy my time like I did with Bryant. This distance thing is going to suck. I hope I didn't do something stupid, ya know? He better be serious this time. I gave up perfectly good, steady sex for him; that I'm sure another girl is enjoying. I've also turned into that lady that sits at home on Friday night in my robe with a pint of *Ben and Jerry's* while I watch all of the best friend and romance movies. I'm pretty positive I could even be a fill-in for a *Friends* cast member now. It's that sad."

I laugh. "Mer," I say in a dramatically saddened voice. "Awe, that's so sad."

"Right. I should end my life. It's never been this bad. I figured I'd be on my way to being a feminine badass right now. For my future I always knew I'd easily be the real life Carrie Bradshaw or Samantha Jones from *Sex and the City*, but no, my life has taken a plunge quickly."

"You're such a diva. Ben may be good but he's not that good. No man can totally tame Meredith Love. How are things going with that? Have you talked to him?"

"God, yes. He calls me like every hour. After every class my phone starts ringing. I bet I know his school schedule better than he does. I've never heard the man talk so much in my life. Totally killed that mystery thing he had going."

"Too much?"

"Yes! Even if I wanted to run back to my latest bang I have no time. I think he's a little paranoid about Bryant. He'd never admit it though."

I don't think he has anything to worry about . . .

"So tell him to chill. I'm sure his frat house is constantly overfilled with drunk girls. It's like a socially acceptable whorehouse. He was probably hooking up with girls just like you were guys."

"No! And stop planting that shit in my brain. Those weeds are not needed. We really need to work on your filter. I'm just a needy bitch that doesn't know what I want. It annoys me until I hear his voice, but I think it's only because it makes me want him more and we are thousands of miles apart. God knows I've always wanted him. It's a shitty card to draw. I even considered flying to Alabama for the weekend. Does that tell you how much I need medication and a big stiff cock right now? I think withdrawals have started."

I scratch puppy's back, listening, and holding back the laughs since this is actually serious Meredith conversation. Meredith could ban Alabama from the United States and never feel guilty. It has nothing to do with the state and everything to do with it being home. Her wings are big and the south is small . . .minded in most cases. It doesn't work for her, and, I can't say that I blame her. I, too, am in no rush to return. "Well, I heard somewhere that FaceTime sex works pretty well."

"Oh my god. That's genius. I don't know why my perverted mind never considered it; although, I'm going to refrain from asking why you know this, because I do not want to know."

"That's a first."

"And the talk of a horny, lonely woman, sitting at home while her good looks go to waste. I'd be mad at the bitch too if I were you. Worst best friend ever. God, I'm starting to hate the sound of my own voice. Come back to me," she wines. "But on a serious note, I'm glad you're having fun. You deserve every bit of it, so stretch out those newfound wings and live it up. I better have lots of stories to live through upon your return."

"You'd love it here. His sister too." That awkward thought returns. Bryant. Okay, maybe not. That sounds like disaster. "So, I need you to help me name pups. Nothing is popping in my head," I say, changing the subject.

"You should name it Sam for shits and giggles. It's a neutral name and it's like meshing Saxton and Kambry together in one love puppy."

"That's perfect!"

"I was kidding."

"I love it."

"Figures. You would."

"Now boarding, flight . . ."

"Are you at an airport?"

"No! That was the television. Gotta go, love. Call me later. Happy birthday. Kisses."

The call drops. Damn shady bitch. She's totally going to Alabama. I glance through my texts, reading the one from my brother.

Ben: *Happy birthday, sis. Make it a good one. Love you.*

I reply quickly to thank him. It means a lot to me that he would text me. Maybe this is a good thing: him and Meredith. I can tell a huge difference in his overall attitude already.

I glance down at Sam in my lap, letting her name roll through my mind a few times. It just fits. I set my phone down and move her to the middle of the bed long enough to grab the spare blanket and put it crumpled in the corner. Then I move her onto the cover on the floor so she doesn't fall off.

It's my birthday and there is one sexy man out there that deserves to see me in my birthday suit. Tynleigh told us on the way home last night that she had to be at work early and stay most of the day anyway since she took off the full day yesterday, so we already expected to be doing our own thing today. Thinking back on it now, and remembering their encounter as she told us, it was probably all planned this way. I may as well take advantage of no one being in her apartment but us.

Luckily Sam goes back to sleep almost instantly after I lay her on the blanket. I tiptoe to the door and quietly lock it, before discarding my shorts and tank top, then step out of my panties, leaving them beside my clothes. The first thing I check off the list is brushing my teeth so I don't forget with other things on my mind.

Thirty seconds. I spit the mouthwash into the sink and rinse it out with water. That's as long as I can hold it and endure the burn. I'm a baby when it comes to the stout alcohol burn of mouthwash. My makeup bag is sitting on the counter. I don't need most of what's in it at the moment. There is one particular thing I'm looking for.

The tube comes into view after moving a few things around. I pull it out and remove the top to the hooker-red lipstick I've never used. It's untouched by a pair of lips. I would think there are others out there like me. I've always been terrified of red lipstick, even when I see someone wearing it and love it. A very fine line in how it's worn makes the difference between a classic beauty and a whore. Then there is the issue of the shade of teeth. Red is a bold color that can accentuate them, for better or worse.

I paint my lips, slowly and carefully to avoid smudging, hoping for the best. My tongue swipes over my top teeth as I toss the lipstick back in my bag. I add some mascara for a little effect to make my face pop, and then brush through my curls from last night, leaving it in a state of long, beach-kissed waves.

I walk to my suitcase and dig through it, my hands settling on the black, patent leather stilettos I'm looking for. I knew there would be a time for these. I grab them by the silver heels and put them on. My heart begins to race. Last thing. The back zipper to my suitcase is already unzipped from me removing things all week. The new perfume I ordered a while ago is still sitting in the original box. I remove it and take the top off, before holding it up to my nose to sample. It smells just as good as it did when I passed by someone not much older than me wearing it, so I shamelessly stopped a stranger and asked her what it was.

I spritz it twice: once on the neck and once on the wrist, before touching my wrists together for transfer. "You can do this," I whisper. "Be everything he wants you to be. Be everything you can be. Just be you."

It's a scary thing: becoming a woman. You're at that bridge between the little girl you've always been and the woman you'll forever be. It's intimidating. There will always be others out there that do it better than you. There will always be men that want sexuality. Last but not least, there will always be a self-conscious backdrop that makes you second guess if he likes it.

To gain your wings of sex appeal is something every girl wants, and a skill she wants to master, but there really is no right or wrong way to obtain it. You never know if you're good at it. It's something I would assume could be self-taught or taught by others you trust. There is no instruction manual. It's a perceptive thing.

But with all that I am I want to be a confident woman. I never want to worry. I want to know that no matter what I'm good enough to be his only. I want to be the one that completes him and his every need. I want to be the woman he'll never forget if I'm gone. So I will be. I may start slow, but I will grow, and over time I'll be exactly the woman I *want* to be.

I grab my phone, fully ready, and turn on the video feature within the camera. Recording begins immediately after pressing the button and I start to speak into the screen with the front facing camera on. "Hey guys. It's Kambry. So, today it's my birthday, in case you didn't know, and Saxton has really outdone himself. See this?"

I rotate the camera and scan the contents of the room: balloons, petals and all, and then end on the small puppy sleeping in the corner, before putting the camera back on me. "Epic birthday, right? I thought so. With every good man stands a good woman, so rewards are equal."

I record the length of my naked body, all the way to my heels, capturing the full view as much as I can, before speaking into it once again. "This is what he gets in return. The code to opening every woman is balance: a little arrogance, some romance, and a lot of lovin'. He made me swoon, so he gets to see me in my birthday suit. Stick around for part two. Coming soon."

I stop recording and ready the video for posting in Tumblr. Once imported, I quickly type out a posting.

#HubbyToBe is #swooning me. Just when I think it can't get any better, I wake up to this . . .on my #birthday! Be jealous. Love life. Cherish each other. #Love in any form is better than none. #RomanceGetsDicksSucked —XOXO, Kam. #SexSessions #Afterthecut #Pornstarlove #BirthdaySuit #LipstickKisses #PerfumeEssence #HesGettingLaid #NewYorkRendevous #PuppyLove #BirthdaySex Stay tuned for #parttwo #WeddingDay

#ComingSoon

I post it and drop my phone on the bed, before making my way to the door. I stop, trying to gather myself. My nerves are trying to get the best of me. This is pre-wedding night practice. I'm not an amateur anymore. I need to get better at this surprise thing. But that's what is hard. Every time I look at him, my words evade me, and I feel like I'm starting back at level one.

Saxton

I flip through the TV guide for the fifth time. Breakfast is made, I've already had three cups of coffee—in which has me shaking like a junkie without his fix—and my anxiety has long before shot through the roof. What the hell is taking her so long? I know she's awake. I heard her scream when she got the puppy, and I heard her on the phone.

There is nothing left to be done. This was all I had in me within the romance department. I figured she needed and deserved to be stunned, so when planning today I gave it all I've got, holding nothing back. The suspense is going to fucking kill me. I know it. What if she hates dogs? I never thought of that. Then I'm going to be stuck with finding a thirteen-hundred-dollar dog a home. All of the research I did when I could sneak a few seconds away from her said Labs were the way to go, so that's what I did with Tynleigh's help. I heard her scream, and I think it was a good one; think being the key word.

Most people have no damn idea how hard it is to *not* eavesdrop on your girlfriend's conversation, but I've been up for hours and she doesn't seem to be coming out anytime soon. I've gone to the door more times than I want to admit to, touched it with my fingers to open it, and then backed away to give her some space. The softhearted boyfriend, nice-boy act is starting to turn to shit.

I toss the remote on the couch and stand, starting to pace. I walk to the window and place my palms on the frame, looking out over New York. "Why are you so nervous?" I mumble, frustrated. "Fuck."

I slap my face to get ahold of myself. "This is not your first time on a horse."

"You wanted me to find you, and so here I am."

"Happy birth—" I turn around at the sound of her voice, only for my fucking eyes to fall out of my head. Oh, holy hell. Thank you, God. I need this vision burned into my mind. I want it seared on my eyeballs. I want to wear it like branding.

I can envision those plump red lips going down on me, leaving lipstick kisses on my body as she does. It complements her light blonde hair and barely tanned skin well. My eyes skim slowly down her body, stopping on the six-inch heels that will soon be pointing at the ceiling instead of the ground.

Her hands move to her hips and she inches one leg out to the side. "You going to come take what's being offered to you or stand there with drool running from your mouth?"

My hand reaches into my pocket and I remove my phone. "Don't move."

A slight smirk appears, puckering her lips a little, making the picture even better. I snap the photo. There are only a few moments in a person's life that are worthy of reminding you they exist on a constant, daily basis. This is one. It should never be forgotten and it should never be blurred from time passing by. I need to remember those *fuck me* eyes and kissable lips forever. I want the memory to encompass me like a second skin. Because in this very moment the female in front of me is no longer the quirky girl I met in the club. She's not the shy girl with an unknown road ahead that I got to know in her apartment. She's not the sassy, lovable, pure-hearted and sometimes-immature girl I've fallen in love with. The little girl has vanished forever. What stands before me is a confident, happy, woman in love. And she looks that way because she's mine. That's a memory worth remembering.

My phone goes back into my pocket where it came from. That one's getting blown up in black and white with her lips staying red. Color pop at its finest. I'm framing it and putting it over our bed, and I'm sharing it with no one. It belongs in the vault of our lives, so that's where it'll stay.

She walks toward me, slowly, her heels tapping against the hardwood floor. She grabs in exactly the right place as she stops in front of me, tightening the fabric of my cargo shorts around my dick. I flinch. Any man would when something comes at his manhood in a quick motion. "I see someone is happy to see me."

"You're naked," I state honestly.

"Yes, but you're extra hard this morning compared to what you normally are at first glance. Tell me," she says in the hottest damn voice I've ever heard. It's laced with sex, enhanced with lust, and wrapped with confidence. "Is it because you're picturing me in this position?"

She drops to her knees slowly, placing her hands on my bare sides. She looks up at me. Her lips are forming a path for a Blow Pop. *Blow* . . . Damn. My heart is pounding in my chest. I'm starting to get dizzy. I can hear my pulse loud in my ears.

She kisses my happy trail as her hands clamp around the front waist of my khakis. She pops the button through the slit, and then lowers the zipper at a snail's pace. "Or is it because you want my fat red lips wrapped around your cock for the world to watch?"

I fight the urge to wrap my hand in her hair. She seems to have a lock on what she wants right now, and I'm not about to stop it. When her lips close, she reminds me just how fucking full her lips really are; not that I've forgotten. "You know me so well."

She smiles, giving me the first glance of her bright white teeth. As she does, she reaches into the same pocket I was previously fishing and pulls out my phone again. "Then you'll need this."

My insides quiver, but my body is smart enough to remain still. I grab it. "But it's *your* birthday."

The selfless part of me won out. The guilt of her giving me an orgasm first on her birthday overtook me. "Just think of it as a personal *thank you* card."

My shorts end around my ankles, my cock in her hand: my favorite view. She's the only woman that's ever made me want to nut by the sight of her holding it alone. "It fits."

She begins to stroke me. "Somehow it always has."

"I guess it was made for you."

"Play a game?"

"Okay. What?"

"How many licks."

"Fuck."

And then she goes at it; at exactly the same time I start recording a video, slowly at first as she wraps her mouth around it for the first time. One thing about her I love: it turns her on to suck my cock. The little moans that come from her throat confirm it. Always following it is a sudden gush of wetness, just like . . .now.

My head falls back against the glass. It's astounding that I never have to ask or hint around for head. Every man likes it. One that says he doesn't is lying. It's filthy, it's wet, and it's fucking hot watching your cock slide in and out of her mouth. She never bitches about not being able to take it very deep or it making her gag. She just opens her throat and breathes through it until my head hits the back; finishing what she can't suck of my length with her hand stroking to the rhythm of her mouth, and then she releases me, starting the entire process all over.

She pulls me into her mouth all the way. I can feel the back of her throat. She makes a noise with her mouth, causing that little dangling muscle in the back of the throat to move, vibrating against my dick. "Holy Chr—"

I grab her hair and pull, letting my phone drop after stopping the recording. Who knows if it's even been angled at the right place . . . I wasn't looking, but I'm not blowing until I have something to replace what I'm about to lose. "Handstand it."

She looks up at me, a little confused, but doesn't stop. "Give me your fucking legs. Now."

She pulls back until I'm no longer touching any part of her, and then turns around and backs toward me. I grab her legs, bringing them toward me until she's standing upside down. I lick between her legs, taking some of the white that's just barely visible at the entrance of her pussy. Her ankles wrap around my head. My arms move to her waist and I lift her off the floor to the appropriate height. "Suck me, baby. I got you."

She starts again as I begin flicking my tongue back and forth over her clit. The vibrating is coming more regular now. It won't take me long. I suck her into my mouth, hard, before licking over her pussy once again. Then I fucking eat her like I'm starving. Her taste, her smell, and the look of her pussy swollen when she's turned on makes it easy.

Just before she orgasms I shift, bringing one hand closer to her ass, pressing between her cheeks until my finger is where I want it. I rub her asshole. It's such a fucking easy orgasm enhancer. A little bit of stimulation and you have an all-consuming, horny-as-fuck woman.

I shove my tongue into her pussy as she begins to orgasm. Like an Oreo the white center is the best part. She deep throats me, moaning around my dick; loud as fuck. I press my thumb into her ass as the first spurt makes its way into her mouth. She takes it all. When your woman is thirsty you quench it.

I lick her once, front to back, and then help her down as she pulls off of me. When she stands I look at her. She sways a little as the equilibrium balances back out. "You swallow?"

Her tongue comes out when she opens her mouth. "Every drop."

I reach out and grab the back of her neck, smashing my lips into hers at the halfway point. I want her so damn bad. My need to have her will never end. Tongue deep and lips raw, I reach down and lift her. She wraps her legs around me as I start to walk toward the couch, laying her down on the cool leather. "You can't have a birthday without birthday sex, baby. I guess it's time to start a tradition."

Her hands rub up my back, nails first, until they're in the back of my hair. She's shaking beneath me. Her nipples are hard against my chest. "Show me the version that filled that room with balloons and gave me a baby. Make love to me. Show me with your body how long you'll want me."

I look into her eyes. She's an open book right now. The floodgates to her soul are open and pouring through her eyes. She's emotional. She's second-guessing herself like she does almost every time she does something bold. That's what I love about her. She's raw. She's needy. She's in love.

"Infinitely," I say as I push inside of her. "Nothing less."

She pulls me closer. "Just like that."

My girl . . .deserves the world.

CHAPTER EIGHTEEN

Kambry

New message from SinisterSlave . . .

I touch the notification on my home screen and it takes me to the Tumblr app. My skin crawls at the sheer thought of what the pervert has to say. Cautiously I open it, unsure of what I'll find.

Happy birthday, slut. Is it okay to call you that? My little slut. Mmmm . . . I like that body. I bet your parents are real proud of what they've created: a product of the Devil. Those red lips did just what they do best. I bet he was thinking the same: being sucked off by a whore. Only whores wear such a sinful color. I was thinking . . . New York might be nice this time of year. Once a whore, what's one more to add to the list? If I come, will you save that shade for me? Name your price. I'll be waiting.

P.S. When it's my turn, I like to be called Daddy ;)
SinisterSlave

My phone falls from my shaky hands as I sit on the bed and wait for Tynleigh to bring what she's been instructed I wear for the night. Where we're going or what we're doing has been a surprise, so I'm not sure how I'm supposed to dress. Apparently, Tynleigh has been assigned to find me something. Saxton left a few hours ago with Bryant so I could get ready.

I grab my freshly dried hair hanging over my bare shoulder, clenching my towel in the hand that's been holding the two sides together. Tears fall down my face. I'm scared. Would he really come here looking for me? That's disgusting. What would he do to me to back up his threats and sly comments if he found me? This is getting to be too much. Should I tell Sax? Will he see it? He'll lose it . . .

I quickly reach for my phone again and delete the message, hoping Saxton hasn't already seen it. He's just a bully. He wouldn't really come here. He wouldn't really harm me. There is no reason to freak out and let him ruin my birthday. Saxton warned me about people like him. How do I even really know it's a guy? It could be some jealous girl or something that's obsessed with Saxton's films. That's possible right?

"Okay. I think you're going to like this," Tynleigh says as the door opens. She walks in holding a long garment bag, the bottom draped over her forearm; the entire thing zipped up so that I can't see what's under it. She looks at me and stops. "Kambry, what's wrong? Did I come at a bad time?"

I brush away my tears. "It's nothing; just a stupid comment online. I'll be fine."

"People are stupid. Do you need me to intervene again? I can raise the bar a little. I'm itching to crush a few balls. It's been a while."

"No. It's fine. I can't depend on someone to come to my rescue every time my feelings get hurt."

"Okay, but Kambry, you do know there is a block feature if someone harasses you right?"

"Block? I thought about that, but not sure how exactly to do it. What does that do exactly?"

"Keeps them from having access to your profile or contacting you usually. It was created for a purpose. Use it. Cyber bullying is way worse than it used to be. Most people think they are immortal sitting behind a computer, using their words like hollow-point bullets. It's no longer target practice when they are bold enough to comment negatively. They are aiming to kill. There are vultures out there, just watching and waiting for a weakling to come along. Be a viper."

"Okay. I'll try that. Thanks."

"Now, back to getting you ready before I have to deal with the wrath of lover-boy. I was put on a strict schedule. He sure is a lot bossier now that he's in love. I don't like it. He's taking all of my older sister privileges."

"I claim no responsibility over his behavior."

She lifts a brow. "Woman to woman, I'm going to need you to fix it. I've turned into a personal shopper, a wedding planner, and a decorator all within a week. Fix. It. Give him some of that porno Voodoo you have."

I kind of already have, all over your apartment . . .

That would probably make for awkward conversation, though. I think in this case it's a matter of what you don't know won't hurt you, so I decide to keep it vague. "If he's not fixed by now he's probably not going to be."

She rolls her eyes. "Fine." Then she lets the bottom of the garment bag fall to just above the floor. "I decided to go back to the basics on this one. If there wasn't something to it, then there wouldn't be a song about it."

"I don't know what that means but okay."

She hangs the garment bag on the top of the door and unzips it, revealing a red silky fabric beneath. When it's completely unzipped, she removes the bag from the hanger and lets it fall to the floor. It's a simple design, the bottom long and the torso solid. There is no pattern really, just a rich red satin. The elegance is in the neckline; a sweetheart one, the boob lift coming from the wide piece of material that runs from one corner, behind the neck, and ends at the other. It's beautiful. "Wow. Love that dress."

"Honey, the wow factor is in the back."

She takes the hanger off of the door and turns it around. There is a lot of missing material up top. The fabric looks like it multiplies just above your bottom, bunching and creating a cascading effect down the center to the floor. "You were right."

"It'll be beautiful on you as light as your hair is."

"Tynleigh."

"What?"

"That's a fancy dress. Where exactly is he taking me?"

"Do you want to get me killed? I've been threatened with my life if I so much as drop a hint. I'm not sure my lips could utter the words if I tried."

I stare at it in her hands. Nowhere back home does a girl dress like that except prom. I wouldn't know a whole lot about that, though. I only got to go my senior year and my parents didn't like it. I begged for months, did everything possible they could think of, and even agreed to let Mom take me dress shopping. I ended up being the most clothed girl there and had to be home by ten thirty. Looking back now I'm not even sure it was worth it. "Please. Just give me something. I've never gotten to dress like that."

She stares at it, and then back at me. "What? Formal?"

"Yeah."

"Did you guys not have winter formals, proms, or charity balls?"

"We had prom. I went once. I never got to wear a dress anywhere remotely close to that."

She hangs the dress back on the door and walks toward me. Grabbing my hand, she pulls me to my feet and walks me toward her full-length mirror, before moving to the back of me. She talks through our reflections. "Leave behind everything you knew before. We can't make corrections on our past, but we can write our future. If you never let anything else I say to you stick, hear this. There is no greater feeling to a woman than watching her man see her for the first time at her best. Watch him. The second you walk out watch his expression. Even if you think he's staring at the girls and being a total perv, watch him. Then, and only then, will you know exactly how he feels about you."

"You're not going to give me a hint are you?"

"Kambry, all that matters is that he told me he felt like he had a lot of making up to do with you. I know he feels like things are in reverse compared to a lot of couples. But one thing I'll never forget is when he told me that most girls don't deserve to be courted based on their behavior, yet they get put on a pedestal, and the one girl that deserves to be treated like royalty was a modern day Cinderella. You really caught this one, sweet girl; so let yourself have a magical night. Let him romance you, even if that dress still ends up torn after the clock strikes twelve." She winks. "Most guys don't give a damn whether they're fucking Cinderella or the bitchy, less attractive stepsister until they have nothing left to do but settle down."

Suddenly, I'm more nervous than I was originally. *Dates* with us have always been things like goofy golf or club nights, and now things like concerts have been added thanks to this week, but I haven't gotten a chance to go to the ball. "Will you make me pretty?"

"No." I nod, just before her smile appears. "I'll make you breathtaking."

"*Well, on a scale from one to* ten, I'm what?" That question has become our thing, so I'm sticking with it.

I stand in the center of the living room as she stows away the flyaway hairs and blends spots on my face with her fingers. The dabbing of lipstick starts as she alternates between two different shades of red. "Give me a second."

I wait patiently as she finishes painting my lips. "This lipstick is smudge-proof and waterproof in case you were wondering. You can kiss him without leaving it behind."

She has my hair pinned at the back just before swooping over my shoulder, where it's been trained to stay. My hair has rarely seen clips and bobby pins. Usually it's up on top of my head, down straight or in manmade curls. I've never been good at the art of hair. Wrapping sections around a large-barreled curling iron is as extravagant as I've ever been able to do. This feels . . . foreign.

She puts away the lipstick and holds out a small, velvet, drawstring bag, pointing at it with her other hand. "Repeat these words after me. I, Kambry Rivers, future Mrs. Saxton Maverick Cambridge, will not come home alive without these very earrings still in my ears."

"What earrings?"

"Repeat now, questions later."

I roll my eyes and do as she says. "I, Kambry Rivers, future Mrs. Saxton Maverick Cambridge, solemnly swear to not show up at this apartment without the earrings I know nothing about in my ears."

"I guess that'll have to do. Continue. And if someone holds a gun to my head in demand of these earrings, I take an oath to sacrifice myself before letting them go."

I stare at her.

"Overkill? Fine, scratch the last part. I would not want you to die. But seriously, look at me. Tough love time." She spreads her index and middle fingers into a V, pointing the double end back and forth between her and I. "Inherited gems. Imagine my best *Dory* fish face. Say it with me slowly. *In-her-it-ed.* These have been passed down since my great, great grandmother. They are irreplaceable. I've had them since Mom gave them to me on my twenty-first birthday. I'm letting you borrow them as my sister because you two hopeless, horny lovebirds deserve it, and I will equally beat your ass as my sister should you decide to be careless with them. Are we on the same page?"

"That's really sweet, but I don't have to wear them. That makes me nervous being responsible for something that valuable. Besides, you're a little scary right now. I'm not sure I'd want to chance getting in a fight with you."

"No, no. Rule number two of dress up: you do not rock a dress like that without diamonds somewhere on your body. Remember: black—diamonds. Red—diamonds. Two colors in formalwear you should not wear out without bling. Pretend my bark is mild compared to my bite, wear them, enjoy them, and bring them back. That's all I ask."

A knock sounds at the door. I feel like I want to throw up. "Hold on," she says loudly, as she takes each diamond solitaire out of the bag and places it in my earring hole, securing it with the back. She grabs the bottle of perfume on the table and sprays me, just before tossing it down and running around me like a mad woman, touching and tugging, fixing and dusting.

"Can I look at myself?" I feel sick. I just pray my skin doesn't start getting splotchy from the nerves. Hives are not attractive.

She runs into the bedroom and comes out with a body-length mirror, holding it far enough away from me I can see my entire body. Who is that girl? She looks nothing like me, but then she looks exactly like me: two contradictions that both make perfect sense. I take a deep breath, taking in my cleavage as it rises and falls: not too much and not too little.

I turn, following the curve of my bare spine until I reach the bright red fabric just above my tailbone. Another knock sounds. "Hold your horses! We are out of time, princess."

She sets the mirror aside and walks toward me, her hands following her eyes without touching me. A smile spreads across her face. "You, my dear, are off the Richter scale."

She pulls me in front of the door and positions me, placing a clutch in one hand without making another sound. When I'm where she wants me I suppose, she grabs just below my lightly shimmering shoulders and gives me air kisses like royalty. "Walk slow and with grace and you'll have no problem in the heels," she whispers. "I'm going to my room to shower while you two do your thing. You'll knock his socks off." She winks at me, but this time it's with different meaning than before. Instead of it being in humor, it's packed with the utmost sincerity.

I reach for the doorknob as she disappears into her room, nervously, and open the door. He turns toward me from the backward facing stance he's in as I do. My mouth falls in surprise when I take him in. This feels like a dream, and one too good to be mine. I can't breathe. "You're so handsome," I whisper, almost so low I can't even hear myself.

He wore a tux . . .for me.

Saxton

"You're so handsome," she says, but I almost missed it. Damn. This is like seeing the Seven Wonders of the World for me. My hand goes to my chest. I work to get ahold of myself. I need all cylinders firing to get through this night without screwing it up.

I thought long and hard about tonight. Long and hard. Thoughts repeated, ideas came and went, and I got aggravated a few times because nothing seemed good enough. Over and over I brainstormed ideas, mad when I couldn't figure out what the perfect date would be. God knows she deserves it. I'm ashamed it's taken me this long. It finally dawned on me at no particular point in time this week.

One phrase I remember my dad saying when it was just he and I stuck out. He wasn't one for a lot of unnecessary words, so when he spoke you listened. He wasn't much of a softy either. He got awkward when it came to sex and always backed away from Mom when we were around. He was private. I never saw him in an inappropriate moment with her. A kiss on the cheek was all we ever witnessed. I joked around with Kambry, but if Dad ever knew either of us had heard them in the most private moments of their lives he'd probably be mortified until the day he dies.

So one day my curiosity got the best of me and I asked how they had been married for so long, immediately followed by the debonair phrase—*in case I ever want a girl.* It was in my puberty phase when all I could think about was how many different girls I could kiss or sneak a feel of something inappropriate. The thought of one woman forever was not cool to a boy hyped up over his own appendage hanging between his legs.

I'll never forget the look on his face. Those dimples that he passed down showed up for the conversation and he put his glove-covered hands crossed over each other on top of the fence post we were fixing. His answer was as simple as he was. *"It's easy. You romance her, son."*

That helped about zero fucking percent back then, but it came in handy all these years later. I figure our generation doesn't know much about the ways of romance anymore, geared more toward sex than any before, so old school it had to be. And with her rather broad yet specific interest, the choice became easy, so here I am in a tux, picking her up at the front door with a single red rose in hand. "You look beautiful," I finally say, after having to pick my jaw up off the floor to speak, holding the rose out for her.

She takes it and brings it to her nose, her eyes closing as she inhales. "Thank you," she says. Her eyes open and she takes a step forward.

I lean in and kiss her cheek, pulling the door shut as she walks out. "You ready to go?" A blush appears on her face. "What?"

"I just can't believe you're mine tonight. I've never seen you like this—all dressed up in a tux."

"What do you mean tonight? I'm yours every night." I look down when my hand touches the small of her back and it's bare. I finally get a glance at the back of her dress for the first time since she opened the door. I owe Tynleigh a hell of a lot for this. "And I could say the same about you."

"Some hot girl could always steal you away." She laughs to downplay her comment, but the paranoid undertone is what I caught.

I grab her hand, pulling her body against mine. The subtle gold shimmer dusted on her chest to match her shoulders catches with the light, making them a focal point, as if her breasts need any more attention to what they will already get in that dress. "You never replace an original with a reproduction, and you obviously have no clue about your worth."

My finger automatically traces along the heart-shaped neckline. I groan, wanting to pull it down. "You, beautiful, are a masterpiece. I'll never let you go. No one or no amount of money can change my mind."

Her full red lips dive into mine, smashing them against each other. Her tongue never enters my mouth and she never makes an attempt to move or deepen the kiss. It's as if she just needs to know they're there when she wants them.

Moments later, after she's had her fill, she leans back. The pad of her thumb rubs roughly against my bottom lip. "We really need to go, baby."

"Okay, handsome. Lead the way."

Kambry

The door opens and I stop walking, my hands immediately going over my mouth, only to drop seconds later. "You didn't have to do this."

Waiting for us is a black limo, the driver standing in a suit with the door open to fit the part of every movie I've ever seen. "Of course I did. It's your birthday. I'm still a little insulted you didn't want me to share this with you."

"This is why." I'm fighting hard not to cry. I don't want to mess up the makeup Tynleigh spent so long perfecting. What part of this not being a normal girl's birthday does he not get? A gift and a card, maybe even a cake, are what I'd always expect to come out of someone making a big deal over my birthday. This doesn't happen to girls like me. "You've done so much already. This is too much."

He grips his hand on the side of my neck, his fingertips pressing into the back. "Says the girl that's never been on a real date. Let me show you what you should expect when someone truly loves you. Even though I admire that you're not a brat, there are times when you deserve to be treated differently than you are on a daily basis. Let me spoil you, Kambry."

"I thought that's what you were doing by bringing me here."

"No, that was us coming to visit family. Stop doing that shit. Every action is because I love you and refuse to exist in this life anymore without you. You're going to be my wife in two days. Everything we do is equally ours, so get your ass in that limo, drink some champagne, and enjoy your birthday outside of the box your parents were keeping you in."

His bossiness is such a turn on. I grip his jacket lapels in my hands and pull him toward me. "I'm so getting drunk sex in the limo on the way home," I say, and then walk past him like the good little fiancé that I'm pretending to be and get in the car, nodding at the driver as I get in. If the eyes were the windows into the mind mine wouldn't be quite so blue, because the thoughts running wild up there right now are filthy.

The ride was pretty uneventful once I got over my kids-first-time-at-Disneyworld facial expression. I've never actually seen the inside of a limo. It still amazes me that there is such an amazing thing in existence. It gave me a tiny taste of stardom. Every time I've ever seen one driving around, my first and only thought was—*I wonder who' s in there and where they're going.* It was pretty cool being on the inside looking out in such an amazing city.

He poured us both a glass of champagne at the start of the ride as he said he would, sipping less on his and watching more on me as I downed mine like Kool-Aid.

My third glass down the limo pulls up to the curb. I lean my head back against the leather seat, waiting for him to get out, and staring at the overhead lights that line the ceiling's outer edge. The slightest glow is created by my tipsy mental state.

I roll my head toward him, watching as he places a glass half full of champagne—his first one—into the holder. "You're not allowed to do that."

"Do what?"

"Let me get tipsy or wasted on my birthday and you be completely sober. It's no fun that way."

"It's your birthday. Someone has to watch out for you."

Without hesitation, I pull my dress bottom up enough that I can move my legs freely and straddle him. "No sir." He stares at me, his hands disappearing under my dress as he finds my thighs. I grind my center against him and lean closer so that he has a better look at my cleavage. I've learned they're my greatest weapons against him. "It's my birthday and I want you drunk."

I place my palm on the outside of his hand and guide it further up my leg, pushing the tips of his fingers beneath the edge of my panties. "Do you want this?" I ask as his fingertips enter the moist center.

"Do you really have to ask?" His breath is short, his words choppy.

I grind against him once more, feeling more of him than I did before. "Today we made love, twice. Tonight I want to fuck, here in this limo, with no thought but each other. I want you to want me so bad you want to rip my dress open. I want you to devour me. Give me my memory of backseat fucking in cars, Saxton. Get your ass drunk, enjoy the date, and then give me that dick. This is my birthday wish. Don't screw this up for me."

Without another word I pull the handle of the door. It opens easier than expected, pulling me forward. The driver was obviously waiting for the cue that we're ready to get out. I stand, with as much etiquette as possible. One word catches my attention as I try and fix my dress before anyone can see me: Jazz.

I blink over and over like an idiot as I read the four letters on the building. He couldn't have known. I try and recall every conversation, every slip of the tongue, and every rambling of words between us since we met. There isn't a time I can remember that we discussed this. My love for music, yes. We've discussed songwriting. He knows I want to learn the guitar. But not once has he met this part of my soul. It's a part that doesn't surface often.

I turn to face him. He's just now getting out of the limo, his eyes locked on me. "How did you know?"

He looks confused. "How did I know what?"

"That I like Jazz. How did you know?" My voice betrays me, flashing the emotions I'm trying to hold back. "Tell me how you knew this."

He stares at me like I've gone nuts. "Kambry."

"Tell me right now. Not even Meredith could have told you this."

I've never seemed to totally fit in. It's like I don't belong in this era. My body acted like a host to a foreigner on most days. I was disguising a poser with the innocent little good girl I never wanted to be. I've always felt like my soul somehow got lost in a time it's not meant to be in. If I wasn't a Christian born and raised, believing it's the truth, I might believe in reincarnation, because all of my life I've believed my soul was old; older than the body it resides in.

There was only one place I truly felt like I fit. On days I needed to get away but had no place to go, I went there. A world filled with Big Band and Jazz music was my hideaway. Swing dancing was something I longed for. The early days I visited in dreams. I wanted the simple life they had back then. The days of technology we know now didn't exist. Pearl Harbor was my favorite movie. It wasn't because of the tragedy that it represents and all of the innocent people that lost their lives, but the time in which it happened.

If I could experience time travel, that's where I would go, and I'd be perfectly okay with getting stuck there. Saxton would fit there too I think. I always pictured myself with someone like him, twirling me around the dance floor with saxophones guiding us. We could go out on Saturday nights and sip tea on the front porch on Sundays. We would love each other and life would be great.

"I don't know what you're talking about, baby. I knew you liked music and I wanted to take you somewhere nice you could dress up. This is what came to mind. New York is famous for it. I didn't know you liked Jazz music."

"Of course you didn't," I whisper. He always just seems to subconsciously know. That's one reason I love him. A solemn tear escapes. "It feels like home."

Saxton

She's been almost silent since we got here and got our table, moving her body along to the music with a smile on her face that never goes away. She looks happy, and for a man in love it doesn't get any better than this. Knowing you contribute to someone enjoying life is the best compliment. I can experience things with her that I never thought I would with anyone, and usually I end up loving it more than I thought when I agreed to do it.

It was just like I said. I chose this because she has a love for music and New York is a famous landmark for Jazz music. It's home to some of the greats. Most people don't leave here without experiencing it in some degree. I've never really been into it myself, but that doesn't mean I don't have a respect for it. It just wasn't a genre I clicked with. My personal likes in terms of music are a little . . .harder. The AC/DC concert was right up my alley, and I like certain styles of country, but that's pretty much where my musical likes sit, never changing or swaying as the years go by.

One thing I'm learning quickly is that compromise in a relationship makes for a more peaceful life. She's happy, I'm happy, and it keeps the world turning with no fights. It was more of a bonus that she actually likes this.

I sip my beer and place my arm on the back of her chair. The pace of the music changes from song to song; some a mellow, romantic Jazz, while some are more like swing music, and others are more instrumental oriented. I lean closer to her ear so that she can hear me. "You having fun?"

"You have no idea," she says, her eyes glued to the dance floor. The couples utilizing it have changed slightly from time to time, but mostly it's the same ones. I am guessing they are probably regulars. The house is full, every table occupied. The lights are turned down low, leaving the room dark, and luckily I got a table in the corner with little traffic.

I figured it was probably easier for her since I knew I was going to have to sneak her drinks. Life will be much easier when she's of age. I never expected to add contributing to a minor to my rap sheet, but to be honest it's always been a stupid law to me. It makes no sense that a person can die for his country and enhance the risk of lung cancer by the age of eighteen, yet can't legally drink alcohol until three years later. The way I see it—if a person can witness some of the things our soldiers witness during a time of war, then you should be able to buy a fucking beer. But that's just my two cents.

I follow her line of vision to a couple that's been out there almost the entire time we've been here. It's an older couple, probably pushing seventy. He's wearing a suit and she a dress made for dancing, her heels low to the floor. Their smiles never fade as he twirls her around the dance floor to the swing number currently playing.

I glance back at Kambry. She's watching them with a longing look, her features relaxed and content as she sits with her hands in her lap, her posture straight. It's amazing to me that another human being can have such a life altering effect on a person. I'll be the first to admit I'm no dancer, much like the fact that I can't carry a tune in a bucket. I've been to proms and formals through my teenage years and survived through it, but it was more of a hands on hips and sway type thing, and not once did I give a shit about what someone thought, but I'm not an attention seeker either. Still, as I sit here, I want to do for her. I want to be the best for her.

The song ends and the band playing announces the next one: a cover of Frank Sinatra's, *The way you look tonight*. I recognize it immediately. It doesn't take a Jazz lover to know Frank Sinatra, or that it's a slower one. He's a classic. I take a deep breath when the instruments begin to play the recognizable tune, trying to mentally sway the thoughts brewing, but immediately could shake my own damn head at myself. *You're totally going to do it and you know it . . .*

I stand and reach for her hand. She looks at it, and then up at me. "Dance with me."

"I don't really know how to dance like that."

"Come on. Dance with me," I repeat, trying to eliminate a lengthy conversation. She takes my hand and stands, her face a little red, allowing me to lead her onto the dance floor. This is one of those times when I'm forced to wing it. Years of movie watching will make me or break me here.

She faces me. I place my left hand on her hip and grab her hand with the right, holding it at the exact place it's supposed to be when two people dance. Surprisingly, she falls into position naturally. I pull her close, our cheeks existing side by side. *Dear God, please don't let me have two left feet.*

My feet begin to move, leading her to the beat of the song. She follows along, and within a matter of seconds it becomes second nature. She pulls back a little and smiles at me. I've always thought her smile was beautiful when it's shining at its brightest. "This is surreal. It's the perfect birthday. Thank you."

I pull her against me again, wanting her close. Our hands remain fitted together, but drop between our chests, slowing the pace a little. What was feet movement in somewhat of a box changes to allow our hips to sway. "You deserve it."

She whispers against my ear. "You always say that, but you deserve things too. I don't know what to do for you that would have the same effect as this."

"You saying yes did, baby."

"Do you really think I would have said no?"

The faces in my direct line of vision become more blurred as I get lost within the song. "You're still young. It wouldn't have been abnormal."

"Since you're such an old man and all . . ."

"I'm old enough to have lived a little. I can get married with no regrets of settling down with you for the rest of my life."

"So can I. People back in the time period we're currently dancing and living in got married young all the time and lived happily ever after together. Just because the world has changed its standards of normal doesn't mean that's what I want."

My hand moves to her lower back, my palm at the small and my fingertips to her backside. I can smell her perfume each time we move to the music. It's a scent I'll likely never forget. "I know. I just want to make you happy. I believe in forever with one person, Kambry. My parents instilled that in me over the course of my life. It's why I haven't dated anyone between you and her. I had the mentality that a girl like you didn't exist and real love was lost in the world. A temporary marriage is not what I'm after, and I can get girls that open their legs frequently anywhere. I really just meant that a person deserves enough time to ensure they don't change their mind. I would have understood."

Her hands inch upward, settling on the back of my neck, and my now free hand moves to accompany the other. She glances at me. "Which is exactly why I want to marry you, Sax."

"Which part?"

She smirks. "Shut up and kiss me."

I inch forward, our lips almost touching. "Your wish will always be my command."

Then I give her exactly what she asked for in the middle of hundreds of people on this very dance floor, because that's what you do when you find the girl that makes you forget everyone else.

Kambry

The driver holds the door to the limo open as we stumble out of the club at closing. My body is consumed with an amazing buzz and my mind with a high that can't be artificially conjured. I'm happy, and it's shown the entire night. We've danced, we've kissed, and we've laughed from the fun the environment has created. It'll be hard for a future birthday to ever top this one. This one is perfect.

He lets me enter first. When he follows behind I grab his black tie in my fist and pull him toward me, messing up his balance. I've wanted to do this all night. There is something extremely sexy about a man wearing a tux and tie. I haven't figured out why. It just is.

He finds a place to break his fall toward me as I pull his lips into mine. My tongue instantly searches for his, the beer on mine mixing with the beer on his. I'm dizzy, and everything in my line of vision is covered with a foggy haze. I want him, right here and now, to end my birthday in a way I'll never forget. For me, and maybe a lot of girls, this is something imperative that I need in our relationship; him reacting to me the instant I initiate intimacy, even when it's not the first time. I constantly need to know that he wants me too. It's a connection that is unexplainable: when your bodies become one. I suppose it was created for marriage. The Bible tells us so. But, I feel that it's just as important if it's someone you truly love. As humans, sometimes we can't wait. It may be wrong, but it's nature.

His body rests on top of mine, the fabric of my dress stretched as far as it will over my legs. "Where to, sir?" the driver asks through the pane of glass that separates us.

He breaks the kiss and I immediately wish he hadn't. "Just drive. I'll let you know when we're ready to go back home."

"Yes, sir," he says, and then the window begins to rise until it's sealed off, leaving us in private quarters.

He looks back down at me. "You really want to do this here?"

"Yes." I sit up and he lets me, going with the flow until he's sitting on the bench seat. "It's just us this week." I remove my heels, one by one. "We may or may not get this for the next half a year. I want this week to be the top memory for a long time."

I hike up the lower half of my dress and pull my panties down my legs, removing them, and then I straddle him. "When you see a limo or hear the word, I want you to think of tonight."

His hands rub up my thighs. "Fuck, baby. I already would without anything more tonight. It's not just about sex with you."

I unbutton the bottom buttons of the tux and push the jacket over his shoulders. He leans up to remove it completely, leaving him in the vest, shirt, and tie. The alcohol starts talking for me. "Shut up, Maverick. Give me what so many girls before me have gotten, only more."

His mouth drops slightly and he blinks at me. "But I've never—"

I press my lips against his. I know where this is going. He probably thought that was a smart-ass remark with his past experience since I have none, but really, it wasn't. I'm just in the mood to be a teenager in ways I've never gotten to be. I heard about the *behind the scenes* of prom night for the four years I was in high school. I was always so jealous that I didn't get to stay late and experience the full night all dressed up with the guy I love, followed by the sex wherever a place was available. Now I have it, and I don't want to miss a thing.

I pull back. My lips feel slightly swollen, tingly, and wanting more already. I undo the hook-and-eye clasp above my right breast on the inside of the fabric, and move the strap around my neck to let it hang on the other side. He looks at my chest and back at my face. "You want me to experience things, well, this is something I want to experience. Be careless with me. Let's pretend we just left prom. What would you do to me if we had?"

He peels the front of my dress down, baring my front. He grips my breasts in his hands as I begin to unbutton the vest, kneading them as I get to his button-down. "I fucking love you," he says when I pull at the knot of his tie, loosening it enough to remove his shirt.

He helps me, pulling the tail out of his pants when it's all that is left. I remove his tie, putting it on me and letting the long portion run between my boobs. "Show me."

He pushes his hips up, shoving me upward, and works his pants open. He then slides them down his legs, me raising enough to get them between us before sitting back down on his lap. His mouth wraps around my nipple, lightly sucking and nibbling. My head falls back at the way it feels. "Put it in," I command, as my center grinds against his length.

He grips my butt and lifts me. When he presses me back down, his head is at my entrance, pushing inside as I lower myself. "I love that you're always wet."

I glance down at my bare bottom, my front dress skirt at my pelvis. I pump my upper body up and down, watching his dick as it disappears and reappears. "I love that you're always hard."

"Only for you, baby."

My pace quickens, my lips lowering to his. "Always and forever?"

His hands grip my butt beneath the back of my dress. "Forever and always."

I kiss him, needing him and wanting him all the same. I feel the closest to him like this. It may seem childish or immature to a lot of people, but when he's inside me, I feel like the bond between us can't be broken. It's a seal between two whole beings. I love him. It doesn't matter where life takes us, because we can always come back here: a place for only us. He's the part of my life I can't go on without, and I never intend to.

CHAPTER NINETEEN

Saxton

"What if they don't like me?"

I wrap my arm around her and pull her into my side as we walk through the airport to the correct terminal. "We've been through this. They will love you."

"Tynleigh couldn't come with us? I feel outnumbered."

I laugh. "She's meeting us at the restaurant. When this is over you'll feel silly for all your worrying."

Her hand slips around the back of my waist. "Well, how would you feel if the situation were in reverse?"

I look down at her. "Meeting your parents? I'm pretty sure I would just have to settle with the fact that they'll probably never like me and move on. That's the only way we'd be happy."

"Good point," she says. She halts, and then tugs on my shirt. "But seriously, what if they ask a lot of questions? What do I say? We need a game plan."

I pull her forward. "Stop worrying. Should they even ask questions, the answers will come, but I doubt they will. You're the smartest blonde girl I know," I tease.

"Ha ha! This is not the time for blonde jokes. I feel like I'm going to throw up."

I laugh again, amused by the fact that she's so nervous. It gives me a sense of satisfaction knowing it affects her emotional state at all. I kiss her temple just before catching Mom out of the corner of my eye, walking beside Dad with a carry-on bag over her shoulder.

She gives me a big smile, glancing between the two of us, and then hands Dad the bag as she approaches. Like Dad always would, he takes it and continues walking behind her as her pace increases, loaded down with both of their luggage. As she closes in I open my arms to hug her, but instead of coming to me she goes straight for Kambry, wrapping her in her arms.

"What the fuck? Mom?"

Dad reaches over and smacks me lightly on the back of my head. "Watch your language, Son."

"Did you see what she did?" I question him, my fingers reiterating what my mouth is saying. "That's so messed up. I'm supposed to be her baby. She hasn't seen me in months, and she's known her for less than a second and giving her all the attention. I'm offended. All those years of sucking up were for nothing."

My tone is dramatic for good measure. I am a little surprised I didn't get the first hug. I've already been replaced as the family favorite, not that I can blame them. She's my favorite too. Kambry looks a little awkward, yet relieved: what my baby does best.

"No, you're not a baby anymore. You're a fine young man. Now you're supposed to be having babies. I'm not getting any younger." Mom releases her and comes at me.

Kambry looks at me with a lined mouth; her eyes narrowing a little in the corners like she's holding back a laugh. "Mom, not the time for awkward conversation. A little too straightforward. You're shot-gunning when you should be sipping."

She laughs; Kambry that is. "Leave her alone. I love it."

I point at her. "First Tynleigh and now Mom. You women are not banding together and forming some kind of an alliance. Dad and I are outnumbered."

"I have no idea what you're talking about." Her lips tighten to form as straight of a face as she can muster.

Mom hugs me. "I knew I was going to like her. Pretty one too."

I settle back into the comfort of home easily, the cocky teenager surfacing. "Are you surprised? I'm a sexy guy, Mom. What is there not to like about this?

And I don't pick ugly girls."

"Are we basing this on track record? Because I'm going to be honest, Saxton, you've had me worried for a long time now." She retaliates with sarcasm of her own.

My mouth falls open.

A tiny speck of hurt registers.

A laugh escapes as I watch Kambry behind Mom battling her inner laughing spell that's all over her face.

"I should place you on the banned list, Mom. Just for that, add about ten years to your first time grandmother status," I tease. "I thought I would at least have thirty minutes of favoritism before you switched to the other team. I'm so hurt."

"Oh, hush, you are not."

"I am. So hurt," I emphasize again. "I could have not called you," I push.

"Saxton Maverick Cambridge."

"Kidding. How was your flight?"

She keeps glancing back at Kambry with a huge grin on her face. "She's not a mirage. Yes, she's still there."

She laughs finally. "It's your own fault that I am this way; you and your sister. The flight was lengthy. Two-hour layover. But I'm here now and ready to get to know my daughter-in-law." She kisses my cheek. "Smartest catch you've ever made, Son," she whispers into my ear.

As she lets go I grab Kambry and pull her against me. "I'll agree with you there."

I weave around her to shake Dad's hand. "Old man. How you been?"

"Busy." He glances at Kambry and back at me. His silence this far is not out of the ordinary. Really, I'm surprised he gets a word in given Mom's talkative nature. "It seems you have been too."

The tell-tell sign comes out that he's pleased: the dimples I inherited. Like a reflection they're returned. "Gotta grab them while in reach. Right, Dad?"

"And hold on tight."

A sense of pride overcomes me. It's funny that no matter how independent you become, a man still wants the approval of his dad. "Dad, this is Kambry. Kambry, this is my dad, Allen Cambridge, and you already officially met my mom, Lori."

He pulls Kambry into a loose side hug. "It's nice to finally meet you, Kambry. It appears you're keeping him in line."

"Trying my best, Sir," she says, her cheeks a little red.

He locks eyes with me. "You've already gotten further than anyone else."

I smirk, placing my hands on her shoulders and pulling her back across the imaginary line. "Would you two stop trying to send her running for the hills? I'd like to still have a wife come tomorrow night if you don't mind."

Mom pats my cheek with a light slap. "Son, if you've kept her this long I don't think you'll have to worry about any running. Her good sense is obviously already gone."

"Gee, thanks, Mom. Love you too."

She winks at Kambry and wraps her arm around her, pulling her away from me as she begins to walk in the direction the two of us previously came. "Where are you going with my fiancé?"

"We might as well go ahead and break her in from the start if she's going to be a part of this family. I need details that I doubt I'll get from you."

"Don't overwhelm her," I call out as she quickly puts distance between us.

Kambry turns her head to look at me, letting Mom tug her along, mouthing the words I want to hear: *I love you.*

"I love you too."

Dad squeezes the back of my neck, reminding me I'm not alone and probably sound crazy talking out loud to myself. "It happens to the best of us, Son."

"Does this feeling ever fade?"

As my eyes set on his aged face, he's looking off at their retreating bodies, a knowing smile spread as if he can see me looking at him. "Not even a little. Before you know it, you'll turn around and it'll be thirty years and two kids later. Even then, you'll want her secured to you just as much as you do today, if not more."

"I'm kind of glad you're here. I know it's not easy for you to leave for extended periods."

"I wouldn't miss this accomplishment. When a man gets married he's crossing over into manhood. I'm proud of you, Saxton. I know you were a little lost for a while, and I can't say that it was the appropriate path to take to deal with your issues, but I'm glad you got it out of your system before you settled down. You're finally finding your way and putting the past to rest. That's something to be proud of."

"*She's* something to be proud of. I really struck gold with this one." I grab the handle of one of the two rolling suitcases standing upright not far from where he stands. "Come on. I'm starving and Mom needs supervision. She's alone with the woman I'm going to marry and has a head full of childhood stories."

The things that could come out of her mouth are enough to terrify even the strongest man.

CHAPTER TWENTY

Saxton

I turn to face her from my spot next to her on the couch, pushing a strand of her hair behind her ear. She's really beautiful like this: those candid moments when she's focusing on something and I get a few moments to just enjoy life for what it has become. There are days when I'm still trying to really figure out my feelings. Not in the way that you don't know if you love someone, but trying to grasp ahold of the depth in which you already do. Some days I wonder if it's all a dream, and others I'm looking for the crack in the ice to avoid the shattering effect. But then there are days like today when everything is completely perfect as it is and I just want time to stand still instead of dissecting why it is.

For lunch we went to Chinatown. I figured it was somewhere Kambry would want to experience before we went home, and I knew my parents would be up for anything. My assumptions were spot on. She loved it. She's so animated in the way that she explores new places.

It doesn't matter if you've ever been somewhere or done a particular thing before, because when you experience it with her, what you knew before seems so dull; a totally different place. Looking through her eyes is like going from black and white to color or standard to high definition. The picture is so much clearer.

I noticed Mom and Dad catching glimpses of her excitement here and there and having their own little private conversation mentally. I knew the second Dad smiled as she jumped up and down pulling me from place to place that they were just as in love with her as I am. She's a limited edition. She's humble and her reaction to others doing for her only makes you want to do more. My heart will never fully understand how her parents could be so harsh to her all of her life. I can't wrap my head around it. It doesn't even take a kind person to recognize the pure heart that beats in her chest. It's one worthy of preserving.

Lunch, hours later, and saddled down with bags from purchases, we returned here while Tynleigh took Mom and Dad to their hotel to check in for the evening. Tynleigh reminded Mom ahead of time that she was taking Kambry out tonight, against my will. This was one situation I was hoping Mom would give her two cents on, but she didn't seem too upset when she mentioned catching a Broadway show while we did our thing. Why is it that I seem to be the only voice of reason on this matter? Beautiful girls don't need to be clubbing alone; mine in particular.

The remote she's holding in her hand becomes a loose item on the cushion. She looks over at me, staring like I've grown a third eye. Then her smile appears. "Tell me what you're thinking. You've been staring at me for a while."

"My parents love you."

She sighs. "I didn't want to say this, because it was something I was kind of dealing with inside, but I really like them. You have no idea. They make me feel like I'm already a part of your family."

"That's because you are," I say simply. "I told you to stop worrying. It was for nothing."

She stands and positions herself between my legs at the front of the couch, placing her hands on my shoulders. Mine settle on her waist, pulling her closer as I look up at her. "Tell me why you love me," she says.

"Lots of reasons. Why?"

"Just name a few."

"You're beautiful, you love me, and I just do."

"Why do you want to marry me?"

"Where is this coming from? If I need to be writing my own vows now would be the time to tell me."

"Just answer the question."

"You make me a better man. I realized that living a mediocre life full of endless sex with random women or film parties with a void in my chest is no longer good enough for me. I want wholesome living. I want two-sided love. I want you. I can have endless sex with *you*, be by *your* side at parties if that's what you want to do, and the hole in my chest was filled when *you* walked into my life. I'm not going back."

One knee at a time she straddles my lap; much like she did last night in the limo before she gave me a night I'll never forget for as long as I live. When the girl says she wants to fuck, she isn't lying. She's quickly coming into her sexuality and I get to be the test subject. It's the best damn job in the world.

My heart is pounding. Memories are circling. Her lips are full and pouty, her long, blonde hair falling in a curtain over her shoulders. "You want to know why I want to marry you?"

"Yes."

She leans toward me, invading my personal space, placing her glossy lips so close to mine I can smell her lip-gloss. It reminds me of peaches. "You breathed life into me. I existed miserably, hoping for a miracle and praying for a change. I was a slave to a dull personality with no strength to escape. I was hollow."

"And now?"

"I'm full. My heart is anchored to you. You resuscitated my soul, Sax. It's never been about age with us, even though you bring it up often. You aren't taking away my freedom, you're giving me life, and that's worth holding onto forever. I need you to understand my love for you will never change no matter what age I am. It's just a number. Stop fixating on it."

"Okay."

"Do you need to know why I love you?"

I return a line that she used last night. "Shut up and kiss me."

When her moist lips touch mine the door to the apartment opens. "Time is up, Maverick."

My head falls back against the couch. Fuck my life. I grip her face. "Stay with me. I don't need a bachelor party, Kambry."

"Fuck yes you do. No normal man ties the knot without one last hoorah. Get your shit together, man. You're coming with me."

I ignore Bryant, looking into her eyes. "Stay with me. I haven't tried to sleep in a bed without you for a while now, except for that one miserable night, and I was drunk as shit and finally passed out. I don't know if I can even try. I won't get any sleep and then I'll look like shit for our wedding."

She kisses me and a horrible sound wafts through my ears. "He's wrapped around that pussy, pussy," Bryant sings in the mocking tone after an old rap song by 69 Boyz: *Let Me Ride That Donkey*. For fucks sake, that's an old song. I flip him off, not knowing exactly where he is. Kambry laughs against my lips, a burst of air pushing against them with force from her trying to hold back and failing.

When her lips leave mine, a smirk is left behind, before narrowing her lips from the state I love them the most. "You should never question the type of weapon you walk around with after that."

"Where are you taking him, Bryant?"

"That depends. Where are you allowing him to go?"

"Where do you want to go? Maybe that's a better question."

"Strip club."

My head whips around her body so that he can get a good look at my face. "Fuck you. You're not taking me to a strip club. That's disrespectful."

"Okay," she says, in the surest tone I've ever heard from her.

I'm a little hurt. I expected jealousy. "What do you mean okay? I'm not going to stare at naked women the night before our wedding, Kambry." I realize that sounds completely different than the way I meant it. "Or ever. What the hell?"

"Oh my god, Sprout! You're turning into a fun-sucking adult."

Obviously one more person was added to this party. "Mind your own business, T."

My eyes stay locked on her face. Her smirk spreads into a grin. "Okay means okay. You're going. I'm fine with it. This is your last night to have fun without me. So we're clear on the boundaries, I'm even okay with Bryant buying you a lap dance as long as your dick stays in your jeans, your hands and lips to yourself, and your body remains in an open area and not a private room. I want you to have fun. I'm not that girl to let jealousy control my happiness. Go and have fun. I just expect the goods to remain mine."

"I love you for that, I do, but I don't fucking want it. What part of this is everyone not grasping?"

"You like boobs. For men a strip club is the equivalent to *Willy Wonka's Chocolate Factory* for kids. I'm giving you permission to go stare at a room full. Why is this an issue?"

"Because the only tits I want to stare at are yours. I'm not going."

She lowers her voice, still staring into my eyes. "Are you scared someone else will make you hard and it'll upset me?"

I'm not having this fucking conversation in front of other people. I'm already pissed off enough. "Get out."

"Come on, Bryant. You can help me pick out something to wear," Tynleigh says, and they walk to her room, shutting the door in somewhat of a slam.

"Talk to me," she says.

I rub my hand on my forehead; aggravated they won't leave me the hell alone, but more so Tynleigh and Bryant than Kambry. "Kambry, I've had other women. If you want to get raw, let's bear all and rub salt in the wound. I've seen more tits in the last four years than I'll ever see in one night at a strip club. I've seen them in every shape, size and color, fake and real. I've touched them, sucked them, and been rough with them for show. For a long ass time I've needed a fucking pill to get up because I was sick of that lifestyle. I thought my dick was broken. It wasn't fun to me anymore. Even if looking at another woman *could* still make me hard, I don't *want* one to. I don't want someone other than you touching me. Furthermore, I fucking like the fact that you're the only woman I get hard for naturally. It shines a little bit of light on the depressing fact that you gave me your virginity and I couldn't give you mine. Look at me. Do I look like I'm bluffing?"

She raises her brow, amused. "Am I scared to watch a woman grind her ass on my dick? No. Pussy becomes second nature when it's part of a daily routine for years; kind of like brushing your teeth. Yours is the only damn one that fazes me anymore. I guess that's because you're the woman I'm supposed to be with forever, so it kind of makes sense that I would actually *like* it forever. I may give in, back down, and shut my mouth a lot of times when it's hard for me, but I'm not a fucking metro man lacking a backbone, and I sure as hell am not afraid to piss someone off. I'm a red-blooded country boy. You can fucking nail my balls to a wall and I'll still feel the same way. Any man that feels like he needs or is entitled to go out and fuck around right before he gets married shouldn't be getting married. I've been on shit like booze cruises and to bachelor parties. I know the kind of shit that goes on behind a woman's back, just like I'm sure there are women out there that do the same. That doesn't make it fucking right."

"So hot when you're angry."

I pause, not expecting the seduction packed into her voice. She rubs her middle back and forth on my lap. "What are you doing?"

She stops and stands before me. "Unbutton your jeans."

"What? I'm not kidding."

"Neither am I." Her hands disappear under her cotton dress and returns with the strings of her underwear hooked in them as she pulls them down her legs, stepping out when they hit the floor. I glance at Tynleigh's door. Her television is on, the volume turned down enough I can barely hear it, and talking is alternating between them. "I'm prepared to bribe you."

I stare at her like a fucking idiot; even knowing her panties are sitting on the floor. "Why do you want me to go?"

"I told you. I want you to go have fun. No one said you have to do anything wrong. Just remember that I make you the happiest."

"I don't have to remember. I'll never forget."

She smiles at me, not holding back. God, she's beautiful. Slowly she stalks toward me and looks down at my still buttoned jeans. I unbutton and unzip them, before pushing them down to my upper thighs. She straddles me once again. "I trust you because you are the way you are. You have a beautiful mind."

She grabs my hand and inches it up her body under her dress, until it's forced beneath her bra. "If I end up in your bed, will you go?"

My breathing is becoming uneven. "You're making this hard."

She squeezes her breast with my hand. "It's just a few hours, women dancing seductively on stage and maybe on you; endless alcohol."

Her voice is thick and low. She starts rubbing her wet pussy along the length of my dick. "Just remember, this is what you get to come home to if you participate. You won't have to sleep . . .*alone.*"

Like a starving fish I take the bait, and my eyes glance down at her bare bottom, hook in mouth and all. I expected stubble. She shaved again. Fuck. "Then what are you doing now?"

"Reminding you of what you'll get to sink into when you get done with your boy time."

Pulling one leg between us, she turns around, her back now facing me. Oh hell . . .reverse cowgirl. She doesn't even wait before grabbing my dick and sitting down on it. It slides in easily, quickly wrapped in a snug blanket of warm wetness. She pumps up and down fast and hard, making it difficult to remain quiet. My hands grip the couch as I work hard to focus on the movement of her shoulder blades to keep from coming.

As if she knew, she bends forward and grips my knees in her hands, arching her back to give me a better view of her ass as she rides my dick, and oh my god. I push the bottom of her dress up to get a better look with no fabric falling in the way. In and out. Up and fucking down. Glistening with her arousal.

My dick contracts, and before I can even stop it my cum has a quick head start inside of her from her grinding against me as she swallowed me whole. I was hoping she wouldn't notice and continue, but almost as soon as I finish she stops. "Why are you stopping?"

She evicts my cock from her pussy before giving me any warning whatsoever and then stands and turns around. I know exactly what kind of grin she is sporting. "My job is done," she says as she scoops her panties off the floor and pulls them back on. I'm working to gather my thoughts as she walks to Tynleigh's door and knocks. "Bryant, he's ready for you!"

I quickly replace my pants where they're supposed to be. "I never said I was going."

Her head cocks to the side, a pleased look on her face. "But that didn't stop you. It's funny how that works."

Why does this seem like two totally different conversations? The door opens to Bryant walking out and Tynleigh in the doorway. "Have fun boys." She pushes Bryant toward me. "I'll see you at closing."

Then she moves further inside and the door slams, the sound of the lock immediately following. "What just happened?" Bryant asks as he points his thumb over his shoulder at the door.

The day I gave her sex before telling her my parents were coming smacks me in the face. I smile, still staring at the shut door. That fine as hell, sweet as candy, sugar rush of a woman that I'm madly in love with just conned me with her body. She actually used me, leaving me confused as hell whether she did this for her or me. "I think I just got played."

"Did I ever mention I like her?"

I stand; mind-boggled over what exactly did just happen. "Who the hell doesn't?"

I walk to the door and turn the knob. It's locked, just as I expected. "I don't even get a bye kiss?"

"More to look forward to later," she calls back. "Love you!"

"Love you too." I laugh and look at Bryant. "Not one fucking word or your ass will go alone."

His grin says more than his mouth. "Wasn't going to."

I walk past him. "Let me get some clothes."

"Stay strong, Bro. Castration can be tough. I'll rub my balls for you."

I flip him off as I enter the bedroom. "Fuck you. Payback's a bitch. Lube up."

"Never. It won't be me."

I'm writing it in the books. One year. That's all I give him until he's groveling in apologies because he's swimming in the same fucking love pool. I'd be willing to bet a hefty sum it'll be with the one he's still fucking. I know her. She's a man-eater. She's deadly, because all she cares about is her career, and her independence will stand between her and being a sappy romantic until the day she dies I'm afraid. It makes her the ultimate hunt when it comes to men, because she doesn't need anyone but herself.

I grab a change of clothes. Twenty-four more hours. That's all I have until she's completely mine in every way there is. The countdown is the part that's going to be hard. Maybe I should get hammered and pass out. I don't need my consciousness if I'm not with her anyway.

CHAPTER TWENTY-ONE

Kambry

Soft fur rubs against my ankle as I finish the last coat of my mascara. Then a whimper follows. I look down as she stands on her back feet and scratches at my leg to pick her up. "Hey Sam. Is Mama's sweet girl awake from her nap?"

I pick her up, hugging her against my mostly bare body; only covered by my bra and panties as I wait on Tynleigh to bring me an outfit as instructed. Again, one that makes me look older so there's no questions once I get on the inside, she said. I figured the smoky effect my eyes were screaming would take care of that, but obviously not. "I promise as soon as we get home I'll give you the attention you deserve, little lady. No more puppy-sitting for a long time. It'll be just us three."

I scratch her back and get a sandpaper tongue to the chin, making me laugh from the tickle. The apartment door opens and closes. It's heavier than the bedroom doors, making it a distinct sound. "Tynleigh?"

I walk toward the bedroom door, almost smacking into a body. "Bitch, call me something besides Meredith again and see what happens."

I stare at her, trying to figure out exactly what I'm looking at. "Meredith?"

She grabs my cheeks in one hand, squeezing my lips into a pucker, and shakes my head from side to side. "Were you expecting someone else, hooker?"

"Yeth," I say in a smothered sound from her clamping of the mouth adding a th sound.

She lets go, that knowing Meredith grin on her face. Sam barks at her. "Calm down, princess. Not your turn."

Then she narrows her eyes. Attitude it coming. "Do you really think you can fucking get married without me? I'm the queen of mischief. You didn't let it slip. Not even once. My innocent little bae is corrupt. Since I have to teach you everything, it's lesson time." Her hand starbursts, palm facing me. "There are five categories in which you fucking stalk me to make sure I know: the need to commit a crime, relationship status change, marriage, birth, and death. I do not appreciate your secrecy. I own you bitch. You're stuck with me till you die."

"Did you really just call me bae?"

I laugh. Her face hasn't cracked yet. "Desperate times call for desperate measure. Next time you keep something this important from me I will whoop your ass."

"You're being a little psycho right now. Just a hair." I use my thumb and index finger as a measuring device.

"Girl, this is mild. No one has seen the crazy I can emit and lived through to tell the stories. The world ain't ready for that."

"Your southern is coming out."

"Don't insult me."

I start laughing. "Oh my god," I yell. "I've missed you!"

Tynleigh walks in. "You made it."

Meredith winks at me in sarcasm. Yes, sarcasm. She has facials for every emotion. "I did. I owe you a few stiff drinks and a big fat vibrator," she says.

"Wait. You are the one that called her?" I look at Tynleigh as she's nodding her head.

"I did. When I found out Mom and Dad were coming for Saxton I asked him if there was someone you would want here even if you wouldn't admit it. When he gave me two names I called them. Victim number one has made her appearance."

Of course he did. He's Saxton and it's thoughtful. How could I have not guessed that in the beginning? An exploding effect occurs in the left side of my chest, leaving a form of pain that I like.

"Who's the second person?"

"Sweet Home Alabama," Meredith sings in the tune everyone knows.

"Really? You're breaking out Lynard Skynard?" It all hits me like a bolt of lightning. "Ben is here!" I scream; a little too excited."

"Yes, he's been instructed to go with the boys for the night."

My face transforms. This situation finally unravels before me for what it is. "Is this going to be awkward?"

"Is what going to be awkward?" Meredith asks.

I look at Tynleigh. "No awkwardness, whatsoever," she says.

"What fucking awkwardness?"

"Bryant is here." The words fly out of my mouth with no remorse.

"You bitch. You invited Bryant before me!"

I shake my head; my mouth lined and pressed shut. "You really wouldn't believe it if I told you," I finally say.

"You better fucking explain. I will stab you in the heart with your sword of betrayal."

"He's fucking Tynleigh!" My hand flies to my mouth as I look between the two of them.

Her and Tynleigh look at each other and Meredith starts laughing. "So?"

"Why are you laughing? Ben will be with Bryant and you'll be here with Tynleigh. You four have shared people. It's like a weird swap."

"My precious. You're so cute and innocent. Is it funny that it's coincidental? Yeah, but we were never an actual couple. I kept trying to tell you we were just friends with benefits. You were the one making it into something more. I messaged him to apologize once the dust all settled, and he mentioned heading to see a friend. He never said New York or that it was Saxton's sister, just an old friend. I took that to mean a girl, but it wasn't my business to ask. It was just a polite way to leave things with no hard feelings. Funny how things work out, but I hardly expected him to be abstinent."

"We actually just met a few days ago," Tynleigh clarifies. "The friend he's talking about is different."

She looks between Tynleigh and I. "I swear this doesn't bother me. I only instantly loathe people Ben has hooked up with. It's a mental illness I caught long ago. My serum for sanity was indulging in a replacement, hence Bryant."

"I feel like our friendship is a lie," I state. I make an O with my hand. "Zero fucking room to talk about secret keeping."

"It's not my fault. You of all damn people should know there is always one dick better than the rest, whether you've actually had others or not. Emotions are little demonlings that have something to do with that. It's nothing personal. Plus, when we started age was an issue. He didn't want to get in trouble or inherit a bad rep. Usually, the only time people can keep those kinds of secrets are when they're dead."

"Don't you dare pretend it's just about the sex. I want to hear you admit it."

"The sex is amazing. It's worth return visits."

"Meredith Rose Love, admit it or I will discontinue this friendship and you will shrivel up and become a cat lady. No one else is crazy enough to put up with your shit forever."

"I have no idea what you're talking about."

I extend my arm, holding Sam closer to her. "Lie to those eyes."

She looks at them. "For fuck's sake, Kambry, don't punch me in the vagina. Please don't make me do it. I can't say it. Those razors will cut up my lady bits forever."

"My heart is forgetting you already."

Her head falls back for the dramatic person she is so she doesn't have to look me in the eyes. Acting really is her calling. "I love Ben Rivers. I always have."

She wipes her tongue repetitively with her fingers. "Was that so hard?"

"My mouth should be washed out with soap."

"You really are a drama queen."

"No, I'm a superstitious person. Once you admit to something it has the power to destroy you."

"I need alcohol to deal with you in love."

"See, you agree. It drives you to drinking."

"I'm going to get your outfit, Kambry," Tynleigh says. "This shit reminds me of college days."

"No! I brought her something from LA," Meredith interrupts.

She rushes out of the room. "She's not normally this crazy." I think about that for a minute. "Okay, yes she is, but you'll learn to love her."

Tynleigh laughs. "No big, sweets. She's great. I just meant if I'm going to referee I need to be drowning myself in shots so that it's a fair match." She winks. "Us old people have to have a head start or we spoil the mood."

Meredith returns with a white one-shoulder dress. It looks short and tight.

"Tonight is your last night to wear white."

"Mer, I lost my virginity. That tradition doesn't count."

She scoffs. "No one else knows that. Everyone is entitled to a scratch or freebie. One person is the same damn thing now days."

"I agree with her there. Just put it on. We need to get going before the club reaches max capacity or he won't look the other way when you show your license. Cops are more likely to hang around. My connections in this city only go so far. Meet you two in the living room in twenty."

Tynleigh walks out of the room, shutting the door behind her. "I still can't believe you were going to get married without telling me."

"Water under the bridge."

"No, it's flooded. This bridge will be out of service until it's cleared. You cannot do that to me again. I would have been devastated, Kam. I've supported this thing since the beginning. Just because I don't travel on the insta-love train doesn't mean I don't understand those that choose to ride on it. You're my best friend. I want to share in your joy the same as your heartbreak."

Dammit. Of course I'm going to feel the ping of guilt. Her voice is clear, her jokes gone, and the face of a hurt best friend remains. "Okay. I didn't mean to leave you out." I shrug my shoulders. "It was just supposed to be a random event between me and him. The rest just happened."

Her freshly manicured nails go to her mouth for a moment. Then, just like Meredith does when the conversation gets too serious for too long, her switch flips and she's back to her normal self: the crazy girl that ordinary people will never forget.

I hold my phone out, front camera turned on, positioning Meredith and I in the middle of the screen. "Take a picture with me."

The music is blaring and I've had two mixed drinks already. We've been here for about two hours and my buzz is now swarming my mind, my body relaxed, and I feel carefree. She uses her finger as an arrow, pointing at the *Bride* sash draped from shoulder to hip at my front. We smile together and I snap the photo, creating a still memory of my last night before I'm a married woman. Tomorrow I become a wife. It's sudden, but it's the perfect storm of crazy love.

I ready the post for Tumblr:

No greater surprise than the surprise of your best friend showing up for your bachelorette party! When she'll fly across the country to watch me walk down the aisle, I know she's a forever kind of love. You're my sister from another mister, Mer! Love you! #BestFriends #BacheloretteParty #Bride #PartyMode #GirlsNightOut #NewYorkLife #IWantToMoveHere #OverThePornHappy #ClubNights #FunTimes #MissinOurBoys #FeeningForTheEggplant #AllHailTheEggplant #HisDickIsBetterThanYours #LuckyGirl #LivinOurLoveStory #PornStarRomance

I post it and scroll down to the selfie I posted from the limo ride here, reading a few of the comments.

Natedog28: *Damn girl. You fine.*
LilaKay.Doug: *Awe, beautiful Hun! Where's the sexy lover tonight?*
ArianaX: *Love that dress!*
DirtyDom: *Following from the Facebook post. Thanks for the tip. Look forward to the X-rated posts. -DD*
SinisterSlave(Just now): *You look almost as good in person as you do in the photos. Deep by Blackstreet is fitting don't you think? I'd even say it's your theme song . . .*

I toss my phone on the table in front of me, my head whipping from side to side. My heart starts pounding against my chest. A bad feeling settles in my gut. This is starting to get really damn weird. Okay, we're past starting. It's been weird for a while. Surely it's coincidental . . .

I go back to my most recent post to ensure I posted a photo and not a video. There is no play option, confirming I posted a photo. How did he know what song was playing? My body is starting to heat, even in this skimpy little dress. I feel dizzy. I look around the room again, searching for any person within eyesight acting weird. Nothing. Everybody is occupied in some form, no one staring at me or lurking that I can see.

"Kambry! Do this shot with me," Meredith says. I look at her. "You've got the drinking cheeks! Good girl." The funny thing: I'm quickly sobering from the fun buzz I had. I glance through my peripheral vision, but still see nothing. Maybe I'm being paranoid. I just need to be drunk. I'm supposed to be having fun.

"Toast time," she says, handing me the tiny glass full of clear liquid. I take the shot glass from her and hold it in front of me to match Tynleigh and Meredith's positions, forming somewhat of a triangle.

"What if I can't drink it?"

"Chase it, love," Tynleigh says. "It's all about the aftertaste. Just open your throat, swallow, and chase it with your little fruity drink there."

"Okay."

Meredith clears her throat; I'm guessing to make sure she can yell over the music. "Kambry, my best friend and soul sister, may you and Saxton have all the happiness in the world, live happily ever after in your porn castle, and have lots of babies after the reign of your sex careers." I roll my eyes. "And if he ever hurts you, I'm just a phone call away. I'll bring the gun and you bring the shovel. Congrats, babe." She raises her glass an inch. "To weddings, marriage, and lovebird things."

We tap our glasses together and shoot. I follow instructions, drowning my throat and swallowing without thought. My face puckers as the liquid fire runs down the back of my esophagus. I feel like I'm being poisoned. Grabbing my drink, I suck from the tiny straw as fast as I can, trying to mask the horrible taste.

My phone vibrates against the wooden table in a burst of two, both short, signifying a text message. I look down and touch the banner message at the top of my screen and it takes me to the messaging box.

Saxton: *Having fun? Please say no . . .*

My face lights up. It's amazing how much I miss him when he's not with me, including days we've been together all day. I hit the reply bar with my thumb, pulling up the keyboard.

Me: *That depends. Lol. Why do you ask?*

Meredith grabs my phone out of my hand. "No ma'am. Tonight is girls' night. You can talk to him later. My god, woman. I'm seriously about to smack that huge grin off your face. It's not healthy. No person should be that happy all the fucking time."

"Give me my phone, Mer. Seriously."

She raises her brows. "Do you really want to battle being the Alpha? No one can defeat me. I am a champion."

"Don't be a bitch. He's going to get upset if I don't answer. He didn't want to go as it is."

"Fine. You have one opportunity to tell him you'll talk to him later. I never get you to myself anymore and it's only going to get worse after tomorrow. We're going to dance. If you try to be sly I'll take it and put it in my purse."

She hands it back to me, the screen still lit up with two messages on the lock screen, both from Saxton. I open them. The first one is a photo. I touch it to enlarge. It's a stage, a little dark, with a pole at the end. The girl is wearing a thong only, turned upside down as she holds the pole in her hands, her legs twisted around the top. I'm a little jealous I can't do that.

Saxton: *Is this what you wanted me to see?*

Me: *Maybe . . . That girl has mad skills.*

Saxton: *This isn't my thing.*

Me: *Just have fun. I promise I won't be offended or hold it against you later if you do. I'm not that kind of girl. Meredith is confiscating my phone. I have to go. Please just relax. I love you.*

Saxton: *Are any guys hitting on you?*

I smile.

Me: *And most people would think I was the jealous one . . .*

"You have five minutes. Wrap it up, sunshine."

I cut my eyes at her, trying my best to give her the evil eye. "I'm going to circulate, loves. Come find me in a few," Tynleigh says, taking off with her drink in hand. My phone vibrates again.

Saxton: *I saw what you're wearing. You're hot as hell. I know what I have and any heterosexual man with a sex drive would look twice. You didn't answer the question.*

I force back the laugh trying to escape.

Me: *I really love your crazy moments, but no. I have not spoken to any members of the male species. You have nothing to worry about.*

Saxton: *I love you.*

Me: *I love you more. Gotta go. Have fun, baby. See you soon.*

Saxton: *Never. And not soon enough.*

I return with the lipstick kiss emoji and put my phone away. "I'm all yours, but I'm taking my drink."

She grabs my hand and pulls me so hard I barely have time to grab it before stumbling. Here we go . . .

I'm drunk.

The music goes in one ear and out the other, but no lyrics come from my mouth. It's taking focus to stand up straight. My hands grip Meredith's hips as she dances against my front with her back. Tynleigh comes and goes; at least I think. I'm not sure how long it's been since I saw her last. I suppose at random times she navigates to people closer to her age. I know she was dancing with a guy . . .if I'm not imaging it.

I tighten my arm down on my purse, ensuring it's still there, resting against the crevice of my armpit. A body becomes flush with my backside. The lack of breasts pressed against my shoulder blades tells me it's a guy. I'm lost in the music, matching my body to the beat. "You're fucking hot."

That voice sounds oddly familiar, though I don't know why. I shouldn't have drunk so much, but the sweet nectar they doused those drinks with was yummy. I move closer to Meredith, and the body behind me follows, not taking the hint. I can feel the denim of his jeans against my thighs at the bottom of my dress hem. The hard area presses into me.

The current song comes to an end. Thank goodness. I push Meredith a few feet in another direction as a new song comes on. She never questions me. We've been doing this for what seems like forever. I'm hot and sweaty, the strobe lights are flashing throughout the room, making everything seem like it's in slow motion, and the music entering my ears feels like the bumping of heavy base through speakers.

I become the meat in the sandwich again. "Not interested," I state.

Instead of backing off he places his hands on my hips, pulling me against him. His face is next to mine. "Damn, girl. Distance has done you well."

Why the hell does that voice sound familiar? His erection is grinding against my backside, making me feel dirty and like a cheating whore. I nudge Meredith forward a little, before turning around to give him a piece of my mind. As my eyes set on the face of the persistent guy behind me, I freeze. "Kyle? What are you doing here?"

"Maybe I should ask you the same question." Again he places his hands on my hips, tugging me toward him. "But whatever the reason, it makes me happy. I've missed you."

I push him off. "Stop, Kyle," I slur. "Why are you here?"

"Kyle?" Meredith asks and walks up beside me. "Oh shit. What the hell are you doing here, Miller?"

"I moved here for school. I enrolled at Syracuse after Kambry called us quits and then stopped answering my calls." He cuts his eyes at me. "Me and some friends came to the city for the weekend."

"Good for you. Have a good night," I say and try to walk away, but he grabs my arm.

I turn to look at him. His brown hair is shorter and his green eyes shine every time the strobe light flashes on him. "Don't leave. These things happen for a reason." He walks closer to me, wrapping his hands around my waist. I can smell the whiskey on his breath. "You never gave me a chance to fight for you, Kambry. I went by your house and your Dad said you took off."

"I didn't want you to fight for me. We were over."

"Why all of a sudden? For two years you were mine. What changed your mind? Did I mean nothing to you? You know, you never asked me why I stayed with you even though you wouldn't give it up."

"I don't need to know."

"Well I'm going to tell you. Maybe that's the problem. I didn't try hard enough. It's because I was in love with you, Kambry. I still am. You were different than all the other girls in school. I knew it then, but I'm sure of it now. I was planning to marry you after college. Even your parents didn't fight us being together."

"Only because you were his puppet," I seethe. "He loves everyone that he can control."

"It's called respect. I knew what I wanted in the end. Those two years weren't easy for me, but I sacrificed things because I wanted you for the long haul. Do you know how many fucking times I had to go home and jerk off to keep my dick in my pants? It was a little insulting for you to just walk away like you barely knew me."

"You're drunk, Kyle. Let me go."

He pulls me tighter. "You heard her, Kyle," Meredith bites out, tugging my arm away from him. "She's done."

"So are you," he says, ignoring her. "I can smell the tequila. You're different."

"That's usually what happens when you escape the very thing that was holding you hostage. Now, if you don't mind, please let me go."

"Did you ever love me? Or was I just the star baseball player to you too just like everyone else, looking for a fun social crowd to make up for your parents?"

"No. Not the way you're asking. I did like you a lot though then, but we're different people. It's not you. It was me. I'm sorry."

He laughs. "That's fucking classic. Maybe I just need to remind you."

He surges forward and presses his lips against me hard, trying to shove his tongue in my mouth. I tighten my lips closed and push him off as hard as I can. "Don't fucking touch me unless I ask you too. This is getting too weird for me. I'm leaving."

He grabs my left hand and looks down at it, shaking his head as he looks back at me. "That's perfect. The good girl runs away from home, leaving everything she knew behind and agrees to marry the first guy she finds. Did you give him your virginity too?"

"That's none of your business."

"You did, didn't you? I never fucking complained, even when I begged and you turned me down. He probably got in your panties on the first date. Tell me I'm wrong. I fucking wish you would."

"Kambry, just walk away. You don't owe him any explanations. He's just being a drunk asshole. Let's go."

I look at her. "No, I think I do."

He struck a nerve, and now I'm pissed off. Call it the alcohol talking or the fact that I'm growing up and finally have a backbone, but I'm really upset that he kissed me without giving me a choice just because he has before. I have to explain this to Saxton and somehow expect him to believe me when this is the one thing he's leery about. And now he's basically insulting me. "No one is entitled to my virginity, *Kyle*. It's mine to give to whomever I want, whenever I want. Yeah, I guess you could say I gave it to him pretty early in comparison to my time with you, and you can take that however you want to. You sure as hell weren't a virgin when we got together. You're holding onto a memory and a fantasy all rolled into one. You wouldn't want me anymore. I'm not the same girl. If you really want to know, I'm a porn star. I'm marrying my co-star. When you know you just know," I seethe sarcastically. "And it wasn't you. Now leave me the hell alone."

"A porn star? Are you fucking serious? I bet your parents will be proud to know what their daughter has become. You could have this, Kambry. Like I said, everything happens for a reason, and I'm standing right here."

"I'm getting married, Kyle. What part of that do you not understand?"

"You aren't married yet. It's never too late to change your mind."

I laugh. My head is spinning. "Nothing is this coincidental."

It all hits me: the comment from earlier with the song playing at the exact same time as the one in the club and the weird parental comments now. My eyes widen. "SinisterSlave?"

He stares at me, not agreeing or denying. My eyes are already welling up. I back up, bumping into a body. "He's not SinisterSlave, but I am. He did make things a little easier for me, though. I knew there was something I liked about him. Was I missed, Sax-Kam?"

He lingers on the username, making sure I heard it. My heart stops. "No.

Please no." I now know there are moments in a person's life when death would be the best option, because the knowledge that you have received is enough to make you no longer want to live. That moment for me would be now. My stomach is rumbling and on its way to expelling the contents. One voice you'll never forget and recognize anywhere is one of your parents', and I just heard mine.

The realization of everything comes crashing down on me.

I want to hurl.

I want to burn my eyes.

I want to erase my memory.

I want to scratch off the very skin I stand in.

Because I don't know what to do from here.

So I do the only thing I can think of. I run. And I don't stop until I hit pavement. "Kambry," he shouts. I glance back to see that he's following me. This is a new low, even for him. The taxi sitting at the curb is the only thing that appeals to me. My heels drag against the cement as I work to keep my balance while I run. My calves are burning, but if I stop, there is no guarantee on what could happen.

The strong girl could fall.

The weakness could return.

The life I've come to love could vanish all together.

The place I call home could become a memory.

I cannot lose him. He's the only thing I have to live for.

I'd rather die than go back, but I can't escape the truth.

My dad is SinisterSlave.

"Drive!" I scream in a panic as I shut the door, looking out the back window. The cab pulls out just as everyone I know halts at the curb, my two lives mixing before me, and staring back at me as I leave them behind. I turn around, focusing on the road ahead. I have no clue where I'll go, or what I'm about to do, but my past will not taint my future. I'll run for the rest of my life before I let it, and that's a promise I intend to keep.

CHAPTER TWENTY-TWO

Saxton

"Dude, you're lame. She told you a lap dance was perfectly fine. Who the hell turns that down?"

"Me. That's who. I'm here, I'm drunk, and I'm watching. Don't piss me off, bro."

The stage has been occupied all night. One after another a girl walks across it in heels, slowly moving her body to the music before she makes it to the pole. Each girl looks different, dances slightly different, and puts on a variation of a similar yet different dance routine fitting to outfit, but to me it's all oddly the same. I personally don't see the hype with men and strip clubs. I can see tits and thongs anywhere with likely a cleaner reputation, but none as clean as the one I lay beside every night.

"Want another drink, cutie?"

I sit back from the elbows to bar position I was in, bottle in hand, passing it to her after finishing it off. "Sure," I say, to the silicone blonde that's been circling all night. I used to like fake tits, until I saw a rack that size that was actually God created instead of manmade. Now they just seem like false advertisement.

She grabs it and winks at me, like she's done all night. Bryant leans over and places his hand on my shoulder, looking back at her as she walks away. "She would give it away for free, bruh."

"Not. Interested," I grind out, teeth clenched.

"If it's on my account and Kambry is cool with it, don't worry about me. I don't take you for a guy that would screw her over now that I've gotten to know you," Ben says.

"I appreciate that, but I'm good."

She returns and sets my beer down on the bar in front of me. "Can I get you anything else?"

I glance at her and toss a bill down on her tray. "Nope," I draw out. "I think that about covers it."

"What a shame," she says, and walks away in her almost completely nude body.

"You've joined the dark side," Bryant says, a laugh in his voice. "Do you still have balls down there?" He glances under the table and grabs my thigh, horsing around. I thrust up with my leg and pin his hand against the underside of the bar. "Ow. Fuck."

"Fuck you, and don't ever touch below the shoulder again unless you grow a pussy and change your name to Kambry."

"Shit, man. Who pissed in your Cheerios this morning?"

"I told you I didn't want to be here."

He pulls his hand free, still running his damn mouth. "Relax, enjoy the view, and remember she wanted you to be here."

"You're an asshole."

He smirks. "Best compliment all night."

I grab my beer and turn it up, guzzling it. If I have to endure this shit for hours still, I need to be hammered. Who the hell cares if I want to stay home or party with my girl? It's my damn business. I don't need to feel wanted by women to know my manhood is still there. I've been there, done that, and earned a degree in it. It's old. And it's fucking overrated.

My phone vibrates continuously in my pocket signaling a call. I reach in and pull it out far enough to glance at the screen. It's probably Mom or Dad.

Meredith calling . . .

I swipe right and hold the phone to my ear. "What's up?"

The music in the building is making it hard to hear her. It's a panicked mumble. "Kambry."

The only word I hear. The state in which the word comes out is what has me on high alert. "What?"

"Ugh. The bird has flown the coop! I'll repeat: the bird has flown the coop!"

I stand and walk toward the door to see if I can get to a quieter place. "What the hell do you mean she's gone?"

"Her ex-boyfriend and dad somehow showed up." More mumbling. "Stalking." A silent pause occurs every few words. "Kissed her." I continue to move around, trying to get better reception in this metal building on top of the music blaring. "She ran."

"Ran where, Meredith? Where is Tynleigh? She was supposed to be in charge. Fuck. This is why I didn't want her out without me." Two words settle themselves nice and tight in my mind. "Wait. What do you mean kissed her?"

"If I knew where she was I wouldn't be calling you!" I stop, finally able to hear in the spot I'm in. "He just came at her when she wouldn't give him the time of day. Then she got really upset. She said something about SinisterSlave—whatever that means—and just went fucking AWOL. Then her dad showed up acting creepy as a damn psycho and she just took off. That's what I mean."

My heart is racing. All of my senses are escalating to dangerous levels. This city is big and she's small. My entire state of being enters into panic. "Why didn't you go after her?"

"You don't think I tried? I've never seen someone run that fast in stilettos. I don't know how she didn't bust her ass and break her neck."

"So help me God, if she doesn't answer her phone neither of you will be taking her anywhere without a chaperone once I find her, and that special person being me."

I hang up the phone and call Kambry's number with shaky hands. "Fucking females—hardheaded and never listen until it's too late." It goes straight to voicemail. I try it again, hoping she's just trying to call me at the same time: same result. My hand clenches around my phone at the exact moment I try to throw it. I guess my subconscious has better sense than the rest of me. "Hey, you okay?"

I look at Ben standing behind me. "Hell no I'm not okay. Your dad showed up and sent Kambry running."

"Dad?" He looks as confused as I feel. "Are you sure you heard her right?"

"Do I really look like I'd have misinterpreted something that fucked up?"

"Dad has his issues, but I don't really see him being that good at stalking, and I sure as hell didn't tell him she was here. He's horrible at everything, honestly."

"If you only knew."

"What?"

"Now is not the time to discuss the secret fucked up life of your dad if I'm right in my assumptions based on that phone call. I need to find her. Do you know what kind of scum waits around in the dark for girls like her to stumble into a vacant alley?"

"You don't think she would just go back to your sister's apartment? She's a smart girl. No one ever really gives her credit, though, including me."

"Are you two going to stand over here and chitchat all night or come join in the fun?"

"Shut up, Bryant! Fuck, think of someone other than yourself. Kambry is missing. I'm hardly in the mood to sit and drool over girls when I might be standing at an alter alone tomorrow."

"Missing? Are you that fucking dense? Kambry is sitting over there."

"What?" I scream, looking in the direction he's pointing, and sure as I have a dick there she sits, in my chair.

"Were you not expecting her? How else would she have known which strip club?"

I rush to the barstool and turn it to face me, placing my hands on the seat to her sides. She's crying, but it's a silent cry, the only sign being the tears that fall down her face from overspill. "You okay?"

"No."

"Tell me what happened."

"Kyle was there. Some guy kept trying to dance on me while I was with Meredith on the dance floor. I tried to subtly move away, but he followed me. When I went to be a little more blunt I recognized him."

I count mentally, trying to stay calm, and guilt suddenly consumes me from the night on the beach when I told her I had been to see Salem. If she felt the way I feel right now I'm an asshole. "How did that make you feel?"

"Confused. He started being weird; saying stuff he's never said and acting in ways he's never acted. It was like a different person using his body." Another set of tears trail down her cheek. "Then he kissed me. I'm so sorry. Please don't leave me. I didn't ask him to, and I don't think I acted like I wanted him to."

Her face genuinely looks confused, as if she's recalling every action or every word spoken. I'm not sure why I'm surprised she would think it was her fault when some douche bag kissed her, but that's just Kambry, and that's why I know she'll make the best wife and life partner. "It's not your fault. I'm not mad at you."

She's looking at my neck instead of my eyes. "I'm so embarrassed," she says, and the waterworks start. This is completely heartbreaking to watch. I don't like seeing her cry.

"Why? You didn't do anything wrong."

"My dad has been stalking our Tumblr page. He's the one that has been making the horrible comments and the crude remarks." She gags. "I don't know if he's that crazy over control that he looked past the fact he was imposing on his daughter's most intimate moments, including but not limited to her naked body, or if he's really that sick and twisted. I didn't even know he knew how to operate the Internet, let alone find me on a social media stage. I'm starting to wonder why Kyle was in on it or how. I thought he hated my dad. I'm so confused."

"Look at me, baby."

She's hesitant but finally does. Her blue eyes are duller than usual, her lips trembling. "Humans do less than honorable things when they're dealing with loss of any kind; whether that be a parent over a child, a scorned lover, or even siblings or friends. I'd even go as far as to say loss of power makes people the craziest. Look at what I went through after heartbreak. Do you think my parents are proud of me, or my decisions? They aren't. They don't have to be to still love me. Their job was to raise me to the best of their ability and then let me go. The rest is on me. The day I turned eighteen their job was done. I think that's the part your dad is having problems with: letting you go. My parents will always be there for guidance when I need them, but it's no longer required. At some point we have to walk on our own two feet, baby, regardless of what our parents would think if they knew how we were living. I can't explain what possessed your dad to take things this far, and I probably will never understand that kind of ludicrous behavior, but just because he's seen your body in a different form than when you were a child or seen you and me love each other in an X-rated way, don't let that change who you are in here."

I point my index finger to her heart. "He'll either learn to love you regardless of how you choose to live your life or you'll go separate ways forever. This is the person I fell in love with and the person that I'll marry tomorrow. She's good, she's funny and loving, and she's naughty at the touch of skin. She's the best damn person I know."

"I'm not that special."

"You did force a grown man to come to a strip club and stare at boobs against his will. I'd say that's pretty special."

She laughs.

"There's that smile." I wipe her cheek. "I knew it was back there somewhere."

She glances behind me at the stage. "Are you having fun looking at boobs and booties?"

"It's terrible. Bryant accused me of being ball-less when I wouldn't flirt back with the waitress."

Her laughter picks up. "You're like the worst porn star icon ever."

"Best compliment all night," I say, stealing Bryant's line from earlier.

"So . . .there is still an unclaimed lap dance on the table?"

I shake my head. "I don't want one."

She wraps her hands around the back of my neck, straightening her posture. Slowly she's coming back. "Who said I was talking about you?"

My jaw drops just enough to cause an opening in my mouth. "Can—" Words fail me.

She laughs. "We could do a double."

I stare at her. "You want a lap dance?"

"Maybe . . . Do it with me and I'll give you one myself after." She pauses. "For all of these people to see."

The dimples come out. I can feel them. "You know the way to my heart. Or I could just bypass the main course and go straight for dessert."

She kisses my nose. "Nope. It's our farewell bachelorhood party. We're going to live it up, old man. You in or out?"

I'm amused. The level in which I am is steadily increasing. "Kambry."

"What?"

"How did you get into a strip club alone under twenty-one?"

Her lips line and her eyes widen, a spark lying within the depths. "See, what had happened was . . ."

"Spill wife."

"Promise you won't be mad? I had to stoop to drastic measures."

"I'm pretty sure you'd be any man's hero for coming here on your own free will anyway, so go ahead."

"Well, after he asked for my ID I handed him the one Tynleigh gave me to use earlier without all the confidence I have when I'm with her. He saw straight through me and denied me entry, so I told the guy at the door there was someone important in here that I needed to see immediately due to an emergency."

"That did not work."

"I never said I was finished. When that didn't faze him I discretely pulled out a small stack of hundreds I had just gotten from the ATM and quietly told him if he'd overlook a few things and let me in I'd never breathe a word and the money was his, along with a nice little bonus. Then, I showed what God gave me that has you so wound up all the time and bam! Here I am."

I'm stressing the ability to suppress laughter right now. "You showed a bouncer at a titty bar a set of tits and that worked?"

"Hey, I just figured if they hooked a famous porn star for life then surely they would gain me entry into a strip club for a few short hours if I were on my best behavior and didn't cause a ruckus."

I glance down at her tight *one-piece* dress that doesn't seem like it has easy access to both breasts. "Are your boobs the only things you showed him?"

"Well I mean . . .I had to pull up my dress to get to them. Does that make a difference? Because he still saw the girls."

I close my eyes and shake my head, biting back the laughter that's getting harder to control with every sentence that comes out of her mouth. I was that poor unsuspecting man that saw her body for the first time once. It's hell on a man, targeting his groin like a damn heat-seeking missile. There is no escaping it. You're going to have a boner.

We're taught through common sense and the sight of eyes that a woman either has all natural curves or skin and bone. Anything else becomes altered content. That's just the way the majority of the gene pool works. But when a man sees a girl like Kambry that has fucking amazing big tits and a tiny frame, it is only natural that he's dumbfounded. It defies everything we know is true. If every woman got the best of both worlds there would be no give and the world would be plastic.

"Did you just go to random strip clubs flashing the staff looking for me or did you somehow know this one was the one I'd be at?"

"I told the cab driver to take me to the most discreet for people that are known publicly and this was the one he chose. I should have given him a bigger tip. Are you mad?"

"Did he touch?"

"No."

"Did he take the money?"

"No. It was kind of strange, actually. As I was pulling my dress back down he asked my name: my real name. I thought he was going to call the cops on me for a minute. When I told him, he got this smirk on his face, let me in, and said I've earned it—whatever that means. By that point I didn't ask any questions. I was afraid he'd change his mind."

A cheesy grin marks my face. "That's all he said, huh . . ."

"Oh, he did say to tell the bachelor to give the club a shout-out. No clue. Just the messenger."

I laugh. Her innocence has always kept me hooked. "It means he recognized you from one of two places, but I'm going to guess it's probably option number one. He was confirming it with your name. By shout-out, he wants me to reference the strip club on my social media platforms like I did the Tumblr account."

"Is that where all of those instant followers came from?"

"Most of them I'm sure. I had a lot of comments and shares on my Facebook post and it had been a long time since I had posted anything on my page other than the link Michael sent for the show. Usually I only post links to purchase anyway."

Her eyes widen and she whispers. "Oh! By recognize, you mean like he watches porn?"

A laugh slips. "Yes," I whisper back. "A lot more people watch it than you think, but why are we whispering?"

She laughs. "I'm not sure," she says, back to her normal tone. "I guess I never really thought about the fact that people could be watching us while we're here. By the way, now what am I going to do with all this money?"

"You're going to need it," I say, a cocky grin on my face. I'm trying to keep my dick in check, but it's getting more difficult with each thought that occurs. "You still want a lap dance? This isn't a male strip club . . ."

She bites her bottom lip and her cheeks become flushed. She stares into my eyes, hesitating. "It's okay to tell me your fantasies, Kambry. I would never judge you for things you want to try, no matter what it is. I'll do anything with you or for you except bring someone else into our sex life. That's the line I won't cross. That's my limit."

"Yes," she breathes out. "I want one. I don't know why. Maybe just for the experience. I don't like girls or anything."

"Stop feeling like you have to explain. That's why it's called a fantasy. You don't have to have a reason to want something. Most of them probably are taboo. That's kind of the point. It's supposed to be something outside of normal."

"Okay. Tell me what to do."

My heart feels like it's about to burst through my chest it's racing so hard. Getting my own lap dance doesn't excite me, but watching her get one has my nerves raging. It's hot as fuck. When this is over we might be having dirty bathroom sex. I can make no promises that I'll be able to keep my hands off of her or my dick out of her. "It's easy. Sit back, relax, and tip. We aren't in a cheap restaurant. Tips are rewards. Use it like a grading scale. The better she does or the more turned on you become—it's okay if it does—the more you tip. I'll give whatever you spend back to you later."

She shakes her head, but I ignore it. I grab the backs of her knees and pull her middle against me. "If you want me to participate, I have one condition."

"What is it?"

"We get a private room together."

"Okay."

Just like that she agrees. I back up and reach for her hand. She takes it, no questions asked. To me, this is what a real relationship is all about; not being in a strip club, specifically, but doing things together that aren't necessarily orthodox. Giving to the other person instead of getting jealous is what truly makes you stand apart from the rest. It's give and take equally. Deep down I want to make her happy. I want to be by her side when she experiences new things. Not only do I love her, but also I love hanging out with her. The girl is my best friend, and the only person I know without a doubt I can't live without.

Kambry

The room is spinning from the alcohol. My nerves are trying to get the best of me. I glance at Saxton across the room, sitting relaxed in a chair facing me. He seems so far away. The longer I look at him the bigger his smile gets. I wish I were as relaxed as he is. I focus on my breathing, trying not to seem so nervous.

The recessed spotlights are dim and the wallpaper is black, covered in a silver pattern that seems upscale. I straighten my posture, sitting upright in my chair from the slight slump I was in, my heels pressed firmly against the hardwood floor between the legs of my chair. I feel like I'm being uptight, but this is the part of me I hate. I find it hard to relax in sensual situations. I want to seem cool and collected, and not like an amateur kid talking to her crush for the first time.

I cross one leg over the other and then uncross it, trying to find a comfort zone. "You nervous?"

I can see his dimples from here, even under his *Cal* ball cap with stubble covering the lower half of his face. Lord knows that man could get anything he wants from me wearing a hat. It's my weakness. Turn it around backward and I'm begging at his feet. I hate the way he can read me like an open book, but I also love it. "No," I lie.

"Liar."

I focus on one thing: him. He grabs the bill of his cap and turns it around backward before slumping down into the chair, folding his arms and grabbing onto the back with his hands. I'm not sure a man could be better looking than the one I have. He's that pot of gold at the end of the rainbow, and he's mine. I'm still not sure how I got so lucky. "I don't know how not to be," I say honestly.

"How do you do it?"

"With everyone else it's easy. I don't care to impress them, so there are no expectations than to simply exist. I'm just myself. With you, I just put on a mask and hope you don't notice."

"You look sexy like that," I interrupt, unable to help it. He's the focal point even in a beautiful room. "It's always been my favorite view."

"Sexy is too mild of a word to describe the way you look, Kambry. You'll always be my favorite view. You're the only person that's ever been able to leave me speechless by your appearance alone. Just know I'm doing this for you. I don't need shit like this to stay happy with you."

"I know. I love you," I say, and then the spotlights dim down until they're off, leaving us in temporary darkness, and the other half that was previously turned off placed throughout the ceiling come on.

Black lights. My dress becomes stark white; slightly glowing like neon does under these same lights.

A strobe light begins bouncing throughout the entire room, creating that same slow motion effect as it was in the club earlier.

Music starts: a sexy, seductive, hip-hop tune.

"Just imagine it being me and you'll relax," he says, a smile evident in his voice. "Or Meredith. Don't forget, you can't touch unless you're tipping. That's the rules." A roll of bills sits clenched tight within my fist. My nerves are not calming at all. If anything they are only getting worse.

The door opens and two girls walk in: gorgeous ones at that. I'm a little jealous. One is wearing a strapless zip up dress, the amount of cleavage implying that only her nipples are covered. It's short, black, and leather, her long red hair cascading over her shoulders to her ribs. The other is blonde like me, her hair long with razor straight layers, wearing low-riding black leather pants and what reminds me of a short version of a biker vest also in leather to cover the black bra she's wearing. Both of them are on the tall side, their bodies so curved it reminds me of an hour glass from chest to hips, but there isn't an ounce of fat present.

My stomach is fluttering wildly. Once they reach the center of the room they part ways, one coming to me and the other going to Saxton. I get the redhead. She stops before me, blocking my vision from anything else. She has the hint of a smile present, her makeup on point to make her eyes the focal of her face.

Her hips start to sway. One foot over the other she turns, slowly and seductively, as if she's giving me a three-hundred-sixty-degree view of the entire product. When she arrives back at her starting point, she lowers the zipper until the dress falls to the floor, leaving her in the tiny string panties that I'm guessing only covers her front.

She walks toward me, her large boobs barely moving at all. By the look of them I'm going to say she's had them done. They're appealing. My heart is racing, only beating faster the closer she gets. My breathing feels out of control, but then the weirdest thing happens. When she straddles me and grabs the back of my chair, all of the nerves go away, and excitement replaces it.

Her body takes on another form, and then she begins, dancing at the pace of the music. At first it's a sweep back and forth, her middle brushing my lap along the way. The music changes and her body adjusts. She begins to roll against me, getting closer with every passing second. I pull a bill free from the roll in my hand and drape it over the front section of her panties, only half showing. She smiles, and then one hand skims down my arm as her hip glides to the right. She lifts my hand and places it on her hip, never stopping the wave motion her body is making, allowing me to touch her as she dances against me.

Each time she starts from the top, her back arches and I can feel her hard nipples against me. It's turning me on, and I'm trying not to think too hard on why that is. She straightens her posture and grabs the back of my hair, tilting my head back so that I'm looking into her eyes as she leans in close to me. Barely any distance apart, she begins grinding and rolling against my entire body. This is kind of hot.

I hang another two bills on the tiny string that sits at her hip. She sits up and releases me, then stands and turns around, revealing her backside. Her ass is smooth and round, completely uncovered, with only the strings to her panties meeting at a T just above it. She drops to the floor, breaking it down in front of me, before standing back up.

She returns to my lap, her back towards me this time. Her back muscles move one at a time as she dances on my thighs, slowly backing up into my lap. I place my hands atop the chair to my sides, trying to remember I'm not supposed to touch unless she places my hands on her. She pops her ass against me, her middle slightly rubbing against my dress. I'm getting hot, and I don't know if it's the temperature or that I'm *that* turned on.

Again, I shove another bill under her panties at the back. Unexpectedly, before I can return my hand to its place, she grabs it and brings it to her front. Slowly she skims it up her body, palm down. I can feel the metal bar through her navel in passing as she continues to ascend. Suddenly my hand is wrapped around a breast as she works her ass against my lap, hiking my dress up: a large, firm one.

Oh my god.

Do I just sit here or do I do something?

Be fucking sexy.

What would Meredith do?

Better yet, what would turn Saxton on?

She's obviously giving me permission to touch her.

I lean in until my chest is at her back and then I lightly squeeze, before rubbing my hand across to the other side. I discretely push my head to the side to see if I can see him across the room.

Our eyes lock just as my fingers brush over her nipple.

He's staring straight at me, despite the fact that a really hot girl is grinding his fucking crotch as if clothes were not in the way. Her body is killer and can move in ways I'm not sure I knew were possible. I'm positive that if something ripped penetration wouldn't be far behind.

I expected him to be more involved in the almost naked stripper in front of him. I foresaw him glued to the chest that sits at eye level had his face been a few inches to the left. I wanted to see that honestly.

I was quite sure if I ever saw something like this I'd be jealous enough to commit murder. The fact that I'm more turned on than jealous is something I don't understand. Maybe it's because I'm here, watching it all happen, knowing nothing will *actually* happen, and maybe it's that I'm getting the same treatment as he is for myself. I don't think I'd have the same reaction if the person grinding an ass in my lap were a guy. I don't want the memory of him dancing on me that night in the club polluted with someone else.

But the way he's looking at me . . .

I'm wet.

I'm hot.

I want to fuck and this girl is not hindering that feeling at all. She's only amplifying it.

Surprisingly, I now see the appeal with boobs. Maybe I just had to experience them from a guy's point of view, touching someone else's besides my own. This is fucking hot: me watching him, him watching me, and both of us experiencing someone else without actually cheating on each other.

I will never be able to live without him. I physically need him just as much as I want him. I love him more than I could ever measure in words. No one else will ever understand me, love me, or complete me the way he does. Him grabbing his girl's ass and squeezing as I grope this one's breast only verifies that we are damn near perfect for each other.

We are explosive.

We are hungry.

We are insatiable.

We are porn stars.

We are Saxton and Kambry.

And nothing or no one can destroy us, because we are in love.

I push her into the bathroom and shove her against the door, keeping it closed. That was the hottest thing I've witnessed in regards to two girls in my entire life. I've experienced threesomes and watched drunk girls hook up, but nothing compared to what I just watched in that room.

My hand disappears beneath her dress; the tips of my fingers skimming up the inside of her thigh until it's at the rim of her panties. I push underneath, immediately met with her wet center. Her head rolls back against the door. "We're in the women's bathroom."

"And I'm supposed to give a fuck, why?"

"Someone could walk in."

She moans as my fingers sink into her pussy. "You liked that didn't you? Touching her tits, feeling her ass, and knowing how fucking hard you were making me when you ran your hand across her chest for me to watch . . ."

I grip her leg and pull it to my waist, opening her up for me. My thrusts inside of her are hard and fast. My adrenaline is raging, my dick hurts, and tomorrow can't come soon enough. "Yes," she whispers, her eyes locked with mine.

I drop her leg and snatch the fabric between her thighs down her legs until her tiny panties are sitting at her feet on the floor. "I'm about to contaminate that white, baby."

Her eyes turn downcast at the sound of my belt as I unbuckle it. I work the button open and unzip my jeans, watching as her tongue grazes her bottom lip, her mouth closing with the skimming of her top teeth on her lip. I grip my dick and pull it out, leaving the rest in place. I grab her leg again, pulling it to my waist for better access. I have to squat a little to match the height of our waists, immediately aligning my dick at her pussy and driving inside, pushing her further up the door from my weight.

My eyes briefly close at the feel of her warmth encasing my cock, but I'm so worked up from earlier that I can't enjoy it for long. I need to fuck her. Before I can process my next action, my free hand is clamped around the back of her thigh, lifting her higher up the door as I straighten my legs. She places her hands on the back of my neck.

My hips buck forward, submerging my dick completely inside of her. Her heels interlock at the small of my back. "Enjoy your last night, Miss Rivers, because tomorrow you're all mine, starting with the name."

Her eyes are heavy, a smile spreading. "Then I guess you better give me a little preview of what's to come," she says, leaning closer to me, her eyes on mine. "For once, fuck me like a porn star." And just like that I let the animal take over, pounding into her over and over, harder with each thrust against this door, because tonight I'm not holding back. I'm going all fucking ten. I'm going out of bachelorhood with a bang.

CHAPTER TWENTY-THREE

Kambry

"I just need your signature on this release form, pretty girl," Tynleigh says, laying a document down in front of me on the table. "And then we'll get started."

I place my palms on the table to each side of the sheet of paper, a pen in hand. Signing legal documents is becoming a pattern in my life. From porn reality television to a major magazine. It's enough to make a person's head spin. A part of me can't help but to be thankful . . .for everything, even though they are both two totally different extremes. The average person doesn't get one of these opportunities, let alone both.

I upright myself before signing my name on the line. "Am I at liberty to ask for something?"

She gets a gleam in her eye. "Depends . . . What is it?"

My thoughts go to the man somewhere in this massive house that is going to be my husband in a few short hours. He's done so much for me. I owe the person I am to him. When I was dull he polished me. He uncovered the real me in such a short amount of time. At every turn I'm surprised. With him my life is whole. He gives living a new meaning. But the problem is he's done everything. He lacks nothing. I feel like I fall short giving to him when he's given me so much. I want to do something for him in return for all he's done for me. And maybe . . .this is my chance.

I'm going to lay down my shy nature when it comes to myself. For him. He did say he wanted memories. "Would you be willing to pick out the best photo and have it blown up and framed? I've never done a real photo shoot. I'll pay you of course. I'd like to give it to Saxton as a wedding gift."

She stares at me. Her expression is blank. Maybe it was too much to ask for. She's done so much already with this whole wedding. She's given us a place to stay, taken off work, and been our tour guide. It's probably rude to ask of anything else. "It's okay if you can't. I probably shouldn't have asked."

She smiles at me. "No, I was just thinking. I don't think I could have handpicked a better girl for my brother given the chance. Thank you for being good to him, Kambry. As far as this, you don't owe me anything. I'll see what I can do on the photo. Let me talk to the photographer. Just take care of him until he's old and gray. God knows I'm not cut out for the job." She winks and I return a smile.

"I plan on it."

"Now sign that paper before I have a bridal shop up my ass."

"Yes, ma'am."

I turn and glance at the piece of paper one more time. Here we go. I scribble my name on the long black line and drop the pen on top. To the start of forever . . .

Turn a little to the right," the photographer says. I do as she says, only moving a little. One thing I have learned about photographers today—when they say move they only mean an inch or so. If she wants drastic she'll come move me herself. "Now line your chin with your shoulder and look at the center of that window. Don't move and relax your lips."

I remember all the tips she went over for facials when we started. I've always wondered what this was like behind the scenes. Here we are in this same room we started in, after what seems like the hundredth pose and twentieth prop. I should be able to navigate around this huge room with my eyes closed at this point.

She walks over and adjusts the bottom of my dress, then pulls the strap off my shoulder on the same side my face is turned. Once she has me positioned the way she wants me, she backs up a little, snapping the first several shots. I hold still as she moves to different angles, capturing many more. The one thing that keeps me from accidentally smiling is that I want these to turn out for Saxton. This is the grown up version of me.

The miles and miles of water on the other side of that window keeps me focused. It's beautiful. And it's calming. I've always found something peaceful about the ocean. The possibility of having one as my front porch view forever with the man I love causes my heart to skip a beat. It's not hard to imagine what that would look like.

Standing on the porch in his arms, watching the waves wash ashore. I'd like a hammock hanging too to lie in on the perfect day together. Maybe even a breeze blowing through to cool the sun beaming down on our skin. Years later, building sandcastles together with our kids or sand angels. Mermaid tales even. To grow old with someone in the same house for fifty years, multiple generations evolving from us. It's a life I want so badly I can taste it.

"You ready to go join your friend?"

I glance back at Tynleigh; not even noticing the photographer isn't near. "I'm sorry. Are we done?"

She wraps her arm around the back of my neck. "We got what we needed."

"Did I do okay?"

"Can't even tell it's your first time. Come on. It's getting close to time. You wouldn't want to be late for your own wedding, would you?"

I smile at her. "I'd never leave him waiting." I turn and hug her, squeezing her tight. "Thank you so much for all you've done. This wouldn't be the same without you."

Finally she hugs me back. "You're welcome, but it's nothing. Family does things for one another. I'm just glad to see the two of you happy."

I close my eyes. Family. It may not have been the one I was born into, but family they'll always be. I release her and run my hands down my dress so that I don't risk crying and smearing my makeup. "Let's do this."

CHAPTER TWENTY-FOUR

Saxton

I pace back and forth, shaking my hands up and down to try and relax. It's not working. What I need is a cigarette the size of my cock. I actually may. It's been a minute since I've had one. That sounds really good right about now.

"Dude, would you sit the fuck down? You're making me feel like I'm the one getting married."

I glare at Bryant in his monkey suit. "Don't tell me to sit down. You can still be uninvited."

"Not according to your hot sister . . ."

"Shut up. Do you have a cigarette?"

"Maybe . . . What's it to you?"

"Fucking fork it over."

"Now, Saxton, is that any way to talk to your best man?"

I sit down beside him at the foot of the bed. My elbows go to my thighs, my palms to my hair. "Do you really want me to walk to the alter like this? Cut me some fucking slack."

He stands. "There is a balcony that overlooks the water. Come on."

I follow behind him until we reach the balcony that he was referring to. I walk through the door and he shuts the sliding glass door behind me. "There is a reason we're friends, you know."

"Well, feel free to remind me. I seem to have forgotten somewhere in the midst of you fucking my sister."

He smacks the back of my head. "Just because you're the groom doesn't mean you don't deserve it. Here," he says, pulling the small box from his inner jacket pocket and pointing the opening at me.

I take one from the box, waiting for the lighter. He places one between his lips and returns the box to his pocket, before pulling out a lighter and bringing it to the tip of his cigarette. "Why are we fucking friends?"

He hands me the lighter as he pulls a drag off the cigarette. I place the filter to my lips and light it, sucking the end until my chest expands. Then I inhale. My head falls back as I hold it in my lungs. Damn, that's good. "Because I'm the only one that stood by your ass when you went bat-shit crazy and became a porn star."

"We weren't even really friends in college. I only saw you when you decided to hang around with your cousin."

"Only because you were stuck up that bitch's ass. But still, you're different with this one of what I know. Joel used to talk about you a lot."

"We all have shit we aren't proud of."

"Yeah, that may be, but I'll speak for all of us when I say you finally leaving her was a good thing. Do you know how hard it is to watch a girl cheat on a guy and do nothing because he already knows she does? Joel told me how she ended up a while back. Said he ran into her at a ballgame and she was hardcore reporter. Girls like that may be successful now but one day karma will have its way."

I look at him, curious; because in all the years I've been doing this we've never had this conversation. I guess I just didn't care about a lot of things. Going through the motions became my daily routine. "Since you brought it up, why'd you stick around? Most of my best friends have dropped off the map. Even Joel drifted away. Back then I rarely was around when you were, and suddenly I take off and you were just there."

"Don't hold it against Joel forever. He's dealing with his own shit. You two were close. At first, it was probably just man-hurt and jealousy that you took off. Then everything happened with Karleigh and he didn't know how to deal with both. You know he's been fucked up since her accident. He still asks about you every time I see or talk to him. At some point he'll return like he never left."

"Yeah, I heard about that. Sucks. I tried to call him but it just wasn't the same."

The awkward silence occurs. He takes another hit off his cigarette. "Oh," he says and picks back up with the previous conversation, "you know, I was an LA boy born and raised. It was convenient when you moved. I only went down there to hang out with Joel."

"Bullshit."

"Saxton, I have a soft spot for good men that are used by women. I watched my own dad literally drive himself insane over my stepmom, if that's what you want to call her. I kind of assumed he knew it was just about the money when he married someone half his age, but obviously for him it was love and her lifestyle. I mean who the fuck hits on her husband's son? A hot girl my age and a quick lay does not reign over fucking blood. Bottom line, I saw someone that needed a friend so I was one, minus judgment on your choice of coping mechanism for the very thing that sent you running. That's just me, man."

"Is that why you keep ending up with independent girls like Meredith and my sister?"

"Probably. They just appeal to me more than the rest."

I utilize the brief silence to gather my thoughts.

"I still have fears, despite everything," I say, finally honest with someone about what's going on in my head.

"Like what?"

"What if five years from now I'm not enough? She's beautiful, she's young, and she has everything to offer someone. What if I piss her off and she realizes she can do so much fucking better?" I take a long drag off my cigarette. "I'm not sure I'd survive it a second time around. It fucks with your head, your heart, and really wipes out your ego."

I put out my cigarette and he hands me another. I take it, well, because why the hell not. I need to get over my nerves now instead of looking like an ass later. "One question is all I'm interested in."

"Which is?"

"Is she worth the risk?"

The fact that I don't even have to think about that startles me a little. "Yes."

He looks at me, legs spread and forearms to his thighs, smoking his own cigarette. “Then nothing else matters. Humans are as controllable as a wild animal. It’s impossible. Look at Meredith, for example. I liked her. I really thought things were going somewhere for a while. It wasn’t love, but it was a whole hell of a lot of liking. Sometimes things aren’t meant to be how we think they are. Then the right one comes along and it all makes sense. Kambry could do that—cheat that is—because nothing is ever certain, but that’s why you spend every fucking day showing her that you’re the best option. Don’t short yourself just because one bitch couldn’t keep her legs closed when someone threw her a compliment. Some girls are easy lays for a reason.”

“I guess you’re right. It’s just scary as hell.” I stare out at the water, boat watching. This place is a different world. The rich really know how to appeal to the less fortunate.

“You really want to know why I tend to fall for girls like Meredith and your sister?”

That statement grabs my curiosity, since he brought it back up. “Why’s that?”

“Because they are self-sufficient. They don’t need a man to be happy. They’re more worried about acquiring things for themselves and just using a man for a good time than mooching off a guy to live the same lifestyle. Those girls are the ones that you make wives, because they’re the ones that see you for what’s inside instead of what’s in your bank account. Even though I don’t know Kambry all that well, I’ve watched her the few times I’ve been around her, and that girl is a gold mine. She’s funny, she’s smart, and her character outwits whatever she’s been through prior to meeting you. Meredith told me a few things here and there in conversation, but for whatever reason she’s completely head over heels for you, and that’s way more than I can say about the first one. I may joke because I’m not ready to take that plunge yet, but if I were you I’d stop questioning it and just do it.”

“I’d give up my own fucking heart for her.”

“Then do it. Give it up for happiness. One thing I learned from my dad before he went completely whack: *there is no greater man than a man in love.* Walk down that aisle, say your vows, and never look back. You become the greatest man for her, and nothing can go wrong.”

I take a deep breath. I never really doubted anything, but once you've been burned the scar reminds you that it could so easily happen again. I take the last drag off my cigarette and plunge the tip into the cement, putting it out. "What ended up happening with your dad and stepmom?"

"Depressing story. Not one for a wedding. I'll tell you some other time."

The door opens and a blonde with short hair peeks out. "What are you two doing out here? Do you want Tynleigh to kill me?"

"Who are you?" I ask, picking up the other cigarette butt.

"Tynleigh's best friend and also homeowner by reproduction. This is my parents' house."

I stand. "Gotcha. I appreciate the hospitality of letting us use your place. Is it time?"

I pass through the doorway, beside her. She waves her hand in front of her nose. "Almost. Geez. Go put some cologne on and get a breath mint. You both smell like an ashtray."

"Yes, ma'am," I say, sarcastically.

"Eww. I'm not old. Don't call me ma'am. Just go before she freaks out that half the wedding party is missing."

I salute her and continue forward. My nerves have subsided thanks to a special asshole that is giving love advice when he's fucking my sister. I glance back at him. "What are your intentions with T anyway?"

"Fuck her till she lets me go. I can't speak for what may happen along the way."

"Seriously," I say. "That's the answer you're going to give her brother?"

"Would you rather me lie and then it not work out? We live on opposite coastlines for fuck's sake. I don't know what she'll decide when it's time to go back. Independent woman. Do you not remember this conversation?"

"Fine. I'm cutting you some slack. If you fuck up somehow I know where you live."

He grins at me. "I wouldn't expect anything less."

"God, sometimes I hate you."

"I'd still be your best friend."

I shake my head, continuing back to the room we've been assigned to. He's probably right. He's been here this whole time. I'm kind of the shitty friend to not know any of the things we've discussed. Before Kambry I was a shitty everything: son, brother, lover, and friend. I appreciate her more than she'll ever know. She's the person that woke me up from a long sleep. She's the woman that stole my heart. She's the woman that will forever call me hers. I'm so ready to make her mine for the rest of our lives.

Kambry

I stare at myself in the mirror, wearing this new white dress. I take a deep breath. In a few short hours I'll be married to the greatest man I've ever known. He'll be mine forever. I'm not sure why I was given this blessing, but I'll never take it for granted.

I'm so ready. I thought he was going to let me have it again once we got home last night after the bathroom quickie, but instead, he took me home and tucked me into bed like an honorable man would do. I'd be lying if I said I wasn't disappointed, but there was a point that it made me feel like a princess. I asked him to get in bed with me, but instead he kissed me on the forehead, told me he'd be on the couch to keep a promise, and that he'd make up for it tomorrow, meaning tonight. He's the best balance. I just hope I'm always enough for him. I never want him to be bored of me, or what we have.

"How you feeling?"

I glance at Meredith through the mirror as she walks up behind me. "Good. I'm ready. I really do love him, Meredith. I know you probably—"

"Enough," she interrupts. "I wasn't going to try to give you a lecture or talk you out of this, Kam. When a girl knows she just knows. Never second-guess your heart, not for anyone. I was only going to give you something."

My brows crease. "Give me what?"

She rubs my bare shoulders. "Last night when you took off I gave your dad a piece of my mind for the first time in my life. We aren't kids anymore. He doesn't control you, my parents don't control me, and there is no one we have to answer to, so I finally told him what I thought after all these years, and to be honest, it was the best fucking thing I've ever done."

I blink into the mirror. "And?"

"He said thank you and left. I gave Kyle a piece too, but he just ran off like a little bitch. I was worried about you, until Ben finally called and said you were safe and with them . . .at a strip club. Pissed off Ben is scary and hot as hell. You put me in a bad situation. I have much to say about that later, but for now, here."

She hands me an envelope. "What is this?"

"I'm not sure. Your dad left it at the front desk of our hotel for you. I will never treat you like the child they did your entire life. You can make your own decisions and you've done a pretty damn good job so far. I've seen *The Notebook* and I would never want to be the person that kept a letter from you knowing the consequences it can hold. Just let me know when you're ready, okay?"

I take it. "Okay."

She walks away, leaving me standing in front of this mirror all by myself. I recognize the handwriting on the front immediately. I close my eyes, trying to stop the nerves from forming. "You can read this," I whisper to myself. "It's no big deal. He can't hurt you anymore."

I turn the envelope over and break the seal. I remove the slip of paper from the envelope and open the trifold, reading the contents before I change my mind and throw it away.

Kambry,

I know there are a lot of things to say that you probably don't understand right now. For that, I'm proud of what your mother and I accomplished. It means we did our job in protecting you from the bad things in this world. But with that, I know there are some things that probably need explaining. Kambry, regardless of what you think, I love you, and so does your mother. We may not have always done the right thing in raising you, but we had your best interests at heart. From the day I found out we were having a girl, I panicked, always wanting to protect you from becoming some of the girls I knew in my lifetime. I have always felt responsible for the way you would turn out. That's being a parent. One day, when you have kids of your own, you'll understand. The world is filled with bad things. As a parent, and as a Christian, you want to protect their innocence for as long as possible. That's what we tried to do with you. Maybe we were a little barbaric at times, but it was all in love; that I promise. As far as the Tumblr account, I shouldn't have been snooping, but when your child runs off in the middle of the night you just want to know that they're safe. I panicked. I no longer had control over the decisions you made. I was merely looking for a Facebook account through a Google search. When I saw what you were doing, it only escalated. I've dealt with the sin of the Internet for a while now, and your mother knows, but when I came across you I lost it. I shouldn't have said the things I did, but at the same time, how could I have not? I want you to know your worth, Kambry. You don't have to stoop to that behavior to get away from your mother and I, or to be happy. You don't have to marry the first guy you meet to get back at us. I know you're angry. I've talked to Ben since Meredith, and surprisingly I listened for once. The photo I sent you wasn't mine. Only a truly sick individual would send his daughter a photo of himself in that context. I wanted you to think. It was just something off the web to show you how dangerous situations can get when you post things that should be kept private. My point in coming to New York was to show you that it's so easy for people to find you based off of what you post on the Internet. Be smart, Kambry. It only takes a second for someone to track you down and pull the trigger when the information is so freely available. I don't want to pay for a funeral for one of my children; regardless of what way they're living. Last but not least, I'm not thrilled about what you're about to do. A wedding isn't something you do on the fly. Divorce is real for a lot of people, and you know how your mother and I feel about that. I wanted you to be a little more concerned about the type of person you're going to marry, but with that said, I wouldn't be a Christian if I didn't believe in forgiveness, so, if this is what you see for your life then okay. I'm backing down. I'd rather live with you making choices I don't agree with than to never see you again. Come home, Kambry, even if it's just to visit. Your mother hasn't been the same since you left. We miss you. Somehow, we'll all work this out. I hope we can move past this.

With love,
Your dad.

I crumble the piece of paper in my hand, my eyes starting to water. "You okay?"

I glance at Meredith, standing behind me once again. "I think my dad and I may have just come to terms with each other and life for the first time . . .ever. Saxton was right. I can't just run back and forgive him this easily, but over time I think we can have some type of a relationship. I'm not sure yet. Right now he needs to know his behavior isn't okay. He's a hypocrite; doing things he's basically told us he'd shun us for our entire lives. Besides, a phone call would have been enough. I listened the first time until he became unreasonable. But after I'm tired of being angry I'll forgive him and move on, because that's what you do when you love someone, and regardless of the way he's treated me over the course of my life, I love him. He's my dad. When someone wrongs you, you forgive them, over and over, no matter what they've done to you. It's the only right way to live."

She kisses me on the cheek and hugs me. "I'm damn proud of the woman you've become. You've advanced miles in such a short period of time. Don't you ever second-guess the type of person you are."

I sink into her. "Thank you for sharing this day with me."

"Wouldn't have missed it for the world, love. You'll always be my best friend. We're in this for life, even if I have to chase you down in your porn mansion." I laugh, the teary eyes disappearing.

"Are we ready?"

I look at Tynleigh. "I think so."

"Wrong," she says. "You have something old, my earrings you wore the other night, something new, the dress, but you're lacking something borrowed and something blue."

"None of that matters?" I question, staring at her.

"Oh yes. Yes it does. We are not starting this marriage out with bad luck. Here," she says, handing me a box. "From the groom." She winks, and my eyes instantly narrow in response.

I grab it and remove the wrapping paper, revealing a large square box made of velvet. I instantly know it's a jewelry box. "Would you tell him to stop spending money on me? Seriously, I don't need this."

"And that's the reason he does it. You don't expect it. Women everywhere would be cursing you right now. Just open the damn box."

I huff. "Fine." I push the top open, revealing a sapphire and diamond crusted necklace sitting inside on a beautifully elegant chain. I rub my thumb over the rather large blue jewel sitting in the center, and close my eyes. "It's beautiful." My eyes open, trying to deal with the emotions quickly piling up. "He doesn't have to do all of this. I will still love him the same."

"Kambry," Tynleigh says. "When a man loves a woman, he'll give her the world, regardless of whether she lets him be a part of it. Your job is to take it, wear it, and show him how much you love it, so he'll do it over and over again."

"But I don't need things to make me happy. I need him."

She grabs the box, removing the necklace, and then places it on my chest, wrapping the chain around my neck to secure it at the back. "We all know. It's easy to see, and also one of the beautiful things that makes us all welcome you into this family so easily. You're a good girl, Kambry, and you love him wholeheartedly. That's why you'll make the perfect wife for my brother, so sit back and enjoy being treated like a princess. That's the kind of guy he is. It's just been hidden for a while."

I touch the necklace with my fingertips. "Just for the record, I'll never understand how she could let him go, let alone hurt him that way. I can't even fathom someone else. I would put that on my life."

She turns me around and hugs me tight. "And that's why you're the one that deserves him. I happen to know you scored the jackpot. Make it last."

She pushes me back. "Now, something borrowed."

"Your earrings serve two purposes."

"I actually have something borrowed."

I turn to Meredith as she rushes to her bag. When she returns to my side, she hands me an antique white handkerchief bordered in lace, daisies marking the cloth in a continuous pattern, all a solid off-white color to make it all the same. An L is monogrammed in sunshine yellow. "What is this?"

"It was my Mom's when she married my dad. It was her *new* to keep the tears at bay, so it's your *borrowed.* I had her meet me halfway with it after Ben picked me up from the airport. She's kept it in her glass wedding cabinet untouched all these years, wrapped around her dried out bouquet."

I try to hand it back to her. "I can't use this, Meredith. I wouldn't want to be responsible for something that sentimental."

She shakes her head. "No, seriously, she was excited when I asked her if you could use it. You know you've always been Mom's adopted second child. There were times that I actually thought she liked you more than me. It goes with your dress. It was meant to be."

I jump forward, throwing my arms around her. "I love you so much, Mer."

She secures her arms around my waist. "Love you too, Kam. Now walk down that aisle, marry the love of your life, and live the smutty happily ever after you deserve; for all of us."

"Okay," I whisper. "Dirty fairy tales are better anyway," I say, laughing into her ear.

"The boys are ready."

We glance at Meg at the same time, standing in the doorway in her red pencil dress and short blonde hair. The diamonds in her ears and the navy heels to accentuate the cute matching belt at her waist make her look every bit of the classy act she puts on the couple of times I've met her.

From what I've seen so far, everyone is in one of those two colors or a combination of the two like her; a nautical feel to match the backdrop of this house that sits walking distance from the water. I've never seen so many lavish homes within such a short radius. *The Hamptons* remind me of a magazine for the elite. This house, and the ones that surround it are things I've never witnessed. I've seen some beautiful places in LA, but I haven't been to many rich neighborhoods. I guess I just never hung around that type of crowd, Saxton being the first in any degree. Sure, there are beautiful houses back home, but the houses here are the epitome of modern: pools for days, sharp lines at every corner, miles of glass, and the amber glow of lights shining through the translucent walls.

Everyone that I've met here has been so welcoming: Meg, Tynleigh, and even Saxton's parents stopped by to see me before finding their seats in the few sitting outside in front of the arbor. This is like a dream come true. I've been lost in the rabbit hole since I met him, and I'm in no hurry to leave.

Tynleigh hands me a short-stemmed, rose bouquet that has a tight-fitted ball of a top made from the many red roses close together. I wrap the handkerchief around the bottom, nod at Meg, and start to walk toward her. Forever here I come . . .

Saxton

I stand barefoot in front of the arch covered in Wisteria vines, my hands deep in the pockets of my khaki slacks, my navy blazer buttoned like it's supposed to be. Luckily for me, and the small army dressed like me, it's nice weather, the breeze keeping it from being too hot. My toes wiggle in the sand, the awkwardness setting in that half of me is attending a party while my feet take on a Jimmy Buffett approach to life. It doesn't seem to go, but like Tynleigh said, shoes and sand don't really mix.

I look out at the few white chairs sitting in an organized manner, somewhat creating an aisle down the center, the house in the background. It's a peaceful view. There aren't many seats because of our lack of guests and short list. We wanted it private and that's exactly how it is, still giving her some kind of a wedding like most girls would want. I owe that to my sister.

Almost everyone has sat down, except for Tynleigh and Ben. Meredith and Ben's seats are on one side with Meg, while Mom and Dad are sitting on the other side behind Bryant and Tynleigh's seats.

I can't help but to stare at the place the girls exited from as I twirl the small ring around my finger in my pocket, feeling every bit of the anxiety building from standing here alone, front and center, with a man I only met a few minutes ago. The man that will soon perform the ceremony and sign off on the marriage license on behalf of the state of New York.

The door opens, making me stand a little taller than I was before. Tynleigh. I breathe and force myself to relax as she makes her way toward us from the house in a navy dress. I let the disappointment settle. I wanted it to be Kambry. I just need to see her. I want to know what look is on her face. I left before she woke this morning to try and keep my sister happy.

We came to a compromise when she found out Kambry had navigated herself through New York to the strip club to find me after the turn of events. She agreed to cave on us sleeping in separate vicinities if I slept on the couch and promised for one night to withstand the temptation of sex. She doesn't have to know about the bathroom at the strip club. I'm a man. We're known for failure when it comes to sex. But Kambry's entire room became off limits after I tucked her in, and because I was raised with some fucking morals, I agreed.

Maybe it was her version of 'sorry that things turned out the way they did' and I'll leave it at that. Tynleigh is never going to admit to total defeat. She's too stubborn, and truthfully, what happened wasn't her fault. If anyone is to blame, it's me. The Tumblr account was my idea. I should have known better having experience in the public eye, especially when it comes to sex. I should have taken the time to discuss the things we should or shouldn't post within the info of the photos. I saw the photo she posted from the limo with the club of choice used as a hashtag, but I didn't think anything of it. For normal people it wouldn't have mattered, but for us, life will always be little different.

Thinking of everything this week has held, at least Tynleigh cared enough to make this special for either of us. It's more than I can say for a lot of people, and she deserves so much more than a damn thank you. It'll take years to truly show her my appreciation, but to start I sacrificed a night of hot, drunk sex at her wish. Yes, sacrifice is the appropriate word, because last night was a night that will replay in my mind for a long time to come, and I could have fucked her over and over for hours after.

It wasn't the strippers or that she was drunk. It wasn't even that I ended up getting my way and spending the night with her instead of apart; nor was it the fact that I was getting a lap dance by a total stranger and my fiancé was completely okay with it. That alone is what most men would consider an answered prayer. It was the fact that the two of us can be totally mesmerized by each other no matter what the circumstances are or the situation in which we are in.

Now, I'm not going to sit back and pretend that watching your girl get a lap dance from another beautiful woman isn't every man's fantasy. It is. There is something hot about two beautiful women sharing sexuality to any degree. I watched my girl touch and grope another woman's breasts last night. I watched her shove one hundred dollar bills beneath panties. I watched her legs spread on reflex as a bare ass rubbed against her lap. For the first time since I met her, I witnessed her turned on from something outside of most people's normal, and something that she most likely would have been condemned for back home. But instead of her hating herself for wanting or liking it, she gave in to her desire and let herself enjoy it.

The hard dick secured and stowed beneath my jeans being ridden by a blonde other than my fiancé was only at attention following the moment I saw her enjoying herself with someone else. She was relaxed and lost in the moment as if no one else was in the room; yet I still knew nothing would fucking enter her. She's claimed territory. And she wants to be. There is no greater knowledge than knowing your partner wants only you. When she looked at me, already looking at her, a crucial moment occurred in our relationship as our eyes locked: mutual trust was earned. What I already knew in my heart was confirmed with the female grinding my lap; what most would classify as sex with clothing. My focus was only on the one across the room. I even grabbed her ass without consent, knowing Kambry wanted some sign that I wasn't angry, so I gave her one, and the result: nothing. Not a damn feeling, want, or need occurred.

I will never physically or mentally want anyone else but her. She will always be the best fit for me out of the billions of women in the world. She's my other half.

I wake up for her.

I live for her.

I breathe for her.

I'll work my ass off from sunup to sundown to support her.

I get hard for her.

I'll never go to bed without her.

She's the one that makes my life worth a damn. She's the one that fixed my broken heart, leaving it in a state better than before, and she's about to be my wife.

Wife. A four-letter word that will change my life forever, and I'm so fucking ready. Tynleigh winks at me as she takes her seat in front of Mom. Instrumental music begins. It's soft, as if it's playing from a distance, but still I can hear it clearly.

My fists clench within my pockets as the door opens once again. My heart is racing, waiting for her to exit. Ben goes first, but then I see her, making her way out the door in a clumsy fashion, as only Kambry would do. Her—the love of my life; the quirky girl that piqued my curiosity, kept me interested, stole my fucking heart straight from my chest, and made me believe in love again.

I can finally see all of her as she begins closing the distance between us, her arm wrapped around her brother's as he walks her down the makeshift aisle. The closer she gets, the better the view. "Damn."

Her body is covered in all the right places and showing in the best spots. She's not sexy right now; she's stunning. I can't take my eyes off of her. If there was ever a woman more beautiful than her, it wasn't in my lifetime.

My hands leave my pockets and one crosses the other in front of me. Suddenly my cheeks begin hurting, and it doesn't dawn on me that I'm smiling until she smiles back at me, our eyes locked together. At the exact moment she's a footstep from the last chair, everyone stands and faces the aisle made of white sand.

My vision becomes a little blurry, but I work to blink them clear. The wet spot underneath my eye confirms I failed. They stop a few feet in front of where I stand. "Who gives this woman to this man?"

"I do, sir," Ben says, and for a single moment in my life I love another man other than my dad. My emotions are crashing down on me like the tide against boulders. I'm forced to stand here in this sand and endure it; even though I feel like I'm drowning with each one that hits. I guess that's what happens when you've closed off a part of yourself with stone, but slowly she's chipped away at it until there is nothing left but raw feelings.

He kisses her cheek and gives me her hand, taking her bouquet, and then walks away to take his seat by Meredith. It takes everything in me not to jerk her toward me. Instead, I watch her as she takes a few steps forward until we're standing under the arch in front of the stranger we'll never forget. The man at my right begins speaking, addressing our guests, but my eyes are locked on hers. I'm forcing the tears back, feeling less like a man, and only allowing the few that slip through the crack the option to break the barrier that would be my tear ducts.

God, her eyes are so blue today. I can almost see my reflection in them. Maybe it's the purple in the Wisteria behind her or maybe it's the overflow of her happiness. I'm hoping for the latter. They scan mine, and then her lips quiver as her own tears fall in a steady trail down her cheek. *I love you,* she mouths.

I love you too. Always.

Everyone else disappears. For a moment time stands still. The memory reels are set to record. It becomes just her and I standing here on this beach, hand in hand. One after the other, as he recites them aloud, we promise to obey the laws of marriage till death do us part, before God, with a simple *I do*. And then I slip the diamond band on her left ring finger as I repeat my vows to her, line by line, after him.

Without a second's lapse, she does the same, staring into my eyes, tears running from hers. She's more beautiful when she's like this than in the most makeup. The best way to see someone is when they're the most susceptible to emotional breakdown. It tells you they're one hundred percent real. If someone had offered me a million dollars to do this a few months ago I would have laughed and told them to fuck themselves, but now, God knows I wish I had saved so much time by meeting her years ago.

My one. I found her, stumbling around that damn nightclub like she didn't belong. Her flirting was nonexistent. She was extremely awkward in conversation and didn't know the very beauty she holds within her tiny little body. Her personality was lost somewhere inside.

But now. Fucking now. God . . . Damn. She's the richest woman in every quality aforementioned. She found her home. It's with me. Her personality is bigger than the person that houses it. The mere fact that I was an inch away from canceling that damn meeting scares the hell out of me now. It just goes to show that every damn move in our life is constructed and played like a board game. We are the pieces, and if it's played right you win by a mile even if realistically it's only an inch.

I almost missed my chance at revival. I'd call it luck, but luck only goes so far and then there's God. Even when we are at our worst he's still there, plotting and planning and moving the pieces in the direction they're supposed to go.

"I now pronounce you husband and wife. You may kiss your bride."

With the change of my face her cheeks flush. I never take my eyes off of her. "I've been waiting for this all damn day," I say, and then grab her face in my hands and take the plunge into forever, starting with a kiss.

CHAPTER TWENTY-FIVE

Kambry

He grabs my hand and pulls me out onto the makeshift dance floor when the music begins—the large square patio that looks out at the pool. The sun is almost completely down, leaving only streaks of pink and orange sketched across the darkened navy sky. It's weird that it looks blue instead of black, but maybe it's the mixture of all the colors swirling into one beautiful backdrop. It's really striking.

We make our way beneath the large Edison-style string lights in white strung overhead in a crisscross fashion, creating a large X out of the bulbs with us at the crossway. He ditched his navy jacket after the ceremony not long ago and added a pair of brown leather flip-flops once we came off the sand. He looks good like this: white button-down and khaki pants. I love that he kept his stubble for the ceremony. Since he found out how much I like it he pretty much just trims it to the skin with an electric trimmer instead of shaving.

"Dance with me, Mrs. Cambridge."

I smile as he turns me toward him, placing my arms instantly around his neck. "I'll always dance with you, husband. All you have to do is say the word."

One hand comes around my waist and the other reaches for a hand that is settled around his neck, before pulling me close to him. The song changes as if it was planned and I immediately recognize the tune of the guitar before the words begin. It's one of our songs. *Stuck on you* by Lionel Richie. I look into his eyes as he starts to sway. "Did you do this?"

"The words are every bit appropriate to the way I feel. I've been stuck on you since the beginning, I'll be with you till the end, and I'm mighty glad you stayed."

The tears fall against my will and I let them, because the man he's becoming with each and every day is far too beautiful for what I ever felt I deserved. "*I've got this feeling down deep in my soul that I just can't lose. Guess I'm on my way . . .*" I sing to him the lyrics along with the song for the first time in our relationship, kind of like he did that night at the club on the bar to me. It's taking a huge step outside of my comfort zone for me. No one ever hears me sing without the music of the song being loud enough to drown me out. It's something I do in private.

We dance beneath these lights, turning in a slow circle, the small lanterns lit up and hanging from the surrounding trees. "Why didn't you tell me you could sing like that? I know you said you love music and want to learn to play for the lyrics that you write, but never did I know you could sing like *that*."

"Music is a part of me I've always kept to myself. It's just hard to free it all at once I guess. It's been smothered for a long time."

"I'll always let you be anything you want to be, but I think you know what you're meant to do, baby. I'll use all of my resources to help you if that's what you want."

"Maybe. Right now I just want to dance with you at our wedding."

"We really did it, didn't we? Somehow I got you and I'm never letting you go. You chose a man like me and all of my flaws when you could have had so much better."

"That's where you're wrong, Sax. You're the best. I mean it. One thing I've loved about us since the beginning is that we love each other for the way we are, flaws and all. I'll never forget the way you looked today. You let me see you cry, and you have no idea how that makes a girl feel. For a brief period of time you let me see you at your weakest emotional moment, and I'll cherish that forever, because that says something about us and about this crazy love that we share. Nineteen or ninety-nine, I'll still want you as mine."

He lifts me off the ground and twirls me around with the best smile on his face: cheeks tight, dimples out, teeth gleaming smile that could send away even the darkest day. "I love you, Kambry Cambridge."

I laugh at my new permanent name. "Only because I love you will I endure that for the rest of my life. This and you are making me feel like Lane and Kelly in *Eight Seconds*."

"I'll make you feel whatever way you want as long as you stay with me."

"Till death do us part," I say.

He looks into my eyes. "You want to get out of here? I think I need some alone time with my wife."

That sounds more amazing than I ever would have thought. We defied the odds. We beat the statistics. We found something and jumped all in, regardless of how crazy it looked. Instead of listening to reason in our heads, we let our hearts lead, and we ended up here, together and completely happy.

Completely in love.

I touch his lips with my thumb, and then take a kiss for the road. "Lead the way."

Saxton

I slide the keycard into the slot and open the door just enough it won't lock again when the green light blinks, unlocking our hotel room. Our stuff is already here. I brought it earlier this morning when I checked in since we will be on a flight back home tomorrow, and then requested a member of staff to help me set up upon my call. All I can do is hope and pray to God that it's done.

After our first dance as husband and wife, the others joined us for one more and then we said our goodbyes. I thanked my sister and Meg for everything they've done and extended a place to stay if they ever want to come to the west coast for a few days. Kambry hugged her brother tight for several long seconds. I believe it was a much-needed moment between them from the way it looked. Then I shook his hand like a man and promised to never make him regret giving her away to me. It was a mature notion and I'll never take it for granted, because if the roles were in reverse I imagine it'd be a hard task to do.

My parents walked us out with smiles on both of their faces, threatened me with my life if I didn't bring Kambry to the house soon, and we loaded up in the limo waiting out front. Now here we are, standing at this very door. I wanted no paperwork standing in my way when we arrived at the hotel.

My nerves are on edge. I want this to be everything she's ever dreamed of. I didn't give her the lengthy engagement or the huge wedding that so many girls require, and she didn't ask for it, but I want this to still be special for her. This is the first and only wedding night for both of us. There is no do-over here.

She takes my left hand, her finger rubbing over my wedding band. I look at our connected hands and then at her. "It's okay. I'm nervous too. It's kind of funny right? Since we've done it umpteen dozen times before . . ."

No words come out of my mouth at first. I silently listen to my heart pounding against my chest. She's right. I'm nervous as hell and I have no idea why. I've had sex more times than I can count, with her and with other women before her, starting at the age of fifteen in my very own bed. All boys suck at first, but each time and with each new person we learn. I've never had any verbal complaints or rumors spread that I was bad at sex. The knowledge that I have is actually the opposite. For me, it's not a proud reflection now that I'm here. I'm ashamed, if I were honest. I wish I could have given her a third of what she's given me.

Even with her, I've seen her body naked more times in the short period we've been together than some couples do in a year. The sex ranges from daily to sometimes multiple times in a day even after this long. There are times we make love, others we fuck. We've savored each other slow and steady and we've gone at it fast and hard. Positions change. We've been vanilla and we've been chocolate, the level of kink varying based on mood. Every single time is engrained in my memory forever, because I'm so far deep in love with her that there's no way out alone and still survive. But in all of those times, I've never been as nervous as I am right now. Not even the first time.

My eyes remain on her, still wearing that dress with her hair hanging over her shoulders in big loose curls. Her cheeks are pink, her lips are full, and her eyes are clear. "Have I ever told you how beautiful you are? Like really made you understand?"

"Almost daily, but even on days you don't voice it aloud, if you look at me like you are now I know just the same, and maybe even more."

I grab the back of her head and force her lips against mine, my back hitting against the door to hold it open and free my hand. It then goes to the small of her back. I clench the lace fabric in my fist. Her breathing is heavy and loud as she kisses me back, turning me on more.

She pushes forward and I let her, the door opening with each step backward I take, until we navigate past it and it shuts behind her. One by one the buttons open down my shirt, our mouths remaining glued together at different points as our heads move.

My hand relaxes a little more with each new touch from the tip of her tongue on mine. A small zipper leads me up her back until I find the start between her shoulder blades. I lower it, unzipping her dress in a fairly quick fashion, and at the exact time that she finishes with the last button.

She pulls away from me and looks up into my eyes. Her lips are the color of Crimson. "Tell me I'm not the only one that's nervous," she whispers.

I grab her hand and place it over my heart, letting her feel my erratic heartbeat. "There isn't a prior time in my entire life that I've been as nervous as I am right now."

"Why are we nervous? It doesn't make sense."

My fingers grip around the wide strips of fabric on her shoulders, as well as the straps of her bra, and I peel them down her arms together, revealing her upper body. Chill bumps become noticeable all over her skin. "I don't know. Maybe it's because there is no more question if you'll be with anyone else this way for the rest of your life and vice versa. Maybe, for me, it's worrying that sex with me will get old for you. Or it could be that the next time we have sex we know it'll be different. We will no longer be breaking the rules set in the beginning of time. I never said I didn't agree with some of your parents' morals, they were morals I was taught too, but only in how they went about teaching them. Husbands and wives are what sex was created for even though we didn't abide by it. Now we get to experience it in the purest form."

I remove her bra. My hands follow the dress to the waist, pushing it over her ass until it falls down her legs to the floor, leaving her in only a pair of heels and panties. She pushes my shirt over my shoulders, letting it drop to my wrists where I finish removing it. "I'll never get tired of sex with you, Saxton."

Her shaky hands go to my belt. She pulls it from the leather loop and toward her, so that she can remove the metal spike from the hole. "You want to know why I'm glad I waited for you? Why I'm glad I married the guy I gave my virginity to now?"

My arms outstretch and my palms press against each wall to my side in the short, narrow entryway. "Yes, because I thought you didn't wait for yourself."

She unbuttons my slacks slowly, and then lowers the zipper, revealing the front of my boxer briefs. "I didn't . . .mostly. I was scared my parents would find out and I'd get in trouble, but there were times that I thought hard about it. I can remember a couple of times that I was able to sneak enough time with him to do it, to get it over with, and one of those times I came really close to just giving in; mostly just to spite them because they were smothering me."

"What stopped you?"

"I knew he wasn't who I wanted to give that part of myself to. It didn't matter how bad I wanted to do it, because I wanted it to be with someone that it was never a question when it came down to actually doing it. I didn't want to weigh the option of yes or no." She strips me bare. I step out when my pants and underwear are in a heap at my feet and then kick them out of the way. "With you I never thought twice about my answer. It was always yes. And let me tell you something. It was every bit worth the eighteen-year wait. I can stand here now and know I'll never get tired of sex with you, because to me it's already the best, and I have no one else to compare it to. You can make love to me and know you're the only one that's been there, and that's special to me."

"I wish I could say the same," I say through gritted teeth, scared to blink, and trying to refrain from letting her see me cry for a second time today. There are very few times a man is allowed to cry: his wedding, the birth of his children, or the death of a parent or spouse. That's it. The first of those three have been used.

"I don't."

Her response throws me off. "What?"

She shrugs. "Maybe it's different for a female, but I'm glad you were with other girls before me, because to know you've been with others, some most likely better than me in every way, and then choose to keep only me forever is the only thing I need to forget that I'm not your first. Being your last is so much better."

"Fuck, Kambry," I whisper, instantly dropping my arms and picking her up at my front. That damn moisture aggravating the hell out of my eye runs from me before I can catch it.

I turn my head toward my shoulder to try and stop it when she wraps her legs around my waist, but she forces me to look at her. "Stop trying to hide your emotions from me. I'm not going to think you're any less of a man for shedding a few tears when we are talking about us. I want to know you're in this as deep as I am. I want to know how you feel. I want to *feel* how you feel."

"I'd rather show you."

Kambry

He turns to walk us further into the room and I look up for the first time, no longer sidetracked by conversation. "Oh, Saxton . . ."

The room is littered with red rose petals, starting on the fancy white comforter in the shape of a heart and cascading across until they drop off onto the floor where they get more scattered the further from the bed they get, the last one at his feet. In the middle of the heart sits a wrapped box. Champagne on ice anchors one side on the nightstand.

I reach over and shut off the lights on the wall, leaving the room in an amber glow from the candles randomly set out in the room. The only overhead lights now on are the two dim spotlights above the bed. My eyes scan the room over and over, unsure of where to start. "Do you like it?"

I wipe my eyes on my forearm. "It's perfect."

He walks me to the bed and lays me on top so carefully I feel like a glass doll. I lock my feet around his waist as he stands upright, but he grabs one ankle, prying it off. One hand cups my calf while the other removes my heel, letting it drop to the floor. Then he does the same with the other side, before peeling my panties down my legs. He leans in and his body comes to stop just above mine. "I have something for you before we go any further."

I shake my head, pointing at the sapphire and diamond necklace still around my neck. "You've given me enough. Between the guitar, the ring, and this necklace, not to mention the dresses, my birthday, and the puppy that I miss already, it's too much. Luckily, I trust Meredith with my life or I would not leave her responsible for ensuring my fur baby gets off that plane in LA. Take it back or save it for Christmas. I haven't even gotten to give you your gift yet."

He smiles at me. "I can't do either of those things."

I narrow my eyes at him. "Stop showering me with gifts. It makes me feel awkward. You know I don't expect them nor do I need them."

"Just open it."

He hands me the black box wrapped with a white bow. "Fine."

I pop it off and remove the lid. A folded up white piece of paper sits inside on top of black tissue paper. My brows scrunch. "What is it?"

"Open it."

I do as instructed. It's a copy of an original document. I skim the wording, gawk at the humongous number nestled in the jumble of words, and end on the signature of a name I don't recognize. "Wait. What exactly is this?"

He flashes me a grin. "I got an offer on my house and I accepted with the stipulation that they close within thirty days max so I can be out."

I blink at him like an idiot. I'm not the smartest girl, but I'm not the dumbest either. "Offer? As in sold? When did you put it up for sale? It's been just shy of a week."

"Monday morning. The second I knew you'd take me back I contacted my realtor. I told her I'd up her commission from the sale a little if she made it a priority. She had it ready for open house within hours. By the time the first offer came in and I realized how fast I could move it we were engaged, so I wanted it to be a wedding present. And because I got two offers I was able to take the highest. I've talked to the homeowner of the other house already and my banker. It wasn't easy, but when I want something bad enough I make it happen, so I worked it out to where we can do a double closing in the same day."

I stare at him; trying to absorb everything he's telling me. "That smaller house on the beach is really going to be ours?"

"Yes," he laughs. "But you do realize that most women want a bigger house and not a smaller one right?"

"I've always been a little weird, but I love that house. It has character. I've thought about it a lot since you showed me the key. I can see our family there."

He kisses me. "I love you, baby, and I'm glad you're not like most girls. I just want whatever makes you happy."

The waterfall that is my tears begins. "I love you too. I'm a little overwhelmed. Happy. I'm happy. It's just hard to believe we are actually starting a life together. A week ago I thought I had lost you forever. Then you came back and it's been full throttle ever since. It's just all hitting me now. I never have to go to bed without kissing you goodnight or wake up alone ever again. It's overwhelming. I'm a wreck."

"I know, baby, and I'm sorry. I should have never done that to you, but it took me a little while to figure out that I'd rather be bad for you than live without you. There's just one more thing."

"Bad or good?"

He smirks. "To me, good, to you, it depends."

I laugh through my tears and shove at his chest. "God, just tell me. What is it?"

"Well, since you're such a simple girl, downsizing and all, and I'm such a frugal guy, I have enough equity from the sale of my house after the remaining loan is paid off and the realtor gets her cut that we can pay cash to get you a brand new car. What's more is that we can still put some back so that we have plenty of wiggle room—meaning we don't even have to touch my existing finances for a while if we didn't make another dime from filming—until we figure out what the hell we're going to do when this porn thing ends with us."

"A car? I haven't even thought of that since I left mine behind."

"I didn't figure you had, but it's a necessity. Not that I mind you driving my truck, but I'm not leaving my wife without a vehicle if I need mine. Period."

My emotions are nowhere close to calming from the raging storm they've become. How we always end up in deep conversations naked I'll never know. It's like things are backward. Adam and Eve wanted clothing and we want nudity.

I can't escape the fact that he spoils me. He treats me like a queen. He's the best man, and I get to call him my husband, but I want to learn to be his partner even when I feel like he's so good at taking care of me. It's hard for me when I've been working so hard to feel independent, but I can also see that it makes him happy. It's really quite unfair to him.

"Then I'll give you what I've made if you want to do that. I can help."

"No. That's yours. You earned it."

I go into panic mode like I used to when my mother wouldn't let me breathe, always hovering over me and checking on me in my room at least every fifteen minutes when I was home. My entire adolescence I had no room to grow, to learn, or to mature. I had no chance at independence. It's why being an adult is still a bit of a challenge for me. It's why I'm scared to spend too much money in fear of having nothing left. Managing finances is like a foreign language because I've never had to do it before. I never had the option of getting a job or learning responsibility aside from cleaning my room. "Same as you. What good is it to me? You won't let me spend it anyway! Please, let me feel like I contribute to our life. It's a part in this I need."

"Why won't you just let me take care of you? It's my job, and one I gladly accept. It's what I want to do."

"Please." I wipe my eyes again. "I want you to feel like I'm your equal. I want you to teach me how to do our finances together. You're smart. I can see that. I don't want you to support me, though. I want us to support each other. I want to feel like an adult. I've been babied all of my life."

His eyes fall. "I'm not trying to control you or what you have. Do I make you feel like you wouldn't have the same access to finances as me even if you were not a contributing income? I didn't want a prenup. It's all ours, Kambry, but at the same time I've had a few years to play with the money I've earned on top of saving it. You haven't. I just wanted you to keep what was rightfully yours."

"No," I whisper. "It's all together or all separate. I'm not going to sit on money while you pay for everything. I can't. I want you to treat me like an adult even though I know you have good intentions. I want responsibility. I physically need it."

His face lights back up as a smile forms. He takes a deep breath. "Okay, hardhead." He kisses my forehead. "Even though it's beautiful. Under one condition."

"What?"

"When you find out what our finances look like before and after we put them together, you can't mentally separate them as yours and mine when it comes to you needing or wanting something. No matter what the number, it's ours. I need you to remember that for a few years I did nothing but work and save. The only two big purchases I made were my house and truck, so don't freak out like you just did when you saw how much the offer on the house was, and I want you to fix up our house the way you want it. The money is yours to use as you see fit."

"You said one condition, but that is two things."

"But they go together."

I glance down the length of his body, sighting between my boobs. Abs. That's what I see. The further down, the closer it is to mine, until there is no gap at the point between my legs where his pelvis connects with my skin. I finally consider this moment for what it is: our wedding night. All I can concentrate on is his naked body over mine and the part of him that is sitting relaxed between my thighs. I toss the paper and box aside, then wrap my body around his. He's still smiling. Geez, I married a hot man. I'm going to love looking at him for the rest of my life. If he wants to talk more it's not going to be for at least the next twenty minutes.

His smile falls and he looks at me. There he is. My large friend that brings amazing orgasms has come out to play. He's hard. His chest begins heaving up and down and it's hard to remain serious. "You just got wet."

"Yes. Does this surprise you?"

"I don't remember a time feeling it actually happen. You've always just been wet when I got down there."

"Well, generally when we're naked we're already turned on. Heavy conversation can be a downer." I laugh, but then it stops when I catch his hand go to his dick from my peripheral vision. My own breathing elevates when the head starts circling at my entrance.

"What were you thinking about?"

He pushes the tip in. The nerves return. "You. The way you look; a little bit of how we look connected at the hips." I pull my bent knees up toward my underarms and place my hands on his butt; the one I love so much. "I was thinking of how sexy you are; even in candlelight with limited visibility."

He places his forearms at the sides of my head, his hands wrapping in my hair, and his open mouth comes down on mine when it opens, his tongue swiping from bottom to top. He kisses me as he slides in slowly, letting me feel every single centimeter.

One hand cups my neck as his kiss becomes more exaggerated. I can feel the contracting of his butt muscles with each thrust. Our lips still wet, he looks into my eyes only a few inches away. "Fuck, I love you, Kambry. It does feel better. It feels final."

And then he kisses me again. He's right. It does feel different. It feels . . . right.

CHAPTER TWENTY-SIX

Saxton

"Who the fuck?"

My anger finally sounds out as my phone rings on the bedside table for about the third time. My eyes don't want to open due to the pounding inside of my head, and that annoying as fuck sound is making my brain feel like it's throbbing.

I reach over and feel around for it, knocking over the empty champagne bottle the two of us consumed when we could no longer deal with the emotions consuming us whole as we made love. Last night I figured out exactly what the term *making love* actually means, and it's nothing like I thought it was. I always thought it was just slow, sensual movement where you make sure you focus solely on the person you're with instead of the sex itself if you love your lover. For steady repeats I thought the same; which looking back is pretty much what Salem was. I'd be lying if I said I didn't use the spank bank a few times during sex with her, so my version of making love then was locking that area of my brain from entry. Really, it's harder than it sounds when you know another man—or men— has been shoving his cock in your girlfriend. It was the only way to still get up.

I was fucking wrong. Even with Kambry I thought I had it figured out, and I was as close as you can get, because you really can't get to that point completely until you've made love to your wife. The act of making love takes your entire being to a whole new level, and the second your bodies become one you realize everything about that person that you love is multiplied by like a hundred. When you're through, your head is so fucked up in love that it's scary.

I forgot how carbonated that shit is. Champagne. Now I know why normal people sip on a single glass instead of consuming most of a whole damn bottle. I pull my phone in front of my face and peek at the screen through one eye.

T calling . . .

I swipe and put the phone to my ear. "What?"

"I swear I didn't say a word, Sprout. Dammit, I had no idea. I swear on my life."

"T, what the hell are you talking about? Can this wait till later? I have a headache and your voice is annoying right now."

"Keep being an ass and my guilt level may decrease."

"Fuck. Hold on." I sit up and let the blanket fall to my waist, rubbing my hand on my face. My eyes remain closed as I move my eyes behind my lids, trying to wake up. "Okay, I think I'm good. What is so important?"

I open my eyes. "Holy fuck."

"Did you see it? Shit. I'm so sorry. I wanted to warn you first. Saxton, I didn't know."

Music starts playing: a guitar. Then the lyrics come. "*Baby, last night . . . was hands down . . . one of the best nights . . . that I've had no doubt.*" This one I actually recognize. *Die a happy man* by Thomas Rhett.

"T, can I call you back later? Like when I'm on my way to the airport."

Kambry is standing in the doorway of the bathroom, butt ass naked, in nothing but a pair of cowgirl boots and a hat. She's staring at me, a very mild smirk on her face. "Makes perfect sense," I whisper, listening to every damn line of this song for the first time. "Come here."

"What? I'm at work. Are you mad? Fuck, Saxton. I swear to God I told no one but Meg you were getting married. I don't know how they knew."

I hear nothing as the words go in one ear and out the other, because the hot as fuck woman I married is walking toward me in nothing but skin. I never thought a true country girl would turn me on way back when, especially not a girl from the south with a southern accent, but this, holy shit. The day we spent at Coney Island and she mentioned this, I thought she'd forget about it. She didn't. She upheld her promise like she always does. I wouldn't have blamed her if she had, and I kind of put it in the back of my own mind, but like me when it comes to her, she remembers things that I like or want. "I'll call you back."

I press that small red button and toss the phone down on the bed when she stops in front of the bed. "You're hot."

One knee at a time, she moves toward me on the bed. "My husband wanted to fuck me in cowboy boots, so here I am."

I grab her waist and kiss her bellybutton, my hands rubbing up and down her body. "I'll never know what I did to deserve you."

I pull her onto my lap, her knees to each side of me on the bed. She rubs her thumbs back and forth across my cheeks. "It was just time for you to stop living in misery, and the person meant for the job was finally grown up."

The song comes to an end and another starts. This one is a quicker tune. I'm guessing she has it on a special playlist. When I realize what song it is I can't help but to laugh. *Save a Horse* by Big and Rich.

"You didn't?"

"I told you I'd show you how country girls ride." Her right hand goes into the air and she mocks a bull rider. "Save a horse, ride a cowboy," she chants in a singsong voice.

"I will gladly agree to that statement." My phone rings again, striking a nerve. "Would people fucking leave me alone?"

We glance at the screen at the same time: Michael. I ignore it and push the blanket down my legs that separates us. My eyes slowly trail up her body before my hands follow behind, starting at her beautiful thighs. My fingers detour to her center and slip inside of her on their own free will. Her head falls back. "Mmm. Do that."

Slowly I fuck her with my hand, allowing her wetness to coat my fingers. My phone rings again. She looks even though I don't. "You should probably answer that," she says, causing me to look. It's Michael again.

I stop movement, but don't remove my fingers. Instead, I answer it with the other hand, aggravated. "Jesus, what?"

"You made the goddamn front page of the paper and didn't give me a heads up? Every fucking media outlet is going to be all over this. Dammit, Maverick, I'm fucking pissed. I don't like to be left in the dark when I own you with a contract. The fucking New York and Los Angeles paper!" It sounds like something being thrown at a wall in the background.

I stare at Kambry, my fingers slowly slipping from her body. Her eyes are wide. She looks a little scared. "Michael, what are you talking about?"

"Have you read the paper?"

"Well, no. I've been a little busy."

"Walk to the damn door and get it. It should be there by now."

Kambry moves off of me, standing from the bed. She grabs a pair of my underwear and hands them to me. I put them on and walk to the hotel door. On the other side lies a copy of the paper on the floor, just as he said. I barely even glance at the photo and recognize what's on the front, but even if I didn't the headline would have been pretty self-explanatory.

Porn king of the west coast marries co-star in The Hamptons over the weekend.

My eyes skim the contents of the article. My name, her name, the details of the reality show, and the name of Meg's dad is listed as the host, followed by details of his social stigma explaining for people that don't already know why he can afford a house in The Hamptons. Every guest is listed with names, leaving no room for privacy aside from Kambry and I since we aren't known by our legal name, or for her, spelling. Thank God Ben's last name is spelled like Kambry's for filming and relationships to wedding party aren't listed. "Fuck. I haven't told anyone."

"You think that's bad? It showed up on my doorstep this morning. You have obviously forgotten that you're the highest seller right now in the porn industry and have been for a while. Why the fuck do you think I wanted you for this project and even made special arrangements I would do for no one to make it happen? Digital sales on you and Kambry are higher than anything else the studio has out currently. Threads are coming in asking when more will be available between episode releases. DVD sales have spiked already. If the two of you weren't making me so much fucking money right now with this show I'd terminate your contracts for this." He takes an aggravated breath. "However, the board thinks this is the perfect advertisement for selling realism, so my hands are tied."

"Why are you pissed off? This is what you wanted technically and there was no clause in the contract that prohibited it. In case *you* have forgotten, I read every fucking line in every contract before I sign my name to it."

"Because now I have no edge and we haven't even started phase two, which is the longer portion of the contract. The last thing people will know is your ass running out the damn door after breaking her fucking heart. And now you're just magically going to return married? The only positive I can use out of this whole situation is that damn Tumblr account. The argument is that married couples get boring, which is why I have a job. You're fucking me over with this, Saxton!"

"I'm not sorry, Michael. For once I did something for me."

Kambry wraps her arms around my waist, mouthing three little words. *Is he mad?*

I nod my head, waiting for the next set of masculine screams through the phone, but instead, a soft groan occurs. "And that's probably the one thing that will save our relationship, so here's what's going to happen. Filming resumes in one month and two days. Exactly one month from today I want both of your asses sitting in my office at 8AM to regroup. It's going to take me that long to figure out what angle we will go at this from so that it doesn't look staged. In the meantime, get your personal matters in order and take that girl on a fucking honeymoon. It's the least you can do."

My smile appears in response to his asshole sarcasm that shows he cares; why he's so good at his job and a damn good friend despite everything that comes from his mouth . . . "I can do that."

"That takes care of it then."

"Sure thing."

"Oh, Saxton."

"Yeah."

"Watch out for the damn paparazzi, because based on that photo it was taken next door. You aren't an amateur. I would have expected it to slip by Kambry, not you. Pay attention. And congrats. Now it begins."

The line goes dead. I shut my phone off and toss it down on the dresser at the front of the room along with the paper. I guess Tynleigh's conversation makes sense now. "Do we need to get ready and go?"

I smirk at her and stalk forward, pushing her backward toward the bed until she falls down on it. I shake my head and remove my underwear once again. "Not until I fuck my wife in cowgirl boots. I haven't had breakfast yet either."

I lean forward on the bed and tickle her so that I can hear that beautiful, pure laughter that only expels when she's caught off guard. Then, I drop to my knees and grip her legs, holding them spread open as I place my mouth on her middle. "Oh . . .wait. Okay. Breakfast. Not what I was expecting. Mmm. Right . . .there."

What I've learned in all of this: don't live an ordinary life, but an extraordinary one. Kiss an awkward girl without asking. Stalk the hot server at the club until she gives you the time of day. Chase someone out of your league. Learn who she is. Be the guy that deserves her. Make her important. Listen to her. Spend time with her, whether it's painting her toes or listening to her read. Have amazing sex over and over again with the woman that had you in a tailspin over all the before mentioned things. Love her. And when she loves you back, never let her go.

CHAPTER TWENTY-SEVEN

Kambry

I glance out the window of the plane, the beautiful sunset set before me. It's surreal I've been in New York City for a week, and all that has happened. I'm sad to leave but happy to start a new chapter. It's an amazing memory for years and years to come. As I reflect on the days past, all that is left are happiness, peace, and serenity. I've never felt so whole in my life. And now, I can really start to live.

I take a photo of the view before me, never wanting to forget this moment. I feel like I'm on top of the world looking out like this. I started scared and ended with a love for flying I never knew I had. There is a freedom, though, to soaring through the sky like this. It's as close to being a bird as I'll ever get.

I prepare and publish the new post to Tumblr as I wait on Saxton to return. It'll automatically post once we land and service is back up. Last one for the trip . . .

> See this? #HomeSweetHome is within our reach. I'm going to miss #NYC and the gorgeous girl that resides there, but that just means more trips are in the near future. I left on a jet plane not knowing what my future held with him, and I'll return with a #ForeverKindOfLove. Thanks to all of our supporters. Because of you there will be a #TakeTwo soon. #DontBreedHate for the rest

of you. #PornBoy and I have had a long talk about things. I will continue to post, as will Saxton, but to keep some our my life private it'll be here and there. Photos galore, but personal information will be cut to a minimum. Thank you for your understanding. For those interested, once some personal affairs are in order we'll be going on a #honeymoon! #DreamsDoComeTrue
He won't tell me where yet, so you'll find out when I do. For now, it's the beautiful state of #California I've come to love so much. Keep an eye out for some awesome photos! Love you guys! XOXO, Kam.
#TrueLove #Honeymooners #PornStarRomance
#NeverGiveUpOnThePossibilityOfLove
#NoTwoLoveStoriesAreTheSame #AfterTheCut isn't over yet ;)

A hand laces with mind, swaying my attention from the window seat looking out over the wing of the plane. I glance back at him as he takes a seat. "Feel better?"

"Yeah, bladder is empty. What are you thinking? You looked pretty intense."

I smile at him. He's always concerned about me when I'm the one that should be catering to him. "Nothing really, but a little bit of everything."

"Tell me. I like to know what's on your mind."

I turn toward him, pulling my leg up into the seat. "I never remember a time I've been this happy in my entire life. I owe that to you, Sax. I can't even begin to explain my feelings about this past week in words. I'm left speechless. I'll never forget this. You really pulled me from the gutter. We went into this for fun and came out with something that's irreplaceable. Thank you for taking a chance with me when you had no hope. I promise to walk by your side each and every day. I love you so much, and I'm ready to do life with you. I just wanted you to know."

He grabs my face in his hands and kisses me, soft and slow. He releases my lips from his, his forehead pressed to mine and his eyes closed. "Life with you has been pretty damn good so far. I can only imagine what's to come."

An amazing story perhaps . . .

He leans back and places his arm around me, pulling me against him. "You ready to go home?"

I snuggle into his side, a smile on my face. "Yeah, I think I am. Our home. Home sweet home."

He lays his head on top of mine, rubbing his hand up and down my arm. "Yeah, baby. Our home."

CHAPTER TWENTY-EIGHT

Kambry

"Okay, so if you could have any car you wanted, within reason, what would it be? Let's save the Ferraris and super cars for later." His tone is full of laughter, as if I would actually choose something like that. Those cars scare me. It's like buying a house that will depreciate. A little too rich-blooded for me.

I glance over at him in the driver's seat of his truck as he backs out of the driveway of our new house, blinking at him like an idiot. "I'd rather you just tell me what to drive and me be happy with it. Then there is no risk of me choosing something outside of your price range."

My fingers go to my lips, my teeth gnawing on my beautifully manicured nails. "That's not how this works, beautiful. When I wanted a truck I got what I wanted, so now it's your turn."

"I don't know, though," I say honestly. "I've never been faced with this kind of decision. I'm still learning . . .remember?"

He reaches for my hand, removing it from the havoc my teeth are wreaking on my costly nails, and laces it in his. "Okay, so why don't we go at this from a different angle. What did you drive back home?"

I think back on the car I left behind. Bertha is probably mad at me, leaving her like that, but there was no way I could bring her. For one, she likely would have croaked before I reached the Alabama state line, and two, my dad would have probably reported it stolen just so he could come pick me up.

He squeezes my hand, pulling me back to present time. I steal a glance out the window as he rolls down the pavement of the road, headed to LA. Car shopping, he called it, but that is something I've never been shopping for in my entire nineteen years.

When I turn back to him, he's looking between the road and me. "Taurus."

He remains silent. "I had a 98 Ford Taurus. A white one."

He continues to drive, his face never taking on any emotion. "That's not exactly what I would call a teenage car."

"Bertha was nothing pretty to look at, but better than nothing I suppose. It was a hand-me-down from my mom. Most girls drove sporty cars or cars that were cute to drive, while I drove the bubble on wheels."

He smiles that genuine smile that still causes my heart to skip a beat when I see it. "You named your car Bertha?"

"Well, I figured a granny name was perfect for the old-timer she was, so yes, I named her."

He kisses the back of my hand. "I'm sorry, baby. No more Bertha. Okay, let's try this. What are things you want in a vehicle?"

I think for a moment. I'm a married woman now, so nothing compact. If we ever want to travel like he often talks about, we'll need room for luggage but still comfortable to make distances in if we don't fly. Then you factor in kids and you really need the extra space, so definitely four door. I would want dependable, low mileage if possible, because there is no need to be getting a new vehicle every couple of years if there is nothing wrong with the one I have. Dad always said that you drive it till you pay it off and then you drive it some more before you even consider buying another. Otherwise it's just nonsense to throw away money. *Don't replace what isn't broken*, were his exact words when I asked for a newer car for graduation.

"Did I lose you?" he asks.

"Sorry. I was thinking. Well, I would want spacious, like a small SUV. I figure at some point we will have kids to factor in on top of other room consuming objects like luggage or groceries. A brand that is dependable so we can get more years out of it. Low mileage if possible. I think that covers it."

"Baby, those things would be the norm for anyone. It's okay to have wants.

I truly get how humble you are, but I'm not your parents. We're partners. You wanted me to treat you as such, so I am. Tell me what you really want and we'll make it happen."

I release the breath I've been holding but have no idea why. "You're going to think I'm stupid."

"Why would I think you're stupid? You're my wife. I love you, and I love to make you happy. Stop holding yourself back when it comes to finances. Let me crunch the numbers for now. Okay?"

"Okay. I can try. Here goes. I like the new Toyota four runners. The pearl white ones with the darker rims. And when I really think about wants I think about us with a family, not me alone. Truthfully, I'd be happy with many different picks. But if we had kids I would want the option of third row seats and a DVD player for travel. I love music, especially while driving, so I'd like the option to be able to listen to my phone music apps when I'm alone. I despise commercials. I don't even listen to the radio anymore. Aside from that array of different things that aren't necessary for a reliable vehicle, there is nothing else I could possibly think of that I'd be lacking if I had all of those things, but I don't have to have them to be happy. They are just nice things; preferences."

He rubs his thumb over mine, still driving. The cab of the truck becomes a suffocating silence—one that makes me nervous anytime I truly speak my mind. He doesn't make an effort to say anything for a majority of the ride, and I wonder what he's thinking. Does he think I'm a brat for giving off such a detailed want list? Maybe I should have just said make and model and left the rest to him. I don't know. I'm not good at this outspoken thing. There is too much about one person that another could dislike. Usually, I just keep to myself. I have for years. I fear that I'll seem ungrateful, and that was something my parents never tolerated.

When I'm about to break the silence, he turns into a Toyota dealership and slowly drives through the huge lot of cars all lined up to make browsing by window easier. The first thing I realize is that he's in the new car lot and not the used. "Sax, where are the used cars?"

"Doesn't matter. That's not where our interests lie."

Panic sets in. "I didn't mean I needed something brand new. You don't have to do this. I'd be happy with anything that runs on four wheels."

He stops and puts the truck in park, before killing the engine. When he looks at me, he places his hand on the back of my seat on the edge of the headrest. I think I just wet my panties, and not in the, *I peed myself,* kind of way. His smile is broad. My stomach flips. "While I don't doubt that's true, I've decided that because you are the way you are, you deserve the best for once in your fucking life, so get your cute little southern ass out of my truck and go look at the car that's sitting right outside the door before I decide to bend you over the tailgate and fuck you into oblivion. Because if one more humble word comes out of your mouth I'm likely to do just that."

I look out of my window, and sitting in the lineup of four runners is the exact one I described; at least from the outside. My stomach is beginning to feel like a bunch of butterflies got loose. And before I know it, my cheeks are starting to hurt from the massive grin I can feel on my face.

In a hurry I grab the door handle and jump out, wasting no time as I rush over to the beautiful white car sitting like an angel under the sunlight. My fingertips begin gliding along the pearly paint as I walk from front to back, admiring it.

I cup my hands around my eyes and peek through the window: dark interior, clean—spotless actually. *That's to be expected with a brand new vehicle, Kambry. Don't be dense.* I continue moving in a full circle as I get the full three-hundred-sixty-degree view.

When I arrive back at the front, Saxton is leaned against the passenger door of his truck, arms crossed over his chest, scrolling through something on his phone. "What are you doing? I ask."

He looks up at me, shoving his phone back in his pocket. "How'd you like it?"

My heart plummets, just before my nerves start. "What were you doing? On your phone."

He smiles at me. Gleaming actually. And I feel sick. "Come here."

My feet begin to move toward him before the thought occurs that I may not want to. It's sad how much he controls my mind, body, and soul. My fingers go for my mouth when he grabs my shirt, pulling me toward his body. "What is it that you think I'm doing?"

"I don't know," I answer honestly. "There is so much you could be doing on a cell phone. The possibilities are endless."

"No. That's not true. What made you question me like that?" He kisses my forehead and then runs his thumb softly between my eyes and down the length of my nose. "Talk to me."

"Do girls ever message you?"

His smile grows, if that's even possible. It's like a laugh without the laughter. My vision becomes a little blurry. "Why is that a funny question?"

He moves aside and opens the passenger side door, before spinning us so that my back is against the seat's edge. And then he presses himself against me: every hard inch. A moan slips. "After all this time, you still have to question my intentions . . ."

"Some would say it hasn't been that much time at all," I argue.

His hand disappears beneath my denim skirt, running up the inside of my thigh, and quickly pushing my panties out of the way to make room for his hand. "Oh, baby, but it's been long enough."

He slips two fingers inside of me. "You're really going to do this? Just ignore the question by getting me off? This isn't the time nor the place for this."

"Quite the contrary. I'm going to remind you of the only girl that interests me and as many times as it takes to drill it into your head. I'll do it anyfuckingwhere."

He grips the back of my knee and pulls my leg into a bend at his waist with his free hand, just as he rubs the tip of his thumb in circles over my clit, still finger fucking me. "Fuck. Someone is going to walk over on us."

"Do you think I give a shit right now?" he grits out. His movements become harder and rushed. It's more like a stabbing motion; only it doesn't feel how I would imagine being stabbed feels. It feels amazing. "No other fucking woman aside from Meredith, my sister, and my mother has my cell number in a personal manner. If a woman calls my phone aside from that short list it's business related. And it will never come in the form of a text message."

He sounds angry, and with every word I grow wetter. My head falls back when his lips brush against my jawline. His strokes against my clit become focused in short hard bursts. "What about social media?" I ask, my stupid mouth opening once again, the paranoia of being married to such a hot man with a reputation getting in the way."

A short, evil laugh sounds against my neck at the same time a deep moan leaves my lips. "I can't control who sends me a message, baby, but I can control what I do with them. I don't respond to them nor do I read them." I start to come around his fingers, hard, my muscles squeezing him tight as I ride out one beautiful orgasm, leaving me breathless. "Because nothing is as hot as the way my wife looks when she's jealous and coming around my fingers so hard I can feel it coating my hand. I'm not interested in any female but you, baby, and any time you want to pick up my phone and dig through it go right ahead."

He kisses me as he pulls out of me, a whimper escaping from no longer being filled. He spreads his two fingers over his mouth, showing me my orgasm, before sucking them clean. "And just so there is no confusion, I was looking up specs on the vehicle. Third row seating is custom but definitely doable even if we have to order, and I'll have to ask about the movie feature, but everything else you want comes included in the *Limited* edition."

I bite my bottom lip. His eyes veer over my head and he clears his throat, no longer speaking in his turned on voice when he glances back down at me in the leaned back position I've been pushed into. "Sales rep. I'll go talk to him while you fix yourself." He smirks. "Jealousy looks damn good on you, wife."

Then he walks away, adjusting his jeans as he leaves me here, pulling down my skirt and fixing my panties. I feel so dumb. Welcome to womanhood. Where girls fight with every paranoid thought to keep their men to themselves. I must admit, though, if that is the outcome of my childish jealousy, I may just make it a regular thing. That was hot.

Note to self: don't wear easy access clothing to public places.

I glance down at myself, hoping I'm fully covered and the redness in my cheeks gone. Just as I shut the door they're both standing in front of me, the sales man dangling a set of keys from his hand. "I'm Josh. Your husband told me you're in the market for a new car. Wedding present. Congratulations. Would you like to drive it?"

I glance at Saxton. He winks at me, his hands crossed over his crotch in the most casual stance he can manage. "I suppose I am. I would love to drive it."

He waves me to the vehicle I was just looking at. Excitement floods my system as I open the door and gracefully get in—graceful in the sense that my excitement didn't result in me flashing the sales person—ending with the huge smile I'm wearing on my face. He hands me the key, showing me how the push start works and going over all of the features. I can't even take it all in I'm so overwhelmed. I've never had something this nice. First the house that now belongs to us in every way possible, and now this.

It's still hard to imagine this is my life. Each and every day I look for the newness to wear off a little in the way he feels about me, and every day I'm proven wrong. Our lives don't dull. They get better.

I look at Saxton in the back seat. "Seatbelt," he orders.

"Yes, sir." I laugh.

"Let's roll, baby."

I love him; so much that life can never disappoint me as long as he's a part of it. I'd be happy in a cardboard box if he's there to live in it with me. I can drive a piece of crap like my Taurus back home and I'd be fine if it's a sacrifice I make to keep him mine and mine only. I'll film porn together forever as long as he doesn't film with anyone else.

Kids or no kids—doesn't matter. I just need him. College graduate or being something like a hair stylist is even fine. I just want to experience every moment of this life with him by my side. Then and only then will I experience life to the fullest. This I know to be true. Because together we're whole, and apart we're incomplete.

CHAPTER TWENTY-NINE

Saxton

I glance over at her, hand in hand, as we stand on the sand. It's very different than the beach at home, and for good reason. I have a limited amount of time before we have to go back in front of the camera, and I'm taking full advantage of it. This will be the privacy we never get, the memories we'll cherish forever, and the beginning of life together as husband and wife. Well, the second half of the beginning. This is just about us. This is the start of our honeymoon.

This is my surprise to her.

We've been going nonstop since we got back to California from New York. Between closing on my house and our new house, and then moving in, followed by getting her the new car and changing over all of her personal matters, there has been little time to just relax. Still, I'm a happy man. She's officially a resident of the state of California and she carries my last name on everything she owns. It's a damn good feeling.

I want her to get the full effect of newlyweds. Newlyweds get a fucking honeymoon to themselves with no outside viewers. So here we are . . .in Hawaii. Out of the country wasn't an option until we get her a passport, which will be remedied soon.

The plan is to spend a few days on each of the few islands carefully chosen by the travel agent and myself, getting to experience all the high points Hawaii has to offer. I wanted wow factor. I wanted unforgettable. I wanted to give my wife something she'll look back on forever.

She's staring out at the water as if she's seen a ghost. I smile. "You going to be okay? I've seen a similar look once. On an airplane set for New York to be exact."

"Is this real?" she asks, her voice sounding reverent.

This is what I love about her. I always will. It gives life more character. There is nothing simple about a simple girl. She's a complex being and that sets her apart from the rest. It's a beautiful thing to be able to give her the world, literally, showing her one magnificent place after another. It's the best fucking natural high there is; second to her pussy that is. That paradise cave is what hooked me to begin with. It doesn't get old seeing her face in total amazement as we experience our lives together.

She finally looks at me. "Why don't you find out for yourself?" I release her hand and give her the extra pair of goggles and snorkel of the two in my hand. She beams as she takes them, and then she takes off running at full speed, kicking up sand as she runs toward the water. Before she disappeared I got a view of her fucking beautiful tits in that skimpy black bikini, already bouncing with just a few steps. I grunt. "No way around it. I'm a fucking lucky man," I mumble.

My heart skips a beat and my cheeks hurt from the smile I'm wearing. She's caught the attention of a few others—men specifically—as she runs past them. Yep, that's my girl. Never a dull moment in life with her.

I shake my head when she stops at the edge of the water to put on the goggles. She's looking down at them, turning them over in her hands, as if she's trying to figure out how they work. Her butt cheeks are peeking out of her swimsuit bottom. And he comes to life with one glance. I adjust myself in the thin material known as my swim trunks; all too fucking telling for a guy like me. Not today. "You've gotten wet twice already. Don't push your luck," I mumble to the object that is my dick. I'm not sure my libido will ever calm down with her if it hasn't by now.

She finally works the goggles over her head, adjusting them around her eyes and nose, before surging forward into the water, splashing as she does. She halts suddenly and turns around to face me, but points at something in the water. "Sax! Hurry! It's a sea turtle! A real one." Her voice has changed into something with a nasal sound due to the goggles restricting her nose.

My smile grows at her choice of words, as if there could possibly be a fake one out there swimming around. I take off in a sprint toward her, pulling my own goggles on. She's jumping up and down in the water's edge, waiting for me to come further. That's my cue. Be the greatest man for her. My wife. Together we'll explore every inch of this island, and then on to the next, because God knows I've never felt more alive than I feel right now. This is what life was made for. The rest is filler to get by while waiting for your purpose to be revealed. She is mine.

Welcome to Hawaii.

Also by Charisse Spiers

Accepted Fate (Fate, #1)
Changing Fate (Fate, #2)
Twisting Fate (Fate, #3)
Lasting Fate (Fate, #4)
Chasing Fate (Fate, #5)
Fated for You (Fate, #6)
Fated For Me (Fate, #7)
Fate By Forgiveness (Fate, #8)
Finding Fate (Fate, #9)

Fight For You (A Broken Soul Novel)

Marked (Shadows in the Dark, #1)
Love and War: Volume One (Shadows in the Dark, #2)
Love and War: Volume Two (Shadows in the Dark, #3)

Sex Sessions: Uncut (Camera Tales, #1)
Sex Sessions: After the Cut (Camera Tales, #2)
Sex Sessions: Passionate Consequences (Camera Tales, #3)

Acknowledgments

I want to say a special thank you to not only the people that contribute to the creative process, but also you, the reader. Seriously, the average reader doesn't really realize how much they matter in an author's life. You are the best motivator, the strongest support, and the part that makes all of the hours, hard work, and heartfelt emotion that goes into these stories worth it. I'm speaking for myself, but I'm sure I'm not the only one that feels this way. There is no greater feeling than writing a character's story and someone loving them just as much as me. Without your feedback I wouldn't grow like I do from book to book. Every message telling me you loved it, to participation on social media as I post things do not ever go unnoticed. I remember those that stay with me through each book, whether you think I do or not.

I also read reviews; even the not so pleasant ones. Growth can come out of constructive criticism. It has since I toughened up with reviews after publishing my first book. I'll give you a little piece of me. As a writer, I pour my heart and soul into my books. I write the story exactly as the characters lead me. I don't write the story that I think everyone will love, but the story that is supposed to be written. I experience the emotions writing and reading it through that you will experience when you read it. Their stories play out in my head as I write it. The characters are very personal for that reason.

Some reviews put a massive smile on my face, some make me laugh, make me cry, and make me proud, and then there are some that give me another perspective from the outside looking in. Sometimes an opinion, and sometimes merely something I didn't see before, and that's when I grow. Then there are a select few that could make a grown man cry, and as much as those few hurt,

I pick myself up and move on – another story, another couple, and remind myself that no two readers are the same, and not every reader will like every book from an author they enjoy. That's okay. The world is a diverse place and everyone is different; has different likes and dislikes. Not everyone will like Saxton and Kambry, maybe even some that like my other books, or some of them. The point in this is I'm going to try something different. Usually I ask that if you enjoyed the book to please leave a review, but that's not really fair, as nervous as writing that very phrase makes me. No author nowhere wants or likes bad reviews. It seems many readers have gotten scared of writing reviews, so I'm asking that if you have the time, even if only a few words, leave a review. There is no requirement in how many words it has to be. Something as short as "I like it," is sufficient. The more reviews for a product, the higher it gets bumped up for someone else to see it and see if they are interested, because the pool of books is vast.

Thank you so much for giving their story a chance, whether you liked or disliked. I hope you loved their personalities as much as I did. I really had fun with this one. I was nervous the entire time I was writing, even though my betas told me I was crazy, but when I read their story as a whole, all of the anxiety about them dissipated. If you did love them, they do have a second book planned...at some point lol, as well as a short of their vacation in New York (if I can keep it short – with me being a developmental writer this is challenging, but surely I can't possibly make a novel out of a week in time). I do skip around with my characters in writing. They choose who is next, so that will answer questions about side characters. Most side characters in each series do have a book planned, it's just a matter of me having a chance to pound out the story.

To my contributors, you are a necessity I cannot live without. Jessica Grover, you know how special you are to me without me having to write two pages. Thank you for helping me eliminate as many errors as possible for a better reader experience. Words fail me here, but you are irreplaceable, as an editor and a friend. Elizabeth Thiele, you are without a doubt the best PA a writer could ask for. Even with a busy home life, you make it easier for me to still love writing by taking some of the burden of marketing and the stress that comes with it away. You bear it with me. I'll always be thankful I found you, as a PA and a friend. Last but not least, my betas, people that I've become very close friends with as well. Thank you for taking the time to walk the journey with me, thank you for loving my characters, and thank you for helping me make it the best possible story I can. Susan Walker, Christina Thompson, Lezleigh Bradley, Nancy Henderson, Heidi Sturgess, Tori Herring, Lacy Waskom, and Keeana Porter, you all are simply amazing and are very much needed in my life.

Thank you Clarise Tan with CT Cover creations for another beautiful cover. It's always a pleasure to call you a friend and my designer. Cheers to many more covers and years to come.

About the Author

I found books when I was going through a hard time in life. They became my means of escape when things got bad. I realized quickly how much I loved to take a backseat to someone else's life and watch the journey unfold. That began my journey with books in November of 2012. I constantly had a book open on my Kindle app. Never in a million years would I have imagined myself as a writer, because I never thought I was creative enough. I'm living proof that things will fall into place when they're meant to be. People will make their way into our lives when we don't expect it, setting the path for what we are meant to do. Never give up on people. Never stop taking a chance on others. Someone took a chance on trusting me with her work when she didn't know me from a stranger on the street and gave me the opportunity of a lifetime as our relationship progressed, which led me to editing and writing as well. This is my dream I never knew I had. As soon as I sat down and gave writing a shot, it was like the floodgates opened. Now, I am lost in a world of fiction in my head, new characters constantly screaming for their stories to be told. Continue to dream and to go for them. No one ever found happiness by sitting on the sidelines. Sometimes we have to take risks and put ourselves out there. Thank you for all of your support, and may there be many books to come. XOXO- C

Stay up to date on release info

www.charissespiers.com

charissespiersbooks@gmail.com

Made in the USA
Columbia, SC
12 August 2024